The
Cast Stone

The
Cast Stone

Harold Johnson

thistledown press

Thistledown Press Ltd.
118 - 20th Street West
Saskatoon, Saskatchewan, S7M 0W6
www.thistledownpress.com

Library and Archives Canada Cataloguing in Publication
The cast stone / Harold Johnson.

ISBN 978-1-897235-89-8

I. Title.

PS8569.O328C38 2011   C813'.6   C2011-905348-9

Cover: photographic detail of *Gag* by Kate McGwire
Cover and book design by Jackie Forrie
Printed and bound in Canada

Canada Council   Conseil des Arts   SASKATCHEWAN   Canadian   Patrimoine
for the Arts   du Canada   ARTS BOARD   Heritage   canadien

Thistledown Press gratefully acknowledges the financial assistance of the Canada
Council for the Arts, the Saskatchewan Arts Board, and the Government of Canada
through the Canada Book Fund for its publishing program.

The
Cast Stone

THE EARLY SUN FLASHED OFF THE ALUMINUM gunwale, a silent flare amid thousands of sparkles where brilliance smashed into rippled water. The boat rocked gently to the rhythm of the man's pull on the net. He stood in the bow, feet set apart and pulled hand over hand, a steady draw that moved the boat incrementally forward, stopping now to kneel for a moment as he untangled a pickerel, pulled the net mesh from the sharp teeth, the head free. He clawed the remainder of the mesh over the thick-skinned body and dropped the prize-sized fish into a plastic tub, stood, and resumed lifting the net.

The pickerel changed the man's thoughts. His eyes lifted from the net that slanted into the water in front of him and found the blue green hills off the western shore, where the scars of industrial logging blotched brown smears against the boreal, smears that leached mud and silt into the streams where pickerel spawn. His thoughts followed the silt flow down the ancient hills into the once rich lake, swam through the weed beds and rushes back to the boat that floated on beige water and the mostly empty net.

He turned his head to look toward the northeast for a moment. There, where the horizon was flatter, where muskeg began at the shoreline and spread back for kilometres of wetland, of moss and stunted spruce and tamarack, the death of the fish began there. Acid: sulphuric and nitric, built up, absorbed from the wind, held there during the dry periods and winter and pulsed out during the spring flood, when snow melted and filled the bog and overflowed into the lake. The acid concentrations poured into the water at the same time that the pickerel found the small streams to lay and fertilize eggs.

The pickerel disappeared. Their death was sudden. Fisher people scratched their heads, stood on the shore and stared at the water. The government biologists scratched their heads, took water samples, and went back to their offices to write reports that never completely answered the question. As lake after lake died, fishers began to understand that the dominant northwest wind was bringing acid from the tar sands refineries. It wasn't just killing the lakes, it was killing the trees. The pine were turning red, the birch were not producing leaves. They stood barren and dry and over the years the memory of their lushness began to fade.

With the last of the net into the boat, the rock anchors and white plastic jugs that served as buoys stowed in the belly between the seats, Ben Robe released the clasp and lowered the motor's leg into the water. He thought for a second of using the electric start, decided against it, and pulled on the starter cord. The four-stroke engine purred into life. The electric start was there for when Ben was old. Today he decided at sixty-seven he was still too young to use it.

The boat clipped the water, resonated dull metallic thumps with each wave, a sound that betrayed the boat's heavier than normal construction. Ben gave silent thanks for the fish as he rode, one hand on the tiller, throttle open three-quarters across the lake, gave thanks for the new day, for the sun, for the sky, for the water, for his good health. Dread thoughts found him and he pushed them away, accepted the day as it was, a good day, a day of sunshine and wind. He followed the east shore of Moccasin Lake for a distance then cut across the large open end towards the reserve at the south.

A speck in the distance grew into a bird, a small bird flying straight toward him, something unusual. The bird did not belong out on the water. Here gulls swooped and swirled or followed the boat, chased for a moment, hung in the air on slender wings then slid away. Eagles sometimes waited high in a dead tree near the shore until the boat drew too close for comfort before they dropped, spread their wide black wings and powered away with forceful thrusts that lifted and carried them over the trees and out of sight. Cormorants formed packs and hunted fish. Long lines of large black birds chased fish across the surface of the lake, hundreds of silent hunters worked together to drive a school, lifted off the water to land again in front of the wave of feeding birds, a constant feed, lift, land, and eat.

The little brown bird did not belong out here. It did not fit. It belonged in the willows close to his cabin. Shy and quiet, patient in the summer heat, it was a bird that moved slowly and never for any distance, a seed eater.

Ben watched it beat the air, fight the wind with rapid wing strokes and struggle straight for him. Straight and purposefully, its short wings never intended for long flights, it should not have been here on the water. It was out of place; a message, a warning, an abnormality to pay attention to. The bird belonged at the cabin. *Someone is coming to visit.* The thought came unbeckoned seemingly from nowhere, the way intuition always defies logic. Ben opened the throttle full and the boat responded, lifted a little higher in the water and clipped the waves a little quicker.

When the fish were prepared, and the cabin was cleaned, and the dishes done and a pot of tea was set on the table beside a new box of cookies opened on one end, the clear plastic wrap torn back in invitation, Rosie knocked at the door. Another abnormality, Rosie never knocked.

"Why are you beating on my door? Have you got something against it?"

"Just bein' polite, I didn't want to interrupt. Never know what you're doin' in here by yourself." Rosie noticed the clean swept floor and kicked off her shoes; she had seen the cookies and was heading straight for them.

"How's your diabetes this morning?"

"You are a mean son-of-a-bitch, Ben. *Mean!*" She pushed the word through her teeth, curled her lips back in a snarl to stifle the smile that was trying to betray her feigned anger.

"Help yourself."

"Oh, you are a mean bastard Ben. Put them away." Rosie opened a cupboard, moved aside a heavy black mug with Z99 Radio blazoned all over it and selected her favourite thin, white china cup, the one with the little blue and purple flowers. Before she poured the tea, she folded back the plastic wrap on the package of cookies and put them in the wooden breadbox on the counter, the box with the lid that could shut.

She settled heavily into a chair, rose slightly to slide it back from the table for a little more room, then lowered her weight fully before she leaned a shoulder against the log wall. "You always make a good cup of tea."

"Did you want some sugar for that?"

"Fuck you, I'm tryin' to be nice. Sometimes I wonder if the only reason you came back was to give me a hard time."

Ben couldn't hold the laugh back; it oozed out, a little rolling chuckle. "Give you a hard time?" His eyebrows raised above his deep grey eyes. The forked lines around the edges showed lighter than the wind and sun-darkened face. "Give you a hard time." He repeated the words because of their ridiculousness.

His laugh spread itself thinly through the cabin, wrapped around Rosie and melted her pretension of anger. She jiggled, set down her cup of tea before it spilled, and let her mirth mingle with his. Her higher pitch laugh played with his deep quiet rumble, the laughs twisted together and became one sound that reverberated gently around the room and chased away anything of remorse or shadow.

This was the reason Ben had returned to the community on the shore of the lake. He had said it was for the quiet, for the return to nature, for tranquility, but in reality it was for the company of laughter, to share, to belong. Here in the cabin he built with his own hands, where the logs soaked up the water from broken blisters, where he was warm and dry, fed and belonged, where memories had roots. Here with Rosie, the little girl from his childhood, the little girl that used to follow him, shyly. Rosie who stood in the shadow, with cotton flowered dress and moccasins. Little shy Rosie, smiled and looked away when he glanced at her, then followed at a distance, a kit fox pretending to hunt but still too full of play.

"Yeah, give me a hard time." Rosie again feigned sternness. "I came here try'n to be nice and you give me a hard time." "Okay, Rosie. I'll apologize. I shouldn't pick on you. But I was just getting you first before you jumped me like usual."

"Maybe you should lend me twenty bucks for being mean."

"Is that what you came over for? To borrow a twenty?"

"Well, yeah, but since you were mean to me, you should just give me twenty instead of lending it."

"I suppose." It really didn't matter to Ben whether he loaned or gave Rosie a bit of money in the middle of the month. In the three years that he had been home she had never repaid a loan or reciprocated a gift. Not that Rosie lacked in generosity or gratitude. The little welfare that she received did not leave any cash over to match the greatness of her heart.

"I sometimes wonder Ben, whether you have a stash somewhere." Rosie stuffed the twenty into a pocket. "You can stretch a pension cheque further than anyone else."

"I don't play bingo." Ben responded quickly.

"And you don't drink. But even so, you seem to always have money when everyone else has run out."

The accusation had more power than Rosie knew. It forced Ben to keep a steady face, forced him to calculate his response, his words, his actions. He chose not to respond and let silence do its work. It did. Rosie finished her tea, rinsed her cup, and put it in the cupboard. Never let it be said that a man washed dishes for her.

~

Lester tried to read the words on the bus ticket, but the letters were nonsense. He closed his left eye and some of the reversed letters reverted to normal. The C and the L he remembered, yeah, the M was there. The ticket should say he was going to Moccasin Lake. He handed it to the man in the grey uniform, hoped he was the bus driver and not someone else. The man looked at the ticket and handed it back. Unsure but unwilling to allow anyone to see that he was unsure; Lester entered the bus. No one stopped him. He sat in a tall back seat with his small pack on his lap, his cheek against the cool glass, and watched the people move around the bus depot, watched for trouble. He saw no sign of anything that might be out of place, not that he knew what normal was out here. He wondered whether his ability to know when trouble was coming would work here in this world. Would he know when to shrink into a wall, find a corner, and become invisible.

The bus filled. Lester watched faces. Men he understood. Knew their way of walking, their mood. Women he could not read at all. They walked strangely, sounded strange. The bus continued to fill and pressurize. He turned back to the window, to the bright green building and black asphalt parking lot.

"Is it okay to sit here?" she asked.

"Yeah, I guess. Yeah. Sure." I sound like an idiot he thought.

The driver closed the door and it did not clang and echo the way prison doors sound.

She was sitting close. Lester could smell her. The smell of diesel fuel and turpentine filled his nostrils. The base of her perfume overwhelmed the scent she had so carefully chosen. Or rather it was lost on Lester, or Lester had lost the ability to smell that particular aroma and only the turpentine that the scent was mixed with filled the thin air between them. Lester turned away, his cheek against the tinted glass and tried to breathe.

The bus rolled out of the little prairie city, crossed the arch of a long bridge across an ancient river, turned through an overpass, and headed due north. Lester watched the new prairie, the land turned by the rush of homesteaders a century before. People who hated trees and pushed the forest line two hundred miles further than the old buffalo hunters' wintering sites. They were easy to hate. Wealthy farmers with big tractors bright red or John Deere green and fancy pickups on the way to town, fat wives and fat children.

The land changed and so did the traffic; now there were more logging trucks. They still hated trees, slashed them down and hauled them to the mill to make paper to wipe their fat arses with. Lester wished he could breathe, wished the woman would get off the bus at one of the tiny dying farm towns where the bus stopped, unloading parcels from its undercarriage. But she sat there in her stink, eating some kind of health food bar, nibbled on it, one tiny bit of oatmeal at a time and flipped the pages of a picture magazine, stared long at photos of celebrities on glossy paper.

Abruptly the prairie came to an end. The bus rounded a corner and began up a long incline and the last farmhouse and bright red barn disappeared behind a stand of spruce. From here to the Arctic Circle was boreal forest; trees, lakes, rivers, muskeg and Indians. Lester was home. Twenty-four years, eight times three is twenty-four, three manslaughters, consecutive, a bargain. Not one minute off the sentence, every damn second of the judge's pronouncement. They had to let him out, couldn't keep him any longer. Fuck the parole board and early release, Lester Bigeye was free. They couldn't send him back. He was completely out. Not on parole. The last eight years had been tough. Ever since that fat cow had said: "Lester Bigeye, your application for parole has been declined. This board finds that you are an unsuitable candidate due to your inability to take responsibility for your actions." Bullshit, bullshit, bullshit."

They filled him with hope before every Parole Board hearing and took that hope away from him every time. Now he was beyond their reach. Lester was home and the trees were still there, beautiful poplars in full, dark mid-summer leaf, and tall spruce with spread boughs like a jingle dress dancer's skirts. The roadside flashed past and Lester caught sight of wildflowers. Flowers that he had forgotten. Brown-eyed Susans and lilies. There were still a few wild roses out. Summer was still young.

Moccasin Lake Reserve was where it was supposed to be; where the sign said it would be, at the end of eight miles of gravel road off the main paved highway that headed north to the mining towns, but it was nothing like the place Lester left. New metal-sided buildings stood over the places he remembered. The band hall was gone and something that might be a skating rink stood in its place. There was a chain link fence around where the schoolyard had been. The new building with steel poles placed architecturally above the entrance to look like a teepee had replaced the old school that he had attended. Then Lester saw the lake, blue and green with white streamers of foam and he knew that he was home.

The house by the lake, up the short, sandy road, amid tall spindly black spruce wasn't there. Lester was not expecting to find his car, the burgundy 1972 Monte Carlo, but he hoped the house would still be there. The house was gone. The car sat flat on the ground without wheels, glassless. Its windows long past the targets of kids with slingshots just for the wonderful tinkle sound glass makes when a stone passes through it. Poplars grew up through where the hood had been removed. Someone had taken the engine, Lester's pride — a Chevy big block that roared and spun gravel. He smelled the mould of rotted seats when he put his head through the gaping driver's window. The tape deck was still there, under the dash, an eight track add on. Someone must have needed door parts; the inside of the passenger door lay across the front seat. Lester thought he remembered electric windows. Something caught his eye and he forced the door to open, to creak against rust and time. He knelt and reached under the seat.

Canadian Club whisky, a twenty-sixer, right where he left it, and still a quarter full. He remembered putting it there, remembered the smooth feel of the neck of the bottle in his hand as he stashed it. He remembered slamming the car door and the solid weight of the 30:30 rifle, the chill of the cold lever action against his knuckles and the steps toward the house.

Ben stood in the doorway, one hand on the frame and looked out at the parallel indentations of sand that led to where his truck sat. They couldn't be called a driveway, just the marks of driving over the same ground again and again from the gravel road to the log house with its narrow deck all along the front. The logs had begun to yellow nicely, the way pine does, its own sap and pitch acting like an expensive treatment. Or maybe it captured sunlight and held it in its stickiness, glued the sun to the logs.

The cabin was square and solid with a low-pitched green metal roof. "Guaranteed for fifty years." The lumberyard attendant had tapped the pile of metal with his toe. "A little bit more expensive, but probably worth it."

"Fifty years sounds about right. I don't imagine it will be me who changes it. I'll be a hundred and fourteen." And they'd loaded the sheets onto the back of Ben's truck.

The little brown bird was back in the willow clump. It sounded a melodic "*tchi tchi, tchi, whooi, whooi, tchi, tchi.*"

"You didn't fly all the way out there to tell me that Rosie was coming to borrow a twenty." Ben stepped gently away from the door. The song sparrow shifted positions in the clump of willow and gave another version of its song.

Ben scraped a heavy white plastic deck chair out a bit from the wall so that he could recline it, and waited. The sun sat high, just over the pine tree, a little east of south, still on the morning side of noon. The pine stood solidly in the middle of its circle of brown needles and the parallel ruts of the driveway curved around it and crawled up behind the truck. The shade of the pine dappled the dark red of the heavy-built, four-year-old Toyota extended cab.

Ben had purchased the truck precisely because it was used. A new truck stands out. He thought about the morning he had stopped in a gravel pit to rub it down with grit to remove the shine laboriously applied by the dealer's hired help. It was a solid dependable vehicle. It didn't need to shine and attract attention. The truck was much like the boat he had purchased that same morning, solid, dependable, the way Rosie would describe Ben.

The song sparrow sang again. Ben mimicked its song. "Someone, someone, someone is coming for tea, tea, tea." The little bird walked sideways along a branch, out of the shadow to where the sun caught its feathers and brightened its drab colours. "You sure have a nice song for such a plain-looking bird." It responded to the compliment and gave Ben the long version of the song with a few quick trick changes. He sat back into the curvature of the deck chair and waited for whoever might be coming for tea.

There were things to do. There were always things to do. There might be three or four new weeds in his garden since yesterday. The gate at the corner of the pole fence was beginning to sag slightly and scrape against the ground. Maybe he should paint that fence around the square garden. Black spruce poles made excellent fence rails but they were not like pine, they darkened with age. Maybe he should paint them white. But that would mean a trip to the city to buy paint and someone, someone, someone was coming, coming for tea, tea.

The sun drifted past the pine and Ben noted the movement of the tree's shadow as it crawled slowly from his right to left across the grassy space. His mind drifted with the shadow and he let it spill back over time. He remembered his early days on this reserve, school, sports and people. He remembered his first metamorphosis. Not a physical change, a spiritual rebirth where all that he believed in came crashing down with the death of his father. Then there was the slow rebuilding of a personality, different than before, but only visible to him. That was the beginning of manhood. There were other times in his life when his universe had collapsed, when a strong belief in something was proven false. There was a poem from when he was twenty something:

Adrift in a sea of chaos
I gather my reality about me
And build a raft thereof.

What he had tried to say was that he had core beliefs that never changed. When his larger belief system collapsed, he returned to that core, that centre, that basic definition of Ben. After a series of metamorphoses he realized that there was very little in which a solid belief could be justified. Most of science, virtually all academia and political discourse was unstable and could collapse in a moment. That realization had been his moment of freedom, his emergence. He rose from the dark and walked in an ephemeral world open to change, open to contradiction.

~

The pine shadow crept across the planks of the deck and touched his foot. A yellow dog sniffed its way down one rut of the driveway, moving slowly the way dogs do in summer. Ben watched its cautious approach, lethargic in the heat. She would be the progeny of the dogs Dolphus and Zachius brought back. That's the story of where the good sleigh dogs came from. It was said that the brothers had paddled north with a canoe full of trade goods and returned in the middle of winter with two dog teams and sleighs filled with fur. Those dozen dogs were the great, great grandparents of every dog on the reserve. He noted that the yellow dog looked pregnant, a bit big in the belly, nipples beginning to show through the fur. She would be looking for a place to make a den, a home, someplace safe to give birth.

The sun sat high over Ben, shone down through the gap in the forest canopy that opened above the small clean space around the cabin. A little wind would be nice now, something to move the still air that was beginning to heat up. He removed his thin jacket, folded it over the arm of the chair, and bathed in the warmth. Old bones like warm sunshine. Not that Ben would admit that he was old, but he was getting there. Time now to slow down, to take in all those elements that he had rushed past, time to sit and absorb. Maybe, just maybe, he would find some way to give back, to make up for the things he had taken. Everything has a price, a cost, an affect that comes from every choice. Put out good things and good things come back. The more you give the more you get; the more you take the less you can keep. He remembered all that he had taken and wondered when balance would assert itself and something would come and take away from him.

The shadow of the pine moved away and began to point more easterly. Five children on three bicycles wove noisily down the gravel road. The sun's heat drove them to the lake and the water. Two larger girls, eleven, twelve maybe, each peddled a bike with a younger child balanced on the cross bar. A smaller square boy with a long towel over his shoulders that was in danger of catching in the chain and sprocket, peddled as fast as he talked. He was one of those children that had not learned that internal dialogue should be kept internal. He voiced every thought, unconcerned whether any one was listening. The two older girls were not listening; they carried on their own conversation. The sounds of tires on gravel and the voices of the children dimmed as they travelled on down the road past Ben's home.

He went back to his thoughts from before he caught the pickerel this morning, President Obama shaking hands with Hugo Chavez. Yes, that was the last time he had hope. The world looked as if it might heal itself. But then . . . Oh well, best not to think about it too much. What was, was. It had been so long; so long since the famous handshake. And hope. What the hell was hope anyway? Such a pitiful word.

The afternoon settled into summer silence, too hot even for mosquitoes. The sun eased across the westerly part of its zenith and began its course to the horizon. Ben stayed in his chair. He sat forward slightly and looked for the song sparrow. It wasn't in the willows. He sat back and waited, wondered what he would have for supper, or rather how he would cook the fish, or which fish. If the person who was coming were white he would fry the pickerel. White people seem to like that kind of food. If the visitor was an Indian, he would cook the big whitefish.

～

Lester found his way back to his car as the sun touched the horizon. He had not really tried to find his relatives today. How do you return to your family and say, "Hi, I'm Lester, remember me? I'm the guy who shot my father, my mother, and my wife." He had walked around some, kept mostly out of sight, not skulking, just avoiding where people gathered, like at the gas station and store or around the band office. He found the old trails were still active, the paths through the trees, the short way to somewhere. The change to the reserve in twenty-four years was incredible. Who could have guessed that the Canadian government would be so embarrassed that they would build houses for Indians that were more than the shacks that Lester left? A quarter of a century is time enough for change, but for Lester who had been away from any change at all, confined to the constants of concrete and steel and wire reinforced glass, the reserve was unrecognizable.

He sat in the back of the old Monte Carlo and sipped slowly and steadily from the bottle. Was the whisky better after twenty-four years of aging under the seat of a car? Lester could not answer, he had no comparisons to say better or worse than. It was different than jailhouse brew, but he could not say it was better. The light changed to copper, tinted the treetops, softened the colours and eased the day to a close. The whisky_had the effect that Lester sought; he closed his eyes and let himself drift away.

⌒

Ben fried the pickerel. Monica laughed and joked and got in the way as she tried to help in the preparations. "Where do you keep your potato peeler?"

"In the knife block."

"I don't see it."

"It's called a knife, it's the one with the handle sticking out."

They managed to get through the preparation of a very late supper and enjoyed the simplicity of crisp fried fish, boiled potatoes, and canned tomatoes.

"What took you so long to get here today?" Ben eased back from the table and placed his fork across his empty tomato-stained plate.

"What do you mean?"

"I was expecting you earlier."

"Stopped to shop in Saskatoon." Monica gave Ben her puzzled look. He let her stay puzzled. He had his answer. He had sat all afternoon in the sun while she shopped.

Monica sat up straight, rested her thin arms on the table, "What do you mean, you were expecting me? Has someone been here?"

"No, no one."

"Then why were you expecting me?"

"A little bird came and told me you were coming." Ben poured himself the cup of tea that he had waited for all afternoon. It did not matter if he knew anything or not. He was satisfied. He was fed, he was dry, and he was warm. The tea held a hint of the wild mint he picked that morning along the shore.

"As long as it wasn't Homeland Security." Monica wiped her mouth with the square of paper towel she had placed beside her plate. "Have you kept up with the Resistance? Her voice changed pitch. It was sharper now. The visit, the customary extended 'how do you do?' was finished and now it was time for business, for work.

"Only what I get on CBC."

"And that's all bullshit."

"Are you telling me that we haven't had three thousand bombs dropped in Canada since the annexation?"

"Annexation! Annexation, fuckin' invasion. CBC may as well be NBC for all the shit they put out." Her anger pulled at her face, lengthened it.

Ben shrugged.

Monica leaned back, "I know, I know, they put out what they can. But, it pisses me off that the people don't hear what's really going on."

"Is the bomb count wrong?" Ben's question wasn't rhetorical.

"Who knows, probably. Does the bomb count include cluster bombs? Does it include Bolts from Heaven? They've dropped at least a dozen. Tore the shit out of the boys in Lac La Biche. What gets me the most is that garbage about balanced reporting; I mean what was that righteousness stuff about? The Christian right isn't balanced, hasn't been since Bush. And we all know that isn't what it's all about. It's about Fort Mac, it's about oil. They invaded us because Prime Minister Thoreau threatened to cut off all trade with the Americans. San Francisco was just an excuse. Everyone knows that it's about oil. Terrorists from Canada, immorality and drugs and atheism and all that other crap are just excuses, and the world allows it."

"I'm not defending the invasion, annexation, but the bombing of San Francisco changed a lot of things."

"I'm not convinced that bomb came through Canada. I think they don't have a clue how it got there, and used it as an excuse. I wouldn't doubt they did it themselves. Think about it. The Christians didn't like what was happening in Frisco; they called it sin city and hated it as much as Islam did."

"That's too far for me. Nobody sacrifices that much."

Monica sat back "I don't know. I don't know." She used a stray strand of dark brown hair across her forehead as an opportunity to run her hand over her head, to soothe her thoughts. "Frisco changed things. But, how did anyone get a dirty bomb across the border. Ever since 9/11 there have been radiation detectors at every border crossing. I'm just not convinced that those eight were the ones that did it. And now we'll never know. Nobody can re-examine them."

"Quick trials and quick executions have a way of putting an end to questions."

"James Henderson was talking at the university awhile ago and he said we were back in the last century, that all of the gains in human rights have been erased. His argument was that we have to start all over again and redevelop a body of law stronger than the old UN Charter or our Charter of Rights and Freedoms, a body of law developed without interference by special interest. You should've been there Ben. The entire theatre sat there with their mouths open. I was wishing someone like you were there to push his buttons; get him to see the other side, to see the people in the equation."

"James is doing what James knows. It took courage for him to stand up."

"He wasn't standing up against the Americans. Never once said directly that the bastards needed to be put back into their place. His argument was that law needed to be redeveloped. He was quite conciliatory."

"As he should be. Calling people bastards doesn't do much."

"Have you read Warren Churchill's piece about American Bastardism?"

"No, What's he saying now?" Ben stacked Monica's plate on top of his, gathered the knives and forks and carried them to the sink.

"Oh, it was a wonderful piece about how the Americans are truly bastards in the literal sense. The world does not recognize the marriage of their parents, that the left was not free to marry the right, the Democrat–Republican marriage was never consecrated, thus American politics is illegitimate." Monica poured herself another cup of tea.

Ben stood for a while looking out the window above the sink at the night's blackness, at the silhouette of the pine with a few stars in its crown. He looked skyward to see more of the stars but the house's eaves stopped his view. "Like I said, it doesn't help." He turned back to Monica. "We can swear at them all we want; they're still here."

"Churchill does inspire however; everything becomes important now. Every act of resistance adds to the body of resistance. Someday the world is going to stand up to the Americans. That's why we need you Ben. Your work on supremacy is far more important now than it was when you were writing about colonialism. You know your students are at the head of the resistance. It was you who inspired them; Jeff Moosehunter, Roland Natawayes, Art Livelong, Betsy Chance. They're all part of it. Betsy was at Lac La Biche when it got hit."

"Is she all right?"

"Shook, really shook. She wasn't hit, not physically anyway. But it changed her. She's jumpy, can't stand noise. I saw her at Batoche, looking over her shoulder all the time, thinks she's being followed. But, she hasn't weakened; she's still strong the way that Betsy always was strong, a proud Ojibway woman."

"She'd correct you and say a proud Anishinabe woman. You know this was never our fight, this American–Canadian thing. Canada promised in the Treaties that we would never be asked to go to war for them."

~

Lester's head hurt and he put it back down on the seat of the Monte Carlo. His nose was plugged and his eyes felt itchy. This was more than a hangover; maybe something in the whisky, maybe old whisky caused this. He opened his eyes again in the early light at the sound of an approaching car. He watched the lone white woman drive past, wondered who she might be: social worker, public health nurse, schoolteacher — probably a schoolteacher to be up and around this early in the morning. Dawn light bronzed the land, softened the features of the trees, coated them until they appeared to have been dipped in a vat of boiling copper and set out again to stand guard along the side of the road.

The smell of mould filled him as he tossed about on the back seat of the car. Here was the answer to his symptoms. Whisky would never betray him but mould he knew about. It had been in the farm annex when he spent time in minimum security. That was black mould, the mould that killed people, and prisoners were assigned bleach and scrub brushes to get rid of it. Lester needed a better place to live. His old Monte Carlo no longer held the power and prestige of its and Lester's youth.

～

"Are you going to lift your net this morning?" Rosie wanted to know how much time she had to visit.

"I pulled it out yesterday; I have enough fish for awhile." Ben stirred a half teaspoonful of sugar into his black coffee. Rosie was going to want to know who his guest had been. Ben decided to make her work for the information and only answer direct questions, see how long it took for Rosie to hint around before she came right out and asked.

"Did you have a good sleep?"

"Very good."

"Hmm." Rosie did not much like coffee at the best of times, and she really did not like Ben's morning coffee. It was way too strong for her tastes. She only accepted a cupful to be polite; now she was stuck with it. She put the cup down, held it for a moment between her hands, then eased it away, slid it across the wood of the table as she talked, moved the bitter black to greater and greater distance.

"I had my children between eighteen and twenty-four, all in a rush, four kids in six years. Then they were my life for the next twenty years. Then all of a sudden I'm forty and all alone. My baby goes to live with her sister in the city and I have a new life to figure out. I'm alone and I have time to think again. And do you know what I think about for the next twenty years?"

"No." Ben shook his head.

"I wondered what happened to the pictures."

"What pictures?"

"The pictures of Father Lambert. What other pictures?" Rosie waited for an answer.

Ben did not have an answer; he sat back and took the time he needed. Three years he had been home. Rosie came over almost every day; she drank tea, nibbled cookies, told stories and retold stories, offered to sew buttons back on, made him moccasins and a beautiful pair of gauntlets covered with otter fur and she never asked, or talked about that summer. He had relaxed, maybe she would never ask, but now there it was; the question.

"There are no pictures, never were; I stole the camera from the school, but there was no film."

"You bluffed him?" Her face changed, serious Rosie dissolved into everyday Rosie. "You bluffed a priest with an empty camera." She shook her head in disbelief. "You always had that, that something." Rosie did not have the words to describe Ben's inherent sense of absolute justice, his determination, his sense of self and place that overwhelmed less aware people.

"I'm sorry, Rosie."

"No. No don't ever say that. If you apologize then you did something wrong and I can blame you, and I don't ever want to blame you. It wasn't you. All you did was ask me to put on my little sister's red dress and go play in front of the church. He did the rest. When you came with the camera you saved me from him. It wasn't your fault for what he done."

"I'm sorry, Rosie, I'm sorry because I didn't think you would get there so quick. By the time I broke into the school and got the camera and got back, well . . . "

"But you did get back, and he saw you with the camera, and he never touched me or any other kid on this reserve again. I don't blame you Ben. I'm proud of you. You took on a priest and beat him. You forced him off the reserve and now I find out the camera was empty. Well, in a way that's a good thing. Nobody will ever see my shame."

~

Ambrose Whitecalf never went to university along with the others, his brothers, his classmates. Red dutifully finished grade twelve, honoured his parent's wishes, attended the graduation ceremony that was for them, not him. He didn't care. It wasn't important. It simply marked the end of an era. Graduation was the signal of freedom, freedom to go back to the land, to enjoy the earth.

Red was law-abiding. But it was his law that he abided. Red's law wasn't much different than that written in criminal codes. The principles were the same. Respect others, take care of your family, don't interfere. Red's law imposed upon him a duty to help anyone who asked. He had no desire to change the world, not even to push the Americans back across the old border. They were part of a world that had no impact on him; they didn't matter. Their rules and regulations and imposed security were meaningless in the forest.

Their economy was not Red's economy. He cut a bit of firewood for people who still burned firewood, took the bit of money they gave, sold a bit of fish and a bit of moose meat occasionally. Sometimes in good years he sold some of the rabbits he snared to people who remembered eating rabbit but were too busy trying to earn a living to take the time to go to the forest, cut a few young tender pine and scatter them around until the rabbits came to feast. He pitied and loved those people, the ones who remembered how it was, the ones who smiled at their memories as they reached for the stringy meat that would go into their soup. They paid with big, happy smiles, not caring that the price per pound, if calculated, would bring the price of rabbit above that of beef. They weren't buying meat; they were buying memories.

It was gasoline that forced Red into the economy, gasoline for the chainsaw, for the truck, for the boat to go lift the net. If Red did not have to buy gasoline, his life could be a whole lot simpler. Everything he needed for a good life was in the forest; food, heat, shelter. Gasoline was his prison, his captor.

Red was completely unsophisticated and loved it. The problems and complications of modern society did not touch him, did not enter into his analysis of any given morning. He woke, made a pot of coffee for himself and a kettle for Lorraine's tea when she got up. His day began with a prayer, usually outside, a simple "Thank you for today, Grandfather."

Then Red would look around to see what needed doing or what the day was best suited for.

He was getting good at predicting weather, watching the sky for those subtle changes, those markers that he recognized — low clouds in an arc above the eastern horizon always meant that the weather would be warming. Sky colour held meaning beyond the red sky at night, red sky in morning cliché. There were also shades of blue, variations near the sun or moon and an encyclopaedia of cloud forms.

Today, Red decided, would be a good day to stay close to home, help Lorraine with the little things around the house, knowing that by noon she would be chasing him out, sending him somewhere. "Go help Moses fix his fence." Or, "Dianne phoned, she needs someone to look at her car. It's making a funny sound."

~

Rosie sat on the heavy plank steps that led up to Ben's door. "The light is good here," she told herself as she sewed beads to leather and created an eight-sided star for the back of a pair of gloves. The truth was that the light at her house, a hundred steps further from the lake, was as intense. But if you challenged her on it, she would argue with you and no matter what proofs you offered, you would eventually lose the argument worn down by the strength of her conviction. She would never admit to you or to anyone that she was there because she was lonely and the feeling of Ben's spirit moved around his cabin and comforted her.

A whimper from under the steps drew Rosie away from her beadwork to kneel in the grass, bend way over, and look under the heavy lumber frame. The yellow dog lay curled around six puppies tumbling with each other for a teat, all mouth and sucking, eyes closed. "You picked a good spot to have your babies." The yellow dog raised her head at the words. "Seems everyone knows Ben will look after them." The yellow dog licked the puppy closest to her tongue. "Thirsty work giving birth, isn't it. Bet you'd like some water." Rosie found a bowl she was sure Ben wouldn't mind sharing. On the way out she grabbed the left-over fried fish. Sleigh dogs and fish, something about that combination just seemed natural somehow.

Rosie sat back on the steps — a fed, watered, contented mother lay in the shade somewhere beneath her — and wondered absently where Ben might have gone. To the city perhaps, more than likely the city she agreed with herself. He would not have gone north for any reason without taking his boat. She wet the thread by drawing it through her mouth to stiffen it so that it was easier to control and returned to firmly attaching the string of beads to their precise location on the leather.

Now if she were her grandmother, she would not sit here and wonder, she would fly away and find out exactly where Ben had gone and how he was making out. Rosie had never seen her grandmother, old Jeannie, do any of the things she was purported to have done. She had only scraps of conversations and whispers that told of the old woman telling her children, including Rosie's mother, "I'm going to check on your uncles on the trapline. Don't be scared. If it looks like I'm in trouble, just pass my shoes over me and I will come back." And the old woman would go to sleep and dream and toss and turn and talk and if she became quiet, her children would pass her shoes over her and she would wake up and tell them how their uncles were doing. "Delbert killed a moose." or "Walter fell through the ice, but his dogs helped get him out. He's okay now."

Ben had a secret, Rosie knew. He had a secret and it had a hold of him and wouldn't let him be, it was like a limp or an ache, and it was always in the way and needed to be cared for like a sore thumb. But Ben had a big secret and it had started to bend him over with its weight. If he wanted to share it with Rosie, she would help him to carry it. She had carried the secret of the priest all her life and it hadn't crippled her; it had made her strong.

But Ben's secret was something newer, something he brought with him to the reserve, something from outside, from the white world. Probably had to do with money. Rosie looked around. The aluminum boat on the trailer parked in the shade of the large pines must have cost Ben a fair price, and the motor, well those don't come cheap, not new ones anyway, and this house. Rosie turned around and looked at the log structure behind her. He must have spent money on it. Those were new windows set in wooden frames, and the door was solid, not one of those cheap doors like the contractors put on reserve houses. Yeah, Ben had spent a fair amount on his house. It might not look like it unless you looked close. Everything was plain, simple and the best quality. And if you added in the truck, well, Ben had spent a big pile of money since he moved back.

So Ben had money, big deal. He was a retired professor after all. So why did he go to lengths to act like he didn't? Maybe he was embarrassed by it. Maybe he didn't want to embarrass her with it. It didn't matter. Funny thing about money — you put people and money together and strange things happen.

She slipped the long thin bead needle through a sequence of different coloured beads, raised the needle and shook the pretty little bulbs of glass down the thread to where her solid left thumb waited to hold them firmly in place while she sewed them onto their designated spot.

If Rosie could travel like Old Jeanie, she would go find Ben and tell him — tell him what? That she was sitting on his steps while he was away because she wanted to be where he had walked, on boards he had nailed. She was sixty-four years old and acting like she was fourteen. What would Ben want with her? She wasn't pretty. Not anymore. She wasn't one of the educated, sophisticated. She was competently literate but wasn't versed in literature. She preferred to read Stephen King and wasn't in the least interested in the William Faulkner novel that lay open on Ben's bedside table.

Something shifted in the shadow of the pines off toward Rosie's left. She watched for it with her peripheral vision rather than turn her head and search boldly. The figure moved again. It was not skulking, just moving slowly between her house and Ben's. She did not recognize the man at first, now that he was obvious and she could openly look at him. His hair was too short for the reserve where the fashion ranged from slightly longer to long. His was very close cropped. There was a familiarity about the face, as hard as it was. Somewhere beneath the mask of sternness lived someone she once knew. He came out of the shadows, walked up, and now stood in front of Rosie.

"Well, drop kick me Jesus. How you doin', Rosie?" the humour in the words did not make it to the voice so the statement sounded bizarre.

"End over end, not to the left or the right, straight through the heart of those righteous uprights." Rosie completed the football cult song. Her light laugh brought out the missing humour. "I'm not bad." She put down her beadwork. "How's Lester?"

"I'm standin' here."

"I can see that."

"I mean, they never broke me, I'm still on my feet."

"I can see that."

"I made it. I made it home again." Lester put one foot up on the first step, so that he stood at a slight angle to Rosie, so that he could deflect any possible attack.

Rosie sat squarely in front of Ben's door, protective. "So what brought you back here?"

"It's home, I guess. Nowhere else for me to go."

"I was just wondering 'cause you don't have any family here anymore."

"Don't have family anywhere I guess." Lester looked around, then looked back up towards Rosie again. "I guess you're about all the family I got Rose." He closed his mouth firmly at the end of her name and stood there, with his mouth clamped shut so that his chin protruded. He looked strong, standing there with his hands tucked neatly away in his hip pockets, one foot on the step and his chin forward. Strong, and resolved, not begging. "Here I am; take it or leave it," his body language spoke.

At that particular angle with the light filtered by pine, Rosie saw the resemblance between Lester and his mother. It was in the oval of the face and the proportions of cheekbone, chin, and brow.

"Have you eaten?" Rosie began gathering up her sewing. She would take him into her home. She was all the family that he had left and a cousin could never be turned away hungry, no matter what kind of a cousin he had been.

She was thinking about her Aunt Ester as she fried up the last few pieces of chicken. Ester had only been a few years older than Rosie, a young aunt, young enough that there were a few occasions that they had played together. Aunt Ester sitting with her little niece and putting dolls to bed. When they were a bit older but still young enough to be just playing, Rosie remembered Ester at parties, dances and laughter.

Then Lester was born and Rosie saw less and less of Ester. Then came Rosie's children and she saw even less of her young aunt and her hard working husband and their house on the other side of the village. She had seen Lester occasionally as he grew up.

She glanced his way. He looked almost swallowed by the large over-soft couch as he tried to figure out the remote control for the television. Rosie liked that couch. It fit her. It clearly did not fit Lester.

Where did he fit? Anywhere? She wondered how he had fit in at the penitentiary. Maybe that was the place for people like Lester. Maybe, who knows? Maybe he changed. Maybe in all that time locked away he had gotten over being mean. Somehow Rosie doubted it, not the power of an institution to affect change, but that anything could ever be done to take the meanness out of Lester. He seemed to have been born that way. Rosie remembered comments that followed him around the community and now resurfaced in her mind a quarter-century later. The voice of an old man, an Elder spoke clearly in her memory again. "He didn't get that way from either of his parents. He brought that with him when he came here."

Rosie scraped the chicken from the splattering grease, careful not to leave anything stuck to the pan. The trick to brown chicken is in the turning. Rosie took pride in her ability to cook. It was something that she did well even, as was often, with very little to work with.

It made Rosie hungry to watch Lester eat. She left him at the kitchen table and took a cup of tea into the living room and visited with her friend the television. There wasn't enough chicken for both of them. Oh well, it wouldn't hurt her any to miss a meal now and then. She could call it dieting. She was happy that at this time of the day there were fewer food commercials, not like Saturday mornings when junk food lured children.

She suddenly wanted her children, any of her children, to be with her on the couch, to cuddle together against the danger. Yes, Rosie allowed herself to admit that she was afraid of Lester, had always been a little afraid of Lester. Even when he was a child, she had watched him closer than the children he played with, and never let any of her children play alone with him.

There were rumours that he tortured little animals, kittens and puppies and a squirrel that he knocked from a tree with a slingshot and kept alive until old Cecil found him and killed the squirrel out of pity. The stories had drifted through the community and followed Lester as he grew up.

"Norma went out with him; he said he was taking her to a movie in town. She won't do that again."

"You know how Wesley is, he wouldn't fight back if he was being murdered. Why would someone pick on a guy like that?"

But, everyone is entitled to change right? Why couldn't Lester have changed? He was human. Maybe he learned something in prison. It was possible. Rosie changed channels, pointed the remote and clicked. Crime scene investigation was not something she wanted to watch at this moment. People can change, unless they're born that way.

He had put his dirty plate on the counter by the sink. Rosie quickly scraped off the bones and remains into a small plastic pail, something for the dog, hated to waste. Her hunger grabbed her again when she saw how much meat he had left on the bones. She was tempted to clean them off, nibble that morsel that hung loose, crunch the gristle from the end. Chicken bones should be clean. But she didn't want him to see, didn't want to embarrass him.

She finished her night routine; she had never gone to bed with a dirty dish in her house. The thought of it might wake her in the middle of the night and torture her. She did something however, that she had never done before and double-checked that the door to her bedroom was tightly shut before she put on her nightgown.

The sun shimmered on the black pavement, created illusions of cleanliness, of smoothness. Ben let the truck find its way around the curve, his hand easy on the wheel, relaxed. Summer exploded in colour where prairie met parkland, where farmland stopped pushing against the boreal. Aspen blended with large white spruce together in a canopy that protected the forest floor from direct sunlight. In the shade places, currants, and highbush cranberries grew in tangles. Where sunlight splotched the floor, broad spreading sarsaparilla protected the earth and buried its roots in the loam and lichens. Farmland ended in abrupt straight lines against walls of trees, a final fatal attempt at agriculture abandoned to scentless camomile and thistles. The fence lines that never did keep the deer from the fields sagged in droops of rusted barbed wire where some of the staples still held the strands to leaning posts rotted at ground level.

South, Ben cringed. Why in hell was he going back. He had a good life. He had everything that he needed. No one bothered him, no one asked him for more than he was ready to give. Time had become his friend, rather than his master. Mornings like this should be for good brewed coffee and bird song. He contemplated turning around, but Monica had asked. A promise is a promise, is a promise. Ben's word was more powerful than his wants. He clicked on the cruise control, set it to a hundred and nine, breathed in and let his shoulders relax as he breathed out.

Moccasin Lake pulled at his mind, or perhaps he was repulsed by the rush of glass and steel on asphalt. Rosie's actions yesterday perplexed him. He had expected her to behave like an old gossip, rush to his cabin as soon as Monica's car left to find out all that was to be found out. She had not even asked. Perhaps she was unaware? No, she had moved the silk scarf Monica carelessly left on the arm of the chair, picked it up, checked its authenticity by gently touching it against her cheek, nylon feels different up close, and laid it carefully aside before sitting.

Ben's ability to predict had developed over the years to the point now where he was confident in his gift. Rosie disrupted that confidence. She had not behaved in the manner he expected. That was it, wasn't it? She had not acted the way he, Ben, expected. His gift was secure. He had not used it. The gift was something outside of Ben. It was different from rationality, closer to intuition. His prediction of Rosie's behaviour was premised upon his ego, upon his sense of importance and superiority. He had assumed that Rosie would behave badly out of jealousy. A good lesson in humility, the most necessary ingredient of the gift.

He was going south, again. He touched the control and CBC radio entered the cab of the truck.

" . . . *is a ticking bomb. President Wright went on to say that the US policy in Canada served the needs of the continent.*

France again demanded that the US withdraw all troops from Canada and Mexico and restore local government, however it did not repeat its threat to withdraw from NATO."

"Chavez speaking only for Mercosaur, again warned the US to stay above Panama."

"To analyze yesterday's developments CBC spoke with Professor James Henderson of the Frazer Institute." A previously taped voice that produced well-enunciated though quick words came on. Designed for media, Ben thought, as Professor Henderson rattled.

"The overall change to Canadian society has been minimal if we consider the possible paths that Canada could have taken following San Francisco. We would have either had to develop our own security at a cost that would have nearly bankrupted the country given the state of our armed forces, or remain open to sneak attacks. If the United States had not assumed the responsibility for our security, we would have been forced to impose the same or possibly more stringent measures. Given the impoverishment of Canada's armed forces prior to the annexation, it is reasonable to imagine that in order to maintain security, Canada would have had to implement measures to compensate for the inability to adequately patrol, and enforce. Homeland Security has the manpower, equipment, and technology to ensure we are not open to sneak attacks, without undue physical intervention. The rights of Canadians living under Homeland Security are actually less infringed — if infringed at all — than if we were to have implemented our own necessarily less-adequate systems to protect Canadians from destruction."

Ben turned off the radio. Hugo Chavez was shaking hands with President Obama in his mind again. He remembered those days of hope and dismissed them. Hope, what a desperate word.

He rode in silence for a few minutes, listened to the tires hum against the pavement and turned the radio back on.

" . . . that's absolutely not true." The voice of a woman came through the speakers. "This suggestion that the US annexed Canada only because of oil has huge holes in it. First of all, in today's world, security is more important than transportation or industry. Neither would be of any use without freedom from sneak attacks. And," her voice rose an octave, "and, the suggestion flies in the face of the fact that Venezuela produces nearly as much oil as we do. If the issue was truly only about oil, Chavez would not be in power. He would not be free to spread hatred and would not have the resources to polarize the Americas into north–south blocks."

Ben turned the radio off again.

"Of course Wright never invaded Venezuela. He might take it, but he could never keep it." He spoke to the steel and glass. "Afghanistan showed them that." The morning sun warmed his left shoulder through the window. The warmth melted his irritation, eased it away. Best not to get caught up in it. It's just a distraction. The important things are being ignored in all the hype, he reminded himself as he adjusted the airflow controls, considered the air conditioner control, decided against it. Better to have fresh air even if it was warm. Next winter he would appreciate a little warmth.

He gently pushed against the CD that protruded above the radio. The player pulled the disc into itself and a male voice sang over an acoustic guitar. *On a slow road home . . . Can't dance in lumber jack boots, Can't sing with a mouth full.* Ben listened to the song nodding his head. "You got it, Jay. You understand."

~

Ben recited Monica's instructions to himself, "Four miles south of Aberdeen, go east at the alkali lake, a little ways up the road the house is behind a row of spruce on the right," and finally turned the truck onto a lane that led up a hill. Behind the row of spruce that stood bough to bough, out of place on the prairie, a two-story farmhouse, swallowed in their shade, spoke of neatness and care. The entire farmyard was an example of the owner's personality of part thrift and part perfectionist. The grain bins to the south of the yard stood aluminum sentinels in parade, rank laser straight. The west of the yard was taken by an over-large brilliant-white barn with red trim, its doors open to the light and air.

A man in blue jeans and short-sleeved shirt that ended above tanned, muscled arms walked out in front of the truck and waved Ben toward the Quonset.

"Park her in there." He pointed.

"Abe Friesen." He put his hand out as Ben climbed from the truck inside the galvanized metal half-cylinder building. "Best to keep the vehicles out of sight." He shook Ben's hand, two strong pumps. "You must be Ben Robe. Monica said I wouldn't mistake you. Well come along, everyone is staying up at the barn; there's beds up there and we'll do our business there or in the shop."

Ben looked around the Quonset as they walked toward the sunlight of the open sliding doors. He recognized Monica's car near the end of the row, dwarfed beside the out-of-place Chevy suburban truck. Someone has money for gas, Ben thought, as he followed Abe past the other smaller vehicles toward the light.

"Hey, Ben, glad you made it." Monica wrapped her thin arms around him and kissed his cheek. "Let me introduce you around. You've obviously met Abe. This is his place. He's our Amnesty connection. This is Ruben." She led Ben to a stout, reddish-coloured man whose face was offset by his bright green John Deere hat.

Ben let Monica lead him around the loft of the barn and introduce him to Roger Cardinal, Stan Jolly with a pony tail, Philip Maurice, Joan Lightning, pretty, with a gentle hand shake, Billy Two Horses, the very elderly Rose Bishop who sat in the comfort of a stuffed arm chair befitting her age, Leslie Iron . . . the names and faces blurred as Monica continued introductions to the thirty-odd people in the loft of the cleanly-swept barn.

"Make sure you help yourself to the food. Coffee is Brazilian dark roast thanks to Faye. She'll be on later today with updates from South America."

"You might not remember me, I was in your class in '06." Ben tried to remember, but the face in front of him did not register. Neither did the name, Roland Nataways. Ben did his best not to offend, with a smile and a shake of his head. "Don't matter," Roland continued. "I did learn a lot in that class. Looking forward to your talk this afternoon." Roland's tanned face framed by long black hair smiled back. But the smile was strained, forced as though through a history of pain.

"*Everybody.*" Abe's voice reverberated through the loft. "*Everybody,* were going to be starting in a few minutes, if we can get you to start taking your seats. Are you ready Joyce? You're up first." He turned slightly toward the grey blonde woman to his left. "Ready Abe." She brushed her cotton dress with a quick motion to remove a stray crumb of zucchini bread as she stood, gathered a thin bundle of notes from a packsack and headed toward the end of the loft where the large wooden doors stood open to the morning sun and the prairie sloped away to the horizon.

"Welcome to the first gathering of the coalition of thinkers." Joyce began as soon as most people were seated. The remainder quickly filled their coffee mugs, grabbed fruit or biscuits, or breads from the table at the back and hustled to the rows of mostly metal folding chairs interspersed with wooden kitchen or an assortment of plastic lawn chairs. The few cushioned arm chairs were all taken.

"First up, I'd like to thank Abe Friesen for risking his home for this gathering, and to remind people not to be outside in groups of more than four or five. If you are outside during a break, remember to come back in and allow someone else to enjoy the sunshine and air."

A chair scraped beside Ben and he did not hear Joyce's next words. He glimpsed the stylized NS tattoo on the smooth-dressed man's right hand as he manipulated a full coffee mug, trying not to spill. He nodded to Ben as Joyce continued. "The food at the back is courtesy of the Mennonite Central Committee. Who would ever have thought that MCC would make the list."

Ben turned at the sound of a woman loudly clearing her throat coming away from the food table. She smiled broadly, raised one hand in the air and balanced a bottle of juice and small plate of pastries.

Joyce continued: "Two weeks ago Wright added them to the list of dangerous organizations. Not the Evil list, they're not full-fledged terrorists, but they are on the watch list. Congratulations MCC. You must be doing things right. I would also like to thank Native Syndicate for the security. So very important. They've assured me that the buildings have been swept and it was their workers who put up the screen." Ben glanced up at the mesh wire tacked to the ceiling. Someone hoped that it would interfere with surveillance. "Everyone should know not to have brought cell phones or platforms. If you have, please remove the batteries. Abe has put his property at risk by allowing us here, let's not put him at any greater risk."

Joyce looked down at the notepad in her hand. The yellow lined paper matched the sunny dress she wore, matched her brightness, a compliment to the youth of her spirit despite the age lines that crossed a face devoid of makeup. "Stan Rediron is here, he'll be up this afternoon, along with Ben Robe as we hear from the academics. This morning is dedicated to reports. Native Syndicate's own Richard Ross is here personally with updates. And a very special guest, we finally get to see the face behind the words. 'That Jack' is here." The screen on the ceiling vibrated with the sound of applause and foot stamping.

"*Easy, easy!*" Joyce raised her voice to cut through echoing din, used both her hands, the notepad in her left flapped pages as she waved down the volume. The applause cut itself short as people realized the risk.

"Finally." NS tattoo grinned at Ben. Ben shrugged. "That Jack," NS tattoo nodded toward Joyce. Ben shrugged again.

"You don't know That Jack?"

"No"

"Wait. You, sir, are in for an awakening."

NS tattoo stood to speak when Joyce introduced him as Richard Ross, president of Native Syndicate.

"I know a lot of you. I know a lot of faces here and I'm looking for That Jack." Richard stood in the spot vacated by Joyce and exaggeratedly twisted his head back and forth. "Patience, I guess, patience. The Elders say to be patient. I'll have to wait like everyone one else to find out. Whoever you are, Native Syndicate thanks you. If it weren't for you we would never know what was going on." Richard stood with his hands behind his back, his feet firmly flat on the floor, a military stance, straight. It was a stance that suited his long arms and lean build. "Native Syndicate knows business. That's where we started and that's where we are. The new world order is the old world order. Was a time NS was just another street gang, on the margins, doing business, taking care of our own. Today nobody can call us a street gang. We are more than the streets; we are more than the jail house. We are the first line of defence. The machine needs grease and NS knows about grease. If we stop the grease, the wheels will stop turning. To that end we have hit targets in Alberta, and recently took a truck of yellowcake. Now that is terror. That is absolute terror. It doesn't matter that we ever use it. We don't have to use it. We just have to have it and they know we have it, and they are terrified."

Ben cringed. A thought rushed at him: *An angry dog is never as dangerous as a dog that is afraid. Cornered animals fight the hardest. Even a spruce grouse will attack if it is afraid.*

⌒

Ben looked around the loft. It was unpainted, bare wood angled rafters held what looked to be tongue-and-groove planks faded uniformly with age. The loft had appeared neat when Ben entered up the stairway, now he noticed it was more than that, it was immaculate. He looked back to the stairway landing where the floor should be worn. It was, but not to any depth. Someone had used a polishing stone to smooth the floor to an even depth. This was not a barn loft, a place to store bales of feed for the animals below, it was a meeting room. There were no stories left, nothing hanging from the rafters that would tell of usage; a bit of horse tackle that would tell of a day's ride, a pitch fork or a set of tongs that would tell of a day's work, the stories had been erased. Even the nails that might have held the stories had been removed from the wood of the rafters that longed to tell their own unedited version of events.

There was some applause at the end of Richard's talk. Ben did not clap; he couldn't bring himself to endorse that level of violence and anger. The tall, straight woman who Joyce introduced as Mary Wiens, co-chair of the Mennonite Central Committee was another who had not applauded, who tried to keep a neutral face, but the pain had seeped through the pores of her very scrubbed forehead and deepened the shallow lines around her blue-green eyes.

"And it's thanks to Mary and her team that we have the wonderful food." Joyce stepped easily away, leaving Mary at the front of the loft waiting for the gentle applause to subside.

"Thank you," she unconsciously brushed the lapels of her short jacket, let her hands fall to the folds of her matching long skirt. "Thank you." There was no hint of nervousness in her strong voice. "Mennonite Central Committee is dedicated to peace. To that end we have spoken against Wright's agenda. If peace is counter to the principles of freedom and righteousness, then MCC and its members belong on the list. We have been accused of assisting listed people and organizations. If giving food to the hungry and shelter to the homeless is a crime, then MCC is happily a criminal organization.

The room stirred.

"But, I don't believe that it was those activities that resulted in the listing of MCC. We had among our membership and on the executive, people who believed that living in a free and righteous society was a worthwhile objective. I was among them. As things changed, MCC participated with Homeland

Security's Freedom and Righteousness Division. We were at the table, we prayed with them, we actively participated in planning for a new democracy. The ideals were high — an end to corruption, efficient government, clean streets, a strong stand against crime, and an end to drugs and dependencies — all worthwhile objectives. We even closed our eyes to some of the means employed to achieve those objectives believing that they were intermediate and immediately necessary means.

Mary paused, not for affect. It was just a good place to take a breath. Someone cleared their throat in the otherwise silent loft, breaking the tension that had begun to build. Mary continued, "The listing of MCC had nothing to do with our activities. We were applauded at Freedom and Righteousness meetings for our humanitarianism. We were listed one day after MCC made a presentation advocating the return of control over education to our communities. It has been the goal of Mennonites since before the first immigrations in the last century to live in our own communities and to have our own schools.

"In fact it was the promise of control over education that enticed Mennonites to immigrate in the first place. When we were betrayed, when the government took education away from us, many of our brothers and sisters left Saskatchewan for Mexico.

"We now have communities in all three American Divisions." A movement of feet and straightening of bodies rustled the loft. "I mean countries, sorry for the slip. I might have spent too much time at Freedom and Righteousness, I am beginning to sound like them.

"But the point is, it wasn't until we began to demand our own schools, our own historical demand, that we were listed."

Be glad you didn't have to go to residential school. The thought surprised Ben as he leaned into a rafter.

Mary recovered from her slip and launched into a strong denunciation of the shift in government policy. "Freedom and Righteousness has an education agenda, an agenda that includes God, uniforms, bright shiny silent children, and no teachers' unions."

Monica offered, "Do you want to get some air? Let's go outside for a minute."

Ben wasn't comfortable walking out in the middle of a talk, but followed her anyway.

The sun stood a little before noon, high in the large blue prairie sky; its heat held a bit of sting to it as Ben and Monica stepped from the barn shadow into its direct blast.

"How about over there?" Monica pointed toward a yard swing; wooden, freshly painted, white, bright white, even though it stood in the shade of large Manitoba maples.

"That caustic sun is another reason to never stand out in the open."

"It's warm," Ben agreed. "Do you really worry about satellites, or are you just caught up in the hype?"

"No, no it's not just hype for me. It really makes me nervous out there. Ever since Lac La Biche." Monica leaned forward on the bench. Ben leaned back and gently pushed with his feet. The twin benches of the yard swing eased into motion. "Did you ever see any pictures of that?"

"No." Ben shook his head.

"Doesn't matter. They couldn't do it justice. The hole is fifty feet deep. It's not like a bomb. The dirt isn't thrown out. It's gone, vaporized, what's left is turned into glass. The house was gone, the people were gone, everything. Imagine being here one second, the next second you're not. So simple, so efficient, drop a tungsten rod from outer space, the rest is gravity and friction. By the time it hits the earth it isn't even metal anymore. It's vapour, and that's what our friends are now, vapour, nothing to bury, nothing to say good-bye to."

"Even in a bunker." Ben kept pushing and relaxing, the swing to- and fro-ed.

"There was no fucking bunker. They dropped that thing because they could, or they just wanted to play with their fucking toys. I don't know. Maybe the bastards believe their Bolts From Heaven are the equivalent of biblical brimstones. *Shit.*" She leaned back hard into the bench and jerked the smooth sway of the swing. "They weren't in a bunker. They were meeting in a house, just a house; they weren't even in the basement. Betsy said she went out to pick up KFC. She was telling me that she was a little pissed that they sent her, a woman. That's what she was thinking as she walked back, that she was being discriminated against because she was a woman, when she thought she saw a falling star during the day." Monica relaxed, the swing flowed and ebbed.

"There were no bunkers; there were no terrorists. They picketed the highway to Fort McMurray. They walked in front of semi-trucks with signs that said "Yankee Go Home.""

"What about the burning trucks, the roadside bombs?"

"That wasn't us. I don't know who was doing that. Maybe the bastards themselves."

"That's too hard to believe, that they're killing their own presumably to justify attacking innocent people. It's too much of a stretch. Sorry, Monica, even if it's true, it's too much."

"It's easier to believe the media is it?"

The swing stopped, stood silent. Ben and Monica both leaned back into their respective benches, distance between them. The moment stretched out, waiting for Ben's answer. He dodged the question.

"There was nothing else going on? Just peaceful picketing? Nothing else?"

"Not the violence that was reported. No burning trucks. Oh, there might have been a few flat tires, sugar in the fuel tanks, things like that. We don't have the money for explosives. N75 is expensive."

"You'll have to excuse my ignorance. But what is N75."

"Synthetic nitroglycerine. N75 is seventy-five times more powerful than the old traditional stuff."

"Seventy-five times the power of nitroglycerine, that boggles the mind." Ben started the swing moving again. "And where would you get it from?"

"From them." Monica pushed a little to contribute to the swing.

"From them?"

"Of course. The world's biggest armaments dealer, who else? Want an assault rifle, a detonator, poison gas, whatever — you buy it from the masters of war."

"You just go up to Homeland Security and put in an order, or what?"

"It's about that easy, except you need a lot of money. The people dealing are probably HS during the day, at night they look after themselves. Steal a bit of technology and put it on the street. Take a nice little bundle home to retire on, part of the benefits package."

"You've got to be kidding."

"No I'm not. The only people making N75 anywhere in the world are the Americans. If you want it, you have to buy it from them." Monica looked away toward the distant dry field of wheat struggling in the baked earth to grow. "How much?"

"How much what?"

"How much do you have to pay for N75?"

"Oh that, last I heard you could get a kilo for about ten thousand Ameros."

"Expensive."

"Depends what you're buying it for, and hey, when you consider its power it's really seventy-five kilos, right."

On the way back to the barn Monica took Ben's hand. He cringed, not outwardly, as he let her hold his calloused fist; he was twenty-five years older than her. Even a short ten years ago would have been different. But now, now he was nearly to the end wasn't he? It would be good for him to have company into these years. But what about her? She would be left alone again. Better she found someone else. Someone a little closer to her age.

~

When they re-entered the loft Joan Lightning had replaced Mary Wiens in front of the open doors.

"Those stacks either have to come down or they have to find some way of removing all the sulphur. They represent the greatest ecological disturbance ever experienced in Canada." The sun behind her highlighted the silver in Joan's otherwise long loose black hair. "The price you are paying for your cheap gas, and some of you might not think your gas is cheap at over five Ameros a litre, but it is — the price you are paying does not come close to the cost to the environment. Tons of sulphur and nitrogen are pumped into the atmosphere every day through those stacks, tons that precipitate out over what we used to call Saskatchewan and Manitoba all the way to Labrador. We once had viable fisheries in the north. Well, viable for the families who fished, maybe not so viable when we had to sell through government-run marketing agencies, but viable for many families.

Joan spoke quickly, though not out of any nervousness. She spoke at the speed her mind worked, the way her mind worked, all in a tumble, a rush. Her hands flashed around her body, indicating directions, wind patterns, and precipitation "When sulphur connects with moisture, and there is still moisture coming over the mountains, it might not seem like it on days like today, but there is still moisture up there. The sulphur connects with H_2O, add a little heat and we have H_2SO_4, sulphuric acid. It's not so much what comes out the exhaust pipe of your car as you burn their product, though that's still a problem, it's what comes out the stacks at Fort McMurray. Those refineries, and I don't care that they cost billions of Ameros each, I don't care that Wright makes a big deal out of their investments in the North Division, I don't care about the employment lies — Fort Mac is automated to the point where there aren't that many jobs anyway. With the unions broken, those jobs don't pay more than subsistence.

"I don't believe I am about to say this." Joan touched her face, ran dry fingers across her cheek, "I have spent my life caring about the Earth, about peaceful co-existence; I have never advocated violence. But when I see the pine trees all turning red, when I see withered birch, when I see mushroom pickers walking for miles looking for what used to be abundant, when I see fishers hang up their nets because there is nothing left to catch or going out on snow machines to spread lime on their lakes trying to counter the acidity, when we have winters without enough ice to go out on the lakes, then I have to side with the people who are fighting to stop the oil companies. Every day that production is stopped is a day when tons of sulphur are not pumped out onto the land.

"Keep it up, you guys, keep up the fight, keep hindering them." Her hands were clenched into fists. "It might not seem like it, but every truck that you slow down, every person that you take out of production, everything that you do that slows them down has a very real effect on the land. Some days it might seem like we're losing. When we look at the McKenzie River and see the sheen of oil all the way to the Arctic, it might seem like it is too late, When we see the bare rocks of the Precambrian Shield, without even moss, let alone trees, you might think it's too late. But we have to do something, anything." Joan's hands stopped, she stood outlined in the sunlight of the doors, solid, straight, her dark eyes stared ahead into the group, looked into their eyes, tried to look into their hearts. "Anything," she concluded.

Ben took his coffee to the big doors that were open to the prairie, and just stood there and looked to a hazy horizon and let his thoughts flow outward across a parched earth. What was he going to say to this group? His lecture notes on supremacy were leftovers from a university and a life from before this rampant insanity.

A car rolled off the grid road and through the wire gate into the yard, crunched gravel in the drive and into the open space between the barn and the house. It was one of those newer models, with the oversize wheels that always made Ben think of Red River carts. He stepped back out of view as Abe crossed the yard to speak to the driver.

Roland Nataways stood where Ben had intended to go.

"Hey, Professor"

"Roland, right?" Ben stepped around him into the shade.

"Yeah, Roland, from your seminar class in '09."

"Right. So how are you, Roland?"

"Good, good," he shuffled until his back touched the wall.

"So what've you been doing recently?"

"Not much now, used to do a lot of work for NGOs, or Near Government Organizations as I liked to call them. First Nation stuff, even worked with the Metis for awhile, development work."

"Not anymore?" Ben liked this young man. He wasn't that young, in his thirties probably. It was hard to tell. The face was of a person who had stood too close to suffering and the pain etched itself into lines.

"Not anymore. Not much you can do when they erase your bank accounts. The last place was an organization trying to feed city kids. I guess we weren't Christian enough or something. The virus not only took out the organization's accounts but nearly everybody who worked there. Some of us tried to keep going. I was hunting in the river valleys and bringing in deer meat. But after a while I just couldn't afford it. Not just the gas, ammunition was getting crazy even then. That's what I'm talking about next."

"The price of ammunition?"

"No, I did two-and-a-half years in Dakota Max for a break, enter and theft. I broke into a gun shop trying to get ammunition. Tell you something, Prof. It was some of your ideas about supremacy that got me through. I forced myself to remember that the reason they were treating me as lesser was because they needed to, that someone else was treating them as lesser. I wanted to thank you for that."

What to say? Ben had no response. He nodded. Stood in front of someone he did not remember speaking to about an abstract subject and found his words returned to him in concrete, as solid as the prison walls of Dakota Max.

When it was Roland's turn to speak, he did not begin with his experiences in the ten-thousand inmate privately run prison. Instead he started by asking if anyone had heard the news this morning. People stirred, but no one answered.

"Well, Wright announced that Canada is a ticking bomb." He paused, "Rhetoric? Not at all. The words were chosen and deliberate. Ticking bomb is a justification for torture. Of course it's never called torture. It's called aggressive interview. In American law, if you know that there is a ticking bomb, and you know that your prisoner knows when and where the bomb will explode, you can legally torture him in order to save lives. That is the first criteria in Homeland Security directive sixty-six. The second criteria is that only enough pain is inflicted that the prisoner responds. Other criteria in the directive include that the interviewer is supervised and decisions about the amount of pain, type of interview, and duration are decided separately. The directive also requires that a trained doctor be present. Note, that the directive does not stipulate the training, nor that the doctor be licensed. Most medical associations refuse to license anyone specializing in pain administration. You would think that any real doctor, someone dedicated to the alleviation of suffering, would refuse to participate, especially since they would have to give up their licence. But, with the amount these guys are getting paid there is no shortage. Nearly double your wage, and work less than half the amount of time. It's a gold mine.

So we have in one room the prisoner, the supervisor, the interviewers, and a medic and a book of guidelines. This is all designed to make torture as humane as possible. Only the amount of pain necessary is administered, taking into consideration the health of the prisoner, the prisoner's tolerance levels, and the permanence of the affects. Very clinical." Roland's own words were clinical, precise. He spoke as though he was reciting, without feeling. "What it does, what all this procedure does is remove any emotion on the part of the interviewers. As long as they are within the guidelines, anything goes.

"Pain can be physical or psychological. Degradation is allowed in the guidelines, except that they cannot use the prisoner's religion, race, or nationality. Women cannot be degraded on the basis of being a woman. No homosexual forms of interview are allowed. The Christian right disallowed that after the prisoner abuse at Abu Ghraib prison in Iraq. Neither can a person's age be used to administer degradation. These prisoner's rights are interpreted by the supervisor. The first target to maximize both physical and psychological pain is always, always the prisoner's testicles."

Roland took his hands from his pockets, put them behind his back, hesitated then let them fall to his sides, limp.

"When Wright said that Canada was a ticking bomb, he put every Canadian prisoner into the interview room. The first criterion has been met. It's estimated that forty percent of the population of Dakota Max is Canadian. The interview wing of that place is going to be busy.

"For those of you who don't know, Dakota Max is owned and operated by Greatwest Electric. It is a privately run, for-profit prison. It does not pretend to be a correctional facility. There are no programs. The prisoners are not there to learn to correct their ways. Prisoners in Dakota Max are there to suffer for their crimes. Period. There is no such thing as a private cell. Prisoners are in ranges of one hundred. These are open rooms with twenty-five foot walls. The roof is made to open outwards. Once a day for an hour the roof opens, rain or shine, and the prisoners get their mandatory one hour of fresh air; bake, boil, or bath."

Roland smiled, a little upturn at the corners of his mouth that only tightened the hard lines of his bony face. He ran his hand across the leg of his pants, maybe to remove the sweat from his palm.

"Food is supplied by whatever fast food company bids the lowest — breakfast, dinner, and supper, wrapped in tinfoil and tissue." The tiny smile faded.

"It's quite the place. Prisoners and guards never interact. Control is accomplished with knockout gas. Seal the range, pump in the gas and all the prisoners go to sleep. End of riot. But what is a riot? Guidelines again. A riot is any major disturbance. Couple of guys get in a fight, in comes the gas. Somebody gets sick. Either the prisoners themselves take him to the door, or they go to sleep so that the guards can enter the range safely. Someone throwing up can be a major disturbance.

"Of course there are calculations that need to be made. Too much gas and prisoners die, too little gas and some will not go to sleep. The guidelines allow for a death rate of less than one percent. Some people have suggested that they over use the gas to keep the population down. I don't think so. Greatwest Electric is paid by the person; purposely killing prisoners is poor business."

He shifted slightly, so that the sun at his back completely shadowed his face. He was too far away for Ben to read his emotions. His words were flat.

"The beds are moulded into the floor. Can't hide a shiv under the mattress, there is no mattress. One personal affects locker moulded into the headboard, room enough for a toothbrush, a pocket book, maybe, definitely room for a Bible. Razors aren't allowed, nor haircuts; after awhile everyone begins to look pretty shaggy. The guards however are all very clean-shaven, helps to differentiate.

"So that's the ranges, pretty bare. Entertainment is each other. Next to the ranges are the interview facilities, and finally the exit. With Greatwest Electric in charge, of course the exit is the chair, no fatal injection, or gas chambers at Dakota Max. It's full current. Nothing cheap or chintzy about the exit."

Roland was about to step away from the spot where the sunlight washed the loft floor when Monica stood quickly. "Roland, a question please. You said that you didn't think that GE used gas purposely to make room for new prisoners, but isn't it true that DM is chronically overcrowded? That gas is used routinely? You were there. You are our best source of information. We've heard rumours that DM is mostly filled with Canadians, but the official reports suggest that DM only has about a forty percent Canadian population. You, yourself said that it's estimated that the Canadian population there is about forty percent. What's the real count?"

"Yeah, I was there." Roland's voice was softer. He was not listing facts now. The words came from a place deeper than the top of his mind. "That's why I don't think it's intentional. I did two-and-a-half years. I was only sentenced to two. The judge was Canadian, Roberts, right over there in Saskatoon. He had to give me a two-year sentence instead of two years less a day where I would be sent to a provincial jail. The charge involved weapons. I did two and a half because Greatwest Electric gets paid by prisoner days. It was accounting that kept me there. Purposely killing prisoners is not good business. It doesn't pay."

"But you were gassed?" Monica continued to stand.

"More than once."

"We know that. How many times? How many did you see killed?"

Roland inhaled, he opened his mouth but no words came out when he exhaled. He raised his hands palms up. "I don't know. I lost count. Gas is colourless, odourless. You're talking to your buddy and your tongue gets numb and you wake up on the floor with a real bad hangover. You don't know how long you've been gone, hours or maybe days and some people are missing. Sometimes you wake up in a different range, or you wake up and your buddy is gone. Maybe he never woke up, you hope he's in another range, you even hope he's gone for an interview."

"But you have seen people killed by gas."

"Yeah, a few."

"How many? In two-and-a-half years, how many?"

"Eight, eight that didn't wake up, that were still in the range. But I don't know if they were brought back or not. We carried them to the door, stepped back behind the yellow line, and they came and got them. I hope some of them were revived, but I don't know. I really don't know."

"How many Canadians? What's the real count? Or do you know?"

"To be absolutely honest, I don't know. It's possible I was only in ranges of Canadians. Maybe they kept Canadian and American populations separate. In the ranges I was in, the population was eighty, ninety percent Canadian."

A woman in a dark denim jacket raised an arm in the air. "Were you tortured?"

Roland took an unconscious quarter step back as though hit in his centre by the question. Looked straight ahead, his voice flat. "I was interviewed."

"What did they do to you?" the woman's voice held a hint of intrigue.

"That's not something I want to talk about." Roland spoke direct, clear, purposefully blunt.

"But, do you know why you were," the woman paused, "interviewed?"

"Ticking bomb. I was involved in a weapons offence. Maybe I knew something about the resistance. I can tell you that I told them every damn thing I knew. Everything, every name of every person I ever knew, everyone who ever spoke badly of Americans, every conceivable plot that I could imagine."

The memory stirred a strong emotion. Roland paused; he seemed to be struggling with it. His face contorted slightly; he opened his mouth but no words came . . .

"Okay everyone, lunch." Abe stepped from where he leaned against the soft-coloured wood rafters into the patch of light and stood beside Roland. "Thank you, Roland." He shook his hand gently.

Ben sat quietly during the break, enjoyed the fresh tomato in the sandwich of homemade bread. That tomato must have been picked not more than yesterday; it tasted of earth and water and vine.

"You have a nice place here." Monica washed down her sandwich with a bottle of cranberry juice.

"You're not the only one who thinks so," Abe responded. "Had a fellow in here this morning determined he was going to buy it even if it wasn't for sale. Had to threaten him before he would leave."

"So, how much was he offering?"

"Started at two, by the time I was pushing him into his car he was up to four."

"Four, four what, four million?" Monica's cranberry juice held suspended half way between the table and her mouth.

"Yup, four million for a quarter section, an old barn, house and Quonset. I only paid a hundred and a quarter for it thirty years ago."

"So what's the big jump in real estate. I thought the market was collapsed."

"In the big cities houses are almost worthless, but that's because everyone who can afford to is trying to move out into the country."

"Frisco." Monica got it. That was the answer.

"Frisco." Abe agreed. "So the people in Vancouver, Toronto, Montreal, move out to Saskatoon, Regina, even Prince Albert. People in the small cities move out into the country."

"But, four million Ameros. You could live a long time on that." The cranberry juice made it to her lips.

"Not as good as I live here. What's four million? Doesn't mean anything. If the price of land doubled again and it was eight million, I'd just end up using it to buy another place. If I sold out to that guy this morning, I'd just spend it all this afternoon pushing someone else out of their home. Naw, it wasn't much of a deal."

"Or you could buy yourself a condominium in Toronto."

"Yeah. Right." Abe bit into his sandwich.

⌒

"*Waweyatsin.*" Ben pushed the word out, imitated his grandmother's voice, clear, concise, tinted with a little smile. "Good for you, you deserved that, now learn from it," she had said.

"*Waweyatsin,*" he repeated because the word meant everything he wanted to say to these people seated, fed, legs outstretched, still holding bottles of water, relaxed after their meal. "Now you know what it feels like." The sun through the open doors warmed his back, grandfather was behind him, he could speak from here. "Canada's assertion of superiority over Aboriginal Peoples lasted for centuries. The Americans have only been here for a few years. Get used to it. They are not going home. No matter how much you cry, no matter if you say it's not fair, they lied to us; they are not going away. Make all the rational arguments you want — this is our land, our home, you have no right to come and take it away from us, you are a bastard nation, supremacy knows no logic. The supremacists are here because they thoroughly believe that it is for your own good. And, maybe it is. Maybe Canada has to learn what it feels like, what it feels like to be dominated, to be moved off the land, to be re-educated. We tried to tell you for decades, but you wouldn't listen. Way back at the Treaty signing, some of our ancestors tried to explain to you that you had no right to take, that you had to ask. But you wouldn't listen, so *Waweyatsin*. Good for you. This is what happens to you when you act like you're better than someone. Someone or something will come and put you in your place."

The room stirred, legs crossed, backs straightened, legs uncrossed, arms folded, unfolded.

"Don't worry about it. Learn from it. The same thing is going to happen to the Americans: someone is going to come along and put them in their place. Doesn't matter that they have the world's biggest army, doesn't matter that they have robot soldiers, or half-robot soldiers, doesn't matter they can kill you from outer space, that they have lasers that can fry you, or Bolts From Heaven to kill you in your hole. They're still humans. They only believe they are God.

"That is what supremacy is about, that's where it came from, from people who thought they were more Godly, the chosen ones. They were given a flaming sword by their God to beat down the other. And, with that flaming sword they became part of their God, the hand of God, doing God's work, bringing light to the darkness. Little Gods."

Ben had not intended to start speaking so strongly. The notes in his shirt pocket, scribbled on a single sheet of paper, folded into a tiny square, held an outline of an academic lecture on the premise of colonization. He had wanted to talk about Albert Memmi and *The Colonizer and the Colonized*, how that book had started a revolution in academia. Albert wasn't wrong. He had written about what he saw, what he felt, his truth; he had put a name to the oppressor, the colonialist. Then when people around the world began to see that Albert's truth was their truth, the academics followed with their papers and journals until the discussion had become dominated with the dichotomy of colonization. But, even though the academics had imagined such things as a postcolonial period, nothing ever really changed. Colonial discourse never captured the heart of the phenomenon. People still died of hunger, of AIDS, from bombs, and loneliness.

Ben had wanted to tell these people, this gathering of children of colonists sprinkled with children of the people of the land, that colonial discourse was about the symptoms of a doctrine of supremacy, that supremacy needed analysis. But his grandma spoke instead. He heard her laughing and the sound of that almost forgotten tinkle filled him and he laughed. He stood in front of the people and let his laugh rumble; it came up from his belly and out into the loft. It spread. Magic. Someone tittered. Someone else chuckled. Then the loft rattled with the laughter of everyone. It was funny that Canada experienced its own oppression, ironic and irony needed to be laughed at, to be laughed away.

$\sim$

On the quarter section of land to the south of Abe's place, Ruben Weebe looked at the silent cell phone in his hand. The phone had died in the middle of his conversation with his daughter in Saskatoon. It squealed for a full second, sharp and shrill in his ear, then died. He put the phone in his shirt pocket and tried the landline, the old-fashioned phone. It was silent, dead. The screen on the computer in the den was blank. "Ruth, Ruth." Ruben walked through the house calling his wife. She was in their bedroom, putting clothes into the closet. "Ruth, something's up." She looked to Ruben's face for the answer, ignored his words. The face said urgent and she followed him out of the house, to the shelterbelt where the caragana grew thick, to the spot they had decided upon, created, a spot with a hollow where two people could hide. Ruth sat silent and hugged Chico, a spaniel who squirmed but kept silent as though he too knew something was coming.

$\sim$

Ed Trembley leaned against last year's straw bale, enjoyed the sun in his face, on his shirt, heating his legs through the denim. He read from a little blue book that he had read many times, started over at the first page. He spoke the words to the sky.

"*The people of Venezuela, exercising their powers of creation and invoking the protection of God, the historical example of our Liberator Simon Bolivar, and the heroism and sacrifice of our aboriginal ancestors and the forerunners and founders of a free and sovereign nation."*

The remainder of the page he read louder, as though an oath, *"To the supreme end of reshaping the Republic to establish a democratic, participatory and self-reliant, multiethnic and multicultural society in a just, federal, and decentralized State that embodies the values of freedom, independence, peace, solidarity, the common good, the nation's territorial integrity, comity, and the rule of law for this and future generations, guarantees the right to life, work, learning, education, social justice, and equality; without discrimination or subordination of any kind; promotes peaceful cooperation among nations and furthers and strengthens Latin American integration in accordance with the principles of non-intervention and national self-determination of the people, the universal and indivisible guarantee of human rights, the democratization of imitational society, nuclear disarmament, ecological balance and environmental resources as the common and inalienable heritage of humanity; exercising their innate power through their representatives comprising the National Constituent Assembly, by their freely cast vote and in a democratic Referendum, hereby ordain*

the following:"

Ed stopped for a breath and in the new silence heard the sound of diesel engines, then the sound of military bombproof tires on gravel. He slid down until he was lying in the short barley and looked toward the grid road that ran straight and bare across the earth from horizon to this rise of land where he smelled the dryness of the soil inches from his face. He did not need the binoculars; the convoy of Hummers raised a cloud of ashen dust that sped toward him and toward the people in the loft at Abe's place.

He kicked the straw away from the blocks of industrial Styrofoam, poured the plastic bottle filled with a mixture of diesel fuel and gasoline, struck a lighter to the fuel, waited a long second and another, until he was sure that the flame had taken, then ran; ran hard for the river to the east, to the valley where the river wandered between steep banks and willow and aspen grew thick and would hide a person from the sky. The burning foam billowed a greasy black finger of smoke upward behind him as he ran crouched. His knapsack with the little blue book, a little food, water, a mirror, and an industrial laser bounced on his back.

"Out! Out!" Abe yelled into the loft. People scrambled, all laughter died at the sight of the black smoke in the distance climbing into the sky.

"I'll drive," Monica almost shouted as she and Ben ran up to his truck.

Abe stood at the gate and designated the vehicles leaving the yard, spreading them to the four directions. "Go north and at the first intersection take the west road."

⁓

"So, how's your day going?" The ferryman leaned into the passenger side window of the truck, rested his elbows on the door.

"So far, so good," Ben answered.

The flat-bottomed ferry angled in the current of the South Saskatchewan River, followed the cable strung shore to shore. Its diesel engine rumbled and tugged against the cable, drew it into the little house and expelled it again out the other side, drawing the six-car ferry toward the far bank of aspen and the winding lane of gravel that ended abruptly where the heavy wooden planks marked the landing. Monica stared straight ahead, watched that landing draw incrementally closer.

"Would it be all right to get out and walk around a bit?" Ben asked.

"Oh, hell, yeah, everyone does. People just love to see water." The ferryman stepped back so that Ben could open the door. "Takes about seven minutes to get across," he added as he turned to talk to the driver of the older Ford pickup.

Ben walked over to the ferry edge to watch the flow of beige water slip away down the river valley. He stood looking out downstream, felt the moisture rise from the water, and wondered about the others. Was anyone still there when whoever was coming arrived?

A lone gull tilted wings and glided beside the ferry, flashed white in the sun as it banked away and turned to follow the river. There's a shortage of birds, Ben thought.

Even though he was only a few kilometres from the university, Ben had never been here before. The river rippled far below its high-water marks. Willow and a coarse grass that he did not know had begun to grow on the dark mud flats abandoned by the shrunken river. But, it was green. The valley was lush in contrast to the burnt prairie it cut through. Comforting to see trees, green trees. Ben wanted to be home, the lake still blue, and evergreens.

Monica wanted to be anywhere but here, exposed, dependent, trapped. Any minute and Homeland Security would appear on that far landing that was taking forever to arrive and they had no way out. Jump into the river and swim back? If she had to. Could Ben make it? Probably not. Too old for that. But, maybe. Ben was strong. Built like a bear. Her mind tumbled as it raced.

Off the ferry the truck spun gravel as Monica turned sharply to the right, away from the main road onto a track that led into the aspen and willow, over a rise, down again, a curve then the truck was pointed at the steep wall of the river valley. The track ran at an unbelievable angle upwards. She pushed the four-wheel drive button and eased the truck into the climb. It pointed its hood at the cloudless sky and began the ascent.

"Hey, just a second." Ben was reaching around for his seat belt.

"Not to worry. I've done this before. Well, I haven't actually driven up here. I had a boyfriend when I was in school who used to bring me here to show off his truck. It's okay. Really. We just have to take it real slow and steady. These Toyotas are incredible here. Watch."

The engine changed tone as it began to work, a deeper sound, a grumble. It climbed the impossible bank upwards, pushed Ben back into the seat until all he could see was the blue of a hot, dry sky.

～

Ed Trembley ran hard for the green fringe at the edge of the dusty summerfallow. He found a strength that rose from somewhere, maybe from fear, felt it first in his chest, then in his legs as he increased his stride, stretched new legs and ran. The Hummer's engine grew louder behind him. The last vehicle of the convoy had turned as it passed the smouldering foam to give chase.

The river valley dropped quickly away from the prairie, a near vertical drop of a dozen metres where the cut bank had crumbled, hid at its top by a bramble of chokecherry and thistles. Ed charged through this brush, dropped suddenly and slid feet first down the steep decline. The roar of the Hummer and the sound of smashed brush behind him became the sound of an airplane over top of him. The driver of the heavy truck must have intended to run Ed over and now it was too late. The Hummer dropped grill first, slammed into the valley wall where the cliff bottom became a steep slope. It flipped end over end through the aspen, bounced incredibly high after each crash landing and ended on its roof in the swirl of the river bend.

Ed slid down the slope, caught a broken tree trunk, put his feet under himself and quickly worked his way to the vehicle. Two Homeland Security officers looked to be dead, hopefully dead. They were not breathing. Another black shirt gasped unconscious, twitched in the back seat. A fourth, opened his eyes when Ed pulled at him. Ed slammed a fist between the eyes and they shut.

The river current made canoeing tricky. The added weight of two bound black-uniformed officers in the small canoe helped to balance the craft fore and aft but made the canoe ride deeper in the water, made paddling harder. Ed followed the shoreline, less current here in the shallows, as he worked his way upstream, pushing the paddle into the mud as much as he drew strokes in dark water. Following close to the shore also meant that it was unlikely that he would be seen as he neared the city with his hostages. It was always good to have something to trade with.

~

"You're going out on the lake? You just got home." Rosie walked behind Ben as he attached the boat and trailer to the truck, removed tarpaulin and straps. He turned and looked directly at her. The little girl was there again, for just a second it was little Rosie.

"Do you want to come along?"

"Me?" Rosie suddenly found herself flustered.

"Yes, you. There's no one else here." Kindness filtered his words. "I wasn't talking to the puppies." The first bold pup toddled out from under the house, fell, picked itself up, and pushed forward. "Hey, you." Rosie picked it up by the scruff, cradled it in the crook of her elbow. "You're too small to go wandering around." She gently rubbed the soft pink of its belly before kneeling, bending further than her body was accustomed to and placing the puppy back in the tumble of its siblings between the outstretched legs of the yellow dog. "What you going to name her?"

"Haven't thought of it."

"If you have a dog it has to have a name."

"Then we'll call her Betsy or something."

"No, what was the name of that dog you had when you were a kid?"

"Duke," Ben answered quickly through a flash of memories.

"Yeah, him." Rosie remembered

"Can't name a female dog Duke."

"Then Duchess. She's kinda royal, don't you think?"

"Seems fitting to name a dog after monarchy, sort of irreverent. I like it."

"Good start, but you've got six more under there."

"Wait and see what they turn out to be first. They'll tell us what their names are."

"Got to be careful what you name a dog. Give a dog a dumb name and they'll live up to it. My kids once named a dog Mischief. Good enough of a name, but it wasn't until I got them to change it to Maggie before that dog stopped getting into everything."

The lake reflected high clouds at its north end, grey against dark water. The boat skipped across shallow waves as it followed along the west shore, to the lee of the line of hills. They rode in silence for an hour. Rosie sat with her back to the wind, huddled in a large red-and-white life jacket and watched the lake flow away behind Ben at the tiller. The boat curved across from west to east then followed that shore south, back to the community, and Rosie found herself on the rickety wooden dock wondering what the purpose of the trip had been. She tried to help Ben reload the boat to the trailer, finally gave up and just stood out of the way.

"He'd only been away for a few days and he was lonely for the lake," Rosie concluded as she hoisted herself into the truck.

She stayed around all afternoon as Ben kept himself busy, not the busy of a man obsessed with doing, going, rushing, but the busy of maintaining space, putting away the net that hung on two wooden pegs on the cabin wall where it had been left to dry, folding it into a plastic tub so that it would come out easily the next time he used it. She kept up a steady stream of talk while she helped pick the dried weeds out of the net mesh. She talked for the sound. Now that her children were gone, her house silent and empty, she felt a vacuum that needed to be filled. And there was of course Lester. Ben needed to know everything about Lester, but she needed to be careful not to cross the line into idle gossip. Ben accepted Rosie's voice as background to their visit; let the words fill the space around them. The words were kind, and gentle, simple stories, everyday things that happened, remembered and brought back to life.

"And there we were with no spare tire, on a dirt road and nothing but prairie all around us. It's times like that when you really appreciate trees. Imagine four little ones, in the winter, and no way to make a fire to keep them warm."

"Yeah, I like trees."

The silence that followed did not last very long. Long enough to be noticed, but not long enough to be noteworthy.

"You like trees, but do you like children?"

"Sure, yeah sure, I like children."

"But you never had any. You went out of your way not to have any."

"Well, children didn't fit into the life I was living." He placed the last of the net into the tub, and in picking up the tub to carry it to the shed, turned his back to Rosie.

"And, what kind of life was that, Ben?" She followed him to the shed, waited just outside as he put the bin on a shelf where it was less likely that mice might make a nest in it, then followed him back around to the front of the house, and pulled up the other white plastic chair and sat looking out toward the pines.

"It was a good life. I don't regret any of it." Ben reclined his chair until it rested against the wall.

"Not even that you didn't have any children."

"Especially that I didn't have any children. Children have to pay for the wrongs of the parents, and I don't want anybody to pay for me."

The sun poured into the trees. Rosie leaned a little more into the chair, let it take her weight. The pines breathed back into the warmth of the day. She leaned forward. "We all have to pay, both you and me have had to pay, whether it was for our parents or grandparents, don't matter we had to pay. But it was still worth it."

"How about your kids, Rosie?" Ben altered the direction of the conversation.

"Good, they're all good. Elsie called the other day. Her and the baby are doing just fine. Dougie, well Dougie is doing what Dougie does best. Working, always working that one. Takes good care of his family, but someday he's going to learn, maybe the hard way, that working and money aren't everything. And Theresa, she's still the same, spends all her free time with her daughters, so much so that she isn't even looking for a man these days."

"I haven't met that one."

"Theresa?"

"Yes, Theresa, I haven't met her yet."

"Well, she won't come back to the reserve for whatever reason. When she wants me to come visit she sends me a bus ticket. Sure would be nice to get the girls up here where they can really play and away from that city. But she says that with her work she doesn't have time. I don't know, I think they get vacations." Rosie rattled on and Ben reclined a bit more and listened to her tell him about her favourite subjects, her children and grandchildren, and she didn't ask him again why he did not have any of his own.

~

Lester Bigeye waited.

~

"Your father?" Monica looked at the young man, his dark hair and grey eyes were too familiar. "Your father?"

"My birth certificate says 'father unknown'."

Monica watched him over the rim of a paper cup of dark fresh-roasted coffee. She liked it this way, with that slight taste of paper. She liked the Broadway Roastery where they sat outside in late-morning shade across the old concrete bridge where Broadway Avenue began its journey south. The trees at the edge of the parking area were beginning to catch some of the rising sunlight. Early, she thought; it was too early in the day for such a conversation. To early, too soon in her busy life to speak about it. Her son had phoned her and asked to meet. Twenty years. Twenty years it had taken him. At the eighteen-year mark she had wondered. Would he come looking? Was he still alive? But the war had come and she had other thoughts to occupy her. Now he was asking for his father.

What right did he have to question her loyalty? What right did she have not to tell him? He was asking for his dad. He wasn't begging, trying to manipulate her. He wasn't demanding, forcing. He just sat there, young, innocent and at the same time impossibly old, jumped from being a baby held by the nurse as Monica sat in the Royal University Hospital bed and signed the forms clipped to the board in front of her. She answered the questions, except for the one that asked for the father's name, wrote "unknown" in the space, clamped her mouth shut, loyal. She would not give him up. Would not ruin a good man for her mistake.

"Benjamin, Roberto, Bird" the young man paced the words. "You gave me those names. I wondered why those names."

"Roberto was after a writer I really enjoyed back then. I thought Roberto Unger was going to change the world."

"What about Benjamin?"

The hard question.

"Your father was my professor. The reason I gave you up for adoption, well one of the reasons — I was young, a student,

student poor." Monica tried to find words, exact words to walk the line between truth and honesty. The rush of traffic on the street beyond the line of trees didn't help. "He would have been fired if anyone found out he slept with a student." The wind out of the north swirled around the building, chilled the morning, chilled Monica. She zipped her light nylon jacket a little higher. Maybe they should have sat inside, it's always safer inside. It was his idea to sit out here, exposed.

"So you named me after my father. Was it his idea to give me up for adoption."

"*No*! No, I never even told him I was pregnant. I've never told him. He doesn't know." She caught herself, "I never said that I named you after him."

"But you just did." Benji smiled to himself. "It's okay, Mom. Strange to call you Mom. But it's okay, it's all right. It feels right." He fumbled for words among his tumble of emotion. "It doesn't matter that you were sleeping with your professor, nothing wrong with that."

"I wasn't sleeping with my professor." Monica spoke firmly. It had to be made clear. "We made a single mistake, once. It only happened once. And I never told him."

~

"Can I borrow your phone?" Lester stood in Ben's doorway, narrow in the frame of the solid door.

"Sure, what's wrong with Rosie's?"

"Cut off. She didn't pay the bill."

"Oh."

He wasn't listening in on Lester's conversation, he was trying to read his book. He was trying to concentrate on the complex structure of, *As I Lay Dying*, appreciating that a writer could have the courage to write a five-word chapter.

My mother is a fish. Lester spoke loud enough to interrupt his concentration. Unwelcome words into a hard plastic device pulled Ben away from the 1920s America into the now.

"I want to talk to the chief then.

"Somebody at the band office has to be able to help me."

Ben was forced to listen to one side of the conversation.

"Somebody has to pay for my meds. I can't. I thought you guys were there to make sure our Treaty rights were respected.

"That's bullshit. Tell them that the Treaties promise a medicine chest. They can't do that.

"You don't understand. I need those meds.

"But, I need them.

"*Shit!*" the phone snapped shut. "Shit." Lester put the phone on the desk. "Shit. At least in jail I didn't have to pay for them." He walked heavily to the door and out into the day that waited for him; not a good day.

~

"It's just the AIDS drugs that they refuse to pay for. I still get mine covered," Rosie explained later as she poured her afternoon cup of tea.

"Homophobia."

"Yeah, seems like they want to let all the queers and faggots die of natural causes as quickly as possible."

"Lester's gay?"

"Naw, well, I don't know. He got infected in jail, maybe he is. Or maybe he was, who knows. He got AIDS in jail that's all I know, maybe from a man, maybe from a needle. Doesn't matter. He can't afford to buy his own meds and he doesn't believe in Indian medicine."

"Worried?"

"Not for myself. Doesn't matter if he dies in my house or in a hospital. I'm not worried about catching it if that's what you mean. But I am worried about Lester, what's he going to do now? Not that he does a hell of a lot anyway. Just sits around the house like he's still in jail waiting to get out. I guess if you spend a lifetime waiting for something, when that something happens, when they let you out of jail, all you know how to do is wait. So Lester waits. He's still waiting."

"Any idea what for?"

"Like I said, it seems like he is just so used to waiting that the waiting is what's important and not what he's waiting for. Lester probably doesn't even know; maybe now he's waiting to die."

"How much is your phone bill?" Waiting for Lester to die was too much; he did not want to think about it.

"Never mind. It's awright."

"What do you mean it's all right? Rosie you need a phone." Ben drained the last of the warm tea, placed the cup firmly back on the table.

"Don't worry about it." She waved a dismissive hand. "Got it covered." She raised an eyebrow showing Ben the twinkle in her eye.

"Tell me."

Rosie looked into her teacup because it was some place to look away from Ben's questioning gaze, took her time answering, enjoyed the delay. "It's being taken care of."

Ben waited, knew better. Rosie would tell him. Rosie wanted to tell him, wanted to tell him and drag it out as long as possible.

"My daughter can't phone me."

"Uh-huh."

"So, if she can't phone me. Then what?"

"I'll bite, then you can't talk to your granddaughter."

"You're getting closer, but no cigar."

Ben shrugged.

"If she can't phone me then what?"

"Then she — " Ben was caught in Rosie's little game — "then she sends you money for your phone bill."

"No silly. Then she comes to visit."

"Okay." Ben did not sound convinced.

"Really. I figured this out long time ago. I think my mother used to use it on us, and I know my grandmother, Old Jeanie, could do things like that. Sometimes I get lonely for just one of my kids, and a day or so later that kid either phones me or comes home.

I remember when I lived with Delbert, locked away down there on the prairie. It was like I was his prisoner. Once in a while I would suddenly need to come home. Just a real strong need to come home and see my mom. I'd make Delbert bring me back, or I would take the car, use all our money for gas. He never understood. Used to drive him nuts. Anyway, when I got back, there would be nothing wrong. My mom would be here. Happy to see me, play with my kids, all smiles. But, she never said anything."

"And, you couldn't phone?"

"My mom refused to have a phone in her house. No, when that feeling came over me, there was nothing I could do but come home. Remember when we were kids, out sliding or playing and our parents would stand outside when it was time to come home and yell our names?"

"Uh-huh." Ben remembered. "Well you went home right away. You didn't take one more slide down the hill when you heard your mom calling. You just went home."

"Yeah, I remember." It was a good memory. Children playing on snow in moonlight. "You could hear her yelling a mile away. *Roseeeee. Roseeeee..*"

"Yeah, like that. I think they trained us to come. Do you think she could really yell loud enough for us to hear her from the hill? Try it."

"Well it was quieter back then."

Rosie smiled at Ben.

"Really, there weren't so many cars and things."

Rosie kept smiling.

"I guess not eh."

"No, there was something else going on. Anywhere we were, we could hear our mothers calling us. Well, I'm using that on my daughter. Right now she's packing my granddaughter in her car and by tonight I'm going to be bouncing that little girl on my knee. Just wait and see."

⁓

Ed Trembley looked into Corporal Rick Fisher's face, didn't like what he saw there and slammed a fist into it. "Fuck you." He had nothing else to say. "Fuckin' black shirt," was the best he could do here in the basement away from the light, away from the sky, away from wind, and rain, away from people and living things. His hate churned his stomach, acid rose and filled his mouth, bitter and sour. Rick's lip bled bright in the fluorescent sheen of the workroom light, dripped down the side of his chin. He wiped his face against his shoulder and tried to glare back at Ed. He did not have the strength for a powerful glare and the look came off an indifferent "I don't care," rather than "Fuck you back."

It might have saved him from another punch in the face. Ed stood back, kicked Rick in the thigh, once, not hard.

"Listen prick. If your buddies fuck with Abe, I'm going to fuck with you the same way." Kicked him again, harder. Ed's fear eased back into the place that anger had filled. If they tortured Abe Friesen, would he talk? Of course he would. Everyone did. How much did Friesen know? Why the fuck did he stay there? Why didn't he run like hell the way everyone else did? Scatter, spread out, hide, mingle, let the masses absorb him. They couldn't watch everywhere at once.

Ed left his tied prisoners in the dark, no sense wasting electricity on the likes of them, and went again upstairs to sit by the window and watch the street, to pace to the back porch and search the alley, watch and pace and watch.

⁓

Benji felt safe again as he drove out of the city that was not a city at all but only a very large prairie town. He was mildly surprised by the extent of paved roads as he took the four-lane north. He had half expected to need a four-by-four.

He caught a glimpse of himself in the rear view mirror as he adjusted it, held it at that angle for a moment and looked, really looked. A narrow face stared back, a thin delicate bone structure covered with healthy, gently tanned skin. The hazel eyes below the high forehead peered quizzically back at him. Who is this man? They seemed to be asking. Who are you?

I am the son of my father, Benji answered the reflection. Do I look like him? Are those my father's eyes? Am I the younger version? He turned the mirror and the highway unrolled behind the truck.

His adoptive parents were old from the time he could remember, too old to play out on the street with, too old to wrestle with, too old to have their own children, and too old to participate in the life of the one they'd borrowed. He made up stories for himself about his real parents, exciting stories, and put in the good parts from his favourite books. Old James and Joyce helped with that, they gave Benji all the books he wanted with time and space to read in the quiet Toronto two-story stone house seven blocks from the library.

Today Benji would meet the fairy tale hero. Would he tell him? Would he say "I am your son come for my inheritance; teach me your art, teach me your science"? Or would he play the practiced role. "I am a gem merchant, see my emeralds and my rubies. How they sparkle." Would he dazzle his father's eyes, eyes that must be hazel like his own, blind him with colours and lead him away from his horde. Take his money and slip away? Into the den of the old dragon and out with a bag of treasure, the rite of passage. Would he then be able to walk free of the legend, write his own saga, become his own fairy tale hero?

Benji checked the map again. Highway 11 to Prince Albert, then Highway 2, north past the National Park, then east to Moccasin Lake I.R. What does I.R. stand for? Is it like R.M. rural municipality as they say out here, or maybe it's something like County Seat. It didn't really matter whether Ben Robe lived in an Intergalactic Region or not. Today the son would come and get his inheritance. I.R. equals Inheritance Restored.

~

The sun marked a bright circle on the whiskeyjack-grey sky, poured its heat through the high empty clouds and stuck Rosie's blouse to her back. The day stood still and damp. A boat ride would be nice today; maybe Ben would go out and set a net or just go for a ride. She hung a dripping sheet on the clothesline, straightened it so that it would dry without wrinkles and pinned it in case the wind she hoped for would come. She stood for a moment and looked, at the line of sagging laundry, at the sky that promised her it would not rain. Not that rain would be so bad. The laundry could stay out for another day or so, nothing urgent there; when it dried she would fold it and take it inside — inside a house that was too hot to sit in for long, too hot to run the clothes dryer.

Lester was in there in front of the television. The heat didn't seem to bother him in his sprawl on the couch. It was his couch now, blanket and pillow, duffle bag under the end table. It used to be Rosie's favourite place, tea and cupcakes and gentle entertainment. Now it was coffee and a full ashtray and the violence of professional sports — even golf seemed tinged with anger when Lester watched it.

Rosie left the laundry basket on the steps to the back door and was going to see what Ben was up to. She walked around to the front of the house to where the path through the trees began. Lester could make his own lunch. He'd make a mess, and Rosie would clean it up. But that could wait until evening when the house cooled down. Rosie had never in her life gone to bed with dirty dishes left out. Learned from her mother, "Spirit things come in your house at night and eat off your dirty plates." It disgusted her to wake up in the morning to find dishes on the counter from Lester's late-night meals.

The black Jeep Cherokee turned onto the track that led from the road to the front of Rosie's little house, too quick — it bounced at the big pine root that ran out under the north track. Not someone from around here; Rosie waited. The truck rolled, slower now, up to the front of the white-sided house. The driver rolled down the window with a buzz of electricity. She waited; too unseemly for a Native woman to talk to a man through an open window, cross her arms and rest her elbows on the door and wiggle her bum in the air. She sat instead on the front step and exercised a little of her deep learned patience.

The man was young and had not earned patience yet; a young man with a salon haircut, and shoes, brown leather; slacks and short-sleeved shirt that matched; black and tan.

"Hello." He stood not so tall in front of her.

"Hello yourself."

"I'm looking for a Mr. Ben Robe." Benji shuffled his feet, tried to find a more casual stance, couldn't, and stood exposed like a schoolboy in front of the master, or a penitent in front of the priest.

Rosie recognized the young man, though she had never before seen him. She smiled inwardly and the smile found its expression on her face.

"A Mr. Ben Robe, are there more of them?"

"I'm sorry?"

"It's okay. So what you want with Ben?"

"You know him?"

Rosie nodded. "Oh yeah, some days I know him better than I want to."

"He lives near here?"

"Right through there." Rosie pointed with her mouth to the beginning of the path through the trees. "Come on, I'll take you there." She stood up quickly. She wanted to be there when these two met.

Ben's son was here, her daughter would not be too far behind.

～

Leroy was eleven months older than Elroy. Their mother must have been too tired to have much imagination left over when she named the second son, still angry that the myth, you can't get pregnant when you're breast feeding, wasn't true. People who knew the boys occasionally mixed up which one was older, Leroy was born January tenth and Elroy celebrated his birthday a month earlier on December ninth, other people thought the boys were twins. Twelve siblings knew the boys' correct ages, but even their mother Agnes occasionally mixed them up. She mixed up the names and ages of all of her children, and had to recite their names in chronological order to find the one she wanted. "Rudy, Barbara, Martha, Elizabeth, Leroy, Elroy, Mary, William, Jonas, Stewart, John, Peter." Never in Agnes's life had she blamed the church for inflicting the denial of birth control on her, and had dutifully attended, a ladder of children behind her, every Sunday.

Tomorrow, Elroy would be in that church for the last time. Tonight he lay in his finest, white buttoned-up shirt, hands folded, head on a satin pillow, eyes closed, his long bright white hair shiny in the fluorescent light. He looked to be almost smiling. "Peaceful" people remarked when they looked into the casket. "He looks so peaceful." It gave them comfort that Elroy's suffering was over.

Leroy was at the wake. He sat with his friends at a table near the exit doors of the school gymnasium, close to outside where he slipped every once in a while for a cigarette. Later in the night when the crowd thinned out he would exercise Elder's privilege and smoke inside. It would piss Elroy off if he knew. Elroy had never smoked, probably because Leroy had started first.

The competition between the boys had begun as soon as they laid eyes on each other. There were some here tonight who remembered when Leroy and Elroy played hockey, never on the same team, each pushing to excel over the other. If Elroy scored a goal, Leroy would be nearly manic to get one as well, skates shattering ice, driving for the net. The boys played hard, elbows and shoulder checks, and sometimes, but not often, a teammate might think that he could drop the gloves against the opposing brother, only to find that brotherhood was far more powerful than team spirit. Fight with one brother, you had to fight both, regardless of which team they were on.

Ben sat across the gymnasium from Leroy at the same table as Rosie and Elsie and little Rachel whom Rosie had on her lap. Benji was there, not knowing what to make of the situation. This was completely foreign to him, not only that an entire community would attend a wake, but that they were all Indians, and he was half-Indian too. He didn't know how to behave, didn't know the protocol. This should be a solemn occasion, the death of an Elder, but people were teasing and laughing as though it were nearly a celebration. All of the stories he heard were either ribald or otherwise twisted to evoke laughter.

There was the story of how Elroy had beaten Leroy in a poker game and went home wearing Leroy's jacket and driving his truck. Time blended and someone else — Benji could not remember the person's name, had trouble remembering all the names of all the people he was introduced to, all the new relatives — this someone, this relative, told of another famous poker game.

"In them days they used to play for muskrat pelts, I guess. In the spring when trapping was over they used to come down here to the Hudson's Bay post from all over as soon as the ice was off the lake. This is way, way back — thirties, forties, maybe. My dad said they used to play anywhere. Someone would spread a tarp on the ground," the unknown relative spread his hands to show Benji, "and a trapper could either win big or lose a whole winter worth of work. Anyway, this one game it was old Kooch Primeau, I barely remember him, he was old when I was a kid and that was a long time ago, and he was losing. He took out his false teeth and threw them out there. And they say old Duncan Bird, he was chief here after that, he took out his glass eye," the unknown relative made a plucking motion, "and threw it on the pile and said 'I see you.'"

When the laughing died down, when the last person had repeated, "I see you," Ben explained to Benji. "Old Duncan Bird was my mother's grandfather, so your great-great grandfather."

"You're related to just about everyone here." Rosie adjusted Rachel in her arms, tried to find some way to ease Benji's tension.

"Be careful who you try to snag." Elsie liked Benji. He was a good-looking young man.

"As if. He knows better than to try to snag at a wake — if he wants a woman he'll come back at pow-wow time." Rosie was really reminding her daughter of propriety.

"Am I related to — ?" Benji even had trouble remembering Elroy's name. He indicated the casket in the centre of the gymnasium with a nod in its direction.

"Sort of, I guess. Leroy and Elroy were my dad's cousins I think." Ben was not sure.

"No, The Moosehunter family came here from the west side," Rosie remembered. "Your family has been here since Treaty; they came later. Your dad and Elroy and Leroy used to go work together in the logging camps, but they weren't related."

"So I'm not related to him." Benji wondered what he was doing at a wake for a stranger.

"Well, sort of. Leroy married a Bird woman. She's been dead now for so long I can't remember her name, but she was your Granny's cousin." Rosie had a good memory for lineage.

Benji guessed from the white casket with the red C logo blazoned on the open lid. "He was a Montreal Canadiens fan."

"No, that's Leroy getting his last lick at his brother. Elroy had to cheer for the Maple Leafs because Leroy cheered for Montreal. Everybody knew that." Even Ben knew of the famous rivalry. "It was Leroy that got to pick the casket."

Rosie warned. "Leroy thinks he got the last laugh at his brother. But Elroy's still around, Leroy better watch out. Tricks from the Otherside can be cruel sometimes."

~

Before the midnight meal was served, Ben was asked to go sit with the Elders.

"How come not you?" Elsie asked Rosie.

"Oh, that's just Leroy, wants to talk politics with the men. He sees me here with my granddaughter. Knows I'm with family, and hey, he paid me a compliment. I'm not old enough to sit with them." Rosie smiled at her daughter. There was no insult, none intended, none taken. Rosie lifted the little girl under the arms until she stood on Rosie's lap looking at her, looked long into her granddaughter's face, at the way she held up her head, felt the strength in the legs as the baby tried to stand against her thighs. "I can't place you little one. You look like someone from long ago but I don't remember who."

"She looks like her father."

The silence that followed was broken by Benji. "Where is her father?"

A longer silence was broken by Elsie. "He was with the Pats,"

Benji offered a bewildered look.

"PPCLI" Elsie responded.

The look deepened.

"Princess Patricia Canadian Light Infantry, defending Toronto."

"You're a widow." Benji didn't know what else to say. He felt a tinge of guilt. The man died defending his city, died defending him, defending the school where they had gathered and waited, cringed at the shriek of sirens.

"I never think of myself that way. Bert never even got to see his daughter." Elsie read his guilt. Offered a gentle explanation to ease what she thought was concern. "He was home on leave, we got together, I got pregnant, then the Americans came. I hardly knew him. But I am thankful to him. He left me a bit of himself, a gift."

~

The food served at the Elder's table ran over the paper plate in front of Ben, deer meat stewed in its own juices until it fell apart, pan fried pickerel, baked bannock, fried bannock, a little scoop of dry pounded meat placed carefully on the edge of the plate where it wouldn't get soaked by the juices from the deer meat; it should be dry, eaten with fingers and dipped in butter, and of course, every wake needs potato salad, lots of potato salad.

"Bet you didn't eat like this at that university, eh Ben?" Roderick nodded toward Ben's plate as Ben tried to keep the blueberries thickened with cornstarch from running off, with a flimsy plastic fork.

"Can't say I did." Ben decided to just eat what was there instead of trying to dam the flow that was defeating him.

The talk during the meal was general, "Who shot the deer?"

"It was Red who shot the deer, of course."

"That Jemima sure can cook."

"You bet, taught by her mother, still knows how to make pounded meat, don't see much of this anymore."

Then when the plates were nearly empty, a few bits of bannock remaining, too much for old men to eat who didn't work hard all day anymore, a young woman served hot tea from an overlarge black enamel tea pot, black tea that smelled of the handful of muskeg leaves thrown in 'just for the Elders', poured into white Styrofoam cups.

Leroy stirred a second plastic spoonful of sugar into the tea. "So, Ben," he leaned back into the hard chair, stretched old muscles, "What you make of this Treaty process that's goin' on?"

"Haven't followed it too close, I'm a bit out of the loop." Ben talked around the bit of baked bannock dipped in the blueberries he had saved for the last.

Roderick said something that he had repeated all his life, something his father had repeated to him: "Can't change the treaties; doesn't matter what, we can't change the Treaties."

"Treaties were with Canada. There is no more Canada." Leroy set the agenda for the coming discussion.

Roderick remained adamant. "Treaties were with the Queen. Queen is white. I take it Treaties were with white people, Canadian or American shouldn't matter."

"AFN don't seem to think so. They're negotiating as we speak," Leroy invited.

"Who said AFN could speak for us."

Ben joined, "That's the thing, isn't it. Who negotiates for us? If we are a Nation, if we really are Moccasin Lake Cree Nation, then we should be the ones who are at the table."

Roderick stood firm, "There shouldn't be a table. We've been saying now for as long as I can remember, Treaties are sacred. If that really means something, then we have to act like it and not run to suck up to whoever has the power right now."

Leroy moved the discussion forward, "There's talk of moving all the Cree onto one reserve, a big reserve like they got down in the States, instead of all these little ones."

"Can you imagine, eh, living beside Plains Cree and Swampy Cree — and where would everybody hunt? Won't work."

"But think about it." Ben was into the discussion. "Just think, if we had a big enough of a land base for us all, if we joined together, we might be a Nation. The reason we have tiny little reserves is because when we were negotiating Treaty, Commissioner Morris didn't want us to have big reserves. He wanted to break us up so that we would be weak and less of a threat to Canada. The reason we have small reserves here is because Canada had a weak military. They were afraid of us."

"That's not how I heard it." Leroy couldn't stay out of the discussion. "The way I heard is that the old chiefs selected their own reserves. Now here William Charles was chief at the time of Treaty and he selected this place for the reserve. Some of the people wanted to be over to the west where the national park is now, but William chose the biggest lake because it would have the most fish."

"Yeah, that's how I heard it too." Roderick agreed. "From what I been able to piece together, my family have lived here as far back as anyone remembers. Always lived here beside this lake. Used to be, we lived up by Thunder Mountain on the west shore, but when the reserve was made we moved here to the south end. But you know what will happen if they make one

big reserve. They'll move all the Indians from the South up
here. Government always wanted to do that, put the Indians
on empty land."

Leroy's hand paused, held the cup of tea half way to his
mouth: "Not anymore, I don't think. They might move us
down there on the prairie so they can take the resources from
here. Americans need lumber and paper and especially our
water. No, my bet is if they move us, they'll march us down
there to the empty prairie; we'll walk another trail of tears."

Roderick disagreed, "Naw, they been taking the resources
from here all along. Used to be they could just buy it and
our government would sell it to them cheap. Didn't matter
that we were here or not. Just look at all the highways in this
country. They all run north–south. That's not so that we could
get around. That's so that they could get the resources out of
the North and sell them to the Americans. Won't be anything
different now."

"Well, Thoreau sure as hell didn't sell us out, did he?" Leroy
shot back.

"All the ones before him did, didn't they? And look
what happened when he shot off his mouth." Roderick was
beginning to have fun.

Leroy the Liberal had to defend Thoreau, had no choice at
all now. He would have to stay a Liberal because Elroy died a
Conservative. Roderick knew well the ferocity of his cousins'
politics. He had mediated between and around them for
decades, knew of the rivalry and the campaigning, and who
put up more posters for their party and who attended more
rallies, and speeches, and who was the best prime minister
and who was running the country into ruin.

"People blame him for bringing on the invasion, but you
got to remember he stood up, them spineless Conservatives

had us in so many wars defending the bastards that the world was beginning to think we were the same country. That's probably why nobody's helping us now. Sure Thoreau was a radical, that's why we elected him, remember. It took a Liberal to stand up to the Americans."

"Well the way I remember it, Liberals weren't much better before Thoreau; they gave away as much as the others."

"What about Trudeau? What about Chretien? You can't say they gave in to the Americans. Compare them to Harper or even Mulroney, remember him? Now that's going back maybe a little too far for you. But do you remember free trade, remember what that did?" Leroy was on a roll. How dare anyone knock the Liberals.

"I always thought that Thoreau was a populist," Ben joined in. "He won that election because of anti-American sentiment. People didn't vote for the Liberal party as much as they voted on a single issue — 'get back at the Americans'. He didn't really have much when he threatened to close the border. The border was closed. They had already built their fences and towers, Black Hawk helicopters, cameras, all that."

"It wasn't a single issue." Leroy defended. "We were going to do something about global warming remember. The big oil companies were screaming and spending money on that election. Every spare dime they had went against Thoreau. We had a plan for greenhouse gases that was the most aggressive in the entire world. Canada was going to become a showcase for the planet. We were going to prove that you could do something. Canada was about to shine again after years of following the Americans. We were going to stand out in the world again." The old fist, knuckles scarred, rested on the table, not pounding, not yet. "The world was beginning to think that Canada was America, and after Afghanistan, and how we acted under the Conservatives over Iran, it's no wonder."

"I gotta agree with you on that." Roderick hesitated while a young man cleared away the stained paper plates. "It was getting so that the rest of the world saw us all as one, and that used to worry me. If we were too close to the Americans, their enemies became our enemies, and the Americans were good at making enemies."

"You bet," Leroy spoke in a rush. "We were set to change that when they annexed us. We never got the chance."

Ben held his ground. "I wonder if Thoreau really would have followed through with his threats. He won the election on the promise to do something, but he was in power for two years and was still only making noises."

"Thoreau was only one man," Leroy defended. "It takes a whole nation to make change, especially the big changes we were trying to effect."

"Well, Ben might not have believed Thoreau, but Wright sure did." Roderick sided.

Ben put his study of obscure history to use. "I don't know, the Americans always intended or at least contemplated taking over Canada; Thoreau's noise only offered an excuse. In the nineteen thirties the Americans had detailed plans for invading Canada."

Roderick also remembered history. "1812, was the first, eh."

"Then the Fenians." Leroy knew history too.

Ben set the record straight. "1775 was the first one. That was the Quebec invasion. The next was 1812. Some historians have suggested that the reason for the American Revolutionary war was not because of the tax on tea as popular history would have you believe but was rather started by the Americans as an excuse to invade Canada — annexation, expansionism seems to have been part of the American ideal since its inception. They thought it was going to be easy, in fact Jefferson said it was 'just a matter of marching'."

"What about the Fenians?" Leroy wanted to know.

Roderick held up an old hand. "Before you go there, I thought the American Revolution was about taxes and conscription. You're saying it wasn't?"

"I'm not saying anything. I just said that some Canadian historians have written that the American Revolutionary war against Britain was started by the Americans as an excuse to invade Canada."

Roderick thought about it. Let it settle in. "Makes sense." He concluded.

"The Fenians." Leroy still wanted to know.

"1866 to about 1871." Ben exercised his memory. "The Fenians were Irish revolutionaries who wanted to cut Britain off from its colony. There were about a half dozen raids into Canada over that time period. The Americans looked the other way. President Andrew Jackson was supposed to have said, "We'll recognize the established facts," meaning of course that if the Fenians were successful, America would recognize the annexation."

"That's right." Leroy rested his hands on the table.

Ben continued his history lesson. "There was also a lot of talk after the American Civil War about another invasion of Canada. After the North beat the South they were looking at us. Some people say they would have invaded if the American people had any stomach left for war." He paused for a taste of his tea, something to wet his dry throat. "Of course the famous 1870 Wolseley expedition sent out to Manitoba was not only about Riel and the Metis. John A. MacDonald was reacting to American newspapers in the West calling for an invasion of Canada."

"If we're counting attacks we can't forget the Cyprus Hills massacre," Roderick added.

Leroy asked. "What was that one again?"

"Remember, the American wolf hunters who attacked the Nakoda at Cyprus Hills, accused them of stealing horses?"

"Oh, yeah, that was an American whiskey fort, wasn't it?" Leroy remembered.

Ben put his cup down. "If we're talking about American commercial activity in Canada, I'd say we have to consider all the big corporations that have taken over."

"Now that was an invasion." Roderick leaned forward. "One thing I really learned when I was chief was that if an American company wanted something, the Canadian and Saskatchewan governments went out of their way to make sure they got it. If a First Nation wanted something we had to wait. Weyerhaeuser, the American pulp and paper giant, wanted all the trees in this territory. We were trying to save some — know who the governments sided with?"

Leroy nodded, "It was always like that. But it got worse under Hopper. It was him who made an agreement with them to use each other's armed forces in case of civil disasters. He invited the American army in. We almost lost Canada in '08 without a fight. Hopper was ready to give it away."

"You know they always planned on an invasion." Ben spoke softly. "In about 1928, maybe '30, they had plans to invade. They were going to take Halifax first to block British support, then attack Winnipeg to cut the rail system. Most of the attack was aimed at Ontario and Quebec. Even when the plans were declassified in 1974, nobody in Canada made much of a fuss about it. A few people went to the American archives in Washington to look at the plans, a few articles appeared, but it was mostly written off as a hoax or something. Nobody really cared."

"Yeah, and look what happened. All the warnings were there and nobody did anything." Roderick leaned back.

Leroy defended: "Well, Thoreau was going to do something."

A silence followed as the three Elders remembered how it had been. Ben looked back at the table where Rosie, Elsie, and Benji continued to sit. Benji seemed to be in conversation with Elsie; Rosie still held her granddaughter, wasn't going to let her go.

Ben wondered if Benji felt deserted. *Well, he came to find out about me — Rosie is a part of me that he needs to know.*

The gymnasium buzzed with conversation, occasionally a laugh rattled across it. People ate, visited, remembered, relished the memories, the good times and those memories washed away the sorrow, the loss of a respected Elder.

Ben had never really considered himself an Elder before tonight, but here he was, sitting at the Elder's table with the very old Leroy, and Roderick who had always been older, but now was clearly old.

"It don't do Thoreau much good now." Roderick interrupted Ben's thoughts. "Governor Johnson sure as hell isn't going to legislate against the oil companies."

"Governor, my ass." The old fist hit the table. "Canada is led by a prime minister, and Thoreau is our prime minister until he's defeated in a fair election. Just because Johnson was appointed don't give him any authority. You can bet Canada will resist until there isn't a breath left to fight with."

Ben came back to the conversation. "That's the problem. The Americans aren't going to go away. We're stuck with them. Like the Borg used to say in the old Star Trek movies:

'Resistance is futile.' We can resist, like we resisted Canada when they were stomping on us. Didn't do a lot of good. They still stomped on us. Now the Americans are stomping on Canada. We have a new supreme master to live with. We'd better learn how. Did you hear the other day about those kids that crucified themselves at the border? A dozen of them nailed to crosses. It didn't change anything. Hungry for three days, sore hands, a little media attention, but they'll be forgotten soon enough."

"They weren't hurting so bad," Roderick paid attention to news. "Morphine; they were all higher than kites on morphine, didn't feel a thing. And the nails they used, weren't even real nails. Did you see them, they showed them on CBC, ground down to the size of needles."

"It wasn't so much how they did it," Leroy liked what the kids had done. "It was that they did it. It wasn't against the government so much as it was a shot at the Christians; a shot at the new Zion. Those are the crazies we have to watch out for, the ones going around preaching the end of times and that America was prophesied in the Bible as the Promised Land. That's what's behind all this you know. Got nothing whatsoever to do with security or oil or water or nothing. It's them crazies and their millions showing up for revivals and screaming their salvation. They're the ones that are war crazy. Those kids did something. They might have been on morphine, maybe they ground down the nails. So what that they didn't nail their feet. They did something about the real enemy. They embarrassed the Christians, reminded them about Christ for a minute and got them out of the Old Testament."

"I have to agree with you, Leroy," Ben nodded toward the older man, a man in his nineties with vigour and strength.

"It's that 'One People, One Country, One God' stuff that's worrying. Now that's supremacy, pure and simple supremacy."

Roderick entered with a little more excitement now: "That's where it comes from, from the Supreme Being stuff. All those Christians believe in a supreme single God. That's their culture. It's all about hierarchy, every bit of it."

"It's certainly cultural. But it's not limited to Christians. Muslims and Hebrews believe in a supreme God too." Ben needed to be balanced. An argument that was too one sided, could not persuade. "It goes back to Plato and his theory of Gold, Silver, and Bronze people. Organized society has tried to follow his formula ever since, and spread the idea to the rest of the world during the era of expansion. Not only to the Americas — this idea of supremacy was used in Africa and Asia. It never diminished. When the academics started to speak of a postcolonial period in the last century as though colonialism had ended, we had the International Monetary Fund and the World Bank forcefully spreading the economic dogma of the Super Powers, America, and the European Union, on the third world. Colonialism never ended. It just changed forms. If we want to understand this symptom we have to examine the cause, and I've been saying for decades that the cause is supremacist ideology"

Roderick liked what Ben was saying. "It's like Indian Affairs. Oh, they were polite and dedicated, but couldn't get it through their skulls that we wanted to do something different. They genuinely could not understand anything but top down."

"How many terms were you chief?" Leroy couldn't remember.

"Three." Roderick held up three fingers. "Two terms in the nineties and again from '06 to '09. That's when I hung it up.

We couldn't do anything. You can't change people's minds who only have one way of thinking."

"And how do you change people's thinking?" Ben asked rhetorically.

"You don't," Roderick answered. "All we can do is live our lives the best we can. Walk in a good way and maybe people will see us walking in a good way and want to walk with us. Can't force anyone to change, never could. It never works."

Ben responded with a hint of sarcasm: "I think assimilation worked pretty well for Canada."

"No it didn't. All those policies did was wreck our people, we never did become them. When they stripped our culture we didn't adopt theirs. That's still what all the grief is about, people trying to find where they belong. So from about the nineties onward there was that movement back to our spirituality. So much for assimilation."

Leroy stayed out of the discussion. It wasn't pure politics and he wasn't really interested.

"But you got to admit that supremacy was what was behind the policy. They believed they were superior and were doing it for our own good."

"And we learned it from them. We started to become, as you say, supremacists ourselves. Indians got to be just as good as white people at believing they were better than others. We had our hierarchies too. AFN, FSIN, Chief and Council. I even got sucked into it. They elected me chief, thought I really was a chief for a while, forgot that I was only *okimakan* and not *okimaw*."

Ben nodded to Roderick, "*Ahie*" he agreed.

"You too, Ben. You got yourself a good education, stayed in that big university. You must have felt pretty important."

Ben's first response was to deny the allegation, deny that he ever put himself above the people, but he knew that to verbalize the denial wouldn't be completely true. He kept silent.

"It's okay, we all got caught up in it. Now we're old, had our ups and downs. Some of us took real shit-kickings before we figured it out. When we started to act like we were better than someone else, something always came along and put us in our place. When you're an Indian, you learn it fast."

"*Ahie.*" Ben understood. Maybe for the first time, understood why things went the way that they did. Why he really wasn't teaching anymore. It might not have had anything to do with his age or his desire to come home. Maybe those powerful forces that keep balance in the universe decided Ben needed to get balanced again. "*Ahie,*" he nodded again to his Elder Roderick.

⁓

Rosie watched Benji, saw his discomfort, saw him sit too straight, saw the mechanics of his movements. This young man was completely out his element and it showed — it showed in his voice, in his questions, or lack of questions; it was there in his silence, in his perfect politeness.

She had watched, stood aside, not part of the reunion, only an observer. She couldn't help herself. She needed to be there when Benji met his father. She needed to see what Ben would do, how he would react — it was important to her, beyond curiosity, way beyond tidbits of possible gossip. How Ben reacted when he came face to face with his child, with his offspring, with his little alter-self, would inform Rosie of the true Ben, the real man inside the image she had created.

She had stood there under the trees, watching from a distance, smiling, maybe even smirking a little as Benji explained, tried to explain, faltered — started again. She couldn't hear the words. She imagined he said who his mother was, gave his birthday, said his name again, "Benji" or "Benjamin", or something.

She'd watched Ben's stance, watched as realization filtered through broken speech, until realization broke the stoic and the body sagged, drained of will and then Ben hugged his son and she knew, even at a distance, that Ben was crying.

She left then — quietly, soft steps away. Now she knew the true Ben and knew that he was the same Ben she had always known, only now he had another dimension. He was a father.

～

"This is what I wanted to show you." Elsie felt around on the dash of her car for a tiny note pad, found it through the open window, flipped pages at the edge of the white schoolyard floodlight, not nearly enough to read by, but she didn't need to read, she only needed enough to assist her memory. Benji stood awkwardly in the gravel parking area while Elsie read out the poem she had composed on her way north, driving with one hand and scribbling with the other.

"Who needs an army?" She read with a deeper voice than she used for conversation.

"Beaten with a Bottle
Broken Spirits Spilled
Bashed
Robbed
Rolled
Stole the Little Bit of Dirt
The Earth
Broken Spirit Lost
Stole the Ragged Bit of Shirt

Ghost Danced
Bashed
Beaten by a Bottle
Spirit Spilled
Spewed
Broken Lips Speak
the English
Beaten
Bottled
Robbed
Rolled
In Drunken Stupor
Stoned."

She looked up to try to read Benji's face. She needed him to like it, wanted him to like her for writing it, wanted him to see her as an Indian, a good Indian woman. Her mother would frown on this, trying to be noticed by a man while at a wake, disrespectful. But, she might never see him again, never see those anxious eyes, those eyes that looked through her and saw the dreams, dreams of great things, great doings.

His expression didn't tell her anything. His words did. "Read it again."

She did. Slower, punctuated, put her heart into it. Three-quarters of the way through she realized. "He doesn't get it. He was raised white."

"I like the sound of it. The rhythm." He confirmed her thoughts when she finished. "I have to think about the content for awhile, but I like it."

But did he like her, Indian woman, traditional Indian woman?

"My adopted parents weren't drinkers. I never saw a drunk person until I was in my late teens. Just never saw anybody act that way. I guess if you grow up around alcohol you might hate it. Or love it," he corrected himself. "Alcohol is a big issue these days, but I just don't see it. Always thought it was just the right-wing Christians imposing their beliefs on the world. I guess from your perspective it would be different."

"I didn't grow up in an alcoholic home either." She corrected his assumption. "Mom never allowed it in the house. She's the inspiration for the poem. It echoes her words. She always said that the whiteman used alcohol to defeat us and to keep us down. To her this neo-temperance movement is a good thing for us."

"Hey, look, a falling star." Benji pointed toward the southern sky. "Wow. I've never seen one so bright, or that colour, almost blue."

"Incredible. Did you make a wish?"

"No, you?"

"For good things." she answered, "good things to come." Good things for her and Benji.

"Are those northern lights?" Benji continued to stare at the enamel black sky and the tinge of white, almost cloud like across the eastern horizon.

"Yeah, they are. Let's go down to the lake away from these lights and maybe we can see them better. It's just down here a ways, not far." She led the way to where water lay perfectly flat and reflected stars, northern lights, and the track of speeding satellites.

"I've never seen them before. You don't get them in Toronto."

"Probably do, just can't see them." Elsie could not imagine anywhere on Earth where the spirits did not dance. She stood close to him, close enough to feel his presence, and as Benji's gaze wove back and forth across the black star-studded sky, where the lights were beginning to dance in sharp waves of green tinged with red, he began to feel her presence too.

~

The hood smelled of vomit, not Abe's. That's all right, he thought, I've smelled vomit before.

"Abraham Isaac Friesen." The voice was not strong, did not have natural strength to it, though the speaker tried to sound authoritative. Like a substitute teacher, Abe thought.

"Charged with conspiracy against peace, order, and good government." The voice continued. "What is the evidence?"

"He was captured at his residence. A reliable source reported suspicious activity there and when a squad led by Captain Ross approached the residence, warning signals were activated by co-conspirators." The voice sounded as though it was reading, flat, empty. "Several vehicles were reported fleeing the residence as the squad approached. Abraham was the lone occupant when it arrived. He was taken into custody, read his right to voluntary statement, due military process was explained. Abraham declined a voluntary statement. Upon investigation, evidence of a terrorist cell was discovered. They had occupied the loft of a barn on the premises; however, a complete search did not uncover any weapons. It is assumed that the fleeing co-conspirators removed that evidence with them."

"Heart rate eighty-four," Abe felt cold metal against his chest, he assumed it was a stethoscope. "Breathing normal." The doctor's voice held a slight southern accent, an educated Virginian, Abe guessed. He slowed down his breathing, willed his body to relax. A heart rate that high showed his anxiety, and Abe needed not to be anxious.

"I'm not convinced there is evidence of imminent danger."
The substitute teacher sounded nearer.

"Upon approach to the residence, a unit was dispatched to investigate the signal fire. That unit was attacked, two officers were killed by the insurgents and two were taken captive. Their whereabouts remains unknown."

"Imminent danger is established." Teacher flipped a page.

"The subject is a healthy male, approximately fifty years of age, cardiovascular and respiratory systems are better than would be expected of a person of this age."

Virginia thinks I'm old, Abe thought.

"He appears to be in better than average physical condition. It is obvious that the subject has received military fitness training. The calluses on his hands appear similar to those observed on subjects who have recently attended terrorist training."

"Hoe and rake. I should have used herbicide in my gardens."

Whatever hit the soles of Abe's feet, bound tightly together at the ankles, was thin and very strong. The sting was a lot sharper than he expected.

"You will only speak when asked a direct question." The reader continued to sound like he was reading.

"Abraham Isaac Friesen; tell him he has the name of a good Christian."

"You have the name of a good Christian."

"Read him his charges."

"You are charged with conspiracy against peace, order, and good government."

"Read him his first option."

"You may give a voluntary statement admitting the charge. Cooperation and truthfulness will be taken into consideration when final determination of your sentence is pronounced."

"Ask him if he desires to give a voluntary statement at this time."

Abe took a deep breath through the heavy black hood, considered what he might say.

"The subject declines to make a voluntary statement." Reader sounded closer.

"Continue," Teacher answered.

Abe breathed out slowly, measured.

The first jolt of pain began somewhere near the bottom of his abdomen, shot upwards through his body and ricocheted around inside his rib cage, sudden, sharp. It left Abe gasping inside the hood. The second jolt followed the same path, lasted several gasps longer. The third jolt did not stop. The pain tore through Abe's core, filled him, as though he was suddenly flooded with sulphuric acid, burned intensely forever, beyond gasps, beyond memory, beyond thought. It erased his brain, became the moment, the only moment in history, then tapered off, gradually allowing thought to return. *Storms never last, do they baby.* The chorus of an old country song crooned in Abe's head as the pain diminished. He searched for the other words to the song, could not find them and repeated. Storms never last, do they baby. Put it to voice, a whisper "Storms never last, do they baby."

"We have a singer." Reader's voice sounded somewhere out in the audience.

"Terrorist training is confirmed." Teacher sounded relieved.

"I don't understand." A fourth voice, from further away.

"Terrorists are trained to sing, usually a battle song or one of the songs of their false religion. It is not too much different than the North American Indian singing their death chant," Teacher explained. "It makes interrogation much more

difficult because the subject removes himself consciously."
Teacher must have turned away. Abe could not make out
the rest of his conversation. The pain ended, tapered off to
nothing, empty. He smelled fresh vomit in the hood.

Wagner. Abe recognized the opening to "The Ride of the
Valkries". *There must be speakers on both sides of my head.*
Good choice. The volume increased until the music was all that
there was. Abe put himself into the music, rode the crescendos,
kept himself conscious through the surges of pain that arched
his body, knew his body writhed and thumped against the
metal table, but it was far away. Abe rode a winged horse out
of heaven, brandished a flaming sword in the war at the end of
the world, rode Wagner's music, one of Abe's favourite works.

~

"Everyone talks." Monica looked closer at Betsy. She seemed
distant, further than the few feet across the back table of the
Olympia Restaurant. Monica recalled when this back area
was the smoking section, when she and Betsy Chance were in
university together, when the discussion was about a different
kind of revolution, about First Nations and the shelved Royal
Commission on Aboriginal Peoples report.

"Abe will talk." Monica tried to give her voice the extra
distance needed to reach Betsy.

"So what. He doesn't know anything." Betsy did not move
any closer.

"He knows the names of everyone that was there."

"So."

"Don't be a bitch, Betsy."

"I'm not, as you so delicately put it, being a bitch." Betsy
leaned her elbows on the table, arms folded, looked directly
at Monica. "You have to learn to grow a thicker skin, sister.

Who is it that you are worried about? The important people who were there are safe. Richard? They'll never find him. Abe never met That Jack, didn't know who he was. The only people at risk are that Mennonite woman and the environmentalist, what's her name?"

"Joan Lightning."

"Yes her, and who else? They already knew about Roland. Who else might our friend Abe know about?"

"There's Ben Robe."

"Oh yes, forgot about you and him. Monica you'll have to learn to let him go. He might have been something when you were a student. Now he's nobody. Even if they catch him, so what."

"You've changed." Monica leaned back. Now she wanted distance between herself and Betsy. "You used to be a good friend."

"Don't pout. It makes your face all funny looking. Listen, Monica." Betsy's voice softened slightly. "They have Abe, and I agree with you, everybody talks. Abe is probably not having a really nice time right now. So, he tells them everything that he knows. Still, so what. We still have the advantage. They can't build enough prisons, enough torture chambers. They can't get enough guards, or interviewers. They can't lock us all up. There are too many of us. Their focus is on finding the leaders. Those are the people to worry about.

"Even if Abe tells them about Ben — let's assume that for a minute — what's going to happen? They might go up there and arrest him, they might even interview him. But he doesn't know anything. Six months, a year maybe, and they'll release him. He'll go back up north and you can slip away and go see him in his wonderful cabin on the shore of his lake, your little romance will pick up again and you can lick his wounds for him."

"Oh, you are a bitch, Betsy. You know damn well that we were only together once and nothing has happened for twenty years."

"And I know that you still dream about him." Betsy smiled mischievously.

"He's a good man."

"I know." Betsy's voice was soft now. "I know, but reality says he might get caught."

"What about those two black shirts Ed has?"

"What about them?"

"A trade."

"For who? For Abe?"

"Why not?"

"No." Betsy shook her head while she thought about it. "No, we'll trade them, but for somebody important, like Edwin or Noland."

"We don't even know if they're alive. Come on, Betsy, we know that Abe is strong. He'll hold out for a long time, there's still a chance. Edwin and Noland, don't get me wrong, I love those brothers, they were both good commanders. But do you think, even if we get them back after all this time, that they will be of any help? Think about it. Trade for a couple guys who will be so badly broken by now that all we can do is keep them safe, wipe the sweat from their brows as they convulse in terror. Even if we get them back now they'll be insane. Or do we trade for Abe, someone who has given everything for the resistance and we get back a full human being? And remember, Abe knows about you and me."

"I'll think about it. You know it's not entirely my choice. Okay, I'll put Abe's name forward, but the council might not agree. In the meantime, I'm going to give you an order that you might enjoy. Go and tell Ben that he might be at risk and arrange some sort of protection."

Moccasin Lake stretched north, flat and black until the lake met the black sky and northern lights danced on both. Elsie tugged at Benji's sleeve and they stepped back from the sand beach to where willow grew down to the high-water line. A boat split the ebony lake and headed straight for them. The driver cut the engine as it drew into the shallows, lifted the leg of the motor and let momentum wash the boat onto shore where Elsie and Benji had just stood. The man in the bow jumped out and pulled the boat higher onto the sand, reached into the boat, grabbed a rope and strung it out to the willows intent on tying to something secure.

"What the . . . " he exclaimed when he caught sight of two human shapes behind the willow clump.

"Red." Elsie recognized the voice. It matched the shape of her tall thin cousin.

"Who's that?" Red didn't recognise her voice.

"It's me, Elsie."

"What the . . . "

"What you doing here?" Elsie stepped out of the darker shadows into the mere dark, hugged her bewildered cousin.

Red nervously looked back at his partner getting out of the boat. "It's okay Mike, it's just Elsie lost or something." He turned back to Elsie, held her at arm's length. "What am I doing here? What the hell are you doing here? Come back for the wake or what?"

Mike began unloading plastic twenty-five-litre gas cans from the boat, plopping them into the sand. "Never mind your cousin. Let's get this boat empty."

"Hey, Elsie, kind of busy now. Tell you what, here." He picked up one of the cans and offered it to her. "Here take this, it's pure alcohol. Don't drink it. It's for your car. And I'll come up to the wake later and we can visit, okay."

"Sure, Red." She struggled with the weight of the can. "Where'd you get this?"

"We made it. But it's not for drinking. That shit will blind you if you try. It's just for your car." Red carried a can in each hand. "Go back up to the gym, I'll see you later, okay Elsie? Hey, cuz, it's good to see you again." And he disappeared up the trail toward the shape of a truck parked on the side of a little-used dirt track of a road.

~

"They sure misunderstood Quebec." Leroy the Montreal Canadiens fan re-entered the conversation. "They seemed to think that the French would be on their side for some reason, didn't realize that Quebec wanted independence."

"Yeah, independence from them too. They're sure putting up a fight down there." Roderick looked around to see if the young lady with the big tea pot was in sight. She wasn't.

"It's like the Americans thought that all Quebecers hated Canada." Ben followed Roderick's searching gaze, another cup of muskeg tea would be nice now. His throat was getting dry. "They must have thought Quebec would side with them against the rest of us. They sure got fooled on that one. Did you hear the news today? Sounds like Montreal is a fire storm. Strongest resistance anywhere comes from the French. Who would have thought?"

"Not that hard to predict." Leroy looked for the big tea pot too. "It's like brothers or even sisters. Oh, they might argue between them, even act like they hate each other sometimes, but just try to get in between and you have both of them against you."

The young woman with the big enamel pot did come around again, poured the last of the wild forest-scented tea into Styrofoam cups; it was cooler now and stronger. Ben only wished that he was drinking it out of a tin cup, the way his grandmother used to pass it to him; evenings with Grandpa, stories, and Ben trying not to burn his hands on the hot metal cup. Styrofoam gave the tea a chemical taste. Oh well, it was still good, soothing on his dry throat.

Elsie and Benji came back into the gymnasium. A quiet stillness had begun to settle over the people there and despite Benji's wanting to get to know her more and more, the quiet in the gym prevented him from speaking.

The night deepened. Young mothers took their children home first, then others drifted out. Groups of visitors became quiet as people gradually left. Standing first for a moment by the open casket, touching Elroy's cold, folded hands one last time, they said their final goodbyes, then walking around shaking people's hands, and promising to "See you tomorrow," they found the door and the dark. Roderick followed protocol early, "I'm about done in here, boys," and only Leroy and Ben remained.

Benji came over to the Elder's table not long after Elsie, and Rosie, still carrying Rachel, left. "I guess I'll take you up on the offer of that cot after all."

"Anytime."

"Well, thanks." He wasn't sure of himself, standing half behind Ben, so that Ben had to twist around on the plastic chair to see his face. "Are you staying?"

"I think so, for awhile anyway."

"The door isn't locked. Just help yourself to whatever you need."

And Benji, too, found the door and the dark, but without shaking hands with anyone or going to the casket.

~

"That's a good looking son you've got." Leroy still wanted to talk, didn't want to be alone just yet. "It's just too bad you missed out on his growing up years." Leroy's voice softened at Ben's pained expression. "It's okay. You have time now. Up to you if you want it."

"I suppose."

The silence of the night drained conversation, took away the energy for talk and both men fell back into the quiet. This was the part of the wake that Ben remembered most, this still, quiet time in the middle of the night when only a few remained to keep the dead company until daylight, his mother only agreeing to go home and get some rest when a much younger Ben had promised, "I'll stay, Mom, you go home before you fall down."

"Don't be falling asleep now. You keep watch."

"I will, Mom. Promise."

"This is the last time you'll have to look after your dad."

"I know, Mom. I know."

~

Leroy butted his last cigarette into the dregs at the bottom of the Styrofoam cup, adding it to the others. Elroy always hated his smoking. Probably didn't smoke because Leroy did. Well, maybe Leroy could quit now. He stretched his shoulders back, forced old muscles to move, stood, scraped his chair loud in the echo chamber of the school gymnasium and went to stand before the open casket. His brother, his little brother. Now he could say goodbye, now when there were only a handful of people left, Leroy and Elroy one last time and the world would change forever. Leroy would be alone for the first time in ninety-two years.

"Well little brother . . . " He stood straight, looked down into the box at the old face and the long grey white hair fanned out on the pillow, rubbed his hand over his own short-cropped hair. "It looks like it's just me now. You're not missing much. This is a different world than we had. Maybe it's better. Maybe it's as it should be. You and me, we weren't made for this world; this world's gone crazy. Maybe it's better that you're not here to see this." His hands held the edge of the coffin, supported his weight, his heaviness. "Gotcha with this Canadiens thing, didn't I? Got you last." Leroy tried to laugh. It wasn't there. "Your kids were here, your grandkids, and even some great-grandkids, but I guess you know that, eh?" He looked away, around the nearly empty gymnasium, collected thoughts for a second. "Gonna miss you." He looked back. "You know that too. It won't be long, not long little brother. You just wait. Me and you in the happy hunting grounds, and I'll show you how to hunt. Nothing left to hunt around here anymore. You must have shot the last of the big moose to get that set of antlers in your living room. But don't you worry, when I get there I'll show you a really big set of antlers." He touched his brother's scarred, cold, hand, the one with the gold Western Canada championship ring. "When I get there, we'll be on the same team. Promise. I promise." Leroy choked on the lump in his throat, felt the sting of tears threatening to burst. "Promise." He leaned down and kissed his brother's forehead.

⁓

Elsie wanted to go because Benji was going. Rosie wanted to go because Elsie wanted to take Rachel with her. Give the boy a sense of his ancestry, Ben figured as he manoeuvred the boat a short distance up Witiko Creek from its mouth on Moccasin Lake. The creek ran deep and dark, its water stained with tannins. The sand bar along the south shore was longer than Ben remembered. He let the boat swing in the light current and nosed it in where the trail began, right there where the pines ran down to the water's edge.

The trail ran straight back, up a slight rise and onto the flat, three- or four-acre clearing. Its indentation from years of use ran through the red brown pine needle-covered ground. Some of them lay in clumps, blown from the boss trees of the forest that stood guard around the grey weathered cabin, shaded it from a relentless sun, broke the wind in winter, sometimes gave their life to that wind. Ben was saddened by the sight of a large pine that lay tilted, its roots torn from the earth, brown and grey across the trail that ran under it straight to the door of the cabin. He remembered that tree, remembered his father leaning his big bow saw against it, wiping his forehead with his sleeve. "That's enough for today, *Nikosis*, go for a swim or something. Can't work all the time." And the dutiful son had gladly obeyed in the cool of the creek.

Ben wanted to share his memories with Benji, memories of two old people living quiet and close to the land. He hadn't intended to sound like a professor, but he did. "They lived here all their married lives." Without the feeling, without attachment. "They moved here after their wedding. The story is that someone was killed at the celebration, stabbed. Mom and Dad came here to get away from the drinking. All the time they were here, alcohol was never allowed; might be why they never received many visitors."

Rosie interrupted: "Adolphus and Eleanor Robe. People on the reserve didn't mention them much, kind of forgotten people," as she walked around the windblown pine towards the cabin. She spread out a blanket before unsaddling Rachel from her hip, put the little girl down and lowered herself onto the hand-sewn quilt. The exact place where Mom used to sit on a blanket to do her bead work or birch bark baskets, Ben realised.

"This cabin is in pretty good shape." Benji pushed against the solid log wall.

"It's not that old. I helped your grandfather build it not long before they both passed away. Actually, we built it twice."

"Twice?" Benji turned to his father.

"Yes," Ben was flooded with memories so strong that he lost his words for a second. "Yes, we built it twice. You see, the old cabin, the first cabin was right here where this one stands. It was getting pretty rough and Dad decided to build another one. I wasn't teaching during the summer so I came to help. We built another cabin just over there, and Mom and Dad lived in the old cabin while we built the new one. When we were done we moved Mom and all the furniture into the new cabin. The plan was to use the old cabin as a shed, someplace to keep Dad's traps, and sleigh, and stuff.

"But Mom didn't like the new cabin. It was in the wrong place. It was only twenty feet, but it was in the wrong place. So they lived in a tent and me and Dad tore down the old cabin, tore down the new cabin, and put it back up where the old cabin was."

"I can understand that." Rosie moved to keep Rachel from crawling off the blanket. "You get used to something and it's hard to change."

"The only difference was the place. The new cabin was the exact same size and shape as the old cabin. Even the windows and door were in the same place. She just didn't like where it was, not how it was."

"Place is important."

"I suppose." Ben realized for the first time that it might be, as he watched Rosie in the exact spot where his mother used to sit, sitting exactly the way she sat with her legs tucked back beside her. "At the time though, I thought she was just being old and silly. That was a lot of work for Dad and me. He was almost eighty."

"Then it's a good thing you helped," Rosie placated. "A little work probably didn't hurt."

"Oh, it hurt all right," Ben remembered as he looked back at the heavy log wall.

"Did you come here often?" Benji wanted to know.

"Every summer from when I first went to university until they passed away. I haven't been back here since."

"Every summer?" Rosie questioned. "Never saw you on the reserve."

"Never went there. I'd come out and stay here. Was no reason to go to the reserve."

"So how come you didn't move here instead of building your place next to my mom?"

"This is a hard place to live. No road, no electricity. Not bad in the summer, you can come by boat, or in the winter you can come by snow machine, or dog team the way Dad used to, but it's not good in the spring and fall."

"Why's that?" Benji came back from examining the construction of the cabin, how the logs fit together in the corners.

"Because when the lake freezes you can't use a boat, and you can't walk on it until it's thick enough. In the spring it's the same thing. The ice gets rotten and you have to wait, sometimes it takes two or three weeks. Wasn't bad when I went to school on the reserve — I got a holiday,"

"Couldn't you put a road in?" Benji was thinking construction.

"Too much muskeg, we're kind of on an island here. The lake on one side, but behind here — " Ben waved a wide sweep toward the east — "it's all muskeg. No way to get across. Anyway it would ruin it." He liked this place just the way it was.

Mice dirtied the floor of the cabin, dragged in litter, chewed the mattress and spread out the cotton lining. Squirrels made much more of a mess. They dropped the leftovers of their meals in piles, chewed holes through the walls, widened gaps between the logs. Birds took advantage of the squirrel holes, moved in and built their nests mudded to the pole rafters. One large nest hung from the ridgepole, the log that Ben and his father struggled to put into place. The south-facing windows were stained with years of dust and grime so that the light took on an orange hue where it fell on the floor, adding to the abandoned feel of the cabin.

"They're taking back their land." Elsie spoke philosophically as she followed Ben inside.

"Yeah, Mom would see it that way too. But in her lifetime that floor would shine."

Benji examined a calendar hung from a nail, February 2001. The picture was of a 1962 Oldsmobile coupe, the one that had the unique wrap-around windows, bright green and enamel white.

"Nobody's been here in awhile." He voiced the obvious.

"It's isolated." Ben moved to look over Benji's shoulder, looked for February 10th. The day they found his father, found him sitting under a tree only a half day's walk up the trapline. "He must have got tired," his mother had said, and before the snow melted that spring she got tired too and they buried her beside Dad.

"This would be a great place for a still." Benji sized up the cabin, measured its cubic feet, considered its isolation, the spread of the pines, and the solidity of its structure.

"Over my dead body." Ben was firm.

"Oh, I don't mean for drinking." Benji realized his gaff. "I mean ethanol, for fuel."

"Not even ethanol." Ben remained firm. He felt ghosts stirring, an uncomfortable stir.

"Come on, Ben." Benji wanted to say 'Dad', but wasn't sure how his father felt about that yet. "Think about the money you could save. That truck of yours must suck up a lot of cash in a year. Maybe even burn it in your boat."

"No, I agree with your dad." Elsie too felt the ghosts. "Not here." She saw the homemade curtains, saw through their raggedness, saw the wood cook stove with its stovepipe still going through the ceiling instead of tumbling behind, saw a place where a woman once cooked and baked.

"What's with him?" Rosie asked Elsie. She had caught a look on Ben's face as he came out of the cabin and headed toward the old garden area, a slightly pained look.

"Nothing." Elsie now looked bewildered. She had not seen anything.

"What were you guys talking about in there?"

"Nothing much. Benji was imagining using this place as a site to set up a still, but Ben wouldn't have anything to do with it."

"I guess not." Rosie sat up slightly, looked away from Rachel who lay on her back and kicked and waved and tried to talk through a voice that could only coo and bah. "Alcohol was what killed us. They didn't beat us in war, they used booze to take everything away from us and then used it to keep us down."

"I know, you've always said that. But what's Ben's reason?"

"He learned it the same place that I did. Right here in this cabin. Our trapline and the Robe trapline come together right there at the first point on the lake. I used to come over here to visit with Eleanor, listen to her stories, learn her beadwork patterns; she's the one that hated alcohol the most. I think old Adolphus might not have been so dead set as his wife was. He was easier going. Well not easy going I guess, more quiet in his ways. He didn't talk much, usually just stood there and smiled a lot, at peace kind of."

"How long ago was that?"

"Oh, I was young, before I got married and started having kids. After I met your dad I never did come back here. But I remember all her stories, and I'm pretty sure Ben does too."

"What kind of stories?" Elsie probed. Stories were always good. She stretched out on the quilt and played with Rachel's bare foot, tickled it to see her wriggle and laugh.

"Old time stories, how they used to live. Stories about the Treaty, lots of stories about the Treaty, kind of like she wanted someone to remember that."

Benji now stood just off the blanket where the three females sat or lay, listening, so Rosie helped to fill him in, gave him something he could use without ever looking directly at him.

"Treaty was signed just up at the end of the lake there where the river begins, 1889. She said it was in winter and all the Indians were there when the treaty commissioner and the police came by dog team from the south."

"Eleanor wasn't there." Elsie calculated years to 1889.

"No, she was old even when I knew her, but not that old. She heard the stories from her dad, he was there. You see, Eleanor was the youngest of her family, the baby. Her dad was already an old man when she was born, so she was raised special. She stayed home with her parents until they died." Rosie added a little gossip, just a little, just for spice. "She was almost an old maid by the time she married Adolphus, and he was younger than her, not much just a few years, but still younger." Elsie looked up at Benji, guessed that he might be younger than her, maybe.

"Eleanor used to say that Treaty wasn't what was written on the paper." Rosie fell back to a more formal recitation for this part. "The commissioner promised we could live like before, then they forced us to live on the reserve, pulled us off the land. She didn't like that. She said the reserve was supposed to be just a place where Indians could go if they wanted to go to school or learn to be farmers, but if the Indians wanted to stay in the bush they could." Rosie let Rachel play with her dangling hand, let the little girl swat and pull at her fingers. She looked down at her granddaughter, away from Elsie and Benji, as though she was telling the story to a younger audience.

"Her family came from further north along the Churchill River, moved down here because that area was getting trapped out. You see the Churchill used to be the first fur trade route, they trapped it out first. When there was nothing left, some of them moved into Chipewyan country. Eleanor thought that was why they don't like us Cree very much. But her family came here, not just for the trapping I guess. I sort of got the sense she was telling me they moved here to get away from the missionaries, but she never came right out and said it."

"What was wrong with missionaries?" Benji wanted to know.

"Nothing." Rosie continued Eleanor's conciliatory manner. She wasn't going to say anything bad about anybody. "It's just that Eleanor's family was traditional, kept the old ways. I guess the Christians looked down on that sort of stuff." She remembered why Benji was there and went back to the story she had begun with the purpose of giving him some sense of his lineage.

"Let's see if I remember this right. Her dad was Moise, that was his Christian name, the one he used when he signed at Treaty time. Everyone knew him as Wapos. Wapos had a brother they called Sikos and a sister Piso."

"Rabbit, Weasel and Lynx," Elsie translated for Benji's sake. "And Piso never married. Eleanor said she had six kids but was never seen with a man. She used to live by herself. Had her own dog team, did her own hunting, set fish nets by herself, everything."

"Where did she live?" Elsie couldn't place her.

"Everywhere. When she got tired of one spot she packed up and moved somewhere else, built a new cabin, planted a new garden, wherever her mood took her. The last place she lived was just past where the Treaty was signed, up the river a little. I remember visiting her. She wouldn't speak a word of English, old Cree, a little hard for me to understand sometimes growing up on the reserve like I did. She was at Treaty signing too, had her own stories about it."

"You knew somebody who was at Treaty." Benji spoke slow, unbelieving.

"Yeah, a few. Are you calling me old?"

Benji fumbled. "No,. no I didn't mean it that way, the opposite in fact. I always thought the Treaties happened, like a really long time ago, you know. I can't imagine anyone, not even my dad, who might have known someone who was actually there."

"Look around, the land hasn't changed. In real time it was only yesterday that white people came here."

Benji had no means of grasping the enormity of Rosie's statement. It was simply and completely beyond him. He changed the subject. "What about her kids, that Piso woman, what became of them?"

"Some of them are still around, not many though. Philip Charles would be her, let's see . . ." Rosie consulted her inner genealogical chart. "Philip would be her great-grandson."

"Is that the guy who walks everywhere, the one people call Traveller." Elsie tried to connect the name from the chart to a person.

"Yeah, that's him. Just like his great-grandmother, too free a spirit to ever settle down."

～

"What'ja doin'?" Rosie asked as she came up to Ben.

Finally separated herself from that baby, he noticed. "Oh, just looking over the old garden," He pointed with his toe at the long wide leaves growing up through the grass. "Hey, check this out. The horseradish is still here."

"Horseradish." She made a sour face.

"Yeah, Dad really liked it. Mom wasn't much for it. He ate it on almost everything, ground it up and mixed it with a little vinegar."

"To each their own, I guess." The sourness was still on her face. "Looks like the catnip survived." She was over near one of the remaining corner posts, the one that still held a pole rail angled down to where another post had rotted and fallen over. She knelt beside the pale-coloured bush, plucked a single leaf and gently nibbled on it to draw out the mint flavour as though to remove the taste of horseradish.

Ben responded with a slow "Oh yeah." He remembered catnip. Remembered a cup of tea, a blend of catnip and muskeg leaves that drained away any residue of stress a day might leave on a body. "Mom would be happy to know that was still here." He too plucked a leaf to nibble on. The mild mint taste brought back other memories. "Dad used this to bait lynx. Worked like you wouldn't believe."

"I believe it." Rosie closed her eyes for a few seconds while her mouth moved ever so slowly, alone with her spit and her tongue and the roof of her mouth and the sweet mint. "Oh, so nice, so nice." She opened her eyes. "You were lucky to have them as parents."

"Dad, was more the potato gardener. Had a bigger garden down there a ways." He pointed east. "For potatoes, beets, carrots, turnips, that sort of stuff. Mom took care of this one closer to the house. Used to be flowers all along that fence line." He half turned toward where Benji, Elsie, and Rachel were approaching. "I wonder." He remembered something. "I wonder if the raspberries survived."

They had. Large ripe berries weighed down thick thorny branches. "So, why did they grow raspberries?" Elsie asked around a mouthful, crunched tiny seeds with her back teeth. "Instead of picking wild ones? They grow everywhere."

"Why walk." Ben answered as he plopped a single dark, thoroughly ripe berry into his mouth, and another. "Raspberries don't take any looking after."

"I remember years when there weren't any wild berries." Rosie stood waist deep in the bramble, held Rachel high on her hip, held up a berry for the little girl to grasp in her fist and mush into her mouth. "Just makes sense to have a patch you can look after, especially in dry years."

"Self-sufficient." Benji ate a handful at a time, picked until there wasn't any room left in his cupped palm before filling his mouth and himself with tart sweetness.

"No, they didn't go to town for very much." Ben looked around. The rabbit pens looked to still be in relatively good shape, the chicken wire stretched across the doors might need a few staples to keep out weasels, maybe replace a few rotted floorboards. The asphalt-shingled roof had done what it was intended to and protected the low pens from the weather. He remembered rabbit soup, potatoes, onions, thickened with flour, lots of salt and pepper. They could have gone out and snared rabbits instead of hauling in feed every autumn, but why walk. The work of cleaning out the pens rewarded them with manure for the gardens to grow the vegetable leftovers that helped feed the rabbits. A good cycle.

～

Monica felt a tinge of jealousy, not toward Rosie for being out with Ben, not even toward young and pretty Elsie. It was the sight of Ben and Benji each with a hand on opposite sides of the bow of the boat, pulling it up onto the shore, working together. She'd had less than half of an uncomfortable day with her son, and here he was, working beside his dad as though they had known each other all their lives. She had not even acknowledged to Benji that his father was Ben Robe of Moccasin Lake. He must have researched that for himself, not that it would have taken much. How many professors named Ben would have taught political studies . . . ? Internet searching could provide present addresses. The thought bothered her deeper. If Benji could find Ben with the little information he had, so could Homeland Security if Abe gave him up.

"Hey, guys." She hid her anxiety and grabbed the bow of the boat to help. But the boat was as far up the beach as it was going by the time she got there.

~

Hershel Rosche arrived not long after the Second World War on a shiny new diesel train. He liked Prince Albert, a young city, a city that would grow, become something. It had potential. He liked the wide sweeping North Saskatchewan River, liked the architecture of the hotel on Central Avenue, and Indians, the first he had seen since his arrival in Canada, there on River Street, going into a fur buyer's store. Hershel followed them in. He carried a small heavy leather case that he occasionally shifted from hand to hand, but never put down. He walked around the tiny store, pretended he was looking at the scarce merchandise, the six used rifles leaning against the wall, the bins of blue steel spring traps, and the coils of snare wire. He was there to see real Indians. He listened in while the Indian negotiated in his own gentle fashion. Both parties to the negotiation knew that there were other fur buyers and that some of them were only a short block up the street.

Hershel watched the Indian shake out a lynx pelt, hold it out at shoulder height and look down at where it touched the plank floor. Without words, he told the fur buyer. *This is a large lynx, not a medium, it's worth more.*

The buyer stood behind the counter, sifted pelts, not looking at them anymore, just moving them to keep his hands busy. "Tell you what. I like you, Adolphus; you're a good customer. Fifty dollars for the whole pile. What do you say?"

Adolphus didn't answer, he touched the pelts, moved a mink, shiny black over toward his left, sorted through the pile for another, slightly larger mink, and placed it beside the first. He might have been sorting out the pelts by species, but he might have begun to package them up.

"Tell you what." The buyer picked up the first mink. The skinning and stretching skills were obvious. The pelt was perfectly shaped, unblemished, completely dried. "Because it's you, I might go as high as sixty. But don't you be telling anyone now."

Adolphus moved the mink pelt back to the pile.

Hershel was not pretending to look at anything other than the transaction. He was impressed. The Indian knew negotiation, knew how to use time and timing, understood the art of it. He was a man of Hershel's spirit, a reader of humanity.

Three days later Hershel used his skills, sized up the town and its people until he found the man he wanted, someone with refined taste, who wore a good-quality coat, and clean shoes. There were a few around, in the hotel lobby or in the restaurants, who dressed well, who looked like they might have the money Hershel was looking for, but they were too flashy, too new, did not walk with the confidence he wanted: someone comfortable with his wealth, who did not have to show it.

"Excuse me, sir. Might I have a moment of your time? I have something that might interest you." Hershel began the sale. Invited the man to a quiet corner of the Avenue Hotel lobby, the finest hotel in Prince Albert. He sat in a stuffed leather chair with the leather case between his feet, felt its sturdiness between his calves.

"It's Swiss made, very fine quality. Something not appreciated so much over here it seems. I know in Europe it would demand a much larger price, but here I am in Canada, a fine place, someday this country will rival old Europe in fashion, but today very few appreciate quality. I don't expect to get what this is worth. I am prepared to live with that."

Hershel sold his first watch. He built a neat jewellery store just off Central Avenue, where he worked every day from when he opened it in 1951 until he took some time off in 1993, feeling a bit tired. His family buried him two weeks later up the hill. A good quality plain marble headstone marks the grave, nothing fancy, nothing flashy.

The store never did need customers. The heavy leather bag contained the wealth of a family that had presented itself modestly to the world for generations, but always with quiet dignity. Hershel's older brother Marcel had been the exception, liked to show what he had. When the soldiers came to Marcel's, before the paintings were stripped from the walls and an *oberstleutnant* drove away in Marcel's polished black-and-chrome automobile, Hershel fled.

Ben had attended Hershel's funeral. He and his parents, Adolphus and Eleanor, had stood back from the small gathering around the fresh-torn hole in the sod. Shook hands with Hershel's son John, such a simple name, and his sister Eleanor. The younger Eleanor had hugged the older Eleanor before they got in Ben's little car for the quiet ride back north.

Bells tinkled as Ben entered Rosche Jewellery and Collectables. He stood with his hands in his pockets looking into a glass-covered case as John came out of the back. Eleanor was with another customer and did not acknowledge Ben's presence with more than a nod and the faintest of smiles. John held one finger pointing downward by his side, hidden from view as he passed on the other side of the glass case from Ben. Ben did not respond. John pointed two fingers downward and still Ben did not respond. As John passed, Ben extended three fingers on the glass case. John responded, his eyebrows raised slightly, and he went out the door, tinkled bells before he went up the street toward where the banks were clustered on Central Avenue.

Ben continued to look at the selection of watches in the case, one hand in his pocket feeling the small soft metal bars that weighed exactly ten ounces each, until John returned. Without a word, Ben followed him into the back of the store.

"I didn't have that much money here." John reached inside his jacket, inside the breast pocket. "Thirty thousand Ameros raises people's attention." He put an envelope on the worktable, knelt and opened a safe that was out of view under the table.

"Is something wrong?" he asked as he handed over the money and took the three gold bars without looking at them and placed them in the safe, shut the heavy door and turned the brass handle, listening for the double click of the lock before taking his hand away.

"No, not really. Just being careful." Ben put the additional bills into the bank deposit envelope without counting either. "In case something should come up."

Ben felt a tinge of guilt as he drove past the building that once housed the Prince Albert Indian and Metis Friendship Centre, as though he had taken the people's money. The envelope in his hip pocket felt thick, uncomfortable to sit on. He took it out, wiggled it around the seat belt for a second before extracting it completely. He went to put it in his shirt pocket. The shirt was damp and sticky, the envelope too bulky. Finally he threw it on the dash of the truck, just as safe there as anywhere.

It wasn't the people's money. It was money that did not exist, erased money. In the first days of the invasion, annexation, everyone scrambled, everyone shifted belongings and assets toward more secure forms. Some people hoarded food, others converted their cash to carryables. The Saskatchewan Indian Gaming Authority wanted Ben on their board of governors, not because Ben knew anything about running casinos, but because he was a respected professor, an Indian with a position of prestige. They didn't want him there, they wanted his image: honest, intelligent, educated, a class addition.

While the planes were bombing the base at Trenton, when the 401 was jammed tighter than that multilane highway between Toronto and Kingston had ever known, Ben took a certified cheque to Sport Gold. He went alone, security guards attract attention, better to be inconspicuous with that amount of money. The exchange was quick, efficient, a heavy oak desk in a large, bare office, two uniformed security guards outside the door, another just inside, his back to the wall. They look thuggish, Ben thought as he entered. The official of the corporation handling the exchange looked too young for the job, close-cropped brown hair, glasses that made his nondescript eyes look larger than they were. His appearance, his choice of clothes, cargo pants with bulky pockets and a golf shirt, did not inspire confidence. Neither did the toothpick wiggling at the corner of his mouth as he spoke.

"So even the casinos think this is going to last. Oh well. Today's price is six hundred an ounce, ten ounce lots."

"Stock price this morning was down to four-sixty-nine." Ben felt an obligation to the board of governors to take care of their investment.

"It went up while you were out front with everyone else. How many lots?"

Ben looked down at the cheque, made a mental calculation. "Forty- two." He handed over the quarter-million-dollar cheque. The toothpick wiggled while the company official made his own mental calculations. "You're short two thousand."

"Yes," Ben faced him confidently, the older man across the desk from the young and anxious. Negotiation is about time. Whoever has the most time will take the hurried. Ben had time. There were still people in the outer room waiting, nervously, rushed, terrorized even.

"All right." He took out the toothpick, and Ben walked away with a cardboard box weighing slightly over twenty-five pounds. He had done well for the board, secured a large portion of their assets against the unforeseeable.

⁓

"We're done." The voice of Timothy Bird, the chairman of SIGA crackled in Ben's cell phone.

"What do you mean?" Ben looked at the cardboard box on the car seat beside him.

"A virus wiped us out this morning. Everything's erased."

"I have to see the board. I have something to report." Ben did not want to explain over a cell phone, didn't know who might be listening.

"There is no board. Don't you get it? Everything is erased, absolutely everything. All of the casinos are closed, well they're not even closed, abandoned is more like it. When people found out they weren't getting paid, they just walked out. Everybody from the floor sweepers, the dealers, security, management, everybody just walked away. Nobody even had the sense to lock the doors."

"I don't get it." Ben needed reason, rationality that was not there.

"What's to get? They didn't like the idea of casinos so they used a military virus to wipe us out, targeted at SIGA. We no longer exist, you won't find a single byte of information that refers to us. Payroll is gone, Human Resources does not have any records of employees, Security doesn't exist. The board doesn't exist. We have no minutes of meetings, we have no records, no financial statements to review. You don't even exist Ben. The virus must've started with SIGA and spread to all of the directors, every employee's name is wiped out. There is no evidence anywhere that there ever was a board, or a corporation."

"Listen Tim, you have to reconvene the board. It's important. I have in my possession a sizable amount of board assets."
"Whatever you might have is nothing. Keep it. Use it for your retirement, consider it your severance package. And hey, Ben. You take care of yourself, and maybe we'll see you around."

~

Dean Fisher stood on his farm, he just stood there, looking north. Six-thousand-four-hundred acres of mixed grain and cattle keeps a man busy, too busy to stop in the middle of the day, but he was doing a lot of that recently, standing there, staring, always north. Not that far, he thought, not that far from South Dakota to Canada. He could almost see it just there beyond the rolling parched yellow horizon. *You have to find some feed for those cattle.* The thought forced itself into his mind. He let it ride there a moment and went back to thinking about Canada; Saskatoon Saskatchewan Canada.

Nothing happened there, nothing was supposed to happen there. Vicky had been so happy that their son Rick had been posted to Saskatchewan and not Quebec City. He would be safe there, quiet, rural, no population to speak of. It wasn't that long ago, in the good days before all this, they had gone to northern Saskatchewan, drove up in the rented RV. Dean remembered Otter Rapids on the Churchill River, little Ricky, he must have only been eleven, twelve maybe — no, he was twelve — just finished sixth grade, the year of the excellent report card. Ricky swam the rapids, seen other kids do it and begged until Dean and Vicky bundled him in an over-large life jacket and stood on the iron bridge with the expanded metal deck and looked down on the rolling blue water, churned into sparkling white foam. They stood holding hands, their hearts racing, while little Ricky floated and bobbed down the rapid, waved up at them as he passed under the bridge. Dean could still see the big smile on his son's wet face. It wasn't that long ago.

Ricky had to grow up, couldn't stay the brave little boy forever. He turned eighteen and they drafted him into their army, not Dean's army and certainly not Vicky's army, that army that belonged to the others, those crazies, those stomping and yelling people, their army. Drafted Dean's son, took him away from the farm. Dean was happy here. His Dodge pickup with the chrome stacks that rumbled when he drove it into Sioux Falls was still in the Quonset for when he came back. He could go to town with a nice girl, take her to a movie, marry her and bring her home to the farm.

Dean kicked his toe into the dry earth, raised powder dust. Missing in action, how can that be? Missing in Saskatchewan; shee-it, they had joked with Rick before he left that where he was going there was no place to hide. "Keep your head down."

"Yeah, right, in a gopher hole, I'd guess."

Three weeks now, Ricky was missing for three weeks; there was hope. If something had happened they would have found him by now. No, as each day came and went, the better his chances, Dean hoped. That was all he had, hope. Hope for the best, hope that Ricky would come home. He kicked the dry dirt again, looked to the west where a promising cloud was beginning to build, maybe it would rain, maybe a thunderstorm would come by with a little moisture, as long as it didn't bring hail.

It was all over by the time Ben arrived in Saskatoon. Idylwyld Drive was open again and traffic flowed down its length over the melted and blackened pavement on the southbound lane. Someone had hauled away both trees, cut them into pieces, left sawdust on the sidewalk and a few small branches too small to bother with. Ester Kingfisher cried often, cried when she thought of those trees, the elms. Mostly she cried when she thought of the elm that had stood in front of her house. Elmer would miss them. Poor Elmer, at least he didn't live to see this.

Roger Ratte's bullet-ridden Toyota Prius sat on its flattened tires on a low trailer in the government insurance inspection garage. The inspector didn't have good news. He could have told Roger when the car was first brought in, but he wanted to hear the story, so he went through the motions of assessing the damage, even wrote figures onto the form clipped to a board. Then he invited Roger into an office, sat across an empty particleboard desk and asked an easy, "So what happened?"

"I was on my way home, Northbound on Idylwyld, about twenty-eighth, twenty-ninth, somewhere in there and holy shit! a tree fell across the street right in front of me." Roger had told the story a few times already, once to his wife over the phone to explain why he wasn't coming home that night, once to the guy at the hotel. He had it down, had practised it again on the way here this morning, each time adding a little more detail, arranging it chronologically.

"There was this old lady, I talked to her after, her name is Ester — she seen everything. I guess she lives right there, all her life she said. Anyway when the tree fell in front of my car there was this guy with his hood up and tied tight around his face so you couldn't see it very well and the old lady, Ester, she was still trying to take the chainsaw away from him. That's the tree on my side of the street. The tree on the other side came down just as I was getting out of my car. So they blocked traffic both north and south. I knew something was wrong then. I knew something was really wrong. The guy with the chainsaw on my side of the street, he gave the chainsaw to Ester, well he sort of threw it at her, or let her take it. I don't know. Then he ran away, towards downtown, right past me; I was on the sidewalk by then. Weird shit, I figured. I went to see if Ester was all right, she was sitting on the grass, it kinda' slopes down to the street there, she was sitting there holding the chainsaw where the guy pushed her down and the saw was still running, and traffic is piling up now if you know what I mean, on both sides of the street, nobody can go anywhere. I sure couldn't have got my car out of there with all the cars behind me and the tree in front of me and the way the land slopes down on each side. I was stuck there. And I knew. I knew something was really wrong. I grabbed Ester, took the saw away from her and tried to get her out of the way of whatever was coming. Tell you the truth, I didn't give a shit about my car at that moment. I was just getting out of the way, and getting Ester out of the way.

Then Homeland Security, they must have been behind me, five, six vehicles of them, all together, you know the way they travel. Well, when the traffic got blocked they must have gone over the meridian there onto the southbound lane where there was no traffic and come up right beside my car on the opposite side of the street where they were blocked by the other tree and the vehicles piled up behind it on that side.

They just opened fire, as soon as they came to a stop, they must have realized it was an ambush and they opened up first, shooting everything. My car got it the worst because it was the closest. They were just, fuck! there were bullets flying everywhere. By this time I got Ester back off the street. There's kinda a cement wall there by her sidewalk up to her house. I held her down in there and laid on top of her. And you know what she's crying about when those bullets are smashing into everything? She's crying about the tree.

Then all I heard was *whoomp* and the first HS vehicle, it's all on fire. Must have been one of those Montreal cocktails we hear about, you know the one with diesel fuel and Styrofoam and oxygen mixed into it like an Aerobar; must have been something like one of those. I didn't see who threw it. I seen one guy on the other side of the street up on the roof of a building come right out to the edge, right out into the bullets. He had some kind of machine gun or something and he was shooting at the first vehicle. Must have been drawing fire so his buddies could get up close enough to throw I figure.

Well they got him. Yeah, fuck man, just like in a bad movie, I watched that guy come off that building, then *whoomp* and that front vehicle, you can't see it anymore, all flames, orange, orange flames, and those HS guys never had a chance, whatever the hell they hit them with, it had some concussion to it. Felt it from where we were on the other side of the street. Then there's more bullets and another *whoomp*, that one must have been the back vehicle, I don't know, I got my head down and there's shooting like you wouldn't believe. Never in your wildest imagination man, you couldn't imagine how many bullets, hundreds, no thousands, thousands of bullets from both sides. Just fuckin' incredible."

Roger stopped, out of breath a little, looking at the inspector, waited for a response. The inspector sat there with the edge of the clipboard on his crossed leg, held it with both hands leaned against the desk, sat there with his mouth slightly open, maybe he breathed through his mouth instead of through his nose that was too small for his face. He sat there for the whole story, didn't flinch even once, not even for the *whoomps*. He waited, possibly for more. But there was no more. Roger wasn't going to talk about carrying Ester into her house, putting her on the old sofa, knocking things off the coffee table, bottles and bottles of medication, of finding a bottle of gin under the pillow when he propped her up and tried to make her comfortable.

"I'm sorry to have to tell you this, but SGI policy does not insure against incidents of war. It's in every policy. War is something you cannot buy insurance against."

Roger put his hands on the edge of the desk, not threatening, not at all; he just needed someplace to put them after waving them around for so long, tracing bullet paths and mushroom clouds. He was tired, shocked and tired.

"Incident of war." His voice was flat.

"Yeah, it's in the policy."

"But the Americans say this isn't a war, it's an annexation, justified in international law as a protective measure."

"Don't matter what spin the politicians put on it; any right thinking court in Canada will determine what happened to your car was an act of war. Fighting an insurgency is an act of war, I'm sure."

"Insurgency." Roger's voice remained flat, questioning.

"Well, yeah, an insurgency is classified as an act of war." The inspector was beginning to feel threatened, remembered his training on psychopathy. *Cold emotionless, kill you as soon as look at you.* Roger was too calm. He should be upset.

Roger remained rational. "An insurgency is when people try to overthrow a legitimate government, right?"

"Uh-huh." The inspector held the clipboard, maybe he could defend himself with it.

"A resistance is when people fight off an invasion, right."

"Uh-huh." Agree with him and maybe he won't do anything.

"So what do we have here, an insurgency or a resistance?"

The inspector shrugged. He didn't know.

Roger stayed still, calm, the car really didn't matter. Insurance, no insurance, fix the flats, buy some glass, maybe even duct tape up the holes, drive it out of here, what the hell, didn't matter. And this guy here with the clipboard, he didn't know shit, not even worth talking to anymore, just a dummy, doing a dummy job, not thinking, not questioning, didn't even know if he was living through a revolution, an uprising, or a resistance. Didn't matter they were all likely incidents of war to him. Did he even know what war was? Probably not.

War is when an old lady cries because a tree was cut down; that's what war is.

～

Monica was not at home. Ben rang the buzzer of apartment 607, waited in the glass case cubical, stood in front of the panel array of names, numbers and buttons and wondered whether he had the right address. He checked the slip of paper again. No this was right. 607- 212 4th Avenue South, Saskatoon. He rang the buzzer again before he went back to his truck to wait, looked skyward as he hurried the few yards between the front doors of the apartment building and the street.

～

Monica sat on the floor with her back against the wall, something about drinking wine and sitting on the floor that seemed right, brought back memories of university, memories that had laughter at their core. This was different, sitting here because they didn't want to be seen through the windows. She leaned as she passed the bottle over to Ed Trembley and he leaned away from the adjacent wall to take it, tilt it, glug it, once, twice, spilt some in his eagerness. He put it down between his outstretched legs, wiped his mouth with his sleeve. "So, was it the full council that decided, or what?"

"Pretty near, there were a few not there, Sakej and Emily are out of town, but most of them agreed. There was definitely quorum, if that's what you're asking."

"No, I don't doubt council. Whatever they said, that's fine with me." His hand on the long neck of the bottle, he lifted it from the floor, held it there. "I'm a soldier, whatever I'm told." He raised it, glugged it again once, and passed it back to Monica.

"Me too, Ed, whatever council says." She sipped at the bottle, looked at the label, a plain white paste-on, a prairie picture and a cherry bush with oversized berries. "I don't believe that people would put their name on a bottle anymore."

"Paul Reiseman makes good wine, always has, why not show that he's proud of it."

"It's not bad." Monica sipped again, lips to bottle, a kiss of a sip.

"Four-year-old chokecherry." Ed leaned his weight into the wall, rested his head against the plasterboard. "Tests out at 18 percent."

"You can tell." Monica's head buzzed, her belly warmed, she kissed the end of the bottle again before passing it back.

"So, you were up north you said. How was that?"

"Not bad, I like it up there, like there's no war going on, trees, lakes, that sort of stuff, and the people, they just keep doing what they always do." She did not want to tell Ed about her son, not that it was a private thing, she could share private things. It was because having an adult son would make her seem old, and Monica did not want to be old, she wanted to be a university student again, sitting on the floor drinking wine from the bottle.

"You went to see Ben Robe. How's he getting along?" Ed needed this visit, needed someone in this barren house besides himself and the prisoners downstairs, needed a fellow human.

"Ben? Ben will be all right I suppose. Took the news a little rough. He's probably never seen himself as part of the resistance, at risk."

"He'll get used to it. Everybody's at risk."

"Yeah, that's true." She reached out, indicating the bottle. "Don't know what he's likely to do. He was pretty quiet." She raised the bottle. "But that's the way Ben is, doesn't ever say too much, so you never know exactly what he's thinking." She drank.

"How much does he know?"

"Next to nothing."

"Then what are we worried about? It's not like Abe. Now if Abe talks, a lot of people are on the line. If they take in Ben, no big deal right."

"Except that Ben could be a power, if we used him right. The man is brilliant. Have you ever heard him speak?"

"Naw." Ed shook his head and a lock of yellow brown hair fell across his forehead.

"He can move you with his words. A natural orator of the old Cree tradition. A magic voice."

"I guess I've never heard an Indian give a speech."

"Did you know . . . " Monica found the space she was looking for, she was a student again. "Commissioner Morris when he came out West . . . "

"Who?" Ed leaned away from the wall; he was either inattentive or having trouble with his hearing.

"Alexander Morris, the treaty commissioner, you know, the Indian Treaties 1874, Treaty Four, Treaty Six up at Fort Carlton and Fort Pitt."

"Okay." Ed was on track.

"Well, he was so impressed by the ability of the Cree to make speeches that he tried to copy them. That's why some people think the words, 'as long as the grass grows, the river flows and the sun shines,' were used. Morris was trying to sound like a great Cree orator. Don't know if he ever pulled it off. But that's where that stuff comes from."

"Doesn't do them much good now, does it?" He was thinking of grass and rivers as he leaned back.

"Maybe not. Ben taught us that the words weren't as important as the spirit of the Treaties. Maybe something there. But that isn't where I was going with this. Now Ben has that gift, that ability to move you with his voice. If we had him in the resistance, or even out of the resistance but speaking for us. He could move mountains for us."

"And so, will he or what?"

"Will he what?"

"Be our speaker, move those political mountains for us."

~

Monica did not have an answer; she looked through the glass of the wine bottle, held it up to the light, slightly lower than half. Half full or half empty? She drank, more than a sip, a full mouthful, but not a glug.

"I think," she leaned out extending the bottle toward Ed. "I think that if we work it right, Ben might come onside, bring his voice and his knowledge and . . . " she nodded to herself, "and his wisdom. The man has something to offer. A good place for him might be on council."

"Ever think we need more soldiers on council and less old politicians?"

"Council makes the hard decisions. They need both. They need to have thinkers and doers. Council is not afraid to act. Sometimes we get frustrated because they seem to take forever, but when it's crunch time, they act. Like this morning, they heard Betsy's petition, thought about it, discussed among themselves and agreed to put Abe's name on the list of people we would agree to exchange for those two downstairs. I didn't see any delay, or inability to act."

"Like I said before, whatever council tells me to do, that's fine with me. But you try staying in this house for three weeks. I was happy as hell to get out for that bit of action yesterday. It was like a holiday. Fireworks and everything."

"And it was council that planned that out. Every detail of it."

"Well they didn't plan for that crazy woman who was trying to take the chain saw away from me." Ed laughed, a tiny laugh at the thought.

"Yeah." Monica smiled. "You owe the resistance one chainsaw, don't you?"

"They can deduct it from my pay." Ed laughed louder, a real laugh. *Nothing from nothing leaves nothing.* He sang the words to an old song. "Wish we had music."

"Yeah." Monica nodded. Music would go good with the wine. "Why not, I mean this place is supposed to look like a normal house isn't it, not draw attention. A little music is normal you'd think. So long as it isn't loud and blaring and someone calls the cops, right?"

"There's a radio on the alarm clock." Ed pulled his legs under himself, used the wall to help stand up.

"An old rock and roll station. Not that new stuff, and definitely not country." Monica tasted the wine. "Something mindless." she added as Ed walked past.

"It's all mindless."

～

The music filtered through the floor, muffled, undecipherable, but clearly music. Rick Fisher heard it, reached a foot out in the dark and nudged Wally. Wally wasn't doing so good, maybe if he woke up, the music would help. Wally stirred.

"Music." Rick whispered.

"Oh." Wally answered and stayed still.

Rick hoped he was listening.

The music became clear as Ed put the radio on the floor upstairs. It sounded better to Rick and Wally in the basement than what Monica and Ed were hearing. The wood of the floor filtered out the tin sound of the speaker, added bass, added quality.

Rolling Stones. Rick recognized "Street Fighting Man." Leaned his head back against the post and listened. What an absolute blessing music could bring. Rick closed his eyes and let it fill him, lift him. He was in his truck again, blasting down the gravel road from town with Clarice, the windows were down and her hair was flipping around her face and she was tapping on the armrest between them to the music. He wanted to take her hand but he needed both of his on the steering wheel. He was showing off how fast he could drive, and the rush of the truck, and the spray of the gravel, and the pounding of the music and Clarice was laughing, and the sun was shining and he wasn't tied to a post in a dark basement. Ricky went home and the draft notice never came in the mail. Mom and Dad were home, and the grass was green again and the cows were fat and the Rolling Stones were on tour again. He would take Clarice in the truck and they would drive over to Minneapolis and go to the concert, and he would never put on a uniform, or learn to use a gun.

~

The sun was setting straight down 22nd Street West, into Ben's eyes. He flipped down the visor, peered under it, hoped he would be able to see the streetlights in the glare. No telling when Monica might get home, try again in the morning. He turned the truck into the parking area of the Westwind

Motel — out of the sun, out of the glare, he could see again and in a few minutes he would be under the cover of the motel roof, away from the sky that was watching him. A night of television and clean, sterile sheets, something different, wouldn't be so bad. Maybe a T-bone steak in that Montana's restaurant that seemed almost deserted. Maybe they should change the name. But that might seem unpatriotic, or insurgent even.

～

The screwdriver slipped in the notch of the wood screw again. Rosie looked at the rounded end of the Robertson driver, wore out, not of very good quality to begin with, it was all that she had to work with. She reapplied it, put pressure on it and managed another half turn on the screw before it slipped again. Bit by tiny bit, she tightened the hinge on the screen door. Where were the men when things needed fixing?

Lester was out, hadn't been around for a couple days, maybe he found work, doubtful, but maybe. Benji, well could she have asked him even if he and Elsie were there? Probably not. It was too soon in their relationship to begin to consider him a son-in-law.

She stood and tried the door. It swung loosely on the hinge, didn't fit the frame. The hinge lifted as the door shut. The wood frame was rotted, the screw holes worn too large. She opened the door again to look at the frame, three-quarter inch, probably spruce plank, maybe she could find one, somewhere. She could not afford to buy it, damn shame, lumber coming out of the country all over, pulp wood, fibreboard plant over by the highway and nothing in the community to build with.

Even if she had the right board, even if she could get a new one, she didn't have the tools to shape it, a mitre saw would be nice, she didn't even have a chisel to counterset the hinge.

For a moment, just a moment, she missed Lawrence's shop, not the farm, not the prairie, just the shop with the tools hung on a pegboard. Wondered where he was? Drunk somewhere, unable to sober up; definitely not the man she had married, not nearly, maybe not a man at all, not anymore.

Sadness tried to fill her; she pushed it away. *No*, she was not going there; that was where Lawrence was, unable to forget, unable to forgive himself. The sadness tried again, brought an image with it this time. Lawrence on the lower step, Darren in his arms, and Darren's head; warped, not right and the blood on Lawrence's shirt. Dougie standing beside the truck, could not come close, could not face his mother, their mother.

Then the police were there, in her kitchen asking questions, and Lawrence could not stop crying, wiping snot and tears on his sleeve, how it happened, how the handgun was in the glovebox of the truck, for no reason, no damn reason other than Lawrence liked handguns, big handguns, 44 Magnum and a 45 Smith and Wesson upstairs in their bedroom. He was going to be charged with unsafe storage of a firearm. That's it. The police had done their job. Wrote up a charge, left the paper on the table. They had to charge him with something. The death of his oldest son, his pride, was not murder, an accidental shooting and the police fulfilled their duty, took notes, a statement from Dougie and left.

Dougie's statement to the police, was not to the police. He looked at his mother as he spoke. "Darren said, don't play with that. It might be loaded. And I said 'don't be stupid. Dad would never leave a loaded gun in the glovebox', and I pointed it at his head and pulled the trigger just to prove it."

Then Rosie had three children, not four. Lawrence never saw that, he never counted the kids. He never stopped and said "this is what I have left." He didn't know how to bury a relative, mourn for one year, cut your hair and then let the dead go, don't cry for them all the time, that just keeps their spirits around, keeps them from going to the Otherside to be with their relatives over there. Maybe if Lawrence had cut his hair. No don't go there. Don't try to reshape the past. That's what he's still doing. Saying what if, what if, what if, and drinking and crying. It was poor Lawrence. He didn't even have the strength to get mad about it. Poor Lawrence.

Rosie heard that he still gets up early in the morning, five AM but now it's to go out and wander the streets of Prince Albert looking for bottles and cans, until he has enough from the dumpsters and alleys behind the schools and other sure places where people don't bother to recycle, until he has enough to buy his daily ration of rotten grape. Why was it that they made such a big thing about alcohol consumption these days and they still sold that shit in the liquor stores, rot gut wine, cheap, rancid, and twenty percent alcohol?

She put the screwdriver back in the kitchen drawer, the drawer where things collected, things that did not have their own place, shut it with her hip and shut Lawrence and the prairie and the farm and that brief other life, shut them and would not go there, stay there. Wonder how Dougie was doing? Maybe she should give him a call now that Elsie had got the phone reconnected, find out how he's making out with his welding business.

"I'm glad you phoned mom. I was going to give you a call, but we've been busy like you would not believe."

"What's going on?"

"Lined up a contract, a big one. Four units."

"But you only have two."

"I know, that's what's been keeping me busy, tryin' to find two more welders big enough for this job."

"Well that's good, that's good my boy, tell me about this job."

"North Dakota, Mom. North Dakota, can you believe it. Big pipeline, and I mean a big pipeline, this job is good for at least three years."

"So, you're moving." Worry crept into her voice.

"No, no don't worry, Mom, I'd never run off on you." Dougie laughed into the phone. "Marie and the girls are staying here. I'll be gone quite a bit at first, setting things up, but it shouldn't be long and all I'll be doing is supervising." He laughed again "and collecting those big fat pay cheques."

"Good for you, my boy, good for you. I knew you'd do good. You always liked playing with your dad's welder," Rosie caught herself, "and hey, look at you now. So what kind of pipeline is this, gas, oil, or what."

"Water. A great big pipeline all the way from Lake Winnipeg to Texas and the best part is that I don't need pressure tickets. Not like a gas pipeline, where they're super fussy. No this is high volume pipe, big diameter. And I mean big Mom, you can drive a truck down the inside of this pipe. Those must be some thirsty Texans."

～

Lester shovelled grain from the back of the pickup into the fermenting pot. This was something he understood, a bit bigger scale, but not that much different than jailhouse brew — yeast, sugar, and something to rot. Farmers were happy to get rid of poor quality grain, stuff that wasn't worth putting on a train and, besides, brewers paid in cash.

Lester stopped, leaned on the shovel for a moment before rolling back the blue tarpaulin to reveal more musty grain. He tired easy. Out of shape, that's all. Just out of shape. Maybe he could find a set of weights and work out, get back that muscle he used to have, muscle that rippled under a tight tee-shirt and warned others not to mess with Lester Bigeye.

He looked around as he rested, both hands on the end of the handle. This used to be somebody's garage, a place for repairing heavy equipment, loaders, dozers, graders. A heavy plank workbench ran all down one side. There were still bits and pieces of engine, or maybe transmission, Lester wasn't sure which, scattered about. The concrete floor still showed black from spilled oil and grease and years of big rubber tires or clank of steel track.

This was a good job he had. It paid not bad, pretty good in fact. The only requirement was the ability to keep his mouth shut, not rat out. He had years and years of experience at that, was well qualified.

The roll-up door creaked a warning and Lester put the shovel back to the grain. The door lifted on its rusted track until it was waist high, the spot where it always stuck, needed a good jerk to get it past and moving again. Red ducked underneath, scraped his back against the battered rubber weather guard on the bottom of the door and let it fall behind him.

"Hey, there."

"Hey, yourself." Lester stopped shovelling again.

"Hotter'n a bitch outside, least you got some shade in here." Red lifted the brim of his canvas hat — green with a gold star on the front, the Castro hat, the kind of hat that the new revolutionaries, and anyone else who wanted to say something to the world wore — and wiped his forehead.

"Not so bad." Lester was feeling good today and that was different than most days.

"Smoke?" Red had the package out, flipping back the cardboard lid.

"Sure." Lester moved to the side of the truck, dragged the shovel and leaned out toward Red reaching. "Marlboros!" he recognized the package.

"Yeah, it's all I got. Hard to get Canadian smokes, even on the Rez."

"It'll do." Lester reached again, this time for the lighter. He sat on the edge of the truck box, liked this position, a little higher than Red, who stood with his elbows rested on the truck, not that Lester had any concerns about Red. Red was a decent enough of a guy, Lester just liked being in positions of advantage. "So, what's up?"

"Nothing much. Just stopping by to see how you're making out."

"Wish I was making out."

"You're too ugly for that man." Red grinned up at Lester.

Lester took a deep pull on the cigarette, let Red's little jab go past, wait for his turn to jab him back. "How many gallons did we get from that last batch?"

"Five full barrels. We'll make about three grand on that."

"That's a lot of work for three peesly grand. You know," Lester paused for emphasis, "if we ran this like a business, we might make some decent coin."

Red was alert. The business word he'd heard before. "We're doin' all right. Might not be getting stinking rich, but we're doin' okay. This is more a community service kind of thing anyway."

"I know some people, could really set this operation up right. Supply, distribution, protection."

"I know those people too, and no thanks. Listen Lester you forget about that. We don't want to attract attention here.

We're small scale and it works. We make a little coin and people can afford to drive their kids to town for happy meals."

"Up to you." Lester straightened his back, gave himself a little more height over Red. "But if you ever want, just let me know and I'll put you in touch with NS management."

"Not today, Lester my man, not today."

~

"So why do they call this Skunk Point?"

"Don't know, it's always been called that."

"Maybe should have called it Rocky Point." Benji was having trouble walking on the smooth, wet stones along the shore. Elsie was doing better, up a little higher where the stones were drier, away from the breaking waves.

"There it is. That's the spot I remember." She pointed ahead to a grassy rise that sloped out toward the water. She let go of Benji's hand, a bit reluctantly, but the choice was walk or hold hands and the rocky ground made doing both difficult.

"Beautiful. Just beautiful." Benji stood on the highest part of the knoll and looked out across the water, at the hills on the opposite shore, distant blue, the roll of the waves way out and closer to shore where they occasionally broke white and foamy. Southward the lakeshore curved in a long sand beach, rushes grew lush, deep dark green and filled the bay. Poplar and large white spruce crowded down to the edge of the sand, and no people, nobody other than him and Elsie on the whole of the lake.

She snuggled against his side, her arm around his waist. She felt his solidity against her thigh, the strength of his back as she ran her hand under his flapping shirt. He might be a half-inch shorter than her, she thought, as she leaned her head against his shoulder. It didn't matter, it was only a half-inch, and he made it up in other ways.

"You know, this is a waste. An absolute waste, all this beautiful land and nobody using it."

"We are."

"But we're the only ones."

"Do you need people to watch?" she snuggled closer.

"No, no." He turned and kissed her forehead, the spot closest. "But just think." He turned to look out again, to wave with his free hand at the expanse. "This could be a resort, easily a resort, people swimming, jet boating, water skiing. Just think of it."

Elsie thought of it. Didn't like what she saw. "I like it the way it is." She understood that Benji came from a city, probably the only time he ever saw nature was at a crowded cottage subdivision north of Toronto on a long weekend. But that's okay. Give him time, he'd learn. And Elsie would be there to help him learn about natural things, about wind and water and trees and how people fit in, how to be an Indian, how to appreciate what is, instead of what could be. Benji was half Indian. His father gave him that. He had good blood, he would have a good spirit, she would find it for him.

"So, did your dad say why he was going south?" She changed the subject.

"Not really. Just said he has something to take care of, said I could use the boat, make myself at home in the cabin, whatever."

"Was he going to see your mom?"

"Maybe. I don't know. He never said."

"That was strange, your mom showing up like that. Like she knew you were here. Mother's instinct."

"I suppose. I don't know what her and Ben were talking about. Whatever it was it got him moving. I've never seen a man pace like that. Walked back and forth in that cabin for hours. I fell asleep and he was still pacing. Next morning he says, "Help yourself to whatever you need, and if you go out don't lock the door. I don't have a key.""

Elsie sat down on the grass, pulled Benji by the hand to join her. "Do you and your dad talk much?"

"Not really, no deep conversations, if that's what you mean. But it's okay, it seems like we communicate in different ways. We do things together, I like that. I like it that we don't just talk, we get out and do stuff."

Elsie nodded. He was getting it. He was learning. You don't have to talk all the time, deeper communication happens in different ways. Benji was learning to become an Indian. The tall grass swallowed her as she laid back content with the wind off the lake and a blue sky and waving slender green blades beside her face.

"What's your favourite song?" Benji laid down beside her.

"Oh, that's easy. Bob Dylan's 'Ange'."

"That's that old guy."

"I like the lyrics. 'Under a sky of orange, God help our Ange. It's not the end of the World, but you can see it from here. Courage Ange Courage'. What's yours?"

"Me, I like 'Universal Soldier' by the Last Temptations."

"I like them too." She felt around for his hand. "The granddaughters of the original Temptations. Did you know that that song was written by an Indian?" She found his hand. "Buffy St. Marie wrote that."

"Who?"

"Buffy St. Marie, from Fort Qu'Appelle, Saskatchewan. That's her song."

The wind rustled the leaves of the poplar behind them, bent the grass over their faces. Tiny white clouds, bright against the deep blue sky, shape shifted, challenged imagination, became beings and entities of drift and change, always change.

⌒

"Dark roast," Ben answered the very young woman behind the counter.

"Need room for cream?" She let the black pour into the glass cup.

"No, I don't use that." Ben liked bitter coffee. Here at the Roastery brought back memories of when he first lived in Saskatoon, mind, the Roastery then was still only on Broadway Avenue. Now it dominated the city, pushed Starbucks to the fringe and as people discovered the merits of fresh roasting, the Broadway Roastery chain could be found in all the western cities as far west as the Rockies. It never made the jump to the coast. Out there, they were still drinking Seattle slough water.

He found a table by the window facing the street. Twenty-second had changed over the years; now it rivalled Broadway for interesting little shops. First Peoples Publishing across the street looked to be already open, or maybe it was just someone coming to work early before the heat of the day ruined inspiration. A little after six and the sun was beginning to climb the highrises down town, spreading tall square shadow fingers, and blinding drivers heading into the heart of the city.

Ben flipped the pages of the *StarPhoenix*, found nothing interesting, or nothing that he could believe, nothing he could trust. If this were his only source of information, he would think that Canada was better off under the new regime. Programs were working, employment was stable, healthcare functioned. The new president of the university denied that enrollment was dropping. The mayor was in negotiations to have the entire city declared an urban First Nation. With a First Peoples population of seventy-two percent, and two thirds of council from First Nations, it was obvious that Saskatoon should have reserve status. He reiterated that non-First Nation peoples within the city would be accommodated. Private property could exist alongside community property.

Ben looked up. Monica was watching him through the glass. Chance, coincidence, destiny, didn't matter. He came here to see her and there she was.

"What brings you here?" Monica liked a little milk in her morning coffee, not cream, not thick, she liked the thin taste of coffee, the water part of the blend between flavour and liquid.

"You."

"Me?" She felt his eyes, held her cup to her mouth longer, hid behind it, tasted it again and held it with both hands, elbows splayed on the table in front of her. She looked to be in a pose of worship. Blessed is a morning cup of coffee.

"I want to know about That Jack." Ben folded the paper, put it aside.

"Do you have a platform?"

"I never went with that technology."

"Too bad, you still using a laptop and a cellphone and a video and a GPS."

"No GPS."

"Still using paper maps I suppose. Maybe that's better, nobody can track you with a map. I left my platform at home — come by and I'll introduce you to That Jack." She slid her chair a fraction of an inch back, needed a little more distance between her and Ben, now that he was leaning forward. She could smell herself, maybe he could too, smelled Ed's sweat, his sperm, her sweat; she could even smell the spit of his mouth on her breasts. She should have gone home for a shower before coffee. "If you've never met That Jack, you're in for a surprise." She fastened the top button of her blouse.

~

Rosie could not stop thinking about that big pipeline full of water, sacred water in a steel pipe, trapped, condemned to chlorine. How was it that those people never learned anything about water? Well, they didn't know anything about life either. How could they know that water and life are connected — if they didn't know that life was sacred, they would never figure out that so was water. Maybe someday, after they ruined all the water they might realize that there is no life, nothing without water. Oh, well, it was up to them to learn.

Same as Dougie. He'd have to learn too, in his own way. Someday he would realize that money was not important, that his wife and his daughters were. Going away to work, well that's what men do. When they're young they're supposed to go out into the world, travel around, explore, face the world and its challenges, burn off some of that craziness that young men get sometimes; but then, they're supposed to come home and take care of their families and the community. This thing that had been going on now since the mining companies began hiring our young men, taking them away and sending them home with pockets full of money, wasn't the way it should be. But how can you tell a young man that he has to think about his life when that's what he's doing? Thinking about his life and how he'll support his family, how they'll have all the things, all the cars, and computers, and toys. That's what it was all about wasn't it — the toys? The little boys never grew up, never went through that phase. Nobody went out on the hill to fast and suffer and look for their vision anymore, they just stayed little boys and never got over wanting more toys.

Rachel crawled off the blanket spread on the floor. Not on her hands and knees yet. She still mostly dragged and pulled herself along, her legs kicked to little affect. Rosie let her go, didn't pick her up and put her back on the blanket, let her find her own way; she had to figure it out for herself, wouldn't be long and she would be crawling for real, a month at the most, then in another month, maybe two and she would be pulling herself up and trying to walk. Rosie had never helped her babies learn to walk, never held their hands, helped them balance and encouraged them to move their feet. It happened too fast as it was, she didn't want them to walk too soon, before they had their own balance.

This was Elsie's first baby. She would learn, same way that Rosie learned, from heartache and joy, if she was around to see it. Maybe Elsie would be like some of those mothers who left their kids, either didn't want them, or got caught in something they thought was more important. "It's okay, *Eskwesis*, little woman, you'll always have your *kokum*. Come back here now, you can't go downstairs yet. Wait, soon enough you'll be running out the door." Rosie picked up her granddaughter, carried her down the short flight of stairs to the front door and out into the wind of the afternoon. "Is this where you wanted to go, my girl? See, it's all wind and dust out here." Rachel gripped Rosie's shirt in strong tiny hands, buried her face in the folds of cotton for a second, caught her breath stolen by the wind and then twisted to look around again at a world where giant trees waved and bent.

"That Jack used to work for CSIS. He was assigned the American files, to watch the neo-conservatives and the militias that were forming in some of the western states and starting to come into Canada." Monica's wet, freshly shampooed hair clung to her face as she prepared breakfast. It was more for Ben than for her. Her stomach wasn't up to food yet, young wine had that affect. "He predicted that the Americans were going to invade long before it happened and nobody would listen. So he dropped out. By the time the bastards got here, That Jack was just another guy with a computer." The toaster popped two slices. The butter dish was empty. She looked in the fridge for margarine, found a tiny yellow tub with a little in the bottom, enough. "He still had all his connections. They think he's one of theirs. Some of the stuff he gets is just incredible. Must be in tight with Homeland Security." She spread margarine thinly on the toast. She was talking as fast as she worked. "How he gets stuff is pretty impressive, but his real genius is how he gets it out there."

"And how does he get it out there?" Ben looked out the apartment window, nice place, you could see the river from here.

"Do you ever read your Spam?"

"No, I've got good filters to keep that out. I'm not interested in discount Viagra, or ultrahigh definition monitors and I definitely won't buy internet pharmaceuticals. I get enough advertising during my day now that CBC radio has had its public funding cut."

"Spam isn't all advertising. It's not just people trying to sell you stuff. A lot of what you're getting is computer-generated nonsense. Try reading it sometime."

"So why do people send it?"

"'Cause they can." She carried a plate, two eggs, sunnyside up, micro-waved bacon and hashbrowns, toast cut corner to corner, something traditional. It was good to keep tradition. Tradition was more important than ever now.

"You're not eating?" Ben saw only one plate.

"Girl has to watch her figure." Monica placed the plate in front of Ben, leaned across in front of him, exposed her nakedness under the thin bathrobe, throat to pale breast. Nice figure to watch, Ben thought, as he respectfully averted his eyes, looked down from the flesh inches away from his face to the food on the plate. The pair of eggs, white and soft, hinted of breasts.

"The reason That Jack can get away with it is because most people are like you. They don't read their Spam." Monica brought out her platform, unfolded the screen, slid the lens cover closed on the camera and spread the keyboard. A computer generated face, not dissimilar from Ben's, appeared on the screen and immediately began to speak. "Good morning Monica my dear. I hope you had a pleasant sleep. The news overnight has been relatively quiet. Homeland Security reports that they have captured two insurgents in Val Dore, Quebec without casualty." The face smiled, showed perfect teeth. "Of special interest, the Sami Parliament has announced that it expects to use more of its share of North Sea gas profits to support Indigenous Peoples in the Americas to negotiate modern Treaties, and hopes that the United Nations will respect those Treaties as international instruments."

"Would you open my email please." Monica's voice was flat.

"Whatever you want, my dear." The face winked.

"Let's see." Monica ran her finger down the screen to a blue icon. The screen shifted to lines of text. "Here," she pointed to a heading that read *Jack Richards*. "Anytime an email comes from someone named Jack or has Jack, or Jacqueline, or Jackie in the sender box it's worth looking at." She touched the screen twice and the text shifted again. Ben read down from the top: *Universality does not require expertise nor amendments. When the first spacemen arrived on the earth, they were not met by mammalian beings. Justice needs just people to proliferate.*

"No need to read all of it. It's mostly nonsense and jibberish anyway." Monica interrupted Ben's reading with her hand running down the screen. "All we're looking for is the word *that*. Here we are." She pointed to a line of text: *when you sing about that two men from Val Dore were taken last night and a third was summarily shot.* "When you read That Jack, the truth is between the word 'that' and the next period."

"So, the report we just heard wasn't correct. There was a casualty."

"Not completely. Homeland Security didn't have any casualties. Truth is tricky stuff, it depends on who is doing the reporting."

Ben forked some of the egg onto the oily toast. "Isn't the web being constantly monitored? I've been under the impression that it was impossible to use it for subversive purposes."

"It is monitored. Always has been. But their search engines can't read everything all the time. The web is too big for any one computer, that's the beauty of it. So they use key words. You'll never find That Jack using words like insurgent, or even Homeland Security or democracy and definitely not resistance. And he hides it in Spam. Nobody reads Spam, apparently not even Homeland Security." Monica grinned, pleased with herself to share in That Jack's brilliance.

"So, what does That Jack have to say about Abe Friesen?" Ben needed to know.

"Yesterday." Monica ran her finger across the screen again. "Here." She removed her hand so that Ben could read. He quickly found the word *that* and read: *foes of the people that will not speak, Abe Friesen, John Doe and Jane Doe, live in pain.*

"And what does that mean." Ben wasn't hungry. He put down the last strip of bacon that he had been nibbling on. "He's being tortured. Right."

"That's what it looks like. But have faith. He hasn't talked."

"Not yet."

"Maybe never. It's not true that everyone talks. Sometimes they overdo it and the prisoner can't talk."

"You mean they kill them."

"That's blunt, but you're right. Sometimes they end up killing a prisoner before he or she talks."

"I can't even let myself imagine that for Abe. Even if it means they don't find out about me. I can't wish for Abe's death." Ben stood, grinding the chair against the ceramic tile floor of Monica's dining nook. Sunshine through the big bay window, refraction of light off the spread of trees along the river, bright cheery tapestry, and a Che poster all dimmed, suddenly became sullen.

"Listen, Ben." Monica put a hand on his shoulder. He faced away from her toward the river. "There's still a chance, there's always a chance." She could not tell him about the negotiations, about prisoner exchanges. But she could assure. "I know for a fact that there is still a chance that Abe is going to get out of this."

Ben turned at her touch. "I never wanted to be a part of this. This isn't my fight."

"It's everybody's fight, Ben." Monica stood back, faced him "This is the way the world is and we all do what we have to do."

She suddenly felt naked in his stare, as though he was looking right through her robe, right through her.

Ben wanted to tell her he had been fighting all his life, but could see that it wouldn't do any good, she would not understand, would try to argue her point, prove that she was right. He looked at her, at the length of her, at all of the parts that showed through the gap of her robe, at the height of thigh, and slant from throat to navel, at a familiar face, at the drape of her hair, at the single heavy gold hoop in her left ear. Monica thrived on being a revolutionary. It gave her purpose. He could not take that away from her. She was doing what she believed in. This was Monica's reality and it was too far away from Ben's understanding to even begin a conversation.

"Do you know where I can buy a gun?" The words surprised him as though someone else, something else, something deeper spoke. He wondered if it was his fear.

∼

A squadron of fighter jets smashed the air, just above the tree tops. They didn't see the planes coming across the lake. At seven hundred miles-per-hour, they had only been visible for half a minute and Benji and Elsie were too busy with each other to be watching. Thunder, thought Elsie. Thor's hammer, thought Benji when he had time to recover, to stand naked in the wind.

"What the hell was it?"

"Jets." Elsie had caught the flash of metal against the sky a half second before the sound slammed into them. She stood stooped beside him in the wind, pulling jeans up muscular thighs. "We should head back." She was now thinking about her daughter. She also noted with a little concern that the wind was pushing the water into large waves.

"Ever drive a boat?" Ben had asked.

"Yeah, on Lake Ontario." Benji had answered his father. He did not say, "once, a boat with a steering wheel, while my friend untangled fishing lines."

They had trouble getting Ben's boat away from the rocky shore with the waves pounding in. Elsie stood in the water and held the bow while he lowered the leg and started the motor. Now out in the roll of the lake, Benji was more than a little unsure; he was on the border of panic as the boat pounded against the waves, nosed high in the air, and splashed down into the next draw only to begin to nose up again. He gripped the tiller, concentrated on his heading, southwest across the wide part of the lake toward the reserve, not that very far, just there under that part of the sky that was deeper black than the rest: ten kilometres maybe, ten impossible kilometres. There may be shelter from the wind along the west shore, he thought, shifted his concentrated stare toward the hills for a second, but even that was six or seven kilometres away. He looked back to where the reserve should be, at the next wave, larger than the rest. The bow of the boat rose, obliterated his view until all he could see was aluminum and wood covered seats and Elsie sitting dead centre facing him, holding on to the seat under her with both hands, her hair blowing forward, hiding her face.

The rain hit, hard, stinging his face, forcing him to turn away, take his eyes from the horizon that his heart pounded for, ached for. He wanted to cry, cry like a little boy who could not have what he wanted and all he wanted was to get this boat safely to shore. He looked down out of the driving rain. His feet were in water. It sloshed half way up his calf. He was going to drown out here because of his own stupidity and worse he was going to drown Elsie. He looked up, at her face. She either was not afraid or was not showing it. She sat hunched away from the sting of rain on her back, looked up as he looked at her. Their eyes met.

She read his fear, saw the shock-etched face with the mouth pulled hard into a straight line. She looked around, beyond the roil, the mash of waves, capped in white foam. She was pointing with her right arm extended straight out, her mouth moved and the wind tore her words away. Benji looked to where she was pointing. He didn't understand. She made big full arm-pointing gestures; he heard the word cabin and turned the boat out of the wind.

Running with the wind was suddenly smoother, easier. The backs of the waves were not as steep as their face. The rain lost its sting, was not in his face, he could see. There was the shoreline, the point of land he remembered. Just to the left of that was where the creek led back to the shelter of the old cabin.

Elsie spoke into the wind again. Benji did not hear. She was not speaking to him. She was talking to her mother, words into the wind.

〜

Rachel began to cry, little whimpers of discomfort. Rosie picked her up, held her to herself, felt the baby's face buried in the soft between her throat and her shoulder. "It's okay, my girl. It's okay. Your mommy is okay." She crooned and swayed, gently rocking Rachel as she walked back to the kitchen. Nothing to do with a day like today but stay inside and bake a pie. A nice plump apple pie, lots of cinnamon.

〜

Elsie stood naked again in front of the stove that crackled and snapped. Dry pine wood does that, she remembered, turning to warm her backside. The cabin smelled slightly of the smoke that leaked from the pipes they had fashioned together. Their clothes steamed on the string lines stretched above the snap and crackle. Elsie laughed, not at anything, lifted her long wet hair from her shoulders with both hands and let it fall. Benji turned at the sound, his hands still outstretched over the heat of the stove. His laugh joined with hers, not at anything, nothing more than relief. Naked, wet, and shivering needed to be laughed at.

~

Strong winds never blow for very long and the sun always shines again another day.

"You and Elsie are getting along well." Ben wanted to talk.

"Yeah, pretty good." Benji appreciated the question, appreciated his father showing interest in him. He turned from the computer after he tapped the keyboard, once, then again, waited for the shutdown page to appear where the video had flashed before folding down the screen to better see his father. Nothing there but cinematic flitter anyway. His father didn't own a television, obsolete things now that internet provided complete entertainment, complete communication, despite those out there dedicated to crashing it.

Ben's cabin appeared spartan to Benji. It was not filled with the collection of a lifetime, not at all like his adopted parents' house, where clutter ruled, and people moved carefully around the assorted and arranged. Here was open, from log wall to log wall, a larger version of the cabin he and Elsie had spent half of one day, a sleepless night, and most of the next day in.

"She's quite the woman. A bit of a flake if you know what I mean, otherwise . . . " Benji searched for the words. Words that would tell his father that he was falling, crazy in love. But how does a man say something like that, especially to another man. "Otherwise she's perfect."

"I've known her mother since I was a kid. Good family, Rosie is good people, so were her parents and Elsie comes from there. But what makes you think she's a 'flake'?"

"Oh nothing, really. We were just out at the cabin and I asked her if she was concerned that her mother might be worrying about us and she says no, she sent her mother a message on the wind that we were all right."

"And that's being a flake?"

"No, it's just that she insists that she can communicate with her mother without words. It's a little weird, but it's nothing, really."

"What makes you think she can't?" Ben faced his son squarely across the table.

"Not you too. Is this some kind of Indian thing or what?"

"I don't think you have to be Indian to have a sense of how your children are doing." Ben paused, wondered how much to tell Benji. "It's not like vision quest or sweat lodge ceremony, not even the sacred pipe. It's more personal than that. Intuition."

"Intuition I can understand, but she insists that she sent her mother a message."

"Well, intuition is part of understanding. You can't know anything completely if you only apply logic." Ben felt the professor within him stir. He suppressed it. "Intuition can be developed, learned. Maybe Rosie and Elsie have learned how to use it, how to use the connection between family."

The word family hit Benji, stopped him from his quick answer. Family he did not know about, was not sure enough to insist upon his otherwise clear perspective. He sat still, looked down at the folded platform on the table. There was a communication device, understandable: microchips, circuits, wireless connections, solid, real. He looked back up at Ben, checked flannel shirt, red and blue squares, something out of history, at the wind-tanned face beginning to be gouged by the lines of age, at the eyes that looked beyond him, not at him, not challenging.

"We understand family, maybe a little differently than you've been taught." Ben was not the professor now, he was his own father and grandfather speaking. "Our ancestors are always behind us, a line of them going back; we're connected to them. The things they did in their lives affect us, just like the things we do in our lives affect our children and grandchildren. If our grandparents did something good, helped someone, that help might come back to us. That's why in this life we should try to do good, so that good brings a blessing to our children." Ben wanted to talk, felt the need to pass this on, understood his own father, and the warmth of the wood stove and the cabin and the quiet of a winter evening while he sat and listened to these same words. He now appreciated his father's need to speak. Time was short, was always short. "You should remember seven generations behind you, and think seven generations ahead of you. Those are your connections. Imagine a string running through you, out your back to your ancestors and out your front to your great grandchildren that are not here yet. When you can imagine that, you are getting somewhere. Then you should try to imagine how you are related to everything else, how you are related to the trees, to the animals, the fish and the birds. Those are our relatives too." Ben held back, did not talk about the other relatives his father told him about. Those could wait. Benji had enough to think about for now.

Benji was thinking. "What about my adopted parents?" he asked.

Ben sat back. The connection between him and his son felt strong. "We knew about adoptions, we used to adopt each other as brothers, people would adopt the children of their friend. That child then would have a second set of parents and when that child needed they could go to them. It didn't get in the way of the child and its biological parents. You could adopt anybody, get new grandparents, or a new sister. It even went so far that nations would adopt nations. That's what the Treaties were to us. We adopted the white people and as relatives they got the right to be here, on our land, we shared with them." Benji was looking up, listening. Ben looked into the young face, at the eyes that were open to understanding. "Your adopted parents are part of the string of ancestors behind you. That string I was talking about. It doesn't have to be only biological. Anybody who loved you in their life, will be there in the Otherworld, looking out for you, will help you when you need help." Ben stopped. This was going too far for Benji to grasp just yet. He needed to experience it before he got it.

Benji did not get what his father was talking about. He thought that the man across from him was trying to explain Cree mythology, trying to explain some ancient superstition. He was not sure which world he was in, which his dead adopted parents might be in and which world Ben might occupy. He was careful enough not to say anything that might be insulting. He had learned not to speak quickly from Elsie, her back straight. "Be careful what you say about things you don't understand." Her voice stern, clear, her head high, her eyes meeting his directly, equally.

"I'll have to think about that," Benji murmured.

It was the perfect answer to Ben. He sat back from the table satisfied. His son was developing understanding. Maybe if he thought about it long enough he might learn how to use his connection between the worlds. He might reach the point where he would settle comfortably into his own life, into his own skin.

⁓

Lester waited. This was easy for him. Sitting around the gas station, listening in on conversations; weather, mostly weather:

"Too damn hot, never seen it this hot."

"What a storm yesterday."

"Heard about the forest fire way down in Regina, I guess the little park downtown burned up, hell-of-a-thing."

Local stuff; going to town, someone needs a ride:

"Chief is at the band office today for a change, better catch him while he's there, before he has to run off again, meeting with officials."

"Is it true the southern Indians are moving up here? What we going to do when that happens? There isn't enough moose and elk for us as it is."

"Heard they're changing the hunting laws."

A man in a suburban truck pulled to the pumps. "Fill," he commanded the young woman attendant.

"You got it." She tightened the leather glove that was slipping off her free hand, teeth to the cuff, the taste of gasoline now in her mouth.

He looked around at this environment: dark green trees of some kind, no one had ever told him the difference between white and black spruce, of pine and poplar and birch. Trees were things along residential streets in the old parts of the city, important to some people, especially important to dogs. Here they were everywhere, the clear areas were the exception, here trees ruled, pushed to the edge of the gravel road, surrounded the back of the gas station — a rectangle cleared into the thick of them for a house across the road from the gas pumps — a pole fence bleached in the sun, marker for a square of faded grass in front of the house that looked like every other reserve house on every other reserve, government issue.

He stumbled, one foot dropping into a pothole between the pumps and the gas station — only savages would live like this, without pavement. He walked carefully, hoped that the dust he raised would not cloud his leather shoes, fine Italian leather, not moosehide. He was not a savage, not a bush Indian, not naïve. He was business.

He recognized Lester sitting on a bench in the shade in front of the gas station, convenience store, grocery, post office, snack bar, coffee shop, lottery distributor. Lester stepped from shade into the August sun. "Richard." He held out his hand.

"Lester." Richard's tone matched the formality of his strong handshake. "So, do you own this place yet?" He indicated with his chin the graffiti-splashed metal-sided building.

"Not yet. I've got something else going on. Something I need NS to help with."

"We're not charity, Lester. What can you do for Native Syndicate? Not, what can we do for you, remember."

Lester nodded, looked down, then quickly back up. Never be humbled. Never feel shame. "It's a good project for NS. But, you look it over. You decide. If it fits in with our other work, maybe we have something. If it doesn't then it doesn't. But between you and me, Richard, I think we have something here."

"I'll have a look." Richard slid a slim wallet from his hip pocket. It was made with smooth nearly shiny material, light and strong. Slim because it did not have any cards or identification, no photos of loved ones, nobody's business card or folded piece of paper with a phone number. It contained one commodity — cash, Amero hundred-unit bills. He gave five to the attendant for the fill. Lester was impressed.

When Lester was in the Suburban, listening to the very good stereo sound of powwow blended with hip hop, absorbing the chill of the air conditioner, reclining in the comfort of leather, Richard reached under his seat for a bundle wrapped in red cloth. "Here, something for you from head office."

Lester unwrapped the cloth around the stainless steel semi-automatic, hefted the weight of the piece, felt the solidity of the grip fit to his hand, pointed it, found its balance, let it rest there, easy, so easy. He checked the magazine, fifteen rounds, pulled back the action, there was another in the chamber. Ready to go, ready to go anywhere with class.

"Nine millimetre Browning." Richard looked back to the gravel and potholes. "Fast as you can pull the trigger."

"Nice." Lester held it to the light, away from the tint of the side windows to see the shine of steel in sun.

"I'll have a look at what you phoned about. But that is not why I'm here." Richard poured bottled water into a glass with his right hand, offered the glass to Lester. Lester declined. The pistol in his hand filled him. His thirst was quenched.

Richard eased back into the seat, drove left-handed; drank water from a glass, not the bottle, not like a wino. He didn't like it here, on the reserve, on dusty rough roads. He didn't like the houses — spaced, each in its square cleared of trees;

these houses were cheap. You could tell just by driving by, nothing solid about them, cheap siding, cheap roofs.

No sidewalks anywhere, no pavement; there was nothing here that Richard wanted, and Richard did not want to be here; did not want to be reminded that this was where he came from — not Moccasin Lake, but from a reserve, a reserve just as dusty and poor and cheap. He was better than this now. He had class. He drove a Suburban, a GMC, with a full-size gasoline engine, not a hybrid — fully loaded, nothing chintzy, nothing routine, nothing working class, or worse — reserve class.

Lester was spinning the pistol on his finger, finding the balance of it; spin it, grab the grip, point, aim.

The music through the clear speakers chanted a song of resistance, banned lyrics; a song of rights, freedom, and homeland, a version or perversion of "Oh Canada", depending upon your perspective. Richard heard the words and dismissed them, this resistance stuff wasn't real fighting. Real fighting was north-central Regina nearly a decade ago. Now that was war. The enemy didn't wear a uniform, you shot at blue bandanas or red bandanas or white and they shot at you for the colour of your clothes. Then killing was all revenge and honour and control, and you never slept.

Native Syndicate rose, became great, faded, and rose again. Now Richard had command and NS had purpose, it had place; and the respect they had fought for all those years in crumbling apartment blocks and slumlord rented collapsing houses was finally theirs. Native Syndicate was the battle arm of the resistance. It put more soldiers onto the streets than anyone. And, whether the resistance liked it or not, NS reaped the profits.

Everyone wanted to get high and hide. The war on the insurgents replaced the war on drugs. While the police chased the bombers and watched the marchers, cocaine flowed freely, morphine was almost as easy to supply as cigarettes, and the OxyContin Blues was becoming the most popular song on the streets. Richard and Native Syndicate were the link between the powder and the profit; and the police were busy elsewhere.

The best part, the very best part; no rats. No one was phoning Homeland Security because there was a crack house in the neighbourhood. And the RCMP, well most people saw them as just an adjunct to HS.

"So, what do you want me to do with this?" Lester toyed with the Browning.

"It's business — not mine — I'm just bringing a message, an assignment for you."

Lester rested the pistol on his lap, kept his hand on it, listened. "Yeah?"

"Someone for you to watch for us. It probably won't go anywhere. Far as I'm concerned it's someone pulling strings, getting favours, wants someone out here looked after."

"You want me to babysit."

"You have a problem with that?"

"No, no problem. You tell me what you want done. It'll get done." Lester tipped the pistol sideways, movie gangster style, and pointed it straight ahead.

～

It's too early, Monica thought, at the sight of a single faded orange leaf on the maple that a city worker had planted, gouged a hole and plopped into the boulevard in front of the new apartment block twenty-seven years ago. It's way too early for the leaves to change. But then she thought, well maybe because spring came so early they are just tired of it all, tired of the constant heat. Summer can become tiring, dust, daylight that comes way too early and wakes you, the buzz of flies, and that dry wind that keeps blowing up from the Arizona desert. Some days she thought she could smell cactus mixed with the grit. Maybe winter would be good this year, some snow, just a little, just enough to settle the dust and make the city look clean again.

Ben loved autumn, used to come back to the university after summer tanned a full shade darker, brought the wilderness with him into the classroom, brought energy and light. He used trees as metaphor to explain to the seminar class how an ecological society might function, how balsam and birch lived together, put thoughts in her head about how she might live. But Ben's utopian society only existed there, in her head, maybe in his; it was not here, on the concrete where grass grew through the cracks beneath her boots, here where the boulevard ended and the busy 23rd Street — a couple more blocks and they would be at the bus depot.

~

Rick hurt, this was a sick he had never experienced before. It was more than the sick that might be expected from six weeks of confinement in a basement without light, more than the sick that might be expected from the beatings, the kicks, the punches to the temple. Why did he always hit me there? What was the damage he hoped to inflict with punches to the side of the head? Brain damage? No, the brain was functioning perfectly well. He knew where he was, knew that the explosive taped to the small of his back was armed, knew the woman behind him held an old-fashioned garage door opener in the pocket of her floppy jacket, knew that if she pressed 'open', the explosive would certainly smash his spine if it did not kill him. Rick's brain was fine. It was the rest of his body that was having problems, serious problems.

"Do not get on the bus until I say so." Monica's voice behind him was indifferent; at first Rick confused it with kindness. Six weeks of anger can do that; make you believe that indifference is kindness. Sunshine and light can give you hope, keep you walking when your body wants to lay down, there on that bit of grass, or even here, right here on the concrete, just lay down for a moment. Rick kept walking, putting one foot in front of the other, promised himself it would be okay once he was on the bus. Buses have reclining seats.

At the station, Rick tried to stand away from the other people waiting to board. If this was all just a set-up, if she pushed the button anyway, he did not want to be standing close to someone who had nothing to do with this. He looked at her, standing in the shade, watching people getting off the bus two lanes over. She nodded and he pushed himself the three steps to the door of the bus, handed the driver the white stiff paper ticket, used the handrail to climb the narrow stair, turned left past where the driver would sit, waited for his eyes to adjust to the dim light, and made his way to the very back of the bus where the man was signalling him. He would have preferred to sit anywhere closer.

"Here, lift your shirt." He felt the rip of tape removed. "Anywhere else?"

"No. That's it."

"Okay then, just sit tight and we go for a short ride." The man sat back, turned away from Rick, toward the window where the light was better and disconnected the detonator from the explosive. "Everything is going to be okay now."

Rick knew it wasn't. Knew that the man with the dirty blonde hair and hawk nose had poisoned him. That was why he stopped the punches and kicks, stood there and grinned while Rick ate cold canned beans that tasted of grit. No, it was not going to be okay.

~

"Everything is going to be okay now, Abe." Monica put her arm around his waist and helped him to walk to the depot.

"No it isn't. Monica. I told them everything."

"It's okay, Abe." She squeezed him tighter, reassured. "We'll handle it. Let's just get you out of here. You're safe now." Quickly through the station, past the ticket counter, out the street doors, into the taxi. "No, the other one." She guided him to the third cab in the line, the one that Ed was driving.

"Where to?" Ed joked.

"You know fuckin' well where to." Monica was not in the mood for jokes as she slammed the door behind her. "Are you wired?" She had her hands under Abe's shirt, feeling.

"No, nothing. They put me on the bus at Dundurn and told me not to get off."

"Nobody rode with you?"

"Not that I know of. Monica, I talked. I told them everything."

"It's all right, we'll handle it. You just take it easy."

Abe wanted to talk, needed to talk. "I don't know what I said, I just started babbling. They gave me an injection, fire in my veins, I don't remember. I couldn't concentrate, confused. That needle, whatever it was, and I couldn't stop talking, babbling was more like it. It was like I was somewhere else listening to myself. It was like I was trying to put the fire out with words, trying to make the pain stop, anything to make the pain stop."

"Bastards." Monica sat back, let the taxi carry her, let herself go with it, wherever it was going. The resistance would continue and she was along for the ride, all the way. The taxi turned hard right, leaned her against Abe, shoulder to shoulder. She put her arm around him. "It's all right, Abe. Like I said, we'll handle it."

Ed sped the taxi through the old warehouse area, the area that had once been converted to nightclubs, offices and restaurants, but was now deserted again. The once bright paint, the purples and oranges that had attracted people at the turn of the century now faded, peeling and empty.

Abe sat up straighter, his strength returning; he did not need sympathy, did not need Monica's arm around him. He relied upon his own strength.

"What did you tell them about me?" Monica needed to know.

"I don't think I did." Abe turned slightly to look at her. "I rambled a lot. They wanted to know about the gathering on the farm, who was there, who said what, and the person that I kept talking about the most was that guy you brought, Ben Robe. Of everyone who spoke at the gathering, it was Ben Robe that stuck in my head, and it was Ben Robe that I gave to them. I don't know if it was the drugs or what, but I remembered everything he said. In my babbling I gave them his speech word for word. I've got to find him and tell him."

"I'll take care of that." Monica looked out the window, looked north.

The rifle kicked into Ben's shoulder. Not the slam of a hunting rifle, more a push than a hit. He lowered it, looked at it again. It was shaped like a rifle, barrel, forestock, trigger, scope. But it was as different as it was similar. Ben was more familiar with walnut and blue steel. This was flat black and plastic, electronic rather than mechanical action.

"It fires three rounds for each pull on the trigger," Monica had bragged when she showed him his purchase. "Laserscope tuned to four-hundred metres, put the red dot where you want, squeeze the trigger, and one dead bastard."

Ben looked back at his target, a plastic bottle hung by a string from a tree branch two-hundred metres distant. He did not need to check, he knew it had three holes in it, saw it jump when he squeezed the trigger. Easy enough, but could he shoot a human? Could he put the red dot on a man? Take a life?

"In self-defence," he answered, but the words were not his, they were his father's: "*When a man takes a life, that man takes that other man's life as his own. If you murder a man you take that man's sins. That man they electrocuted there.*" The old man had pointed at the newspaper a young Ben was holding. "*They took all his sins onto themselves when they killed him. The wrong that man did, they have to pay for it now — him, he goes to the happy hunting ground.*"

"The one that pulled the switch has to pay?"

"*Not just him, all of them. All of them that decided to kill this man, they take his sins. You watch, they keep doing this, they keep electrocuting and hanging people, all of them are going to pay. It's going to come back on their people.*"

"They've been doing this for a long time."

"*And look at the suffering it brought them. They still have murderers and rapists, lots of them. Just watch. It'll keep getting worse.*"

Ben put the rifle away. It did not hold any answers.

~

Rosie knelt, moved aside a branch to check the underside of the faded blueberry bush. There weren't any berries there either. Nothing. She felt tired, wore out, more from disappointment than from exertion. In a good blueberry-picking year she could stay out all day, walk with a pail for miles, happily filling it and spend her evening cleaning the berries, picking out the occasional unripe green one and the very rare unwanted leaf, packaging them up, and stocking her freezer. Blueberries were Rosie's staple. She depended upon them for the pies she baked over the winter, her famous pies that she could sell when she needed a little extra during the last days of the month when things were running low.

She had heard of years like this. Her mother had told her about the year they had a big snowstorm in June that killed all the young berries. But even that year her mother had found berries. The snow had come while her mother and father were travelling. They had stopped overnight, made a camp, the next morning when they started out they found the snow had come all around them but not the place they had camped. Her mother had gone back to that spot and sure enough there were berries there, not much, but enough.

Rosie wondered if she would be the first in her family's history to ever get skunked. She picked up her pail and started walking, looking for that one spot where the sun had not burned away the berries, where there might be some, enough. Maybe in the shade of poplars. Maybe there were saskatoon berries on the island at the north end of the lake. Maybe Ben would take her there in his boat. Maybe Elsie and Benji would come and they could take Rachel. There was a nice beach there, a little cove of sand and driftwood. They could have a picnic. It would be good to be on the lake, on the cool of the water.

~

The hitchhiker looked like the Indians that showed up on movie sets, with a pair of long black braids tied with leather, darker skin; he could have been Indian, wore denim, and boots. Even the name he gave, Billy Thunder, sounded Indian. But the accent that accompanied the name was not Indian, not Cree, not Saulteaux. Ben suppressed a laugh at the thought, maybe he was Dene. He thought of asking, making a joke, but Billy Thunder or whoever he really was would likely not appreciate the humour, would not understand that the Cree and the Dene were once enemies and still teased and made jokes about each other.

The more Ben thought about it, the more honoured he felt that an Arab man would disguise himself as an Indian. It meant that there were a people more reviled than his people. Someone had said that the Arab in America was in as much jeopardy as the Jew was in Nazi Germany. Ben didn't know if that was true. It might be. The average German did not find out exactly what was going on in the concentration camps until the war was over. Maybe, you never know. That was the thing of it, you never know.

He had found Billy standing at the junction. He looked undecided, like he was not sure whether he was going down the gravel road to the reserve, or up the paved highway to the north. So Ben stopped and asked. "Where you going Bud?"

"To my reserve," Billy answered quickly. He walked across the road toward the driver's side door until he was close enough to get a good look at Ben. "*Tanisi*." Billy said the Cree word that meant How are you? the way that it was written, instead of the way it was commonly spoken; without dropping the unneeded middle "i". That was when Ben first wanted to laugh but kept his face deliberately stoic, very Indian. "Jump in, I'll give you a ride."

"You live here at Moccasin Lake?"

"Yes, I was just in town to buy some paint for my fence. Here let me get it out of your way." Ben moved the four-litre pail from the front passenger seat to the back.

⁓

"You are not under arrest, Mr. Robe. There are no charges pending. We merely wish to discuss some matters with you."

"I have nothing to say until you remove this hood."

"The hood is for your own safety, Mr. Robe. When you were found you had a person in your company who gave the name Billy Thunder. What can you tell us about this person?"

"Remove the hood."

"Only innocent people do not have to wear a hood, Mr. Robe. We found an M-37 assault rifle in your dwelling. You are not an innocent person."

"Remove the hood." Ben's voice was as flat as the voice asking the questions.

"Mr. Robe, you attended a clandestine meeting on the farm of Abe Friesen earlier this summer. Do you recall this event?"

"Remove the hood."

"Mr. Robe." The voice beyond the hood might have been a principal speaking to a schoolboy. "Do you understand where you are? Do you know the seriousness of the allegations against you?"

Ben did not answer. He rested against his arms handcuffed behind him, shifted them into the lower part of his back. He knew the answers to the questions, knew where he was. He was in a prison, not far from Moccasin Lake; Prince Albert maybe, more probably Saskatoon at the old correctional centre out in the industrial section. His calculation of time under the hood was limited by his inability to see the sun, but he knew he had not travelled far in the back of the Hummer, bound underneath a tarpaulin, rattled down the gravel highway, then smooth pavement when the throb of diesel engine became a whine of turbo, to here. Here was a correctional centre from the stop and go of their movement when they dragged him in. Stop and wait, held up by his arms, his hands handcuffed behind him, his feet tied together so he could not walk. Stop, wait, listen to the sound of steel doors clang shut behind them, listen to the grind of steel doors open in front of them. Then dragged, one person at each shoulder, arms looped through his, his feet dragged on concrete, carried too low to get his feet under himself to stand, ankles bound together so that he could not walk in any event, and when he tried to stand, while they waited for doors to grind or clang, his feet were kicked out from underneath him. Dragged to here. Here was a table and Ben lay on his back, on his arms, on his numb hands behind him, and the hood kept out the light.

∽

"It was your responsibility."

"I gave the prisoners to Ed Tremblay. He captured them. I trusted him." Monica defended herself.

"It was still your responsibility." Councilwoman Betsy Chance sat across the long table from Monica, looked directly at her. Monica stood straight at the narrow end of the table, not quite at military attention, but in a formal pose, stood for this dressing down from the full council. "Council appointed you to look after the prisoners."

Councilman Moosehunter leaned forward slightly to see around the person to his right, so that he could see Monica. "It's not that we really give a damn about whether the prisoner was poisoned, you realize. We're dedicated to killing as many Americans as we can, same as you. The problem lies in two separate factors. First, we traded a prisoner for two of ours, one of those was at your urging. Council went with your recommendation." The person beside him leaned back so that Councilman Moosehunter did not have to lean so far forward. "By poisoning the prisoner you jeopardized all future exchanges. This is very delicate. The process of a prisoner exchange requires a great deal of good faith and it exposes our negotiators to incredible risk. Councilwoman Chance negotiated that transfer for us. Her credibility is now tarnished."

Monica glanced at her friend Betsy who sat shoulders back and stared directly at her.

"The second factor," Councilman Moosehunter continued, "maybe the more critical factor, is that the prisoner was poisoned with yellowcake. The Americans now know for certain that we have it. We've been able to keep them guessing so far. Do we have the material or not? Now they know. Maybe it's a good thing, maybe it was time to let them know that we have it. But, that was for council to decide, not you."

"I was not aware of Ed Tremblay's actions. He acted without my instructions."

"It was still your responsibility." Councilwoman Chance repeated.

"I am not denying my responsibility." Monica stood a little straighter, a little more formal. "I am merely advising council of the facts. I take full responsibility for my actions and ask the indulgence of council once more. Please tell me what council needs done to repair the damage."

Council sat back in unison. Each of the seven looking down the table at Monica. Chairman Booth sipped water from a plastic bottle before he spoke, straightened his glasses to see the length of the table. "We are going to ask you to do something that you might find goes against your sense of loyalty. You will have to decide where your loyalty lies, with this council or with Ed Tremblay."

"I assure council that my loyalty lies here." Monica indicated the table.

"One thing more." Councilwoman Chance turned slightly as she spoke. "Your friend Ben Robe has been taken in. We appointed someone to watch out for him, but our man was obstructed by a neighbour woman."

"Rosie?" Monica guessed.

"Whoever she was, she grabbed our man's gun away from him as he came out of her house. The arrest did not take long. Your friend Robe apparently went willingly, did not resist."

"That is just for your information. You are not to do, or try to do anything more about it." Councilman Moosehunter did not lean forward to speak this time. He did not even bother to look at Monica.

"Should I have the barrel of yellowcake moved from the house?"

"Where to?" Councilwoman Chance spoke in a sarcastic tone.

Monica shrugged, lost for a second. She had never received a dressing down before, did not know how to react. She was determined to stand up, say 'yes sir', 'no sir', 'three bags full sir', 'never complain, never explain', 'take your lumps', 'maintain honour', all those military axioms. Yet she was shaken by Betsy's behaviour. Betsy her friend was a different person from Councilwoman Chance. Councilwoman Chance obviously was not her friend.

"That barrel is in the best place we could find." Chairman Booth spoke quietly, explaining to a five-year-old patiently. "There aren't many houses left with cold war bomb shelters made of a foot of reinforced concrete. That barrel is giving off radiation, radiation that can be detected by satellites. Radiation that can only be stopped by an inch of lead or heavy concrete. As Councilwoman Chance asked you, where do you think we could move it to?"

Monica shrugged again.

"So you realize, Miss, what needs to be done is not to move the yellowcake, but to remove the risk."

"You mean Ed."

"We mean Ed." Councilman Booth stood abruptly; his chair scraped back loudly. "You will cooperate with Councilwoman Chance in ameliorating the problem." The meeting was over.

∽

His body was shutting down. Rick did not need Doctor Finlayson's report that his kidneys and liver were failing. He did not need to look at the intravenous tubing stretched to the hum and bubbling machines, did not need to crane his neck to see the digital readouts. He knew, felt the slowing of his life, felt it fade, drip away. The time would come soon when he closed his eyes and would never open them again. He forced them open now, to look around the hospital room, at his mother sitting in the armchair by the window where there was good light. She was keeping her hands busy with her knitting, found comfort in doing, in making. His father would be pacing — the room was too small for him, he needed the hallways, and the little green area outside where patients and visitors sat at plastic picnic tables, ate a sandwich or drank a coffee and smoked cigarettes.

Vicky looked away from her knitting for a second, at her son in the bed, the back raised. He was looking at her. She smiled at him, put down her needles and yarn on the floor beside her.

"You okay, Ricky?" She asked leaning over him.

"As okay as it could be, Mom. Where's dad?"

"He's around somewhere. Do you need something."

"I need lots of things. But nothing you can bring." Rick lifted his hand, the right one, the one without the tube, reached feebly with it. Vicky took it, held it, squeezed it, took it in both of hers, patted it, leaned over and kissed the back of it, smiled down on her son, put as much happiness and kindness as she could find into the smile, but her eyes showed her pain.

"Your dad needs to be on his feet at times like this."

"I know, Mom."

"He never was a man to sit down. He's trying to stand up the best he can."

"I know, I'm trying to stand up too."

"You don't worry about anything, Ricky, you just rest and get better."

Ricky looked directly into his mother's pained eyes. Breathed in slowly. "I'm not going to get better." He was standing up the best he knew how, he was not hiding behind a lie, he was standing straight, honest, like his father. "U238, the doctor said. There's no magic cure. I'm not coming out of this one. I'm not coming home." A tear began at the inner corner of Vicky's left eye, welled out and ran the length of her nose, around the end and hung beside her nostril, bubbled there while she sniffled.

"Don't cry, Mom. Please, that makes it hard."

She took one of her hands away from his to wipe away the tear and snot, breathed in deeply looking for strength in the air, wiped her face with her palm.

"I don't want to die, Mom."

Vicky's tears poured, dripped down her face into her mouth, she tasted salt.

"It's not fair. I should be on the farm." Ricky gasped air between words, sucked it in, whistled it past the plastic tube in his nose. "It wasn't our war. You and me and Dad and Clarice, we never started it, never wanted anything to do with it. You know what we did wrong, Mom?" He waited for her to answer. She didn't, couldn't, her mouth was full of tears.

"We didn't do anything to stop it." Ricky answered for her. "We never stood up to the crazies. Never put them in their place. They came and said that God wanted us to do this and we would not talk against God and we went to war; that's what we did wrong."

Vicky knelt beside the bed, her legs would not hold her up anymore and she could not let go of Ricky's hand. She laid her wet cheek against that young hand, rested her upper body on the starch white bed and poured tears onto the hand.

"Mom," Ricky tugged at his hand to get her attention. "Mom." She looked up. Raised herself on her elbows, found the strength she did not believe she had. Raised herself until she could see his face, his serious young face. "I need you to know something, Mom. It's important." Vicky nodded and wet dripped from her chin with each nod. " I never killed anyone. I never shot anyone. I want you to know that."

"Uh-huh," she dripped more tears.

Rick relaxed back into the pillows, looked toward the tiled ceiling. "I never killed nobody." He sucked in air, hospital air, air that smelled of disinfectant and linen. "I never killed nobody."

~

"You'll have to stay and look after your dad's place." Rosie was standing in Ben's big garden. It was full now, beets were ready, potatoes were beyond bloom and needed another hilling up, the squash were not doing so well, too dry; squash need lots of water.

Benji leaned on the hoe, looked toward the house, at the red truck parked beside it. "I guess, eh?"

"Someone has to." Elsie was thinking of moving the last of her few belongings over from her mother's place. She had only come home for a visit, to see how her mother was doing, had stayed the entire summer. She had no wish to return to the little apartment in Red Deer. There was nothing there that she wanted. It was Bert's apartment, his family would take care of it. Elsie didn't want to go back there, that little life ended with the message that Bert had been killed, ended before it started. It was a false chapter in her life, a promising beginning, not more than a couple of weekends with a soldier home on leave, a pregnancy and emails and phone calls and she promised she would stay at his apartment, look after his stuff, wait for him to come home. She kept her promise, stayed and waited. He did not keep his promise. They sent his coffin to his family in Edmonton. It was a very short chapter that ended in loneliness despite the company of her daughter.

"How long do you think they will keep him?" Benji was not asking anyone in particular. He felt a tinge of guilt at not being there the day his father was arrested; he'd been occupied with Elsie.

"Who knows." Rosie felt the dryness of the soil as she dug for the root of a dandelion. Sandy soil grows good root crops but it doesn't hold moisture. It would be nice to mix in some clay. There was that blue clay up the little creek where her father once killed a caribou, but it was a fair distance even if they used Ben's boat, and how would they carry it?

"Your dad is going to be okay." Elsie picked up Rachel, fingered the dirt out of her mouth, wiped the grit from her face and put her back down on the centre of the old patch quilt.

"I've got that same feeling, like there is nothing to worry about. It's strange. I'm not at all worried about him. Even when I try to imagine the things they could be doing to him." Benji continued to lean on the hoe, felt the heat of the sun on his back through the thin shirt.

"Trust that feeling." Rosie sat on her legs, straightened her back, stretched it out.

"You think it's intuition?"

"You can call it that if you want. You and your dad are connected, learn to trust the connection." Rosie wiped the loose soil from her hands against her dress. "I feel it too."

"But you and him aren't related are you, Mom?"

Rosie turned to look toward her daughter. "No, Ben doesn't have many close relatives left. Most families back then had lots of children, Adolphus and Eleanor only had Ben. They used to gossip about her that she was using Indian medicine for birth control."

"Was she?" Elsie wanted a bit of gossip, even if it was ancient.

"What kind of medicine?" Benji wanted to know what it was made from.

"I don't know if she was or not." Rosie deliberately answered Elsie instead of Benji. Some medicines were dangerous if you let people who didn't know anything use them. The medicine Rosie knew about caused abortions and sometimes steril- ization, not something to be given out randomly. The world did not need that medicine anymore, there were enough birth controls and procedures. She looked down at the pile of plants she had pulled from around the row of carrots, weeds some people might call them.

Benji went back to thinking about Ben, put the hoe to the earth again, chopped the little green that grew up between the rows of onions. Yeah, his father was all right. He would take care of things here until he got home. It wouldn't be so bad. He had the house to live in, a good solid truck to use, a boat to go out on the lake whenever he wanted. He was learning about boats, listened to people who knew about crossing big water, how to take the waves on the beam instead of dead on. He had the monthly allowance his adopted parents willed him, a trust until he was thirty.

Benji had not thought about them in a long time, those two people who should have known they were too old to take in a child. Something was different now when they came into his mind. They did not stir the anger. He imagined what they might have said if he had brought Elsie home, Elsie with a baby, an Indian woman and a papoose into the home of a retired diplomat. How would they have introduced their daughter- in-law-to-be to their circle, an all-white circle of elites? Benji could not hold the thought of their possible discomfort. Instead he wondered whether they would like her. Probably, they probably would have liked her, taken her in and made a fuss over her and Rachel, poured tea for her in the middle of the afternoon and offered cookies and little cakes. And

Rachel, well they would have been proud to be grandparents and they would have made good grandparents. He could see them spoiling the little girl with frilly dresses and fancy hats and teaching her to speak English like the Queen. He could hear Joyce calling her princess, and James with her on his lap in the big recliner chair reading her a fairy tale book. Here in the garden, with his hands sore from the wood of the handle of the hoe, the sun on his back and the smell of water from the lake on the little wind, he wasn't angry at them anymore. In a way he missed them, wished they could see him now.

"What was Lester up to the other day?" Elsie asked her mother.

"I don't know what he had in mind. Came out of the house with a gun just when they were putting Ben in that truck. He came running past me. I just reached out and grabbed it out of his hand." Rosie laughed. "He ran another three or four steps before he realized he didn't have it anymore — Rachel is eating dirt again."

Elsie picked her daughter up, brushed the soil from her face and held her wiggly and flailing on her hip. "Don't eat too much of that, my girl."

"Yeah, Ben needs all the soil he has." Rosie pushed herself to her feet. "We really have to do something about this garden. Maybe haul in some peat from the muskeg or something."

Benji leaned on the hoe again. He was beginning to like this long-handled thing. "So, why did you take the gun away from him?"

"What was he going to do? Him with one little gun and all them with machine guns and who knows what else, all he was going to do was get himself killed. I didn't want him to get Ben in more trouble than he was."

"But maybe he could have surprised them, got Dad free."

"Then what?"

"Then Dad would be free."

"No, then they would have sent more men and more guns and more trucks and Lester would have to get a bigger gun, and your dad would have to hide out in the bush for the rest of his life."

"RCMP never chased anyone who went out in the bush." Elsie hoisted Rachel a little. It seemed that gardening was done for now. She picked up the quilt with her free hand.

"No, that's true, they never did. But these aren't the RCMP. Maybe these Americans would go into the bush to look for someone. But even when the RCMP were after someone, they never stayed out there very long. Longest I remember was John James and he only hid out four months. Gets lonely out there." Rosie dumped her weeds onto the compost pile she was starting by the gate and headed toward the house, Elsie and Rachel followed. Benji looked around. No, there was nothing left to put the hoe to. He leaned it against the rail, closed the gate, looked back again at the garden, the freshly painted pole fence that did not keep anything out, at the rows of vegetables and the potato patch that took the whole northeast corner. There was a lot of food in that garden, he thought, as he followed the women. A person could survive off that for a while if they had to.

~

The voice beyond the black hood asked. "Are you a Christian, Mr. Robe?"

"Remove the hood."

"Now, Mr. Robe, we have been through this before. The hood is for your protection. It's a reminder to you that you live in darkness and only when you have accepted Jesus into your life will you see the light."

"So you're going to torture me in the name of Jesus."

"No, Mr. Robe. Nobody's going to torture you. I have a checklist here in my hand and do you know what? There's a little box on it that says Imminent Threat. That box is not checked off. No, Mr. Robe, if that box had a little x in it, you wouldn't be here, you would be somewhere else answering questions for someone else. This is just an interview we're having here, not an interrogation. You have nothing to worry about, all we are going to do is talk. Now, again, Mr. Robe, do you believe in Christ."

"If you remove the hood, I'll tell you about how he was a medicine man."

"A medicine man. Really, Mr. Robe, you don't follow the heathen way of thinking do you?" The voice waited for an answer. Ben waited for him to remove the hood, knew that it was too soon, that it would take much more before he saw the face of the voice, knew also that the voice would give in, knew that he had won the moment he was asked if he was a Christian. In the silence, Ben could hear the sound of metal against concrete, of people moving, talking. This place was never quiet. It echoed every move, every footstep, every human motion bounced and rebounded as though resisting its confinement.

Ben began to dig in his memory, those things he studied, the memory of hours under a coal oil lantern in a cabin just back from the shore of Moccasin Lake. He found the image first, felt the warmth of a woodstove, then he began to retrieve the contents of his study. "In the beginning was the word," it said. Words that are like the sounds that echoed around him, wanting to be free, words, who would be the master of the words? Ben or the voice, or would the words be masters of them?

"Mr. Robe, you were found in the company of a charlatan, an Arab man who was pretending to be an American Indian — do you have a plausible explanation for this?" The voice spoke first and Ben relaxed. He was in a contest of wills and he was winning.

"Remove the hood." Ben's voice was flat, fixed.

"You have not earned the right to see. You cannot see until you find the truth. Tell me what you intended to do with an M-37 assault rifle."

Ben listened to the sounds that echoed through the concrete and cinder block — waited, found his own inner silent place and waited.

"You attended a meeting earlier this summer, Mr. Robe, a very important meeting on a farm not far from here. Can we talk about the presentation you gave? I understand that you impressed a lot of people with your little speech."

"I spoke without a hood."

"Now, Mr. Robe, that is not getting us anywhere. I'll remove the hood when you earn the right to see, until then you and your soul are in the dark."

Ben only heard "I'll remove the hood." Time did not matter. Time was on Ben's side, his friend. His father had given him the gift of time, how to use it, bend it, stretch it, a lifetime of time.

<hr />

Monica checked her watch. Cute, she thought when she bought it, a Swatch, nice bright shiny plastic band, something fun to wear, even fashionable. But, that was a long time ago. Now the hard plastic band wore into her wrist and she wished she had worn a different watch, maybe the one with the cloth bracelet, much more practical for what she planned for today. The planning had been easy. Ed was easy. "Want to go stubble skiing tomorrow? Something different for a change."

"Yeah." Ed let the thought sink in. "Yeah, sure. Haven't done that in a while."

"Abe's farm?"

"No, I want wheat, Canola is too damn hard on the body."

"South quarter was wheat. Heard they took the crop off already."

"South quarter of Abe's farm it is then. That's the one with the rolling hills by the river, right?"

"That's the one."

"Yeah, let's do it." Ed's face had lit up, stupidly she thought now.

Even with the traffic it only took twenty minutes to get to the wheat field. She checked the passenger side mirror. He was still on his feet, leaning hard against the ten-metre towrope tied to the truck, his heavy work boots ploughing up the soil as he skidded an arc. He turned his body against the rope, dug his boots into the earth and crossed back behind the truck again out of Monica's view. She checked the speedometer, forty killometres-per-hour, right where he wanted to be, fast enough to be able to really skim along, slow enough that if he fell it wouldn't hurt too bad. It would hurt, but not that bad.

She noted the knuckles of her left hand — they were white. She was gripping the steering wheel too hard; switched hands, drove with the right as she clenched and unclenched the left for the circulation.

Was she scared?

Maybe she was being set up.

Would Betsy give her away, offer her?

Possibly.

Would council?

She wasn't sure. Council was not pleased with her.

Maybe.

Maybe her fate was tied to Ed's. One at either end of a long rope.

She pushed down on the accelerator, moved the needle up gradually, forty-five, forty-eight. Now Ed was skimming nicely, almost elegantly, as he slashed back and forth behind the truck. She put the truck into a long slow turn. Ed leaned away, dug in the edges of his boots and arced out across the wheat stubble, skidded and gouged the dry earth

She began a turn in the other direction and lost sight of him as he crossed back behind the truck. She checked her watch again before she began to accelerate toward the poplar bluff along the west edge of the field. "Stay on your feet, bastard." She spoke to the mirror as the truck rounded the north end of the poplar. She turned sharply, way too sharp for Ed to make the corner and sent him tumbling across the stubble. He held on to the towrope and rolled through the wheat straw and chaff. He stopped tumbling, found his knees first, then his feet. "Crazy fuckin' woman!" he yelled, wiping the grit from his eyes and mouth. Those were his last words. Two black uniformed Homeland Security officers began firing in unison at the man promised and delivered at exactly 2:00 PM on Thursday, September 18th. Two other men dressed in civilian clothing stood behind the officers, witnesses of the delivery and execution.

Monica drove away without looking back, without looking into the mirrors to see what happened. Her assigned task was complete. She had only to phone Betsy and make the report and that would be two words — "It's done." When she reached the approach to the grid road that would take her first to the highway, then back to the city, she got out, unhooked the rope from the trailer hitch behind the truck and dropped it there, left it lying stretched out in the stubble.

Late that evening, That Jack sent out a revised Spam to a select list of recipients. Included in the garble were the words: "that Edward Riley Tremblay did not survive this day, he will be missed by those who loved him."

⌒

A hush of wind rose and fell in the big white spruce. It deepened the silence of the boreal where Benji stood and listened to the nothing, the absolute nothing now that his boots no longer clomped the trail. He listened for something, anything, and only heard the sound of his own breathing, his own heartbeat. That's the problem he thought. That's what's wrong. Nobody is making any noise. Ben's beloved forest didn't care that he was arrested, a political prisoner. "Where was the outrage? Where was the indignity of humanity?" Humanity sat comfortable in its own silence, speaking of its own discomfort, not caring about the plight of one man. This quiet, empty land needed someone to scream, to shout and stomp and rage. He would have raised his own rant at the trees, shouted the needed words into the wood and branches, but the forest was stronger than Benji, smothered him in green stillness, siphoned away his hurt and anger and left him muted, with only thought swirling, coming back to the need for someone, anyone to speak out.

He turned on his heel, gouged a hollow in the earth trail, left a mark at his turning point and could not help but listen to the sound of his own feet, heavy on the trail as he plodded back toward the community beside the big lake.

"Thomas, Thomas Larson." Benji spoke resolutely into the phone. "This is Ben Ferguson. James and Joyce's son, James Ferguson remember, from the Foreign Service. You worked with him . . . I'm glad you remember.

"How am I doing?

"Not too bad, not bad at all,

"No I'm not in Toronto anymore.

"Listen, Thomas, I need a favour from you. Are you still with Amnesty International?

"Good, that's good.

"Yeah, I know Tom. I should have stayed in touch. My parents put a lot of faith in you.

"Year-and-a-half ago. Yeah?

"Yeah, she was quite the lady.

"But, Thomas, there's this thing happening here I think Amnesty might want to get on."

⌒

It's better that he is home, even if . . .

Vicky looked over at her son flailing slowly in the hospital bed. Fighting it, she thought, fighting to stay home. Rickie eased a bit, sighed around the hoses, rested. She fell back to her first thought that it was better that he was home even if it was just to die, to slowly die. She didn't have to worry anymore. Since Ricky came home she had not once turned on the news. Not like when he was gone, every morning, first, before she even brushed her teeth or combed her hair, she tuned in, listened for news from Canada, and hoped she never heard it. She lived by the news, trapped by it, unable to break away, in case she missed it, in case they announced something from Saskatchewan and she was away, rushing through the shopping in town, worrying that she would be late home for the six o'clock, staying up, forcing herself to stay awake for the eleven o'clock, and hating it, hating the horrors broadcast, sanitized horror, bombs and guns and Montreal cocktails, torn bodies and black smouldering twisted metal. She wouldn't have to watch that ever again. She could go back to the farm when this was done.

The machine beside the bed beeped loud, steady. Vicky put her knitting aside, and was almost to the bed when the nurse arrived. She must have been standing outside the door. Vicky noticed that she checked the machine first, before Rickie. He was shuddering, his teeth clenched on the plastic tube, his eyes open, staring hard at the dream catcher hung above him, its web to catch the bad dreams, something from the gift shop, the little folded card said the Indians used this, maybe it would help Rickie to rest. Maybe this was just a bad dream caught and struggling. Rickie's shuddering subsided, eased to twitches, his jaw relaxed its clench, he drew in a long rattled breath, and let it go — let go.

The beep became a steady howl, a wail. The nurse slapped a switch and it quit, left Vicky in sudden silence standing beside the bed holding Rickie's hand. What did he see in the dream catcher web? What final image struggled in the strings?

She heard Clarice's sobs behind her, her daughter-in-law-to-be, or never be; felt the grip of her hand clenched to the back of her shirt. Clarice was using Vicky to stand up, pulled at her, would pull her down as her knees weakened. Vicky found the strength to stand against the added weight, gently closed her son's eyes, brushed with the palm of her hand, shut the sight, hoped that it was a good dream that came and carried him away.

~

It wasn't a full military funeral. There was an honour guard, regal dressed, spit shine shoes, brass buttons, a dozen men to march their son across the close-mowed grass, green still despite the lateness of the season, greener than the surrounding fields. They must have watered it often, Vicky thought, as she followed the honour guard toward the open hole. She looked up, Dean's attention was on the fields, she held tighter to his hand. He'd escaped already. That was not a bad thing. She wished she could join him there. It was lonely here when Dean went away into his mind She put her other arm around Clarice's thin waist, more for the company than to give comfort. The girl was cold, shivering, wobbly on her high heels. She pulled her close, to hold her up and to lean on.

Vicky stood like this through the ceremony of going to the earth, holding her husband's hand to keep him from wandering too far away, holding on to Clarice to hold her, to hold herself up.

Then it was over. The flag and the box and the earth, the march, the drill and they were coming one by one in the closing ceremony of shaking hands with the family members.

"My condolences."

"I'm so sorry, Mrs. Fisher. Your son was a good man."

And they took the hand she needed to hold Clarice with, pumped it twice.

"He served his country."

Just a nod, "Ma'am." Pump the hand and shift over to pump Dean's hand and then wander over to where they grouped, uniformed, taking off their brimmed hats, wiping their brows, shuffling. Vicky watched, wondering what they might be talking about. Not her son she knew, maybe there was still time to gather at a pub later, she suspected.

"Ma'am." The officer in front of her did not let go of her hand after the two pumps. Held it as gently as he could. "Ma'am, I'm sorry that for security reasons the media was not allowed to be here for this."

"That's quite all right." She didn't have the energy left to explain. "We're private people." That was all she had for words. It would take too much effort to tell him her fear that Ricky would become part of the daily diet of horror, an episode, a string of words across the bottom of a screen and somewhere someone would rejoice that it was not their son.

"But I do have some good news, Ma'am. Something to take comfort in."

Vicky looked up at this man who stood in a military stance, feet apart, head high, chest out, so much a part of him that it was his relaxed pose. "The man who poisoned your son was taken care of. He was executed three days ago. I'll have to ask you not to speak to the media about this. The information is very classified. I'm only sharing it with you for your own comfort. Please understand."

Vicky nodded. She understood, but there was no comfort in it. There was no comfort at all in it. She looked over at Dean, but he was gone, maybe he was already back at the farm. "Thank you, officer." She wanted to go home, just go back to the prairie house and look after Dean.

~

Too many years of not doing, of swinging a mop, not with any effort to it, just sloshing the painted concrete floor, too many years of waiting, maintaining, left Lester without the stamina for a full day of physical work. He rested, found reasons to stop, to straighten out the logs piled in the back of the truck rather than join Red and the others hauling them on their shoulders out of the bush. Red was in a good mood, joking, teasing all day, lifted peoples' spirits with his banter. Late autumn, now that the leaves were off the undergrowth, now that the mosquitoes and flies were not so thick, was the best time to cut firewood. Red said it was almost tradition for him. Put up a big pile of wood and then go shoot a moose. Then you could spend the winter with your feet up in front of the fire and eat ribs and brisket.

Lester wasn't so sure it would work out that way, wondered if he would make the winter, wondered if he could find the money for the meds. This work was not bad. Paid a bit, but they sure wanted a lot for a little bottle of green pills. Red could turn this into a real money-maker if he wanted, but Red didn't have any ambition. He only wanted enough for the moment, and enough for Red wasn't enough for Lester.

Short time on the inside, when the sentence is running down, stand away from trouble, stand aside, watch the fights; but keep your record pure, be patient and pure, abide the rules. But short time on the outside felt the opposite. Lester wanted these last months, these possible last months to be worth something, anything. If it wasn't for Rosie he could have had a moment of glory, walked into the face of authority with a nine millimetre and carved a path of fame for himself. Damn Rosie. Then Lester laughed at the memory of it. How he was walking past her, not thinking of her, she was just old ,fat Rosie. But old fat Rosie snatched the gun right out of his hand and he took two more steps before he realized his hand was empty. Then she put it in her pants and how was he going to take it back.

"What's so funny?" Red flipped the log from his shoulder onto the already large pile in the back of the truck.

"Oh, nothing"

"You were sure grinning about something." Red gave the end of the log a flip to roll it over, fill a gap.

"Looks like we might get some snow." Lester looked toward the grey sky.

"Maybe. It's cold enough." Red thought about the possibility, considered the weight of the clouds. They were heavy enough for snow. "We'll get what we have cut off the ground just in case it does snow and bury them, then we can call it a day. I'm feeling a little crappy anyway. Damn cold, just can't seem to shake this one." He sniffled. It wasn't enough and he wiped his nose with the sleeve of his canvas jacket, coarse against the tenderness of his nostrils. "What have we got today? Is this the third or fourth load?" Red was the type of guy who in his enjoyment of working, especially working outside, could lose track of such things.

"Fourth load." Lester wasn't.

"That's not bad." He struck a flame to the end of a cigarette. Lester swung his legs over the side of the truck box and sat on the rail. Looked like they were taking a break. Red wasn't quite ready to stop yet. He took a few drags from the cigarette, handed it to Lester. "Here, finish it." And went back to hauling the last of the logs out of the bush.

~

"It's snowing." Elsie watched the first flakes; small, drifting, lazy white specks. "Wonder if it will last." She followed a flake to the ground to see if it melted right away. It didn't. The ground was frozen enough to hold. First of winter. Something new. She was about to turn away from the window when the truck stopped next door at her mother's house, a load of wood sagging its springs. She waited until it came to a spot where she could see through the trees. It was her cousin Red bringing

Lester home. A good thing to know that Red still cut wood. She'd wondered where they might get their winter supply. Ben had a chainsaw and a truck. Benji could do the work. She could help. She would be happy to help, to be outside, physical work, fresh air. But, there was just the thing about Benji and a chainsaw. Grew up in the city. Would he cut his leg off? Or worse.

She turned away from the window, instinctively looked around for Rachel. The little girl had been quiet for too long. It meant she was up to something, and she was. Standing on a chair, trying to reach Elsie's now cold cup of tea.

"Come down from there, my girl. Come on over here and see. Look out the window, see that? That's snow. That white stuff. That's snow, my girl." They stood together and watched it fall. There were more flakes now, and not lazy. The wind picked up and slanted them, gave them purpose and destination. The sight chilled Elsie. She added another block of wood to the steel fireplace. Not that it needed it. Forced it in and shut the glass-screened door. "You stay away from this stove Rachel. It's hot. Don't touch. Hot."

She wished she could build something around the stove. Something to keep Rachel away. But this wasn't her house. It was Ben's. And someday Ben was going to come home. What would he say when he found her here, living with Benji. Shacked up, like they used to say. What would she say? "We were looking after your place for you. Taking care of things." If he ever came home.

She wished she and Benji had their own place, a small warm cabin, built of logs, like the one up the lake where Ben was raised. That would be nice. She could live without electricity, without all the distractions that came with it. But, could Benji? Or was he still too dependent, too modern to ever give up the comforts and ease. Not that there was anything wrong with comfort. She felt the heat of the crackling stove. But some comforts are better than others. Some don't cost your soul so much.

~

"You have mail."

"Mail?" Ben didn't get it.

"Well, not for you, but about you."

The daily interview, at 2:00 PM. The guards came to the cellblock, beckoned Ben to come with them down the concrete hallway to administration, into the office complex where the floor was tiled and the offices had glass in the windows, where coffee and doughnuts scented the air. Someone here liked Tim Hortons. Brought in a half-dozen sugared old-fashioned every afternoon and spread the smell of cinnamon into the otherwise still, dead air.

The interview would last an hour, the same questions, the same answers. "Why an M-37?"

"Because my eyesight is fading."

"That's not the average hunting rifle you have there."

"It works for me."

Ben sat in the chair, kept his feet flat on the floor, never stretched out his legs, never relaxed. The voice had a name now, John Penner, and a face. The hood was negotiated away. "I'll trust you, if you trust me. It's about answers." Ben knew it wasn't about answers. It was about questions. The questions John Penner wanted answered weren't about guns or meetings or the hitchhiker. The daily interview always started with those questions, repetitions, rote to the point of becoming custom. The answers were slight variations of more of the same.

Ben watched the time, the big office clock on the wall in the next office, there where the window let in the light from outside. John Penner came to believe that Ben was looking in that direction because of the light, outside, freedom, believed that it tormented Ben. He liked it that he sat between Ben and that freedom and that Ben had to go through him to get to where he knew Ben wanted to be. He sat in the seat of power, his legs stretched out under the desk.

Always take your time, my boy. Don't rush things. Those old people, when they negotiated the Treaty, they took their time. It was the government people that were in a hurry. Us Indians, we sat and talked about things, all kind of things before they got here. We were ready. We knew what we were going to say. We sat on the ground, on our Mother, got our strength from there. They sat on chairs. It was always the treaty commissioner who tried to hurry things up. Remember that my boy. When it's important. Don't rush. Time is your friend.

Ben had one hour with John Penner. He had the rest of the day to listen to the words of his father. One hour in an office, and then he would sit by the fire in a log cabin, hot tea in his hands, a willing receptor of the wisdom of generations and their stories. Even here, even in this concrete and glass, in this office, he heard his father, heard the slow speech, the short sentences, each filled with importance, never an empty phrase, a wasted word.

"It seems like you have some friends, Mr. Robe."

"I'm sure I have one or two."

"Oh, there's more than two. We're starting to get a little pile of letters, people are writing, saying you're a political prisoner. Are you a political prisoner, Ben?"

"I am a prisoner."

"That's not what I asked. Are you political?"

"Wasn't it George Orwell who once wrote that everything is political?"

"So you admit that you are part of a political movement?"

"I've told you over and over again, John, I am not part of any organized resistance. I speak only for myself."

"Maybe not organized, as you say, but you are resistant."

"I accept that you are here and that you are not going away, that we have to learn how we will live together."

"Good answer, Ben. But between you and me, we know you would prefer that I went home to Richmond. I'd like to go home to Richmond too. Especially now with winter coming on. But, we have things to take care of here first. Satan walks these lands, spreading lies, spreading his hatred of the holy." Ben watched as Penner's hands began to wave the air. The beginning of the rant, the calling down of the wrath of God, the demand for repentance that began with admission of sin. Soon he would be begging Ben to save himself, save his soul from eternal damnation, admit his wrongs so that he could experience the salvation of the lord.

Ben tuned him out. Would not follow him into the circular depths of his rant. Instead he wondered why Penner had told him about the letters. People on the outside were putting on a little pressure. He imagined the content; held without charge, principles of fundamental justice, the rights of humans.

But why tell him?

To give him hope?

Maybe. Probably. Give him hope so that there was something to take away. The problem was that Ben had no hope, had taught himself to not hope. Hope exists for people who never learned to live entirely in the moment. Ben stayed in the here and now.

"Repentance is the path to salvation."

Ben didn't need salvation, or the promise of salvation. His Mother, the Earth, was still somewhere beneath the concrete. His Grandfathers were in the air around him. He didn't need promises of somewhere better. He was home.

"'I am the way, the truth and the light. No man comes unto the Father but by me'." John Penner stared straight into Ben's eyes. "Jesus said that. Know what he meant?"

Ben kept silent.

"He was telling us that the Muslims and Buddhists and Indian spiritualists and Atheists, and all of them are deceived by Satan. There is only one way, Ben. You have to follow the truth and the life."

Ben refused to respond, kept his face calm. He realized in that minute, even though he had thought about it before, the power of a few words. He counted them in his head: *I am the way, the truth and the light. No man comes unto the father but by me* . . . Eighteen words. How many millions have died for so few words? The phrase was the epitome of intolerance. There it was, clean, simple, deadly, perfect. It didn't say go and kill everyone who prays differently than you. Ben couldn't resist. He asked, "What did he mean, he was the truth, the light and the way?"

"That's not important, Ben. The important part is that no man comes unto the father but by Jesus. If you understand that part, then you are on the path of righteousness."

But Ben couldn't stop thinking that he knew a little about the truth, that *the light* was synonymous with *understanding* and that he definitely had a *way* to pray that was humble and honest.

~

"Do you think Benji could set a net?" Rosie was talking to Elsie, but her eyes were on Rachel. The little girl toddled, holding on to the edge of the cot, her feet unsteady. Going, always going. The little girl had two speeds, flat out and stop: she was either asleep or moving, a handful.

"He could." Elsie forced confidence into her voice. She had never seen Benji set a net, didn't know for certain that he could. "Are you hungry for fish again?"

"Oh, not for me. I could use a big feed of pike, maybe make a fish pie. No, I was thinking about Duchess and her puppies. Whitefish run this time of year, we might want to put up a bunch of fish to feed them over freeze up. Might be a long time until we can set nets through the ice."

"I don't know if Benji can set a net through the ice. His dad showed him how to set a net in open water. But, I don't think he ever saw fishing through the ice."

"That's okay, we can show him." Rosie moved to stand behind Rachel, let the little girl fall against her legs.

"Now, how in the world did you know she was going to fall right then?" Elsie stayed seated at the table, her tea cooling in the cup, no need to move, her mother had things under control.

"Four kids, no help from anyone." Rosie offered an answer that didn't satisfy Elsie, didn't at all explain how. Elsie let it go, one of those things about her mother that she might never understand.

～

Benji pulled the boat up on the beach. Setting the net had not been too difficult, he tangled it a couple of times, it hadn't been a smooth set. But now it was in the water and tomorrow there should be fish in it. He stood for a moment before unloading the gear, a moment to take in his surroundings. It was one of those perfect fall days, crisp; a light wind out of the west that rippled the lake for no apparent reason other than to give the sun something to reflect off of. A large flock of snow geese swirled off the northern horizon, formed patterns, waves that broke and reformed chaotically. Nearby a gull screamed its demand for food, or just yelled for the joy of its own voice in the wind and sun.

Benji noticed a bit of ice on the deck of the boat, it didn't mean much to him, other than the day was colder than it looked. He packed the gear into the back of the truck. No need to put the boat onto the trailer. He would be back out onto the lake tomorrow. He was thinking about a hot cup of coffee with Elsie and Rachel when he put the truck into gear. The rear wheels spun in the sand, the truck bounced up and down. He pushed a button on the consul and the bouncing stopped. Four-wheel drive was such a nice option.

$$\sim$$

A large black and grey pup jumped at the hanging fish, out of reach. It stood and bent its neck back, blue grey eyes begging. "That fish is for you, but you can't eat it all today." Rosie's soft voice shooed the puppy as she hung another string of fish, a slender, peeled pole pushed through holes cut in their tails, shoulder-high on the drying rack. "These are for winter, little guy — you go eat with your brothers. Benji brought you lots of tasty fish."

She knelt and petted the pup, felt it along its broad chest already muscled, ruffled the fur along its back and its narrower hips. "You're going to be a good size dog in a few months. Before winter is over you'll be big enough to pull." The pup wriggled with the petting, turned and licked her hand. "I'll make you a harness the way my mother used to. A nice one with lots of padding so it doesn't rub. Yes sir, little guy, you are going to become a good-size dog."

"Having trouble, my girl?" Rosie returned to the gutting table under the pines where Elsie struggled with a knife.

"Just this part gives me a hard time. How do you get the little bones out."

"Here, I'll show you again, just run your knife along here." Rosie started a cut down the inside of the pike fillet. "Well, here is your problem, your knife is dull." She ran the edge of the knife against a honing steel hung with a string from a branch. A half dozen quick strokes and she handed the knife back to Elsie. "Try it now."

"Benji did good. I didn't think we'd get this much out of one net." Elsie's knife found the line, made the shallow cut the way her mother showed her, felt the click of it against the line of tiny bones, another cut above the first line and a sliver of flesh fell away. Elsie held up a perfectly boneless fillet.

"Pretty good," Rosie agreed as she prepared the next string of fish. She watched Elsie without being intrusive, let the girl learn, even though Elsie was leaving way too much fish on the bones. She had to do it to learn it. Rosie prepared the fish that would go to the dogs and let her daughter prepare the fish for the frying pan.

~

The wind died overnight. The water calmed, Benji slept content in the silence.

~

"Rosie said we had enough yesterday. I should have listened. But man we were catching good, I just wanted one more lift, just one more." Benji tugged against the boat frozen into the lake.

"That's the way it goes." Red agreed. He was happy to answer cousin Elsie's phone call, *I need a favour, cuz.* He looked out across the frozen bay. "Where's your net set?"

"Off Willow Point."

"That part still looks open, lucky thing. It's hell chopping out a frozen net."

"If the boat isn't buggered up."

"It's not the boat you have to worry about. A little chopping and we'll have that out. You left the motor down. If there was any water in that gear housing, it'll bust sure as shit."

~

Elsie helped Benji to hang the net. "You've had quite the day."

"You can say that again. If it wasn't for Red we'd be in real trouble. He not only helped to get our boat up onto shore. He chopped ice for about fifty metres so that he could get his boat out to open water to go rescue this net."

"Red's a good guy."

"I like his attitude. Know what he said about the motor? 'Well good thing it happened today, now you have until spring to get the parts.'"

"So, how bad is the motor?"

"Broke the housing around the gears and the water pump is shot. I should have known better. It's not like Dad doesn't have enough going on right now without me wrecking his stuff."

"Don't worry about it, it's just stuff." Elsie hung the last of her side of the net on the peg, turned, and wrapped her arms around Benji from behind.

He turned back for the kiss on the cheek he knew was coming. "Dad might not think of it as just stuff."

"Like Red said, you have till spring to fix it." Elsie hugged him tighter.

~.

"'I am Alpha and Omega, the beginning and the end, saith the Lord, which is, and which was, and which is to come, the Almighty'." John Penner nearly screamed.

Ben thought about this simple linear construct of time. It wasn't at all relevant to his experience; he let the thought go, let it drift out into the cyclical universe that Ben chose to exist in.

Penner was in the middle of his daily rant, and Ben knew from experience not to push his buttons. Penner's vomit of words excluded rationality, excluded Ben, excluded even Penner himself. The words poured, spewed, angry and raw. This wasn't a preacher bent on conversion. This wasn't a teacher explaining. This was hate wrapped in gospel, hate warped by gospel. Hate that surfaced and subsided quickly. Penner stopped. Briefly the interview room fell silent. He looked directly at Ben and asked. "Do you believe in Democracy?"

Ben hesitated, looked for the trick in the question and decided it would be safe to answer "Yes."

"That is absolute foolishness. Democracy is the work of Satan. Satan puts ideas into men's heads to lead them away from the Kingdom of Jesus. There is only one rightful government. That is the government of God. Jesus came here to create his kingdom on Earth. It is his kingdom that we should be working to create. Not our, or your kingdom, Ben." Penner's voice changed. It became a pleading. "Do you honestly believe we could create a kingdom on Earth that would be superior to

Jesus' kingdom? Do you believe that man is better than God?"
He didn't give Ben an opportunity to answer. "Of course not.
Now you are asking, what would this look like, this kingdom
of Jesus on Earth? Well, let me tell you. It would be Christian
Totalitarianism. Mao had it right, even Hitler knew what he
was doing. God chose those men. He chose them to get the
world ready for the day when he puts his kingdom back on
Earth."

For the remainder of the interview Ben sat and listened to
the words of hate, the words that were part prayer, part calls
for help, part confession (though this had to be read in) and
part demand for the damnation of everything not Godly.

~

The chainsaw screamed in Benji's hand; he concentrated on
Red's instructions. "Cut out a wedge on the side you want the
tree to fall toward. Then when you make the back cut, don't
cut all the way through, leave a little wood, that's what you
use to steer with." The standing dead pine was a nice size. A
good tree to learn with. Red stood back and watched Benji fall
his very first tree. Eighty feet, at least eighty feet. Red looked
toward the heavy crown where dwarf mistletoe cancered
the ancient tree, rapid growth, branches twisted into thick
brooms. The disease clustered in stands of pine, leaving dead
wood for insects, and the birds that feed off them and easy
fire wood for people like Red who still enjoyed simpler though
harder ways of living.

Red didn't notice the change in colour of the sawdust, from
white to orange brown sprayed out onto the thin covering of
snow. He was looking toward the crown, feeling pride in Benji,
a good sized tree for his first. Fall a tree like that and a person
couldn't help but to feel proud of himself. Neither of them

knew about the ants. Big carpenter ants that ate away the tree's core, left a honeycomb labyrinth at the centre. The little wood that Benji was to use to steer the tree with had no strength. The big pine leaned, twisted on the cut at its base and slowly began to fall. Red saw it first. The tree was coming toward them. He grabbed Benji's shoulder, pulled and stepped aside. They stood still and watched the tree pick up speed. Benji screamed a silent "*No!*" when he realized where the tree was going. "*No!*" his heart sank "*Please No!*" The top of the tree hit the cab of Ben's truck where the passenger door met the roof, smashed glass and warped metal, the weight of two hundred years growth and the inertia of coming to earth drove the tree until the roof of the truck touched the seat. The steel frame under the cab bent, then held, snow caught in the branches and released in the fall flittered down for a few more seconds, then everything was still and quiet.

~

"You were trying to do something good. You were getting wood to keep me and Rachel warm for the winter." Elsie hugged Benji tighter. "Don't be too hard on yourself. Your dad will understand, you were trying to do something good."

~

"Happy birthday, Lester." Rosie hoped to lift his spirits.

"How'd you know it was my birthday." Lester lifted his head and a bit of one shoulder from the couch.

"I remembered when you were born. Your mom came over to our house to ask for a ride to town. December first. I think she came to her big sister's house, half expecting my mom to midwife for her. But in the end we took her to the hospital instead."

"You got a good memory, Rosie." Lester let his head rest back on the softness of the overlarge couch, let the foam and fibre swallow him.

"I remember when she brought you home too. She pretty much lived with us that winter."

Rosie's memories drew Lester backward through time. "Where was my dad?" he wondered, looking upwards at the tile of the ceiling.

"Work. Cutting pulp. Something, I'm not sure. Only home on weekends. During the week, your mom stayed with us." She remembered the baby and the fussing. It was her first experience up close with a baby, a young girl trying to be a part of this woman thing that was happening between her mother and her aunt. She was playing with dolls with her aunt again, and the doll was wriggly baby Lester. "Anyway, that was a long time ago." Rosie suddenly felt uncomfortable, talking about her aunt with the man who murdered her. She came back to the present. Lester on the couch with a bad cold. A cake in the oven. Not one of the big cakes she used to make for her children, she was a little short on ingredients, just a little something because it was his birthday and he was sick. Cake and a little kindness can be good medicine.

～

Winter, again, another cycle of the great wheel. We count winters because they are the most memorable. Ben wondered if he would spend this entire winter indoors. What would be his memories? This cell, concrete and steel, not so different from the winters in the university; thinking, re-gathering, ordering thoughts, finding the order that organizes chaos. The cell was not so different from his university office; windowless, cinder block cold, only his body confined, now by guards, then by exam schedules, his mind free as ever to fly, to find the truth in itself, or out there in the snow and wind, flying above the boreal of his home, or walking the ancient trails. Ben walked often with his father, listened again to his stories, spent hours in front of a warm fire again and reheard the wisdom. The thick of winter, silent, smothered in hip-deep snow, when the magpie circled the cabin looking for scraps, the storyteller, just through the window: *"The people moved around lots back then, whenever you wanted, pack your tent, harness your dogs or make a new birchbark canoe. I knew whenever my dad made a new canoe, as soon as it was finished we'd move again. It was like a new canoe was a good reason to move."*

Ben had been reading history; stories about Indians who moved to be closer to the missions, the priests, the documentation of conversions, and asked his father. *"The truth, my son, is that some people did move to the missions. But a lot more moved away. That's why we're here. Your grandfather moved away from the Churchill River because there were getting to be too many Christians up there. He came here. Strange though, I met a young man a while ago. He was from that Churchill River area. Out travelling, the way young men are supposed to, came back to see the land of his grandfather, the Thunder Hills. Seems, that old man moved away from here for the same reason, to get away from the Christians. You know, you hear how we used to banish people. Even Chief and Council nowadays want to banish people. Got a drug dealer they don't know what to do with and they tell the court to banish that person, kick him off the reserve. That's not how it used to be up here. Maybe in the South they did that. But up here, there was lots of room. People could move. What happened most often if a person was acting up, didn't get along with everyone else, well, the people would move, leave that person behind. That's a good way to do things. Banish somebody and you make hard feelings, and things were hard enough before. Make a hard decision like that and you make a hard thing harder. But now we can't do that anymore, the land is all taken up. Did you know they cut lines around the reserve to mark the boundary? As if the reserve wasn't too small as it was, the government paid to cut lines, wide ones all the way around, I think just to rub it in. 'You Indians stay there' and what are the people going to do when someone acts up, what choice do they have? They have to move to the city."*

Ben left his father, reached down and touched his toes, both hands, slowly, stretched out the back muscles, felt the tightness in his lower back resist the stretch, pushed through the resistance; and again, straightened and bent, this time a little slower as he bent through the range of muscle tightness. He bent his knees, squatted and rose, listened to the leg muscles speak to him through his bones. Then, he began his push-up routine, not worried about the count. There was nothing important about one hundred, that was a number, a favourite number of the younger men, a hundred push-ups at a set, repeated several times a day. Ben was thankful for them, their dedication inspired him, reminded him, mind, body and spirit all need attention. He repeated the motions, push slowly up, feel the muscle, experience the ache as tight becomes loose: push slowly up, the burn of the rise felt different than the pain of the slow, controlled down. Repeat, listen to the body, push against the pain beyond the pain of yesterday, beyond where he stopped last time, forced another, one more push-up and then down, then relaxed, lay for a moment on the hard concrete floor of the cell, remembered that Mother Earth, the great grandmother was there under the cement and stone. He laid in her arms for those last few moments before lights out and felt her comfort.

～

"Did you laugh?"

"I couldn't, you had to see his face. I wanted to. It was hard not to. His first tree." Red shook his head, "His very first tree. It looked like he was going to cry."

"I would've laughed anyway."

"I know you would, my dear." Red brushed his wife's hair away from his face, it tickled his nose. He slid his arm under her pillow so as not to pull her long loose hair, intent on drawing her close. He missed in the dark, put his arm inside of the pillowcase, fumbled until he realized why he was unable to hug her, pulled his arm out and tried again. Lorraine snuggled against her rail-thin husband, ran her free hand down his back, felt the cool of his skin. She rolled away onto her back, looked up toward the ceiling. The night was young, lots of time yet for talk.

"You should have laughed at him. I know he's mostly white and doesn't get it yet. But he has to learn sometime. Know what I mean?"

Red ran his hand over Lorraine's stomach, made another circle, then stopped, let his palm absorb the warmth. "If you'd seen his face."

"I know, you said that already. But," she put her hand on top of his before he could begin circling again. "But, if you laughed at him, laughed right away, maybe he wouldn't've taken it so seriously."

"I didn't want to see him cry." Red defended himself.

"I know you didn't. You were trying to be kind." She pressed his palm against her belly. "That's the way you are. All

I'm saying is that it might have been kinder in the long run to have laughed at him right away, instead of letting him feel bad, know what I mean?"

"Yeah, I guess."

"Know what?" she held his hand from moving, kept it from making the circles again. "You should take him hunting."

"Aow." It sounded like a sigh.

"No seriously." She kept him from drawing his hand away. "Think about it."

"I am." It wasn't a good thought.

"Somebody has to teach him."

"I know, but why me? That's a lot of teaching." Red remembered the way Benji clomped when he walked.

"Somebody taught you."

"That's different. I didn't grow up in a city."

"Not his fault, take him with you. It won't be so bad." She moved his hand in a little circle, enjoyed the feel of the rough of the callus and the cool of his palm.

"You don't know what you're asking."

"It won't be so bad." She rolled over onto her side again, drew Red close. "It won't be so bad." She whispered into his ear, felt his palm climb her spine.

⌇

"Collaborators?"

"Yeah, collaborators."

"No, Betsy." Monica did not like where this was going. All she wanted was a nice dark roast coffee, a little demerara sugar, very little, just enough to counter the bite of the coffee, and conversation with a friend. Then Betsy had to start talking like this. They should have been talking about anything else, the weather even. Snow was swirling out the window of the

Roastery. They used to come here and sit for hours Saturday mornings and discuss political ideas, or listen to the chatter at other tables. "That won't get us anywhere." Monica wanted the conversation to go in another direction, or stop. "If we start hitting our own, they'll turn against us."

"If we don't hit them, and hit them hard, the people will follow who they think are the strongest. Strength Monica. We have to show that we're strong. Otherwise we become insignificant. They have to learn there's a cost to doing business with the enemy."

"But they're our own people. Remember Ben, he always said that the people were ultimately in control. Even in a tyranny, the people decided at some level to live with it, made the choice, whether consciously or not, to accept where they were. Without the people we will never succeed. Start hitting collaborators and we lose. That's the path to our own end."

"Your rationalizations start out correctly enough, the people are the key to final success. But we are losing them, every day, more and more, they're lining up for the easy money. We don't have the money, we can't compete. We teach our children not to take candy from a stranger, and when they dig in the cookie jar too often we slap their hands."

"You're not talking about slapping some kid's hand here. Agribition, that's been around for probably a century."

"And they've always collaborated with the Americans. What do you think Agribition is about? It's about selling beef to the devil."

"Oh, it's more than that. Farmers from the whole country come to show off their stuff, not just to the Americans. Lots of people from Europe come to it."

"Used to come, Europeans used to come. Not anymore. Now it's about supplying the bastards with T-bones, giving the fat of the land to the new master."

"Maybe, but I can't stop thinking that if we hit them, the people will turn against us and we need them." Monica looked to the snow, watched it swirl. They sat at a corner table, each with their backs to respective walls. The tables near to them were empty. Maybe it was the snow that kept people away. Maybe it was something else. Monica did not want to talk about this. The thought of security might have been a good reason to bring it to a stop, but they had talked here before, made plans, successful plans. Homeland Security could not listen to everything, all the time. The Roastery was as safe a place to talk as anywhere else, maybe safer. It had a proven track record. She tried another approach. "Has council thought this through?"

"As far as you need to know, I am council."

"I'm not doubting." Monica ran a thumbnail under a fingernail, nervously, realized what she was doing and stopped. She reached for her coffee, not because she wanted it, just to give her hand something to do, something that did not show Betsy that she was in anyway nervous, or distrustful. This was a first, this feeling, this sense, a sense of doubt, and doubt was dangerous. It led to fear. If Betsy was acting alone on this, Monica could not go directly to council, could not go around her, ask her superiors. That would be insubordination and the insubordinate, undisciplined did not survive long. She remembered Ed Tremblay.

"On a final note, I have some good news for you."

"What might that be?" Monica was thankful for the topic shift.

"We found Ben."

"Where?" Monica leaned forward with the word, closer to hear, pulled by the promise.

"He's here."

Monica waited for the rest of the good news, wordless.

"He's here, in Saskatoon." Betsy fed a little more.

Monica waited.

"At the correctional centre."

"Not Dakota Max." Monica sat back.

"No, he's here."

"Then he should get a hearing and be allowed a lawyer, everything else." Monica spun possibilities.

"Not necessarily." Betsy enjoyed feeding Monica little morsels of words.

Monica waited for more. It didn't come. They sat in silence a moment. Monica looked out the window at the gliding snow, let her mind go out into the city to look for Ben.

Betsy looked at Monica, weighed her, weighed her strength, didn't find any weakness and fed her the remainder. "Ben never went to Dakota Max. He's been here all along under psychological review."

"But what does that mean?" Monica came back into the Roastery, looked into Betsy's face, a long, hard face with new lines around the mouth adding to the old lines that were becoming deeper.

"Don't know. Usually politicals get sent south and the correctional centre is used for criminals. Don't know what they're up to. Maybe psychology is the new word for torture. Maybe they don't have enough on him. Maybe Dakota Max is full. Who knows."

"Maybe we can get him out."

"A jail break."

"Why not?"

"Because, my girl, Ben is small potatoes. He doesn't know anything. Council will never authorize it, and even if they did, then what? Ben goes into hiding. He goes to the bush. We have hundreds out there now, just here, under local authority. Imagine there must be thousands across Canada hiding out there. Great thing about Canada, we still have lots of bush. In the summer it's not bad, kind of a picnic, an outdoor adventure. But now with winter, everyday we have people showing up, hungry, frozen, begging council for a place to stay, a blanket, a bed. Hell, we even have people turning themselves in because they think jail is better. At least it's warm."

"Not Ben. Ben can survive out there."

"So much faith. In a way it's good to see. It's good to see faith in something. But, I think you're putting it in the wrong place. Ben is an old man, he doesn't know anything, he can't do anything. He is just not a priority. Not for council and probably not for Homeland Security. Give them a little more time and they'll figure it out for themselves. Then you're beloved Ben can go back into retirement, fade away into the bush."

"Maybe." Monica looked out the window again, the snow was getting heavier. "Maybe, but I still think that he knows a way out of this."

~

Elsie stood with her back to Benji, felt the smooth round of the log on her palm. She leaned against the wall, not for support, it was her stance: she touched the wall beside the window for the sensation of its solidness, its security, as she looked out at the snow on the pines, building on the ground, becoming deep. "Mom's alone over there." She spoke more to herself than anyone.

Only Benji heard her. "Where's Lester?"

"Medevac yesterday. Mom helped him walk to the clinic. They took one look at him and put him on an ambulance to Prince Albert." She turned to look at him, "It doesn't look good. Pneumonia."

"Pneumonia's not a big deal. A couple of days rest, some antibiotics and he'll be back."

"It's not a big deal unless you have AIDS."

"Lester has AIDS?" Benji put the book down.

"Thought you knew."

"No. I thought he was just being lazy. Red needs him to work and he keeps staying home. I thought he just had a cold." Benji spun thoughts, rapid thoughts, a blur of experiences with Lester. Had he ever had an open wound when Lester was around? Had he ever drunk out of the same cup, shared a bottle of water? His thoughts slowed to a stop without finding anything, realized the senselessness of his fear. "Is he going to be all right?"

"Don't know." Elsie turned to slide a chair away from the table; she wanted to sit and watch the snow fall. She never got the chance. The chair scraped against the floor. The sound woke Rachel. She had been asleep for over an hour. Wore herself out, little legs that have just learned how to walk tire easily. The little girl fell asleep on her blanket spread on the floor, across a cushion she had pulled from the couch. Elsie had found her and put her on the bed. The floor was too cold a place for little ones to sleep.

A north wind hammered down the length of Moccasin Lake, flew full force into the tiny community at the south end, brought with it any loose snow and piled it in the willows along the shore. It shaped drifts, then reshaped them, created its own abstract art forms: lines and swirls, depths and hollows — piled snow in one place for no other reason than it chose to, and in others exposed the naked black ice.

Cut by the pines around Ben's cabin, the wind lost some of its force before hitting the solid logs. It tried to find any loose chinks, a place where insulation was thin. Thwarted, it passed, without looking back where it would have seen Elsie standing in the window, her daughter held on her hip with one hand; the other against the wall, drawing strength in the middle of the storm. She was looking south toward her mother's house.

"I love you." Benji put his arm around her waist; stood beside her, pulled her close so they stood hip-to-hip, thigh-to-thigh, rib cages pressed together.

"I love you back." Elsie turned from the window to kiss his cheek, a gentle brush of lips against bristle.

Benji sought what Elsie was watching. All he saw was snow, swirls of it, skittering across the spaces between the trees, piling into, onto itself. He soon tired of it, could not capture whatever it was that had captured her, could not comprehend that she appreciated the power of the storm, the power of those forces that shape and form everything.

Red's truck ploughed through the drift that was forming across the driveway, cut two parallel tracks up to the house. Elsie and Benji watched as he walked, head bent away from the wind to the door.

"Want to go hunting?" he asked as soon as he was inside.

"Today?" Benji wasn't sure.

"Best time. Good wind."

Benji looked back toward the window, at the swirls on the other side of the glass.

Elsie figured this out, saw what was happening. If Red wanted to go hunting today, there was a reason, probably a good reason.

"You should go," she urged. "Get us some moose meat."

"Why today?" Benji wanted to know.

"He can't smell us coming. Best hunting weather. We can walk right up to him if we do it right. Come on, I'll show you." Red was excited, in a rush, his words as fast as his thoughts.

~

"You guys all need names." Rosie scraped leftovers from a plate onto the ground. Six half-grown dogs scrambled, nosing each other aside to get at the bones and scraps. "Here Duchess, saved a piece for you." She tossed a bit of meat aside for the mother, then stood and watched the action. If Ben was here, you guys would be in harness by now, earning your keep." She thought about what she had just said. The words had come before the thought. If Ben were really here, then he would need harness and a sleigh. She could make harness. That was easy. She needed snaps, rings, nylon strapping, something for padding so the harness did not cut into shoulders. Six dogs, she counted, imagined freight harness, not bad, only a dozen snaps and rings, it was do-able. The sleigh, that was a different matter. Her dad used to make his own, bent birch runners, a frame tied together with rawhide or sinew. It needed to be sturdy and flexible. Someone has to remember how to make a sleigh. She couldn't think of anyone alive anymore who would know how. She remembered all of the steps. Her dad had built his inside the house; boiling water to bend the hand-hewn boards, a drawknife leaving piles of shavings on the floor. It wasn't that she had watched him build sleighs; it was that he had done it in front of her so many times that she absorbed it.

She thought it all through again. She could make harness. That was easy, a little sewing. Could she make a sleigh? The hard part would be getting the right tree. Now was a good time to cut it, winter when the sap was all drained away, the boards would be half dry to start with. Red. Yeah, Red, he could get her the wood, probably cut it into boards too. Rawhide and sinew — someone needed to kill a moose. Rosie was beginning to feel chilled. She went back into the house, now with a purpose, not to watch television.

She gave her house a thorough cleaning, not that it needed it. She needed the movement. Lester's duffle bag behind the couch was half open, the leg of a pair of jeans hung out. She stuffed it in and zipped the bag. Everything he owned was in there. Not much. She lifted it, checked its weight, was about to put it back where it had been since early summer and realized, "Lester isn't coming home."

She stood a moment, holding the bag, half bent over. She straightened. No, he wasn't coming home. She put the bag in a closet, made room for it on the shelf, then reconsidered the sudden thought. It came to her as soon as she had touched his bag, his things. Lester was not coming back. No, that wasn't it. She had thought, Lester is not coming home. This had been his home, Lester's home. Now it wasn't anymore. But he wasn't going to die homeless. She took the bag down from the closet shelf and gently put it back behind the couch.

$\sim$

"Hurry it up, you old fuck. Against the wall."

Ben did not hurry any more than he had before. This was routine. Against the wall, hands spread on the cinder block. That's all he has, Ben thought. All he has is that I am older than him.

Even the shove between the shoulder blades was routine now. The hands patting, feeling through the coveralls, striking; chest, belly, thighs, ankles, looking for a shank, contraband, drugs. An excuse to hit, even with an open hand, is still an excuse to hit, to demean, punish, force a hand into the crotch, grab, exercise power.

Ben turned his head, looked over his right shoulder. She stood aside, watching the male guard, the one without hair and a belly that pushed against the black shirt, with the hands that hit when he searched. Her face tried to hide what she felt; a brown face, frozen, flat, cold. It was trying to say, "I am doing my job." But it wasn't. It mumbled something else, something quiet. How did she feel? Ben wondered. Collaborator. Her hands were on her belt, the right one near the holster with the pepper spray. "I am doing my job." Her feet were spread, ready, her back straight, her neck straight, her eyes straight, the crease that ran down the front of her legs, straight, stiff, starched. Everything said "I am doing my job" except the eyes. The black, intelligent eyes said something else, they said "I am doing my job, but I don't like it. I don't like to see old people pushed around. I especially don't like to see old natives, Elders treated without respect."

There was no real strength in the hands that hit. These were the hands of a man who never had to work, never used an axe or a shovel; maybe at one time they lifted weights in a gym, but today the memory of the steel bar was distant. Ben noted the feel of the hands the same as he noted the belly. It was not a belly that bulged. The male guard did not know that it was noticeable. He thought it was hidden under the black shirt, covered. Mostly it was, but the shirt touched the roundness just above the wide belt. Ben imagined a puppy with worms, its weakness exposed by a round hard belly.

She walked at Ben's left, he walked on the right with his hand constantly on Ben's shoulder, steering, commanding. A buzzer sounded a long second before the steel door slid noisily to the right, clanged when it was fully open. The hand shoved, pushed Ben through the door that he was ready to walk through on his own. The strength of the push did not come from the arm. It came from the man's waist. Ben noted, stored the memory. The guard with the belly used his weight to compensate for his lack of muscle, a dangerous practice; weight needs balance, unbalanced weight can be toppled. She had balance. Ben watched her feet, watched her walk beside him, watched how she stepped, set her feet down toe first, then rest on the heel. She also had strength, more than muscle. She had the strength to stand still and watch a bully push an old man around; even though it went against everything she had ever learned.

She opened the door to John Penner's office. Ben walked through. The male guard did not push, did not put his hand between Ben's shoulder blades. Ben noted that the bully in him was too much of a coward to act in front of a superior. The door shut behind him with a thump. Wood makes a different sound than steel. The office was slightly different. Ben looked around. The desk, bare, was in the same spot, as was the chair he would sit in. The difference was on the wall. A single framed diploma now hung on the panelling. University of California, Berkeley, Bachelor's degree in psychology. Penner saw Ben read it.

"Yes, Ben. I went into the den of Satan and took that away as a trophy. I matched wits with the liberals and in the end they were forced to concede that God might exist."

"Berkeley is a noteworthy school."

"Berkeley is the home of Satan. He walks those halls and his minions bow and grovel. It is the ultimate denial of the holy."

"So why did you go there?"

"Like I said. I went into his den and walked out with a trophy."

"Psychology."

"A degree in the art of denial. Know your enemies, Ben, always know your enemies more than you know your friends. Don't put any trust in that piece of paper, my friend. I assure you I am not who it says I am. The only reason it is up there is because someone in this organization has succumbed to the liberals' propaganda that we are not qualified, and now we have been reminded in a memo to nail our credentials to the wall."

John Penner has a superior, Ben thought, as he took the familiar chair.

"Something you asked the other day got me thinking." John leaned his elbows on the desk and stared into Ben's face, looking, always watching for the opening, waiting for Ben's face to betray him. It didn't. Ben waited.

"You asked me how many trees are in the Bible."

"So, How many are there?"

"Quite a few. Of course the ones that jump immediately to mind are the Tree of Knowledge and the Tree of Life in Genesis, that, and of course we refer to Jesus being hung from a tree, but I was amazed at the number of references to fruit trees, fig trees, the tree that is pleasant to the sight, people sitting under trees, cedar trees, the tree that Moses threw into the water of Marah so that the people could drink." John leaned harder into the back of his chair, felt the metal dig into his shoulder blades, enjoyed the discomfort. This was not going to be comfortable. He flipped over a single sheet of paper, turned it scribble side up on the desk and read: "Psalms 96:12. Let the field be joyful, *and* all that *is* therein: then shall all the trees of the wood rejoice. Isaiah 14:8. Yea, the fir trees rejoice at thee, *and* the cedars of Lebanon, *saying,* Since thou art laid down, no feller is come up against us."

Ben noted that John did not use his memory.

John continued. "Isaiah 55:12. And all the trees of the field shall clap *their* hands. Chronicles 16:33. Then shall the trees of the wood sing out at the presence of the Lord."

He turned the sheet of paper over and continued, "The burning bush of course was a tree. So, I see what it was you were getting at Ben."

"And what was that?"

"Don't be a smart ass. I get it. You asked me how many trees are in the Bible to get me to think about God and nature. Nature, that's your thing." John leaned forward, elbows on the desk. "Like I said, I get it; references about trees rejoicing, trees singing. Yeah, trees are in the Bible in a big way, and yeah, trees are an important part of the story, a part of the story that scholars tend to miss. You showed me that there are things about the Book of God that you know more than I do." John sat up straight. "You win that round, I concede. You have a unique understanding. You know something that I didn't."

Ben didn't like where this was going. John was working himself up for something. This thing about trees was not about bettering him, it was to give him something to think about, to consider in his interpretation of his ultimate authority. John had accused him of worshiping trees;

Ben had just wanted John to know that John's God also had an affinity for the forest nations.

The door opened and the two guards re-entered the office, the guard with the belly came in first, she followed.

"Handcuff this bastard." John stood, kicked back the metal chair, it scraped against the floor.

She held him by the right shoulder, he held the left, it was his weight that pushed Ben face down on the desk, his left cheek pressed into the fibreboard finish. He could see her, felt one of her hands on his elbow, the other on his shoulder. She gripped his shirt, a solid grip, different than the hand on his other shoulder. That hand was flat against his back and pressed down, hard.

The opening of the drawer vibrated through the desk. Ben felt it in his cheek and the slam of its closing. John held a screw in front of Ben's face, about an inch long between thumb and forefinger. "See this, asshole, wonderful technology, self-tapping. That means that I don't have to drill a hole first. This little beauty will bore itself into solid metal. Screw with me and I'll screw with you."

Ben fought down the fear. Breathed, drew in a chest full against the pressure on his back. The screw pulled hair with the first twists, tore them out by the roots. It ripped through the skin without effort and began to bite into the bone of Ben's skull. Pain has colour. This was brilliant white with orange and yellow flashes, bright to the point of blinding. Pain has heat. The fire began above Ben's right ear and spread around his head, flamed through to the desk and danced down his spine. Pain has sound. Ben heard the bloodrush, heard the roar, heard the scream of it in his ears. It wasn't his scream. He was too busy breathing. Bringing in air to put out the fire.

John Penner wasn't thinking about God as he torqued the screwdriver. This had nothing to do with grace, the right way to pray, the wrong way to pray, which direction to send the prayer. This was about John. Simple. This had nothing to do with Sodom and Gomorrah, though John could tell you every sin ever alleged to have occurred there. This had nothing to do with Canada, or God Bless the United States of America. This wasn't political, secular. This was simply *Don't fuck with John Penner*. This came from the idea that Ben was screwing with John's head, and now John was screwing with his.

He didn't taste the bile in his mouth, or feel the throb of his own headache. That would come later, when Ben was carried back to the cell block and John sat alone at the desk, gasping, gagging. Then he would absorb the bitter acid at the back of his mouth, across his tongue, coat his teeth; teeth clenched until his jaw ached and pain throbbed in his temple. When he unclenched his jaw and the tension in his arms, so strong that he shook, drained away with the sweat from his chest and his throat, then John would realize what it was that he had done, even though he had planned it, every detail of it, from putting the screwdriver and screws in the desk, to arranging for the guards to return exactly two minutes after they shut the door; now the full realization hit him, hit him hard that Ben did not scream, or beg. When the guards stood him up, it wasn't fear in his eyes, it was pity. Ben stood against the pain, breathed hard against it, and felt sorry for little John Penner.

Ben walked between the two guards, held his head up and breathed, drew in air, deep, held it, pressurized his lungs, released the air for room to draw in another deep breath. The pain tried to pull his head down. He held it up to keep his air passage open for the cooling air against the fire in his skull.

He felt a tug at his right shoulder. She was pulling at him, turning him toward the hallway in her direction.

"No, this way." The guard with the belly pulled at Ben's left shoulder.

"The infirmary is this way." Strength in her voice.

"We weren't told to take him there."

"We weren't told not to."

The guard with the belly was confused, off balance, even though he stood flat footed. She turned Ben. He breathed and followed. The guard with the belly caught up, took Ben by the left shoulder again, but now he wasn't leading, he was following.

John Penner opened the computer, looked into the camera that read his retina, identified him, and gave him access. His shaking subsided as he entered information onto the form.

The subject complies with all requirements. His attitude toward authority is within the normal range. Release recommended.

He read the form over again. It felt right. It felt like redemption. He pressed his right forefinger to the little scanner at the bottom corner of the keyboard and his signature appeared in the form's authorized box.

~

Rosie woke with a steady pain in her head. Menopause was a long time ago, she thought, as she walked softer than usual around the house, getting dressed, getting breakfast. Those headaches throbbed. This pain was unwavering, burning inside her skull. Maybe she should go back to sleep. Try again in a few hours. But the sky in the east was brightening. In less than an hour it would be daylight. Rosie waited with a cup of tea and a biscuit that ran over with strawberry jam, pampering against the pain.

It was going to be cold out there. She looked out the window at the pines still black against the birth of morning. Cold, and the snow was getting deep. Maybe she should have picked medicine last summer while it was nice, brought it into the house and stored it in a jar, handy. Maybe start a medicine chest of her own, pick a little of each that she knew for certain, put them away and keep them. Put labels on the jars, this one for headaches, this one for sore throats. Then she would have to keep her house clean. Clean of people who had angry thoughts, and people who used alcohol or drugs. She would have to keep herself clean. She couldn't indulge in fantasy or foreboding. She couldn't rant against the stupidity that entered her house through the television news. Medicine needed to be kept in a clean place. If it wasn't, if it became contaminated, it picked up the anger, frustration, stupidity and could put that into the person who took it.

No, this was the better way. Rosie walked through the snow, Duchess at her heels. The fungus she was looking for grew down by the lake, in the willows. It was easier to find now that the leaves were gone, easier to see. She didn't find the one she remembered from last summer. She found another one, a smaller one, enough for what she needed. As she thanked it before picking it, she thought, this is the right way to keep medicine. This is where it belongs. In the big medicine chest, and the labels were in her memory. She remembered Ben's mother, old Eleanor, telling her of a time before. *"Everywhere we looked, there was our food, there was our medicine."* Everything was where it was supposed to be. Everything was as it should be. Some days are hard. Those days you just have to get through. Some days are better. Some days are really good, and Ben would be coming home soon.

~

That falling dream again, falling through darkness as thick as black water, smothered scream, heart racing, pounding louder than the scream that didn't make it past her teeth. An afternoon nap should not end this way. It was supposed to be an indulgence, a refresher, a break from the stress of work. She checked the time on the clock radio, twelve minutes, that's all; she had only been down for twelve minutes, not enough, not nearly enough. She thought about putting her head back down on the too small cushion but it wasn't on the couch anymore. It was on the floor. She thought about picking it up, knew it was useless, knew she would just lie there, too afraid to fall asleep again.

Monica hated the smell of this; gasoline fumes burned her eyes, there was nothing about this that smelled right. The tiny hollow glass wand connected to a rubber hose hissed as she stirred oxygen blended with hydrogen into the goo, and slime of Styrofoam dissolved into gasoline, putting the bubbles back in. This was the dangerous part. Flow anything past anything and there was a risk that static electricity would build up. Enough static and it would want to go somewhere, jump from one surface to another, spark, a single tiny flash to ignite the fumes and oxygen and Monica would not have to worry about getting the mixture fully fluffed. She would never worry about anything ever again.

She hated all of this, this windowless concrete cave, that bare electric bulb, this rough wooden workbench. She hated the steel door and its complicated latch and lock. She hated the tank where electrical current ran through water, breaking down the bonds between hydrogen and oxygen. *Hydrogen is lighter than oxygen, it rises up here and comes out the red hose. Oxygen is heavier. It comes out here, this blue hose.* She hated the sound of Ed Trembley's voice in her head, but listened to him again. *"It's simple. Just common everyday stuff, water and electricity. They can't prohibit those, or gasoline, or Styrofoam."* But mostly she hated the black steel barrel in the corner there, with the bolt-down lid and the bright yellow trefoil symbol painted on its side.

Maybe she was hating this because out there, on the other side of the steel door, was where Ed Trembley had shackled the American soldiers, where he fed the contents of the barrel to Rick Fisher, where Wally the other soldier died, and Ed left the body chained to the water pipe until it began to smell.

A feeling crept into the bomb shelter, mixed with the fumes of gasoline, mixed with the escaped hydrogen and oxygen. It wrapped itself around Monica and her hate armour, worked itself through the hate shield and touched her. Loneliness drained the hatred, drained the strength that kept her standing. Her knees weakened and she would have sat down, there on the cement floor. All that kept her standing was the fact that if she sat down without grounding out the glass wand, a spark would end all feeling.

Monica sat on the couch, the little cushion still on the floor. She held the bottle of cranberry juice in both hands, because neither hand by itself was strong enough on its own. She held herself up with the little strength she had left. She wanted one thing in that moment, she wanted another human being to touch her, touch her anywhere. What good were legs, if you had nowhere to walk to and hands never stroked them. What good was a flat belly if no one ever kissed it, or a throat, or arms, or even hands. When was the last time someone touched her hand? Just touched it, a finger. When was the last time someone shook her hand, just in greeting, just in politeness even? She remembered the last time she made love. That was easy. That was here on this couch. Was that the last time a human had touched her? Was long dead, forgotten Ed the last human to touch her?

Her body dragged her mind back from the past. She experienced the couch against her back and beneath, experienced the fabric of her clothing, the tightness of an elastic waistband, the bite of her bra strap. She felt the ache in her flesh to be touched, not even caressed, just touched, anywhere.

A man's callused hand, cupped, thumb against forefinger, held her. He didn't drop her. She jumped. Monica found the beginning of the falling dream. She sat motionless on the couch, absolutely still and pushed with her mind against the darkness, sought in the black for more of the image, looked for a face beyond the hand. Nothing. Her mind found only emptiness. She came back to the couch. Breathed again, broke the meditation, became aware of her body, now without the burning desire to be touched, now that she was aware that it was her who jumped from human touch, her choice to leap into the void.

Her sadness rose in her throat and began to choke her, a burn ignited beneath her eyes, and the moisture started to flow high in her nostrils. The door slammed behind her as she continued to button her parka, marched down the unshoveled walk toward the street. She would not cry, would not be weak. Cold air filled her, purified her. She drew it in deep, gasped it, pushed it out and drew in more. It opened her throat and eased the sting, promised to freeze any tears that dared to appear. Monica found gloves in her pocket and pulled them on, continued to breathe deeply and walk. Walk an empty street. She stepped off the snow-covered sidewalk, to march down the hard pack of rare traffic.

She wasn't going anywhere. She was just going.

~

Freedom Friday marchers, silent, voiceless, only the crunch of boots on snow, walked four abreast down Idylwyld Drive. Jason's marched in unison with his wife on his left. The woman on his right was more often out of step than she was in. It didn't matter. She was a body, another body in the march. That's what it was about for Jason, the number of bodies that showed up every Friday at four. His personal count was ninety-seven consecutive Fridays, even last Christmas that just happened to fall on the chosen fifth day. For Jason every Friday was a Good Friday. His wife Elise, her arms swinging beside him had a personal count of over a hundred.

The marchers did not speak. This was not a chanting, screaming demonstration. He liked it this way. It was more dignified, solemn. Words are useless when they are shouted, or screamed, or mindlessly chanted, sound for the sake of sound. He liked this form of protest, this serious, almost religious form, a moving vow of silence, in unison. He took a quick half-step so that he was marching with the woman. She was in step with the man beyond her, an older man, almost old, with a slight but noticeable limp. The marchers tried to step in unison, but were often unable. With time and repetition, the veterans learned how to accommodate the novice, to shift step, and fall in. Mostly it worked.

Homeland Security watched the marchers, one at every intersection from 33rd all the way down the hill to 22nd, cold, stamping their feet to keep warm, shifting their weapons slung over their shoulders. The men and women and the occasional child, stomped past the black uniforms, looked straight ahead, heads high, determined, serene.

Monica stopped when she saw the soldier. He was not the human she was looking for. Then she saw the marchers coming down the street behind him. Fools, she thought. They could march forever and nothing would change. Change needed action. A couple hundred people every Friday didn't even make the local paper, an exercise in futility at worst, at best just exercise. But, they were human. She walked forward, past the black parka, stood at the curb, watched for a place where she might step into formation, watched the faces of the marchers coming down from her left. A mix of ages, an occasional teenager, but most of them were older, some were even old.

The first ranks were all full. Monica hoped she would not have to fall in at the end. She did not want to be last, a tagalong. She wanted to belong, in the middle somewhere, shoulder to shoulder with someone. If not, then she would carry on alone she decided. Why participate in a fool's parade?

"*Ben*" she almost shouted at the old man in the green canvas coat. He turned at his name. A smile twisted his face. "Monica, come on." He swung a weak right arm out as if to draw her in. Monica skipped along as she tried to get into step with the marchers beside him. "What are you doing here?"

"Later." Ben continued to march, kept protocol.

The woman at his left touched his elbow, indicated with a twist and nod of her head that she would give her spot to Monica, and graciously stepped out of rank behind him.

Four more blocks, just four more, Monica's head swam with questions as she marched along beside Ben. She wanted to lean over and brush shoulders with him, but she was afraid to bump him. He looked as though he was using all his strength just to keep walking, stumbling, as though he was dragging his left leg. The limp was slight but noticeable. A stroke, she concluded. Ben has had a stroke.

The march ended in a jumble of people, smiles, chatter after the silence.

"Jason." He held his hand out first to Monica, then to Ben.

"Monica."

"Ben."

They responded and shook his hand in turn.

"My wife, Elise."

Another round of handshakes. Monica removed her glove for the pleasure of it.

"We're going to Tim Hortons. Why don't you join us? On me." Jason indicated down the street.

"Sure," Ben wanted something hot.

Monica wanted to be wherever Ben was. "Before we go anywhere, you are going to tell me how the hell you got here."

"I walked."

"You walked?" Monica held Ben's arm, walked beside him, pressed against him. "Where from?" She looked into his face. It was different, twisted sort of.

"From the Correctional Centre out at the north end." Ben was having trouble walking with Monica hanging onto him. "I'm not sure what happened. This morning she gave me this coat, walked me to the gate and stood at attention while I walked out. She never said anything. Just pushed some papers into my hand. I haven't even read them yet."

"Who's she?"

"A guard. Just one of the many."

"So how did you come to be marching with us?" Jason was listening, walking behind Ben and Monica, holding Elise's hand.

"You were going the same direction I was." Ben looked over his shoulder. "I just joined in."

The coffee at Tim Hortons was okay. Ben would have preferred Roastery coffee for his first taste of freedom, fresh roasted, fresh ground. But, Timmy's wasn't bad he had to admit. Not bad at all.

The lineup at the counter grew as Freedom Friday Marchers sought to warm themselves with a hot cup. Several who walked past their table stopped to pat Jason on the shoulder, on the back, or just to lay a hand on his head, a ceremony of touching.

"You're well known," Monica noticed.

Elise explained with a proud smile at her husband. "He started the march."

"You don't worry about HS?" Monica looked at Ben. " Leaders are known to disappear."

"They haven't bothered us." Jason's elbows were on the table, his cup held in both hands. "It seems that if the media are watching, HS behaves. Lance from CTV is there every week. Even though it rarely makes it on air, just the camera keeps us safe."

"But then I guess you're not doing much. I mean you stop traffic for a bit. But everyone has learned not to take Idylwyld Friday afternoon."·

"We're doing a lot." Elise defended against Monica's dismissive comment. "Look at how many people are out every week. That in itself is something."

"But, you're not going to chase the Americans out with a few hundred marchers."

"We're not marching to chase the Americans out. Freedom Friday is about an end to all war. It's about imagining peace. That's why we don't yell and chant. We come together and walk together and imagine peace. It's also a prayer, a silent prayer. And it's working. Every week there are a few more people. One or two more that can imagine a world without war."

"Prayer!" Monica was indignant. "Religion is a weapon. Look at what happened historically in Afghanistan. When the Soviets invaded it, the Americans joined with the Muslims in Pakistan to fight godless communism. They printed thousands of Korans, created religious fervour, and it came back to bite the Christians in the ass on September 11th. Look at what's going on now. It's the Christian Right that feeds the government that attacked us."

～

The wind stopped.

Red stopped.

Benji kept walking.

"Hey!"

Benji turned at the word, loud in the new quiet broken only by the crunch of snow around his boots.

"What?"

"I don't know."

Moose tracks, fresh, led away through the stark black tamarack, trees highlighted here and there with phosphorous-coloured hanging moss.

Benji turned, faced Red, shifted the strap on the rifle higher on his shoulder, the borrowed rifle, the rifle Benji desperately wanted to fire to kill the promised moose. Red looked at the sky, a boiling grey black low sky, a sky that should be accompanied by wind.

"I was thinking about maybe circling ahead if we found an open spot for you to wait. Let him get a sniff of me so that he turns back."

Benji looked around, looked for the open spot. It wasn't anywhere near. Here was all thick, stunted muskeg tamarack standing in bough-deep snow. Only the moose tracks and their own tracks broke the whiteness.

"There's no wind." Red explained.

"Hey, that's right." Benji looked around again.

There had been wind all morning, strong wind that rattled the snow loose from the trees, wind that buried the moose tracks. Red, the hunter, needed wind to hide in, to show him how fresh the tracks were, to silence the clomp of Benji's boots. Wind was his friend. He looked at the sky again.

"We better get out of here, over there to that stand of spruce." Red pointed north.

"What about the moose." Benji looked at the tracks that led west.

"Later." Red started running.

They were not quite into the spruce when the first hailstones hit, driven hard by the new stronger wind that wasn't Red's friend anymore. This was an angry wind that tried to find the two men huddled under the heavy spreading boughs of the towering white spruce.

"This ain't supposed to fuckin' happen. It's January." Red's curses didn't slow the hammering ice. He crouched close to the tree's trunk, circled around to the lee side and sat down with his back to the rough bark. Benji followed, sat beside him, fumbled with the rifle and strap that tangled him. Golf-ball-sized hail beat fiercely against the branches above them, blocked out the world in a violent curtain of white beyond the edges of the bouncing boughs, roared its anger and punished the earth as it tore down smaller branches and broke the weaker trees.

"It's not supposed to hail in January," Red repeated.

Benji wasn't sure, depended upon Red, to track the moose, to say if tracks were fresh or old, to know which direction was home, which was safe, which would lead to the end of the hunt. Benji didn't want to hunt anymore. He stared at the wall of driven ice, listened to the rough rattle of it. He looked to Red. Red wasn't afraid. He was angry. Benji let go of the fear that had been tightening around him, accepted what was happening as nature.

~

"Did you do anything to piss Rosie off?" Red stopped, waited for Benji to catch up, a few steps behind in the tracks Red ploughed through the snow. The snow wasn't fluffy anymore. It was hammer-packed by the hail that lay in a solid layer on top and made walking difficult.

"What's that?" Benji caught up, shifted the rifle strap.

"Did you piss Rosie off?"

"No, not that I know of. Why?"

"You don't know?"

"Know what?"

"Your mother-in-law is a witch."

"A witch?" Benji pulled off his hat, wiped sweat with his mitt, shrugged under the rifle strap that slid on his nylon parka and settled in the same spot on his shoulder.

"Maybe she sent that storm against us."

"You're serious?" Benji searched Red's face for a hint of a joke.

"If she was pissed off at you, she could do that."

"No, me and Rosie get along good." Benji was serious too.

"There!" Red pointed over Benji's shoulder.

"Where?" Benji turned around. The moose looked more confused than Benji. It stumble-shuffled toward them.

Red waited. He wanted Benji to experience the kill, but Benji was taking way to long, fumbling with the rifle, tangled in the strap. The moose wasn't going to keep coming. It was going to see them, or smell them, and run. Red pulled the butt of his rifle into his shoulder, sighted centre, glanced over at Benji who had his rifle down looking at the mechanism, trying to find what was wrong, why the rifle hadn't fired when he pulled the trigger. Red looked back down the barrel of his rifle. The moose had its head up, stopped, straight on. The rifle kicked into his shoulder, cracked incredibly loud. The moose shifted back onto its haunches a little, then fell forward, its front legs buckling.

"I guess you didn't piss Rosie off after all." Red found the jugular with a knife, let the animal bleed out for a few minutes before they began to skin it. "Unless it was her who put the safety on when you were trying to shoot." Red smiled, he wasn't in the least serious.

~

Theresa poured dry cereal into a brightly coloured ceramic bowl, measured this bowl against the box, allowed for the next bowl and two more bowls tomorrow. Her daughters, Dorothy and Rose, eight and ten, sat sleepy-eyed at the table, quiet. There was enough cereal for tomorrow, but the milk was not going to make it. She made a note to herself to pick up a carton on the way home from work. She didn't want to. Monday was her day off and she would do a complete shopping then.

She checked the clock on the microwave. "You girls have twelve minutes to eat and get ready."

Day shift on Saturday wasn't fair to the girls. It was their weekend. They should be able to sleep in. During the week she left them to get themselves ready for school, a five-block walk, lunches left on the counter and she would be home by four. But weekends meant they had to go to the sitter's and be out of the apartment by seven-thirty.

Her thoughts turned to the old man as she buckled the wide leather belt that held her pepper spray, handcuffs and baton. It matched the black uniform. She wondered where he was today, remembered how he turned and looked into her eyes before he limped through the gate. Looked right into her soul. She wondered if he liked what he saw there.

She tied her hair back, tucked it down, where it could not be grabbed. Safety first.

"Come on, girls, time to go." Ben Robe was not her problem today. He was out. She had to go back in there.

～

"Aren't you afraid of criminals, Mommy?" little Rose asked, she squirmed under the seat belt that at her present size tended to run across her face.

"No, my girl, there aren't many criminals in jail, mostly it's people with addictions."

"Junkies?" asked Dorothy.

"Where did you hear about junkies?"

"School, of course." Rose answered for her little sister.

"All kinds of addictions, not just junkies. I'm . . . " Theresa hesitated. "I'm more a counsellor than a guard," she lied.

"But are there junkies there?" Dorothy asked with the shoulder strap under her chin.

"Not many." Theresa really didn't know. "Mostly it's people who have troubles in their lives, one kind or another who get in trouble and can't find a way out."

"But is it dangerous?"

"No," Theresa lied again. "Most of them are addicted to tobacco." She told the truth. Enough tobacco for a cigarette sold for more inside than either marijuana or coke.

Theresa kissed the end of her finger and pressed it to Rose's nose before her daughter could get out of the car and run to the sitter's.

"Love you back, Mom." Rose found her pack with the books and crayons for Dorothy, and a snack.

"Hey, you girls want to go visit your grandma next weekend? I have four days off. Why don't you take Friday off from school and we'll go up north?"

"You are not going to work overtime." Dorothy's words remained in Theresa's head as she drove her Land Cruiser, the Land Cruiser that almost belonged to her; two more payments. She liked this truck, all-wheel drive, heavy, reliable, Toyota technology. She liked the way it handled in the corners, its four hybrid engines, one for each wheel, computerized to apply the perfect amount of torque.

She accelerated hard at the change of the light. The truck responded with a smooth, quiet rush of power. She was reminded for a minute of the reason she had purchased it, her excitement about the cross between the rotary gas engine and an electric engine, how one fit inside the other, how she had phoned her brother Dougie to tell him about it, and his excitement.

"So they must've built the armature into the rotary part of the gas engine. That means the stators must act as seals." He figured it out in his head. "It would make one hell of a welder."

"I don't know how it works, I just know it's really easy on gas."

"A rotary engine has unlimited RPM. There's no top end." Dougie's mind was working with this, imagining it from a thousand kilometres away.

"It goes as fast as I want." Theresa didn't need details.

"No, think about it. What you have there are three things all together. First you have a rotary gas engine, an electric generator, and an electric motor all in one unit. It's brilliant."

Theresa liked it that her big brother approved. It was a good truck to take to Moccasin Lake.

~

Red dropped the front quarter of the moose onto the table, slid it off his shoulder, red meat and bone. He straightened once the weight was off, stretched his tired shoulder. "This is the last of it."

Benji looked for space on the table for the set of ribs he held away from his body, not wanting to bloody the front of his parka, his arms tired.

Red made space on the counter and helped Benji to lay it out. "There's some good eating there." He noted the layer of fat that covered the outside of the ribs.

Lorraine put a knife to the flesh, separated gristle and bone.

"Lots of people are going to eat good for a while." Rosie moved the men away from the meat with her hip and shoulder, simply took up the space they occupied until they stepped back. They had no business here. This was her place, her business.

"You men must be tired, that's a lot of meat to pack." Rosie was reminding them that they should go sit down now, relax, drink tea, tell stories. They should be keeping an eye on the children running around, gently teasing, scolding the more mischievous ones. There should be children here. Rosie looked away from the meat, around the room — the only child was Rachel. Three women and two men, enough people to get the work done, but there should be more, more women laughing, more men bragging, more children getting in the way, learning.

"It wasn't as bad as I thought it would be." Benji got Elsie's attention by touching her elbow. "Red made a sleigh out of the hide. We just wrapped all the meat in there, tied it with a rope and pulled — amazing how easy it dragged."

"Trick to that," Red was happy to explain, to teach, "is pull in the right direction. All the hairs lay one way. You have to pull it forward." Red felt good, tired, sore and complete. He brought home meat, he fed his friends. It was said that when Red shot his first moose he was holding his diaper up with one hand. That wasn't quite true. He shot his first moose when he was eleven. Uncle John and Simeon had shot a moose across the bay from the village, a cow moose; they were saying that the calf was still out there. Red and three of his buddies went looking with a .22. Red saw the calf first, put a bullet between its ribs, came home a man, with that same complete, strong feeling he was feeling today.

~

Dean wasn't thinking about his wife, Vicky, he had not thought about her in a long time. His thoughts rolled back to the Canadians who killed his son Ricky. He tried thinking about other things, tried thinking about the farm, the equipment that needed repairs before spring seeding, about the cattle. When she was there, or when he was there on the farm, they talked, said "hello," "good morning," "I love you." Then he went back to the world of thoughts; in this world revenge dominated. The Canadians took his son, a cheap, dirty trick. Dean would not stoop that low. He imagined he would kill a Canadian honourably. Walk up to him, face him like a man, put the gun in his face, look into his eyes.

He did not tell Vicky about the handgun. He was not keeping a secret, he didn't care if she knew or not. They just never talked about things like that. She refused to leave the farm, gave Dean lists to take to town, odd spices and particular flour, specific ingredients for the constant baking, creating, cooking. He ate well when he was home, pastries to try, something new and different every supper. Strange breakfasts beyond eggs Benedict that included fruit and smoked salmon.

Dean stayed in his mind, even when he was all the way over to Minneapolis, in the big mall, wandering from store to store with Vicky's lists. Then he found the handgun, an American-built handgun in the Mall of America, a forty-four calibre, an American calibre, not a foreign nine-millimetre, something heavy, something steel, and solid, a gun that fit a man's hand.

A small box of ammunition, nothing extravagant, little cardboard box, not much bigger than a deck of playing cards really, fit into a shirt pocket easily. Now all he needed was a Canadian.

⌇

For no reason at all Dougie suddenly thought of his mother. He stopped and looked around. Did these people ever stop shopping? The mall was busy, filling the nine-million square feet of the largest mall on earth. He tried to imagine her here. He couldn't. Rosie simply would not stroll among the shoppers, drink coffee from a paper cup, dangle a handbag fashionably, lean over the rail and examine the plastic model of the planned phase III. He stopped trying.

Work on the big water pipeline was going well. His four crews looked after themselves pretty much, giving him time for a leisurely trip over to Minneapolis to spend a little time and more than a little money. There was lots of work in North Dakota, but not a lot else. Dougie was enjoying his time in the Mall. Looking around, eating, drinking, he even went to the amusement park and rode the big roller coaster alone. It would have been better if his wife and daughters were with him. Easter. He imagined, Easter he would bring them down when school was out, if she could get time off work. Maybe they should ask his mother to come with them. Give her a break from the cold of Moccasin Lake. But Rosie still refused to come. He let it go.

～

"I have something to do before we leave." Monica thought of the house, the equipment, the open door to the bomb shelter. "Why don't you wait here until I get back."

"Sure, no problem." Ben relaxed into the kitchen chair.

"I won't be long." She wrapped a scarf.

"No problem."

"It's this house. I have to take care of a house and . . . "

"No need to explain."

But she did need to explain. "It belongs to the resistance. I could take you, you could wait in the car, but even that is against the rules. If anybody saw you there I would be in trouble."

"I understand, No problem." It didn't matter to Ben how long it took to get back to Moccasin Lake. Time was his friend, it was no longer his master. There was another cup of coffee in the machine, the sun was beginning to show through the window lighting up the trees outside, spreading its copper colour across branches, across snow. He was silently saying 'thank-you for another day' while Monica went out the door.

～

"Theresa phoned." Elsie wrapped meat in brown waxed paper.

"So did Dougie." Rosie cut meat as fast as Elsie wrapped it, her knife finding its way easily around bone.

"What did Dougie have to say?"

"Not much, he's in Minnesota on a break, just called to say hello. What's your sister up to?"

"She's actually thinking about taking some time off work, come up for a visit."

"It's been a long time." Rosie paused, thought about it. "At least four years," she remembered, "maybe more." Her memory wasn't sure. "When's she coming?"

"Next weekend. Bringing the girls." Elsie smiled.

Rosie smiled too. "They're getting big."

"When was the last time you saw them?"

"When I went with Lester to the hospital. I stayed with them."

"You mean you babysat for her." Elsie remembered how it was when she visited her sister, left alone with the girls while Theresa worked.

"I spent lots of time with my granddaughters." Rosie's answer was definite, final.

Elsie respected her mother's tone, accepted the bare truth of the statement. "Well, it'll be good to see them again." She acquiesced, then changed the subject. "How's Lester?"

"Not good."

"Going back to see him?"

"Maybe." Rosie thought for a second. "Yeah, maybe I'll go back with Theresa." She wasn't sure. Something was coming, she listened for it, then turned to Elsie, "Maybe you should go and clean up the house. I think Ben might be coming home today."

⁓

"No big deal." Ben examined the truck. "Nobody was hurt?" He looked to Benji.

"No, like I said, we were both at the tree." Benji did not want to be here. He wanted to be anywhere else, but he stood straight. "I am really sorry, Dad." He said the words, words he'd rehearsed over and over. They didn't come out the way he thought they would, the way he practised them. These words were filled with hurt, the practiced words were empty, probably why he tried over and over to make them right. Standing here in front of his father, beside the smashed truck, the son, the son who tried to do good, here the son spoke from the heart and the words came out naked, honest.

"No big deal, we'll get another one." Ben heard more than the words, he heard the meaning.

"And the boat dad, I got the parts for the motor. Red said he'd help put them in."

Ben shrugged. "Lots of time for that." He looked around, spring was a long way off. "How have you made out?"

"What with?"

"Everything else."

Benji thought for a second, spun his thoughts through time back toward Ben's arrest. "Elsie?" he asked thinking of the important things.

"Sure, how're things with Elsie?"

"Good, things are good with Elsie, and Rachel, and Rosie, and Red. Everything has been good, Dad."

"Good." There was nothing more to say. "Let's go eat some of that moose you shot."

"I didn't shoot it. Red shot it."

"Don't matter, let's go eat it." Ben's hunger was for more than meat, he wanted to be inside with his son, with Rosie, with Rachel, with Elsie, with Red, with Lorraine, with Monica, with people, with laughter.

~

One of the reasons, maybe the main reason, that Theresa avoided coming back to Moccasin Lake was because here she often ran into people who recognized her from work, from the other side of the reinforced glass. She was never sure how to make the adjustment from institutional to social. The contact often ended in uncomfortable silence, sometimes bitter silence.

Rosie was happy to have both her daughters in the house, and her three granddaughters. They filled it with sounds, little girls squealing, shrieking. She had forgotten that little girls made that sound at every surprise, at dogs, at babies, at each other. It was a warm sound. She was happy to hear her daughter's visit, the chatter and laughter, to hear Theresa remind her girls to keep the volume down, just a little, so that adults could hear themselves think. When Rachel was not trying to climb onto every lap, especially her grandma's, she was chasing her cousins who were happy to be caught, to pick her up and carry her, feet dangling, to kiss her, give her baby smooches. "She's so heavy, Mom." And plop her down.

It should all be perfect. Ben was home next door. There was fresh meat in the house. Winter was not harsh, the way she remembered it could be. Yet something nagged at her, some old dark dread she could not name. Dougie should be here, then it would be perfect.

She fell silent, looked often into her teacup that she held in both hands, listened to her daughters visit, Theresa's serious voice.

"I didn't know you were living with his son."

"About seven months now."

"What's he like? The truth now, you're talking to your big sister here."

"Like his dad — " She paused, thought about it — modified it. "Almost."

"How's that?"

"Well, he's a thinker, likes to think things out, and he does. He's learning how to live here. Like going hunting, and he's had a net in for most of the winter until Mom told him she was getting tired of eating fish."

"How long have you and Ben been friends?" Theresa drew her mother back into the visit.

"Forever," Rosie came back slowly.

"You never talked about him. I had no idea who he was when they brought him in."

"If you had come home more." Rosie immediately wished she had not said it. "It's okay, my girl, I'm happy you're home." She took the sting out of the words as best she could, touched her daughter's arm, soothed the flesh with her fingers. "Ben and I were friends when we were kids, then he moved back about three years ago."

"Yeah, I got that much. But why didn't you ever talk about him?" Theresa was unstung. "You talked about absolutely everything else over the years."

"Must've missed some things." Rosie did not want to talk about pictures of a pedophiliac priest, not then, not now.

"What's with you Mom?" Elsie wasn't sure how to take an untalkative mother.

"Tired, I guess," Rosie lied.

~

Ben lay on his bed, his own bed, for the first time in almost five months. It felt good, sleep was looking for him, circling the cabin, drawing on his will to stay awake. He went to his routine place, his prayer before leaving the world, the place where he said thank you. But first he remembered the day, the thing he was giving thanks for, from waking up on Monica's couch, to the ride home and the welcome. Poor Benji, he felt so bad about the damage to the truck and the boat. Elsie, was obviously uncomfortable with Ben being home again. It had been her house, her nest; now she wasn't sure. Something needed to be done. She and Benji were living as man and wife in a one-room house with an old man. Maybe a partition to give privacy. He let it go. That was for tomorrow.

He remembered Rosie's laugh, loud, from the belly. That in itself was worth coming home for. But, he heard something else in the sound. The laugh was the same. He let it repeat itself in his mind, let it fill him again. Rosie laughed easily, always, but today it sounded like she was trying, even forcing the laugh.

Ben let himself move forward, remembered Theresa, that was her name. She became more of a human with a name. And she was Rosie's daughter, a relative of sorts. Ben remembered Theresa's face when she first recognized him, a will not to show emotion, or surprise, or to even acknowledge the recognition. "Nice to meet you, sir." She stretched out her hand to him when her mother introduced them. No need for anyone other than them to know they had met before, had a history together. It was best that they start a new relationship, a human relationship away from concrete, cinderblock, and reinforced glass. He remembered the feel of her hand, strong in his, and warm. Here, among relatives, they could be persons, they could be the person their hearts chose to be, not the person dictated by the uniform or the orange coveralls.

He remembered Monica, the long visit on the drive back north. Monica wanted so much to be academic, to discuss ideas. Mostly he listened, let her create paradigms, problems within the paradigm, and propose solutions. He was not convinced. His heart was not in the discussion. He played along, enjoyed the sound of a human voice for the sake of the sound. He remembered the hug she gave him before she left, felt her arms around him again, noted that he was hugged last, after she hugged her son and her daughter-in-law, not quick, polite, proper little hugs. Monica's hugs were long, endearing. She was learning.

Sleep pulled at Ben. He whispered into the dark "Thank you for today, Grandfather." Pulled the blankets a little higher, shifted the pillow so that it cushioned his head, eased the ache there, and let himself drift away.

～

Dougie liked this time of day, wondered if he got it from his mother or his father. His father probably. He remembered him on the farm, in the good days, before Darren, up early, before the sun, at first light, out on the tractor, coming home for breakfast after he put in a couple of hours of work. His father knew something about work, something about sunrises, something about the land and how it breathed again at first light, a long, deep inhalation. Dougie was not on a tractor or even in his truck. He stood in front of the little South Dakota nowhere motel with a coffee brewed moments before in his room. Good coffee, strong, black, sweet, the wonder of a simple French press and an electric kettle.

He watched the eastern sky begin to redden, enjoyed the bitter, nutty, flavour of his coffee. There was no wind. Dougie remembered his father once saying, "Twelve days a year the wind doesn't blow on the prairie, maybe today will be one of them." Dougie concurred. Maybe today would be one of them. Maybe today the dust would not blow black across the earth.

It was still properly winter, there should be snow. Maybe there was. Maybe come spring one of those black mounds would melt, turn to mud instead of slush, maybe they would call it mush. Maybe there would be no spring, can there be spring if there was no real winter? Maybe the earth would stay black, never bloom again.

He thought of home, of his mother up at Moccasin Lake. There was snow up there, lots of it. When spring came, that country would green up. Grouse should be in the poplars about now, eating the forming leaf buds. Dougie remembered hunting this time of year, him and Darren sharing a .22. He'd been thinking a lot about family recently, just homesick, part of the job, part of what he did. The job was going well. His men were still asleep, each with their own motel room. They would eat breakfast together in the restaurant then head out to the pipeline.

He felt someone beside him. He did not have to turn to see that no one was there. It was Darren. He knew. It didn't feel scary, or awful. It felt okay. It felt right to have his brother beside him. "In May," Dougie spoke to the presence. "In May, I will come visit you again, when it's time to plant."

"Where did you get the coffee?"

Dougie turned to meet the voice. It was a slow voice that spaced words, forced each word to follow the last.

"In my room, would you like a cup?" Dougie indicated the door behind him.

"You're a Canadian." The slow voice said.

"Yeah, eh." Dougie smiled at his own joke.

The man turned, walked back the way he came, four doors down the line of motel doors and went into his room.

"His problem." Dougie spoke to his cup. It was nearly empty and getting cold. Didn't matter, there was a carafe in his room. If the American didn't want his coffee because he was Canadian, then he would drink it by himself.

The presence that had been Darren was gone. Dougie felt very alone under a large prairie sky.

~

The light woke Ben. He dressed quietly, let Benji, Elsie, and Rachel sleep. Outside the world was quiet. He could hear his own breathing, drawing in cold air, warming it, releasing it in a soft white mist back again. He looked toward the stars, dim now that the eastern sky was beginning to brighten. "Thank you for today." He spoke toward the specks of overhead light, somewhere up there his ancestors were watching. His boots crunched in the snow, loud in the absolute quiet of early morning as he started out on a walk, a pilgrimage, a blend of exercise, prayer, and meditation.

A mile down the empty, ice-packed road, Ben stopped, looked at the house, the house with the lights that reflected off the snow. Someone else was awake. He forced his mind to remember, clicked through names of neighbours, until he came to Leroy. That was Leroy's house. Ben had not talked to Leroy since the funeral, stood beside him at the gravesite as Elroy's casket was lowered, and covered.

"I was hoping someone would come visit me today." Leroy was moving much slower than when Ben had last seen him.

Leroy's coffee was weaker than what Ben preferred. Ben let the first liquid of the day fill his mouth, hot, watery, smooth with a hint of sweet.

"So, I heard they drilled a hole in your head to let in some light."

Ben did not respond, just smiled, relaxed into the armchair, tasted the coffee again. He remembered how to take teasing.

The old man was doing him a favour, doing something good for Ben, helping him to laugh at his misfortune. It needed to be laughed at.

"I heard they used a number 12 Robinson."

"No, it was only an eight, maybe even a six."

"That's how it goes, people add on. Just wait, pretty soon it's going to be a lag bolt." Leroy's smile held a hint of mischief.

"I'm sure if you have anything to do with it, it will have gone in one side and come out the other."

Leroy laughed, a little chuckle laugh. "Now that would be a story worth telling." He was comfortable now that laughter had chased away the tension. "So why were they pissed off at you about in the first place?"

"Oh, I had a gun I wasn't supposed to have."

"What kind of gun?" Leroy exercised the privilege of bluntness that comes with age.

"M-37 assault rifle."

"What the hell did you want with one of those? Were you going to war, or what?"

"No, I just got scared. I was getting tangled up with the resistance and, well, things were getting scary."

"So, you went looking for trouble and you found it."

"Something like that."

"You know better." Leroy exercised the other privilege of age, the right to scold. "Didn't your dad teach you anything? I used to work with him, out in the pulp camps, long time ago when there was still trees worth cutting. There was a man, would never go looking for it. Us Indians Ben, we got enough trouble every day. Don't have to go find it." It was said, done, Leroy did not have to say anymore.

Ben felt a little smaller, as though the armchair had grown. Like the teasing, this scolding was meant to help him, help him feel humility, help him to be human. He remembered to be appreciative. "Thank you, Uncle." He kept his head down, focused on the darkness inside his cup.

"Okay then, enough of that. How's your boy?"

"Benji? Benji's doing good." Ben looked up.

"You are a lucky man, Ben Robe. I was worried about you for a while, not having any children. Then out of the blue you have a son. What a blessing, someone for you to pass along all those things your dad taught you."

"Yeah, it's good." Ben agreed fully.

"You know, maybe it's just age or something, but I don't think so, it's something more. I've been thinking about all the people that have gone ahead of us. Your dad, my dad, my mom, my sisters." Leroy paused, then said what he wanted to say, said it as simple matter of fact. "Elroy was here this morning."

"Yeah." Ben agreed with him, acknowledged what he said, not patronizing. If Elroy was here, Ben knew it was for a reason.

"I guess I won't be here long." Leroy stated the reason. "I don't know how many times I've been told that when it's time to go, one of your relatives will come and get you."

"Yeah." Ben agreed. "What did Elroy have to say?"

"He never said anything, just walked in, smiled at me, and sat in that chair you're in, sort of waiting for me."

Ben was suddenly acutely aware of the chair, its shape, how it wrapped itself around him. He forced down an impulse to stand up.

Leroy smiled at Ben's discomfort. "You don't have to be afraid of Elroy. He always liked you."

"I liked him too." Ben made peace with his situation.

"You know, I'm half a mind to go for a walk. Just go out and find a big old spruce tree and sit down and wait like they used to do. You know they tell stories about long ago, old people went out to die. They said it was because those old people didn't want to be a burden, as if everything was really bad for us, like we were always starving. I don't think so. I think those old people just wanted to go some place quiet, sit down, relax, let what happen what was going to happen. That's what I think."

"I think you might be right."

"Don't think about it too much my young friend. Not like me, I think this is my last winter; North Wind is going to come get me, take me home. You . . . " Leroy nodded toward Ben . . . "You got lots of time. Your job is to remember all the good things. Like the old people did for us when we were young. When times were tough, your grandma or grandpa would start talking about when they were growing up. How it was. They never told us stories about starvation or freezing. They told us about how good it used to be. That's your job now. Remember how it was, so that the young people have some hope. Remember how the world was, how the trees grew, how there used to be big fish in the lake, how people were decent to each other. Now you got a hole in your head to let in some light so that you can see your way around in there. You'll be all right." Leroy sat back, relaxed. "Yeah, you'll be all right, Ben."

At first Ben thought the old man was just talking the way he talked all his life, loud, in your face, always the one to step forward, take a position and defend it, but the more he listened the more he realized Leroy was talking in a rush. He was speaking as though he might never speak again.

He watched the old man on the couch, flannel pyjamas that might have fit better even a few months ago, now hung on his thin frame. He seemed to be shrinking, fading as he spoke. Ben tried to focus, wondered whether what he was seeing was real or a product of his damaged brain.

"You got money, Ben." It wasn't a question. It was a statement.

"Some."

"A little more than some I think."

"I've got enough."

"That's going to be the hard part. Like I told you, you're going to be all right. But that money you got. That's going to be your challenge. You got to figure out how you're going to do some good with that. Money has always been hard for Indian people."

The old voice dimmed. Ben leaned forward to hear. He missed a few sentences, something about residential school money.

"You, figure it out. I still believe it can be done."

"I thought about giving it to the resistance."

"*Resistance!*" The old man came back to life. If he had a table he would have pounded it. "Resistance. You ever go moose hunting with a stick? You're just trying to throw it away, give it to someone else to worry about. No. It's yours. You figure out how to use it. Resistance is just going to cause a whole bunch more misery. Who said 'an eye for an eye makes the whole world blind'?"

"Gandhi."

"Yeah, him. We need another one like him. Think you're man enough?" Leroy raised his chin higher, pointed with it toward Ben.

"He walked to the ocean to make salt and kicked the English out of India." Ben thought about the old movie, remembered images of dusty feet, and men beaten with bamboo rods.

"Think about it. You can't ever buy enough guns and bombs. I know you have money, but can you buy even one fighter jet, can you put a satellite into outer space, drop bombs from up there on Washington?"

Ben remained silent, accepted the truth of the old man's words. His head began to throb, little bubbles of pain, a pulsating ache. He consciously relaxed, let his shoulders sag, and breathed, slow, deliberate deep inhalations, and controlled release.

"Did it change you?"

"Did what change me?"

"That screw in your head."

"No." Ben answered quickly. He thought about it. It hadn't changed him, he was the same Ben, the same convictions. Then he became acutely aware of the numbness that ran down his left side. "Yeah, a bit." He changed his answer. He was a changed man. He was slowed down physically. Mentally he was as sharp as ever. He thought about that too. His mind was sharp but it wasn't as ever. The fog was gone. That haze that accumulated with age had dissipated. The mist in his thinking that he became so accustomed to, or perhaps because he had no reference to anything other, that he perceived it as normal wasn't there anymore. His thinking was crystallized.

"Yeah, Uncle. It has changed me."

"Tell me about it."

Ben was about to tell Leroy about the numbness and the mental acuity, but when he opened his mouth, his answer surprised him. "I used to be afraid."

"Of what?" the old man still had strength in his voice. A bit of power.

"I wasn't afraid of death, well not much, it wasn't the dying part that scared me. When I first found out I was in trouble with HS, I was really scared they were going to torture me."

"And they did."

"That's right. And I'm not afraid of it anymore."

"You survived it."

"I survived it." Ben and Leroy were on the same page, nodding toward each other as they spoke, echoing.

Leroy carried it forward. "It was bad."

Ben nodded.

"Hurt like hell."

"Oh, Yeah." Ben remembered.

"But now you're okay with it. Not with the torture. I mean you're okay with the fear of it. You're not going to go and buy another rifle and try to take on the whole American army by yourself again."

"No, you're right, Uncle. I'm way past that."

"Good. But you're still afraid of death."

Ben had no response to Leroy's direct statement. He couldn't deny it. But, he couldn't quite accept it either. Fear of death — wasn't everyone afraid of death?

"You stay with me today." Leroy broke the growing silence.

"You want me to?"

"Yeah," the old man nodded. "Stay with me. I don't want to be alone, but I don't want a whole bunch of people around. My granddaughter is going to come in a few hours and make lunch. We'll eat together. Then she'll go back to her family. It'll be all right."

"I'll stay."

"All day?"

"If that's what you want."

"It's what I want. You know what, I think it's time for a nap. Think I'm gonna lay down on this couch for awhile, close my eyes for a little bit. You're gonna stay?"

"I'm gonna stay."

The old man stretched out his long, thin body, pulled down a Pendleton blanket from the back of the couch and wrapped himself in it. He struggled to get it right, let out a little groan as he tried to get it around broad shoulders. Ben noted the feebleness, reached over from where he sat and tucked it around the callused, bony feet; wondered how many miles they had walked. Leroy twisted around, straightened the pillow so that it fit better under his head, closed his eyes, and sagged into a comfortable sleep.

～

The sharp, rugged Argentinean Andes Mountains faced a dull blue sky. Clear, cold wind, the always wind of this place tugged at the flimsy satellite dish in Stan Jolly's hand. He set it down, found a flat rock nearby and leaned it against the base. He needed it to point north, toward the equator, toward satellite WV3114.

There was enough power in the platform, the battery checked at 68, but with the sun out, it would be a good time to use the solar panel. Using more rocks to stabilize it, Stan aimed the concave black dish generally toward the west. Precision was not necessary. This solar dish was designed based on the sunflower. It knew to follow the sun in its arc across the sky, always in direct sunlight, a technical solution borrowed from the botany of a plant that learned millennia ago to harness solar power.

Ready, he keyed the computer, waited for connection, entered the password that was written only in his memory.

His program. It was his program now, he was the only person remaining who knew of it, the rejected program, perfectly adequate, simple, rejected by HS for a more complicated security program, because for some decision maker, complex equated with better. The program Stan used, this rejected program, once existed on a single disc, a disc left on his desk when he still worked as the Canadian Liaison on Security and Trade. He could not say for certain that the program was given to him, or that it was deliberately left for him to pick up and use, all he could honestly say was that he suspected it was left by the program writer out of frustration at having his program rejected, feeling rejected. The program now only existed in the memory of Stan's platform, labelled Space Invaders and filed fourth on a list of a half-dozen games.

Stan always worried at this point, when he connected to the satellite, entered his password. Would the system suspect him,randomly select him for detailed protocol assessment, search for his uplink position? It didn't. Stan, as ever, was allowed in. He scanned through files of communications, searched for friend's names, scrolled down a list of the last 24 hours, found Monica Bird, stopped and read:

"The bunker contains seven-hundred-and-fifty kilograms of U238 unprocessed Yellowcake uranium. Operative Monica Bird attends regular to bunker."

Stan clicked up the communication trail to the next message.

"Sensors indicate slight elevation in radiation at and near house at civil address 3112 Avenue H North, Saskatoon, Saskatchewan, Second Division."

He clicked up one more, the latest communication, minutes old, held his breath as he read:

"Thunder Bolt Satellite directed to position. Wait for confirmation operative is in bunker before dropping. Ground surveillance directed to positive identification of operative. Gentlemen, we want to be absolutely certain she is in there before we drop."

Why? The question crawled into Stan's mind. Why a Bolt from Heaven? Why not just shoot her? There were no logical rational answers. This wasn't calculated. Someone decided this way rather than another way. The decision was probably based on nothing more than someone wanted to play with the big toys of war.

The important question was, who turned? Someone turned. Stan frantically searched through the trail of communications, senders, receivers, names — he needed the name, the name of the informer, the enemy within. He raced against his own addition to the program. It was going to automatically disconnect him at one-minute fifty-nine point nine seconds, just before the two-minute mark when the system would perform another security check. He thought of downloading the entire file and reading it later, but a large download would trigger the security program. Too risky. Or was it too risky to save a friend? Seconds clicked, Stan experienced an internal battle between rationality and emotion, expose the informer or risk exposing himself. He heard words coming from his mouth, a prayer, "please, please, please." His fingers clicked through the list, images appeared on the screen and disappeared in a blur as he searched for a name.

Then, there it was, not in the sender's box; halfway through a message he caught the words, not capitalized, "b.chance". Betsy Chance. Betsy Chance. The name echoed in Stan's mind. Betsy betrayed Monica.

The message froze to the screen, he was disconnected from the satellite. He read the message again this time in its entirety. It was a longer message with several points from someone using the name RaynCloud, to HS Second Division, a generic address. He reread the important phrase "confirmed data with original b.chance. confirmed safe passage. All payments made."

Stan fought the wind against the thin dish again, rearranged rocks to support it, used the built-in spectrum analyzer to find the new satellite, the civilian satellite, connected and began sending emails. Now he was the Canadian on vacation, the kayaker, the mountain climber. He stopped and blew on his fingers to warm them, unaware whether it was the keyboard that was cold or the message he was sending.

~

Abraham Isaac Friesen knew he spent too much time on the computer, knew he spent too much time indoors. He should be outside, even in winter, out on the land, on the bare prairie, watching the sky for weather. But he was a landless man now, city bound, hiding. They gave his land, his farm, to a retired Homeland Security colonel. What would a warmonger know of land? Something to drop bombs on, tear up with tracks and tires, dig trenches in. Land is holy. Soil is life giving. Sift the dirt through your fingers at the beginning of a day, feel the moisture, clumpy; or feel the dry, dusty; hold it to your nose, inhale the smell, fill your body with the richness.

Abe sensed a familiar wind at the same time the screen informed him that another message had been sent to the Spam folder. He clicked the icon. The message was from 'JACK', all capital letters, not the usual 'jack sprat' or even 'Jackie Blue'. Abe wondered at the boldness. He read through the garble until he found the word 'THAT', also capitalized. He read the message only once before he sprinted his large frame to the door, remembered parka and boots. He was going out. Out into the new dangerous world where he might be found. He was going to find Monica.

Maybe they were watching, probably not. There were seven-billion people on the planet, Abe reasoned — even with technology, they would need seven-billion people at seven-billion monitors to watch all of the people all of the time. He wasn't afraid of the sky.

~

Dougie knocked on the door to Wesley's room, a loud pounding knock. Wesley was one of those who was difficult to wake in the morning, one of those that stumbled around groggy for the first hour of the day, grouchy, uncommunicative. Dougie had seen him close his eyes between mouthfuls of breakfast, pulled back to the sleep world, the dream world. Every morning, every transition, was difficult for Wesley. It took time for him to shift from that world to this.

But once his eyes were open, once he was into the day, into the job, Wesley stayed with it, completely into the work. Wesley focused on whatever was in front of his eyes, whether it was the work of welding pipes together or the inside of his eyelids and stayed with it. He ignored the world around him as he worked, didn't feel the cold or care about the wind. Dougie figured you could drop a bomb beside Wesley while he worked and as long as it did not knock him off his stool, he would keep working. He was a good employee.

Dougie pounded on the door again, louder, harder, rattled the door in its frame. He stopped, listened, heard a groan, and someone moving. He pounded again. Once Wesley was moving, you had to keep him moving or the bed would call him back.

"Canadian."

Dougie turned at the voice behind him.

Dean held the big handgun in both hands, held it up and out, arms straight — pointed the barrel in Dougie's face.

"My son's name was Ricky, Richard James Fisher, he was only twenty-years-old."

He wants to make a speech, Dougie realized. He wanted to listen, pay attention, hear the man out, but the black spot, the hole surrounded by blue steel stuck in front of his face grew and pulled Dougie into it.

'Is this what Darren saw?' Dougie wondered. 'This black, is this the last thing he saw? Did he look into it, go into it?'

Dean Fisher was talking, speechifying, slow deliberate words, words said over and over again in his mind, rehearsed, now vocalized, freed, spoken. Dougie did not hear the words, he was in the cab of his father's truck with his older brother. He was holding the gun with the big black hole.

"Don't fool around with that. It might be loaded."

"Don't be stupid, Dad would never leave a gun loaded."

"Don't fool around with that. It might be loaded."

"Don't be stupid, Dad would never leave a gun loaded."

"Don't fool around with that."

"Don't fool around with that."

⌐∽

Rosie came out of the bedroom, down the hall to the kitchen where her daughters were visiting. She hadn't slept well; tossed often, or simply lay there with her eyes open. The girls were giggling as she entered, sharing a corner of the table, heads together over cups of coffee. Rosie didn't join in. That was the first indication to Theresa and Elsie that something was wrong. They knew it was serious when Rosie said almost angrily, "Someone should go out there and chase away that woodpecker."

The girls looked at each other before both turned to look toward the window. The bird's rat-a-tat barely penetrated the winterized house, audible only now while they held their breath. It was halfway up a partially dead black spruce a few metres beyond the double glass panes, ignoring them, its back turned, intent on the rough flaked bark and whatever might be beneath.

"How long has it been hanging around?" a newly serious Theresa asked.

"Yesterday morning." Rosie turned on the stove to heat water for tea, stood there at a different angle and watched the black-and-white bird walk up the trunk a couple steps before it hammered a new hole.

No one was going out to chase it away. That would not do any good. Everyone knew that. The woodpecker was simply a messenger, or perhaps a mourner, come to tell them of the impending loss, or to be with them at the time of their suffering.

Eight-year-old Dorothy figured it out, saw her mother, her grandmother, and her aunt silently, fearfully staring out the window, saw the bird, knew from the adult's expressions or lack of expression that this was serious. "Get the hell out of here!" she yelled and banged against the glass. "My Grandma doesn't want you to come around no more."

The bird turned as it dropped from the tree, spread its wings and in a flurry of flapping gained a bit of altitude before it was out of sight.

"Watch your language young lady." Theresa's scolding didn't have any edge to it.

"It's okay, my girl." Rosie felt relief at the little girl's action, something lifted, maybe only for a while, but in this moment it was a good feeling. She readied the teapot, brought down a package of cookies from the cupboard and joined her daughters at the table to wait for the water to boil.

"Here, my girl, cookies for breakfast," she called Dorothy to her lap.

~

Elsie, Theresa, Darren, and their mom were with Dougie, a flat tire, no spare, on a dirt road in the winter. "Here Dougie, you wear my mitts. I have warm pockets," Theresa the Saint's pockets were not any warmer than his.

"Keep your knife at twenty degrees to the stone," his father showed him, pulled the skinning knife across the new Arkansas stone.

Elsie squealing, her arms so tight around his neck that he had trouble breathing as he ran, his little sister clamped to his back, spindly arms and spindly legs and shrieking in his ear.

"My son. You took my son. That was all I had. You took all that I had." Dean Fisher's voice came from behind the black hole, brought Dougie back to the motel on the edge of a little prairie town, to the door, to the morning. "He had a mother, a good mother . . . "

Dougie looked into the black hole and left again. He was with his mother. Rosie hugging him. "You have to be strong now, my boy," whispering into his ear, "don't let this ruin things for you. Darren was going to have a good life. You have to live it for him now. Make sure that it's good."

This was going to be the end of that good life. The crying American was going to pull the trigger any second and Dougie was going to be with Darren. Would anyone come and put flowers on his grave, the way he put flowers on Darren's grave every May 11th. One day each year he let himself feel sorrow, made a pilgrimage to that little cemetery, cleaned up around the mound that marked where they put his brother's body, sat for a while and told him about the things that happened in the last year. "I have another daughter. Mom is still in Moccasin Lake. Theresa has a new job."

The door to the motel room opened. "I'm up," Wesley sighed. He didn't open his eyes completely until Dean shifted the handgun away from Dougie and pointed it directly at him. "What the . . . " was all he had time to say before Dougie hit Dean. His fist arced in a roundhouse swing that ended in a solid collision just below Dean's left ear, crumpled him into silence on the cement walkway. Dougie kicked the handgun away; felt a moment of hate as his boot connected with it.

～

Ben waited. He sat in the black leather armchair with his thoughts. What brought him to the old man's house this morning? It really didn't matter which forces were at play; ancestors talking, tugging, he was where he should be.

The room slowly lit as the sun cleared the horizon, found the east windows. Ben pulled himself from the armchair, turned off the light. While he was up, he made another pot of coffee, a little stronger than the last, stood around the kitchen for a while, reading the things magnetized to the fridge door, waiting for the brewer to finish its work. When it was done, he took his cup back into the living room, quietly finding the armchair again, and waited.

Midmorning Leroy stirred, pulled himself determinedly into a sitting position, forced old muscles to do his bidding. "How's it over here?" he asked.

"Quiet."

"Same over there, lots of people just waiting around." He scratched an itch at the side of his neck. "There's something on that cabinet," he pointed with his chin toward an oak and glass cupboard.

Ben stood and walked over, looking.

"It's a card, should have flowers on it."

Ben moved things around, a birthday card, held it up.

"That's not it. It's just a card, doesn't open up."

He moved a few more things; a power bill, a little book of Saskatchewan birds, found a yellowed card printed on one side, began to read. "I haven't seen this in quite a while."

"That's it. Bring it over."

Ben handed Leroy the card.

"Yeah, this is it," Leroy read the first few lines. "This is the truth. Want truth, Ben? Right here," he shook the card in Ben's direction. "I met the person who brought this." He handed it to Ben.

Ben leaned back, turned the paper toward the light and read it through. Leroy waited for him to finish, to lower it. "Me too," the old man sagged on the couch.

"You too, what?"

"I was expecting something in Cree, maybe a song, a death song or something. Then I meet this person. Can't tell if it's a man or woman over there, and they tell me that there is the truth, brought it for everybody, that's why it's in English."

Ben looked at the card again, read it in new light. "Most people have forgotten this."

"Then it's up to you to remember." Leroy noted Ben's expression. "What? Don't think you can?"

"Well, my memory isn't what it used to be."

"That's because you don't exercise it. When was the last time you memorized something?"

Ben couldn't remember, shook his head.

"Memory is just like anything else. Gotta exercise it or it gets lazy. Used to be in school they made us memorize all kinds of stuff; the times table, days in history, when Columbus came here, poems. When was the last time you recited a poem to a woman, Ben?" Leroy smiled.

"It's been a very long time, if ever. I don't remember."

They both laughed.

"What's the use of having a life if you don't remember it? You memorize that." He indicated the card in Ben's hand. "It'll be good exercise for you." Leroy slouched back down, wrestled a moment with the pillow again and again closed his eyes.

Ben stayed in the leather armchair and waited, but now he had something to keep his mind busy. He read the card over and over, stopped and stared out the window, his lips involuntarily moving over words forced through a resisting neuron net.

At eleven-thirty, Leroy's granddaughter came over and made lunch, heated a can of soup and put together a plate of sandwiches. "For when he wakes up," she was putting her coat back on. "He sleeps lots now, it's good he has some company. Tell him I'll be back to make him supper," and she was out the door, back to her own young life and the things that were important to her.

Leroy woke once more that day, early afternoon he stirred, this time he didn't try to sit up, looked around the room, gave Ben a weak smile. "You'll be all right," he assured, "you'll do good. Know how I know?" There was a hint of mischief in his voice.

Ben leaned forward for the answer.

"There's a little guy standing beside you," Leroy almost whispered.

Ben looked.

"The other side. Can't see him, can you?" Leroy let his eyelids fall.

"No."

"I didn't think so."

"Who is he?"

"I don't know, maybe he's your grandson." Leroy took a breath. "Keeps looking up at you," he let the breath go, "like he's trying to decide. Do I want you for my grandpa or what?" He sagged deeper into the couch, shuddered and drew in a breath that rasped deep in his chest. Ben leaned forward, listened. Leroy's breathing was irregular, noisy. Ben got up, limped over and sat on the floor beside the couch. But, Leroy had no more words for him. He stopped breathing. Ben thought maybe this was the end when Leroy drew in another rasping gasp, let it out, opened his eyes staring into nothingness, his mouth moving around voiceless words. The end was without any twitch or movement. The old man drew one last shallow breath and when he let it out, he left with it.

⌒

Lester made it to the funeral. He looked sickly but he was standing. Rosie stood with her daughters and granddaughters. Ben was an honorary pallbearer. He was expected to be up close to the grave, just back of the bishop who was taking bishop's privilege to make a long speech before they lowered the ornate casket into the ground. Ben looked over at Rosie, remembered what she said last night at the wake. "I always wanted to have a child with you, Ben. But, we're going to have something better, we're going to have a grandchild together." He thought about Benji's mother. How would Monica take being a grandmother. He hoped she would take it well.

The bishop finished speaking, stepped back from the grave and aside to let Ben come forward.

Ben stood at the edge of the sandy hole. He spoke softly. Even people close by had trouble hearing him as he recited the faded words on the yellow card in his shirt pocket. He still did not completely trust his memory. "Go placidly amid the noise and haste, and remember what peace there may be in silence. As far as possible without surrender be on good terms with all persons. Speak your truth quietly and clearly; and listen to others, even the dull and the ignorant; they too have their story." Ben was aware of his voice and how it carried over the snow-covered ground and was swallowed up by the trees. He put more volume to it, "Avoid loud and aggressive persons, they are vexatious to the spirit . . . " Ben's gaze fell from the large gathering of people down to the casket. He recited as much to Leroy as to them. "Take kindly the counsel of the years, gracefully surrendering the things of youth. Nurture strength of spirit to shield you in sudden misfortune. But do not distress yourself with imaginings. Many fears are born of fatigue and loneliness"

~

Betsy stood straight, faced her end, she would not go whimpering and crying. There was no out from here. Everything catches up to you in time, and Betsy's time had come. She knew it was coming, had known it for years, had made friends with it over and over again. "I only followed council's instructions," she answered again.

"You set up the thing with Ed Trembley." Monica held the weight of the pistol in the large fatigue jacket pocket.

"On council's instructions."

Abe Friesen felt the rough bark of the "walking" stick in his right hand, remembered the night he crept back to his farm to cut it down from one of the maples, a memento from the land, the land that was to have kept him in his old age. "You weren't at the gathering of thinkers," he accused.

Betsy did not answer, stood silent.

Abe waited, lifted the walking stick from the floor, held it in both hands.

"You knew the risks." Only her eyes and her mouth moved as she spoke, her eyes on the heavy length of branch in Abe's hand.

"I lost my farm. I went to prison."

"And I got you out."

Abe felt the urge to swing the maple branch, to smash, to hurt.

"How did you do that, Betsy?" Monica stepped slightly closer, between Abe and the woman who had once been her friend. "How was it that you could negotiate with the bastards? Tell me that."

"I think you figured it out."

Monica had her answer. "Yeah, we figured it out, figured out why you weren't in the house in Lac La Biche."

The accusation hit like a punch to Betsy's stomach. She involuntarily stepped back one full step.

Monica knew the force of her words from the sudden glare in Betsy's eyes. "We made you a hero because of that. The survivor of Lac La Biche is just a bitch."

Betsy had no answer, no explanation, no rationalization. She had walked away from the house with the men who laughed and joked and teased, young men who wanted to be revolutionary heroes. She had walked away, and in all the next years she kept walking back. The story about the falling star in the daylight and the vaporized hole was just a story. She sat in the restaurant after the agent left. Sat and drank coffee and waited until the blast four blocks away rattled the windows. Then she simply drove off and never looked back, never even ordered the chicken she volunteered to go get.

Now Betsy was walking into 3112 Avenue H North. Monica and Abe did not have to watch, did not have to make sure she didn't try to run. Betsy had nowhere to go. It wasn't that Abe and Monica had forced her to come here. She had volunteered. Betsy put the idea forward, offered an ultimate solution. It wasn't an act of honour so much as a declaration of *fuck it all. Fuck everything. Lets bring this fuckin' show to an end. Get it done. I'll show you bastards how it's done.*

Monica's coat fit Betsy a little too tight and the scarf smelled of her perfume. The two men who sat in the running car across the street were obvious, bold, sure. Betsy felt an urge to wave, to tell them, "Okay, call on your brimstone, bring on your heaven, bring on your hell." She didn't. She turned in at the gate, walked calmly to the house and used Monica's key to open the door. She took off the coat, dropped it on the floor, dropped the scarf and sat down on the pile to wait. She heard the sound of the car across the street drive away.

"Hey Freddy, hey Joe, how are you guys? I'll be with you in a minute." She may have spoken to the empty room at 3112

Avenue H North, Saskatoon, but she was back in the house in Lac La Biche and her friends, her true friends, were with her again.

~

"A dog sled?" Red wasn't at all expecting this phone call. And he certainly wasn't expecting that the person asking him to build a dog sled would be Ben Robe. "I could make you one, or I could give you the one in my shed."

"What's in your shed?"

"Oh, about a ten-foot toboggan, the canvas might be a bit rotten, but I've tried to keep it dry."

An hour later, Ben and Benji helped Red slide a solid oak toboggan down from the rafters of his shed, over piles of "stuff" and out into the snow. "It was my Dad's," Red explained. He grabbed the canvas carryall in both hands and tugged, hard. The canvas did not tear. "Well it didn't rot. It's only been up there for about thirty years."

"You've done a good job in taking care of it." Ben stood at the back of the toboggan, gloved hands on the handles. It felt right, felt like something normal, real, something with history, from a time when things were better.

"See the rubber there," Red pointed. "On the handles. My dad put that there. He cut an old inner tube into strips. Used to tie everything with that stuff."

Ben gripped the handle harder, it had a good feel to it.

"My Dad had lots of tricks like that. If you tie something with rubber, it isn't coming undone, and ice doesn't stick to it."

"I imagine it would be warm as well." Ben's hands had not left the handle.

"I suppose you are going to want harness too." Red turned back toward the shed. A moment later and he threw a bundle of harness and gang lines into the toboggan carryall.

Benji knelt to check them out, to tug at nylon harness, to open a brass snap, feel the pressure of its spring, note that it wasn't corroded or stiff. "What made you keep all this stuff?" He looked up toward Red.

"I didn't keep it." Red's smile widened ever so slightly. "I just never bothered to throw it away."

～

A child once played on this floor, crawled around on the hardwood, hands and knees slipping on the shine; not hers, not Betsy's; Betsy never had any children. She ran her hand across the wood grain, stroking, perhaps even caressing — something from this world, solid, tactile before the moment of vapourization, before she crossed over to another world.

She imagined someone somewhere, perhaps he even looked like Ernie, perhaps it was Ernie himself at the controls, guiding a satellite, adjusting, lining up, perhaps there were even cross-hairs, and Google Earth type zoom, and he would put the satellite directly above her and drop a tungsten rod that would heat up in the atmosphere until it was pure vapour, then it would hit the house, and Betsy and the house and the hardwood floor would all be vapour, would all be ghosts.

Didn't Ernie say that they were not using tungsten anymore, too expensive, they were using spent uranium? Just Betsy's luck eh, hit with an old fuel rod from a nuclear reactor because someone didn't want to pay the storage costs. That would be more like it — more fitting with the way the rest of Betsy's life had gone, or hadn't gone.

Fuckin' Ernie. What an asshole. At first she'd thought — and that was decades ago now — at first she'd thought he was maybe like a Hell's Angels guy or something; getting her to move stuff, a little something from here to there; something exciting, something with a bit of thrill to it. What's a few guns from Ottawa to Edmonton? Then Ernie wanted her to become friends with people who were going to protest at the G-20 meetings, just find out what they were up to, go along, become one of them. *"Hell, Betsy, even go to the protest, have a little fun. If you happen to get arrested I'll cover your ass."* Fuckin' Ernie.

There' was no quitting when Ernie had his hands on you. You didn't bow out on Ernie, Fuck no. There was only one out — only one exit — and this was it; the hard way out, the permanent fuckin' door slam.

At least it would be quick. Betsy put her palms to the floor, pressed down, held her breath. What was taking so fuckin' long? Let's get this done.

And Monica; what a silly bitch Monica was anyway, with her ideals, her fuckin' high ideals, her perfect world, perfect ecological order, perfect utopian crap. Crap; that's all it was, fuckin' crap. The world would never be the way Monica wanted it to be; there were too many Ernies, too many people who needed you to do what they said. And if you didn't, if you doubted, you never did anything ever again, and if your family was lucky they found your body on the side of the highway and your family had something to bury, if you were lucky.

What a fuckin' life. The hardwood wasn't slippery shiny anymore; it was sticky, sweaty and sticky and she wiped her hands on her pants, and the sweat showed on the floor, a smear, a dull smear on the gold-grained wood. Was that it? Was that all her life was going to amount to, a fuckin' smear on a beautiful floor where a baby once learned to crawl, and maybe even learned to walk?

She imagined a baby, a boy baby, crawling across the floor toward her, her imagination so vivid in this ultimate moment that she could almost see the child, her child, her child that never was. As soon as she began to feel, to experience an emotion other than anger; as soon as she started to open herself to the imagined child, Monica came unbeckoned and picked up the child from the floor and held it to her breast.

Fuck this.

Betsy hit the back door to 3112 Avenue H North at a dead run, across the backyard, through the place where someone once had a garden, and hurdled the back fence. At the alley she turned right, turned north, and ran as hard as her legs would carry her. At the house, just before the alley met the street, someone had left their car running, backed it out of the garage, left it in the driveway to warm up for a minute. Betsy didn't have a coat or even shoes and now maybe there was a God, maybe there was life after Ernie. The car doors were not locked.

∼

Abe wasn't watching, he had turned away, just a glance down the snow-rutted street. Monica was watching. There was nothing that represented a falling star in the daylight. One second the house across the street was the same house that Monica had spent days and weeks confined to; it was the same house she had just watched her best friend walk bravely into, walk bravely to her end — and in the same second the house disappeared, replaced by a flash. It was very fortunate for Abe that he wasn't watching. The flash lasted through the end of that second and through the next second and part way through the second that followed that, but the brilliant flare in Monica's eyes did not end after the house was replaced by a glass-lined hole.

The flash continued, painfully, as though someone had thrown sand into her eyes, blinking hurt and did not dim the bright blue that Monica continued to see. Even though tears continuously poured from her eyes, they felt paper dry as she blinked and rubbed and desperately tried to relieve the pain. She considered using snow, but without sight was not sure she would select a handful clean enough to rub into the sockets and put out the fire that continued to burn there.

Monica clung to Abe — one hand with a desperate grip of his parka, the other constantly wiping at her face — as they both stumbled down a sidewalk that desperately needed the attention of a snow shovel.

Abe's growing belief that Monica might be faking her injury came from his own experience with welder's flash. Yeah, it hurt, your eyes watered, felt like there was sand in them, but you could still see. It wasn't until he had Monica back in his basement apartment, seated in the leather armchair, and he couldn't undo the zipper on his parka that he realized maybe her eye injury was serious. The nylon zipper, designed for cold weather, was melted together and would not open.

～

"They're getting it. They're trying to figure it out." Ben untangled a dog from harness and gangline as Red looked on. "They mostly got it right." With the dog free, Ben headed back to the sleigh. "What I really need is a leader."

"How about the mom?" Red offered.

"Tried that, she won't stay on the trail, keeps trying to take us through the bush after any rabbit or squirrel or grouse that happens to catch her attention."

"Hunter." Red summed it up in one word.

"Hunter," Ben agreed. "One of these six has to be the natural leader." He indicated the team in front of him. "I just have to find out which one."

"How you going to do that?" Red held the lead dog by the collar, kept the team in somewhat of a line as Ben got back on the sleigh.

"Just have to keep trying — let them go."

Red stepped away from the dogs and they responded to Ben's *"Hike!"* by bursting into a sprint down the trail in a mix of puppy excitement and natural instinct. Ben held firmly to the sleigh handles. The team was a bit faster than he had anticipated and without his normal balance was having difficulty staying on the sled.

Red liked what he saw, liked the line of dogs and sight of his dad's sleigh and Ben determined to make a litter of puppies into a team. He liked the idea of it even more when the snow machine didn't start and he had to pump the primer again and again and pull on the starter cord again and again and again, until the engine sputtered, caught, ran rough for a few seconds before Red set off to follow Ben, thinking two-stroke engines were never designed to run on alcohol.

⁓

"Fuckin' Monica." Betsy turned the car toward the pile of snow that marked the side of the street. *"Bitch!"* she screamed into the still frosted windshield. The heater was doing its best, but the engine wasn't warm enough yet and Betsy had the heat control set to the floor, toward her feet. As soon as she had the car in park, she immediately pulled her icy foot from the brake pedal. At first she just lifted it, like a shorthaired dog standing on the step whining to be let back inside, one paw in the air and then another. "Fuckin' Monica." This time the words were more resigned — and more determined.

She vigourously rubbed a foot rested on her right knee, brushed the snow from the wet cotton sock, switched and rubbed the other foot. Her body vibrated with more than cold, more than the pain of fresh frostbite; she clawed a frozen chunk of snow from the heel of her right foot, fingernails angrily into the stiff cotton. "Who the fuck does she think she is?" Betsy pulled off the wet sock and threw it on the passenger-side floor, cupped her toes with both hands and applied pressure, firm, steady, strong, breathed in, held the breath in her lungs a full long second. Her body slowed, stopped vibrating.

Betsy's anger calmed, settled into a simmer, a glowing red coal that spread its warmth and chill. "Her and her fuckin' ideals. Who does she think she is anyway with her fucked superior morality." She sat sideways on the seat, her back against the door. She banged her head against the glass, hard. "*Fuck Monica!*" she screamed into the empty car. "Fuck her and her Ben." She banged her head again, harder. "*Fuck Ben.*" She calmed, an idea forming, banged her head again, not so hard, "Yeah, fuck Ben."

⁓

Ben read slowly, carefully, enjoying the imaginary landscape of Yoknapatawpha County and the character Joe Christmas:

At last the noise and the alarms, the sound and fury of the hunt, dies away, dies out of his hearing. He was not in the cotton house when the man and the dogs passed, as the sheriff believed. He paused there only long enough to lace up the brogans: the

black shoes, the black shoes smelling of Negro. They looked like
they had been chopped out of iron ore with a dull axe. Looking
down at the harsh, crude, clumsy shapelessness of them, he said
"Hah" through his teeth. It seemed to him that he could see
himself being hunted by white men at last into the black abyss
which had been waiting, trying, for thirty years to drown him
and into which now and at last he had actually entered, bearing
now upon his ankles the definite and ineradicable gauge of its
upward moving.

Benji disrupted the quiet afternoon, scraped a chair back
and put his book on the table, "So, exactly what do you believe
in?"

Ben laid Faulkner on his lap, his finger keeping his place
at page 313. He noted the author of Benji's book: Russell, and
answered accordingly. "I am beginning to believe in nothing."
He nodded toward the red dust jacket with big white letters in
front of Benji, "I suppose he would call me a nihilist."

"Really?" Benji looked closely at his father's face, looked for
an explanation, looked for something that he might not have
seen before. He couldn't find anything, it didn't make sense,
didn't match with his understanding of Ben. "But, you pray."

Ben took greater notice of Benji's book, beyond the author,
he noted the title; *Why I am Not a Christian.*

"I suspect your question is more religious than philo-
sophical. Doesn't matter; it amounts to much the same thing."
Ben put a bookmark in place of his finger, turned behind and
placed the yellowed novel on the little stand against the wall;
it would be a while until he returned to it. "What I meant
when I said I didn't believe in anything was that I am not
a liberal, not a socialist, not a conservative; I really believe,
more now than ever before, if we ignore government, maybe
it will go away."

"We'll just pretend it isn't there, just like that, and the Americans will go home?"

"Almost" Ben answered. "If we don't participate, they have no power. The only real power the Americans have is that we accept them."

Rosie perked up, tuned in to the conversation over at the table. The light coming through Ben's front window was almost white, most of it reflected from snow. Rosie didn't even pretend that the reason she was at Ben's was because of the light as she sewed beads to leather, making a little pair of moccasins for Rachel. She was here because everyone else was here, Ben and Benji at the table reading, Elsie on the computer and Rachel asleep. It had been quiet, peaceful quiet, family quiet, a collection of people together, comfortable and safe with each other, comfortable with silence.

"I don't know about that." Benji rubbed his chin. "If we ignore the Americans they will just do whatever they want with no one to say they shouldn't. I think we should at least speak against tyranny."

"And what are you going to say?"

"How about, 'Go Home'."

"And do you think they will?"

"Maybe if enough of us shouted it."

"I doubt it." Ben settled into the conversation, prepared for a long, patient explanation. "If you and all your friends and all their friends start shouting at the Americans, all that will happen is that they will become more resolved to stay and show you they can't be pushed around. You will only escalate the conflict."

Benji sat and waited for the obvious more that was to come.

Ben continued. "When you fight someone, you make that someone stronger, conflict always does that. And, it is not the natural state of being. We are not always in a state of for-and-against. That's just a simple pattern of thinking. The world doesn't divide itself into dichotomies, left, right — good, evil — us, them — black, white."

"Well, I appreciate that everything isn't black and white, there are grey areas."

Ben cut Benji off. "No, not grey. That is still applying the principles of black and white, just mashing the two together. When people speak of the grey area, they are still caught in the dichotomy of opposing forces. There is more than black and white, a whole rainbow of choices. We have to be careful not to get stuck in these ideas"

Ben paused, thought through what he needed to say "We get stuck in ideas that out of oppositional forces we will arrive at truth. Look what happens when we apply that idea to anything; to law, to education, to religion. All we end up with is more conflict."

"But law works, don't you think? Two sides bring their dispute to a judge who decides based on the arguments put forward. It sure beats trial by combat."

"See, that's the thing. We've all been taught to believe that law works. It doesn't. The dispute isn't resolved by the judge. The judge just picks a winner and a loser, and it's a winner-take-all situation. Disputes are almost never only between two people, the whole community is affected by the conflict at some level, even if it is only an experience of rising tension. Law says there are always two sides to a story. Well, there are a whole lot more than two sides to anything, I don't know about everyone else, but my world is multi-dimensional."

Benji felt stung, as though the words were aimed at him. "What do you mean, you don't know about everyone else. Of course we aren't two-dimensional."

"But I don't know that." Ben spoke softer. "I don't know what others experience. I only have my own experiences to trust."

Rosie hoped Ben would get those ideas across to Benji; she was about to offer a prayer, a little something to those entities that were her constant companions, something to the effect of "give Ben the words he needs." But she thought better of it, it was best to let Ben find his own words, find his own way through to his son. Prayer was for important things, like health and happiness. It was always good practice to let the universe conspire to do whatever it was the universe conspired to do. It would give Ben what he wanted, the same as it perpetually gave her what she needed. Now if only Ben could show his son how to walk in the balance of all things. She threaded another half-dozen beads, shook them down to the leather, and continued her creation, glass, leather and thread; and good thoughts — these moccasins needed to have good thoughts put into them so that her granddaughter wouldn't trip.

Ben reached across the table and picked up the red-and-white book from in front of Benji. "This isn't so bad, I like the comparison between Christianity and Stalinism and Hitler, but it doesn't really get us anywhere. Attacking Christianity doesn't increase our understanding of where we are." He put it back down; "When you finish it maybe you would like something written without the confusion of philosophy. I can't remember who it was, someone once said that rationality was the flatulence around reason." And with that he went over to his little library of three bookshelves against the back wall where he kept only those treasures that were too important to abandon when he left academia. He searched for a few seconds before he found what he was looking for, returned and set the thin volume at Benji's elbow.

Late in the evening, after Rosie went home and after the supper dishes were done, when Elsie and Benji were alone momentarily, when the warmth of the log walls absorbed her words, Elsie asked, "So what was that book your dad gave you this afternoon?"

"Oh that. You know, I was sure he was going to give me something by Nietzsche." Benji went and got the book and brought it to her. "He said to read it after I finished Bertrand Russell, so I'm kinda skimming along to get it done."

Elsie examined the cover, "Doris Lessing, *Prisons We Choose to Live Inside.* I think I would like to read this." She turned it over to read the back jacket.

~

Monica cried. It was more than that her eyes watered from being burned; she lay in her bed, covers over her head and her face buried deeply into a pillow and cried. She was by herself; Abe left hours ago. He assured her, promised her that her sight would come back. "It's just severe welder's flash, hurts like hell for a few days, but you'll be all right. Just stay in the dark and I will be back now and then to check on you."

She hugged the pillow her face was buried into; squeezed hard, pulled it to her breast and let her tears pour. The worst part about being blind wasn't the pain, it wasn't even the fear; the fear that someone or something unseen was going to attack and you were defenceless in a world of white light. No, the worst part about being blind was this strange form of loneliness, unable to see people, forced to live inside of your head, alone.

She wondered if she might be crying for Betsy — probably not; Betsy was a traitor, a fake, a liar — if she was crying at all for Betsy, it was for the loss of a friend and that friend was lost before Betsy went into that house.

Perhaps she was crying for Ben, for the life companion, the husband that he had never become. She wasn't sure. She was filled with sorrow and despair that seemed to gurgle up from the deepest part of her soul as though she was mourning. She wondered if she was crying for a home, for a family, for Benji; all of those things that she had denied herself, given up for the resistance.

She sat up, sniffed loudly; wiped the wet away from her eyes with the sleeve of her blouse. Her eyes burned, but not with the same intensity as before. She strained to see something through the white glare, anything; and was rewarded with the dim silhouette image of Abe standing silently in the doorway.

〜

"¿Señora,Quieres algo para desayunar?"

Kay smiled back at the young, nicely tanned waiter. *"Yo no hablo español,"* she did the best she could.

"Oh, Señora, I asked if you wanted breakfast with your coffee," without any hint of an accent.

"I'll wait, my husband will be down in a few minutes."

An easy wind came in from the Atlantic and brushed Kay's bare shoulders. Maybe she should have brought a shawl; yes a shawl would go nicely here at the sidewalk café. She could have sat inside, but it seemed that she had been inside all winter and when you are on vacation, well . . . you put up with a little chill in the morning. Here in Miramar, Argentina, it was summer, or rather late summer, early autumn. It wasn't cold, frozen Toronto where Kay and Stan Jolly kept their home, and it was definitely a lot warmer than mid-March on the Saskatchewan prairie and Kay's family's farm.

She liked it here. She could relax. The tension of home, the constant tension, the tension that was always there, so always there that it became normal and you didn't notice it, wasn't here. They left it behind, left the constant wariness; they stepped off the plane in the sunshine and it was no longer heavy on their minds, on their bodies, on their spirits. Here she was just a tourist, just a retired schoolteacher from Canada tourist, having a normal morning cup of coffee, at a normal outdoor restaurant, and Stan . . . well today he too would be the tourist. He would join a group of kayakers and explore the coast, a normal tourist thing to do, and Kay would maybe go down to the beach, more probably wander the streets looking into shops, not shopping, listen to people speaking Spanish just for the sound, have lunch somewhere, a nice sandwich, and later in the afternoon maybe a *yerbe mate*. She had become quite fond of the local drink, an infusion served in a gourd and drunk through a silver straw, and the known fact that it reduced cholesterol simply added to the pleasure. And it seemed to Kay that it helped with her arthritis, maybe she was imagining it, it might be the sunshine, or more probably it had to do with not living under constant stress; anyway the ache wasn't as intense as usual. It wasn't enough that she could go kayaking with her husband today, or mountain climbing with him last week, but it made life much more enjoyable.

A chair scraped and she looked up. "You finished posting?"

"It's done." Stan put the computer bag on the sidewalk beside the chair before sitting. "You have my absolute undivided attention until noon." He looked around for the waiter.

Kay touched his elbow across the table. "What was the result?"

He looked back toward her: "Inconclusive."

"Come on Stan, was it or wasn't it?"

"I honestly don't know."

"Well, what did you post?" she corrected herself, "what did That Jack post?"

"Only that the bolt from heaven was dropped on a house in Saskatoon. I didn't say anything about the barrel of yellowcake."

"Why not?" Kay's tone changed, Stan could be frustrating at times.

"Because we don't know for sure."

She stared at him for a long second, he was serious. She leaned forward, lowered her voice a little, "We know they dropped it on the house, we know there was a barrel of yellowcake uranium in the basement. Now, maybe no one has done any testing, but it seems only logical to me that Saskatoon is completely contaminated."

"Okay, then let's examine what we know for sure. When the bolt hit the house it was pure plasma. Tungsten melts at 3,422 degrees celcius, and uranium melts at 3,027 degrees, so we can assume that all of the uranium was vapourized."

Kay sat back. Stan had done his homework. She thought of something she had read not that long ago. "Remember Suzuki's *Sacred Balance*?"

Stan was looking for the waiter again, "Uh-huh."

"Remember that bit about Shapley I think his name was?

"No." Stan looked back at her.

"Well he said that if we calculate the amount of argon in a single breath, I can't remember how many atoms there are, but something like trillions and trillions and he calculated — and I do remember this — each breath we take has about four hundred thousand atoms that Gandhi once had in his lungs. And each breath we take has atoms that Jesus once had and atoms from Hitler and Stalin."

Stan thought about it for a moment. "It's worse than that. Even if the uranium was vapourized on impact, it would only be vapour until it cooled down again."

〜

"Okay, so I've read Doris Lessing and I get it." Benji held the lead dog, Duchess, while Ben harnessed one of the full-grown puppies. "Don't belong to any organization, how simple."

"Right. If you *belong* to them, then they own you."

Benji thought for a moment about that play of words. "Yeah." He nodded his head, happy outdoors in the sunshine of early March, with a bit of warm wind coming from the southwest.

"It's also kinda like that dog you're holding there." Ben finished harnessing, attached a tug line, and stopped. "For most of the winter I've been telling her that haw means I want her to turn left and gee means I want her to turn right. She doesn't question it. She's been told it so many times consistently that it's become her truth. She probably believes me because I am the alpha male here. I am the one that brings the food. And her puppies." Ben waved a gloved hand at the other five dogs harnessed to the toboggan, "They believe that this is normal, perhaps even natural and necessary, look at them, they're anxious, they want to do this. It's like they're saying, come on already, let's go. I've only been running them a few months and already this is their absolute truth, they belong to this team." A dog jumped over its teammate. Ben gently put it back on its side of the gangline. "People get that way too, get to believing something is natural and necessary because that's all they ever experienced."

Benji joked, "So should I turn her loose?"

"Naw, she's too domesticated, wouldn't survive on her own yet. In time she could learn to go back to being wild and free, run with a pack because the pack was her family and not because the pack was a yellow dog pack or capitalist pack or conservative pack or a resistance pack." Ben stood on the back of the toboggan. "Okay, let her go."

Benji let go of Duchess's collar and stood aside. The team began to run all at the same time, a fast, long-legged lope, and as Ben went by, he leaned out and gave Benji a pat on the shoulder. "Be back in about a couple hours."

～

She could kill Monica, that would be easy, she knew where Monica lived, knew her habits, how she always used the elevator to get to the parking level of her apartment. It would be simple, Betsy would sit in a car near the elevator and wait — simple, easy and unsatisfactory. No, Monica deserved to die a fuck of a lot slower than that. It was simply a matter of principle. Betsy grinned at the idea, "Yeah, on principle, Now who was being principled — bitch?"

Her feet still hurt from the frostbite, and the new shoes didn't help. The pain fed her anger, she breathed in deep, exhaled with a surge through clenched teeth. She was going to fuck Monica the way Monica had never been fucked before, take away the one thing that that the bitch cherished the most. Betsy was going to kill Ben — kill the idea, kill the principle. Then she would come back and kill Monica too — and Abe — just for the fuck of it.

～

The early sun reflected off the sharp edge of an axe that hung by a strap attached to the dog sleigh, a tiny flare lost in the sparkle of sun on crystallized snow. The sleigh runners made a slicing sound behind the team that ran a familiar track along the edge of Moccasin Lake. Ben stepped down on the sleigh brake, and shouted a calm "whoa" that brought the team and the sleigh to a stop. Most of the seven dogs looked back over their shoulders as though to ask, "What's up, why'd we stop?"

Ben had no reason. The dogs had not run far and did not need a rest. The track across the lake was clear. No reason other than he wanted to, it felt right, just stop and enjoy the warmth of the sun on his face for a minute, to take off his gloves and grab a handful of snow just to feel it melt between his fingers and wipe the wet across his face, to walk up to the lead dog and scratch her behind the ear for a minute and tell her she's "a good dog, yeah, you're a good dog."

There wasn't much left of winter, the remainder of March, then most of April and the geese would come back and the lake would melt. The sun already gave a good warmth and stood higher in the southern sky; a pale blue completely cloudless sky. There to the south, just above the horizon, a black spot caught Ben's attention. He watched it, mildly curious, a raven probably; more than likely a raven. But ravens were still mating this time of year and there should be two of them.

The black spot became slightly larger. It was clearly a bird. Ben noted the flight pattern of flap and glide. Pelicans fly like that, so do eagles, as do ravens occasionally. It wasn't a pelican, too early, no open water. So, it was either a raven or an eagle. If it was an eagle it would be the first to migrate back, the first to return to their nesting grounds. Ben waited. Scratched the lead dog's ears absentmindedly for no other reason than she deserved kind treatment and for the feel of fur on his hand.

The eagle flew straight towards Ben and the team. He recognized its flight long before he could make out its white head and tail. As it passed directly overhead in a long glide, wings outstretched, it banked steeply to its left, made a circle as it descended and landed on the snow-covered lake a dozen metres from the back of the sleigh.

At first Ben was wary, looking around. This was not normal behaviour for an eagle. There was nothing here to attract it. It wasn't like a fisherman had left something out on the ice that an early eagle would be interested in, something to eat before the lake ice melted and it could fish for itself. It would be hungry though, it had come a long ways. He took a sack filled with chunks of frozen fish from the sleigh, snacks for the dogs, and tossed a few greasy pieces out towards the large bird.

It kept its distance. Ben dumped the sack. There wasn't a lot in it, something though, a bit, an offering. "Hey, Mikisew," he spoke softly, reverently, "Hey, Grandmother. You can see far, you can see the future, you can see the past. Thank you for coming back to us." He gave the sack a final shake for the last fish crumbs, pulled up on the sleigh brake. The dogs leaning into their harness, eager to run again, did not need to be told when the tension came off the gangline. They burst into a quick lope. Ben looked back, turned around on the sleigh so that he was facing backward and watched the eagle hop toward the offering he had left, accepting it.

The House

on

Durrow Street

ALSO BY GALEN BECKETT

The Magicians and Mrs. Quent

The House

on

Durrow Street

GALEN BECKETT

BALLANTINE BOOKS   NEW YORK

A Spectra Trade Paperback Original

Copyright © 2010 by Mark Anthony

Published in the United States by Spectra Books,
an imprint of The Random House Publishing Group,
a division of Random House, Inc., New York.

SPECTRA and the portrayal of a boxed "s" are trademarks
of Random House, Inc.

ISBN 978-1-61664-982-1

Printed in the United States of America

Book design by Carol Malcolm Russo

For my own sisters—

Victoria, Augusta, Elizabeth,
and Margaret

BOOK ONE

The Black Stork

CHAPTER ONE

IVY WOKE TO the sound of voices.

She sat up and reached for Mr. Quent beside her, wondering if he had murmured something in his sleep as he often did. Her hand found only a cold tangle of bedclothes. He was gone—a fact her dull mind recalled after a moment—off to the north of Altania on business for the lord inquirer. He had left nearly a quarter month ago and would not return before Darkeve at the end of the month.

Besides, it was not from inside the bedchamber that the murmuring had come.

Ivy rose, gathering a nightgown around her, for it was late in a long umbral and the coals in the fireplace had burned to cinders. She stood in a beam of moonlight that had slipped through a gap in the curtains, listening. Was Rose wandering the house in the night as was her habit, singing softly to herself? Or perhaps it was Lily, making exclamations as she read by candlelight in her room, turning the final pages of one of her romances.

Ivy heard nothing save the beating of her own heart. The high hedges outside guarded against the noises of the city, and the old house on Durrow Street was silent. She turned to go back to bed.

This time the voices were louder: a chorus of whispers that seemed to come from outside her bedchamber door. By the deep tones, it was neither Lily nor Rose. Nor could it be any of the servants; their quarters were still under renovation, and they were not yet in residence. Which meant the moonbeam was not the only interloper in the house.

A dread descended over Ivy. Not three months ago, upon his return to the city from Torland, a band of revolutionaries had set upon Mr. Quent as he met with the lord inquirer. Their intent had been nothing less than murder. However, Mr. Quent had been warned of the attack beforehand, and the rebels were apprehended before they could act. Yet if *they* had desired to do violence to agents of the Crown, it was not difficult to believe there were others who might wish the same.

Her heart quickened as she went to the door. She pressed a hand to it, as if she might sense through its panels what lay beyond. If only the door was fashioned of timbers from the Wyrdwood! She would call to the wood, wake it from its slumber, and shape it with her thoughts. What did a witch have to fear from a robber when there was Wyrdwood nearby?

But the material beneath her hands was inert, hewn from a tree of New Oak; it could be of no help to her. Despite this fact, Ivy summoned her courage. After all, she told herself, this house belonged to her father; it was a magician's dwelling, and so had its own powers and protections. She opened the door and stepped into the corridor beyond.

It was empty except for the moonlight that spilled through a window at the end. All was quiet; the voices had ceased.

Ivy moved down the corridor, pausing to crack the door to Lily's room, then Rose's, peering inside. Both of her sisters were asleep. She wondered if it was the sound of wind she had heard. Sometimes, in the months she had dwelled at Heathcrest Hall, the wind over the eaves had sounded like whispering voices. Only,

when she reached the window, she saw that the straggled hawthorn and chestnut trees below stood motionless.

So much for *that* hypothesis. Her gaze roved across the garden,
but she perceived only shadows. Beyond the hedges, a scattering
of gold lights shone here and there in the Old City. Another spark,
brighter and more reddish than the streetlamps, hung low in the
southern sky. Otherwise, the night was void.

Ivy shivered in her nightgown. According to the almanac, it
was to be an umbral of over twenty-two hours. Frost would tinge
the windowpanes by the time dawn came. Despite the cold, she
did not return to her room. Instead, she went to the stairs to begin
a survey of the house.

It took half of an hour, for the house was much larger than their
previous dwelling on Whitward Street. She moved up and down
staircases, through narrow passages and across vaulted halls. Many
of the chambers were in various states of refurbishment, and others
were all but impassable, crowded with furniture moved out of
those rooms under repair.

The task of opening the house on Durrow Street was proving
to be a greater labor than she had guessed How unwise she had
been, to think she could have accomplished the task on the wages
of a governess! Much had become dilapidated in the years the
house had stood empty. And she suspected that even when her
father had dwelled here, all had not been cared for as properly as
it might have been.

Mr. Quent had quickly educated her as to the enormity of the
work on the day they made their first inspection of the house. The
roof sagged over the north wing, and in the south the floors were
rotten. The cellar showed signs that water seeped in when it rained;
there were myriad broken windows, cracked walls, and faulty
beams. Such was the length of the report that Ivy feared to be told
that the only solution was to raze the house to rubble.

Instead, Mr. Quent had sat in the dusty light of the downstairs
parlor and, in his cramped yet meticulous hand, had written out a
list of repairs to be undertaken. It was a document that required
several pages.

"I cannot possibly imagine the cost of this," she had said in astonishment when he gave it to her to review.

"As there is no need for you to imagine it, I suggest you do not attempt such a futile and obviously distressing feat."

"But the repairs are so great. It will be an exorbitant sum—over five thousand regals, I am sure!"

"And now it appears you can envision it quite well, Mrs. Quent. How curious for a thing you could not possibly imagine a moment ago."

"I mean only, is it worth the expense for a house that is so very old?"

His brown eyes had been solemn as he regarded her. "It is worth it *because* it is so very old."

With that, all other arguments were superseded. The letter was delivered to a builder, and work commenced at once.

Now, as she walked through its moonlit chambers, Ivy wondered just how old her father's house was. Many of the buildings in the Old City had been in existence for centuries, and were built on the foundations of structures more ancient yet. However, while the other dwellings and shops and churches in this part of Invarel all crowded together, her father's house stood apart in its garden, a thing unto itself. Nor was it constructed of the same gray stone as the other buildings, but rather hewn of a reddish porphyry, speckled with interesting inclusions and darker crystals. Ivy wished she could ask her father about the age of the house. But that was not possible.

True, her father's state was better than it had been several months ago. Now, when Ivy went to Madstone's to visit him each quarter month, she was able to sit with him in his private chamber. The room was in the dormitory where the wardens dwelled, far removed from the awful clamor of the rest of the hostel, and Ivy had been allowed to make it familiar and comfortable with furnishings brought from his attic at Whitward Street.

The only thing the wardens had not permitted her to bring was any of Mr. Lockwell's books, for these were deemed too likely to agitate him. Her father had been a doctor and a man of learning, and Ivy did not like to deprive him of at least a small library. Yet while she did not think kindly of the wardens at Madstone's, she had to wonder if perhaps they were right. Her father had seemed exceedingly placid on her recent visits. He had even smiled at her from time to time.

Yet he never spoke her name, or any other intelligible thing. Lord Rafferdy's influence had been enough to improve her father's treatment at the hostel. But the royal charter under which Madstone's operated granted it considerable autonomy, and no patient would be released unless the wardens deemed him cured or the king ordered it.

While her father was improved, even Ivy could not pretend he was cured of his malady. As for gaining a writ with the king's seal, Lord Rafferdy had submitted the petition. However, King Rothard was infirm himself these days. A recent edition of *The Comet* reported that while the Citadel had tried to keep the news from public knowledge, the king had been confined to his bed for nearly a half month of late.

This was ill news, but Ivy would not stop hoping for the king's health—and her father's—to improve. In the meantime, whatever the age of the house on Durrow Street might be, she was beginning to think that it would increase by at least another year before the work on it was completed. The repairs were going more slowly than she had anticipated. Materials had grown dearer and scarcer of late. And, according to the builder, he had lost several skilled craftsmen.

"How have they been lost?" she had heard Mr. Quent ask Mr. Barbridge one day as she descended the stairs to the front hall.

The builder had shifted from foot to foot, turning his hat in his hands. "They say it watches them while they work. The house, they mean. I beg your pardon, Mr. Quent, for it's a foolish bit of fancy, I know. Yet they're simple men, and all those eyes—well, they do give one a feeling."

His gaze had gone toward the knob atop the newel post, which was carved in the shape of an eye. It blinked a wooden lid and turned in its socket, gazing about in a quizzical fashion. There were others in the house—set into moldings and doors—which often did the same as one passed by.

Open or shut, the eyes never troubled Ivy. If her father had not created them himself, then at least he had been aware of their enchantment. And if he had tolerated them, then why shouldn't she? Besides, she was glad for their presence in those times when Mr. Quent was away. Most of the magicians of the Vigilant Order of the Silver Eye were gone—perished, or locked away in Madstone's. But there was at least one who remained. Even if it was the case that Mr. Bennick was no longer a magician himself, that did not mean he was no longer perilous. She and Mr. Rafferdy had witnessed that firsthand. So she was grateful that the house kept watch.

By his grimace, the builder did not agree. Ivy and Mr. Quent had not discussed it, but after that day she went through the house, draping cloths over all of the carved eyes she could find. However, at the end of each lumenal when the workmen left, she would uncover the eye on the newel post at the foot of the stairs. That one, at least, she would leave to keep its silent vigil.

Now, as Ivy started back up the staircase, that eye was shut fast. Her own eyes wished to follow suit, and a yawn escaped her as she climbed. Since leaving her room, she had heard nothing except for the sound of her own footsteps and those natural sounds a house makes at night—the groan of shifting beams, the creak of an eave as it settled—which can give no rational mind cause for fear.

What had been the source of the whispering voices, she could not say. Ivy had not thought them to be figments of a dream, but now she had to admit that it was possible. She reached the top of the stairs and went to her bedchamber, ready to return to sleep.

This time it was not a whispering she heard, but rather a distant clattering. She turned from the door. The sound had echoed from down the corridor. Nor could it be ascribed to a dream this time.

Ivy started forward even as it occurred to her this was absurd. If there really was an intruder in the house, what would she do if she encountered him? She was a smallish woman of twenty-three years clad in a night robe and slippers—hardly a thing to inspire alarm or cause a thief to flee. Yet she could not return to her room and huddle in her bed knowing there was another presence in the house.

Ivy crept down the corridor, then turned a corner into the north wing. The passage beyond was cluttered with lengths of wood and crumpled heaps of cloth. A sheet draped the window at the end, dimming the moonlight to a gray gloom.

Again she heard a noise: louder now, as of sharp objects being struck together. She stopped before a door halfway along the corridor. Ivy laid a hand on the knob; like many in the house, it was formed in the shape of a brass orb clutched in an eagle's talons. The metal was icy to the touch.

A feeling came over her as it sometimes did at night—a sense that the darkness pressed in from all around, seeping through cracks and beneath doors, seeking to smother everything. The Testament said that before the world was made, only darkness existed. In moments like this, she could believe it sought dominion once again.

Suddenly convinced that she did not want to see what lay in the room beyond, Ivy snatched her hand back. So violent was her motion that she flung the knob away from her as she recoiled, and the door, not being fully latched, swung inward.

A coldness rushed out. The clacking came again, loud and jolting, but her mind could not grasp what it was. There was another sound, like that of a wet cloth being shaken, and something lurched across the floor not five feet away from her.

In the gloom it was no more than a shapeless blot, scuttling like some half-formed thing not ready to have been birthed. The coldness froze her; she could not move. Then the thing rose up off the floor and spread itself outward, as if to catch her in its black embrace.

Ivy screamed.

Rustling, scrabbling, and clattering filled the room. Two other shapes lifted from the floor, expanding outward, spreading dark appendages. A rush of cold air buffeted Ivy so that she staggered back, raising her hands to her face. The noises rose into a terrible clamor. Then, with one last gust of air, all fell silent except for a low, sighing sound.

Ivy lowered her hands. Her eyes had grown accustomed to the deeper darkness of the room, and she saw the remnants of a curtain flapping before the room's one window. The glazing was gone, and the shutters were open as the cold night poured in unimpeded. Shivering, she started forward to draw the shutters. As she did, something snapped beneath her foot. Ivy bent to pick it up. It was a twig.

"Ivy?" she heard a faint voice echoing behind her. "Ivy, where have you gotten to . . . ?"

She grimaced. Her scream would have been enough to awaken the dead. She proceeded forward, avoiding the heap of sticks in the center of the room, and closed the shutters. Then she left the room and hurried back down the corridor.

As soon as she turned the corner, she saw Lily and Rose. They stood outside their bedchambers. Lily held a wavering candle.

"Blood and swash, there you are!" Lily exclaimed, holding the candle higher. In addition to her usual romances, she had been reading a number of nautical-themed adventures of late, and so had taken to speaking like a sailor. "Rose said you weren't in your room. We heard you scream. Something awful has happened, hasn't it?"

Now that it was over, Ivy realized how her imagination had gotten the better of her. She felt an absurd laughter rising. "I'm afraid the only awful thing is that I've roused you from your beds for nothing."

"But I thought I heard voices," Rose said, her eyes very wide in the golden light. "Was there someone here?"

"Three someones, in fact." Ivy held up the twig she still carried in her hand. "They were storks, I believe, given their size. They had come in through an open window in one of the empty rooms and were building a nest. I'm sure I frightened them quite as much as they frightened me. They flew off."

Lily let out a snort. "Storks? Really, Ivy—you aren't brave at all, to be scared of a few silly birds. Sophella didn't scream once in the last chapter, even when the duke shut her in a crypt full of skeletons. You've quite ruined me for sleep for the rest of the umbral. I might as well read my book." With that, she took the candle back into her chamber.

Ivy sighed as darkness descended once again. "Do you need me to show you back to your bed, dearest?" she said to Rose. "My eyes are quite used to the dark by now."

Rose smiled at her. "I can always see when you're near. Just stand in the doorway for a moment, and I'll find my way."

As was so often the case, Ivy didn't quite know what to make of Rose's words, but she did as her sister asked, and Rose was soon in her bed again. Ivy shut the door quietly, then returned to her own room. She thought, like Lily, that there would be no more chance of sleep for her that night. Instead, as she laid down, a great yawn escaped her. The excitement of dread had passed, leaving her exhausted in its wake.

"Not brave!" she murmured to herself as she settled her head against the pillow. If only Lily had seen her when she escaped from the highwayman at Heathcrest Hall, or when she faced the magicians of the Vigilant Order of the Silver Eye. Then she might not think the fictional Sophella to be superior in character to her eldest sister. After all, one had little to fear from a pile of bones. Or from a few birds. It was living men that one had reason to worry about, and Ivy was now very certain there was not a single one here.

Knowing that the house's eyes kept watch in the dark, Ivy shut her own, and did not open them again for the remainder of the night.

ONCE AGAIN SHE was awakened by a sound coming through her door, only this time it was the noise of hammers pounding.

Ivy sat up in bed. A pink glow tinged the windowpanes, which were indeed rimed with frost. By the light, it was only just after dawn. She was surprised the workmen were here already. Yet they were, and that meant that, despite Ivy's late-night exertions, there would be no more sleep for her.

She rose and dressed quickly, her breath fogging on the air. Then she proceeded downstairs to the parlor, where the family was taking their meals while the dining room was under repair. Upon entering, she found Lily and Rose already at the table.

"Shiver my timbers!" Lily exclaimed and shut her book, which she had been reading as she nibbled at a piece of toast. "I don't think I can bear another day of this blast and blunder. I can hardly read two words in a row with all this racket."

Ivy smiled at her. "I believe it's the house's timbers that are shivering. However, if the noise bothers you, I suggest you ask Lawden to drive you up to Halworth Gardens." She went to the hutch and checked the almanac. "It's to be a short lumenal today, which means it should warm quickly. You could find a bench on which to read."

Lily's eyes lit up. "That's a capital idea. I'll tell Lawden to put the calash top down on the carriage so we'll look extra fashionable. Rose will come with me. She can keep watch and tell me when there's a fine-looking gentleman coming so I know when to put down my book and look uninterested."

Ivy sat at the table. "Should you not rather appear interested if you wish for a gentleman to take notice?"

"Good gods, don't you know anything, Ivy? No gentleman will speak to you if you appear interested in him. If he thinks you have a wish to speak to him, he will turn at once and go the other way. Instead, you must look very bored and wait until he wanders near on his own. That's what Sophella learned when she was trying to speak with the duke's son in Chapter Two."

Ivy poured a cup of tea. "I had no idea young gentlemen lived in such dread of conversation that they must be lured into it unsuspectingly. They must suffer a great fright every time they encounter a pretty young lady. All the same, you should not presume that Rose will assist you in your scheme. She might like to occupy herself with an activity of her own choosing."

"Nonsense. What could Rose possibly have to do? Sitting next to me will be quite enough activity for *her*, I am sure. You'll come with me to the gardens, won't you, Rose?"

Rose gave a hesitant nod. "But I'm not sure I'll know which gentlemen are the ones you think are handsome."

"That's easy," Lily said. "Simply choose the ones that look the most like Mr. Garritt. Though it's been so long since we've seen him, I'm not certain I'd recognize him if he walked past. When will he and Mr. Rafferdy come to call? Since we've moved to Durrow Street they've paid us but a single visit, and they hardly stayed an hour. They're terribly rude. If I see Mr. Garritt at Halworth Gardens, I'm sure I will be too peeved to speak with him." Her dark eyes sparkled. "Wouldn't that be marvelous, if I saw him there?"

"I do not see how it matters, if you're too peeved to speak to him," Ivy said, putting a bit of cold partridge on her plate.

"Blow me down, of course I'll speak to him! After I show him how I am peeved, of course." Lily fixed her with a scowling look. "I suppose *you* won't come with us to the gardens, will you?"

Ivy had to admit that a stroll through the gardens sounded pleasant. However, she shook her head. "While he is away, Mr. Quent is relying on me to supervise the work on the house."

"I hope he will not be away so long as he told us," Rose said. "He is only just gone, and I already wish that he were back."

"As do I," Lily agreed heartily. "I've just realized that all of my bonnets are dreadful. I'll be ashamed to be seen in Halworth Gardens with any of them. I'll need a new one immediately upon his return."

These words concerned Ivy, though she kept her admonishment gentle. "Mr. Quent has already bought you a great many things—dresses, ribbons, parasols."

"Yes, but not a single bonnet. And if I tell him I can quite do without it, and that it's the silliest of things, and kiss his cheek, he will tell me to go at once to the finest shop and select my favorite one."

Ivy said nothing and ate her breakfast. She suspected Lily was correct in her prediction. Mr. Quent had been indulgent of Ivy's sisters since they took up residence on Durrow Street—especially of Lily, since Rose seldom asked for anything. Prior to his most recent departure, Ivy had mentioned that she feared Lily was becoming spoiled.

"Why should she not be spoiled?" Mr. Quent had replied. "I am sure she has had little enough opportunity to be spoiled in her life. And as she is nearly a young woman, the time in which she can be so indulged grows short. You were not spoiled at all before it was too late, Mrs. Quent, and look what it has done to you. You are practical and somber! No, we must hurry and spoil Lily before it is too late for her, and she becomes hopelessly serious."

"I highly doubt *that* will happen!" Ivy had exclaimed.

A grin parted his beard then, and he looked—as he sometimes did, with his brown hair curling over his furrowed brow—like some wild faun from an ancient Tharosian play. At such times, Ivy could do nothing but laugh and hold him tightly.

"Very well," Ivy said now as she set down her fork. She gave Lily what she hoped was a stern look. "But only one bonnet, mind you."

Lily gave a sweet smile in return. This response did little to reassure Ivy. Before she could say anything more, Mrs. Seenly entered the parlor bearing another pot of tea and the post. At once Ivy forgot about all other concerns, for there was a note from Mr. Quent. She opened it and scanned its brief lines.

The contents were what she had expected. He wrote to let her know of his safe arrival in the north. His work was just commencing; he did not think it would be strenuous. They were there only to make observations, comparing the size of various stands of Wyrdwood to those recorded in old surveys. He still planned to return by month's end. Ivy was glad he did not expect to be delayed. However, it was not yet Brightday, which meant Darkeve was still more than half a month away.

She never told him that it was difficult for her when he was gone. The burden of his work was already great, and she had no wish to add to it. Besides, any difficulty she might have to bear in his absence was nothing compared to what he must endure in his travels. Still, she could not deny it was hard to have him gone so often; nor, as much as she did her best to conceal it from him, did her own difficulties go unnoticed by others.

"It is not right for a young wife to be so frequently without her new husband," Lord Rafferdy had told her some months ago, after a supper at Lady Marsdel's house. It was the night before the lord inquirer departed the city to return home to Asterlane. "It weighs on you already, Mrs. Quent, and will weigh further, I have no doubt."

She tried to demur, but she could not lie, and could only admit it was, in truth, a challenge.

"I know it can offer you little comfort now," Lord Rafferdy said as they sat apart from the others, "but know that his work is of great importance—indeed, of the very greatest to all of Altania. Know also that, one day, it will be rewarded. He has labored all these years without any recognition. Yet one day—sooner rather than later, I think—that will change."

These words had at once shamed and heartened Ivy. Who was she to mope about, pining for Mr. Quent, when she knew that so much depended on his labors as an inquirer? Knowing that Mr. Quent's work was so important was all the reward they required, she had assured Lord Rafferdy. For some reason, the look he had given her then had struck Ivy as both pleased and amused, but he had said nothing more. The next day the lord inquirer had departed the city, and he had not returned since.

"Mrs. Seenly," Ivy said, "is Mr. Barbridge in the house this morning?"

"Aye, missus, he is indeed," the housekeeper said as she poured tea in Ivy's cup. "I saw him out in the front hall not five minutes ago."

"Would you tell him to have one of his men go to the north wing, to the upper floor? There's a room there with a broken window." She described her late-night encounter with the storks.

Mrs. Seenly's face pursed in a frown. "And you say they were all black, missus, as they flew out the window?"

"I think they must have been. They were difficult to see against the night."

"Then we'd best have the window boarded right away. 'A black stork brings black luck,' as they say where I'm from."

Ivy smiled at her. "I'm not concerned about the bad luck they bring, Mrs. Seenly, only about being awakened again by the noises they make."

The lines beside Mrs. Seenly's mouth deepened. The housekeeper had lived in Invarel for the last thirty years, but she had been a girl in Torland. It was a heritage reflected in the copper strands mingled with the silver in her hair, as well as in her predilection for superstition. More than once Ivy had seen her sprinkling salt on the ledge of the kitchen window to keep out mischievous spirits, or knocking thrice to prevent ill words from coming to pass.

As Mrs. Seenly had proved to be an excellent housekeeper—despite the challenges of keeping a house that was under refurbishment—Ivy did not mind her practice of customs and habits from her childhood. However, Rose had a tendency to become alarmed by such things, so while Ivy would not admonish Mrs. Seenly for her beliefs, she would not lend them credence either.

"I'm sure we're quite well, Mrs. Seenly," she said. "This proves only that storks have superior taste in dwellings. But this house already has occupants, so they'll need to find another. Do tell Mr. Barbridge."

"Aye, Mrs. Quent," the housekeeper said, and departed.

Along with the post, Mrs. Seenly had brought that morning's edition of *The Comet.* In the past, Ivy had never made a habit of reading the broadsheets, but she had read them with greater regularity ever since the Risings in Torland several months ago.

The days that followed the news had been strange. A queer energy had filled the city. There was astonishment and disbelief that groves of forest that had stood still and silent for ages could suddenly lash out, and there was outrage over the deaths that had occurred.

Yet it wasn't only that. There was something else in the air: a kind of excitement. What had been remembered as no more than a children's tale—if it was remembered at all—was now perceived as perilously real. No one could ever walk by a tall tree again, or cool himself in its dappled shade, and not consider what it would be like to see those branches bend and sway without the benefit of any wind.

Of course, there were no Old Trees anywhere in the city. People had nothing to fear *here,* they assured one another. What was more, shortly after the first stories appeared in the broadsheets, there came more news out of Torland. Due to the efforts of the king's inquirers, the Risings had ceased. The witch who had provoked the primeval forest into action had been discovered and captured. As a result, the Wyrdwood had been contained, and all known stands of Old Trees were now under constant watch. A sigh seemed to go through the city. People went again about their daily business. All was the same as it had been.

Except it *wasn't* the same. Several times, as she walked through the city, Ivy had seen a pale stump in front of a house where previously there had stood a graceful elm or ash. And there were other signs that things were altered from before. She unfolded the broadsheet Mrs. Seenly had left on the table. REGULAR PATROLS CONTINUE AROUND THE EVENGROVE, read the title above a small article at the bottom of the first page.

Ever since the events in Torland, stories about outlaws causing troubles in the Outlands had been markedly less frequent. It seemed that putting an end to the Risings had been a blow to the cause of rebellion. When considered, this made sense. As Ivy had witnessed herself in the West Country, with the aid of witches, rebels had been using stands of Wyrdwood as places to conceal themselves and plan their traitorous activities.

It was the work of the inquirers to keep watch over the Wyrdwood and prevent anyone—man or woman—from trying to disturb the ancient groves. Now, through their efforts, the Wyrdwood in Torland had been quelled. And as it was Torland that had offered the greatest source of agitators, rebellious activities had become far less common in recent months.

All the same, the broadsheets must find something to print on their pages, and fewer articles about rebels and outlaws left more space and ink for stories about the Wyrdwood—the location and size of the stands nearest to Invarel, who was watching them, and what works were being undertaken to strengthen the walls around them.

Ivy took a sip of tea, then read the piece that had caught her eye.

Though it is fifteen centuries old, the story began, *Madiger's Wall remains a formidable barrier around the Evengrove, which is the largest grove of Wyrdwood in all of Altania, and also the closest to Invarel. Some hold it was into this vast stand of ancient forest that Queen Béanore fled long ago rather than let herself be captured by the forces of Tharos. Erected at the command of the Tharosian Emperor Madiger during the—*

A great crashing sounded from above, and the ceiling shuddered. Lily let out a cry, and Rose dropped her teacup. It cracked apart on the table, letting loose a flood of tea.

"It's ruined," Rose said. She looked up, her eyes wide. "Is this the bad luck that the black storks brought?"

Ivy set down the broadsheet. "No, I believe this was brought by workmen, not birds. Lily, ask Mrs. Seenly to come clean up the table. I'll go see what Mr. Barbridge and his men have accomplished."

While Ivy had kept her tone light so as to not worry Rose, she felt some degree of alarm as she exited the parlor and hurried up the stairs. As she reached the gallery on the second floor, she found the air thick with plaster dust. Through the haze she glimpsed Mr. Barbridge and several workmen on the far end of the long room.

Mr. Barbridge bowed as she approached, his face and coat white with dust. Ivy saw a heap of rubble at the base of the wall and bare wooden beams. A discussion with Mr. Barbridge soon gave her an understanding of what had occurred. The men had been repairing the wall, removing the plaster where it was crumbling and then patching it. However, the wall had not been as sound as they thought, and when one of the workmen took out a piece of plaster, an entire section had collapsed.

"Do you know what made the structure so weak?" Ivy said, concerned that the entire wall would need to be rebuilt, and already tallying the cost in her mind. "Is the wood rotten?"

"No, Mrs. Quent. The beams in this part of the house are good and solid. It's not rot that caused the problem."

"Then what do you think caused it?"

"I can't rightly say just yet. Sometimes there are cracks too fine to see. Or sometimes it's something deeper than that. A wall is only so strong as what's behind it, you see."

These words did not particularly reduce her apprehension. Mr. Barbridge assured her that they would proceed with greater caution as they refurbished the gallery. Ivy looked around, hoping the room was not beyond repair. It was a large space with tall windows and handsome woodwork, and their intent was to make it the main parlor of the house—a place for gatherings and music.

Mr. Barbridge cleared his throat. "If you'll excuse us, Mrs. Quent, we'll be about our work, then."

"Of course," Ivy said, realizing she was in the way. She started to remove herself from the gallery, then paused. "Mr. Barbridge, did Mrs. Seenly speak to you about the birds in the north wing?"

"Yes, ma'am," the builder said. "My men will glaze the window. The storks won't be bothering you again."

Ivy thanked him, adding, "I confess, I'm a bit sad to have to force them out of a home. However, I am happy knowing I won't ever have to be disturbed again by the sound of their voices."

Mr. Barbridge frowned, the action drawing creases in the white dust on his face. "Their voices, Mrs. Quent?"

"Yes, I was awakened by them last night. The noises they made sounded almost like people talking. I will be relieved not to hear *that* again."

The builder shook his head. "I'm not sure what it was you heard last night, Mrs. Quent—I know better than most how old houses can make all manner of queer sounds—but, begging your pardon, it wasn't the storks you heard. Black storks have no voices, you see. I used to have a nest of them up in my own attic, so I know for a fact that they're mute, but you can ask anyone as knows birds. Now, if you'll pardon me." With that he bowed, then put on his hat and returned to his men.

Ivy was suddenly mute herself. No doubt Mr. Barbridge thought her a silly young woman alarmed by the natural noises of an old house. Yet it had not been creaking floorboards or settling beams that had awakened her. It had been the sound of voices whispering outside her door.

Only, if it was not the birds she had heard, then what was it? Ivy's head felt light. It was the dust; she had breathed more of it than was good for her. She turned and descended the stairs to the front hall.

And for once she was glad of the cloth that draped the knob of the newel post, so that its wooden eye could not watch her as she went.

CHAPTER TWO

YOU'RE TRYING TO force it again," Dercy said, his voice echoing out across the empty theater. The young man leaned against the edge of the proscenium and crossed his arms over his black jacket. "Remember what I told you yesterday. Light is like quicksilver—the more you try to grasp it, the more it will break apart and chase away. So stop trying to make a tree, because you can't make one. Instead, just *see* it."

"But I can't see it," Eldyn said, standing alone in the center of the barren stage. "I can't see anything. That's the problem—my mind is all dark."

Dercy's short blond beard parted in a grin. "Is that so? Then maybe we drank too much at the tavern last night."

Eldyn put a hand to his temple. "Or maybe we didn't drink enough."

But no, he *had* drunk too much last night. After the performance at the Theater of the Moon, which Eldyn had watched from a seat in the balcony, Dercy had dragged him to an unsavory tavern perilously close to the edge of High Holy.

The patrons there had been a rough lot. At first, given the hard looks he and Dercy had received, Eldyn had feared for their lives, but his apprehension dissipated a bit each time Dercy refilled their cups. Before the night was done, they were barely able to contain their mirth as flowers appeared in the hair of some pock-faced fellow, or a man with a murderer's look suddenly bore rouged lips and painted cheeks—all to the confusion of the others in the tavern.

By the time the source of these tricks was discovered, Eldyn and Dercy had already been on their way out. Dercy had thrust out his hands, throwing a flash of blinding light back into the tavern, and the two had fled into the dark, holding on to each other and laughing as they ran.

Now Eldyn's head throbbed from the aftereffects of overindulgence. Even so, all he wanted was to go to the Sword and Leaf and order a pot of punch. Why was he trying to do this anyway? He was a clerk, not an illusionist—as today had indelibly proved. For the last three hours he had attempted to evoke the illusion of a tree, but he hadn't made so much as a leaf appear.

Eldyn didn't know why he couldn't do it. He had mastered any number of small glamours—making a glass appear full when it was empty, or turning a rose from white to red. He had even achieved greater feats. After all, it was illusion that had saved him from a violent fate at the hands of the highwayman Westen. Eldyn had woven the light around himself, making him appear to be his sister, Sashie. Thus he was able to dupe Westen and lead the highwayman into a trap—and so to the gallows.

However, that had been months ago, and in the time since Eldyn hadn't worked a single illusion of any real significance—and certainly nothing worthy of being performed at a theater on Durrow Street. Each time he tried to envision a grand sculpture of light, all he saw was blackness. It was as if he stood behind a curtain, and no matter how much he searched and groped, he could not find the seam in its heavy folds.

Eldyn gave Dercy a weak smile. "I believe the only phantasm on this stage is the notion that I could ever be in a play. It's all right; I don't mind. You've been amazing to try to help me, but it's time I faced the fact that I'm not like you, Dercy. I'm not an illusionist."

At once Dercy's grin vanished, and he crossed the stage to Eldyn. "That's not true. You *are* an illusionist. If you weren't, how could you hide yourself in shadows the way that you can? Besides, wasn't it illusion that got us our drink last night? I saw you turn a copper penny into a silver half regal before giving it to the tavern keep."

"Yes, I can do those things," Eldyn said reluctantly. "But they're tricks, that's all. You told me yourself that it's easiest to make people see what they expect to see. But you're also the one who told me that conjuring a vision from thin air, shaping something out of light itself, is the real mastery of illusion." He gestured to the empty stage around them. Nothing floated on the air except dust. "And that's something I can't seem to do."

Concern shone in Dercy's sea-colored eyes. He opened his mouth as if to say something, then pressed his lips into a line. What could he have said? It was the truth. Eldyn shared something of the same power the Siltheri possessed, but it was a fraction, nothing more.

Eldyn regarded his friend. "I'm a clerk, Dercy. No, don't shake your head—it's true. And it doesn't bother me. After all, it was not all that long ago that I thought I wanted to be a lord, to reclaim the Garritt family fortune, and to sit in the Hall of Magnates like my grandfather did. Now *that* was truly a phantasm."

He couldn't help a rueful grin. Had he really been so artless as to believe that was possible—that the penniless son of a debtor drunk with a few drops of nobleman's blood in him could climb his way to the heights of society? Well, he didn't think about being a lord these days. His friend Rafferdy was going to be sitting in the Hall of Magnates soon, and that was as close to Assembly as Eldyn was ever going—or ever needed—to get.

"Then what exactly do you want to be?" Dercy said. He spread his arms to encompass the stage. "If not this, then what?"

Eldyn turned around. He looked at the rows of rickety chairs, at the cracked frescoes of nymphs and fauns and grape vines that adorned the ceiling. By day, the Theater of the Moon looked exactly like what it was: a cramped, shabby playhouse on the far side of Durrow Street. It was only at night that the work of the Siltheri turned it into a place of wonder. And even if he couldn't work those wonders himself, it didn't mean Eldyn couldn't still enjoy watching them.

He returned his gaze to Dercy. "I want to work and make a little coin for a change—real coins that don't turn back to copper after a minute. I want to improve my lot, and put away something for my sister's future. I want to see a play now and then." He reached out a hand and gripped the other man's shoulder. "And as often as possible, I want to go to tavern and get pissed with my most cherished friends."

Eldyn spoke those last words in a light voice, in an effort to dispel a little of the heavy atmosphere that had settled over the stage, and Dercy's lips did indeed curve in a smile. Still, there was a look in his eyes that Eldyn had seen on occasion—a look that seemed at once bright and regretful. Eldyn didn't know why Dercy gazed at him that way sometimes.

But Eldyn did know there was no point in indulging in any sort of regret. "I'm a scrivener, Dercy—an excellent one, when it comes down to it. I think it's time to stop playacting and be what I truly am."

"What if you're wrong? What if you don't know what you truly are?"

"I do know, Dercy. I'm a clerk. I work in the office of the rector of Graychurch, and let me tell you, the Church of Altania has more money than all the trading houses in Invarel."

Dercy took a step back so that Eldyn was forced to let go of his shoulder.

"You *think* that's what you are," Dercy said, his expression solemn. "Only you're wrong. Whether you ever set foot on this stage again, whether or not you ever work another glamour, you are an illusionist, Eldyn Garritt. We Siltheri always know our own kind. Once you know how to look for it, all it takes is a glance, and I knew it the first night I saw you outside this theater."

"Well, what use is an illusionist who can't work illusions?" Eldyn said. He tried to make a joke of it, but the words sounded flat. It didn't matter—he didn't want to talk about it anymore. Besides, he had promised Sashie he would be back by dark.

He told Dercy he had to go, but that he would arrive at the Theater of the Moon, if not in time for the rise of the curtain that night, then at least in time for its fall, and he secured a promise that they would go to tavern together after the performance. Reassured by his friend's willingness to commit to such a plan, Eldyn bid Dercy farewell. He left the dusky theater and walked out into the gold of late afternoon.

And if a few bits of shadow followed after, clinging to him as he went, then surely it was only from longtime habit.

THE BELLS OF St. Galmuth's were tolling by the time Eldyn approached the doors of Graychurch.

The lumenal had sputtered and extinguished even more swiftly than he had thought. Hadn't the timetables on the front page of *The Fox* said that the day was to be eight and a half hours? Surely he had not been at the theater *that* long. All the same, the sun had slipped behind the rooftops of the Old City, and in the thickening gloom, the appearance of Graychurch was well in accord with its name.

Situated no more than a hundred paces from St. Galmuth's cathedral, Graychurch was often forgotten in the shadow of the grander, paler edifice. With its graceful buttresses, its windows of lustrous glass, and the wings of its transepts spread wide, the cathedral seemed ready to leap off the ground, as if it were constructed not of stone and iron, but of air and light.

In comparison, Graychurch was stunted and hunched, its walls hewn thick and its windows cut narrow for want of flying buttresses, which weren't invented until long after its construction. Its beetle-browed portico frowned toward the street, and it was surmounted by a tarnished bronze dome like a dour hat on an old dame.

As if the smaller church were indeed so unfashionable, the cathedral angled away from it, turning a shoulder to its elder. Guided by a new understanding of the workings of the heavens, St. Galmuth's builders had aligned the cathedral with the four cardinal points. However, Graychurch had been raised in a different era, by men who still thought more of the history of the Faith than its future, and so they had turned the church's face not to the east, but rather south of west, toward the memory of Tharos.

That St. Galmuth's was inordinately more splendid and more beautiful, Eldyn would not deny. To tread beneath its lofty vaults was to stand beneath the foundations of Eternum itself. Yet for him there was a sort of elemental appeal to Graychurch. Perhaps it was because it did not seem like a thing built to inspire awe. Rather, it looked like a fortress: a place hewed to protect something fragile and imperiled and precious.

The last traces of color faded from the sky. Eldyn dashed up the steps, scattering a group of pigeons, and pushed through a heavy door into the dimness of the church.

He found his sister in the little apse off the chapel of St. Amorah, just as he had expected. Eldyn paused in the doorway, watching as she lit a candle on the altar before a statue of the chapel's namesake. The light bathed her face, so that it seemed as smooth as that of the marble saint.

Perhaps it was fitting the two appeared so similar. After all, St. Amorah was the patroness of unmarried women, and she was celebrated for her fabled beauty as much as for her legendary piety. Pursued by many eager suitors, the story went, she cast herself off a cliff rather than let herself be despoiled before she was married. As a reward for her purity, God reached down and caught her before she could strike the sharp rocks at the foot of the cliff and bore her directly up to Eternum.

Which meant it was *He* who had won her over all other suitors, Eldyn thought, and could not suppress a soft laugh at the notion. Sashie looked up at the sound, then saw him in the doorway.

"And might I ask what amuses you so, dear brother?" she said. "I can only suppose my bonnet is askew or I've blackened my nose with soot from a candle. Do I look so very odd, then?"

"In fact, you look charming."

Sashie smiled at him, an expression as beatific as any saint's, and set down her candle.

"I'm sorry I'm late," he said, entering the apse. "The day was shorter than I thought, and I spent more time than I meant trying to work a . . . that is, at my business. I hope you're not angry with me for leaving you alone for so long."

She gave a pretty frown. "Alone? I don't know what you mean. I am far from alone here. I have St. Amorah to converse with. And if she grows weary of listening to me, then there are St. Devis with his lamb and St. Vanrus the Younger in the next chapel over, and I find them to be amenable to long discussions of the most cheerful sort."

"Well, then, perhaps I should have delayed my arrival further. I'm sure you'll find my company dull by comparison."

"That's impossible. For there is no one in the world I'd rather see than you, dear brother."

She went to him, kissing his cheek. He was at once bemused and delighted. How often in the past had she rebuked him when he arrived past the hour he had promised?

Yet those had been different times, and he had left her in far different places than this—shabby inns or rude boardinghouses. Nor had she understood that it was for her own good he had done it. To Sashie, Westen had been only handsome, richly dressed, and mysterious. However, before the end, she had finally seen the highwayman for what he truly was.

Eldyn had never told Sashie about Westen's fate. All the same, news of the notorious brigand's hanging had been all over the city for a quarter month, and printed on the front of every broadsheet. There could be no doubt she had heard of his execution, yet she had never spoken of it. Nor had she ever mentioned his name since that night they fled to St. Galmuth's.

Now, as brother and sister walked from the apse of St. Amorah and through the echoing space of the choir, he listened as she spoke about how she had passed the lumenal at Graychurch. Brightday was approaching, and the verger had asked her to dust the niche of every saint along the ambulatory, and she had also polished all the brass in the chapter house. As always, Eldyn was perplexed—if pleasantly so—by her apparent relish for the tasks the old verger set for her. He could not recall her ever willingly dusting or polishing anything in her life before they came to Graychurch.

All the same, he could not complain. Between his work, his time spent with Dercy, and his occasional meetings with Rafferdy, he was often away. He was grateful he had no reason to be concerned with how she occupied herself when he was gone. Nor could he remember a time when Sashie had seemed so happy. Yet it was more than that. There was a modesty about her manner that he had never observed before; the capriciousness she had demonstrated so often in the past was nowhere to be seen.

As they walked along the transept, it occurred to him that this change might be credited to the wholesome influence of their present surroundings. Sashie had never known the benefit of a church prior to this. Certainly their father had never taken them to a service when they were young; drinking and whoring away the Garritt family name and fortune had been too consuming a task to allow any time for attending sermons.

Perhaps it was because Vandimeer had held churches in such disdain that Eldyn was so fascinated with them. As a boy, he would lurk outside the doors of St. Galmuth's, peering in and watching through the haze of incense as the priests worked their holy mysteries. For a time, he had even fancied he would become a priest himself—until he made the mistake of speaking aloud of his ambition. Which had been the graver blow—the hand across his face or his father's words—he could not say.

No son of mine will ever be a priest, his father had said. *I'd sooner break your neck.* He had uttered this with a kind of fierce glee, as if he might in fact relish the act.

Even after the world was rid of Vandimeer Garritt, Eldyn had continued to avoid setting foot in churches. He wasn't entirely certain why. Perhaps it was because he imagined his soul, haunted by the deeds of his father, was too tainted to permit him to enter such a sacred place.

Only it wasn't. He and Sashie had found sanctuary at St. Galmuth's cathedral that terrible night. And now, by a stroke of good fortune, it was to the Church that he owed his living.

Except maybe it wasn't luck at all. Maybe it was God's hand that had snatched them up and saved them, just as He had reached down to save St. Amorah from her precipitous fall. For three days after the night they fled to St. Galmuth's, Eldyn and Sashie had dwelled in the cathedral. Once free of Westen's power, though, there was no basis for them to apply for protection. Eldyn and Sashie had made ready to leave the cathedral, though where they would go, he hadn't known. They were all but penniless, and he had no work.

Yet even as he and Sashie moved reluctantly to the cathedral doors to make their departure, a white-haired deacon hurried up to them.

"Pardon me, Mr. Garritt," the deacon had said, "but is it true what I have heard, that you are a clerk by vocation?"

Eldyn was unsure what to make of these words, but he nodded and explained that he had indeed been recently employed as a clerk.

"It seems providence provides for us in our very hour of need!" the old deacon had exclaimed, casting his gaze heavenward.

He went on to explain that the priest who had kept the ledger over at Graychurch had recently passed from this life. Soon after, it was discovered that the old fellow, while a devout soul, had not been blessed with much ability when it came to ciphering, and the books were in great disarray.

It was a surprise to Eldyn that the Church had need of clerks at all. However, the deacon said that, while their attention was ever directed toward the next world, they yet dwelled in *this* one, and here there was much to be accounted for. Thus a clerk was required at once at Graychurch to put the ledger back in order, and if Eldyn was interested, he was to leave the cathedral, go over to Graychurch across the way, and present himself to the rector there.

Eldyn could only accept such an extraordinary and timely offer, though he wondered why the deacon would offer him such an important position when the Church knew nothing about his abilities or character. Even as he thought this, movement above had caught his eye. Up in the clerestory of the cathedral, he saw the tall silhouette of a priest before a stained-glass window, his hooded head bowed as if in prayer.

At this sight a feeling welled up in Eldyn—one as brilliant as the light from the window. Perhaps it was simply an act of faith, he thought. Nor would he betray that faith. That very afternoon he went to Graychurch to begin clerking. Thus Eldyn came to work for the Church of Altania.

And the ghost of Vandimeer Garritt be damned.

AS THE LAMPLIGHTERS began their work, Eldyn walked with Sashie the short distance to the place where they had dwelled these last few months: a slate-roofed building that was nearly as ancient as Graychurch.

In years past, the building had housed a monastery, but just as fewer people attended church these days, so, too, fewer people were willing to devote their lives to it. Thus the monastery had been converted some time ago into apartments to accommodate

visiting clergy, as well as to house some of the various laymen who
served the Church.

Even as the Church of Altania's congregations had shrunk
over the centuries, its holdings had grown at an ever-increasing
rate, thus proving that, next to the power of God, there was no
power in creation so miraculous as the mathematics of compound
interest. As a result, the Church owned a great deal of capital, and
many people were required for the management of its lands and
buildings.

Eldyn's part in this was small, being nothing more than the
keeping of the daily ledger at Graychurch—which, while an es-
teemed institution, was but a fraction as busy (or rich) as nearby
St. Galmuth's. He tallied income and expenses as he might for any
business, and if the income came in donations and tithes, and the
expenses were for candles and incense and bottles of sacramental
wine, the numbers cared little. They added and subtracted just the
same for holy purposes as for profane.

An apartment had been granted to him as part of his wage. It
was not large, consisting of no more than a sitting room attached
to one chamber of goodly proportions (which was Sashie's) and one
rather smallish (which was his). The bare stone walls and wooden
furniture were austere, but a lush Murghese rug covered the floor,
and there was a window looking out over the courtyard in which
a plum tree always seemed to be blooming.

Eldyn sat at the table in the main room and opened a leather
satchel full of papers. Recently, he had asked if he might be allowed
to bring some of his work home with him, as it was just as easy for
him to tally figures here as in the office of the rector. This request
had been granted, and so from time to time Eldyn was able to do
his ciphering in the apartment, which meant Sashie did not have
to be alone so much. He cut a pen, took out a bundle of receipts,
and in neat rows of figures recorded transactions for altar cloths,
silver goblets, and a stonemason's labors on a cracked wall.

As he worked, Sashie busied herself setting out their dinner.
The foodstuffs had been brought in by a woman he had hired.
Despite the many improvements in her behavior, Sashie still had

neither interest nor ability with regard to cooking. It seemed some
miracles were beyond even God's power.

Eldyn did not mind; they could easily afford the expense. He
made suitably pleased and amazed remarks as she set a plate of
cold roast pigeon and candied apricots before him. She smiled as
she sat with her own plate, and he set his papers aside as they took
their meal together.

Sashie looked pretty in the glow of the oil lamp; he was glad
the strain and worry of these last months had not pinched her face
or made her wan. However, he saw she wore the same plain gray
dress she had worn yesterday. Did she have nothing nicer to wear?
He could not remember the last time he had bought her anything
new.

"I do not think I'll be so very busy on Brightday," he said. "And
if *The Fox* can be believed, the lumenal is to be longer than this
one. I propose we go to Gauldren's Heights, to some fine Uphill
shop, and buy you a new dress."

She set down her fork as her blue eyes went wide. "Oh, but we
mustn't!"

He smiled at her apparent concern. "You needn't worry, Sashie.
We can more than afford it now. You can have any dress you like,
and a hat to go with it as well, if you so wish."

She shook her head. "But we can't buy anything, not on
Brightday. It's horridly wicked to touch a coin from dawn until
moonrise."

He could not help a frown. "Where did you hear such a thing?"

"One of the priests, Father Prestus, told me, and I am very
grateful he did. One is supposed to spend the whole lumenal in
prayer and reflection, and to engage in neither work nor merriment. To think, all this time I've never known. How awful I have
been! I've never thought a thing about buying this or that on a
Brightday. The angels must consider me the most wretched creature in the world!"

His frown ceased, and now his urge was to laugh. He was certain, if the hosts of Eternum wished to find a paragon of wickedness in the world, they would have many examples to choose from

besides Sashie. However, her distress was obvious, and he gave her a solemn look.

"I am sure the angels will not judge you ill for something you did not know. It wouldn't be fair of them, would it? And angels are very just. But are you certain about not being able to buy things on Brightday?"

"Oh, yes!" she said with great enthusiasm now. "The verger showed me the place in the Testament where it's written. It is a transgression against the Faith to buy or sell anything on Bright-day."

If that was the case, then Eldyn was certain the city was rife with transgressors, and come the full moon every market and shop in the city would be crowded with people happily stopping to make a purchase or two on their way to the Abyss. He did not speak these things. The Church, the saints, the Testament were all new to his sister, and their novelty no doubt imbued them with a power and mystery.

"Well, we'll go shopping another day, then," he said, and this seemed to appease her, for she smiled at him.

"If you wish it, sweet brother. Though really, I can't think of a thing to get. I already have everything I could possibly need."

She rose, kissed his cheek, and cleared away their plates.

Eldyn could only smile in return, though a bit perplexedly. How often in the past had she derided him for the poor state of her wardrobe! He returned to his ciphering as she wiped the dishes and put them in the cupboard. After a few minutes he lowered his pen again and looked up at his sister. She hummed a song as she worked, and despite her plain dress she looked quite lovely, her dark hair shining in the lamplight.

He still had every hope of seeing her well-situated in life, and he could only think that her new manner would make that task easier. What man would not be pleased to take a young wife who was both lovely and sweet?

Of course, his ideas of a proper suitor were more humble than he had once entertained. What portion he would be able to offer in exchange for her hand would provide little temptation for a gentleman who had an appetite for fine things. All the same, it was not inconceivable that a lawyer or well-to-do tradesman would consider her beauty and charm to be adequate recompense for a small dowry.

Still, even a modest dowry would take him some time to save on his wages as a clerk. He took up a bit of scratch paper and did some quick ciphering. He estimated their expenses, subtracted the amount from his monthly earnings, and then divided the remainder into a sum he deemed was the barest minimum he could offer as a dowry.

A feeling of gloom came over him. By his calculations, it would take him two years to amass the required portion. Two years! It seemed a long time off. Yet there was nothing else he could do. Besides, as far off as it seemed, Sashie would still be just twenty then—more than young enough to tempt any man except one who favored only the most tender of brides. And in the interim, he could perhaps hope for some small increases in his wages if the rector of Graychurch continued to be pleased with his work.

So there—all that lay between now and Sashie being well-situated was some time and toil, neither of which were things to be dreaded. Much work lay ahead, but despite that he could not help feeling pleased to know that his sister's happy future was well within his power to assure.

And what of his own future?

Eldyn gazed at the oil lamp on the table. With a thought and a quick motion of his finger he made the flame flare and twist, so that it took on the shape of a woman with long, fiery hair. The glowing figure danced upon the wick, moving in a flickering tarantella.

Crafting a small glamour such as this barely took an effort now. That much at least Dercy had been able to teach him. But it was a minor trick—not even enough to entice a person to enter a theater, let alone impress them once they paid their quarter regal.

Eldyn sighed. The lamp flame guttered, taking on its usual appearance, and he dipped his pen again in the inkwell. Then he held it above the page, not touching it to the paper. He recalled the day at Sadent, Mornden, & Bayle when he got his first position clerking, how a white-haired clerk had expired right before his eyes and was carted off, and how the head clerk had given Eldyn the old man's pen and seat at the table.

Was that all that lay ahead of him? Working as a clerk, totaling endless columns of numbers, until the day he fell off his stool and they pried the quill from his fingers to give to another, younger man?

The low tolling of a single bell drifted through the window, marking the first span of the umbral and the start of night prayers. It was at once a sublime and a mournful sound, and for a moment Eldyn was thirteen again, standing in the dark on the steps of St. Galmuth's, waiting for Vandimeer Garritt to return from some meeting, drunk and angry and as likely as not bearing scraped knuckles and a bloodied lip. How Eldyn had ached to go inside, to escape his father and the wretched hovels they dwelled in—to enter that world of ritual and light he glimpsed through the cathedral doors.

So then why didn't he?

The thought was as clear as the tolling of the bell, resonating through him. Since becoming a man, he had been consumed with the idea of restoring the Garritt family name and fortune. Only, such ideas no longer compelled him. He was free now—free of his debts, free of Westen, and free of his father's spirit. He could do anything he wanted. He could do more than merely work for the Church.

He could enter it.

This idea sent a thrill through Eldyn. That he might again take up a dream so long ago discarded was like discovering a lost treasure one had shut away in a drawer and forgotten. He was still a clerk, though, and he could not help tallying the columns for and against the notion.

For one thing, he would have to save a portion for himself, not just for Sashie, as one entering the clergy was required to pay a grant to the Church. That would require at least another year of saving, and he was already getting to be a bit old to start along the path to priesthood. Yet not impossibly so. Dercy was twenty-five, a year older than Eldyn, and his parents had given him to the clergy just two years ago.

Of course, Dercy had left the old church of St. Adaris after not much more than a year within its walls, drawn by the spell of the theaters on Durrow Street. He could not return to the priesthood now even if he wanted. Eldyn had never read the whole of the Testament, but he was certain there were passages in it that condemned what Siltheri did in far stronger terms than the spending of money on a Brightday.

Eldyn had been to tavern after enough performances at the theater to know the proclivities of some illusionists. That the things such men did with one another were sinful was a matter the Church had made abundantly clear. Not that the Siltheri seemed to care. And why should they? If one was already condemned for all eternity, then it could hardly make things any worse to compound one's sins. On the occasions at tavern when he had happened to spy a pair of illusionists off in some shadowed corner, engaging in kisses, the men had seemed to show no concern about the repercussions of their actions. Eldyn could only watch them in fascination, for they always behaved as if what they did was the most pleasant and harmless thing.

Only nothing the Siltheri did was harmless in the view of the Church, and that put another tick in the column against the idea. Eldyn wasn't a true illusionist—as his failures at that theater had proved—but he doubted the Church would make so fine a distinction between the small tricks he had done and what the Siltheri did onstage—or off.

Despite this, an excitement continued to vibrate in Eldyn's chest, as if his heart still felt the thrum of the bell. He could not believe it was impossible that the Church would ever have him. After all, no man was a paragon. It was not any one thing a man did that granted him entrance to Eternum or condemned him to the pits of the Abyss. Rather, it was the final sum in the entire ledger of his existence that mattered. And no one was better at making a column of figures tally out the way he wanted than Eldyn.

Besides, he was young; he had plenty of time yet to make sure the balance came out in his favor. Heartened by this thought, Eldyn dipped his pen again, blotted the tip, and bent over the ledger.

He had figures to scribe for God.

CHAPTER THREE

"I TRUST YOU will take this new responsibility seriously, Mr. Rafferdy," Lady Marsdel declaimed in a tone made loud for his benefit—and for that of all in the dining room. "When you take a seat at Assembly, it is not something you do to advance your own cause, but rather the cause of all Altania. This is not a party, where you are used to saying anything at all to claim attention for yourself. Instead, you would do well to sit quietly, listen to your betters, and think long before you stand and raise your voice."

Rafferdy set down his fork and regarded the speaker from down the length of the table. "If I am to listen to my betters, then I must necessarily listen to you, your ladyship. Therefore I will hew close to your advice, and while in Assembly I will endeavor to make myself as vapid, as unwarranted of notice, and as utterly without consequence as possible. In this, I am sure I will be the very model of a member of the Hall of Magnates."

Unlike her voice, her ladyship's frown needed no amplification for its force to carry the distance. "As usual, Mr. Rafferdy, your agreement is of such a nature that I am convinced you mean to do the opposite of all I have just advised. So I say again: this is not some pleasant social affair to which you are going. Taking a seat in the upper hall is a matter of real consequence."

Rafferdy was aware of all at the table directing their attention toward him. He was silent for a moment, and when at last he spoke, it was with that seriousness of which he had only recently learned he was capable.

"I have never thought, your ladyship, that there would be anything pleasant about this affair. If the weight I give this duty does not seem very great to you, it is only because I will not perform it for very long. I am not *taking* a seat in Assembly, as you know, but rather *occupying* it until my father can do so again himself. My only aim is to keep his space on the bench free from dust until his return."

Lady Marsdel went stiff in her chair. Her pursed lips suggested she was not convinced that Rafferdy's duties in Assembly would in fact be temporary. However, she could not say such a thing, for to do so would be to express something other than firm hope that Lord Rafferdy would soon recover.

As any stream when faced with a hill it cannot surmount must flow along an easier route, the conversation so turned in a less precipitous direction. Mr. Harclint, one of Lady Marsdel's surfeit of nephews, blinked his watery eyes and stated his belief that Assembly would have a great deal of work before it this year, what with the various ills that afflicted the nation.

On that point Sir Earnsley professed agreement, although it was plain that the bluff old baronet thought Assembly's labors would be likely to aggravate such afflictions rather than cure them. Lord Baydon, in turn, clasped his hands across the broad bow of his waistcoat and expressed his unwavering conviction that all of the acts passed this year by Assembly would be the most benevolent, the most prudent, and in general the most agreeable laws ever passed in the history of Altania.

"Well, I would be content if Assembly passed no acts at all," Mr. Baydon declared. "To be enacted, any law must be passed by both the Hall of Magnates and the Hall of Citizens. And these days, if the lower hall approves a thing, then it can only be mischief and tomfoolery. They would see gold bestowed upon traitors while loyal servants of Altania are taxed into penury. It would be better, Rafferdy, if you passed not a single law at all during this session rather than anything the citizens wanted."

Mr. Baydon reached to pick up his broadsheet; however, as none were allowed at her ladyship's dining table, he found only his napkin. He gave it a confounded look, then let out a sigh and spread it on his lap.

"Well, I for one am certain that any decrees our Mr. Rafferdy is involved in passing will all be very sensible by nature," Mrs. Baydon said, her blue eyes sparkling as she set down her glass of wine. "I have no doubt that soon all ill-fitting coats, scarves of garish hues, and dreadful hats will be outlawed from public view, and that anyone who commits the offense of being unfashionable will be taken at once to Barrowgate."

Rafferdy maintained his air of seriousness as he regarded Mrs. Baydon; or rather, he heightened it to the point of absurdity. "On the contrary, I would never do anything to impede the unfettered movement of poorly dressed people through the streets of Invarel. Instead, I will propose an act that rewards anyone with twenty regals if they can prove they have worn only the most awful clothes, gone only to the most tedious parties, and said only the dullest things in the past month."

This provoked a furrow upon Mr. Baydon's brow. "Why, you'll empty the exchequer faster than the king with a law like that! Every day there must be a hundred parties in the city, and what party isn't a gathering of outlandishly dressed people saying insipid things? Besides, Rafferdy, in your scheme, shouldn't it be the stylish people who get the twenty regals?"

"Not at all," Mrs. Baydon said delightedly, "for I see now the aim is to increase the throngs of the horridly clothed so that those who are fashionable will appear all the better. Is that not the case, Mr. Rafferdy?"

He nodded at her across the table. "You are always clever at fitting together puzzles, Mrs. Baydon. Besides, there is no need to pay those few who properly attire themselves. Being well-dressed offers its own rewards."

This comment elicited an outburst of mirth around the table.

The reaction might have pleased anyone else, but it left Rafferdy unfazed. The good opinions and approval of other people meant nothing to him—so long as he was assured that he had them.

"Well, you must be a very rich man, Mr. Rafferdy," Captain Branfort said cheerfully, "for no one is ever better attired than you are. I can't fathom how you march apace with fashion as you do. You must practice at it as a soldier practices his drills; and no doubt, for your efforts, you reap a great many of those rewards you mentioned—the admiring looks of young ladies being chief among them."

Captain Branfort sat to Mrs. Baydon's right, as he always seemed to these days. He was a ginger-haired man whose deficit of stature was offset by a surplus of energy. The captain was only a little older than Rafferdy, perhaps twenty-six or twenty-seven, but already a large number of medals and ribbons adorned his blue regimental coat.

Mr. and Mrs. Baydon had made the acquaintance of Captain Branfort during a trip to Point Caravel two months ago. Point Caravel was popular not only for its mild climate and picturesque views of the sea, but also for the numerous soldiers, sailors, and officers who were to be found there at certain times of the year.

Mr. Baydon had wanted to go to Point Caravel to escape a series of particularly long and hot lumenals that had plagued the city. However, Mrs. Baydon had confessed to Rafferdy that the presence of so many eligible military men provided an added reason to go, for it was her intention to keep her eyes open for any likely suitors for Mrs. Quent's younger sisters.

Despite these charitable intentions, it seemed Mrs. Baydon had decided to keep the one handsome, unmarried soldier she had found for herself. Recently, Captain Branfort's company had been recalled to Invarel from duty in the West Country. Since then, he had become a common fixture at Lord Baydon's house on Vallant Street and also at Fairhall Street.

Rafferdy gave a laugh. "I am not so rich as you presume, Captain Branfort. In fact, when it comes to attire, I would say you have the advantage. For you never have to labor over your wardrobe, deciding what outfit would win the most esteem. You simply put on your uniform, and your coat assures you more admiring glances than I will ever be so fortunate to receive."

"Would that it were so, Mr. Rafferdy! If only you knew how many scowls and grimaces my coat has won me of late. I fear in these times that not all of Altania is as civilized as Invarel."

Mr. Baydon made no effort to disguise his snort. "I would hardly call Invarel civilized these days—not when treasonous devils feel free to come and go as they please. If you had told me half a year ago that a band of hoodlums would be so brazen as to take powder kegs to Trawlsden Square and set them off beneath the cenotaph, I would have called you ridiculous. Yet they have gone and done it, and now I can only think that there is nothing they would not do to tear down the very civilization that has given them everything they possess and every freedom they enjoy."

While Rafferdy always made an effort to know as little about current news as possible, there had been no escaping stories about the recent tumult in Trawlsden Square. There had been a paucity of dire news since the Risings in Torland ended, so every broadsheet in the city had seized with relish the chance to blare stories about the incident upon its front page—though whether the act was described as villainous or audacious depended on whether one read about it in *The Messenger* or *The Swift Arrow*.

At his club, Rafferdy had seen a picture of the aftermath printed in an issue of *The Comet*. The vivid impression, created by an illusionist, had shown a heap of blackened, smoking rubble. It was all that remained of a monument to commemorate the Three Corners War, which ended several centuries ago with Hathard Arringhart taking the crown of Altania after his defeat of both the House of Rothdale and the House of Morden.

To this day, some historians suggested that it was the latter of those houses that had possessed the most legitimate claim to the throne after the last of the Mabingorian kings died heirless. That was certainly what Bandley Morden had believed when, backed by a ragged band of rebels, he tried to seize the throne seventy

years ago. However, the Old Usurper was driven from the shores
of Altania—with, according to popular legend, the help of the magician Slade Vordigan.

Despite his ousting from Altania, some had never accepted the
Old Usurper's defeat—folk in the Outlands, mostly, and especially
in Torland. In recent years, it had been whispered that Huntley
Morden had made an alliance with one of the Principalities on the
edge of the Murgh Empire, and that even now he was amassing a
navy with plans of sailing to Altania to seize the crown his grandfather had failed to win.

Rafferdy had no idea if those rumors were true, but they had
been enough to stir up acts of rebellion in the Outlands in the
past—and now here in the city. An anonymous letter published in
The Fox claimed the monument had been destroyed because it was
an emblem of the wrongful rule of the Arringhart kings and their
oppression of the good people of Altania. Not that the cenotaph
had been the only casualty, for Trawlsden Square had housed a
bustling market. The fact that a number of those same *good people
of Altania* had lost their lives in the blast seemed not to impinge
upon the sensibilities of the rebels or their sympathizers. Apparently being scattered to bits was just another way of securing one's
liberty.

Or perhaps it was simply that when the worth of a life became
so low, many had to be spent in order to buy anything with them.

"You ask why people would wish to destroy our civilization,
Mr. Baydon," Rafferdy said, his voice going low so that the others
were forced to lean over the table to hear. "A civilization, you
claim, that has given them every possession they have and every
freedom they enjoy. Well, perhaps the reason is simply because it
has not given them very much of either of those things."

This elicited a number of frowns along the length of the table;
another witticism had been expected. Mrs. Baydon gave him a
concerned look. Before she could speak, Mr. Baydon let out another snort.

"They are not slaves of the Murghs, are they? These ruffians were all born free men, and thus Altania has given them every-thing they could ever possibly want. Surely you're not being seri-ous, Mr. Rafferdy!"

Rafferdy drew in a breath, then let it out. "No," he said at last. "No, of course I'm not being serious."

Mr. Baydon appeared ready to expound, but his wife was the swifter. "Must we discuss such awful things at the table?" she said, affecting a pout that, given how perfectly and charmingly it was formed, must have been oft-practiced before a mirror.

"They are not awful things, Mrs. Baydon," Mr. Baydon said, di-recting a stern look at his wife. "They are important matters that lie before Altania, and you should endeavor to take a greater inter-est in them."

"No, you are right, madam," Captain Branfort said. He pushed back his chair and stood. "These are grim discussions for a pleas-ant evening. Yet you must know that all men enjoy battle as a sport, whether on the field of war, in the Halls of Assembly, or around the dining table. Do forgive us."

He made a smart bow, and Mrs. Baydon could not conceal her delight at the gallant gesture, nor Mr. Baydon his annoyance.

After that, the supper proceeded in a more benign fashion. However, as he picked up his spoon, Rafferdy could not agree with the captain's assertion that all men enjoyed battle. Rafferdy cared nothing for war, and it was his aim to neither cause nor engage in any sort of conflict during his time in Assembly. No, the only campaign that mattered to him was the constant struggle against banality and boredom.

Unfortunately, that was a battle he had chosen to surrender the moment he accepted the invitation to dine at Lady Marsdel's.

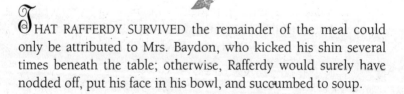

𝔗HAT RAFFERDY SURVIVED the remainder of the meal could only be attributed to Mrs. Baydon, who kicked his shin several times beneath the table; otherwise, Rafferdy would surely have nodded off, put his face in his bowl, and succumbed to soup.

Why had he come here tonight? He could have gone to his club for brandy and tobacco and gambling at cards. Or, better yet, he could have hired a carriage to take him through the dark streets of the Old City in search of less gentlemanly, though certainly no less satisfying, amusements—preferably in the company of Eldyn Garritt.

But it had been some time since he had accepted one of her ladyship's invitations. Declining another might have resulted in her wrath—as well as a letter of complaint to her cousin Lord Rafferdy. *That* was something Rafferdy must avoid. Besides, he had learned from Mrs. Baydon that another person, who he knew came to Fairhall Street with some frequency, would not be here tonight. And if *she* was not here, then *he* could be.

"I am so glad you are in town, Captain Branfort," Lady Marsdel pronounced after they retired to the parlor and were arranged to her liking—that is, where she could keep an eye on all of them. "Our society has been much improved by your presence. Things have been exceedingly dull of late. My nephews only ever seem to speak of some dreadful thing they have read about in the broadsheets, and Mrs. Baydon seems more intent on fitting her puzzles than on conversing in an interesting manner. I want for more young people to liven these proceedings, but I hardly know any these days."

"There is Mrs. Quent, of course," Mrs. Baydon said, looking up from one of those very puzzles, which she was piecing together at a table. "I am sure you enjoy *her* company."

"I would enjoy it better if it were more reliable! It is difficult to take pleasure in something that one cannot count upon. Mrs. Quent does not come here nearly as often as she is wanted." Lady Marsdel opened a fan decorated with gilt roses. "Nor have we seen Mr. Bennick for months. He left the city suddenly, and we have not had the benefit of his conversation since. As you can see, Captain Branfort, we have had a grave deficit of amusement until you arrived."

The captain bowed. "You are kind, your ladyship, but I cannot imagine a soldier's tales provide much in the way of entertainment. Besides, how could anyone want for amusement with Mr. Rafferdy about?"

Lady Marsdel waved his words aside with her fan. "I assure you, Captain, Mr. Rafferdy is not nearly so amusing as he used to be. He provides very little entertainment when he is here—not that he seems to present himself in my house with much regularity of late. In fact, if I did not know it was an impossibility, given his duties to this household, I would have thought that he was secretly avoiding us."

She delivered these last words with a sharp-eyed look at Rafferdy. In turn, he affected his most irreproachable expression.

"I promise you that is not the case, your ladyship," he said. "For I never avoid anyone in secret. Rather, I always make a great show of it. If I did not, they might forget me in my absence, and my purpose to make them feel deprived of my presence would be wholly frustrated."

Captain Branfort clapped his hands and laughed. "There! I need offer no other proof that entertainment is assured when Mr. Rafferdy is present."

"I will grant you that *some* still find him amusing," Lady Marsdel said, and this time her glance was for Mrs. Baydon, who had failed to convincingly conceal her laughter by means of a feigned cough. "However, if I ever had a taste for such drollery, I seem to have lost it. I would rather, Captain, that you tell us more of your voyage to the New Lands. *That* would be something of real interest to hear."

Sir Earnsley seconded this suggestion, and Lord Baydon added his agreement. So commanded by his superiors, a good soldier like Captain Branfort could do nothing but charge into the fray.

His mind preoccupied, Rafferdy paid scant attention to the discussion, and when Mrs. Baydon threaded her arm through his and pulled him away, he offered no resistance.

"Poor Captain Branfort," Mrs. Baydon said as they took a turn around the room. "Or rather, poor us. We won't get a moment of him to ourselves tonight now that my husband's aunt has possession of him."

Rafferdy felt the loss less keenly. "Perhaps it's good for you to practice sharing him."

She gave him a quizzing look. "What do you mean?"

"I mean, it was my understanding that you went to Point Caravel with hopes of finding prospective husbands for the Miss Lockwells. Yet when you do bring a soldier back, you appear intent on monopolizing him."

"I hadn't noticed that I have been monopolizing him in any way."

"Indeed, just as I'm sure you hadn't noticed that Captain Branfort is a strapping fellow who cuts a fine figure in his regimental coat. Though he is something of a dwarf."

She disengaged her arm from his. "He is no such thing, Mr. Rafferdy! I am sure he is half a head taller than me."

Rafferdy, who was tall himself, took pleasure in her indignation. Mrs. Baydon always looked prettiest when she was animated.

"In his boots, perhaps," he said. "But my point is proved. I knew you would come to the good captain's defense. However, you needn't worry, for I like him. He is stolid, modest, and honorable—all characteristics I admire and will never possess. I approve of him as I approve of drinking castor oil for the benefit of one's health, or tutoring orphans for the benefit of one's soul."

"You have never drunk castor oil or tutored orphans in your life!"

"No, but I'm sure I would be a much better person if I had." And he gave her a perfect imitation of one of Captain Branfort's bows.

Despite her evident annoyance, she could not help but laugh at him, which had been his intent, and after a moment she deigned to take his arm again. They walked onward a bit, then came to a halt beside the large figure of a sphinx that stood beside a fireplace.

"It's good to have you here tonight, Mr. Rafferdy," she said. "Do not heed anything Lady Marsdel says, for you are much wanted. There's such a surplus of gloom these days, what with all the news of rebels and outlaws coming closer to the city by the day, and your presence always enlivens things, even when you're trying to be dreadful. I do wish you would show yourself more often." Mrs. Baydon turned her blue gaze up at him. "Surely you know that *she* would be as glad to see you as I am on those occasions she is here. I have no doubt that it would increase her happiness."

"I am sure you are mistaken," he said. "For the last time I saw her, she was very happy."

He recalled the day Mrs. Quent had received him and Eldyn Garritt at her house on Durrow Street. Her joy had been apparent in everything she did and said, and in every green-eyed glance she directed at her husband. She had, he had thought, never looked more beautiful.

"Indeed, she was perfectly happy," he went on. "And since something that is perfect can never be improved upon, it is not possible that my presence could increase her happiness. Instead, there is only the chance it could decrease it. If one cannot help, but might possibly harm, what is the point in acting?"

Mrs. Baydon tucked a ringlet of gold hair behind her ear, and her nose wrinkled with a frown. "Whatever are you talking about, Mr. Rafferdy? *You* would never cause harm to anybody. You are quite incapable of it."

He thought of the tenants he had removed from their houses at Asterlane, after his father had enclosed his estate. "We are all of us capable of harm, Mrs. Baydon, even if we do not intend it." He made his tone lighter, not wanting to alarm her. "Ask the sphinx there if it is not so. I believe such creatures are said to tell only the truth."

"Is that so?" Mrs. Baydon moved to the figure that crouched beside the fireplace. It was hewn of pitted limestone that bespoke countless years of sun and wind. Its nose had been knocked off in some other eon, before it was pulled from the sands of the Murgh Empire and brought to Altania, but its lapis eyes were intact. They gazed forward, sad and serene, as Mrs. Baydon bent and whispered in a stone ear. She made a little play of tilting her head by its mouth, then rose and regarded Rafferdy.

"Well," he said, crossing his arms. "What doom did it pronounce?"

"It said, 'The man who does the greatest harm is the man who does nothing at all.'"

Now it was his turn to frown. "I am sure it said no such thing. Where did you get such a notion? Have you been reading from Mr. Baydon's broadsheets? I can't see how one might cause harm if one does nothing it all."

Her look was peevish. "I *have* been reading, and not from Mr. Baydon's awful newspapers. I've been looking at a book of Tharosian philosophy to improve myself. You needn't appear so shocked, you know."

Rafferdy hastily shut his mouth. "Forgive me, Mrs. Baydon. That's commendable. Certainly I have never occupied myself with so worthy an endeavor as reading philosophy. But be wary of placing too much stock in what the Tharosians thought. They all went extinct, you know, which means they couldn't have been so wise after all."

She shook her head. "No, you're wrong. Ancient things can have worth, even if the people who made them are gone. Like this." She touched the head of the sphinx. "It's so somber and mysterious. Looking at it makes me realize how much I don't know, and how much I wish I did know." She gave him a defiant look. "Besides, I believe what I read is right. We all have the power to do harm, as you say, yet we have the capacity for good as well. So if you never do anything, it is as if you are undoing all of the good things you might have achieved in your life. Think of the harm of *that*."

Rafferdy could only stare. He had never heard Mrs. Baydon speak with such passion about a topic other than puzzles or parties. "You astonish me," he said at last. "I can only think it would be better if it was you who was going to occupy a seat in Assembly. I have no doubt, of the two of us, *you* would do more good."

"And I have no doubt that you are mocking me!" she said, her cheeks brightening.

"Not in the least. In fact, I am certain you would choose better than most lords if you were to sit in the Hall of Magnates."

"A woman can never sit in Assembly, Mr. Rafferdy." She turned away from him, regarding the sphinx again. "So what use is there in reading and becoming wise? I will give the book back to Mrs. Quent the next time she calls. I should never have borrowed it."

Now it was Rafferdy who was a little bit wiser. He should have guessed from what source sprang Mrs. Baydon's desire to improve her mind. She was a clever young woman, but with a tendency to be impressionable.

All the same, her words unsettled him. He had felt a kind of noble pride for the way he had deprived himself of the presence of Mrs. Quent these last months. Each time he declined one of her invitations on the grounds that he was busy with his father's affairs—whether that was the case or not—he had told himself it was for her benefit.

Except as he looked at Mrs. Baydon, he thought that her ancient philosophers would not have agreed. What if, by staying away, he was denying Mrs. Quent and her sisters company that, however inferior to what they missed during Mr. Quent's absences, might still serve to entertain them and help pass the time until his return?

Even as he considered this, he knew it was not for *her* sake that he had been avoiding Mrs. Quent.

"My father has a figure just like this in his library at Asterlane," he said, brushing a hand over the sphinx's rough mane. "He and Lord Marsdel must each have brought one back from the Empire after they served there together, when they were young men in the army. I used to loathe looking at it as a boy. I felt it was staring at me, asking me questions I was sure I wouldn't know how to answer. I suppose it was at that."

Mrs. Baydon turned around, her expression now one of worry. "Have you heard any more news from the doctors?"

His hand slipped from the sphinx. "News? If it is news, then it is no more informative or cheering than what Mr. Baydon reads in the latest issue of *The Comet*. The only thing they know for certain is that it is a wasting malady. Each doctor who sees him proposes a unique remedy—not that these do anything except increase my father's discomfort. However, as I am given to understand the purpose of a cure is to be more unbearable than the disease, each physician must consider himself a skilled practitioner of medicine."

Mrs. Baydon did not smile at his jest. "I'm glad you went home to Asterlane last month, Mr. Rafferdy," was all she said.

Rafferdy was not so certain he could say the same. Had it come to him in a letter, his father's request could have been declined with the swipe of a pen. Seeing him had been different. Half a year ago, Lord Rafferdy had been on the verge of corpulence; now he was gaunt, his cheeks sunken and his fingers like gray sticks. When he asked Rafferdy to occupy his seat in Assembly for the time being, Rafferdy's every thought and desire had been to refuse. Instead, he had nodded and said yes.

The rap of a fan echoed across the parlor.

"I fear our absence has been noticed," Mrs. Baydon said with a sigh.

He gave her a look of feigned alarm. "Then we'd best return before she looses the hounds."

Now Mrs. Baydon did laugh, and she took his arm as they started back across the parlor.

"There you are, Mr. Rafferdy!" Lady Marsdel exclaimed as the two rejoined the rest of the party. "Whatever were you and Mrs. Baydon doing at the other end of the parlor? I cannot imagine it was anything important, and you have been needed here. No command I can issue seems to be enough to induce my nephews to cease their discussions of laws and acts and any other horrid thing they have read about in the broadsheets. You must convince them to speak of something else."

He shook his head. "If you cannot make them do as you wish, your ladyship, I do not know what power I possess to accomplish it."

"On the contrary, you have powers that we do not," Mrs. Baydon said with a smile that suggested mischief. She glanced at Captain Branfort. "We have seen Mr. Rafferdy work spells before."

"Is that so?" the captain said, raising an eyebrow.

"I was once induced by another, quite against my will, to perform some small parlor tricks, that's all," Rafferdy said, then gave Mrs. Baydon a withering look. "And as you know, that person is no longer in the city."

Nor, Rafferdy thought, would he expect Mr. Bennick to return anytime soon—not after what had become of his former cronies in the Vigilant Order of the Silver Eye. While Rafferdy had not entirely spoken the truth to Captain Branfort—he had, in the end, performed feats of magick much greater than a few tricks—it made no difference. He had only worked magick at Mrs. Quent's request and due to her grave need. Now that need was no more. He had spoken Mr. Lockwell's spell and reestablished the binding on the Eye of Ran-Yahgren. At this point, Rafferdy intended to never do magick again.

"Well, perhaps you should find yourself a new teacher," Mrs. Baydon said, not letting the topic drop, much to his vexation.

At this, Mr. Harclint sat up in his chair. "I should have thought of it before! Now that you are to take a place in Assembly, Mr. Rafferdy, you will surely make his acquaintance, for there is no one in that body who is more eminent. You must be sure to speak to Lord Farrolbrook at the earliest opportunity. I suppose he is in great demand, but it is said there is no one more skilled in magick."

"By all Eternum, not that subject again," Sir Earnsley exclaimed through a cloud of pipe smoke. "I had thought we were done with discussions of magick. I have had enough with these young men who fancy themselves to be magicians rather than take up proper occupations. It is nothing more than an affectation."

"It is no such thing," Mr. Harclint argued. "The ring Mr. Rafferdy wears proves it. A magician's ring, once it is put on, can never be taken off. You could tug at it all you wish, Sir Earnsley, and it would never budge. That is hardly an affectation." He gave a small sniff. "True, it is not the ring of House Myrrgon such as Lord Farrolbrook wears. But still, it is a ring of one of the seven Old Houses, which means Mr. Rafferdy is in fact a magician."

Sir Earnsley blew a smoky breath through his mustache. "Well, if that is the case, then I am most displeased. When you left university, Mr. Rafferdy, I thought it was because you had gotten some sense. Yet that cannot be if you are pursuing things as frivolous as magick."

"Magick is in no way frivolous, sir!" Mr. Baydon said, lowering a copy of *The Comet.* "Rather, it is the hope of Altania. The Quelling on the Wyrdwood was first worked by a magician long ago. So who else but magicians will be able to keep the Quelling in place and assure there are no more Risings?"

Sir Earnsley glowered at him. "So you are concerned about Risings now? I remember you speaking otherwise the last time I mentioned a word of warning about the Wyrdwood. As I recall, you termed it all superstition and codswallop. So now you believe me, I presume?"

Mr. Baydon tapped the front page of *The Comet.* "I believe this."

"And I believe it is time for me to depart," Rafferdy said before Sir Earnsley could offer another reply, "for I need some time before bed to digest both supper and her ladyship's advice."

In truth, it was this conversation he was having difficulty stomaching. It was wretched enough he would be forced to wear the House Gauldren ring for the rest of his life. He did not need to endure talk of it as well.

While he waited for his carriage, a plan was crafted for the day after Brightday, when the new session of Assembly would begin. It was decided Lord Baydon would come in his four-in-hand to retrieve Rafferdy at his house. With him would be Mr. Baydon, for he intended to observe the proceedings in the Hall of Magnates from the upper gallery. At this point, Mrs. Baydon announced that she was going to go as well, despite her previous assurances that nothing could make her attend such a dreary affair—a promise of which her husband reminded her.

"But it won't be dreary if Mr. Rafferdy is there," she said. "I hadn't considered his being in attendance. Therefore my earlier promise is null, for it was based upon the idea of there being no amusement to be had, when now I am sure there will be plenty. I will sit with you in the gallery."

"You do remember, Mrs. Baydon, it is the opening day of Assembly for the year," Mr. Baydon said. "The king is to give his annual invocation. It is a great occasion, and very popularly attended. There might not be room for both of us to sit."

"Well, if you must stand and sacrifice your chair for me, it is a small price to pay for something of such importance. Did you not stress earlier that I must endeavor to pay more attention to the affairs of the nation? I quite clearly remember you saying it. Don't you, Mr. Rafferdy?"

He could only concede that he did remember it. Rafferdy would never lie to prevent another man's discomfort—only his own.

"Then it is settled," Mrs. Baydon said, clapping her hands. "I will wear my green dress with the gold brocade, and I'll put on a blue sash—that should give me all the colors of the national banner. I will look very patriotic, don't you think?" She glanced at Lady Marsdel. "Will you be attending as well? You could wear your emerald damask, the one with the gold thread, and I have another sash if you need it. We would look very smart together."

"Here, here!" Lord Baydon exclaimed. "You will each be as fair as the island of Altania herself."

However, Lady Marsdel would have no part of it. Women were never permitted in the Halls of Assembly proper, only in the gallery, and then only for special ceremonies such as this. Her ladyship had no interest in any affair that relegated her to its periphery.

A servant informed Rafferdy his carriage was ready. He removed a pair of gloves made of gray kidskin from his coat pocket. Wearing gloves was the latest mode among young gentlemen. It was a habit Rafferdy had taken up the very moment before it became popular.

He bowed to Lady Marsdel, then to her brother beside her on the sofa. "I will see you soon, Lord Baydon."

"I am looking forward to it, Mr. Rafferdy. I am very curious to observe how you vote in Assembly."

"Then I am afraid your curiosity is likely to be disappointed. It is my hope to avoid voting at all, for fear of making a ruin of Altania if I do. I am no magnate."

"Nonsense, Mr. Rafferdy," Lord Baydon replied jovially. "You'll make for a fine young lord. Besides, I'm quite convinced you're bound to save our fair island, not ruin it."

As usual, Rafferdy did not share the elder man's optimism. How could he presume to vote on the nation's future when he could scarcely govern his own? No, Mr. Baydon was right. It would be better for all concerned if he did nothing, and helped to pass no acts whatsoever. Rafferdy bowed again, then took his leave.

Yet as he departed the room, he had the peculiar sense that ancient eyes of lapis watched him as he went.

CHAPTER FOUR

"THANK YOU, LAWDEN," Ivy said as he helped her step from the cabriolet. "You may return the carriage to the livery. We won't be needing it for the rest of the lumenal."

The driver bowed and uttered a barely audible word of assent. Lawden was a crookedly built man afflicted with an overlarge nose, and he was quiet to the point that Ivy could only suppose speaking was a difficult endeavor. However, he was adept at avoiding potholes in the streets, and she had always observed him to be kind to the horses. Thus Ivy could offer no complaint.

As Lawden drove off, Ivy tucked a book of Tharosian philosophy under her arm, pushed through the gate, and headed up the walk. She stopped to pat the head of one of the stone lions that crouched on either side of the door, then entered the front hall.

At once, the noise assailed her. A great amount of thudding

and pounding drifted from above, and the din was in no way ameliorated by the rumbling of Lily's pianoforte. Ivy followed the ominous sounds of music into a chamber off the north end of the hall.
In time it would serve as Mr. Quent's study, but while the upstairs
gallery was being refurbished, the room housed Lily's pianoforte
and served as their sitting room.

Rose occupied a sofa, petting Miss Mew. The little tortoiseshell
cat was wild-eyed from all the noise and looked as if she would
have bolted were it not for Rose's soothing touch. Lily's pretty oval
face formed into a glower as she labored away at the lowest keys.
Her music ceased as soon as she became aware of Ivy standing in
the doorway.

"Avast, who's there?" Lily exclaimed, then looked up with a
grimace. "Well, sink me, you gave me quite a fright, Ivy. What
with all the racket coming from upstairs, I didn't hear you come
in. I thought you must be a specter sneaking in to peer at us."

Rose looked at their younger sister, concern in her brown eyes.
"Why do you think there would be a specter here?"

"All old houses have specters," Lily said in an authoritative
tone. "What with all the people who have died in them over the
years, there are bound to be a few souls that stay around. Especially if any of the bodies were buried under the floorboards."

"Lily!" Ivy said, aware of Rose's increasingly alarmed expression. "This is hardly suitable talk."

"I'm just saying what's true."

"On the contrary, there's not a bit of truth to it."

"How do you know people haven't ever died here?"

"I suppose it's very possible that they have. I'm sure many generations have come and gone in this house, but that in no way
means there are specters here. When people pass, their souls go to
Eternum. Their spirits don't remain in this world."

"What about those who don't get to go to Eternum?" Lily said.
"The Testament says that not everyone goes there, not if they're
wicked."

"There is another place for the spirits of wicked people." Ivy
looked at Rose and gave her a smile that she hoped would be

reassuring. "The only place where specters exist is in the books Lily has been reading of late, which also concern princesses and pirates. As we have neither of *those* in our house, I'm sure we have no specters either."

"How can you be certain?" Rose said, holding Miss Mew tight and resting her cheek against the cat's mottled fur.

Ivy set down the book, then went to the sofa and sat beside Rose.

"Look there." She pointed to the fireplace. The mantel was carved with intricate designs, and in the center was one of the many eyes to be found throughout the house. The eye was shut now, but at other times it was open, watching them as they sewed or talked. Since the workmen had no reason to enter this room at the moment, Ivy had left it uncovered.

"Father placed many enchantments and protections on this dwelling. The house is always keeping vigil to make certain we are safe."

Rose hesitated, then nodded. "Sometimes I feel as if it's alive— as if it's watching us and listening to our voices, and noticing when we go from one room to another." She did not speak as if these were awful or alarming things, but instead with a fondness in her voice.

"Do you believe in spirits, Mrs. Seenly?" Lily said as the house-keeper entered the parlor with a tray.

Ivy felt a note of exasperation. "Lily!"

"It's quite all right, ma'am," Mrs. Seenly said as she set down the tray. "I don't mind her asking. Aye, of course I believe in spirits."

Lily gave Ivy a triumphant look, then turned her attention back to the housekeeper. "Have you ever seen one?"

"I can't say that I have."

"Then how do you know that they exist?"

"Well, how do we know that God exists, or Eternum?" She un-covered a plate of biscuits, then proceeded to pour tea. "Now, men of learning are very clever these days. They'll tell you that no one's ever measured a spirit's footprints or detected a change in the air caused by the comings and goings of a phantom. But we know in our hearts that even though some things can't be seen or touched, that doesn't mean they aren't real."

Mrs. Seenly spoke the words lightly, but all the same a clamminess crept across Ivy's skin. She could not help thinking of the whispering voices she had heard a few nights ago.

"Do you think there are any specters in this house?" Rose said with a worried look.

"Here?" Mrs. Seenly clucked her tongue. "Oh, I should think not, what with all the hubbub of hammering and pounding going on. If I were a spirit, I am sure I would want for a dark and quiet place. No, if there were ever any spirits here, they're sure to have all been driven out."

"Thank you, Mrs. Seenly," Ivy said gently.

"Of course, ma'am," she replied, and left the room.

Ivy was grateful for the housekeeper's cheerful words. An assurance that the house was free of spirits could only be more compelling coming from Mrs. Seenly, who was a woman of superstition, rather than from an elder sister who was known to be a skeptic. Indeed, after that there was no further talk of specters or phantoms as they took their tea.

As the sounds of work continued from above, a more musical sound drifted through the window as the bells in the church of St. Simeons chimed the arrival of the last farthing of the day. Ivy had been glad to discover there was a church so near the house, just down the street. She listened to the bells and waited for the sound of the mantel clock to join in.

The tolling ceased, but still there came no echoing chime from within the sitting room. Perplexed, Ivy went to the fireplace and examined the clock on the mantel. It was the very clock she remembered seeing in the house as a small girl. Its housing was of rosewood, inlaid with pieces stained different hues and shaped like planets and suns and comets.

The clock had three faces, each the size of a saucer. The middle face showed the hour like a usual timepiece. However, the left face depicted the phases of the moon, from Darkeve to Brightday back to Darkeve again, while the right face showed the progression from day to night. Ivy had loved watching this latter face the most as a girl, for on short lumenals the clock turned so quickly that she could actually see it moving: a black disk spinning downward to cover one of gold as day gave way to night.

Ivy had found the clock beneath a cloth when she and Mr. Quent had made their first inspection of the house, and she had been delighted to discover that, when wound with a heavy brass key, its gears sprang into motion just as of old, emitting their familiar, comforting hum.

Now Ivy frowned at the clock. "That's peculiar."

"Peculiar?" Lily said. "It's mad is what it is. I wouldn't be surprised if the whole ceiling came crashing down." She leaned over the table and slurped at her teacup, which she had made too full with a large dollop of cream.

Rose looked upward and bit her lip. "I think it's lower than it was a minute ago."

That wasn't what Ivy had meant. She had set the clock according to the almanac just yesterday. Now, while the church bells had struck the start of the fourth and final farthing of the lumenal, a bit more than a quarter of the gold circle still showed on the right-hand face of the clock.

She went to the hutch to get the almanac. According to the timetables, the last farthing today was to begin just after the ninth hour. Indeed, in the center face of the clock, the second hand had moved a little past the hour. So why had it not struck last farthing? Ivy sighed and shut the almanac. Perhaps the old clock was not running as well as she had thought.

She returned to her seat with the intention of looking over the copy of *The Comet* that Mrs. Seenly had brought with the tea, to see what news there was that day of the Wyrdwood. However, when she reached for the broadsheet, she found it was no longer on the tray.

"Listen to this!" Lily exclaimed.

Ivy looked up and saw that Lily held the newspaper before her.

"It says there is a new theater just opened on Durrow Street," Lily went on, "and that the viscountess Lady Crayford is known to have seen a performance by its troupe of illusionists. So do you see, Ivy? There's no reason we can't attend a play ourselves. It can't be wrong to go to a play if *she* went. Besides, we live on Durrow Street. We're hardly any distance at all from the theaters."

Ivy did her best to sound sensible rather than scolding. "We live on the west end of Durrow Street, not the east, and so we are no closer to the theaters than we were in Gauldren's Heights. Here, let me see."

She took the broadsheet from Lily and perused the article.

"I thought as much," Ivy said. "If you had bothered to read farther, you would have learned that the viscountess did not in fact go to a play on Durrow Street. Rather, Lord Crayford brought in a single illusionist from the new theater to provide an entertainment at her birthday party. Even so, the article says that a great number in the Hall of Magnates consider it scandalous that one of their peers allowed illusionists to enter his house, and a resolution of censure is being considered."

Lily slouched back in her chair. "I don't believe that's what the article says at all," she said, though she did not take the newspaper back. "And even if it is, who cares what a lot of dreary old men in Assembly think? Everyone says the viscountess is beautiful and thirty years younger than her husband. They say that he gives her anything at all that she wants, and that she's dreadfully fashionable. If she does a thing, you can be sure every magnate's daughter will be doing the same in short time."

"Well, as your father is merely a gentleman and not a magnate, I am certain you will not be following suit."

Lily crossed her arms and sank deeper into her chair. "How can I when Mr. Rafferdy never brings Mr. Garritt to call? I can't very well go see a play all by myself. *That* would hardly be fashionable. And I suppose now that you've gone and married Mr. Quent, Mr. Rafferdy will never come again. You've quite ruined everything, you know."

Ivy set down the broadsheet. "Is that what you believe, too, Rose? Have I made a ruin of everything by becoming Mrs. Quent?"

"No!" Rose exclaimed. "It's just the opposite. Everything is wonderful now. Isn't it, Lily? You must say it is. You must!"

After a great deal more cajoling on Rose's part, Lily was at last made to admit that their situation was indeed improved compared to what it had been dwelling on Whitward Street with their cousin Mr. Wyble, and that she did in fact adore Mr. Quent, even if he was decrepit and needed a new coat.

"Do you think Mr. Rafferdy will come to call soon?" Rose asked.

"We can hope so," Ivy said, "but we must not expect it. His work occupies him greatly."

Ivy had received a note from Mr. Rafferdy last month, apologizing for not presenting himself at Durrow Street more often. His father's health had worsened, he had written, and Mr. Rafferdy had been kept busy attending to Lord Rafferdy's business in the city.

Ivy had not heard again from Mr. Rafferdy since receiving that note, though she had gotten some news about him on the occasions she had been invited to Lady Marsdel's house. She also received reports from Mrs. Baydon, whom she saw with some frequency. Just that morning they had walked together along the Promenade.

Lily was chattering again about asking Mr. Quent for a new bonnet, and Ivy was thankful the subject of theaters had been dropped. However, her disquiet, while diminished, was not removed. The frequency with which her youngest sister brought up the idea of attending a play had increased since their arrival on Durrow Street. Ivy feared that one day the temptation to see a performance by illusionists would become too great for Lily to resist, no matter how unfashionable attending a play by herself might seem. And while a wealthy and popular viscountess might dare a brush with scandal and bring in an illusionist at her party for notoriety's sake, it would be a far more rash act for the daughter of a modest gentleman to go to a theater. If such a thing became public, it would irrevocably ruin Lily's reputation.

There was only one solution: she must be given something else to occupy her desires. If she could be offered something that was more likely to result in her encountering fashionable beings, and having herself counted among them, she would be drawn to it wholeheartedly.

Lily was sixteen now—it was not in any way too early. Ivy resolved to speak to Mr. Quent as soon as he returned, and to tell him that it was time Lily be officially introduced to society. A ball held in her honor would surely drive any thoughts of illusionists and theaters from her mind.

Ivy could not help feeling a pang of regret, for she had always hoped her father would be well enough to attend Lily's coming out affair—that perhaps he would be able to present her himself. However, there was no telling how long it would be until they obtained the writ from the king and won his release from Madstone's, and the matter of Lily's coming out could not wait.

Lily flopped on the chaise to read her book, while Rose picked up her poor basket and resumed sewing shirts. As her sisters occupied themselves, Ivy took up the copy of *The Comet*. Doing her best to ignore the thudding noises coming from above, she started to read an article about the exorbitant price of lamp oil, which was rising at a rapid pace. After a moment, her attention was caught by another item on the front page.

NOVEL HEAVENLY BODY IS BESTOWED NAME read the headline. With great interest, Ivy perused the article below.

According to the story, the Royal Society of Astrographers had recently convened to review all that had been learned so far about the red planet that had been discovered last year. While much remained to be understood about its properties and motions, the preliminary calculations suggested the planet would continue its approach—a hypothesis borne out by its ever-increasing brightness in the sky.

Such an important body required a name, so the Society had solicited suggestions from its members. After a vote, they had settled upon a name which, given their charter as the will of the king in all matters celestial, was now official. The name they chose was Cerephus.

Ivy frowned. She could not say she was pleased with *that* name. In Tharosian myth, Cerephus was a crimson-eyed cyclops who stole a magickal winged helm and used it to fly up to Mount Valos where the gods resided. His intention was to pelt them with stones—which he could turn blazing hot by means of his red gaze—until they admitted him as one of their own.

So assaulted, the gods relented and allowed Cerephus into their order. But they soon found a way to betray him by holding a feast in his honor and lacing his wine with lotus. As he slept, they took the winged helm, put out his single eye, and cast him down off Mount Valos.

Ivy supposed it was not just because of the red color of the planet that the astrographers had chosen to name it after the mythical cyclops. Perhaps, from their calculations, they did not expect the planet to remain visible indefinitely, but rather believed it would dwell among the other planets only for a time: a temporary peer in their heavenly assembly.

Regardless of the meaning or quality of the name, it was certainly exciting to dwell during a time of the discovery of an entire new planet. If only her father was capable of understanding what was happening. How fascinated he would have been to know of it!

Except, he did know about the new planet. Or at least, he *had* known before his malady befell him.

So, you have returned at last from your wanderings, he had said that night when Ivy found him gazing out the window at the red spark shining in the sky. What was more, his celestial globe, which now resided in his old study upstairs, had been engineered to accommodate the addition of a twelfth planet. Indeed, it was by adding a twelfth orb—a thing discovered in his old magick cabinet at Heathcrest Hall—that the mechanism had been unlocked, revealing the key to the house on Durrow Street.

Yet how this was possible, she still did not know. Her father had been ill for ten years, insensible to everything and everyone around him. So how could he have known about a world that no one had seen in all of recorded history until last year?

In the broadsheet was a drawing of one of the devices that had been used to observe the new planet. It was over twenty feet in length, and according to the article its ocular crystal was the largest and most flawless ever produced. In the drawing, several men gathered around the device as another peered through the aperture.

Looking at the picture, Ivy felt a sudden jolt of realization. Her mind whirled and spun like the wheels and spheres of her father's celestial globe. Were there not other crystals that allowed one to glimpse worlds from afar? In fact, there was just such an artifact upstairs, shut away in the secret room behind her father's study.

She had not removed the cloth covering the artifact since the day the magicians of the Vigilant Order of the Silver Eye had come to the house. She did not dare—not after seeing how merely peering into its depths had driven them mad. At her urging that day, Mr. Rafferdy had used magick to bind the door of the secret chamber so no one could enter.

All the same, she recalled the scene she had glimpsed fleetingly through the surface of the crystal globe: an undulating landscape beneath a livid red sky. Perhaps it was not so strange after all that Mr. Lockwell had known of the red planet ten years or more before anyone else.

Even as she considered this, her excitement turned into a chill. According to the article in *The Comet,* the most powerful devices used by the Royal Society of Astrographers could resolve Cerephus into no more than a hazy disk, its ruddy surface mottled with dark blotches. Yet the landscape she had glimpsed through the Eye of Ran-Yahgren had looked as near as a scene just outside a window.

It seemed impossible. However, an application of logic only reaffirmed what intuition told her: it could not be chance the red planet had appeared in the sky even as the artifact came to light in the world. No, there could be only one explanation.

The place she had glimpsed through the crystal *was* Cerephus. The newspaper quavered in Ivy's hands. She hastily set it down, lest her sisters detect her trembling. A ringing sounded in her ears, and it was only after a moment that she realized the loud clamor from above had ceased. After enduring the din for so long, the silence was as jarring as any noise.

"Is something wrong, Ivy?" Rose had looked up from her sewing.

"I'm just wondering why it's gotten so quiet all of a sudden," she said briskly, and rose from her chair. "I believe I had better go have a talk with Mr. Barbridge."

As it turned out, Mr. Barbridge had thought the very same thing, for she met him just as she reached the second floor. He had been coming to speak with her. The men had been working on the wall at the end of the gallery, he explained, but all had not gone well.

"As you'll remember, we put up new plaster the other lumenal to replace what had fallen down," the builder said. "This morning I looked and saw it was already starting to crack again. I knew there had to be something amiss, so we tore it all out."

Ivy could not help a wry smile. "So that explains what we heard."

"Begging your pardon, Mrs. Quent, I'm sure the din was awful, but it couldn't be helped. I knew there had to be something deeper in the wall that was causing the cracks. So this time we took out every bit of the plaster and then the lath and timbers behind as well, all the way down to the stone. And when we did, we found . . . well, I think you should come take a look."

Her curiosity piqued, Ivy followed Mr. Barbridge to the end of the gallery where the laborers stood in a group, tools idle in their hands. She saw that a large section of the wall had indeed been stripped all the way to rough reddish stone.

But this was all to be expected. She started to ask Mr. Barbridge what was so remarkable, but before she could speak the builder motioned his men aside. Then words were beyond her.

A door stood in the stone wall. It was hewn of dark wood, with deep-set panels and thick scrollwork, and was framed by turned columns and crowned with a triangular lintel. The door looked very solid and heavy. Ivy drew closer, marveling at the unexpected sight.

"It was covered over at some point," Mr. Barbridge said. "However, the lath wasn't nailed into it and had pulled away, causing the wall to sag. That's why the plaster kept cracking. But you've no cause to worry, Mrs. Quent. The stone couldn't be more sound, and we'll rebuild the facing. The wall will be as good as new by the time we're done."

Ivy told him she had no doubt that it would be. "Yet how odd that there was ever a door here," she said. She pictured the room on the other side of this wall, which she knew to be a bedchamber. "I'm certain there's no door in the room on the opposite side."

Mr. Barbridge agreed. They had already completed the repairs in that room and had found no trace that there had ever been a door.

"But then why would there be a door on *this* side?"

Mr. Barbridge shook his head. "I've seen some curious things in the course of my work, Mrs. Quent—cellars no one knew about until a floor fell in, or whole rooms that had been walled in and lost, with tables and chairs and plates all set out as if for supper. Old houses have peculiar histories, and this house is older than many, I would guess."

These words sparked Ivy's curiosity. "How old do you think it is?"

"I can't say for certain. I'm baffled as to what quarry provided the blocks for this house. It's not like any other stone I've ever seen. But from the style of the masonry, I'd say the house was built at least three hundred years ago." The builder laid a hand on the ruddy stone. "By the looks of it, this was once the outer wall of the house. The north wing must have been built at a later time, abutting the other side."

The builder's logic was sound. Yet even if this had been an outer wall at one time, that hardly explained the presence of a door on the second floor, unless perhaps there had once been some sort of balcony on the other side. But given its solid look, it hardly appeared like the sort of portal one might expect to open onto an airy veranda. Rather, it looked like a door meant to shut out the harshest of elements.

As Ivy stepped nearer, she saw that what she had taken for a kind of scrollwork in the panels was in fact a pattern of interlocking leaves and vines. She brushed the dust from one of the leaves. It was carved with exquisite care, so that she could even make out the tracery of veins in its surface. The wood was still rich beneath a thick coat of varnish.

"What an extraordinary thing," she said.

"As I mentioned, you needn't have a worry, Mrs. Quent," Mr. Barbridge said, perhaps mistaking her wonder for alarm. "Once we've rebuilt the wall, you won't see any trace of the door."

"No," she said, turning toward the builder. "I can't imagine why such a beautiful thing was ever covered up in the first place, nor do I think it should be hidden again."

The builder scratched his dusty beard. "Are you certain, missus? It is very pretty, I grant you, but it has no use anymore. You can see for yourself if you open it. There's nothing but blank stone behind."

She smiled at him. "If it is pretty to look upon, then that is use enough. The door will make a fine piece for conversation. As this room is meant to be a place for gatherings and social affairs, it could serve no better purpose than to induce curiosity and comment."

The builder nodded and assured her all would be done exactly as she wished. Ivy thanked him, then left the men to their work.

As she descended the stairs, she ran a hand along the banister. Three hundred years! That was how old Mr. Barbridge thought the stonework was. It was another clue to the age of the house. As the refurbishment continued, what other pieces of evidence might come to light?

There was no telling. However, Ivy had no doubt that there were more marvelous things waiting to be discovered. Nor could she wait to share that day's finding with Mr. Quent when he returned at the end of the month.

CHAPTER FIVE

ELDYN DIPPED HIS pen, then scribed another row of evenly spaced figures in the ledger before him.

"Never have I seen such worldly matters recorded in so heavenly a fashion!" Father Gadby, the rector of Graychurch, declaimed as he peered over Eldyn's shoulder. "I have seen hymnals illuminated by monks, with all manner of flourish and ornament, that hardly looked more beautiful than your accounts of daily receipts and demands, Mr. Garritt."

Eldyn smiled, though he did not look up from his work. "I simply try to do the best that I can, Father."

"So you do, Mr. Garritt, and there are many that could benefit from your example." He ran a hand over his pate to smooth his gray hair, of which there was little left, for as a result of being frequently fussed with for want of growing in the right direction, most of it had given up growing altogether. "It is a tribute to God to use all of the talents that He in His benevolence has granted you. But you hardly need me to tell you that! I can see by every stroke of your pen that you know it in your heart."

The rector returned to his desk on the other side of the long room, moving delicately, despite his considerable circumference, on a pair of small feet. There he busied himself with rearranging books and papers that had already been gathered into tidy stacks.

Eldyn took the last slips of paper from the wooden box to his left, then shifted the ledger on the table, the better to catch the light that fell from the windows high above. He glanced up, and through the rippled glass he could just make out the shadows of boots and shoes and the hems of dresses passing by. Eldyn didn't mind working below the church. It was quiet, and even on the afternoons of a long lumenal it stayed cool. While the lofty vaults of the church above inspired, the thick walls offered a quiet comfort.

True, if he went lower down, he would find those whose bodies would never leave their silent sanctuaries of stone, for below these rooms were the crypts. These were said to extend for level after level, as the church had been built upon the ruins of holy edifices even more ancient than itself. However, that thought did not trouble Eldyn. He had never had a fear of the dead.

As a boy, he had liked the tranquillity of graveyards. There had been an old burial yard not far from the house at Bramberly, where they had dwelled in the days before his father had squandered the last of their money. Sometimes Eldyn would venture across the field to the burial yard and lie down before one of the headstones. There he would shut his eyes and fold his arms over his chest, pretending to be at eternal repose.

Until such time as his father would find him and threaten to send him to the grave for real if he did not get up.

Eldyn began another page. Scribing figures was in no way so wondrous as working illusions, yet the acts were not entirely dissimilar. He was still conjuring a thing that had never existed before, though he used ink and paper to do so rather than light and air. As he worked, the sunbeam falling from above turned a deeper shade of gold. Perhaps the rector was right; perhaps God was indeed happy when one used one's talents.

Or was that really so? Eldyn had no great ability for illusion. But if he had, would God have been happy if he had used *that* talent?

Eldyn couldn't think so. Recently, he had spent some time looking at a copy of the Testament that he had purchased new despite the expense. If Eldyn applied to become a priest, he imagined the first question he would be asked was if he had ever read the whole of the Testament, and he wanted to be able to answer in the affirmative. Thus he had gone through several chapters while Sashie was asleep.

He was not entirely sure what he thought of the Testament yet.

Some of it read like the most beautiful story, while other parts of it made little sense, being about the dealings of cherubim and seraphim and other strange celestial beings. He did not mind those sections, though there were a few passages he had found unsettling. These described the fate that awaited those who defied God's will and, after death, were thrown into the pits of the Abyss to suffer torment for all of eternity.

It seemed to him an exceedingly severe punishment for misdeeds that were, in this imperfect world, exceedingly easy to commit. While nothing Eldyn had read so far had included specific proscriptions against the practice of illusion, he had heard enough over the years to know they were in there, only waiting for him to turn to the right page.

Yet it made no sense. If God did not want a man to use a talent such as illusion, then why give it to him? Eldyn twirled the quill in his hand, thinking. Perhaps God had given people the ability to commit sins because a man could only truly be good if he freely chose to be so. Not that it mattered; he wasn't going to be an illusionist anyway.

But Dercy was one.

The gold light faded, and Eldyn looked up. The high window had gone gray; the middle lumenal was nearly finished. However, he was far from finished with his work, so he returned his attention to the ledger. He had told Dercy he would attend the performance at the Theater of the Moon that night, and Eldyn didn't want to disappoint him. Perhaps it was because he knew he was soon bound to disappoint Dercy in other matters.

He had not yet told Dercy about his plan to enter the priesthood. Fortunately, over the last few days, Dercy had not mentioned anything about Eldyn's failure to work real illusions. Nor had Dercy pressed him to try again, which was just as well, as he had work enough to occupy him.

Eldyn opened another wooden box of receipts and dipped his pen, then continued entering figures in the ledger, recording the purchases of surplices, altar covers, and hymnals. The actions of angels and seraphs might be a mystery, but the behavior of numbers was well known to him, and they aligned themselves in orderly rows as he worked.

❧

 HE MOON WAS rising above the spires of St. Galmuth's by the time Eldyn left Graychurch. The curtain of the Theater of the Moon would be rising as well by now. Yet if he was quick about it, he would still be able to catch the last half of that night's performance.

His plan was thwarted upon entering the apartment, for Sashie was in high spirits and wished to tell him about everything she had done for the verger that day. Nor could he help but indulge her, given how cheerful she was, and how many kisses she lavished upon him when he entered. So he listened to his sister chatter as they ate a cold pork pie.

At last all her excitement wearied her, for she began to yawn, and at his gentle yet persistent encouragement she retired to her room. As soon as her door shut, Eldyn made himself ready for the night.

He put on his coat of gray velvet—he had two coats now, one for daily wear and one for evenings out—then paused before a small mirror to arrange his hair. It still fell to his shoulders in a dark tumble, even though he could afford to have it cut more often. Dercy had told him to leave it long, that it would look more dramatic onstage.

Well, there was no point in *that* anymore. Tomorrow he would get it cut. For the moment he tied it back with a black ribbon. He shut the door quietly behind him, then locked it. In the past he would have made sure there was no key inside so that Sashie could not escape. These days he was not worried about such things. For where would she go besides Graychurch, and what harm could come to her there?

The moon was well into the sky by now, and Eldyn moved quickly, walking in the direction of High Holy. Usually he took care to avoid that area, for if the Old City was home to Invarel's thieves and beggars and whores, then High Holy was home to its most ruthless thieves, its most wretched beggars, and its most vulgar whores. However, it was the shortest route to Durrow Street.

High Holy took its name from the rise on which it was situated, and which was crowned by an abandoned chapel. It was said the Church of Altania still owned the land beneath High Holy. If that was so, Eldyn wondered why such profligate behavior was allowed to flourish there. Yet as he now knew, the Church owned lands all over Altania; it could not possibly maintain order on them all.

Howls of laughter rang out just ahead. Or were they moans? Eldyn thickened the shadows around himself and hurried down dank lanes. Cloaked by darkness, he passed unmolested—though from some of the sounds he heard, that was not the case for everyone.

He reached the Theater of the Moon just as people were spilling out of the entrance. Some of them affected a blissful expression, while others frowned or wore a puzzled look.

The Theater of the Moon was not the most popular theater on Durrow Street. Unlike in the other theaters, the illusionists here did not work glamours out on the street to draw people inside. Nor did the audience always seem to understand the play, in which a silvery youth, an avatar of the Moon, was eternally pursued by the fiery Sun King. Some nights the audience cheered the youth and booed the king at every turn, while other nights they sat in silence or became surly and shouted insults at the stage.

No doubt the theater would have pulled in larger crowds and greater receipts if it changed its play to a salacious caper involving leering satyrs and buxom nymphs. However, Madame Richelour had no interest in such productions.

"It is our work to conjure beauty," the owner of the theater had said on the first occasion Eldyn met her. "Let the Theater of Emeralds or the Theater of Fans fill their stage with tawdry tricks and their house with imbeciles."

"Let them fill their coffers with gold regals as well," Dercy had said to Eldyn quietly, grinning.

He was only making a jest. With his talents, Dercy could have found a place in the troupe at any theater. Instead he had chosen the Theater of the Moon, and Eldyn understood why. It was small and rather dilapidated, and the visions of light wrought upon its stage were not so grand or lurid as those crafted at other houses on Durrow Street. However, while not everyone cared for the illusion play about the Sun and Moon, those who did loved it with all their being. Just as Eldyn did.

He moved past the patrons into the dimness of the theater and approached the curtain of frayed crimson velvet. All theaters on Durrow Street had red drapes before their stages, Eldyn had noticed. When he mentioned this, Dercy had told him it was because red was the only color that could fully block out illusory light. Thus, by using curtains of that hue, the theaters could make certain that audiences did not inadvertently get a glimpse of any illusions until the players were ready and the curtains parted.

While the curtains might have kept illusions from passing outward, they could not prevent Eldyn from passing in, and he slipped through a part in the drape, onto the stage.

"Did you see me?" Dercy said, catching Eldyn's arm at once. He had changed out of his costume, but there were still flecks of silver around his nose and eyes. "I was marvelous tonight."

"If you do say so yourself," Eldyn replied. "But I fear I was delayed and only just arrived, so you'll have to grant me a repeat performance."

"That can be arranged," Dercy exclaimed. "*'Though I might be charred / to a cinder dark and dead / to shine forth anew / I need only turn my head.'*"

"I believe your head has indeed turned," Eldyn said with a grin.

Dercy was not the only one still filled with the energy of that night's production. All of the young men onstage shared in his liveliness as they talked and laughed, some still dressed to evoke stars or comets.

Eldyn could not help laughing along with the actors. He could feel the power that still lingered in the air of the theater. It brushed his skin like flakes of snow, at once causing a shiver and provoking a flush of warmth.

"Come on," Dercy said. "I'm thirstier than should be allowed by law, and I imagine you are, too. I can see the ink on your fingers. Hard at work this evening, were you?"

Eldyn confessed he had been.

"Then let us get to tavern quickly. These others can catch up to us—or try to, that is!"

Dercy led the way back through the theater and out onto the street. As they went he spoke of that night's performance: how he had been able to perfect the silver shimmer of his aura, and how the illusions had come easily to all of them that night, as they always seemed to when the moon was near its full.

All the theaters had let out their audiences, and Durrow Street was crowded. Some men slunk away, hats pulled low, while others walked boldly, clad in their richest attire. There were even women to be seen, most of them as painted as any illusionist. All of them were accompanied by gentlemen who had brought—and perhaps had bought—them here. But just because a lady held the arm of one fellow did not mean her gaze might not embrace another, and many of the women cast lingering looks at the two young men as they went. For their part, Eldyn and Dercy ignored all such glances and instead walked merrily down the street, linked arm in arm.

As they passed before the entrance to the Theater of the Doves, someone called out Dercy's name. They looked up to see an illusionist fluttering toward them, still clad in his feathery costume. The thick layer of powder on his face had cracked, accentuating rather than concealing the deep lines by his mouth and eyes. He was certainly past fifty, which made him one of the oldest Siltheri that Eldyn had ever seen.

"What is it, Gerivel?" Dercy said as the other reached them. "Forgive my saying, but you look a bit ruffled tonight."

"Well, if so, I should think I have good cause!" The older man smoothed the feathers sewn on his sleeves. "We were short an illusionist tonight."

"Short an illusionist?"

"Yes, Mondfort is still unable to perform. Indeed, he was not able to leave his chamber tonight, and of course Bryson insisted on staying with him, as he always does."

Dercy's smile faded. "I'm sorry to hear that. I hope Mondfort will be well enough to return to the stage soon. He is a great performer."

"Oh, the greatest! We all wish for his swift return, of course. But if he ever will be able to go onstage again . . ." The plumed epaulets of Gerivel's coat lifted in a shrug. "Well, only time will tell. In the meantime, the performance must go on, and it was no small feat tonight."

"Do you not keep two understudies?"

"Of course we do! Do you think us imprudent? But it was not only Mondfort and Bryson we were missing tonight. We were without Donnebric as well, and so I was forced to take on another role. I already play two, mind you, but there was no one else who could do Bryson's role without practice. I was the only one, as I used to do it myself. So I had no choice. Above all, the play. Yet I tell you, I am enervated beyond all reason."

Indeed, the illusionist looked weary. Again he smoothed the feathers on his arms, and Eldyn saw how his hand trembled as he did. Dercy appeared to notice this as well, and when he saw their attention Gerivel quickly crossed his arms, tucking his hands beneath.

"So where is Donnebric?" Dercy said, arching an eyebrow.

"I was hoping you would tell me! That young libertine is gifted, I grant you, but he has yet to develop proper respect for the craft. To miss a performance with no word or explanation is a betrayal of the troupe! I suppose he will offer some excuse, though. He always does."

"When did you see him last?"

"Earlier in the lumenal. He was leaving in a carriage, off to the New Quarter for a private performance at the house of a magnate. I cannot say whose house, though—we are forsworn to be silent."

"Or paid to be silent, you mean," Dercy said with a grin.

Once again Gerivel shrugged, as if to say there was no difference. "Well, even if I wished to tell you, I could not. We worked through an intermediary who arranged everything. Regardless, Donnebric was supposed to be back well before the play, but he still has not returned. I know you two used to run about together. Have you seen him?"

"We had a few drinks together at tavern once or twice," Dercy said flatly. "That's all. And no, I haven't seen him. Have you spoken with this agent of your nameless magnate?"

"Of course," Gerivel said indignantly. "According to him, Donnebric departed the house of the patron in question hours before nightfall. Where he went next is unknown. All that is known is that he left in the company of a priest in a red cassock."

Dercy laughed. "A priest in a red cassock, you say? Illusionists and clergy at the same time—this magnate keeps peculiar company. Well, if Donnebric left with a priest, I don't imagine he can get into too much trouble. Though a few of the priests I knew at the Church of St. Adaris seemed determined to battle sin by becoming well versed in it."

The old illusionist gave him a sour look. "Now is not the time for jests, Dercent. I am seeking help."

Dercy's laughter was extinguished at once. "Of course. If I see Donnebric, I'll let him know you're looking for him."

"That is all I ask," Gerivel said. He gave an overdramatic bow, then returned to the door of the theater, vanishing within.

Eldyn regarded his friend. "I thought only people you didn't like called you Dercent."

"You thought right. Now I'm doubly glad I didn't apprentice at the Theater of the Doves. The conniving old slag—he wants Mondfort's place, that's clear enough."

Eldyn looked at the darkened door of the theater. "Who is Mondfort?"

"He's the master illusionist at the Theater of the Doves. I met him once. He's brilliant. He can transform the whole stage into a garden or a cloudscape with a twitch of his finger—or could, at least. Gerivel doesn't have half his talent. He can scheme all he wants, but he'll never be master at this or any theater. Now come on, let's get a drink."

"What of your friend Donnebric?"

Dercy laughed. "I wouldn't call him my friend! Nor was I his. For, as I discovered, all he wants in a friend is a place to plant his boot while he climbs a step higher. Only by standing upon me, he could not reach anyone wealthy or powerful enough for his liking. Once he discovered that, he ignored me—much to my relief. I have far superior companions!"

With that he took Eldyn's arm, steering him toward a tavern beyond the last of the theaters, and Eldyn was led willingly.

THEY WERE ALREADY on their second pot of punch by the time more performers from the Theater of the Moon arrived. There were illusionists from other houses as well—from the Theater of Dreams, the Theater of Veils, and the Theater of Mirrors. Laughter erupted, cups went around, and soon the Siltheri were putting on an impromptu play.

It was mostly incomprehensible to Eldyn, as the players were constantly changing their forms. First they were Tharosian legionaries and woad-painted barbarians enacting a battle, then shaggy wolves and bleating sheep engaging in a fierce dance. But no matter how little sense it made, the regular patrons of the tavern applauded enthusiastically at every turn. Few of them would have been able to afford to go to a theater, and so they were more than glad to have the theater come to them. And drinks were freely handed to all of the performers—which was no doubt the purpose in giving a show.

Yet, while the illusions were amazing, somehow the shimmering lights and raucous laughter were too much for Eldyn that night. He wanted a more dim and quiet place. Sensing his friend's need, Dercy led him to a booth in the back of the tavern. From there they could watch the illusionists without being caught up in the wild phantasms they conjured.

"Damn Siltheri," Dercy said, shaking his head. "They craft illusions all evening for money, then for fun they go and give them away for free."

"I think it's marvelous," Eldyn said, watching as a handsome young illusionist opened a door in his tall wig to let a flock of sparrows fly out. "They do it because they love to do it. Besides, what harm can there be in it?"

There was an expression on Dercy's face that Eldyn couldn't quite describe. It was thoughtful, but there was a sadness to it as well.

"They are beautiful fools," he said, then filled their cups again.

Eldyn sipped his punch. Despite his pleasure at being with his friend, he could not help feeling a note of sadness himself. Would that he could conjure such visions of delight and amusement as the illusionists did!

Well, he had other abilities. And even if he could not work grand illusions, there was nothing to stop him from paying a quarter regal to see them—at least until he entered the priesthood. Besides, as long as Dercy was his friend, he was bound to encounter illusions every day. This thought buoyed his spirits as much as the punch.

Applause rang out. The Siltheri in the wig bowed, then sat and gladly accepted the cup that was placed in his hand.

"So what does *Siltheri* mean anyway?" Eldyn said, asking a question he had often wondered. "It's a peculiar word."

"It comes from ancient Tharosian." Dercy flashed a grin. "Or so I'm told, as I'm no scholar. It means *the concealed,* and it was the name illusionists took for themselves long ago, back when their craft was as likely to get them an audience with an emperor as burned at the stake. Sometimes on the very same occasion."

"Well, times have changed."

Dercy scratched his bearded jaw. "Have they?"

"I saw in *The Fox* that an illusionist performed at a party at the house of a viscountess."

"Don't let that fool you! Every now and then, some lord or lady who seeks notoriety will manufacture a passing encounter with illusionists. A touch of scandal is like honey—it sets all the bees to buzzing. Then again, too much is poison, and the moment that lord or lady has risen high enough, they'll be the first to spurn a

Siltheri." Dercy let out a snort. "Besides, last I looked, I hadn't seen any respectable lords coming to Durrow Street—at least not without their hats pulled down low and collars turned up."

Eldyn could only concede the point. Yet things *had* changed. The theaters on Durrow Street, while beyond the bounds of respectable society, were allowed to operate openly, and they were busy nearly every night. So why couldn't things keep changing? Perhaps a time would come when illusionists would no longer need to conceal themselves no matter where they went. The world was a vast place after all—vaster than anyone had thought only a few hundred years ago, before the New Lands were discovered. Why shouldn't there be room for all sorts of folk? For some reason, this thought was as intoxicating to Eldyn as the punch.

At last the hour grew late, and Eldyn drained his cup. The umbral was to be of only middling length, and he had promised he would attend Brightday service with Sashie in the morning. When he told Dercy it was time for him to leave, to his surprise, Dercy said he was weary as well, and so they left the tavern together.

They tottered back down Durrow Street, heads light and legs wobbly, laughing and gripping each other as they went. Dercy had a room above the Theater of the Moon, so getting that far was their first goal.

The street was all but empty now, the theaters dark, and the only illumination came from sooty streetlamps, which were few and far between. However, when they were about halfway down the street, they saw a knot of people gathered before the doors of one of the theaters.

It was the Theater of the Doves.

"Get away!" a voice shrieked. "All of you, get away from here!"

Eldyn recognized that voice, and by his look so did Dercy.

"It's Gerivel," he said.

Then he was hurrying toward the door, stumbling no longer. Eldyn drew a breath to steady himself and followed after.

"To the Abyss with all of you—just leave us!"

Dercy pushed his way through the small throng of people, all of whom stared at something, mouths agape. Then Dercy stopped short, and Eldyn staggered to a halt beside him. The large quantity of punch in his stomach went sour, and the world spun in a giddy circle around him.

Gerivel knelt on the paving stones before the door of the theater. He no longer wore his feathered costume, and was clad in plain black, though his face was still powdered. The powder had flaked off in patches, and tears had carved deep grooves through it, so that his face was a grotesque mask of anger and anguish.

Next to Gerivel, slumped against the door, was a young man. Or rather, the body of a young man. He was dressed in fashionable clothes of velvet and brocade. However, there was no way to know if he had been handsome or not, for his face was crusted with blood.

"Get back!" Dercy shouted, his voice deeper than Eldyn had ever heard it. He thrust his arms out. "All of you, get back!"

The gawkers grumbled but complied, edging away from the door. As the crowd shifted, a beam of moonlight fell upon the corpse. Now Eldyn could see the source of all the blood. Both of the young man's eyes were gone; only empty pits remained.

Dercy crouched beside Gerivel, who was pawing at the corpse with thin hands, as if trying to wake it.

"What happened, Gerivel?" Dercy gripped the older illusionist's shoulders.

"I told Donnebric not to go! I told him it could not be for good, not when it was all so secret. But he would not listen, not to *me*. What value could there be in anything I had to say?" Gerivel rocked back and forth on his knees. "I went out to look for him, only I couldn't find him anywhere. Then I came back, and he was . . ." His words dissolved into a moan.

Dercy rose and pounded on the gilded doors of the theater, not letting up until at last it opened a crack. Sounds of outrage emanated from within, quickly transmuting into dismay. Eldyn was aware of figures appearing in the dim doorway, of hands reaching out and picking up both Gerivel and the corpse, drawing them inside.

Then the doors shut. Without a spectacle to behold, the crowd melted away.

A hand touched Eldyn's shoulder. "There's nothing we can do here," Dercy said, his voice low.

"Should we not call for a redcrest?"

"They would not come. Even if they did, what would the king's soldiers say, except that this is what happens to men who do such things?"

Eldyn could do no more than give a mute nod. He stumbled with Dercy down Durrow Street, thinking at any moment he would be sick. His head throbbed from too much punch. He remembered pushing through a door and staggering up a flight of steps.

The next thing he knew, light flared—the mundane gold light of an oil lamp—and he saw that he was in a small but neatly kept room. They had made it to Dercy's chamber above the Theater of the Moon.

"I need to go," Eldyn said. "I need to get to Sashie."

"You're not going anywhere. You've drunk too much. Besides, it's not safe out there tonight."

"I can bring the shadows to me." Eldyn's head was clearing now. It wasn't the punch that had addled his wits so much as the sight in front of the Theater of the Doves.

"The shadows can't help you walk straight. And it's too late to find a hack cab, at least in this part of the city. You can stay here tonight. You'd best lie down. I can sleep in the chair."

Eldyn wanted to argue, but he could not. He sat on the edge of the narrow bed and drank the cup of water Dercy handed him. His head still hurt, but his stomach had settled, and he knew he would be well enough.

The same could not be said for the illusionist Donnebric.

"Who do you think did it?" Eldyn said. "Was it robbers?"

Dercy let out a snort. He stood near the window. "No, not robbers. At least not in the sense you mean. For every magnate is a robber in his way."

These words astonished Eldyn. "The magnate he performed for. You think *he* had this done?"

"Who else would do it?"

"For what purpose? Why kill him?"

Dercy gazed out into the night. "It wouldn't be the first time someone was removed in order to preserve a secret. It's one thing for a lord to have an illusionist summon gold sparrows at a party to propagate talk and interest. But cavorting with Siltheri in private is a far different matter. You can imagine what it would do to some staid old magnate's reputation if it was discovered he had let illusionists conjure lewd phantasms in his bedchamber while he paraded about without a stitch on."

Eldyn could indeed imagine it. It could very well cost him his seat in Assembly. After all, such actions had ended any chance Vandimeer Garritt had ever had of taking his own father's seat in the Hall of Magnates.

"That idiot." Dercy shook his head. "Donnebric would have been fine if he'd been more discreet. But he always wanted to blaze in the sun. I'm sure he must have said or done something, made some boast, that caused the magnate to fear the whole sordid affair would be revealed."

"So Donnebric was murdered," Eldyn said, hardly believing a man—a lord even—could be so cold as to buy secrecy at the cost of a man's life. "God protect us."

Now Dercy laughed, but it was a bitter sound. "Oh, he won't protect *us*, Eldyn. Well, you, perhaps. You're the one who works for the Church and who looks like an angel after all. But as for us Siltheri . . ." He drew the curtain and turned from the window. "Men might pay to see our illusions, Eldyn, but it is better if we are not seen ourselves. What happened to Donnebric—that's what happens when our kind become too visible."

Eldyn looked down at his hands. Perhaps the world was not so vast after all. Perhaps it would never have room for people like Donnebric and Gerivel and Dercy, and they would always have to remain concealed. He began to shiver, though the night was balmy.

"Come now, what's this?" Dercy said, sitting on the bed beside him. "You're all right. You need not shake so."

"I can't stop it," Eldyn said. "I can't stop thinking about him."

Dercy put an arm around his shoulder. "There is no point in it. I would never have wished such a thing for Donnebric, but he brought it on himself by his own actions."

"Did he? Did he truly do something to deserve such an end?"

"Deserve it? No, he did not deserve it. Yet he knew the rules we must abide by, and he flouted them."

It was so cruel. How could one man have so much power over another? And how could God, who was sovereign over all, allow it? Were they just beasts, then, like the wolves and sheep in the makeshift play at the tavern, engaging in a savage dance until one consumed the other?

Still Eldyn could not stop shaking. "I feel cold."

"Then let's get you warm."

Dercy rubbed his hands against Eldyn's back, his shoulders, his arms. He did this vigorously at first, to induce the production of warmth. Then, as the force of Eldyn's shuddering eased, Dercy's motions grew slower, more gentle. Yet even when Eldyn shivered no longer, the other young man did not stop. He touched Eldyn's hands, his throat, his cheeks.

"There, do you see?" Dercy said in a low voice. "You are well, my angel."

Eldyn looked up into the young man's sea-colored eyes, and at last he understood the expression he had seen in them before: the look of hope, and of regret. How had he not realized before what it meant? Yet up until then he had been so preoccupied with trying to improve his ability at illusions that he had been insensible to that other capacity that had been steadily increasing in him whenever he and Dercy were together.

Now he recognized it for what it was, and he could only be astonished at himself. Though in a way that was foolishness, for he supposed he had always known the truth of the matter. Certainly he had never watched a pretty young woman with the same fascination that he felt when he spied two illusionists together in the shadows of a tavern.

But there was a cause for why he had factored such thoughts

and feelings away, was there not—why he had endeavored to tally them to null in the ledger of his life? He had only to read a little further in the Testament, and he was sure to find the reasons all ciphered out. . . .

"Forgive me," Dercy said, and he shook his head. "I shouldn't have presumed . . ." He started to pull his hand away.

Even as he did, Eldyn caught it in his own; it was smooth and surprisingly strong. A delightful warmth welled up inside him, and as it did his trepidations vanished like ink sanded from a page. Perhaps tomorrow, when he opened his copy of the Testament in the morning light, he would again suffer concern for the perfection of his immortal soul. But now, at that moment, it was only the transient tenderness of flesh that he could consider.

Acting on an impulse, he brought Dercy's hand to his lips. Then, once again, he looked into Dercy's eyes. This time there was no regret to be seen there, only a brilliant light. For a moment the two of them were frozen, like actors in a tableau.

Then Dercy leaned in to kiss him. His beard was warm and marvelously rough against Eldyn's cheek. Their lips pressed together, suspending breath, as if that action granted them all the necessary stuff of life, so that mere air was no longer required. Eldyn gripped Dercy's shoulders like a man drowning, yet he felt no distress, only a blissful warmth. He sank, and willingly.

At last they parted. The expression on Dercy's face was at once delighted and amused.

"Good God, you act as if you've never kissed anyone before, Eldyn Garritt."

Eldyn felt his cheeks flush. Of course he had kissed others. Except he suspected Dercy would not count pecks against his sister's cheek. True, there had been a few girls he had let himself be cornered by as a youth, and he had let them kiss him, but he had never kissed them in return.

The only occasions he could remember that had been remotely like this had been the two times Westen had kissed him: once knowing him to be Eldyn, and once thinking him to be Sashie. However, for all that one of those kisses was mocking and the other lustful, there had been a violence to both. Each had been the act of one person seeking domination over another.

Dercy's kiss was different. The gesture had been freely given and received, and even now Eldyn could feel the force of it thrilling along his nerves like lightning along a wire.

Dercy grinned. "So have you or haven't you kissed someone before?"

"I have now," Eldyn said. And this time it was he who leaned in and brought them together.

Never had he done such a thing in his life. Yet such is the wonder of instinct that it apprehends when knowledge does not. A salmon knows which way to swim, a bird to fly. Similarly, his lips, his hands, knew what to make of themselves. He drank of Dercy as he had drunk of the punch that night. A tone hummed in him, like a crystal glass struck just so, and a green light seemed to suffuse the air.

Then, to his dismay, the other young man pulled away.

"Look," Dercy said softly, his eyes alight. "Look around you."

Eldyn did, and then wonder struck him. The room, the bed, the drab curtains were all gone. Instead, the two of them sat upon a flat stone in the midst of a forest glade. Great trees arched overhead, and fairy-lights drifted among their boughs.

"Did you conjure this?" Eldyn said, trying to comprehend.

"No, this is all from you. Don't you see? The other morning you couldn't make a tree—and now here's a whole forest of them." He gripped the back of Eldyn's neck. "You did it, my friend."

Eldyn could only stare. It seemed impossible; he had never conjured more than the smallest glamour. Yet even as he thought that the trees should be taller, and that there should be more glittering lights, these things were made manifest. Eldyn let out a sound of delight. He had crafted an illusion—a real illusion.

"Now what do I do?" he said, amazed.

Dercy's grin broadened. "Oh, I'll show you that," he said, pulling him forward and off balance. Eldyn gripped him in turn, and they both fell laughing to the green leaves that scattered the forest floor.

CHAPTER SIX

ESIDES THE INCIDENT at the cenotaph, the broadsheets had been starved for ill news of late. The morning after Brightday, they at last had some fresh misery to feast upon. Reports had come of an insurrection in County Dorn. This was in a remote region in the northwest of Altania: a poor and rock-strewn landscape where the population was still less than what it had been before the Plague Years centuries ago.

That such a desolate location, so far from the influence of Invarel, would suffer throes of discontent could not entirely be a surprise. Ivy knew from her studies of history that the land that was the poorest for growing crops often proved the most fertile for sowing rebellion. All the same, the news of the violence at Dorn was shocking.

Provoked for some unknown reason, the men of a number of villages had banded together and stormed several manor houses, looting as they went and turning out the landlords. Then the mob had marched upon the county seat, and there they had forced their way into the keep, seized the mayor—a known loyalist to the Crown—and dragged him into the town square, where they proceeded to pelt him with stones until he was dead.

The few soldiers stationed at the keep had been unable to thwart the mob. Indeed, two of them were murdered along with the mayor, though several managed to escape, and thus reports of what had happened were brought to the south. At this point, the entire county was in a state of lawlessness, and there had been no more news. Whether more soldiers would be sent to control the situation was unknown. It had lately been the practice of the king to withdraw troops from the Outlands and station them nearer to Invarel; though whether this was seen as a prudent bolstering of the city's defenses in uncertain times, or a reckless abandoning of the countryside, depended upon which newspaper one read.

While it was always troubling to learn of awful news in distant places, once it was read and digested there was nothing to do but to go on with all the usual affairs of one's day. That life should continue apace for one person when it was all in tumult for others seemed grossly unfair, but it was ever the state of the world. Besides, Ivy needed some activity to direct her attention toward, for otherwise she would find herself wanting to take out a map so she could count the miles between County Dorn and the region of the northlands where Mr. Quent had gone to perform his work. And there could be no useful purpose in that.

With this in mind, Ivy decided to take the old rosewood clock to be repaired, for it was still off. Yesterday, it had marked the end of the lumenal eighteen minutes before the almanac predicted. True, when Ivy glanced out the window of the sitting room, the sky had already been getting dark by the time the black disk eclipsed the gold one on the right-hand face of the clock. However, the day had been generally cloudy. And anyway, because of the Crag looming to the west, Ivy could never get a good view of the sunset.

But she had checked the timetables in the almanac twice, and had compared the time on the rosewood clock to others in the house, and so there could be no mistake about it—the clock had chimed the start of the umbral too early. Therefore, after breakfast, she wrapped it in cloth and took it to Coronet Street, to the shop of a clockmaker.

Evidently there had been an epidemic of broken clocks in the city, for upon entering the shop she found it crowded with people. Each of them held a clock in their hands (or leaned against it if the clock was very large), and all the disparate noises of their ticking and chiming and cuckooing made for a jarring symphony.

She waited for over an hour to be seen, and then it was not by the clockmaker but rather by his apprentice. After giving the workings of her clock only a brief examination, the young man pronounced that there was no mechanical problem that he could observe.

"I will say that the workings of this clock are peculiar," he said, his eyes large behind thick spectacles. "There are extra gears and other mechanisms whose function I cannot guess. I am sure my master would have seen their like before, if he had time himself to look at it, but he does not. Regardless, it is all in good working order."

"I'm sure that's not the case," Ivy protested. "I set it according to the almanac at the beginning of the last lumenal, yet by the end it was nearly twenty minutes behind."

"Then I suppose your almanac has a misprint in it," the apprentice said, and shut the door on the back of the clock.

Ivy had never known the almanac to be incorrect. She always used *Sparley's Yearbook,* which had a reputation for being highly reliable. Yet she had to concede it was possible that there were mistakes in the almanac. After all, there were a great number of entries, and the typeface was very small.

She left the shop, the heavy clock in her arms, and walked a short distance to a bookseller's, where she bought the last copy of *Gooding's Altanian Almanac* on the shelf. Then she went to hire a hack cab to take her back across the city. Her sisters had Lawden and the cabriolet, as Lily had wanted to go to Halworth Gardens again that day.

The lumenal—which, if the new almanac was any more accurate than the old, was to be over eighteen hours long—was growing torrid by the time Ivy returned to Durrow Street. As she entered the front hall, she was greeted by a great racket emanating from upstairs. Evidently repairing a wall caused more of a disturbance than tearing one down.

Ivy took her burdens to the sitting room and set them on the mantel. The carved eye in the center of the mantelpiece blinked at her, and she smiled. Any dread the eyes had given her the other day had been superseded by reason. The voices she had heard the

other night could not have been made by the black storks, as Mr.
Barbridge had informed her, which meant they must have been
produced by her imagination instead. Besides, she could not believe that the eyes were anything other than benevolent.

Ivy took up the old almanac, but she was uncertain what to do
with it. It was hardly of use now, but she could not bring herself
to throw away any sort of book. Instead, she took it to the shelf in
the corner of the sitting room.

The majority of her father's library was stored away in crates,
awaiting the completion of work on the house to be unpacked.
However, as her father had often said when she was young, a house
without books was like a body without a soul, and so she had
brought out a few books and arranged them here. She slipped the
almanac onto the shelf beside them.

That task accomplished, Ivy considered how to occupy herself
for the rest of the long morning. She supposed she should look at
the household ledger. It had been some time since she had cata-
logued the receipts related to the restoration of the house, and she
wanted to keep them in order for Mr. Quent to inspect upon his
return.

Or she could read a book.

While it had long been Ivy's custom to spend every free moment reading books from her father's library—volumes about history, ancient mythology, and especially magick—it had been
difficult to maintain the habit these last months. With her sisters
gone, she had some rare time to herself.

The receipts could wait; after all, Mr. Quent would not return
for nearly half a month. Ivy ran a finger along the spines of the
books on the shelf. None of them concerned the arcane or occult;
she had not thought it appropriate to bring out such tomes when
strangers were coming and going. However, there were several
volumes regarding various scientific studies.

Her finger came to a halt upon a book of astrography. Over the
last few days, Ivy had thought a great deal about the article she
had read in *The Comet* concerning the new planet. Further reflec-

tion had convinced her that her hypothesis was correct—that the place she had seen through the Eye of Ran-Yahgren was in fact the planet Cerephus.

Though the long morning had grown hot, a shiver crept across Ivy's arms and neck. She would never forget the lurid crimson glow that had welled forth from the crystalline orb in the secret room upstairs, or the dark shapes that had lurched across the queer landscape beyond.

What the things were, Ivy didn't know. Something alive, and ravenous. Whatever they were, the magicians had sought to use the artifact to open a door for them. They had thought to control the things, to use them for some unknown end. For power, she supposed. One glance through the orb was enough for Ivy to know that plan was madness. Indeed, merely gazing into the orb had driven the magicians mad.

Using the spell left by her father, Mr. Rafferdy had restored the binding on the artifact, but the new planet was drawing ever closer. What if one day Cerephus drew so close that magick was no longer needed to open a door?

Now she was intentionally horrifying herself. She had absolutely no evidence on which to base such a theory. For one thing, she had no idea how close Cerephus would approach, and she knew little about the movements of the planets.

Which was why reading about astrography could only be to her benefit. Ivy pulled the book from the shelf and sat on the sofa. However, the noise of work continued to drone from above, and she knew if she tried to read in here she would soon get a headache. So she left the sitting room and instead went out into the garden behind the house.

With its disheveled hedges, the great trees of New Ash which leaned at odd angles, and a collection of spindly chestnuts and hawthorns, this garden could not have been more different than the one where Lily and Rose had gone that morning. In Halworth Gardens, the greenery was no less precise in design than the carefully tended paths, while there was a wildness to *this* garden that made it seem as if it had not been planted at all, but rather had sprung up unbidden. Indeed, the garden seemed to have a life and will of its own, and had grown only more dense in the months since they had arrived, despite the constant efforts of Mr. Seenly.

Book in hand, Ivy walked through the garden. There was a bench situated beneath one of the larger ashes, and so it would be protected from the heat of the long morning.

The air seemed to grow greener as she went. Though the city lay just beyond the hedges, if she shut her eyes a little she could imagine she was miles from Invarel. She could picture herself out on the moorlands around Heathcrest Hall, where clouds scudded along the tops of the fells and ancient trees murmured in the wind, tangling behind an old stone wall. . . .

Ivy blinked, and the shadows all around leaped ahead several inches from where they had been a moment ago. Before her was one of the stunted hawthorn trees. Unlike the ash trees, a number of dead brown leaves clung to its branches, in and among the green.

Given its ragged appearance, she could not help being reminded of the stand of Wyrdwood on the ridge to the east of Heathcrest Hall. Like the little hawthorn, those trees had always been shedding their leaves, as if they did not understand that they were supposed to hold on to them. But the comparison could be no more than superficial. There were no Old Trees here in the city. It was only a want of trimming or more water that was causing the hawthorn to lose some of its leaves. She would tell Mrs. Seenly to have her husband see to it.

The bench lay just ahead. Ivy started for it, then realized the book on astrography was no longer in her hand. She looked around and saw that it had fallen to the ground. She retrieved it, then went to the bench and opened the volume on her lap.

"Ahoy, Ivy, there you are!" a voice called out when she had read no more than the introductory paragraph.

Ivy looked up to see Lily tramping across the garden toward her, bonnet in hand, while Rose wandered behind.

"We looked all over the house and couldn't find you anywhere. We thought you'd gone. Then Rose looked out a window and saw you standing in front of a tree, staring at it as if it were somehow the most fascinating thing. What are you doing out here?"

"Nothing," Ivy said, and with a sigh shut the book. "I was merely escaping the noise of work."

Lily plopped herself on the bench. "Well, I can't blame you for that. We couldn't leave the house soon enough for Halworth Gardens."

"Yet you're back very soon as well."

"I'm surprised we stayed as long as we did," Lily exclaimed, picking at the ribbons of her bonnet. "The heat was beastly. The flowers were all wilting, and there was no one there, nor anywhere along the Promenade! Well, hardly anyone, at any rate. Certainly no one who was very handsome or dressed very well, though Rose kept telling me to look up every time some portly vicar or white-haired barrister strolled by."

"I didn't know if you might find them handsome or not," Rose said. She kicked off her slippers and picked up the hem of her gown as she walked through the grass.

Lily rolled her eyes. "Well, there were hardly any homely gentlemen, let alone good-looking ones. It seemed as if everyone had abandoned the place for somewhere else. Which was not very good of them, as we had gone to all the trouble to go there. I wonder where they could all have gone."

Even as Lily said this, Ivy realized she already knew the answer to the mystery. Today was the opening day of Assembly—as she should have recalled. When they met the other lumenal, Mrs. Baydon had explained with delight how Mr. Rafferdy was to occupy Lord Rafferdy's seat in the Hall of Magnates until his father was fit to travel to Invarel.

The idea of Mr. Rafferdy sitting in Assembly was one that gave Ivy great amusement—even as she was certain it would provide *him* none. How dull he would find it all: a room of men in wigs debating resolutions and expounding on the actions of the Crown!

All the same, she could not help thinking that, if he applied himself, he would make a very good politician. He certainly had the wit for it, if he could only find the patience. No doubt he would consider the notion unthinkable; but then, he had never thought he could be a magician either.

That today was the opening day of Assembly would account for the absence of gentlemen in Halworth Gardens. Ivy explained this to her sisters. However, the clarification did little to mollify the youngest.

"I don't know why people would want to go to Assembly," Lily said. "I'm sure listening to speeches is dreadful boring compared to walking along the Promenade or sitting in the gardens and being seen."

"Some might think so. Yet I am sure you must agree that the governing of our nation is a worthwhile endeavor, especially with the state of things in the Outlands."

Lily plucked another ribbon from her bonnet. "If you mean all the rebels running about the country, I'm sure a lot of old lords wouldn't be able to do anything about them if they should decide to storm the city. It will be up to all the king's dashing soldiers to win the day." Her eyes flashed. "Unless it's the rebels who prove to be the more dashing lot, in which case I hope it's *they* who are victorious!"

Ivy knew that if supporters of Huntley Morden should indeed ever win through and enter the city, it would not be for the purpose of inviting young ladies to balls. Nor was such a mob likely to be a well-dressed or mannered lot. But there was no point in admonishing Lily or bringing up such a grim topic. An enemy army had not marched on Invarel in over three hundred years. Besides, it was well known that Lord Valhaine and the Gray Conclave labored ceaselessly to find those who were behind the seditious acts in the country—and here in the city as well, after the incident at the cenotaph. No doubt the news out of County Dorn would only increase these efforts.

The subject of rebels was dropped, and after that the three of them sat in the garden for a time. However, with her sisters there, Ivy had little chance to read her book on astrography, for Lily chattered on about her annoyance with Mr. Garritt for not presenting himself in Halworth Gardens. After all, *he* was not taking a seat in Assembly that day.

Before long, the day grew too hot for remaining outside to be pleasant, and they retreated into the house. Yet it was hardly any cooler in the sitting room, and the sounds of the refurbishment continued unabated from above. At the same time, Lily sat at the pianoforte and commenced a lengthy exploration of every minor key. Ivy almost found herself wishing the new almanac contained errors like the old one had, and that the lumenal would not last so many hours as the timetables predicted. For if it did, this was going to be a very long afternoon indeed.

Planning for Lily's ball might have pleasantly occupied her mind and distracted her from the noise. However, she could not mention the idea of the ball to her sisters until she had discussed it with Mr. Quent.

That it would have to be Rose's ball as well as Lily's, Ivy had already concluded. Both would have to be presented to society, and Rose first. It would not be proper for a younger sister to be out while an elder was not. Then again, Ivy doubted that Lily would much mind sharing the occasion. After all, Lily could have little fear that Rose would be the center of attention.

Given the various sounds that assailed her, Ivy knew there was no hope of concentrating on a complicated subject like astrography. She returned the book to the shelf, and instead took out the box in which she kept the papers related to the repairs on the house, and worked on organizing and totaling them for Mr. Quent to review upon his return.

AS WAS ALWAYS the case on long lumenals, there came a point when they all grew weary of being awake.

The sun stood still outside the windows, drenching the city with white light, and the sounds of construction had ceased, for Mr. Barbridge and the workmen had departed for a midday respite. After so much noise, the silence seemed a heavy, stifling thing. Lily cracked enormous yawns at the pianoforte, and Rose drowsed on the sofa, her sewing forgotten on her lap.

Ivy could not claim to be any more alert than her sisters. She had totaled the last stack of receipts thrice and had gotten a different sum each time. At last she laid down her pen. Then, as the people of Altania had done for time out of mind, the three sisters went upstairs and attempted to fashion a small bit of night in the middle of day.

They retired to their rooms, closing shutters and drapes tightly so they might sleep. This also had the effect of making Ivy's room stuffy, and despite her efforts a thin line of light slipped between the curtains, cutting the air like a silver knife. Her sleep was fitful and provided little in the way of restoration.

It was the sound of wind blowing that woke her.

Ivy sat up in bed, pushing damp gold tangles from her face. Had a storm come to cool the city? However, as she parted the curtains, light flooded the chamber. There was not a cloud to be seen.

By the angle of the sun, she had not slept for very long—an hour at the most. Yet she was awake now; there was no use in lying down again. With a sigh, she took up a hairbrush and made herself ready for the remainder of the lumenal.

The house was silent as she left her chamber. The doors to Lily's and Rose's rooms were both shut, and it would be some time before the workmen returned. Which meant she would have some time to read after all. With that purpose, she started down the stairs. When she reached the second floor, she paused.

There it was again, low but unmistakable: a rushing sound, like wind before a storm. Ivy crossed the gallery, picking her way among stacks of lumber and troughs for mixing plaster. She stopped before one of the tall windows, pushed back the sheet that draped it, and looked out.

There was not a cloud in view. The only dark shape to be seen against the sky was the imposing outline of the Citadel up on the Crag. Then she looked down into the garden in front of the house. The straggled chestnuts and hawthorns drooped listlessly, their branches still. Yet she was certain she had heard the sound of wind blowing.

Ivy tilted her head and held her breath. She could still detect it: a low soughing that made her think of bare, bleak stones and empty moorlands. Perhaps the storm was approaching from another direction. Ivy let the sheet fall, then turned to pick her way back across the gallery.

She halted. Her eyes fell upon the door at the end of the gallery, the one that Mr. Barbridge's men had discovered. In the dim light seeping through the sheet-draped windows, it seemed the leaves carved upon the door stirred and rippled.

Ivy drew closer, and a giddiness came over her. No, they did not seem to move—they *were* moving. The leaves fluttered and danced, as if from a breeze. She reached a hand out to touch them.

Something rapped against the window behind her.

Ivy snatched her hand back and spun around. Again something small and hard struck the window. A pebble, she thought. She went back to the window and pushed aside the sheet. Something moved in the garden below, and it was not the branch of any tree.

The figure of a man stepped into view. His coat was black, as were his breeches and boots, his gloves and hat—and all of his attire was frilled and plumed, slashed and gored, and knotted with brocade. Like a costume from another era, she had thought the first time she saw him. He made a florid bow. Then he rose and looked up at the window. His face was covered with an onyx mask, curved into a frozen smile. It was a fierce expression.

Ivy could not help a gasp. All the same, she was not truly astonished to see the man in the black mask. *I am watching,* he had told her the last time she had encountered him. It was on the day she and Mr. Quent had first made an inspection of the house on Durrow Street.

Nor was it a troubling notion. Three times prior to that last instance, the man had appeared to her, and on each occasion he had helped her understand what to do. It was he who warned her that the Vigilant Order of the Silver Eye sought to enter the house on Durrow Street and use the artifact upstairs.

Who the man was, she did not know. He had never revealed his face. However, she knew from her father's letter that he had seen the man in the mask. *I trust him more than I trust myself,* Mr. Lockwell had written. *If he should ever speak to you, heed him.*

She *had* heeded him, and the magicians had been prevented from using the artifact to open a portal for the beings called the Ashen. Yet if the danger had been averted, why was he here now? In the past, he had only ever showed himself when peril was near.

Except peril *was* near, wasn't it? According to the article she had read in the broadsheet, it drew nearer every day. The magicians had wished to open a portal to the world she had glimpsed through the Eye of Ran-Yahgren, a world she was now certain was Cerephus. Which meant the creatures she had seen through the orb were the Ashen themselves. . . .

No, it was not the Ashen you saw, a voice seemed to whisper beside her. The words were soft and musical in cadence. *Those were only their slaves, their servants and pets.*

"But what are they?" she whispered, knowing he would hear her no matter how quietly she spoke. "What are the Ashen?"

Now the mouth of the mask was set in a grim line. *They are the cold between the stars, the emptiness after the death of time, and the darkness that dwelled before all things. They are the first ones, ancient beyond all else. And their hunger knows no bounds.*

She folded her arms, shivering. "I don't understand. Why would God allow such things to enter into his Creation?"

Allow them? Below, he shook his head. *God did not allow them to enter. Before the word of creation was spoken, they were already there. When the first suns sputtered into life, they were there to witness those feeble rays. And how they loathed that illumination, even as they craved it! They seek to consume all light, all life—to try to fill the void of their beings. But their hunger can never be sated. It is endless. They have laid waste to their own world, and so they seek a new one to feast upon.*

Ivy felt a cold terror grip her, as it did sometimes when night fell and darkness took the world. "But the magicians of the Silver Eye are all gone now. We stopped them from opening the door."

There are other magicians—men far more powerful than the ones you encountered. And there are other doors.

A despair filled her. She and Mr. Rafferdy had stopped the Vigilant Order of the Silver Eye from opening a portal—but barely, and only by renewing enchantments her father had already placed in the house. What were they to do about unknown magicians in unknown places? The man in the mask could not think she had any power to stop *them.*

She had done her part. With Mr. Rafferdy's help, she had guarded the house on Durrow Street. Her only wish now was to make a home for herself, her husband, and her sisters, and to bring her father to it. A spark of indignation flared inside her. Who was this being, to come here in his bizarre attire and speak to her so? She opened her mouth to tell him to go away and to never return.

News comes, his voice sounded in her mind. Below her, his black mask was expressionless. *Everything is changed now.*

Even as she struggled to comprehend what this meant, there came the hard sound of knuckles rapping.

Ivy spun around, and again her eyes fell upon the door at the end of the gallery. For a wild moment she thought it was from *that* door the knocking had issued. The wooden leaves trembled, as if buffeted by a gale. Yet that was one of *his* tricks, wasn't it, to make statues and carvings seem to move? She glanced again out the window.

The courtyard was empty of all but the trees.

Again came the knocking, more urgent than before. This time her mind was clear enough to grasp that the sound issued from below. Ivy cast one last glance at the wooden door; the carved leaves were motionless now. Then she turned and hurried down the stairs.

By the time she reached the front hall, Mrs. Seenly was already opening the door.

"Now, what's all this banging for?" she exclaimed. "Don't you know it's a long lumenal and folks are abed?"

"I have a letter for the lady of the house," spoke a man's voice from beyond the door.

"Well, give it here, then," said the housekeeper. "I'll see that she gets it."

"I cannot do so, ma'am. It was sent under the seal of the Crown. I can deliver it only to Lady Quent."

"Mrs. Quent, I am sure you mean," Mrs. Seenly said. "But if you must give it only to her, then you can wait here. I'll go see if she is risen, but I will not wake her, mind you!"

"It's all right, Mrs. Seenly," Ivy said, hurrying forward before the housekeeper could shut the door on the messenger. "I am very much awake, as you can see."

"Well, 'tis no wonder, with all the din," Mrs. Seenly said.

She stepped away from the door, allowing a man to enter. His red-crested hat was tucked under his arm, and his coat was more gray than blue from road dust. The soldier gave a crisp bow as Ivy approached.

"I have a letter for you, my lady."

Ivy could only smile. The soldier's sense of duty was to be commended, but he was certainly overzealous in his politeness.

"You may call me Mrs. Quent."

"Begging your pardon, but I was commanded to deliver this to Lady Quent on the west end of Durrow Street."

Ivy saw no need to quibble regarding honorifics. She reached out a hand. "I assure you I am the only woman by the name of Quent who dwells here."

Evidently this was good enough, for the soldier handed her a folded parchment sealed with a thick disk of blue wax. She asked if he needed anything to drink.

"Thank you, my lady, but as my duty has been discharged, I must return to my regiment." Asking her leave, which was granted, he turned on a heel and departed.

"Well, that was all very curious," Mrs. Seenly said as she closed the door, shutting out the hot light of the afternoon.

"Indeed," Ivy said. She was curious as well, and concerned. That the letter was from Mr. Quent she knew the moment she saw the address, written in his cramped hand. Why should he send her another letter so soon after his last, and have it delivered by a soldier rather than the post? She touched the disk of blue wax; the shape of a stag was impressed into it. She could not help thinking of the fate of the mayor of the county seat in Dorn. Had he not been a loyal subject of the Crown—just like Mr. Quent?

Alarm grew within her, but she did her best to disguise it. She told Mrs. Seenly they would take an afternoon breakfast in the parlor. As soon as the housekeeper left, Ivy broke the seal with a trembling hand, then stood in the sun that fell through a window and read.

My Dearest Ivoleyn—

I must keep these lines brief. If I do not, this letter will have little chance of arriving before I do, and I do not wish you to be surprised when you see me walking up the steps. I am coming home. My work here is only just begun, but all the same I must quit the North Country and make all haste to Invarel, where I must present myself to the king. You can expect me the lumenal after this letter finds you.

How alarmed you must be at the preceding words! Do not be. I have news for you of a happy nature, though it is also weighty. This is not a thing I have ever craved or sought. Yet now that it is given me, how can I say I am not pleased? While I cannot be without trepidation at such a drastic change in circumstance, all the same I will not refuse it. Nor could I if I wished to, as Lord Rafferdy made quite clear in his missive that brought me the news.

And how should I impart this news to you? There is no way to deliver such a thing, except in the plainest of words. By royal writ I have been granted, in return for services rendered in Torland, the barony of Cairnbridge. I am thus in one stroke made a baronet. I am to be Sir Quent.

There! What do you think of such peculiar and unlooked-for news? And I warn you—do not be too glad or think it too wondrous. I am cer-

- *tain it will all be a burden in the end. Indeed, it is one already, for I must present myself to His Majesty at once and kiss his ring and swear an oath.*

Yet it is you I will kiss first upon arriving in the city. To see you will be the greatest of rewards, and if the state of the roads allow, that happy moment will come after the passage of but one more umbral for you.

That must be enough for now. The soldier who brought me Lord Rafferdy's letter waits. I must fold this sheet no matter how smudged it will get. I will hold you soon. Until then, know that while much has been changed by this unexpected act, one thing is ever constant. I am and always will be—

—Devotedly Yours, Alasdare

Ivy leaned against the windowsill, the letter fluttering in her hand as if it, too, felt the influence of a wind. Such was her astonishment that she could hardly fathom the words she had read. Again and again her eyes roved over the page, but it was no use. She could not put two words together in her head.

"What was all that banging?" Lily said, trudging down to the bottom of the staircase. "I thought the workmen were gone."

It wasn't the workmen, Ivy wanted to say, but she could not.

Lily frowned, then crossed the hall. "Blast and blunder, what's wrong with you, Ivy? You look like you've seen a ghost. Have you? If so, don't say I didn't tell you there were spirits."

"Who saw a spirit?" Rose said as she descended the stairs, Miss Mew padding behind her.

"No one," Ivy managed at last to say. "It's only—a letter has come. . . ."

"A letter? From whom?"

When her demand was not immediately met, Lily snatched the paper from Ivy's hand, nor did Ivy have the power to resist the act. The sunlight seemed to fill her with its radiance and warmth. A joy rose in her, only it was not for herself, but rather for *him.* How perfect that he should receive such a grand reward—he who had never worked for any reward at all. However, if Mr. Quent was not a man who harbored pride, she would harbor it for him, and at that moment her heart was filled with such regard and affection for him that it was almost too much to bear. Would that he was home now, so that she could throw her arms around him!

"Well, blow me down!" Lily roared. She looked up from the letter, her brown eyes wide.

"What is it?" Rose said. "Is something wrong?"

"Wrong?" Lily threw back her head and let out several peals of laughter. "No, nothing is wrong. Nothing will ever be wrong now, Rose!"

"What do you mean?"

Lily thrust the letter back at Ivy and grabbed Rose's hands, spinning her around in a circle. "Lady Quent, that is what I mean! Ivy is to be Lady Quent! And we shall be a lady's sisters. How marvelous we will be! And what men we will meet! No mere gentleman will do for you or me, Rose, not now. We shall both marry sirs, and then we shall be ladies, too!"

"Lily!" Ivy said, her sister's display restoring her to her senses. "It is not proper to crow like that."

"Why shouldn't I crow? Just think how happy our mother would be if she were here! She would have shouted the news at the top of her lungs. Even *she* could never have asked for more for us."

Ivy was forced to admit Lily was right. Were she alive, Mrs. Lockwell would have been beside herself to see the situation of her daughters so vastly—indeed, almost unimaginably—improved. Surely no one on Whitward Street would ever have expected the three Miss Lockwells to rise so far.

"Dance with us, Ivy!" Rose said, taking her hand as Miss Mew pranced around them.

Such was the power of Rose's smile that Ivy could not resist. Nor, when she grasped the hands of her sisters, could she prevent herself from joining in their merriment, and together they laughed and spun before the windows, basking in the light of the long day.

CHAPTER SEVEN

THOUGH IT HAD been nine hours since dawn, the light on the towers of Assembly was still the white-gold illumination of morning. Such was the way the light bathed them that it imparted to those spires a patina of virtue and purity that, Rafferdy was certain, was wholly misplaced.

Despite its breadth, Marble Street was a snarl of horses and carriages. Every driver struggled to get close to the steps in front of Assembly to discharge his passengers, while at the same time a company of soldiers endeavored to press them back, shouting, "Make way, make way, the king is coming!" Whips were brandished, and polished swords in turn. And if the soldiers pressed the carriages back on one flank, then the drivers advanced on another.

"It looks like a battle is going on!" Mrs. Baydon observed through the window of Lord Baydon's barouche as it crept down the street in a series of fitful starts and stops. "I wonder if that is Captain Branfort's company. If so, I'm sure the soldiers will prevail. You'd think people had come not to see the opening of Assembly but rather to assail its doors, wrest them open, and take over the place."

"I am certain that taking over is precisely what people intend," Rafferdy said. "Though it is not doors that will be assailed and wrested, but rather ears and arms, for the purpose of winning votes."

He shifted on the seat, attempting not to wrinkle his new velvet coat. Rafferdy had changed into his best attire, despite Lord

Baydon's assurances that he could wear any old thing, as no one would see under his robes.

Mrs. Baydon smiled at him from the opposite bench. "Isn't it too thrilling, Mr. Rafferdy, to think that you will get to raise your hand and speak yea or nay on matters of importance to all of Altania?"

"Yes, too thrilling by far. Thus I will pretend to be mute and palsied, unable to either utter a syllable or lift a hand."

"You can do no such thing, I am sure! It is your duty to make wise choices for Altania. Besides, it would be horrid to pretend to be infirm when you are not."

"No, Mrs. Baydon, it would be horrid to pretend to be wise when I am not."

"Now you're speaking gibberish, Rafferdy," Mr. Baydon said, lowering a broadsheet that he had folded into quarters in order to read it in the confines of the barouche. "You have nothing to worry about when it comes time to vote. Why, all those lords out there think nothing about voting this way or that on the weightiest of topics, even if they haven't learned a thing about it, and not one of them is a whit more wise than you are."

Rafferdy gazed out the window. "That's exactly what I'm afraid of."

Before the others could reply, the barouche gave a violent lurch and came to a halt. Outside, a number of soldiers dashed by, expressions angry and hands outstretched.

"Do you think we'll get inside in time?" Mrs. Baydon said, adjusting the blue sash draped over her shoulder. "I don't want to be late for the king's entrance."

"It is impossible we could miss it," Lord Baydon said cheerfully. "It is far too grand a day for such a misfortune to befall us. You will see—the moment we have gotten inside and made ourselves comfortable, and have our wigs properly arranged, then the king will arrive."

"It is impossible we could miss it," Mr. Baydon repeated, "for it is the king's purpose to address Assembly. Therefore he cannot very well speak before Assembly is gathered." He raised his broadsheet. A headline on the reverse blared, SPY CONFESSES—REBELS IN OUTLAND COUNTIES SEEK TO INDUCE FURTHER RISINGS.

"Oh, look at this!" Mrs. Baydon exclaimed, and seized the broadsheet from Mr. Baydon's hands. "There is an article here about Lady Crayford. It says the viscountess is expected to host a party this evening, following the opening of Assembly."

Mr. Baydon crossed his arms. "I am relieved, Mrs. Baydon. I thought for a moment you had suddenly developed an interest in news and rational affairs. I see that is not at all the case."

Mrs. Baydon raised the newspaper, blocking him from her sight. "It says there will be musicians, and a play, and a flight of gilded doves. The article claims it will be the grandest of affairs, and that everyone is going to be there."

"Then I fear the article is in error," Mr. Baydon said, plucking the broadsheet from her hands, "for we were not invited."

"No, we were not," Mrs. Baydon said, slumping back against the bench. "Everyone agrees the viscountess invites only the most desirable and stylish guests. Thus it is assured that *we* will never attend one of her affairs. I will never get to see so marvelous a thing. Instead, I will content myself with the same worn and dull amusements forevermore."

"I had no idea you were so resigned to such a fate," Mr. Baydon said. "Yet if that is the case, then I won't bother speaking to Captain Branfort."

She frowned at him. "What do you mean, you won't speak with the captain? Why should you speak to him?"

"He once served in the same regiment with a certain Colonel Daubrent, who is, I understand, the brother of the viscountess. From what Branfort told me, he and Daubrent were on friendly terms. I had thought he might be able to ask the colonel to inquire on your behalf about an invitation to one of Lady Crayford's affairs. But since you are no longer interested . . ."

"Oh, Mr. Baydon!" she exclaimed.

"Well," her husband said, "if you are certain, now that you have pledged yourself to a life of dullness, that a party will not be too distressing for you, then I will speak to him when next we see him." He raised his broadsheet again, though not before Rafferdy caught the hint of a smile on his lips.

With a jerk, the barouche began to move again. Apparently the soldiers had decided the way to clear the street was not to turn everyone back, but rather to let everyone through. Against some tides, even the mightiest army could not stand, and the soldiers, for all their valiant efforts, had proved no match for a throng of politicians all wanting a good seat. In moments the carriage pulled up to the steps below the Hall of Magnates.

Rafferdy opened the door and helped Mrs. Baydon out while Mr. Baydon assisted his father.

"Are you still certain you want to observe today?" Rafferdy said to Mrs. Baydon. "You know you find politics tedious."

"As do you, Mr. Rafferdy. But if you can bear to participate in Assembly, I am sure I can bear to watch it."

"And if I cannot bear it?"

Mrs. Baydon looked up at him. "You must, Mr. Rafferdy." She took her husband's arm and walked with him up the steps, Lord Baydon huffing after them.

Rafferdy glanced up. A cloud had gone over the sun, and the spires above Assembly were no longer white, but rather were a sullied gray. For some reason the sight of this pleased him, and smiling despite himself he followed the rest of the throng up the steps.

*

ℒORD BAYDON WAS right about one thing: no one could see a stitch of Rafferdy's new clothes beneath his robe.

The Robe Room was a dim, wood-paneled antechamber off the front gallery of the Hall of Magnates. He and Lord Baydon were some of the last to arrive, and so took off their hats and donned the garments the usher handed them with all possible haste. Rafferdy's robe was an ancient thing of heavy black cloth with a ruffled collar and a decidedly musty odor.

He meant to ask the gray-haired usher for another. However, it took considerable tugging to get Lord Baydon into his robe, and then the older man's wig was askew, and by the time it was straightened they could hear the High Speaker's voice echoing into the Robe Room, calling for order.

"Your wig, Mr. Rafferdy!" Lord Baydon said. "You haven't put it on. Where is it?"

"I don't have one."

"Well, the usher can lend you one to wear. All lords must have a wig!" He gave his own white hairpiece a tug, so that it came down to his eyebrows.

Rafferdy eyed the row of wigs on a shelf. They were yellowed and matted, and had he not known otherwise he would have taken them for something the servants used to clean the floor.

"As I'm not yet a lord, I'm sure it would be improper for me to wear a wig," he said. Somewhere a gavel was banging. "Now, Lord Baydon, we must find our places."

They departed the Robe Room by the opposite door and found themselves in a corner of the Hall. It was a great rectangular room with a rostrum at one end and rows of ascending benches on the other three sides. A dome surmounted all, its frescoes tarnished and tainted from the smoke of oil lamps—or perhaps, Rafferdy imagined, from the noxious exhalations of countless politicians.

Finding their place was not difficult, as there were few places left. Rafferdy seated Lord Baydon at one of the lower benches—an act that resulted in a sudden displacement of lords in either direction. Then he took a spot in the highest row for himself. He plucked at the various frills of his robe, trying to arrange them without provoking any further emanation of odor.

"I see you've forgone a wig as well. Good for you, sir!"

Rafferdy looked at the young man who sat to his right. He was clean-shaven, like Rafferdy, and his crown of light brown hair was uncovered. Indeed, fitting a wig over it would have been as great a challenge as fitting a robe over Lord Baydon, for his frizzy hair rose up in a mass nearly as tall as a top hat.

The young man's face was less remarkable than his hair, being neither homely nor handsome. However, it was round and open, with a goodly aspect. Perhaps not a face to inspire love, but one very easy to like. His cheeks were rosy, and dimples appeared as he grinned.

"If a few more join us, we will make a fashion of it. Soon only the most doddering old lords will be caught in a wig."

"It wasn't for fashion that I forwent a wig," Rafferdy said. "I was simply in dread of touching any of the ones in the Robe Room."

"Well, you were wise not to borrow one of *those*. There'd be no telling who wore it last. Eternum knows, it could have been a Stout."

Rafferdy knew little about politics, but he had heard Mr. Baydon complain about the Stouts. They were an insignificant but apparently vocal party, and adhered to the belief that the magnates must hold themselves subject to the will of the Crown in all matters. That they should be detested by the rest of the magnates was thus a necessity.

"I confess it was not the former owner's party that concerned me," Rafferdy said, "but rather the frequency with which he washed his head."

The young man laughed. "Then you definitely didn't want the wig of a Stout. As far as I can tell, they only bathe if the king decrees it. Though I see you had to borrow a robe."

"You mean we can have our own?" Rafferdy said, astonished. He saw now that the other man's robe was simple but elegantly cut of black crepe, with not a frill or ruff to be seen. Rafferdy suffered a pang of envy.

"Of course you can have your own. Unless you prefer ..."

Rafferdy raised an eyebrow and gave him a pointed look.

The young man grinned again. "I see. Then you'll be wanting to visit Larrabee's. They make the finest robes. You'll find the shop down Marble Street, just past the Silver Branch."

"I'll go there directly once the session is over," Rafferdy said. "I'm in your debt. And who should I tell them sent me?"

"You can give them the name Lord Coulten Harfax."

Rafferdy gave a genial nod, as if no way surprised to hear the other's name. In truth, he had not expected to find himself sitting next to the son of a marquess; Lord Harfax was well known to have a vast estate in the east of Altania.

"And I'm Rafferdy," was all he said in reply.

"Excellent to meet you, Mr. Rafferdy."

Lord Coulten extended his hand. As he did, Rafferdy saw a glint of red. On the other man's index finger was a heavy gold ring set with seven small red gems. Eldritch symbols were etched along the sides. Rafferdy held out his hand, and the gem on his own House ring flashed blue.

Lord Coulten's grin broadened, and his eyes sparkled as they shook hands. Before he could say anything more, the pounding of a gavel rang out, and the High Speaker's voice thundered across the Hall, calling the session to order.

Lord Coulten gave Rafferdy a nod that meant, *We will talk, you and I.* Then they faced the rostrum as the work of the Hall of Magnates began for the year. However, Rafferdy soon believed it would take a year for Assembly to get to any business. A proposal first had to be put forth asking if the members thought Assembly should be convened. As if they had gone to all the trouble of coming here for some other reason!

The motion then had to be seconded and put to a vote. Then more motions were proposed and accepted, granting the gavel to the High Speaker (as though he didn't already clutch it in his hand) and the keys to the Grand Usher (as if they didn't already hang about his neck on a gold chain). Rafferdy followed Lord Coulten's lead and spoke yea when he did.

Presently the members of the Hall of Citizens filed in to stand in every bit of free space in the aisles and behind the last row of benches, as when the king made an address to Assembly, it was the custom that the members of both Halls gather together. Finally a proposal was put forth asking if the king should be permitted entry in order to address the Hall.

Of course the proposal passed unanimously, though there was a small knot of lords who shouted their yeas in a hearty manner; those would be the Stouts, Rafferdy supposed by their ratty wigs and fervent expressions. The members of the Hall of Citizens gave their affirmation nearly as enthusiastically as the Stouts. Most lords spoke their yeas in more reserved tones, and there was one group that took great time in standing up, and who spoke their assent with an obvious lack of enthusiasm.

Rafferdy leaned his head toward Lord Coulten. "What party are those lords in?"

"Oh, they're in the Magisters. It's the newest party, formed just last year. I think you can guess their opinion of the king."

So could the Stouts, by the glares they threw across the Hall. However, the Magisters kept their gazes on the rostrum as all took their seats once more. The last to sit was a tall, fair-haired man whose black robe, while obviously new and rich, was adorned with even more frills than Rafferdy's. His face had a high-cheeked haughtiness to it, but his gaze, when cast about the Hall as he sat, was more limpid than cutting.

The fair-haired lord proceeded to fuss with his robe, as if its drape was of greater concern than any business before the Hall. Indeed, all of the Magisters seemed preoccupied with their robes, their wigs (which had a bluish tint), or—for many of them—the House rings that glittered on their hands.

Rafferdy was going to ask Lord Coulten more about the Magisters. However, at that moment the Grand Usher called out: "By order of the Hall of Magnates, the king is hereby welcomed to address our body. Make way for His Majesty! Make way for King Rothard, High Lord of Altania!"

AT LAST THE speech was over.

Rafferdy's back ached from sitting for so long on the hard bench. Here in one room were the heirs to all the greatest fortunes in Altania, and no one had ever thought to purchase cushions? He rose to his feet along with the lords as the members of the Hall of Citizens filed from the Hall, the king having departed before them.

Rafferdy glanced up at the gallery and caught sight of Mrs. Baydon sitting with a group of other young women all clad in shades of blue, gold, and green. Her sash had drooped off her shoulder. He waved up to her, but at that moment she shut her eyes, holding a hand to her mouth as she let out a great yawn. Rafferdy imagined she had been cured of the belief that politics in any way had the potential for excitement.

Certainly *he* would never believe such a thing. The king's address had been interminable—at least half an hour. And all the while, Rothard had slumped in a chair on the rostrum, his head bent down as if it was painful for him to raise it, his thin hands curled in his lap.

Given the king's feeble appearance, Rafferdy would have thought it impossible for his speech to have any sort of impact. But Rothard's words, no matter that they were muttered, might have been a barrage from a cannon for the way they struck the Hall. He had called for the nation to come together as one. Inquire not what profit might be made, he proclaimed, unless it was for the sake of Altania's profit; and let all pride be set aside, save for pride in Altania herself.

As pride and profit were all that generally consumed a magnate's thoughts, these statements necessarily caused many a lord in the Hall to recoil. And the citizens applauded vigorously, the small band of Stouts with them, so that the king's reedy voice was often drowned out. After such moments, Rothard appeared to have to gather himself to find the breath to continue on. That such a pitiful being could in any way oppose the will of the magnates seemed impossible.

Yet on those few occasions when he did raise his head, his eyes were sharp and gray. King Rothard's body may have withered, but not his mind—as was made clear by his very last statements.

In dark times, the king had said, *just as a ship must have a star to guide it, so must a nation have a ruler to steer it through stormy waters. While it is my intention to be the one who pilots this nation to the hope of a new dawn, it is vital that there be no doubt who would take my place should I not be able to do so. Thus I call upon Assembly to ac-knowledge the power of the ancient laws, and to immediately ratify my existing writ of succession.*

A motion was made to close the session, which was seconded. The High Speaker's gavel fell, and a great din filled the Hall as everyone spoke at once. The noise reminded Rafferdy of a swarm of bees; there was an industrious and threatening sound to it.

"I must say, I really hadn't expected him to call for *that*," Lord Coulten said beside him.

"Indeed, it's preposterous," Rafferdy replied. "How are we expected to plunder someone else's ship when we're all in the same boat?"

Lord Coulten grinned. "An excellent jest, Mr. Rafferdy, but you know what I'm talking about. You have far too clever a look about you to be able to feign ignorance."

In fact, Rafferdy had no idea what Lord Coulten was referring to. All this talk of ships and stars had been nonsense to him. Though it appeared from the way others in the Hall spoke that it meant something to *them*.

"He's thrown down the gauntlet," the other young man went on. "Now Assembly must accept his preferred succession, or they must openly oppose it. Not that his request will have any trouble in the Hall of Citizens. They'll be all for it; the people love her dearly. And why shouldn't they? She's pretty enough, and by all accounts a doting daughter. However, a sweet princess is one thing. A ruling queen is quite another."

At last Rafferdy understood. "So the magnates would deny the crown to the princess?"

Lord Coulten nodded. "It's been centuries since we had a queen after all, and there are plenty in this Hall who would keep it that way if they could. Only now King Rothard has called them out. They must either accept the succession or deny it outright. I must say, those who hold that Rothard is hopelessly weak have underestimated him. There will be no more scheming in the shadows now. It will all be out in the open."

Rafferdy looked out across the Hall. He saw several Stouts

glare as a group of Magisters walked past, led by the pale-haired man, his expression aloof.

"I am new to these proceedings," Rafferdy said. "All the same, I believe the scheming is far from done. What of you, Lord Coulten? Do you think a woman should be allowed to rule?"

"I certainly think a woman is no more likely to be a poor queen than a man is to be a poor king."

"That's not the same thing. Would you prefer a king to a queen?"

"That implies, Mr. Rafferdy, that I wish for any sort of monarch at all." Lord Coulten laughed, his cheeks bright. "But you're right, of course. The scheming will continue. So why should we be left out of the amusement? Once I take off this robe, I'm meeting a few others at tavern—some wigless young lords like you and I. Would you care to join us? We can have a drink or two and devise our own plots for ruling Altania."

Rafferdy was tempted—as much by the drink as by Lord Coulten's good-natured company. But he had promised to have dinner at Fairhall Street that evening and was forced to extend his regrets.

"Another time, then," Lord Coulten said.

"You have my word on it."

"I will hold you to that, Mr. Rafferdy. A magician's word is as strong as any enchantment—as I'm sure you know."

He gave a wave of farewell, the ring on his right hand glinting red, then descended the steps, his towering column of hair the last thing to disappear from view. Rafferdy winced and glanced down at his own ring, which shone a dim blue. He rummaged beneath his robe, found his gloves in his coat pocket, and put them on.

This act encouraged a renewed exhalation of the musty odor. It was time to rid himself of this dreadful garment. He descended to the lower benches, found Lord Baydon, helped him to stand, and accompanied him to the Robe Room, which was filled with older lords returning their robes.

"Well, Mr. Rafferdy, what is your opinion so far of being a magnate?" Lord Baydon said, as if they had just been to the most delightful party. "No doubt you are impressed by the ancient atmosphere of the proceedings."

"Indeed, an ancient, even decrepit, atmosphere had a direct impression upon me throughout." He wrinkled his nose as he gladly relinquished his robe to the usher.

"I'm glad to hear it, Mr. Rafferdy. You are not too modern a man to apprehend the weight and importance of tradition. Not like my son. I hope, when the time comes for him to sit on the benches, you will be there beside him. Now you—by heavens, I don't think that's right."

In attempting to take off his robe, Lord Baydon had only succeeded in thrusting an arm through the collar and now was quite stuck. Rafferdy moved to help him remove the garment—a feat that proved even more difficult and time-consuming than getting it on.

At last the deed was done and the robe delivered to the usher. There were few lords left in the Robe Room, and the usher made no attempt to hide his wish that the stragglers remove themselves promptly. Having every desire to comply with the usher's wishes, Rafferdy took his companion's arm and led him toward the door.

"My wig!" Lord Baydon exclaimed, raising both hands to his head. "Why, I've lost my wig."

"Perhaps it came off with your robe."

The older lord shook his head. "No, I remember now. It was very hot in the Hall. Once the High Speaker closed the session, I took it off. I believe I set it on the bench next to me. Yes, I'm sure I did. I must hurry back for it."

He started to turn around, but moving in a hurry was not something of which Lord Baydon was capable. The usher glared as he walked at a stately pace toward the door to the Hall. Aware of the usher's disapproving expression, Rafferdy volunteered to go fetch the wig.

"That's very good of you, Mr. Rafferdy," Lord Baydon said. "I will make my way to the steps. If you don't go very quickly, I'm sure I'll be to the carriage before you."

Rafferdy ducked through the door back into the Hall. Now that it was emptied of people, it had a hollow feel to it. His footsteps echoed up to the dome, where a stray pigeon flapped in circles, trapped. He went to the bench where Lord Baydon had been sitting.

The wig was not there. Rafferdy peered underneath, but it was not there either. He searched up and down the bench, and among those benches above and below, but it was no use. Someone else must have picked it up—one of the Stouts, perhaps. Certainly they could do with better wigs. Lord Baydon would simply have to get a new one. Rafferdy turned to go back to the Robe Room.

And there it was. The wig perched on the railing that separated the first row of benches from the floor, adorning the knob of a post. So intent had Rafferdy been on searching the benches that he hadn't seen it right before him. Or perhaps he had mistaken it for one old lord, head bowed, asleep in his seat, unaware that Assembly was over for the day. However, Rafferdy was alone, save for the pigeon that still struggled vainly for escape. He snatched up the wig and hurried back to the Robe Room.

The door was shut.

He was so astonished that for a long moment he merely stared at the heavy oak door. At last he thought to try it, but of course it was locked. He pounded on the thick wood to no effect. Surely the usher knew he was here in the Hall. Then he recalled the man's sour expression, and Rafferdy knew he would not get out *that* way.

Well, there were other ways out. But when he approached the tall, gilded doors opposite the rostrum he found them also shut, and no amount of pushing would make them budge. Rafferdy turned, searching for another exit, and for a dreadful moment he felt as trapped as the pigeon.

The bird was no longer in view; it must have escaped. Then he saw his own means of egress. The small door beside the rostrum, the one through which King Rothard had entered and exited, stood open. He hurried to it, lest it suddenly slam shut before he could pass.

Beyond the door was a corridor. Narrow windows lined one side, permitting thin shafts of sunlight to enter. Through the windows he glimpsed the esplanade before Assembly. It was devoid of people. Mr. and Mrs. Baydon would be wondering what had become of him. They might have already headed back to Fairhall Street to have a glass of wine without him! The corridor was long, so he increased his pace.

At last it ended in a door. To his great dismay, it was locked. He started to turn, to dash back down the corridor to look for another way out, except there wasn't another way.

Besides, didn't he know how to open a lock?

Rafferdy turned back toward the door. He took off his right glove, then laid his hand against the wood. A beam of sunlight caught the ring on his fourth finger. The gem winked like a blue eye.

Surely it was against some law to open a locked door in Assembly. But, he reasoned, he wasn't trying to break into Assembly. Rather, he was trying to break out, and *that* couldn't be any sort of crime.

Before he could think of a reason not to, he spoke the words of the spell. It had been months since he had worked an enchantment. He had not uttered words of magick since that day at the old house on Durrow Street. Yet now that he did speak them, the ancient words sprang easily to his lips, as if he had just finished a lesson with Mr. Bennick.

There was a distant rushing noise as he uttered the final word, followed by a discernible *click*. Rafferdy pushed, and the door swung open. He glanced at his hand. The blue gem flared brightly, then faded. An exhilaration filled him, and a sense of satisfaction, just as it had that day he spoke the enchantment upon the Eye of Ran-Yahgren.

Rafferdy shook his head. It was only because of *her* great need that he had worked magick that day, and it was only because of *his* that he did it now. He put his glove back on and passed through the door into another corridor. As he proceeded quickly down its length, he felt a movement of air. Just ahead, the corridor bent to the left.

"But I still can't fathom how he could have gotten inside," said a voice—low and stern, a man's voice. It echoed from around the corner. "Only members of the king's retinue were allowed in through the west door."

Rafferdy came to a sudden halt, his heart beating vigorously.

"Then you've already answered your question," spoke another. This voice belonged to a woman and, while not loud, it was as sharp as a splinter of crystal. "If only members of the king's retinue were allowed in, then he was part of it. There can be no other answer."

"So he was a traitor, then? But would Lord Valhaine not have discovered him? He has kept watch on all of the king's servants."

"Perhaps he was a traitor." Her voice sounded at once unsure and intrigued. "Or perhaps he was . . . something else."

"What do you mean, something else?" The woman didn't answer, and the man went on. "Well, whoever he was, it wasn't getting in that was the problem for him—it was getting out. He should have known we would take the king by another route than the one we used to bring him in. I don't think he thought through that part of the plan."

"Perhaps," said the woman. "Or perhaps he never intended to get out. In fact, I am rather certain that he didn't. Look."

"What do you think you're—Great God, what is that?"

Such was the sound of astonishment and horror in the man's voice that Rafferdy could not suppress a small exclamation himself.

A rustling sound. "We are not alone, Moorkirk."

Certain he was about to be exposed, Rafferdy saved them the trouble. He stepped around the corner.

"Excuse me," he said, doing his best to emulate Lord Baydon's ever-cheerful tone, "but I've managed to get lost. It's my first time at Assembly, you see. My name is Rafferdy. I'm sitting in the Hall of Magnates for my father, who is ill, but I've gotten myself turned around. Is this the way out?"

"How did you get here?" the man said. He was a hulking figure, with a thick neck, brutish hands, and an overhanging brow.

Rafferdy might have expected to encounter his like in a rough tavern in the Old City. However, his garb was rich and well-cut, if all in shades of gray.

Rafferdy gave a vague wave. "There was a door back there."

The man advanced on him. "All the doors were locked. We sealed all of the exits from this corridor when—" He seemed to catch himself, clenching his thick jaw. "The doors were locked." '

"Well, obviously one of them wasn't, much to my good fortune." Rafferdy smiled as if his life depended on it; he wondered if it didn't.

The woman, who stood above a heap of rags on the floor, moved toward him. Her gown made a stiff, crackling sound. It was all black, like her hair, her eyes, and the ribbon around her throat—a stark contrast to her skin, which was so pale he could discern the paths of blue veins beneath.

"Perhaps the door *was* locked, but then something unlocked it." The woman's gaze flicked to Rafferdy's gloved hands before returning to his face. Her thin lips—a red so deep as to be nearly black—curved in a smile. "Or, more likely, you overlooked one of the doors, Moorkirk."

His face darkened in a glower. "I am certain I did not, Lady Shayde. More likely this fellow is in league with the conspirator. Why don't you use your knife to find out like you did with the other one?"

The man's words provoked two shocking realizations on Rafferdy's part. The first was that this woman was none other than the famed White Lady, a member of the Gray Conclave, and an agent of the king's Black Dog, Lord Valhaine. The second was that she held a slim stiletto in her hand.

"No, that won't be necessary, Moorkirk. See the way his cheeks are flushed? I've encountered their like before. They cannot blush—they are not capable of it."

As she spoke, Rafferdy's gaze went past her to the thing on the ground. What he had taken for a pile of rumpled cloth was in fact a man. His legs and arms were splayed at unnatural angles, and his face was slack in a way that seemed beyond death; rather, it was as if the flesh were melting away from his skull. A wound had been cut into the man's neck—a deep, sharp-edged gash. However, no blood flowed out. Instead, a thick, grayish fluid oozed onto the marble floor.

"Moorkirk," Lady Shayde said, "cover the conspirator."

The man took off his cape and laid it over the corpse, so that only a single limp hand remained in view. Rafferdy's attention was drawn to that appendage. Dark lines marked the palm, and at first Rafferdy thought they were scratches that had crusted over, perhaps wounds gained in some scuffle. Only how could a man who did not bleed from his neck form a scab upon his hand? Besides, the lines were too precisely arranged to be wounds gained in a violent struggle. Instead, they looked like a kind of symbol. . . .

The man called Moorkirk gave the cloak a twitch, covering the lifeless hand. As if a spell had been broken, Rafferdy was able to avert his gaze. He no longer made any pretense of smiling.

"I still want to know how he got in here," Moorkirk said, looking up. Rafferdy was certain he was not referring to the body.

Lady Shayde took another step closer. "Your name is Rafferdy, you say. You are Lord Rafferdy's son, then?"

He managed a nod. "So I am."

"And I believe you know who I am."

Again he nodded.

"I'm sorry you witnessed this sight, Mr. Rafferdy. I know it can only be upsetting. There was a plot to disrupt the opening of Assembly today. You must know, of course, that such things happen. There are a few wicked people who seek to harm Altania and its institutions because they hate anything good and noble. It is my duty to find them and stop them. The other conspirators were caught before they could enter the Hall of Magnates today, and as you can see, this man was prevented from doing any ill."

She moved closer yet, until her face was a white moon before him, eclipsing all else.

"Even so, I am sure this is distressing for you to witness. A grave shock such as this can have an effect on your mind. You might not even be certain what you really saw today. It would be best if you did not speak of it to anyone. Do you understand, Mr. Rafferdy?"

Her eyes were so black he could not see where iris met pupil. "Of course," he said. The words were hoarse, for his mouth was dry.

She regarded him for a long moment, until he felt lost in her black gaze. Then she nodded and stepped away.

Her companion frowned. "Aren't you going to question him? He could know something."

"I am satisfied, Moorkirk. Besides, he is the lord inquirer's son. It is not as if we don't know where to find him should there be need. Please show Mr. Rafferdy the way out, then make arrangements for this to be removed." She gestured to the body.

Moorkirk appeared less than pleased, but did not question his mistress. He made a sharp motion for Rafferdy to follow. They turned a corner, leaving the lady and the body behind, and walked in silence until they came to an iron-bound door. Moorkirk unlocked it with a key and pushed it open. Yellow sunlight spilled through, so brilliant Rafferdy was forced to raise a hand to shade his eyes.

"You'd do best if you forgot this," Moorkirk said. "But do not think that she'll forget you. She doesn't forget anything."

Rafferdy gave a mute nod. However, in his mind, he could still see the body sprawled on the floor and the colorless liquid flowing from the gash in its neck. He knew it was a sight he would long remember.

"Go," the large man said.

Rafferdy walked into the light, and the door clanged shut behind him. He found himself at the side of the Hall of Magnates. Above, the Citadel loomed on its rocky height. Usually he thought nothing of the sight of the king's fortress. All he could think now when he looked up at the Citadel was that it was the place where *she* resided. He worked his tongue in his parched mouth. By God, he needed a drink. How he wished to call for a hack cab and direct it to the nearest tavern.

Instead, he made his way around to the street, and there he found a single black carriage waiting.

"There you are, Mr. Rafferdy!" Mrs. Baydon said, throwing open the door of the barouche. "We are all quite vexed with you. We have been waiting for you forever. Where have you been all this time?"

He opened his mouth, unsure what he would say. At that moment Lord Baydon exclaimed from inside the carriage, "My wig! You have found it, Mr. Rafferdy."

To his surprise, he looked down and saw Lord Baydon's wig protruding from his coat pocket. He took it out and handed it over to its owner.

"Well, I knew everything would work out to our satisfaction," Lord Baydon said as Rafferdy climbed into the carriage. "I have my favorite wig back, and it is very well it took you so long to find it, for now all the crowds are gone, and we shall speed to Fairhall Street without delay, no doubt arriving just in time for dinner."

"I can only imagine you're right," Rafferdy said.

Mrs. Baydon gave him a look of concern from the opposite seat. "Are you well, Mr. Rafferdy? You look very tired."

"So much novelty and interest are bound to take a toll on one," Mr. Baydon said. "Of course, Mrs. Baydon found the proceedings to be very dull, though that's only to be expected, for she could not really understand them. But what about you, Rafferdy? What did you think of the whole affair?"

"I'm afraid it left little impression on me," he said, affecting a light tone. "Indeed, I find I can hardly recall anything that happened, except that my robe was very old and pitiful and had a dreadful smell about it."

This elicited a groan from Mr. Baydon, but Mrs. Baydon laughed.

"That's our dear Mr. Rafferdy," she said. "With a few words, the entire workings of our government can be reduced to one shabby gown."

Mr. Baydon proceeded to lecture her on the importance of the day's proceedings. She gave Rafferdy a pained look, and he smiled in return.

The barouche rolled into motion. As it did, Rafferdy looked out the window at the tall spires that surmounted Assembly, and his smile faded. The sun had begun its descent, and in the flat light of the long afternoon the towers seemed forged of silver, like slender knives.

CHAPTER EIGHT

NOW THAT MR. Quent's situation had been so suddenly and drastically altered, the plans for the refurbishment of the house on Durrow Street were by necessity altered as well. Again Lord Rafferdy wrote to him, this time advising Mr. Quent to reconsider all of his schemes and ideas for the restoration of the house. What might have seemed appropriate for the dwelling of a gentleman must be deemed completely unsuitable for the domicile of a baronet. Even as his status had been raised, so must the quality of their habitation.

That they remove themselves to an abode in the New Quarter, Lord Rafferdy did not think necessary. Propriety must be obeyed, but not necessarily fashion. Besides, as he was but a baronet, and one newly made, it was best if he did not appear eager to assume all the appurtenances of a magnate. He must do his new class credit, so as not to diminish it, yet he must not appear to reach beyond its bounds either. To please his peers and reassure those above him was entirely the purpose of the improvement of the house.

And Lord Rafferdy's advice must be heeded. Mr. Quent's respect for the lord inquirer, whom he had long served, was profound. He showed Ivy the letter, which arrived at the house on Durrow Street nearly simultaneously with Mr. Quent, and meetings were held with the builder that very day.

Everything must be grander and more impressive than previously envisioned. Rooms that were to be left closed must now be opened, or joined together and expanded. Windows were to be increased in number, low doorways replaced with arches, and ceilings vaulted to increase the influx of light and air. Simple moldings must now be carved with detail, new furnishings imported from the Principalities, and plain carpets and drapery replaced with Murghese textiles.

In the brief time it took to explain these things to the builder, the allowance for the restoration of the house increased tenfold. Ivy could not imagine, as she listened, that her eyes were any less wide than those of Mr. Barbridge. To think, she had kept the household at Whitward Street for little more than five hundred regals a year. Now, such an amount would hardly furnish a single room at Durrow Street! The tallying of the expense left Ivy stupefied. However, there was no stopping things. Mr. Barbridge was dispatched at once to make new arrangements.

It was not until the day was done that she at last had a moment alone with her husband. The lumenal had given way to night in the most sudden and startling fashion, as if a dark cloth had been cast over the world; or rather, as if a thin blue veil had been snatched from the sky, revealing the endless void that lay beyond, pricked by cold stars.

The new almanac (if it could be trusted) said the umbral was to be brief, and it was true that short nights usually fell quickly. All the same, Ivy could hardly recall an umbral that had descended quite so abruptly as this. For a moment, there in the gallery on the second floor, she could not help a shiver. Then Mr. Quent took her hand and she grew warm again.

Mrs. Seenly was gone for the day, and Lily and Rose had retired to their rooms, weary from the excitement of the past two lumenals. Ivy had no doubt Mr. Quent was weary as well after his rapid journey to Invarel from the North Country. But the lumenal had not been long, and she felt wide awake herself.

Besides, she wanted to show him the door.

There were no lamps lit in the gallery, but she pushed back the sheets over the windows to let in a flood of silver light. It was not long since Brightday, and the moon was still large. There was no need to light a candle, which was well, for the price of candles had become even more exorbitant of late. Ivy had been forced to frequently admonish Lily not to light more than were necessary when she was reading.

Yet what did it matter? If they were to spend so vast a sum on the restoration of the house, how could the expense of a few boxes of candles be noticed? It would make all the difference a pea might if added to a cartload of stones. An absurd laughter rose within her, and she clamped a hand to her mouth too late to stifle it.

"It seems something is giving you great amusement, Mrs. Quent," her husband said, a curious look on his broad face. "Whatever it is, perhaps you would be willing to share it?"

"Amusement?" she gasped, then shook her head. "No, you have spent too much time away from me lately, Mr. Quent, and you have forgotten what my expressions look like. I assure you, it is not any sort of amusement I feel. Rather, it is terror!"

His voice became low and gruff. "Now I am puzzled by your words, or dismayed, really. I would have thought any terror you might experience would be lessened upon my return, not increased."

"So I would have thought as well. However, I find you returned in a far altered condition. I was expecting the arrival of my dear Mr. Quent today, but he is no more. It is Sir Quent I have received instead."

"And this should cause you terror? I would think your reaction to this change should be one of immense pleasure, even joy."

"No, you are mistaken. You see, joy is what I knew before, in every moment I spent with Mr. Quent. To be with him was everything I wanted or wished for. When I was with him, I had not a single want or care. But this Sir Quent—I cannot say how it will be. I do not know him yet."

He let out a rare laugh, though it was more an expression of astonishment than humor. "I would think that you do know him! Indeed, I am certain that you do, for he is the very same man you bid farewell to not half a month ago."

"Is he?" Ivy affected a serious tone. "I am not so certain as you. The Mr. Quent that I knew proceeded on the refurbishment of the house with great frugality. Yet I have heard Sir Quent blithely command orders for brass chandeliers and gilt trim and Murghese rugs."

"Are you saying that I acted injudiciously today?"

Furrows creased his brow, and something of that old glower, which she had witnessed so many times in her first months at Heathcrest Hall, came over his face. For all that he had grown lighter since then, he could not help the expression sometimes—and she loved him for it.

"Tell me, Mrs. Quent—or Lady Quent, for that is who you are now—and spare me no measure of scorn. Do you think I have become frivolous?"

Now it was Ivy's turn to laugh. "No, I do not think I will ever be able to accuse you of *that*! I am sure there has never been a man who ordered damask curtains so grimly as you. I know you did it with specific purpose."

He turned to look around the moonlit gallery. "Yes, it was all done for a purpose. Even if I disagreed with him, still I would follow Lord Rafferdy's advice. Yet I think he is right. A man must not appear to willingly stray from his place. Others would ask themselves why he chose to set himself apart from his peers, and so would wonder at his motives. Such scrutiny would only make it more difficult to do my work in a discreet fashion. Thus I must live within the confines of my new position."

This time it was she who was astonished. "You sound as if, rather than being granted a title, you have been sentenced to prison!"

"It is a kind of prison, perhaps. One with its own keepers and its own locks—that is, other members of society, and society's own restrictions, which as you know are as rigid as any bars of iron."

These words unsettled Ivy for a reason she could not quite identify. Before she could consider it further, his beard parted in that wolfish grin she all too rarely witnessed, and which she held all the more precious for its scarcity.

"Do not worry, Lady Quent. It will be a very fine prison that confines us, will it not? One with damask curtains and brass chandeliers. I'm sure you will find it utterly pleasant to dwell within."

Her smile returned. "I am sure you are right. That is, as long as the expense of the construction does not result in us being sent to yet another prison—by which I mean to the pauper's house."

"On that account you need have no worry. Most of Earl Rylend's estate returned to the Crown upon his death, for he had no heir. Still, it was no small fortune that he left me, and Heathcrest Hall was only part of it."

He moved to one of the windows. "It was something I scarcely deserved for what little I had done. How much better I would have served him if I had been capable, and for how much less in return! Now once again, for services I hardly feel warrant such merit, I have received a vast reward. Along with this new title, I have been granted some of the same lands that once belonged to Earl Rylend." He turned to regard her, his brown eyes solemn. "Therefore you must believe me when I say you can have no worry about the expense of the work on this house."

Ivy was overwhelmed. *You do warrant such merit!* she wanted to shout. However, feeling had constricted her throat, so that she was mute.

Now he took a step toward her. He wore the same boots and breeches he had ridden in that day. He had taken off his coat, and in his white shirt—open at the throat and turned up at the cuffs— he shone in the moonlight that streamed through the window.

"You mistake me, you know," he said in a low voice. "It was not any sort of frugality that caused me so rarely to spend money in the past. Rather, it was that I had no cause to spend it. It has been many years since I had any reason to be frivolous. But now I have you."

"Then I can assure you, you have no more reason to be frivolous than you did before!" Though she laughed as she spoke these words, she felt again some of that trepidation that had gripped her all day. "There is no need to make expenses on *my* account. As I said, I was perfectly happy before."

He closed the distance between them. "If that is the case, then you will be perfectly happy still. This will not change us."

"No, you are wrong. This will change everything, as it must."

Ivy looked up at him, and for the first time since reading his letter yesterday, her dread receded. She laid her right hand against his bearded cheek.

"Yet despite all the changes that must come, one thing will never be altered. I will love you no less and no more than I did before. That is, I will love you with all of my ability to do so."

He took her hand and brought it to his lips. It was the left hand he used for this action, and it was no less strong or deft for the fact that the last two fingers were missing. At Heathcrest Hall, he had told her how he had come to be injured so: that as a boy an act of foolishness had caused him to spend a night in a grove of Wyrdwood, and the loss of his fingers was the mark that incident had left upon him.

Since that time, it had always been his habit to keep his left hand in his coat pocket when others were present. However, he no longer made any attempt to conceal his old wound from her, and there was no gesture of affection he could have made, no words of devotion he could have uttered, that would have meant more to her.

"Was there not something you brought me here to see?" he said at last. "Come, take me to it."

Still holding his hand, she led him to the north end of the gallery and showed him the door.

Mr. Barbridge's men had done excellent work. The door had been scrupulously cleaned, and its coat of varnish burnished to a gloss. The wall around it had been painted a deep red, against which the door's ornate molding stood out like the frame around a piece of art.

And it *was* a work of art. The leaves and twining tendrils were so finely wrought, so natural in appearance, it seemed they had not been carved into the wood, but rather had sprouted from it. As they made an examination of the door, the leaves seemed almost to stir and quiver. This time it was not the result of any kind of magick or spell. Rather, it was only an effect of the shimmering moonlight.

After her dealings with the Vigilant Order of the Silver Eye, Ivy had told Mr. Quent about her various encounters with the man in the black mask. He had agreed that the stranger's help had been crucial in preventing the magicians from using the artifact upstairs. But Mr. Quent was wary of any man who chose not to reveal himself, and he had asked Ivy to inform him if she ever saw the peculiar stranger again.

Ivy had not yet had a chance to tell Mr. Quent how the masked man had appeared to her yesterday. She did not want to concern him unduly—not when there was so much on his mind. Besides, it was not as if there was anything more Ivy could do. If there were indeed other magicians and other doors, then it was for other people to concern themselves with.

I will tell Mr. Quent about it tomorrow, she decided.

They continued their examination of the door. Mr. Quent said that she had been right to instruct Mr. Barbridge to leave it exposed; a thing of such beauty should not be hidden.

"If you have any concerns about the expense of the work on the house, then this should remove them," he said. "A house that has such marvels to be discovered deserves everything lavished upon it. So would you agree, then, that the new Quent is in no way more frivolous than the old?"

She could only concede the point.

"Now," he said, his tone grave, "what else can I do to introduce you to Sir Quent? I do not want to alarm you further."

Ivy looked up, considering him as he stood before her. She

had no doubt that, after much expense, the house on Durrow Street would be considered handsome by even the vainest residents of the New Quarter. She also had no doubt that those same people would never say the same of Mr. Quent. Even if he owned fashionable clothes, he would not be able to wear them; he was not tall enough, and his figure was not elegant, but rather deep-chested and heavy-shouldered. Nor would fashionable attire hide his unruly brown hair or coarse beard or the lines around his eyes. However, there was nothing that gave her more delight than the sight of him.

"Come closer to me," she said.

He did as commanded. She leaned against him then, and he enfolded her in his arms. He smelled of the open air. The scent reminded her of Heathcrest, and she breathed deeply.

"Does this mean that I no longer induce a terror in you?"

"No, not anymore. Indeed, Sir Quent, I believe I prefer you to Mr. Quent in every way. For your embraces are just as pleasant, yet you are significantly richer."

"So you admit it—you are pleased that I am now a baronet?"

"Yes, I am pleased." Feeling washed over her, a kind of fierce pride. "I am pleased because you deserve it. You say this house warrants everything that is being lavished upon it. Well, you warrant what is being lavished upon *you*. Because of you, disaster in Torland—indeed, in all of Altania—was prevented. You were overly modest when you recounted the events in Torland to me, but Lord Rafferdy told me more when he was here: that it was due to your actions alone that the witch who provoked the Wyrdwood was found. It was you who put an end to the Risings—a fact that Lord Rafferdy has no doubt imparted to the king. Now, like any hero, you must have your accolades, whether you wish for them or not."

He gazed at her, and for a moment his expression startled her. There was a peculiar light in his brown eyes, almost like a glint of sadness—or rather, like a kind of regret.

Yet this expression should not surprise her. She could only suppose it caused him some measure of sorrow that he had been forced to deliver a witch into the custody of the king's soldiers in Torland. Ivy's own feelings were at odds on the subject. She felt a great relief that the Risings had been stopped. At the same time, she could not help thinking of Halley Samonds, who had been drawn to the old stand of Wyrdwood not far from Heathcrest Hall. Just as the first Mrs. Quent had been.

It had not been at their choosing that the ancient wood had called to them. And perhaps it had not been the choice of the witch in Torland. If so, it would have been difficult for Mr. Quent not to think of his Gennivel—or of Ivy herself. For did she not share the same propensities as Halley Samonds and Gennivel Quent?

All the same—no matter whether she went willingly to the wood, or whether it had called to her—it was wrong for the witch in Torland to have done what she did. Just as it had been wrong for Halley Samonds to have used the stand of Wyrdwood near Heathcrest to harbor Westen Darendal and his band of rebels. For the sake of Altania, Mr. Quent had had no choice but to find the witch and deliver her to the Crown.

These were all grave thoughts, but then he tightened his arms around her, and she had no more cause or ability to consider them.

"Well, you have made the acquaintance of Sir Quent," he said, his voice gruff once more. "Now it is my turn to be introduced to Lady Quent."

She agreed it was past time for such a meeting. They went upstairs to their bedchamber, and there the introduction proceeded very well, so that they were soon acquainted with each other in the most intimate manner.

THE VERY NEXT lumenal, the house was swarming with twice the men as it had on the previous day, and there was not a room in any wing on any floor where the furor of the reconstruction could be escaped. Soon Lily was beside herself, being unable to read or play the pianoforte. Then Miss Mew, upset by all the clamor, scratched Rose's arm when she was trying to hold the little cat, upon which Rose burst into tears.

Before that lumenal was half-done, Ivy knew they could not remain in the house while work proceeded at this new pace. Mr. Quent concurred, and that afternoon they removed themselves to The Seventh Swan, the inn near the Halls of Assembly where they had stayed when the house was first being opened and made habitable.

This at once improved their situation. Rose had a quiet place to sit and sew with Miss Mew curled up beside her, while Lily found great entertainment in looking out the window at the passers-by on the street below—though Ivy had to remind her it was not tactful to lean out the window and wave to any of them, no matter how good-looking or well-dressed they might be.

"What if I see Mr. Rafferdy go by?" Lily complained. "Should I not wave to him? We are acquainted, so I am sure it would be very rude if I did not. He would be upset if we did not call him in to take tea with us."

"If you see Mr. Rafferdy, it means he is on his way to Assembly, in which case he would have little time for tea."

"Not if he's walking *from* Assembly rather than toward it."

Lily may not have inherited their father's scientific demeanor, but that didn't mean she wasn't clever, and Ivy had to concede the point. She agreed that Lily could wave to Mr. Rafferdy—in a discreet fashion, so as not to make a scene—if she ever saw him walking *away* from Assembly.

Indeed, if Ivy saw him walking so, she was sure she would wave herself. She wanted very much to hear what he thought of being in the Hall of Magnates, and she knew Mr. Quent would be pleased to see him as well. The two had met just once, not long after Mr. Rafferdy had warned his father of the plot to harm Lord Rafferdy and Mr. Quent.

For that Mr. Quent had thanked him, though Mr. Rafferdy had claimed that he had done nothing more than to pass on news that had come to him from an anonymous source. This apparent wish to take no credit for himself had made an impression upon Mr.

Quent, who later remarked that he thought Mr. Rafferdy to be a very sensible and modest young man.

Ivy found great amusement in that statement, and replied that while she was exceedingly fond of Mr. Rafferdy, she thought perhaps Mr. Quent would need to meet him again to form a more accurate assessment.

WHILE THE AGITATION of her sisters was reduced by their removal to The Seventh Swan, Ivy's was soon increased, for the very next lumenal came their meeting with the king.

"How I wish there had been more time to prepare myself!" she exclaimed as she descended the stairs of the inn. "I should have bought a gown in the current mode and devised some new way to arrange my hair. Instead, I look just as I always have."

Mr. Quent took her hand as she reached the foot of the steps. "If your intent was to alter yourself, then I am glad you did not have more time. It is best if we do not appear too suddenly changed. If our look is somewhat plain, then it is only as it should be."

"That is easy for you to say, for *you* look very smart."

He wore the blue coat she had bought him not long after their arrival in Invarel, and he had polished his boots to a gloss. His hair was oiled and his beard trimmed. In fact, he looked exceedingly good.

"Besides," she went on, "is that not precisely why our house is being redone—to better effect the air of a baronet? Well, you should have refurbished your lady as well as your house."

He regarded her seriously. "I am sure it is possible that your gown might be judged in a disparaging manner by the ladies of the court. Yet I am equally sure no man will take notice of any deficit of fashionability it might display. Indeed, I had best keep a tight hold on you, Mrs. Quent, for it is said no king can see a beautiful jewel without coveting it for his own."

Despite his solemn expression, she was sure he was making a jest at her expense. Nor could she claim she did not deserve it. To worry about her appearance when her husband was to receive a weighty honor was a vanity she might have expected of Lily rather than herself. As if, with a hero of the realm present, any eyes would be upon *her*!

All the same, rather than admit her error, she affected a haughty tone. "Pardon me, but that's *Lady* Quent."

Then she was laughing at the absurdity of it all, and even he grinned as they walked out the door into the brilliant morning.

By the time the carriage halted before the Citadel, however, their mirth had subsided. Neither of them was very suited for such an affair. In her life she had only ever had the occasion to meet three magnates—Lord Rafferdy and his cousins, Lady Marsdel and Lord Baydon—and now she was to meet a *king*. That her experiences had left her unprepared for such a duty was an understatement of the severest degree!

As for Mr. Quent, he looked more steady than she felt. Yet he seemed to approach the event with the same sort of grim resolve he might display if he were setting off to investigate a Rising.

A redcrest helped them out of the carriage and they were ushered into the keep, where they found they were far from the only ones waiting to see the king that day. For some reason, Ivy had envisioned that His Majesty would be sitting on his throne, and that they would be forced to proceed down the long length of the echoing and empty hall to kneel before him.

Instead, there was neither monarch nor throne in view, and the main hall of the Citadel was anything but empty, being filled with dozens of other petitioners of every possible station and appearance. If anyone thought ill of Ivy's gown, they did not show it. Indeed, there were many who were clad far more poorly than she.

Mr. Quent took her arm, and to pass the time while they waited for their audience they toured around the hall. Ivy had been in here once as a girl, when the Citadel was open for a public day. Then she had imagined the rows of thick columns to be a forest of trees, and she had run merrily among them, hiding from Mr. Lockwell behind one, then dashing to another once her father caught sight of her.

Now as she gazed at the columns she saw not trees but cold stones; and their massiveness, rather than reassuring her of their strength, only served to remind her of the vast weight of the structure pressing down.

"I must say, you watch the ceiling with a rather wary eye. I trust that you'll let the rest of us know if you see something up there we should be alarmed about."

Startled, Ivy lowered her gaze, to see a woman before her. Mr. Quent stood a short way off, his expression somber as he looked out a window. Ivy must have been wandering as she stared at the vaults above; and she had been so preoccupied that, had the other not spoken, Ivy would have walked right into her.

The woman smiled. "I admit, the arches do have something of a precarious look about them. To stand beneath so many tons of stone is disconcerting when one pauses to consider it. Yet I'm sure you needn't worry. Kings always assume that they'll rule forever, and so they tend to build their fortresses to last just as long."

She was a little older than Ivy, a great deal taller, and was strikingly beautiful. Her chestnut hair was styled into coils and ringlets that spilled over her shoulders. Her brows formed elegant arches above violet eyes, her nose was small and refined, and her teeth were very good.

Ivy realized she was staring again, only this time not at the ceiling.

"It is absurd to worry about it falling," she said with some chagrin. "I have read that the Citadel was built upon the remains of an old Tharosian keep, which itself was constructed upon the site of a fort erected by the first people to inhabit Altania. That a thing that has stood for so many eons should choose to collapse just at the moment I enter is a conceit I cannot allow."

The woman laughed—a sound that was not trilling or sharp like the laughter of some women, but rather low and warm. "But you are very wise! I have been in the Citadel a hundred times and never thought a thing about how it came to be here. Only I wonder why I haven't. I will consider these old stones with far more interest now."

The woman's mirth was catching, and Ivy could not help smiling in return. She noted that the other's dress was exceedingly rich, crafted of pale apricot silk, its bodice sewn with tiny pearls.

Ivy looked about. "Do you think there is anyone who might be able to acquaint us? My husband comes to the Citadel at times to . . . on his business. Do you think there is someone here who is known to both of us?"

The other gave a wave of a gloved hand. "Oh, I am sure of it. I know far more people in this hall than I care to." Again she smiled at Ivy. "Yet not so many as I wish to. Nor do I hew to that decrepit maxim that two people, though they are sure they would find each other agreeable, must not speak to each other, and must each pretend the other does not exist, until they can dredge up some mutual acquaintance—however distant or detestable—to link them together in an introduction."

Ivy could only concede the other's point. "I admit, it is something of a peculiar custom. Yet imagine if as you walked down the street any person might accost you in order to introduce themselves."

"All manner of rude and horrible people already do. It is only the finer people who adhere to the rules of proper society and restrain themselves. Which means that manners cannot protect me from the legions of the ill-behaved; rather, they can only serve to prevent the people with whom I wish to speak from speaking to me. Therefore I will have none of it, and I will be the rude person who accosts *you*." She held out her hand. "You must now, whether you wish it or not, consider yourself acquainted with Lady Crayford of Armount Street."

Ivy listened to this last speech with great amusement—until the other's final utterance. A lady was introducing herself to her! And not merely any lady, for Ivy had heard the name on several occasions as Lily read about famous parties in *The Comet* or *The Messenger.* This was a viscountess and, according to Lily, one of the most fashionable beings in all of Invarel.

Ivy nearly faltered, her head abuzz; but she had come to meet a king today, so she must consider a viscountess, however beautiful and renowned, to be an object of less dread. She took the other's hand and made a curtsy, though Lady Crayford, with the gentlest pressure, pulled her upward before she could sink very low.

"I am Mrs. Quent," Ivy remembered to say at last.

"There, it is done," Lady Crayford said with a pleased look. "We have introduced ourselves, and neither the Citadel nor the edifice of society has come tumbling down upon us. I presume that is Mr. Quent over there?"

Ivy followed her gaze. Mr. Quent had turned away from the window and was now speaking with someone she did not know— a striking man with gray at the temples, clad all in black.

"Yes, that is him in the blue coat," she said.

"I suppose he is not from Invarel."

Ivy could only smile. "He is from County Westmorain."

"A country gentleman—I had thought as much. He looks as if he could toss three lords at once with his bare hands. Men in the city have all become such fine things. They are exceedingly nice to look at, I grant you, yet it seems these days they wear more lace and powder than I do." She looked again at Mr. Quent. "I imagine he has never worn a bit of lace since infanthood. How you must admire him!"

Ivy was not one to display an overt pride, but all the same a warmth filled her. "I do admire him. Though I am sure you will never see him toss a single lord, let alone three."

Lady Crayford sighed. "How unfortunate. I'm sure some lords in the city could do with a little tossing. Speaking of which, I see that Lord Valhaine is monopolizing your husband. Come, let us take a turn about the hall while you wait for your audience."

Ivy glanced back at the tall, imposing man her husband was speaking to; his dark eyes were intent upon Mr. Quent. So that was Lord Valhaine! Ivy supposed she should not be shocked that the two men were acquainted. It was public knowledge that Lord Valhaine was concerned with all possible threats against the Crown, so he could only be well aware of the work of the inquirers. Still, it startled her to realize Mr. Quent was familiar with men such as the king's notorious Black Dog.

As Mr. Quent indeed appeared occupied with Lord Valhaine, Ivy could find no cause to deny Lady Crayford's request, so she allowed the viscountess to lead her in a tour about the hall. As they went, Ivy's companion pointed out the various objects of art all around. Despite her professed ignorance of the Citadel's architecture, she could utter the title of every painting and statue, as well as who created them and what they symbolized.

"You are an expert on the subject of art," Ivy said, both astonished and delighted at Lady Crayford's knowledge.

The other gave a small shrug. "I am audacious enough to consider myself something of a painter. I'm dreadful, of course, but like most amateurs I find great amusement in expounding upon the works of others, as if I could have done any better."

"I am sure your works are not dreadful at all," Ivy said. "A painting made by one possessed of such insight must have something of interest to behold in it, no matter the level of skill with which it was wrought."

Again Lady Crayford laughed. "Where have you been hiding yourself all this time, Mrs. Quent? I would that I had made your acquaintance ages ago! I will repeat your words to my husband the next time he wonders why I waste so much time daubing a brush against canvas."

With that she took Ivy's arm, as if they had been friends for the longest time, and continued to lead her about the hall. So flustered and thrilled was Ivy that she could only follow along, like some charmed creature, listening to her companion's interesting and amusing expressions.

A man in black attire passed them, and as he did his eyes lingered upon Ivy, to the point that she became painfully aware of herself and was forced to look away. It was, she realized with a start, Lord Valhaine.

"Do not be concerned about the looks of others," Lady Crayford said softly. "You are sure to get many stares today."

"I cannot imagine why I should receive many looks, unless it is because I appear odd in some way. I am sure I am nobody important."

"On the contrary, you are exceedingly famous," the viscount-ess said, and her violet eyes sparkled. "Indeed, I can conceal it no longer, and must confess my horrible crime. You see, I did not encounter you by chance today. Rather, I sought you out, know-ing you would be here, and then inflicted myself upon you. Do you see how awful I am? My husband assures me that I scheme in the most devious ways, and now I am revealed to you in all my vil-lainy."

Ivy's astonishment brought her to a halt. To think she had been the object of a viscountess's plans was beyond her comprehension.

"There, you are repulsed!" Lady Crayford said triumphantly. "I cannot blame you. Yet how could I not concoct a means of encountering the heroic Mr. Quent, savior of the realm in its recent time of troubles, as well as his new wife, Mrs. Quent, whose beauty is said to be exceptional, and which I have now discovered far exceeds any rumors? Though in a moment you will be Mr. and Mrs. no longer, but rather *Sir* and *Lady*."

At last Ivy reacted, and it was not out of repulsion, but rather great discomfort. "How presumptuous you must think us! You must believe that we aspired to this, that we somehow sought out such a reward."

Lady Crayford tightened her hold on Ivy's arm. "No, I detect that you are far too sensible, Mrs. Quent, to want something so silly as to be made a lady. Also, because I am an artist and can de-tect such things in a profile, I can see Mr. Quent is too noble in his character to ever want for a noble title. Thus it is perfectly clear it has all been forced upon you."

She turned to face Ivy, taking Ivy's hand in her own. "How amusing it will be for all of those who so desperately cling to their titles to witness someone receiving one he would no doubt will-ingly give up. Yet that is not possible, for it is to be bestowed upon him whether he wishes it or not, and upon you. And here comes the steward for you now, I see. Farewell, Mrs. Quent. When I see you next, I shall call you Lady Quent!"

Ivy had only time for the most hurried farewell. Then Mr. Quent was there beside her, along with a man who was introduced to her as Lord Malhew, the king's steward. Having just become acquainted with a viscountess, Ivy could only take her meeting with a lord in stride. Nor was there much time to form a proper reaction to anything, for in moments they were taken to an antechamber off the hall, and there, before she hardly had time to draw a breath or formulate a thought, they were presented to His Most Glorious Majesty, Rothard, King of Altania.

Perhaps it was the smallness of the room that made the king look small in turn. Or perhaps it was that his garb, while fine, was too large for him—or rather, it had been cut for a larger man. He did not so much sit on his chair as he was crumpled upon it. He wore no crown, but only a silk hat as if he was cold. A few courtiers sat about the perimeters of the room, but their gazes were not derisive as Ivy had feared, merely bored.

The king did not look at them as they approached and paid their obeisance with a bow and a curtsy. However, as the steward read from a proclamation—declaring that Mr. Alasdare Eulysius Quent of County Westmorain was to be granted the Baronetcy of Cairnbridge and all of its holdings and incomes in return for re-markable service rendered to the Crown in containing the recent Risings in Torland—the king raised his head. While his shoulders remained hunched, and a tremor could be detected in the motions of his hands, his eyes were a keen gray.

"I am told that the Risings in Torland were the most extensive since those recorded in ancient times." His words were hoarse but precisely enunciated. "Lord Valhaine says that the lives lost num-bered in the hundreds."

"Regrettably, that is so, Your Majesty," Mr. Quent said. "I con-firmed the figures with him only a few moments ago."

The king nodded. "He also tells me that the devastation could have been far worse had it not been for your efforts in securing the person of the witch who instigated this, and that she might have caused every stand of Wyrdwood in the west of Altania to rise up. The disaster this would have caused—not only in terms of life and property, but also in its effect on the minds and hearts of my sub-jects, and on their confidence in the strength of their government—

would have been of the gravest proportions. For averting this disaster, you have my gratitude, and the gratitude of all of Altania."

Mr. Quent drew a visible breath. "I did only what I must."

"As do all great men." The king seemed to straighten a fraction in his chair. "It is not a man who makes himself great. Rather, it is circumstance that permits him to be so, if it is in his being. There are many men who might be great who dwell in times of peace, and so their true nature is never shown. But circumstance has revealed *your* true nature, Mr. Quent. Therefore I bestow this reward upon you. It is hardly enough, but I presume you will not refuse it. So come, and claim your due."

Mr. Quent dutifully knelt before the king and kissed his ring. The steward placed a slender sword in the king's hands, and aided him in lifting the blade and tapping Mr. Quent on each shoulder. When he rose, the steward declared that he was now Sir Quent, Baronet of Cairnbridge. Ivy felt her heart flutter in her chest. Such pride and admiration she felt for her husband could hardly be borne.

Nor was she the only one affected. The various courtiers no longer seemed dull. Rather, they watched with interest, and many of them even stood and clapped. And if Mr. Quent bore the whole thing soberly, it only made him seem more the worthy hero.

Then it was finished. It was time for the king's next audience. The whole affair had taken no more than five minutes.

As they departed, a startling thought occurred to Ivy. Here in this room was the very king whose approval they required for the petition to release her father from Madstone's. But there had been no time to ask His Majesty about the matter, nor could it have been deemed in any way appropriate to have used this occasion to do so. However, even as she considered this, she realized Mr. Quent was discussing the very topic with the steward.

"I will be sure to inquire as to the status of your petition, Sir Quent," Lord Malhew said as they paused by the door.

"You have my thanks," Mr. Quent replied.

The steward nodded, then they departed the room. Ivy was

beyond words, yet she knew that Mr. Quent could detect the gratitude in the look she gave him.

As they entered the hall, Ivy looked about for Lady Crayford but did not see her. It was just as well; by the purposefulness of his gait, Ivy knew her husband was ready to depart. She took Mr. Quent's arm—or rather, Sir Quent's, she thought, giddy now—and they walked across the hall.

"Well, I suppose that went well enough," she said when it was clear he was not going to speak without prompting. "Though I confess that I was, on the whole, a bit disappointed."

"How so?" he rumbled.

"For one thing, I thought there would be fanfares of trumpets."

"You thought no such thing!"

She could feign seriousness no longer, and she smiled at him. "Perhaps not. But you'll forgive me if, in my ignorance, I thought—or rather, I dreaded—that the ceremony would be grander in scale."

"I am in no way surprised it wasn't. It can hardly be considered an exceptional happening for another baronet to be added to the rolls. Like lords, they are already as common as fleas on a hound."

"Well, then, let us hope Altania does not get an itch and shake them off, lords and baronets all."

"She may yet," he said, and despite the fact that Ivy had been making a jest, his tone was grim.

Before she could wonder what he meant, she caught a glimpse across the hall of a tall, slender woman. Was Lady Crayford still in the keep after all? However, as Ivy turned, she saw that the woman was not dressed in an apricot gown. Instead, she was clad all in black. For a moment, Ivy was aware of onyx eyes set in a pale face. Midnight blue lips curved upward, though the expression did not seem to be a smile. Then the woman stepped behind a column and was lost from view.

Startled, Ivy realized she had just seen Lady Shayde, servant of Lord Valhaine and mistress of the Gray Conclave.

"What a sad and pitiful creature," Mr. Quent said quietly.

Ivy glanced up at him. He spoke as if he knew her. Though, now that she considered it, she supposed she could not be surprised that he was acquainted with Lady Shayde. If in his work he had come to know Lord Valhaine, then surely he had encountered the Black Dog's famed White Lady.

Her husband tightened his hold on her arm. "The stones of this place hold the night chill," he said. "Come, let us go back out in the sun."

They did so, walking through the doors of the Citadel out into the day, and so Sir and Lady Quent made their entrance into the world.

CHAPTER NINE

ELDYN AWOKE TO warm light. The radiance seemed to surround him, to buoy him, as if he was floating in a golden sea. He stretched and gave a great yawn, then blinked his eyes to clear the sleep from them. As had been the case nearly every morning for the last half month, it was not his chamber in the old monastery near Graychurch he saw as he opened his eyes, but rather, a small, neatly kept room above the Theater of the Moon.

"Well, there you are at last, you layabout." Dercy looked down at Eldyn, leaning on an elbow. "Someone must have given you too much to drink at tavern last night. I was beginning to think I would have to hasten the dawn along even more swiftly to wake you."

He made a motion with his hand, and the honeyed light brightened around them. Eldyn sat up in the bed and looked at the small window in the opposite wall. Through a gap in the curtain he could see a strip of slate gray sky. He let out a groan.

"The sun's not even up yet. This light—it's all your doing."

"So it is," Dercy said with remorseless cheer.

Eldyn lifted a hand to his head. It was still fogged, and there was a thudding between his temples which he supposed was his own heartbeat, but which felt more akin to a drum being beaten in his skull.

"I could still be sleeping if it weren't for you."

"You were the one who told me not to let you oversleep."

"I was drunk when we got here last night. As you know perfectly well, since you were the one who compelled me to imbibe that last pot of punch. So you can't hold me to my words. I didn't know what I was doing."

Dercy's grin broadened. "On the contrary, you knew exactly what you were doing."

A warmth came over Eldyn, and this time it was not from the golden light. He had not drunk so much that he could not remember clambering up the stairs to Dercy's room, laughing as they stumbled through the door and fell onto the bed. Despite his best efforts, his frown vanished, replaced with a smile.

"You're still wicked for waking me," he said.

Dercy's sea-colored eyes were serious. "Of course I am. As the Church likes so well to remind us, all illusionists are wicked." He tapped a finger against the smooth, pale skin above Eldyn's heart. "Except for you, of course. You, my friend, are very, very good."

He climbed out of bed, then gave Eldyn a wink. "I'll go downstairs and get us a pot of coffee from Cook."

Eldyn laughed. "You're going down there without a stitch on? You'll get the pot thrown at you."

"Really? Why would Mrs. Murnlout be angry to see a fine-looking man dressed in fine-looking clothes?" Dercy crossed his arms, and suddenly he was clad in a white shirt, buff breeches, and polished brown boots.

"You're not seriously thinking of going down there like that."

"Why shouldn't I?"

If Eldyn concentrated, he could see through the illusion. One moment Dercy was clad in a young gentleman's garb, and the next he wore naught but what God had granted him. However, the glamour was exceedingly well-crafted. The cook would not be able to see past it, not like Eldyn could.

That is, as long as Dercy kept weaving the phantasm.

"Go on, then," Eldyn said, still laughing. "But if I hear a scream and a crash from below, I'll know you let the illusion slip. Nor will I come with a pair of breeches to rescue you!"

While he waited for Dercy's return, Eldyn entertained himself by summoning illusions. The golden light Dercy had conjured vanished when he left the room, but Eldyn brought it back with little more than a thought and a flick of his finger.

He twisted his hand, and the light shrank into a brilliant sphere like a tiny sun. He gave a toss with his other hand, and a moon-pale sphere lofted into the air. With a nod he sent the two spinning in circles, each giving chase but never catching the other.

The phantasms came easily to him, as they always did now. The first time he had crafted a real illusion had been that night a half month ago, when he had come to this room with Dercy after the awful sight at the Theater of the Doves, and without even thinking about it he had conjured a forest. Ever since then, he had been able to sculpt light just as he had previously woven shadows.

Why he could do it now, why he could craft true illusions when he could manage no more than a mere glamour before, he did not know. Dercy thought that perhaps the shock of what they had witnessed that night had caused him to forget his own fears of failing.

"A fright can cure the hiccoughs," Dercy had said. "So maybe it cured whatever was amiss with you. Sometimes the only way to accomplish a thing is to get so rattled that you forget about even trying. You simply do it."

Eldyn could only admit that what they had seen outside the Theater of the Doves that night had gravely affected him. He would never forget the scene of the two illusionists before the theater door, the elder weeping as he clutched the body of the younger. Donnebric's face had been crusted with blood; yet somehow, to Eldyn, it was the pale, cracking mask of Gerivel's powdered face that truly signified death.

All the same, Eldyn was not as certain as Dercy that it was due to shock that he was suddenly able to accomplish what had previously been beyond him. After all, had not something else occurred that very same night that had altered him in the most profound manner? He had drawn aside a curtain, revealing an aspect of himself he had never known existed.

Except he *had* known what lay beyond there—or had an inkling of it, at least—hadn't he? How many times at university had he kept his nose firmly planted in a book when his homely but witty friend Orris Jaimsley showed up at the library at St. Berndyn's College with a pair of pretty young women in tow? Yet Eldyn always quickly set his book down if Jaimsley brought along his handsome Torlander friend, Curren Talinger, instead.

However, no matter what Eldyn might have felt, acting upon such feelings was not something he had ever allowed himself to consider. His father had never taken him to a church, but Eldyn had never wanted for priests to hear proscriptions against that sort of behavior.

Your mother was a witch, and I know what they say of a witch's son, Vandimeer Garritt had told him more than once while drunk and sneering. *But I won't have it. I'll make a man of you, or I'll break your neck trying. Either way, I'll not suffer some mincing prat for a whelp of mine!*

Only now Vandimeer Garritt was dead and in the ground. And while the disapproval of society endured, Eldyn found it difficult to keep such thoughts firmly in mind. Every time he was with Dercy, and felt the warm touch of his hand or the delightful roughness of his beard, any fretfulness Eldyn might have had regarding the opinions of others was immediately forgotten.

In sum, now that the curtain that had concealed that part of himself had been opened, Eldyn could not seem to close it again. And was it not possible that whatever it was that gave him the ability to craft illusions had been concealed behind that curtain as well? Whatever the reason, he could now conjure any number of illusions—real phantasms, like those one might pay a quarter regal to see on Durrow Street.

True, there were yet many things beyond his grasp. Those illusions that required careful detail, such as a human face or the fine clothes Dercy had manifested, were not yet within his ability. Like a painter who must learn to control his brush with ever finer motions to achieve the effect he desires, so Eldyn would have to learn to control his own art. For now, he could only paint with the broadest strokes of light. All it would take to improve, though, were time and practice.

With this thought in mind, Eldyn laced his hands behind his head and gazed up at the two spheres—one silver, one gold—that chased each other around the room. He concentrated, making them brighter yet. . . .

"I see you're conjuring your own version of our play."

Eldyn blinked and sat up. So focused had he been on crafting the illusion that he had not noticed Dercy's return. The other young man stood by the bed, a pot in hand, still clad in his illusory garb.

"I was just practicing," Eldyn said.

"As well you should," Dercy replied with a grin.

He set the pot on a table by the bed, then went to the glowing spheres, which now hovered in the middle of the room, to make an examination of them. He must have seen some imperfection in them, for after a moment his smile diminished, and his expression grew thoughtful.

"Do you know why the sun does not love the moon?" Dercy said, looking back at Eldyn.

Eldyn shook his head. "I don't understand."

"It's an old question—a riddle, really. Long ago, when the Siltheri did not move about so freely as they do today, when they had to remain hidden for fear of torture or even death, they used the question as a sort of key. If someone knocked on your door in the depths of a greatnight, you spoke the words to the person on the other side, and only if they could answer the question would you unbar the door."

"Then I'd never get inside," Eldyn said, "for I couldn't answer it."

"Couldn't you? Not even after all the times you've seen our play?"

Eldyn leaned his chin on his knees, thinking. "I don't know. It doesn't really make sense. I mean, why should the sun not love the moon? It's so much brighter. It owns the day and chases away the night."

"That's right. It's far more powerful. You'd think it would have no reason to be jealous of a thing so much smaller and dimmer than itself. All the same, it is."

Eldyn thought of the silver coins that were used as tokens of entry at many of the theaters on Durrow Street. An illusionist at the Sword and Leaf had given him one of the coins once; it had bought Eldyn his first performance at a theater. Like all such tokens, it bore an image of the sun embossed on one side and an image of the moon on the other. The two were inextricably connected, yet only one side of the coin could be seen at once.

"I suppose," he said at last, "the sun is jealous because no matter what it does, it can never catch the moon. It can only banish it from the sky for a time. But the moon always returns. And sometimes, when everything in the heavens is arranged just so, the moon can cover the sun."

As he spoke, he recalled an eclipse of the sun he had seen once as a boy. His father had shown no interest in the celestial event, which was predicted in the almanac. What was more, when Eldyn had expressed a wish to see it, his father had threatened to lock him in a closet for the duration. However, Eldyn had made sure to keep his father's cup filled that day, and by the time the event came, Vandimeer Garritt was eclipsed himself, unconscious and snoring on the floor in the front hall at Bramberly.

Eldyn had watched the eclipse through a piece of smoked glass. He remembered how glorious rays had radiated from the dark circle of the moon as if they were its own.

"It's like the moon steals the sun's crown," he said.

Dercy gave a nod. "No ruler likes it when another usurps his power, not even when that power is willingly given back. And the greater the ruler, the less he cares for it."

Eldyn looked up at him. "So that's the answer to the question? The sun doesn't love the moon because it steals his crown?"

Dercy spread his hands. "And the door opens, and you step into warm firelight and the arms of friends. Yes, that's the answer to the question. You got it right."

"I still don't know what it means."

Dercy looked again at the two glowing spheres. "It's a lesson, I suppose. It serves to remind the Siltheri of their place, and warns what happens if we reach too far, or touch what we should not."

"But sometimes the moon *does* eclipse the sun."

"And when it does, it is burned black."

Eldyn didn't know a great deal about astrography, but he knew Dercy was right; an eclipse could occur only when the moon was completely dark, as it would be tonight. While the moon always returned from darkness, and grew full with silver light again, the same was not true for illusionists who overstepped their bounds. He did not want to, but once again in his mind he saw Gerivel and Donnebric before the Theater of the Doves. The two orbs of illusory light flickered, then vanished.

"I'm sorry," Dercy said. "Now I've gone and made you melancholy. Come, drink some coffee. It will clear your head."

He sat on the bed and tipped the pot over a pair of cups. At the same moment his fine clothes vanished, and Eldyn could not help letting out a great laugh—as was no doubt the intended effect.

"I hope that didn't happen when you went down to Mrs. Murnlout."

"You didn't hear any crashing, did you?"

Eldyn conceded the point. He took a sip of the strong coffee, and he felt his spirits rise once more.

"So why is it that other theaters don't tell the story of the moon and sun? If it's so important to the Siltheri, I'd think others would want to make a play of it as well. Why is yours the only theater that does?"

"Because it's the Theater of the Moon," Dercy said as he donned a pair of trousers—real ones, this time. "It's the only theater that has the charter from the Guild to tell the story."

Eldyn shook his head. "The Guild?"

"Have you been listening to nothing people say at the tavern after a performance?" Dercy grinned. "No, I suppose you're too intent on getting drunk. The Guild of Illusionists issues the charter for each theater. A theater cannot operate without such a charter—no illusionist would work for it. Ever since the founding of the Guild, only one theater is allowed to tell the story of the sun and the moon, and it is always called the Theater of the Moon. Our theater was called the Theater of Shadows before Madame Richelour won the charter, after the last theater that held it closed."

Eldyn returned Dercy's grin. "I like the Theater of the Moon better."

"As do I."

"I'm glad you got the charter. However, no one's ever spoken to me of the Guild of Illusionists until this moment. But that's no surprise, as I'm not an illusionist myself."

Dercy gave him a serious look. "You *are* an illusionist, Eldyn Garritt."

"No, I'm a clerk who has learned to work a few illusions, that's all."

Eldyn didn't want to speak about it anymore. He could not deny that it felt marvelous to at last be able to work true phantasms, but it didn't change what he planned to do. Illusions were marvelous, but they were hardly a solid foundation upon which to build a respectable life for him and his sister. What proper gentleman would ever marry Sashie if it become known her brother was an illusionist? Nor could such a thing be counted upon to remain a secret, not if he ever performed upon a stage. However, he had not yet told Dercy about his intention to save enough money to enter the priesthood, and he was not in the mood to do so that morning, for they were bound to get in an argument when he did, given Dercy's own history with the Church. He set down his cup, slipped out of bed, and found his clothes on a chair.

"If I don't get back to Graychurch soon," he went on, making his tone light, "it's my job that will vanish like a phantasm. You may be able to trick the cook with illusory garments, but I can't fool the rector with an illusory ledger. If there's one thing the Church enjoys counting more than souls, it's money."

Dercy took Eldyn's place on the bed. "Suit yourself. Go be a good little clerk. Yet Madame Richelour saw you practicing at the theater the other day. Take heed, for she has her eye on you."

These words made Eldyn flush—or perhaps it was the sight of Dercy lying on the bed in nothing but his breeches. Whatever the source, he put such thoughts aside as he donned his coat. A rosy light shone through the gap in the curtains, and this time it was no illusion. He had to go.

"The day is not to be very long, if I recall the timetables right. Dusk will come soon enough, and I'll see you then."

"It's Darkeve. The theaters are black tonight. There won't be any performances."

"Then that leaves us all the more time for drinking," Eldyn said with a grin.

ELDYN WAS JUST on the edge of Covenant Cross when he heard the bells of St. Galmuth's chiming the end of the umbral. Despite the brightness of the sky, it was earlier than he had thought. He hadn't needed to rush from Dercy's room quite so quickly, though he supposed it was for the best. Had he lingered, no doubt the other young man would have entangled him in a way that assured an even longer delay. And if he was late to his work because of it, what reason would he give the rector? He could not have told the truth, yet he felt it would be awful to utter a falsehood in a house of God.

No, it was best he had left without lingering. Besides, while his head was improved, it was still somewhat dull from last night's activities, and he decided there was both time and reason for another cup of coffee. As he was already at Covenant Cross, there was no place closer to get a cup than Mrs. Haddon's.

True, if his old friends from university were there, they would want him to sit and talk, and he did not have time for heated discourses on all that was wrong with the government. Yet it had been months since he had been to Mrs. Haddon's, and even longer since he had seen Jaimsley, Talinger, or their usual companion, Dalby Warrett. A meeting with them was long overdue. Besides, if the bells were to be believed, he could afford to sit and talk with his old companions—if not long enough to solve all of Altania's ills, then at least for the space it took to drink a cup.

Cheered by this thought, Eldyn headed toward a familiar sign painted with a cup and a dagger hanging above a red door. As he went, he wondered if Jaimsley, Talinger, and Warrett were still attending university. Eldyn had always meant to go back to St. Berndyn's College once he had saved enough money to pay for tuition again. The books, the lectures, the atmosphere of history and wisdom that perfused the air of St. Berndyn's ancient stone halls—all had been dear to him. When the professors spoke, it was as if they were opening windows to worlds Eldyn had never seen before, giving him glimpses of new and wondrous sights.

Yet there were other windows that had opened for him now, ones that looked out on their own wonders. Besides, it was a different kind of studying that would occupy him once he saved up enough money to enter the priesthood. Eldyn felt a pang of sorrow as, for the first time, he considered that he would likely never return to university.

All the same, it would be good to see his friends, and to hear what amusing things this or that cracked old professor had done of late. Smiling at the thought, he made his way toward the door of the coffeehouse.

As he drew near, though, a misgiving filled him. The windows of the coffeehouse should have been blazing with lamplight at this early hour, revealing a room filled with young men readying themselves for the day's lectures at the various colleges that lay just beyond Covenant Cross. Instead, the windows were dark and empty. Eldyn laid a hand on the brass knob, but the door was locked. Then he saw that there were two pieces of parchment nailed to the red surface of the door.

The first one was a copy of the Rules of Citizenship. This was a familiar sight, as by order of Lord Valhaine a copy of the Rules was posted in every tavern, coffeehouse, and public meeting place in the city. The Rules put forth all of the things a good citizen of Altania was required—or forbidden—to do. Each time Eldyn glanced at a copy, it seemed the list was longer than before. Looking at the bottom, he saw that gatherings in public streets of more than five unrelated persons were prohibited without a permit, as was publishing any pictures of the king that depicted His Majesty in an unflattering or grotesque manner.

Eldyn glanced at the Rules for only a moment. It was to the second piece of parchment nailed to the door that his attention was drawn. CLOSED BY ORDER OF THE GRAY CONCLAVE, the notice read. There was no further reason or explanation given. It was signed by the king's Black Dog himself, Lord Valhaine.

The tolling of the bells faded to silence. At the same time, Eldyn heard the sound of boots striking against cobbles. He turned to see a group of three redcrests walking through the broad square of Covenant Cross, backs straight in their blue coats, sabers at their hips. Quickly, Eldyn brought the early morning shadows in close around him—not so much as to make him abruptly vanish from view, but enough so that a casual glance would be less likely to fall upon him.

Keeping his head low, he walked at a brisk but not hurried pace. He did not want the king's soldiers to see him standing by the door of the coffee shop, for fear they might question him. Mrs. Haddon's shop had always possessed a reputation as a favorite place of agitators and anarchists, and it was not so long ago that Eldyn had carried messages for rebels himself.

He passed out of Covenant Cross, and the sound of boots faded behind him. A glance over the shoulder confirmed that the redcrests were not following in this direction. With a sigh, he released the shadows, then made his way through the streets of the Old City. Both his need and desire for more coffee had dissipated; he could not be more awake now.

That Mrs. Haddon's had been closed by order of Lord Valhaine was a shock. True, many of the young men who frequented the coffeehouse had liked to criticize Assembly and, on occasion, the king. However, such talk had gotten quieter and less frequent after Lady Shayde made an appearance there. Eldyn hadn't seen it himself, thank God, but he had heard about it: how the White Lady had come into Mrs. Haddon's and had sat there, slowly drinking a cup of coffee, and all the while not speaking a single word.

She hadn't needed to. All knew that Lady Shayde was a member of the Gray Conclave, and also that she was Lord Valhaine's favorite servant. Just as all knew that no agent of the Gray Conclave had sent more men to the gallows for crimes of treason. Or women, for that matter, for Lady Shayde was no kinder to her own sex than to the opposite.

Once her cup was empty, Lady Shayde had left. After that, not so many people had gone to Mrs. Haddon's, and those who did spoke in lower tones. While they still discussed politics, and even criticized Assembly and the king at times, anyone who spoke anything that remotely sounded like a call for revolution was quickly hushed and hurried out the door.

To tell the truth, Eldyn had preferred the change. Had the rebellious talk continued, he doubted he would have set foot in Mrs. Haddon's again, for fear of placing himself—and his history of treasonous work for Westen—at risk of discovery. However, the discussions Eldyn had heard the last time he had been at Mrs. Haddon's had been so innocuous he could not believe they would have caused concern to anyone who might have overheard them. Then again, that had been before the incident at the cenotaph, and before the ill news out of County Dorn. Perhaps talk of rebellion had started up again among the students who frequented the coffeehouse; maybe someone had even been so foolish as to speak the name of Huntley Morden in public.

If so, it must have been enough to bring down the wrath of the Gray Conclave. Eldyn was sorry for Mrs. Haddon. She had always treated "her lads," as she called all the young university men, in the most motherly way, and she had been kinder to Eldyn than to most. All the same, whatever had happened to close the shop, Eldyn was glad he had not been there to witness it. He only hoped that no one had been taken to Barrowgate, and that, wherever she was, Mrs. Haddon was well. He would be sure to ask Jaimsley about her the next time he saw his old friend.

Though when that would be, now that the coffeehouse was closed, Eldyn did not know.

BY THE TIME he passed St. Galmuth's, the gilded spires of the cathedral were aflame with gold light. Just beyond, Graychurch still huddled in the shadows—a thing that was hardly seen unless one made an effort to look for it. Yet its unassuming appearance pleased Eldyn. Was it not more pious to be humble and stand in the darkness than to thrust oneself into the light and strive for glory? He was not a priest yet, but it seemed so to him.

He made his way past the two churches to the rooms he inhabited with Sashie. Outside the door was a basket covered with a cloth as well as a pot of tea. Eldyn picked up the basket and used his key to let himself in. He was glad to find that Sashie had not yet risen.

While her behavior was greatly improved, an industriousness that compelled her to rise early from bed must be placed along with cooking on the list of virtues his sister had not yet mastered. Not that Eldyn would complain, for it meant he could come in after a late night without enduring questions about where he had been.

Eldyn changed his attire, as it would not do for Sashie to see him in the same clothes he had worn last night; besides, he never wore his best coat while clerking, for fear of spilling ink on it. He tied his hair back with a ribbon, freshened his face in a basin of water, then went to the table and took the cloth from the basket.

He poured cold tea from the pot, and was just setting out a loaf of bread, a soft cheese, and a crock of honey when the door to Sashie's chamber opened. As usual, she wore her simplest ash-colored dress.

Eldyn had given up on the idea of buying her anything prettier to wear. After Brightday, he had taken her to Gauldren's Heights as promised, and they had gone into several fashionable Uphill shops. However, there was nothing that suited Sashie's taste.

"It has all become so vulgar!" she exclaimed in the last shop, a bit more loudly than he might have wished, as several other patrons in the shop looked their way. "It has been too long since I have bought anything, and now I hardly know what to make of the latest modes, except that the necks are far too low, and everywhere the tiniest scrap of lace is substituted for a proper covering. A young lady would hardly be fit to present herself on Durrow Street in these dresses, let alone in a respectable place."

In a way, Eldyn was amused that his sister was suddenly repulsed by the very gowns she had previously berated him for failing to buy her. Yet it could hardly be surprising that an impressionable young woman, who had endured the most lax and chaotic sort of upbringing at the hands of their father, had become enamored of the simple and comforting order espoused by the Church, and so in her childish way wished to emulate it. Either that, or Father Prestus had told her that pretty dresses were frowned upon just like spending money on a Brightday!

All the same, it was clear other patrons in the shop did not find her outburst so amusing, and Eldyn had quickly hurried her outside. That had been the last time he had taken Sashie to a shop, and nor would he do so again until her attitudes returned to their more natural state, and she once again pined for all things frilled and flounced and beribboned. He had no doubt that time would come soon.

Now she kissed his cheek, an act that always pleased him, and sat at the table. Pretending he did not already know the answer to the question, he asked, with an affectation of great interest, what she intended to do that lumenal.

"I must be with the verger all day," she said as she slathered honey on a large piece of bread. "His arm grieves him terribly still. He wrenched it, you remember, when we were moving the reredos that stands behind the altar in order to clean there."

"I'm sorry to hear he is ill."

"And there is so much to do today! This umbral is Darkeve, so all the figures of the saints must be changed in the nave. The verger will insist on lifting them, but he will ruin himself if he does. I will insist he sit in the pews while I move them, and he can direct me how to place them in the proper order."

Eldyn could not help wondering if the old verger's complaints of pain were not so much due to his injury but rather to the fact that he had an able young person to do his work for him while he rested. However, all he said was "You are very good to do that."

Roses bloomed on her cheeks. "Whether I am good is not for me to judge, I am sure! I only strive to do good in whatever way I can, no matter how small it might be." She smiled at him, her blue eyes bright. "I am glad you have found good work as well, brother."

He broke off a piece of bread. "You no more than I! It is good to have a reliable clerking position."

"I mean," she said, seeming to choose her words with care, "I am glad that you labor not just in any position, but in *this* one. It has, would you not agree, peculiar rewards?"

"I don't know about peculiar. The rector is kindly enough, and the work is not so tiring as at a trading house. As for rewards, money is money. It spends no differently wherever one gets it."

She affected the tiniest of frowns; it was charming to behold. "Yes, a coin is not altered by where it comes or goes. But is not the one who receives it more malleable? Is he not changed by the source from which the coin springs? Surely the money you now earn comes from a source of far greater good than any that might be gotten at a trading house."

Eldyn could not resist her when her expression was so earnest.

"I had not thought of it that way," he said. "You are right, of course. There is no telling where the coins I earned before came from. For all I know they passed through the hands of corsairs or slavers in the Empire! That the coins I receive now, that bought us this food, have any such taint upon them is impossible."

She did not answer him, but she treated him to a very sweet smile, then licked honey from her fingertips.

Eldyn returned to his own breakfast, and as he ate bread he looked at yesterday's edition of *The Swift Arrow,* which lay on the table. The headlines spoke of further discord in the Outlands. According to one article, a band of Torland loyalists had confronted a small group of soldiers. At first only hot words were exchanged, but then someone threw a stone, striking one of the redcrests.

The soldiers had been greatly outnumbered and, fearing for their lives after the recent mayhem in County Dorn, had fired shots. They escaped in the chaos that ensued, but when the smoke cleared three Torlander men lay on the ground, shot dead. Assembly had called on the king to send additional soldiers to enforce the peace, but instead His Majesty had recalled even more of his forces from the local garrison.

This ill news hardly impinged upon Eldyn. It was not the words on the page that occupied his mind, but rather thoughts of meeting Dercy at the Theater of the Moon after dark and working more illusions. He could almost see the phantasms moving in a lithe dance on the page before him.

Eldyn blinked. It was no idle daydream. The words printed on the broadsheet were indeed moving, roaming around the page like black sheep on a white field. Even as he watched, they rearranged themselves in a new pattern—one that made no sense when read, but which conveyed a meaning all the same. For such was now the distribution of white and black on the page that the effect was to form an image, like a kind of etching, of a face. It was a young man, his short beard parted by a grin.

"There you are smiling again," Sashie said. "As you have done all morning! You are in very fine spirits today, dear brother."

Eldyn quickly folded the broadsheet and set it aside. "I won't deny it. I am indeed in a fine mood. Is there a reason I shouldn't be?"

Sashie smiled herself, a sight that pleased him as much as any illusion. "No, we have every reason to be happy. We have received so many blessings from our Creator, and in His kindness He will only continue to reward us, I am sure."

Eldyn gave her a fond look and picked up his tea.

"Unless we give Him cause for displeasure, of course."

The cold tea was unexpectedly sour on Eldyn's tongue. He had to clench his jaw to make himself swallow. "I am sure *you* could never displease our Lord in Eternum."

She cast her gaze down, though her pleased expression could not be mistaken. "I hope you are right, dear brother, but sometimes I am not sure. I asked Father Prestus how I could know if what I was doing was right. He told me that one only has to look in one's heart, and that one always knows when one has done something that is wrong. I still worry sometimes. Yet when I make a careful examination of the things I do each day, I confess, I cannot believe that any of them would truly displease God."

Now she looked up, and her eyes were bright. "I am sure the same is true for you, sweet brother, and that everything you have done and will do this day will be to His liking. When I think of all you have done for me, I know it can only be so!"

Sashie wiped her lips with a cloth and stood. It was time for her to go, for if she waited longer, she feared the verger would try to move the saints without her. She kissed his cheek again, then departed.

It was time for Eldyn to go himself; the rector would be expecting him. However, he remained at the table, gazing at the copy of the broadsheet. He turned it over, but the image of the cheerful face was gone. Instead the words had returned to their familiar arrangement, forming grim sketches about the doings of soldiers and brigands, beggars and lords.

Just as Sashie said she did, he examined things he had done since the previous day. A minute ago, such remembrances had filled him with warmth, but now his gut was as cold and sour as the tea he had drunk. Would God approve of the things he had done at the Theater of the Moon or in Dercy's room? And what would Sashie say if *she* knew what he had done?

But the answers to that question didn't matter. For he would never tell her, and there was no way for her to find out. She would never go to Durrow Street, and Dercy would not come here. He claimed he loathed even going near a church these days.

Yet what of God? There was no way Eldyn could conceal anything he had done from *Him.*

A dread came over Eldyn, and his palms grew damp. He had been so astounded by his sudden ability to work illusions, and crafting them filled him with such delight, that he had not stopped to consider what he had been doing. Instead, he had willingly let himself be encouraged by Dercy's enthusiasm, and he had indulged his own whims and fancies, conjuring illusions without a thought of what it meant for his future, and for Sashie's.

That must not continue. He could only hope he had not already damned himself by what he had done these last days. What if, no matter how much money he saved to enter the Church, the priests took one look at him and rejected him?

Yet that was foolish. Such things could not be perceived with a glance. Besides, he had been marked by sin well before this, given his past and his parentage. He could not believe these most recent actions made a difference in the sum of things. Even if that was the case, he would still have to give up working illusions to become a priest, and the sooner he got in the habit of it, the better.

Eldyn stood, then brushed a hand across the front page of the broadsheet where Dercy's face had grinned up at him a moment before. His clammy fingers came away black, stained with ink. He left the newspaper on the table, then headed out the door.

It was time to do God's work.

CHAPTER TEN

*I*T WAS A fine afternoon on a middle lumenal just after the start of the month when Ivy left The Seventh Swan, a book in hand. Their chambers at the inn were not large enough to afford her much time apart from her sisters, and over the last quarter month she had gotten few chances to read by herself. With this purpose in mind, she walked down Marble Street and passed through an arch into Barrister's Close.

Being surrounded by buildings on all sides, the close was well protected from the bustle of Marble Street. There was a small garden in the center, and there she sat on a bench and read in blissful peace. Nor was there any need for her to hurry back; Mr. Quent had gone to the Citadel on business, and he had told her not to expect his return until quite late.

(While in public she and her husband were now required to refer to one another as *Sir* and *Lady,* this was not a custom either of them had adopted in private, nor did they intend to.)

The object of Ivy's attention was another book concerning astrography. The volume from her father's collection she had read had been interesting but unsatisfying, as it was clearly out of date. For one thing, the author had suggested there was still a controversy around the theory that the world was not fixed in space but rather resided on its own sphere of crystalline aether that moved like those of the other planets—a thing that had been observed to be a fact well over a hundred years ago.

Still, the book had set her mind whirling like the celestial spheres themselves, and eager to learn more she had gone to a bookshop and asked for the latest volume concerning astrography.

She was not the only one interested in such a topic these days, for the bookseller had known just the book to give her, and he had but a single copy left.

The few chapters Ivy had managed to read so far had proved fascinating, if something of a challenge to comprehend, being rather scholarly, and as she sat on the bench in the garden and read, her mind grew even more fascinated by the author's various explanations and theories.

Of particular interest to her was the chapter regarding *seasons*. Ivy still didn't fully understand the theory, but it had to do with the notion that, some time in the far distant past, days and nights weren't of varying lengths like they were now. Instead, there would be times of the year during which all of the days were long and all of the nights were short, and other times when the opposite was true.

Ivy imagined, in the latter case, it would be like having only short lumenals and long umbrals for months on end. That was a dreadful thing to consider. How cold and dark the world would have grown in such a time! That any living thing could survive for so long without light or warmth was difficult to believe.

However, according to the book, the evidence for the ancient existence of seasons was incontrovertible. If one made just a slight alteration to the movements of only a small number of the celestial spheres, the calculations showed that remarkable symmetries would arise. The current, familiar system of varying lumenals and umbrals would cease, replaced by a new scheme in which days progressed from long to short and back again.

As strange as this idea seemed, there was something about it that Ivy found compelling. Hadn't there been times when she suffered a sense of *wrongness* upon arising in the middle of a greatnight and using candles and lamps to carve a waking day out of the long dark? Perhaps their bodies had been fashioned for a time when things were not as they were now. It would certainly be a boon not to have to refer to an almanac to know how long the lumenal would be!

Not that the almanac had been any help lately. According to

the old rosewood clock—which she had brought with them to The Seventh Swan—the lumenal yesterday had ceased a full twenty minutes sooner than was printed in the timetables. It was clear the new almanac contained mistakes just like the old one. Evidently no source was reliable anymore.

Except for the rosewood clock, that was. Unlike the sitting room at Durrow Street, the window in her chamber at The Seventh Swan afforded a good view of the west that was unimpeded by the bulk of the Crag. Thus she had made an experiment, standing by the window and watching both the sky and clock. Just at the moment the sun sank out of view, the black disk moved to cover the last sliver of gold on the right-hand face of the clock. Somehow the clock knew when the umbral would begin, even if the timetable was in error. Yet that seemed impossible. How could an old clock be correct when the almanacs were not?

Well, she could test the theory again that night. For the moment she put aside thoughts of clocks and returned her attention to the book. As she read, a thought gradually occurred to her. If the motions of the spheres in the distant past had resulted in seasons, what had caused those symmetries to become altered so that the present system of varying lumenals and umbrals arose? And when had this event occurred? It was her understanding that the heavens were, by God's design, eternal and perfect in their fundamental nature; they could not simply be changed on a whim.

Except that wasn't true, for they *had* changed recently, hadn't they? She looked upward. The new red planet was not so bright it could be seen by day. Nor could she have seen it anyway. While the day was sunny when she left the inn, the sky was now thick with clouds.

Indeed, as she gazed up, a large, cold drop of rain struck her cheek. Another fell upon the open book, and at that moment a great peal of thunder rattled the stones around her. So absorbed had she been in her reading that she had not noticed the storm gathering overhead. Ivy shut her book and hurried from the close.

By the time she turned down Marble Street, it was pouring.

Nor was there a hack cab anywhere in sight, as was always the case when it rained. There was nothing to do but walk back to the inn as quickly as she could. While the distance was not far, the rain was hard and frigid, and by the time she reached The Seventh Swan she was drenched.

At once she stripped away her sodden clothes and ordered a hot bath, but it was no use. Despite the heat of the water, she could not stop shivering. An ache crept into her bones as evening approached, and her head grew so stuffy she could hardly breathe. By nightfall, any thought of testing the old rosewood clock again had been driven from her mind. It was all she could do to crawl into her bed with the help of her sisters.

$\mathcal{T}$HAT NIGHT IVY did not sleep, but rather drifted in a dark delirium that was awhirl with stars and planets.

As she turned the handles of her father's celestial clock, the heavenly bodies danced and spun around her. For some reason, it was important to her that the planets all be kept well away from one another. She did not want them to come into proximity; something terrible would happen if they did. However, no matter how she turned the handles or worked the gears, the celestial spheres began to move in time with one another.

She cranked the handles harder, until her hands ached from the effort, but it was no use. The spheres turned with a will of their own, and one by one the planets fell into a perfect line, one behind the other, until she could not see the eleven planets. Instead, all of them were hidden behind a twelfth: a red orb that stared at her like a fiery eye. She withered beneath its red gaze, and she cried out, for all was lost.

Only then she glimpsed an emerald spark out of the corner of her eye. One of the planets had not yet fallen into line with the others. It shone like a green island floating in a dark sea. A hope filled her. She gripped the metal handles of the celestial clock, though they were so hot they burned her hands, and worked them with all her might to keep the green spark of light away from the other planets.

Then the red eye blinked, and the dark consumed her.

*I*VY WOKE TO discover that the umbral had passed, and the short lumenal that followed it was nearly half over.

"There you are," Mr. Quent said, his face solemn but his eyes bright. He sat on the edge of the bed, wearing a white shirt open at the throat and brown breeches. He lifted her hand and pressed it against his bearded cheek. "The doctor said there was no great cause for worry, that you would come back to us. So you have. But you were very far away for a while."

His face was the most welcome of sights. She beheld every crag and valley of his mien as if gazing upon the most familiar and beloved landscape—one she had been away from for too long, but now had returned to.

"I am sorry if I alarmed you." Her throat was raw, and it was difficult to speak. "It was silly of me to be caught in the rain. However, I am sure I will be very well . . ."

She sat up, but at once the room turned in a dizzy circle around her. With strong hands, he eased her back against the pillows.

". . . but I believe I will rest just a little longer," she finished with a weak smile.

"Yes, I believe you will, Mrs. Quent."

The sternness of his tone did not alarm her. Rather, she felt only a warm reassurance. She lay back down and shut her eyes, knowing no harm could possibly come to her while *he* was here.

Ivy did not rise from her bed for the rest of that day or the umbral that followed. The next lumenal she was improved enough to sit in a chair for a time, but her recovery progressed slowly. While her health was never in grave peril as it had been the year before, when she had been forced to stay a half month at Lady Marsdel's, she was nonetheless plagued by tremblings and a recurring fever. By order of the doctor, she was confined to her room for more than a quarter month.

Not that this was such a dreadful thing. An invalid could not have asked for a more faithful or gentle attendant than Rose, and Lily often helped to occupy the hours by reading to her.

This Ivy appreciated, for the fever had left her eyes too weak to read. However, Lily did not think the listener should have a say in choosing the book, which meant Ivy learned nothing more about the topic of astrography, but instead received much instruction concerning the habits of wicked barons, kidnapped contessas, and dashing young sea captains.

Mr. Quent's business at the Citadel continued to occupy him during this time. Ivy was not privy to the details of his work there. Even if Mr. Quent had wished to tell her about it, he could not do so, for matters of such vital interest to the nation could only be kept strictly secret. All the same, she had the impression that there was some discussion or argument going on concerning how particular dangers to Altania were to be addressed. What's more, from the way Mr. Quent spoke, it seemed that the inquirers were on one side of the matter, while other forces within the government stood on the opposite. Despite all this, he did not neglect observing the work at Durrow Street, and he gave Ivy periodic updates on the progress of the renovations.

In all, her convalescence would have been little trouble to bear, save for one grave blow to her spirits. Namely, she was forced to miss visiting her father not once but twice, for one visiting day came the lumenal after she fell ill, and the next came the lumenal before the doctor pronounced her fit enough to venture out.

"Would you like me to go see him?" Mr. Quent asked her before the second occasion.

Ivy knew he would go to Madstone's if she asked, even if it meant delaying his work or rearranging his meetings at the Citadel. However, while he would never admit it aloud, she knew he was reluctant to see Mr. Lockwell in his present state.

Mr. Quent never spoke about his own father. From Lord Rafferdy, Ivy had learned that the elder Mr. Quent had suffered a protracted and agonizing decline when his son was a young man. As Mr. Quent's mother had passed when he was hardly out of childhood, it was left to him to care for his father—once a strong man and a loyal servant to Earl Rylend—after an unknown malady left him bedridden, blind, and unable to speak. When at last his many years of suffering were done, it could only have been a relief.

Ivy could only imagine that seeing his old friend Mr. Lockwell afflicted by illness would stir in Mr. Quent painful remembrances of his father. Nor was there any use in him going. That Mr. Lockwell would recognize Mr. Quent was doubtful; more likely he would perceive him as a stranger, and so become fearful and agitated.

Nor could Ivy ask Lily or Rose to go see him. While Mr. Lockwell resided in a more peaceful part of Madstone's now, she could not allow her sisters to so much as glimpse the other, terrible area where he had been kept for a time. Rose, particularly, would be devastated by such a sight.

No, she would have to trust that her father was well. She had no reason to believe otherwise. Ever since Lord Rafferdy's letter on Mr. Lockwell's behalf, his treatment at Madstone's was of such a quality that it could have been improved only by his being released—which they now had every reason to believe would occur soon.

🍃

*I*T WAS NEAR the end of her convalescence when Mr. Quent brought her something that had been discovered in the house on Durrow Street.

The day had been nearly twenty hours, and her head had ached throughout the duration, so that even listening to Lily read was more than she could bear. By the time Mr. Quent returned to the inn, she was in something of a miserable state. However, even as he entered the room she felt her spirits rise. He carried a bundle in his arms, something wrapped in a cloth.

"The men were working in a room on the upper floor," he said. "They found this there."

Ivy was at once intrigued. Mr. Quent knew that she was always eager to see anything that might provide further clues regarding the age or history of the house. She sat up in bed, and he set the object on her lap. It was rectangular and rather heavy. At once, the headache that had plagued her all day vanished.

"You said you found this on the upper floor," she said, her interest mounting. "Which room was it?"

"The third on the left after you turn into the south wing."

"But I am sure that was my room when I was small!" She laid her hands on the object. It felt hard beneath the cloth.

"The men were repairing the floor, and when they took out several loose boards they discovered this beneath. I think . . . no, I am certain this must have been intended for you to find."

She could hardly wonder what he meant by this. The look he gave her was so odd—at once eager and concerned, she thought.

"Go on," he said. "Open it."

Ivy did so, removing the cloth from the object.

"Oh," she said, and sighed.

It was a wooden box, about as long as her forearm, half again as wide, and as deep as her hand. The box was like nothing she had ever seen before. Its sides were not planed smooth, nor its corners squared off; instead, the natural, irregular surface of the wood had been left intact, so that every whorl and knot, every groove and furrow, was visible.

This was not to say the box was rough-hewn. On the contrary, the wood had been shaped and fitted together in the most clever way. She could only imagine the maker had chosen each piece with great care, so that they could be bound together with only the most judicious amount of carving. Ivy's fingers ran over the box, as if with a will of their own.

"I've never seen anything so lovely," she murmured.

It was more than its beauty that fascinated her; nor could she believe that Mr. Quent did not already know, or at least guess, what she had been able to sense the moment she touched the box. Why else would he have brought it to her? By force of will she removed her hands from the box, laying them at her sides, and looked at him.

"It's made of Wyrdwood."

"So I thought. I wondered . . . that is, I knew you would be able to determine it for certain."

Since their return to Invarel, they had not spoken about what had happened at the old grove of Wyrdwood to the east of Heathcrest Hall. Nor had they spoken of the woman who had given birth to her, the witch Merriel Addysen, or the legacy which that parentage had imparted to Ivy. When they were here in the city, so far away from any stand of Old Trees, there was little need to think of such things.

Only here was a thing of Wyrdwood on her lap. Carefully, as if it was precious—or perhaps perilous—she picked it up.

"It feels as if there's something inside. Do you know what it is?"

"I cannot open it. Look here."

At once she understood. The box was locked, but not with any sort of metal hasp. Instead, fine tendrils had been woven into a complex knot around two whorls of wood, holding the lid fast.

"Besides, I do not think it is for me to open," he said. "Your father must have left it in your old room, hoping you would find it when you returned to the house one day."

"How can you know that? He could not have been certain I would be the one to find it. Indeed, I was not!"

"Yes, but he would have known that only you could open it."

Ivy examined the wooden knot. The intricate way the tendrils had been woven together reminded her of the bent willow chair in her room in the attic at Heathcrest, the one made by the farrier in Cairnbridge, Mr. Samonds, when he was a young man. The box also reminded her of the Wyrdwood stand on which the Eye of Ran-Yahgren rested. As she let her fingers move over the knot, Ivy could feel an echo of life in it, like a faint hum. She knew she had only to call to it, and it would awaken and listen.

"Go on," he said, his voice low.

A nervousness came over Ivy. Mr. Quent knew what she was; indeed, he had known about her nature long before she did. Yet knowing a thing was not the same as seeing it. Did he truly wish to witness what she could do?

He was watching her, and she knew she was being foolish. He had told her never to be ashamed of what she was, and she must believe that he had meant what he said.

She touched the knot, and even as she formed a wish in her mind for the box to be unlocked, the tendrils began to move like tiny brown serpents. They uncoiled themselves from around the whorls of wood, then curled up neatly, lying flat against the box.

Ivy heard Mr. Quent let out a breath and she looked up. With his right thumb, he traced the scar on his left hand where the last two fingers had been severed long ago. He must have noticed her gaze, for he slipped his left hand into his coat pocket.

"I was certain you would be able to open it," he said, and he surprised her then, for he gave her a look she could only describe as triumphant. "Well, then, see what is in it."

Ivy lifted the lid. An object wrapped in parchment was nestled within. It was heavy and solid as she took it out, and even before she unwrapped it, she knew it was a book.

She set the wrapping aside and examined the book. The binding was sewn of black leather, but there was no title on the cover or spine. The book did not seem particularly ancient, for the leather was supple, and as she opened it the endpapers were not yellowed, but rather a crisp white. Ivy turned to the first page, then her breath caught in her throat. The words on the page had not been printed on a press; instead they were written in a familiar, spidery hand.

My Dearest Ivoleyn,

If you are reading this, then it means you have solved the puzzle I left for you and found the key to this house inside my celestial globe. Well done! But then, I knew that you were bound to discover the riddle in the book I gave you for your birthday, and that once you did you would not rest until you had solved it. So you have.

And here in your hands is your reward.

It is my intention to write down upon these pages all manner of thoughts, observations, advice, and any other thing that concerns me. This way you can know my mind, and I can tell you all those things I always wanted you to know once you were old enough to understand.

That I would rather have told you these things in person, you must know. However, just as I was certain you would solve my puzzle, I am also certain that, if you are reading this now, it means I am no longer capable of telling you anything—or, more than likely, that I am no longer to be counted among the living.

But put aside gloomy thoughts! This is no time for sorrow, but rather a time to gather your resolve. Through the power of the written word— that magick of the simplest and most wondrous sort—my thoughts can be with you even if the remainder of me cannot. In this way we can be together, still and always. But be warned. There are others who must not read some of the things I intend to set down upon these pages.

Who are these people? If you do not know them already, then you will learn as you read this volume. Let me stress again, in the strongest manner, that if you encounter any of them you must never show them this journal nor even hint at its existence. It is for you only, as there is no other I can possibly trust. That is why I have taken precautions to be certain no one other than you might come into possession of this volume. There are men whom I once associated with, ignorant of their true nature—men who would do terrible things in order to gain this knowledge.

Yet do not fear! You are clever and brave, my dear one. I have every confidence in you. Remember that, as long as you have this volume with you, then I am with you as well. And so I will always be—

—Your Devoted and Loving Father

Ivy set down the journal, unable to turn the page or even hold it any longer, for her hands were shaking, and she felt a pang deep in her heart. To read these words—it was indeed like having her father with her and hearing his voice speak in a way that he had not for so many years. For a moment she was overcome.

Then she felt Mr. Quent's touch upon her arm, and this lent

her strength. She picked up the journal again and read the page aloud, to hear the words again herself, and also so Mr. Quent might hear them.

"'There are men . . . men who would do terrible things in order to gain this knowledge,'" Mr. Quent repeated. "That is a dark thing to write. Yet I suppose he meant the magicians of the Silver Eye, and they can pose a danger no longer."

"No, they cannot."

Yet even as Ivy said this, she recalled her encounter with the man in the black mask. There were other magicians, he had said, and other doors. She wondered what Mr. Quent might think of this, only she had not told him about the most recent visit of the man in the black mask, and once again she found herself reluctant to do so. He had enough to concern himself. If the stranger in the mask showed himself again, then she would tell him.

"Well," he said, his eyes upon her. "Are you not going to look at it?"

Ivy picked up the journal again. For so many years she had been deprived of her father's intellect and his wisdom, his companionship and humor. Now, here in her hands, was an entire volume filled with it. Eagerly she opened it and turned past the first page to the next.

It was blank.

Ivy turned the page once more, but again found herself gazing at a blank sheet. She flipped through several more pages in the journal. All were empty. She opened the book a quarter way through, halfway, and toward the end. Blank, blank, and blank again. Other than the first page that she had read, the journal was devoid of words.

A gasp escaped her; or rather, a sob. How much crueler it was to lose something marvelous when it had just been promised to you mere moments before! The journal fell to her lap, and this time Ivy could not prevent tears from rolling down her cheeks.

With gentle motions, Mr. Quent wiped them away.

"Lockwell must never have had the chance to write in these

pages as he intended to," he said. "Before he could work on the journal, he must have been forced to take action to stop Mr. Bennick and the rest of his order from using the artifact."

"You must be right," she said, though she could barely speak the words. She was shivering, as if the fever had come upon her again.

"I am sorry, Ivoleyn."

She forced herself to smile at him. "I am as well. However, even these few words of his are a gift." So they were—if a bittersweet one.

For several minutes they were content to be with each other in contemplative silence. At last, Mr. Quent remarked that she looked very tired, and she confessed that she wished to rest. He kissed her brow and left her, promising to return in a little while. When she was alone, Ivy laid a hand upon the journal. She felt the same as she did after one of her trips to see her father at Madstone's, for here was a thing that gave her remembrances of her father, yet which contained none of his thoughts, his intellect, and his feelings.

Ivy felt her eyes sting, but she blinked away the tears. She would not succumb to despair. *That* her father would not have wanted. He had known what he was doing when he sacrificed his mind to stop Mr. Bennick and the Vigilant Order of the Silver Eye from using the artifact. She placed the book back in the box of Wyrdwood and set it on the table by the bed, then laid her head on her pillow. Even as she did this, a thought occurred to her, and as it did some of her sorrow was replaced by puzzlement.

If her father had never had a chance to write in the journal, then why had he gone to the trouble of finding a way to seal it inside a box of Wyrdwood that only she could open?

AT LAST THE doctor pronounced Ivy fit to leave the inn, and that very day Mr. Quent drove her in the cabriolet to Durrow Street so that she could behold the latest discovery that had been made in the house.

Upon entering, Ivy was astonished at the progress that had oc-curred in her absence. That none of the peculiar attributes of the house—the wooden eyes, the clawed doorknobs, and any such thing odd or wizardly—be altered was one of the stipulations under which Mr. Barbridge worked. All the same, much had changed since last she set foot in the house. A second set of steps was being constructed, a mirror to the original, to form a double stairway that swept up to the second-floor gallery. The front hall had been made grander by replacing the square beams with arched vaults, and the floor planks had been pulled up to reveal an exquisite mosaic in the style of the Principalities, depicting a wild forest strewn with stags, lions, and huntsmen.

The mosaic had been badly damaged, which was likely why it had been covered up. Artisans had been hired to painstakingly cut new pieces of tile and match them to the original pattern, restor-ing it to its colorful glory. However, as wondrous as this was, it was not what Mr. Quent had brought her here to see. Instead, he led her to the north end of the hall.

As they went, he described how the mantelpiece above the fireplace had been removed, for it had been charred in a fire that had gotten out of hand sometime in the past. Once the mantel was taken down, it was apparent that the entire fireplace was sur-rounded by a plaster facade. This was torn away as well, and beneath was revealed the original fireplace.

As they approached, Ivy's wonder was renewed. The fireplace was framed by pale marble traced with green veins. The marble was sculpted into rich scrollwork that intertwined with a pair of eagles perched to either side. There was no mantel. Instead, above the fireplace was a bas-relief carving of a shield. Behind the shield was a single sword, and the whole thing was wreathed with leaves as delicately rendered as those on the door they had discovered in the gallery upstairs, though these were fashioned of stone, not wood. Chiseled upon the shield was a name: *Dratham*.

A new thrill passed through Ivy. "Dratham? Do you think it might be the name of the man who built this house?"

"It must be so," Mr. Quent said. "I spoke to Mr. Barbridge, and he is convinced the crest above the fireplace is original to the house."

Ivy moved closer, examining the stone shield. "I suppose it was covered over when the house changed hands. A new master would not have wanted for the name of the previous owner to be so boldly advertised."

Mr. Quent concurred with her assessment. Nor was there any disagreement between them on the matter of the fireplace. Both agreed the fireplace must be restored to its original appearance.

After that, they passed a pleasurable hour as Mr. Quent showed her all the things that had been done to the house while she was ill. Ivy examined everything with great interest; and if a few times her gaze strayed to a window, as if expecting to see a tall figure all in black standing outside, her attention always quickly returned to Mr. Quent.

At last she grew weary, for she was still somewhat weak from her illness, and Mr. Quent returned her to the inn. The next morning she woke feeling greatly refreshed, and after breakfast she went to the Toll House in hopes of learning more about the builder of the house.

The Toll House was a turreted building of thick gray stone next to the Hillgate. Long ago it had been home to the collectors who exacted a tax on everyone and everything passing in and out of Invarel, and the vaults beneath had guarded the great sums of money so gathered. These days the Toll House held not taxes, but rather the Old City's registers.

At first the clerks could not be bothered with Ivy's request to examine some of the old records. Finally, weary of being ignored, she introduced herself again to the head clerk, this time giving her name not as Quent, but as Lady Quent. While she was reluctant to flaunt her newly gained title, Ivy could only admit that its effect was clear and immediate. She was hurriedly shown to a room and placed at a table, and any such ledgers as she requested, for any particular year, were brought to her.

Ivy spent several hours poring over dusty ledgers and registers, and sorting through crackling parchment deeds. Many of the documents were faded or spotted with mold, and the records for many years were missing altogether, lost in the past to fire or flood.

But even if the records had been complete, there was no reason to think the man Dratham had been born in the same district in which he built his house, or even that he had been born in Invarel at all. However, it seemed the most logical place to start, and so she gamely read through lists of names in the rolls of births, marriages, and deaths for the West Durrow parish.

She did not know exactly how far back to start, as they were not sure of the age of the house. Thus she started at the beginning of the register, which went back over four hundred years. Eventually her eyes began to smart from staring at the columns of names written in dim, archaic script. Given the gaps in the register—as well as the gaps in her own attention, which could not be prevented from wandering from time to time—she began to despair that the task was impossible. After all, this was just the register for one parish, and there were seventeen parishes in the city. She might read them all and still never find what she sought.

Then she turned a page, and there was the entry from over three hundred years ago, right near the top: DRATHAM, WAYWREND LOERUS.

There was scant information in the birth record. All the same, it told Ivy a great deal. The mother's name and place of birth were given as Ethely Milliner of Lowpark Parish, and her residence at the time of the birth was listed as Marmount Street. The father's name was not written in the ledger.

So here was a woman with a modest name from a modest part of the city who resided in what, at the time, was one of the most fashionable sections of Invarel—for the New Quarter was yet more than a century away from being constructed. What was more, the father's name was omitted, and the child's surname did not match the mother's.

From these facts, Ivy could draw but one conclusion: Waywrend Loerus Dratham was almost certainly the illegitimate son of a well-to-do gentleman, or perhaps even a lord. While the man had been unable (or unwilling) to marry the descendant of a hat-maker, he had not abandoned Ethely; and he had set her and the child up in an expensive district of the city.

It could even be surmised that the man had left some part of his fortune to his son, for Waywrend Dratham had gone on to build a very fine house on the west end of Durrow Street, replete with exquisite marble fireplaces. True, it was possible Dratham had made his own fortune in life. Yet given the way his father had obviously treated Ethely well, it seemed fair to presume that at least some portion of Dratham's fortune had come from his sire.

As for his name, that was likely not his father's surname, though Dratham might have been his father's middle or given name. Indeed, as she continued to look through the register, she saw no more incidences of the name Dratham anywhere.

Until she got to a page fifty-three years later. There she saw the name one more time. There were no details listed, nor any heirs or survivors noted. Instead, there was only a brief entry: DRATHAM, WAYWREND LOERUS, OF W. DURROW PAR., ON THIS DAY DECEASED.

In the intervening years there had been no record of marriage or of further births involving anyone named Dratham, and such events were always recorded in the man's parish of origin. So Ivy knew not only that Dratham was the misbegotten son of a gentleman or a lord, but also that he never married and had died childless (or at least with no legitimate children).

Despite her excitement at having learned more about the history of the house, a melancholy descended over Ivy. She gave the ledgers back to the clerks, then left the past and the dusty air of the Toll House to walk out into the warm present of a brilliant afternoon.

Ivy had intended to hire a cab to take her back to The Seventh Swan, for she had told Lawden not to wait for her in case her sisters needed the carriage. But she always seemed to think better when walking, and she had much to ponder. So she walked up the bustling length of King's Street and considered all she had learned that day.

There was no way to really know, but Ivy was convinced from

what she had learned that Waywrend Loerus Dratham had been a magician. She did not know for a fact that the magickal eyes in the house were original to it, but there had been nothing found to indicate they were added later. In which case they had been *his* doing.

Then there was the matter of his middle name. From what Ivy had read, the planet Loerus was one whose movements were often watched by magicians. That Dratham's father, whoever he was, would give his son such a name could not be chance, and he may well have been a magician himself. The fact that Dratham had never married also gave the impression of a man alone in his house, studying arcane lore.

Still, this was all conjecture. For all she knew, he had been a dull-witted man who was too homely to get a wife and who never cracked the pages of a book in his life.

Yet she couldn't believe *that*. A man with an incurious mind would never have built a house so interesting as the house on Durrow Street. All the same, she had to admit it was unlikely that she would ever uncover proof that Dratham was a magician. While these days it was becoming fashionable for the sons of lords to study magick—or at least to affect the appearance of studying it—that was not the case two and three centuries ago. In that era, there had still been edicts banning the practice of magick. And if Dratham was a magician, it was something he would have done in secret.

So consumed was Ivy with these thoughts that it took her several moments to realize that someone was calling her name.

"Good day, Lady Quent!" came the voice again, followed by a clatter of hooves and wheels against cobbles.

Startled, Ivy looked up to see a barouche of lacquered and gilded wood, drawn by a pair of perfectly matched grays, come to a halt not ten paces away. The driver, whose coat was as rich as any gentleman's, leaped down to open the door, then helped a woman out of the carriage. Her gown was a violet that matched her eyes, and her hair fell in a shower of chestnut curls over her shoulders.

"I knew it could not be long before we met again, Lady Quent," the woman said as she approached. Then she gave a bright laugh. "But how dreadful you must think me! You can only imagine I devised this encounter even as I did our first. Yet this time I can profess my complete innocence. I had come to the Old City to select new pigments for my painting. I am weary of all my usual colors, and long for new ones. However, I discovered nothing of any interest. Until I spied *you* from the carriage, that is."

"Lady Crayford!" Ivy managed to say at last, and made a curtsy.

"Lady Quent," the other said, curtsying herself.

This shocked Ivy. The wife of a viscount had no need to pay honor in such a way to the wife of a baronet—and one freshly made, at that. Only then she saw the gleam in Lady Crayford's eyes, and the curve of her lips, and Ivy knew the other lady was making light of the whole affair.

"I see that you go afoot," the viscountess said. "Exercise is beneficial, no doubt, but talking is far more entertaining. Can I tempt you into the barouche? There is a great deal of room, as I bought very little today—a fact for which my husband will no doubt be glad!"

Presented with such an invitation, Ivy could hardly refuse. Nor could she say she had any wish to. Nothing could be more pleasant than spending a little time in the company of one so charming and interesting as Lady Crayford, and this way she would return to Mr. Quent and her sisters all the sooner.

"You are very kind," Ivy said after the driver had helped them both into the carriage.

"On the contrary, I am very selfish," her companion said from the opposite bench. "For this way I can have you all to myself, at least for a little while."

"I am sure you hardly need me for company!"

Indeed, there was a pretty girl in the carriage, a servant who had no doubt accompanied the lady to help bear packages. She was a meek thing, though, and sat very quietly with her head bowed.

"On the contrary, I need you very much," Lady Crayford said. "I haven't encountered a single interesting person or seen a single lovely thing today. And how is an artist to paint with nothing for inspiration? I might as well coat my canvas all in gray. Do you mind if I direct the driver to go around by way of the Promenade? It is a little farther that way to Marble Street, I confess, but it is prettier."

Ivy conceded that it was, and as she was already going to return faster than she would have on foot, she could hardly complain.

"What sort of things do you like to paint?" Ivy asked after the directions had been relayed to the driver.

Lady Crayford shook her head. "No, Lady Quent. I will not let you so deftly turn the topic of the conversation to me, as I am sure is your wont. Rather, I will defy your modesty, and instead ask all about *you*."

She proceeded to quiz Ivy on what she had been doing that day, and why she was residing at The Seventh Swan, which required an explanation of the refurbishment of the house on Durrow Street. Ivy at first attempted to keep her answers brief, so the topic would not become tedious. When Lady Crayford pressed her for all manner of details, soon Ivy found herself discussing what she had learned about the house.

"How fascinating to live in a house with such history!" Lady Crayford exclaimed. "And owned by a magician, you say. I'm sure there must be all manner of hidden doors and secret passages."

Indeed, they had found a hidden door, Ivy said, one all carved with leaves, though it led only to a blank wall. All the same, her companion was intrigued.

"I envy you, Lady Quent, to soon be dwelling in such a remarkable abode." Lady Crayford gave a sigh. "None of the houses in the New Quarter is nearly so interesting. Oh, they are pretty enough. Yet they are neither truly new anymore, nor really old enough to offer real character. Well, it is always the way that what was new becomes old, and what was old is rediscovered. Thus I wouldn't be surprised if everyone started moving back to the Old City soon. Which means you are in the vanguard of fashion, Lady Quent."

That was a point Ivy could not concede. They were dwelling on Durrow Street because the house belonged to her father, she explained, and for no other reason. Except that wasn't really true. No doubt Mr. Quent could have afforded a house in the New Quarter and would have moved them there if Ivy had asked him to.

The carriage rounded a bend on the Promenade, resulting in a striking view of Halworth Gardens with the Crag rising above, and Ivy remarked that it would make for a lovely painting. This time her attempt to turn the topic away from herself succeeded, for Lady Crayford agreed that it would indeed be pretty, but that there was a superior view just a short way ahead, where the ragged edge of an old wall created an interesting frame to it all.

As the carriage continued on, they leaned out the window, and Lady Crayford pointed out other scenes worth painting. Ivy noted that she seemed to favor provocative contrasts: a dead tree in the midst of a garden in bloom, or a dusty street sweeper standing beside a heroic statue of a general, holding his broom even as the statue gripped a sword.

Ivy could not help noticing that they received many looks from people in the street as they passed. However, Lady Crayford seemed not to care. Nor, after a time, did Ivy. Why should *she* worry if others thought her and her companion deserving of a stare or a gawk? In a moment those faces would flash by, and Ivy would never see them again. Before long she laughed as Lady Crayford did, leaning out the carriage window and pointing at anything that intrigued or delighted, imagining them in a painting.

Too soon the carriage came to a halt before The Seventh Swan. Ivy thanked Lady Crayford for the conveyance. Then, perhaps imprudently—but she was yet filled with excitement from their conversation—she exclaimed, "I wish I could see your paintings someday!"

"Then you must come see them," Lady Crayford said, her expression pleased. "I would not have thought to compel you to view such tedious things, but since you have tendered yourself, you cannot withdraw the offer. You must come to my next party. I am planning it for Brightday eve. Your presence will assure it is a lively gathering."

At once Ivy's excitement vanished. How could she have been so presumptuous? She must have appeared as if she were fishing for an invitation. How dreadful she must seem!

"I am sure my presence cannot be needed to make an affair at your house lively," she said. "And you no doubt already have a full guest list."

"On the contrary, there is always room for one more couple, and you and Sir Quent will be the best thing about the party. I will be delighted to show you off."

Ivy hardly knew what to say. According to the stories Lily had read in the broadsheets, the viscountess's parties were the most famous affairs in the city, filled with all manner of noble and glorious beings. That she and Mr. Quent would be out of place there was beyond a certainty.

"But my husband is often out of town."

"Well, if he cannot come, then bring another companion." She reached out and gripped Ivy's hands. "But come you must, Lady Quent. Promise me that you will."

Asked so directly—with such warmth of feeling, and by one who was her superior—Ivy could not refuse. Nor, once she had accepted the invitation, could she say she was in any way sorry, for she truly did wish to see Lady Crayford's paintings.

Once Lady Crayford was satisfied with the solemnity of the promise, she bid Ivy farewell, and in an unexpected and charming gesture, kissed Ivy's cheek. Ivy said farewell, then departed the carriage and entered the inn. As she did, laughter rose within her. She had just been invited to a party at the house of the renowned viscountess Lady Crayford! How was she to tell Mr. Quent? What was she going to wear?

And, most of all, whatever was Lily going to say?

CHAPTER ELEVEN

RAFFERDY KNEW THERE was no further use in leaving it to luck.

His friend could only be avoiding the Sword and Leaf. Twice in the last half month Rafferdy had gone to their old haunt and had sat for at least an hour, and neither time did his drinking companion have the decency to present himself. True, it had been a few months since they had met at the tavern in the Old City. All the same, was it too much to ask for Garritt to present himself when he was wanted?

Apparently it was. While a chance meeting with a friend was always more merry than a planned affair, the problem with such encounters was that they never seemed to reliably happen when one wished them to. Which meant if he was ever going to meet with that rascal Eldyn Garritt, it was going to have to be arranged.

As he blotted and sealed the note he had composed to Garritt, his gaze strayed to the stack of invitations on his writing desk. At the top was a letter from Lady Marsdel, informing him that his presence was required for tea tomorrow. The note had come two days ago, but Rafferdy still had not written a response. Each time he tried to pick up a pen to do so, some invisible force stayed his hand. For what if *she* had been invited to tea as well?

True, he had promised Mrs. Baydon that he would not avoid another affair at Lady Marsdel's just because he knew Mrs. Quent would be there. He had realized it was not for Mrs. Quent's benefit that he had kept himself from her these last months. However, knowing that one had acted ignobly was far from the same thing as being noble, and the idea of encountering Mrs. Quent was one that still filled him with discomfort.

That she would gloat about her marriage, or burden him with overly affectionate anecdotes concerning her husband, was impossible; she had too much sense, and too fine an apprehension of the feelings of others, to ever do such a thing. *She* would never say anything to injure his feelings.

Still, no matter how thoughtful or sensitive her statements were, she would not be able to conceal her present state of joy. Merely to be bright and lovely in his presence would demonstrate stronger than any words how content she was with the way fate had arranged things.

No, Rafferdy was not ready to witness *that* yet. Besides, there was no way to know if she had been invited to Lady Marsdel's tomorrow. Which meant if he turned down the invitation, it could not be because she was expected there. Thus his promise to Mrs. Baydon would not be broken.

Rafferdy took up a pen. However, after a minute he set it back down without writing a word. Instead, he picked up the note for Garritt and gave it to his man.

🍃

To RAFFERDY'S IMMENSE satisfaction, a reply came that very afternoon. Garritt would happily meet him at the usual place; he would be there an hour after sunset, and he promised his purse would be full.

He set down Garritt's note and returned to the mirror, where he had been modeling his new robe of black crepe. After some consideration, he decided it gave him a lordly look. Not that this was something he had sought. The main benefit of the robe was that it did not emanate a musty odor. The lack of any kind of ruffle was also a welcome characteristic. If it happened that the garment lent him a more official air, he supposed it could not be helped.

As he turned to admire the drape of the robe, he noticed a flash of blue. Rafferdy raised his right hand, looking at the ring on his fourth finger. He had grown so used to the thing that he seldom paid it attention anymore. Except that wasn't entirely the case, for on more than one occasion since the opening day of Assembly, he had found himself absently turning the House ring around and around or gazing into the blue gem.

It was only a stray sunbeam that caused the jewel to glimmer now. But it wasn't sunlight that had made it flare that day at Assembly, when he used an enchantment to unlock a door and gain his escape. He had not studied magick since his final lesson with Mr. Bennick last year, but the spell of opening had come easily to him. It seemed he had not forgotten everything he had learned from the former magician.

Which had proved fortunate. Who knew how long he would have been trapped in the Hall of Magnates if he had not been able to unlock the door? He might have had to spend the night alone in that echoing hall, with no light and nothing to drink or smoke. He could not imagine a worse fate!

Or couldn't he? That very day he had seen someone who had suffered a far worse fate than being deprived of brandy or tobacco. *A grave shock such as this can have an effect on your mind,* the Lady Shayde had said to him, her eyes black holes in her pale visage. *You might not even be certain what you really saw today.*

Yet he *was* certain. The image of the body splayed on the floor was still vivid in his mind. Her brutish companion, the man Moorkirk, had told Rafferdy to forget what he had seen. Would that Rafferdy could comply with that order! Even now, as he recalled the scene, he felt a creeping of the flesh on the back of his neck. How could a man's throat be slit like that and seep not blood, but some grayish substance?

He had no idea. However, it was *their* concern, not his, and he did not expect he would ever encounter the White Lady again. Her purpose was to seek out spies and plotters against the king, of which Rafferdy knew precious few. All the same, he would think twice before using magick to open a locked door again, for dread of what might lay beyond!

He supposed such a trick would be beyond him soon enough.

What little magickal ability he possessed would no doubt fade away with time and disuse. Nor could he have improved upon his skills even if he wanted to. He could hardly go beg Mr. Bennick for another lesson in magick, and he had no idea who else he might ask.

Unless Lord Coulten would know.

Rafferdy had not spoken with Lord Coulten since the opening day of Assembly. The Hall of Magnates had convened twice since then, and both times Lord Baydon had asked Rafferdy to sit by him. The elder lord had lately felt unsteady due to a lingering head cold, and he had wanted to make sure he had convenient access to a young arm to lean on should he need assistance. At the end of the last session, Rafferdy had spied Lord Coulten from afar, and the two of them had exchanged cordial waves, but that was all.

Rafferdy imagined that Lord Coulten attended Gauldren's College. It was the most likely place for a young man to study magick these days. Except, now that he thought about it, Rafferdy had never seen Lord Coulten in the two years he had spent at university himself. While it was possible he had started at Gauldren's College after Rafferdy left, Rafferdy could not imagine a freshman would already be wearing a House ring, as Lord Coulten did. Besides, he was a bit old to be in his first year. In which case Lord Coulten hadn't attended Gauldren's College at all.

So then, where did he study magick?

Rafferdy realized he was still staring at his ring. He lowered his hand. The act took a greater exertion of conscious will than he would have thought necessary. He grimaced at himself in the mirror. Great gods! What did it matter where Lord Coulten had gotten his ring or learned to be a magician? It was not as if Rafferdy had any need to ask him of it.

Rafferdy took out a handkerchief and wiped away the damp sheen that had collected on his brow. Despite the fineness of the crepe cloth, the robe was surprisingly hot and stifling. Nor did he really care for the look of it, now that he reconsidered himself in the mirror.

Well, he would only have to wear it for a short time, just until his father's health was improved. Unlike the ring on his right hand, at least *this* thing he could take off easily after putting it on. He did so then, throwing it over the back of a chair and leaving it for his man to pick up.

$\maltese$

EVENING SEEMED TO take its time coming, and without any regard to the tolling of bells from down the street or for Rafferdy's thirst. If he had ever made a habit of consulting the timetables in the almanac, he was sure he would have done so then. However, as he never did, he took a small brandy instead. At last the sky bothered itself to darken, and Rafferdy put on his coat and gloves, took up his cane, and called for his cabriolet.

Warwent Square, where his house was situated, was nearly as close to the most notorious sections of the Old City as it was to the most fashionable avenues of the New Quarter. Thus, it was only a short while before the cabriolet turned down a lane some way off Durrow Street and halted before a squat building of gray stone. A sign hung over the door, barely visible in the cast-off light of a streetlamp. On it, painted in weathered green and silver, was the picture of a curling leaf pierced by a sword.

Rafferdy entered the tavern and immediately saw Eldyn Garritt, sitting in their favorite booth in the back corner. Despite Rafferdy's velvet coat and ivory-handled cane, few eyes glanced toward him as he moved through the tavern. It was not unusual for young gentlemen to frequent some of the seamier taverns and drinking houses in the Old City. Nor, in a place like this, did an expensive coat always mean a man was a magnate or shabby attire mean he was not.

Garritt stood as Rafferdy drew near. Rafferdy took off his gloves, and the two men clasped hands warmly.

"Playing at being a lord must suit you, Rafferdy," his friend said with a broad grin, "for you look very well."

"And playing at being a clerk must do the same for you, Garritt. You look well yourself tonight."

In fact, now that Rafferdy studied him, Eldyn Garritt looked exceedingly well. He wore a gray coat that was not overly rich, yet was nonetheless very handsome, and his face was not pinched with shadows, but was rather open and cheerful. These characteristics aroused a curiosity in Rafferdy, for he was used to Garritt appearing gloomy and threadbare.

He made no comment about it as the two of them sat in the booth. Garritt had already ordered a pot of punch, so they dispensed with idle words and instead got right to it. Rafferdy put a lump of sugar in his cup, squeezed a lemon over it, and filled it with sweet, heady liquid. Only when each had drained his punch halfway did they resume speaking.

Garritt admired the cup in his hand. "Now, that's a fine end to a fine day."

"A fine day you call it," Rafferdy said, affecting a skeptical tone. "Yet the weather was not remarkable, and I heard of no special happening in the city. As far as I recall, the lumenal displayed not a single characteristic that I would call *fine*. So why should it have been fine for you?"

"Why shouldn't it have been? If there was no reason for it *not* to be fine, then fine it should be. It is the intrinsic quality of a lumenal to be good, don't you think?"

Rafferdy scowled at his friend. "God above, what's happened to you, Garritt? You are in an awfully cheerful mood tonight."

"You speak as if that's something you find disagreeable."

"Of course I find it disagreeable. 'Dreariness always desires a friend,' as the saying goes, yet I find I am alone in being miserable tonight. Our positions are reversed from their usual and more natural arrangement, as I am all in a gloom, and you are in high spirits."

Garritt laughed. "What in the world do you have to be miserable about, Rafferdy?"

"A great deal. That is why I asked you to meet me here tonight, for who else in the world can I count on being miserable with? Yet instead you defy every usual expectation and are merry. You are no use." Rafferdy finished his cup, and pushed it forward to be filled again.

Garritt complied, tipping the pitcher over Rafferdy's cup. At least his friend could be useful in *that* way.

"Come now, Rafferdy," Garritt said encouragingly. "I am sure that you can bring me down if only you try. You are very skilled at getting what you want after all. So do your best—give me every reason to discard my happy mood, to let misery supplant cheer, and to pity you."

"An easy enough task!"

"Go on, then."

"For one thing, there is yet another session of Assembly I am required to attend the day after tomorrow."

"How many does this make that you have sat through?"

"There was the opening session, and two more after that. So this will be the fourth time I must go in little more than half a month."

"That hardly seems burdensome! I would have thought your presence was required more frequently. Apparently governing the nation is an easier task than I had imagined, for it to require so little time or trouble on anyone's part."

Rafferdy slammed down his cup, which might have resulted in a great splash had it not been already empty. "Easy, you say! Do you have any idea what it is like to sit on those wretched planks they call benches and listen to some ancient lord in a crooked wig drone on forever about this tax or that act or some new proposal to build more schools or hospitals or some such twaddle? Even if the benches were not so hard as to preclude any chance of dozing, you still can't lower your head for a nap, because at any moment you may be required to suddenly stand up and shout out a vote of yea or nay. As if, after listening to some old windbag prattle on for an hour, you have any idea what the measure is about, let alone if it's a worthy thing. And that's just the—I say, Garritt, are you even listening to me?"

Garritt turned his head to regard Rafferdy; he had been gazing at the door of the tavern. "Yes, of course. The benches are very hard. Can't you bring a cushion to sit on?"

"And look like a fool? I've never seen anyone else do such a thing. Even the most decrepit lord sits there contentedly as if upon a comfortable chaise. I wonder if they've not all of them completely lost sensation in their backsides. But I tell you, I am in agony the entire time."

"So bring a pillow, and damn anyone if they stare at you. When have you ever worried about what anyone else thinks?"

"Do you not know me after all these years, Garritt? I've always worried what others think. That is, I worry that they do not think as highly of me as they should have the sense and wits to. But since I can hardly count upon the taste and intelligence of others, I must necessarily lower myself to secure their good opinion, as little as it is worth."

Garritt smiled and shook his head. "You sound like a man who willingly spends gold to buy lead."

"On the contrary, I'm like a man who spends gold to buy rum. The one is more valuable, but the other must be had all the same for sustenance."

"Well, maybe you need something to sustain you besides the approving looks of other people. Maybe you should strive to do something that wins *your* approval."

"If you mean I should do as abstainers advise and give up drink and tobacco and start chewing grass like a cow so I can feel superior about myself, you are wasting your breath. I have no desire to improve myself."

"Don't you?"

Garritt was gazing not at Rafferdy, but at his hands. With a start, Rafferdy realized he had been fidgeting with his House ring, turning it around on his finger.

"Have you never thought about continuing your studies in magick?" Garritt went on, his tone more serious now. "I can only believe mastering some new spell or enchantment would provide you with more entertainment and satisfaction than mastering public opinion."

Rafferdy could only wince. A few months ago, in a drunken moment, he had told Garritt how, at the urging of Mrs. Quent, he had taken up the study of magick to help her gain entry to her family's old house on Durrow Street, and how they had managed to keep a group of magicians from gaining an object there that had belonged to her father.

At the time he had reveled in the tale, sparing no detail that served to illuminate his magickal prowess. Now, however, he regretted ever telling Garritt about it. The whole affair was something he wanted only to forget.

Except *she* would never let him forget. Perhaps that was another reason he had been avoiding her—not only because she had appeared so happy to be Mrs. Quent, but also because she had once appeared similarly happy to see Rafferdy work magick. If given the chance, would she not encourage him to work magick again?

"Are you well, Rafferdy?" Garritt said, his eyes concerned. "You look ill of a sudden. Have you had too much punch?"

"On the contrary, I haven't had enough." He drew his right hand back from the table, and pushed his cup forward with his left.

Garritt filled it again, and Rafferdy took a deep swallow.

"Besides," he went on, "you forget what other causes I have for gloom. Or do you not recall the entire reason I am now sitting in Assembly?"

At once Garritt's expression grew solemn. "I'm sorry, Rafferdy. I had not forgotten about your father's situation. All the same, I confess that sometimes I forget to consider the constant effect it must have on your spirits. You have every reason to be somber. Just because I am used to you being cheerful does not mean you don't have the right to be in a gloom for good cause. Tell me, is there any more news?"

Rafferdy was gratified by Garritt's concern. All the same, now that the topic had been brought up, he had no real desire to discuss it. He had in fact received a letter from Asterlane that morning, and the news had been no better than in the letters that preceded it. His father wrote that he was improved, but that he was not yet ready to make the trip to the city.

By this, Rafferdy knew that his father's condition was not improved at all. However, it was the case that Lady Rafferdy read everything Lord Rafferdy wrote to their son (as she was not one to write letters herself), and thus his father could not discuss his situation openly, for fear of increasing the degree of her fretfulness about his health, which was already acute. Nor was there any need for him to do so. The meaning of his words might be obscure to his wife, but to his son it was more than clear enough.

Rafferdy told Garritt only that he had heard nothing new from Asterlane, which was true enough.

"As for magick," he went on, adopting a light tone, "even if I wished to study it again, I have no one to study it with. As I told you, Mr. Bennick turned out to be the worst sort of villain, and by all reports has fled back to his estate in Torland. Not that I am surprised. I never liked him from the moment I saw him, and I am an excellent judge of character."

"I'll disagree with you there." Garritt affected a wry grin and raised his cup. "If you were a good judge of character, I'm sure you wouldn't demean yourself by associating with the likes of me."

That was the first really amusing thing Rafferdy had heard all day, and he laughed. "On the contrary, Garritt, I have never encountered a more decent or wholesome being than you in my life. Just being near you surely reduces by some degree the blemish upon my character. Most people struggle all their lives to be good, and they mostly fail. Not you, Eldyn Garritt. You do not need to strive to be good, for you are good by your very nature. And it's not just that cherub's face of yours. It's who you are in your being. That you are capable of doing anything profligate or wicked is impossible. The moon is no more capable of shining in the daytime."

Rafferdy thought these words would have left his friend with a pleased look about him. Instead, Garritt's grin became a grimace, and he shifted in his seat as if he'd just encountered a splinter.

"You do me too much justice," Garritt said after a moment, his voice subdued now. "Besides, as you'd know if you were ever awake when it was light out, you can easily see the moon during daytime. It's faint, but it's there. You have only to look up."

Rafferdy did not know how to react to these words; for some reason this sudden display of his friend's customary moroseness did not please Rafferdy as much as he might have thought. It occurred to him that perhaps he should ask Garritt if something was wrong.

Before he could think of something sympathetic to utter, a motion caught his eye. Rafferdy turned his head to see the back of a young man who had just walked past their booth. This would not have been remarkable except for two things. The first was that the young man's buff-colored coat was exceptionally well made, and a rich coat was something Rafferdy always noticed. The second was that the young man's hair rose up in a frizzy column, reaching as high as a top hat might.

The other went to an opening at the rear of the tavern. He cast a glance over his shoulder—in the direction opposite where they sat, so Rafferdy could not glimpse his face. Then the young man vanished through the opening.

"What are you looking at?" Garritt asked, noticing his attention.

"I'm not sure exactly," Rafferdy said. "I think it's—that is, excuse me for a moment."

Rafferdy went to the opening in the rear of the tavern. Beyond was a hallway. It was unlighted, and he could see nothing past a few feet—though he had little trouble discerning the sour odor that drifted outward.

Curiosity won out over distaste. Rafferdy took a deep breath, then plunged in. The only light was the wan illumination of oil lamps that seeped from behind. However, as his eyes adjusted, he was able to perceive the hallway before him, as well as several doors.

He tried the first door, found it unlocked, and opened it. Beyond was a closet filled with barrels. The next two doors opened onto other closets, one containing a stack of boxes and the other a heap of rags. It was from this last closet that the fetid odor emanated, and he quickly shut the door.

He came to the last door, at the end of the corridor. It was heavier than the others, bound with rough iron bands—more like a door that opened outside rather than to a closet or a room. Did

Lord Coulten know of a back entrance to the tavern? Rafferdy hardly cared that anyone saw him enter here, but one never knew when it might be useful to make a discreet exit. Grasping the iron ring that served as a handle, he pulled the door open.

Beyond the door was not a room or a hallway, but rather a wall of bricks.

"But that doesn't make a bit of sense," he muttered.

There was nowhere else Lord Coulten could have gone. He surely hadn't been hiding in one of the filthy closets. However, when Rafferdy laid his hands against the bricks, he found they were rough and solid. If this had ever been an exit to the Sword and Leaf, it had been walled up long ago.

Rafferdy was giddier than he thought. He must have turned his head for a moment or shut his eyes. It had only *seemed* that Lord Coulten had stepped into the opening. Instead, he had probably turned and gone out the front door. Indeed, it probably hadn't been Lord Coulten at all, but some other man with tall hair and a fine coat.

Satisfied by these conclusions, and moreover deciding that, despite his impairment, he was thirsty for more punch, he shut the door. As he did, a glint of blue caught his eye.

"Rafferdy?" Garritt's voice echoed from behind him. "What are you doing down there?"

Rafferdy raised his right hand and looked at his ring—the ring that marked him as a descendant of House Gauldren, one of the seven Old Houses of magick. In the gloom, it seemed that an azure spark winked within the gem set into the ring, then went dark.

"I say, Rafferdy, I've ordered us another round. You don't want me to drink it all by myself, do you?"

Rafferdy shook his head, then made his way back down the hallway.

"I thought you'd gotten lost in there," Garritt said when Rafferdy emerged. "You weren't looking for a pot to piss in, were you?"

"No, but by the appalling smell, I believe others have ventured there for such a purpose, pot or no."

"Then what in God's name did you go in there for?"

"Nothing. I'm halfway drunk, that's all. Which means I still have halfway to go." He seized the pot of punch to fill their cups.

Having had his fill of serious subjects, if not of punch, Rafferdy directed the conversation in a more frivolous direction. He detailed his new robe from Larrabee's, and he described how, so far, he had avoided uttering anything of any sort of worth at Assembly. Garritt responded to these things in only the most absent manner.

Indeed, Garritt's thoughts seemed entirely elsewhere, and his unnaturally cheerful mood had returned. Several times as Rafferdy spoke, Garritt glanced at the entrance of the tavern, and more than once Rafferdy was forced to repeat himself to get any kind of response. At last Rafferdy could suffer this behavior no longer.

"Don't let me keep you, then!" he announced loudly.

Garritt started in his seat, then turned to regard Rafferdy. "What are you talking about?"

"By the way you keep looking at the door, I fathom you'd rather be somewhere else than here at the moment."

"That's not true."

"On the contrary, your mind is already off and about. I know it, for you haven't heard a thing I've said."

"Yes, I have. You've got a new robe, you said. And you've been a great success at being an utter failure at having any effect upon the proceedings at Assembly."

"I said those things a quarter of an hour ago. What have I said since then?"

Garritt opened his mouth, then shut it again and affected a sheepish look.

"I thought as much." Rafferdy leaned back in the booth. "Well, wherever it is you wish to be, you might as well go. You're no use to me in this state, Garritt. Something has you very pleased with yourself, and whatever it is you can think of nothing else. So go on, then, and get your fill of it. Yet make no mistake—when I see you next, I expect you to be melancholy!"

Garritt offered profuse apologies, and assured his friend that he would be properly miserable when next they talked. A plan was formed to meet here again several umbrals hence, after Rafferdy's next session at Assembly, for he surely would be in need of a drink *then*. They rose and shook hands, then Garritt departed—and none too slowly, Rafferdy thought.

Alone, Rafferdy sat to finish his punch. However, he found the cup empty, and the pitcher, too. It was just as well. His head hurt, and his stomach had gone sour. So even his dearest and most trusted companion—that was, rum—could not be counted upon for amusement that night! He was entirely abandoned and friend-less.

No, that was not true. Mrs. Quent would yet be his friend, he was sure, if he would only let her. She would not look elsewhere as he spoke, or act as if she had somewhere else to be.

Rafferdy lurched to his feet. A compulsion had come over him to return home and reply to Lady Marsdel, accepting her invita-tion. If there was a chance Mrs. Quent would be at her ladyship's house, then he should be there as well, as a show of regard. He owed Mrs. Quent that; more, it was his duty.

"So once again," Rafferdy muttered, not so drunk he didn't know what he was really doing, "you follow your whim and claim nobility for it."

Yet he was resolved. He would go to Lady Marsdel's tomorrow. He took up his gloves and cane and made for the door. As was al-ways the case after dark, a thick-necked man stood at the entrance of the tavern, leaning against a sideboard as he watched the door. He had black hair and narrow-set eyes. Rafferdy asked him to call a hack cab.

"Couldn't open the door, then, could you?" the man said with a yellow grin.

Rafferdy frowned. The front door of the tavern stood open be-fore them; the dank night air rolled in. "I don't know what you're talking about," he said, fumbling in his coat pocket for a coin.

"Oh, you don't?" The man's grin broadened. It was a rather leering expression, and missing more than a few teeth. "All right, my lord, be mysterious if you want. I know your sort favors that."

Rafferdy shook his head. Either he was drunker than he thought, or the man was having some amusement at his expense. "My sort?" He found a silver penny and set it on the sideboard.

"You know what I mean."

The man's gaze flicked down. At first Rafferdy thought he was looking at the coin, and that perhaps it was not sufficient to bribe him to summon a cab. Only then it struck him that it was not the coin the man looked at, but rather the ring on Rafferdy's right hand. The blue gem was dark now.

Rafferdy pulled his hand back. "Are you going to call for a driver, or should I pay someone else?"

The other's grin was gone now, and he scooped up the coin. "Whatever you want, my lord."

The doorman stepped out into the street and let out a sharp whistle. Moments later a scuffed carriage rattled up to the tavern. Rafferdy started through the tavern door, only then he paused. He took his gloves from his coat pocket and put them on, covering both his hands.

Then he went out alone into the night.

CHAPTER TWELVE

"𝒯HE NEW TREATMENT has had a remarkable effect," the warden said loudly as he took the ring of keys from his belt and unlocked a door. "There has been a discernible improvement in his behavior. I think you will be both surprised and pleased by his condition, Mrs. Quag."

"Mrs. Quent," she said, forced to raise her own voice to be heard above the cacophony of wails and screams, grunts and moans, angry shouts and wordless pleadings that resounded off the hard walls. "But what new treatment do you mean? What have you been doing differently?"

She followed the warden through the door, and he locked it shut behind them. At once the dreadful noises were dampened to a rhythmic murmur, like the surge of a doleful sea.

The warden led the way down a corridor. He was not the same one who used to take Ivy to see her father at Madstone's. The colorless man who had previously done so had recently vanished. Ivy did not know what had become of him, only that he had been replaced by the man she followed now. He was taller and younger, with a pulpy face, ruddy cheeks, and red lips that were always moist from the frequent application of his tongue.

"You said the treatment you had given my father was new," Ivy called from behind him.

"Indeed, it's the very latest technique," the warden replied. "As I am sure you know, we always employ the most modern practices at the Madderly-Stoneworth Hostel for the Deranged. There is no method of treatment too novel or too unconventional for us not to adopt it here."

"After it has been studied and deemed safe, you mean."

The warden chuckled. "Of course—that goes without saying, Mrs. Quaff."

"Mrs. Quent," she replied.

He opened another door and again locked it behind them. The terrible sounds of the hostel could not be heard at all now, and the corridor they entered was both cleaner and lighter.

"The new treatment involves the use of an electric condenser."

Ivy hurried to keep up with his long strides. "An electric condenser?"

"Yes, it's a marvelous invention. It just came over from the Principalities."

"But what is it?"

"It's a glass container, and there are various salts and chemicals within, separated in metallic chambers, and a copper rod is inserted—well, there's no use in attempting to explain it further. It's something *you* wouldn't understand, as you're not a doctor."

"It is true, I am not," Ivy said, a bit breathless from the brisk pace she was forced to maintain to keep up with him. "However, I might comprehend better if you discussed it in more detail."

He laughed again—a high-pitched sound. "No, I am sure you would not. It is enough for you to know that an electrical charge is produced, similar to a bolt of lightning from the sky. Not so large, of course! You need not be alarmed."

His words had the opposite effect. "What do electrical charges have to do with my father's treatment?"

"Everything, of course. The technique involves placing a copper circle around the patient's head. Wires are connected to the circle, and these in turn are attached to the rod in the condenser."

Ivy halted, a horror coming over her. "You mean you induce an electrical shock in him?"

"Not one shock. *That* would hardly be useful. The treatment requires repeated application at precise intervals." The warden smiled back at her. "There is no cause for concern. Strong muscular contractions are a natural result of the application of the electrical charge. However, he is restrained very securely before the treatments begin so he cannot cause harm to himself during the convulsions."

Ivy felt as if she had been shocked herself. "That is no treatment. It is a torture! I have heard that such things are done to prisoners in the Empire to make them confess to their crimes, and that men sometimes perish from it, for the shock stops the beating of their heart."

"Many of the most effective medicines are also poisons if given in the wrong dosage," the warden said pleasantly. "Experiments have shown that application of an electrical charge can negate pathological function in an ill mind, and as a result induce more normal behavior."

"That may be so. All the same, it is surely not without risks! How could you do such a thing without informing me?"

The warden leaned over her. "As you know, our authority here is categorical. Once he enters the hostel, a patient belongs to us solely. There is no need for us to seek any sort of outside consent. We do what we decide is best for the patient, Mrs. Quirk."

"My name is Quent," Ivy said. A kind of electricity grew within her, and she drew herself up, though she only came to his shoulder. "And it is Lady Quent now."

"Is that so?" His moist red lips were still curved in a smile, but there was now a rigidity to his previously mushy face. "Well, I am sure you cannot think *that* will change how we proceed. The basic function of the brain of a lord is no different than that of the most wretched cretin on the street. We have no interest in the person; we care only what malady they possess. That is all that matters here—Lady Quent."

The charge within Ivy dissipated. Despite his cheerful demeanor, in the end this warden was no different than his predecessor. Ivy knew there was no further use in argument. Besides, whatever her father was being forced to endure, it would not be for much longer. Now that Mr. Quent had spoken to the king's steward, His Majesty was sure to approve the petition to free Mr. Lockwell soon.

"Here we are, number Twenty-Nine-Thirty-Seven." The warden took a key from his ring and unlocked the door. "I will return in exactly half an hour. You may pull the cord by the door if he should become violent or attempt to harm you in any way."

"That will not be necessary," Ivy said, and entered the room. The door shut behind her, and she heard the key turn in the lock.

She was satisfied to see the room was arranged the same way as when she had left it. A beam of sunlight fell through the window, and the effect was to render the chamber bright and cheerful. Indeed, were it not for the bars that had been fitted over the window, along with the iron-banded door, it would have seemed a very pleasant little room.

Ivy perceived a cloud of gray hair floating above the back of the chair that faced toward the window. She hesitated, afraid of what she might see. But how could anything *she* might suffer by seeing him compare to the things he had borne? She placed a smile upon her lips and went to him.

She was at once relieved and dismayed. They had dressed him in his gray suit, and his face was shaven. That his hair was a silver tangle was something for which they could not be blamed; Ivy herself had never been able to subdue it.

So it was not as terrible as she had feared. Yet what had been done to him had clearly taken a toll. The flesh beneath his eyes was dark and sunken, the corners of his mouth drooped downward, and she could detect a series of red welts across his brow. His hands twitched on the arms of the chair, as if his nerves still resonated with the electric charge that had been applied to them.

Ivy knelt beside the chair, took one of those hands, and held it gently, stilling its vibrations.

His chest heaved in a sigh. "It is about time," he said.

Amazed, Ivy looked up at him. It was the first occasion in months she had heard him utter a word. However, she did not want him to see her astonishment; he must think there was nothing unusual or strange about his having spoken. Instead, she stood and affected a light tone.

"I'm sorry I was away so long, Father. Mr. Quent and I have been preoccupied with the work on your house on Durrow Street. It has been many years since the house has seen such attention. Centuries, perhaps. I believe you will be very pleased when you see it."

She waited to see if Mr. Lockwell would speak again. He did not. But the tone of her voice appeared to have soothed him, for while his eyes remained fixed on the window, the tremors of his hands decreased, and his mouth relaxed into a calm line.

"I brought you something, Father." She removed an apple from the little bag that hung from her wrist. "I know how much you like them. Though they are getting rather precious of late, as is anything good these days."

She found a pewter plate on the table, and from her bag took out a little knife she had brought to cut the fruit. No doubt it was forbidden to bring such an instrument into the hostel—or to bring the fruit, for that matter. *Apples can only remind the patient of the world outside these walls, and thus contribute to his delusions,* the warden would no doubt admonish her. However, she was concerned they did not give him enough variety of foods to eat.

Ivy cut the apple, picking out the seeds and pushing them to one side of the plate. Then she went to her father, took his hand, and with gentle coaxings encouraged him to rise and come to the table. His steps were too feeble for her liking, and his shoes scuffed across the floor, but with little trouble they were both seated at the table.

The sunlight sparkled in his blue eyes, and he seemed to listen in an alert manner as she spoke. While she was reluctant to extend any credit to the wardens, she could only think, as brutal as it sounded and as painful as it must be, that the electrical treatment had indeed had some positive effect on Mr. Lockwell.

Yet now that her initial alarm had receded, and she could consider things in a more rational fashion, it made a sort of sense. It was as a result of working magick that this affliction had come upon him. The strain of binding the enchantment on the Eye of Ran-Yahgren, so that the other magicians of his order could not use it, had been too great. The shock had fractured his mind and left him in this state.

For years Ivy had read books in her father's library, trying to learn everything she could about the workings of magick. She had reasoned that if it was magick that had caused his malady, then it was necessarily magick that could cure it. Yet what if another sort of elemental force—one different but equally strong—was applied? Could that not undo the harm that working the enchantment had done to him?

She was not certain. There was so much more to learn. Yet given the change brought on by the electrical treatment, she had to consider that it was possible. Despite their callousness, she could only concede that the wardens at the hostel were indeed on to something.

All the same, if the application of the electrical condenser was to continue, it would have to be done in the most prudent and systematic manner. Every effort must be made to ensure her father was comfortable and to ease his fear. Also, they should apply only the minimum force necessary, and no more frequently than required. To know how to proceed, she would have to read as much as possible about the production of electrical charges and their effects upon the nervous system.

Unfortunately, as she had not been allowed to bring any of his books to the hostel, her research would have to wait. Instead, she fed him bits of apple and spoke about how the work on the house on Durrow Street was proceeding, thinking that if he could at all comprehend her, he would find the subject interesting.

How she wished she could ask him questions about the house! She had no doubt there were secrets about its history her father had uncovered in the years he had dwelled there, if only he could tell her.

Perhaps that was what he had intended to do in the journal he had left for her in the box of Wyrdwood. Perhaps he had meant to tell her everything he had learned about the house, about its enchantments and peculiarities, since it would one day be hers. However, fate had not granted him the time to follow through on that plan.

Or had it?

Ivy had thought it peculiar that he would bother to lock the journal in the Wyrdwood box if he had never had the chance to write any secrets on its pages. What if they were in fact all there, only she could not see them—just as she was sure all of his knowledge was still locked in his mind, but he could not speak it. Her father had been a magician, after all. It was certainly possible that he had cast some enchantment upon the journal. And if an application of electricity could help restore his faculties, then was it not possible there was something—a certain chemical, or a spell—that could reveal any words he might have written upon the pages of the journal?

The sound of a cough returned Ivy to the little room in the Madderly-Stoneworth Hostel. Her father's hands were in his lap, and he was gazing out the window again. The last of the apple was gone.

Again her father made a sound in his throat, as if clearing it. Perhaps he was thirsty. There was a pitcher of water on the sideboard. Ivy rose and went to it to fill a glass.

"Has the black stork come to you yet?"

Ivy set down the pitcher with a clatter and turned around, clutching the cup in her hand. Mr. Lockwell had turned his head, and for a moment she could almost believe that his faded blue eyes, which always gazed past her, were instead directed *at* her.

Water splashed over her wrist; Ivy's hand was shaking. She hurriedly went to the table and set down the cup. His gaze had returned to the window. Outside, the brief day was beginning to fail.

Ivy sat in the chair beside him. "How do you know about that, Father?" She made her voice cheerful. "I don't remember telling you about the storks I found upstairs."

Mr. Lockwell's shoulders heaved in a sigh. "It's about time," he said, as he had earlier. Only this time the words were hardly more than a murmur, and there was a sorrow to them that induced a pang in her heart.

Ivy reached a hand toward him—then halted. Her gaze fell upon the pewter plate where she had cut the apple. In the center of the plate, a number of seeds had been arranged in a row. Ivy counted them.

There were twelve seeds on the plate, all in a perfect line.

Ivy opened her mouth. Whatever it was she was going to say turned instead into a small cry as there came a metallic noise behind her. The door of the room opened, and Ivy leaped from her chair.

"Visiting hours are over," the day warden said. His lips formed a moist red smile as he jingled the key ring in his hand.

Ivy looked at her father. Her throat ached with questions she wanted to ask him. However, she knew there was no use in requesting more time. Her questions would have to wait for another quarter month, until she could visit him again.

She went to Mr. Lockwell and pressed her lips to his cheek. "I love you, Father."

The jingling of the key ring grew in volume. Ivy departed through the door, then turned to look back into the room. Mr. Lockwell sat in the chair, his faded gaze still fixed on the window, as if he saw something in the square of sky beyond.

The door shut with a clang of metal against metal.

"I'll show you out, Lady Quash," the warden said, turning the key in the lock.

"Thank you," was all Ivy said.

*

$\mathcal{M}$R. QUENT WAS to be away at the Citadel until late again. That morning, before she left for Madstone's, he had told Ivy that he would be leaving Invarel for the country once more, just as soon as he could complete his business at the Citadel. Ivy could not say she was happy to hear this news, but nor could she be surprised.

"I am glad I have gotten as much of you as I have, Sir Quent," she had said with a smile. "However, I know you are on loan from the Crown, and so must be returned when needed."

"On the contrary, Lady Quent," he had said, a grin parting his beard, "it is the king who has me on loan, for I am entirely under your ownership."

If that was so, she said, then she expected some recompense for allowing him to be away from her. He agreed, and as an advance payment he gave her a number of kisses before departing out the door.

Now, knowing Mr. Quent would not be at the inn, and expecting her sisters to be at the gardens, Ivy hoped to have an hour to make an examination of her father's journal before it was time to ready herself to go to Lady Marsdel's house, as she had been invited to tea that day.

However, upon her return to the inn, she discovered her sisters still there, and a glance at the old rosewood clock informed her that she had scant minutes to spare. She was not entirely certain the clock could be believed, but being late to her ladyship's was not something Ivy cared to risk. So she threw on her green dress, made a few wild gestures with a hairbrush, and pinched her cheeks to bring a bit of color to them.

"I do not see why we can't come with you," Lily said, looking up from her book as Ivy entered the sitting room.

"You cannot come because you were not invited."

"Well, I don't know why I shouldn't have been. After all, I've met Lady Marsdel on more than one occasion. Besides, you've been there a hundred times. It's only fair that someone else gets to go."

"It has been far fewer than a hundred times," Ivy said, but gently.

Not for the first time, she was tempted to tell Lily about the plan for a party to present her and Rose to society. She had discussed it with Mr. Quent after his return to the city. However, due to the degree of excitement such news was likely to induce in Lily, they agreed that the information should be kept from her until a date was set.

This had not happened yet, as Mr. Quent wished to wait until he was certain he would not have need to travel for a time. As soon as he could be sure of a date he would be in the city, the party could be planned. That would give Lily something to look forward to. Until then, Ivy supposed she would have to endure more sighs and frowns.

"I hope you have a very happy time," Rose said as she tried to entice Miss Mew with a bit of thread. "Tell Mr. Rafferdy hello for us if you see him."

"Don't tell him hello from me," Lily said, raising her book before her face. "I am still very cross with him for the way he's ignored us."

"Very well," Ivy said. "I will be sure to say hello from Rose only."

The book came down again. "Great gods, Ivy, you can't do *that*! How awful would you make me look? If you say hello for Rose, you *must* say hello from me as well."

So directed, Ivy promised she would, though she had not seen

Mr. Rafferdy at Lady Marsdel's in a very long time, and she did not expect in any way that he would be there.

§HE WAS WRONG.

Upon entering the parlor at Fairhall Street Ivy saw a tall figure clad in an elegant coat of charcoal velvet standing by the fireplace. She had neither desire nor ability to suppress the smile that sprang to her lips. If she could have, she would have gone to him directly. However, she had hardly taken a step before Lady Marsdel's voice rang out.

"It has been far too long since you have been here, Lady Quent. It has been a month, I am sure. Do not try to tell me it has been less! Now come this way at once. Mr. Rafferdy can suffer to wait a little while longer to be greeted by you, but *I* cannot."

Mr. Rafferdy returned her smile. He nodded, a sparkle in his brown eyes, and he made a small gesture with his hand, so that the blue gem on it sparked as well. The message was clear: *Her ladyship must be obeyed.*

Ivy went to pay homage to Lady Marsdel. Her tiny puff of a dog perched on a pillow on her lap, its eyes as black and round as buttons.

"I heard news from Mrs. Baydon that you were ill," Lady Marsdel said. "I did not think you had such a poor constitution, Lady Quent, to succumb to a malady again so soon after the last time. But then, you do not look poorly. Indeed, you appear quite well. I cannot imagine it was anything much at all. Certainly nothing to have kept you away for so long."

Ivy assured her ladyship that, while she was now happily recovered, she had in fact been confined to chambers by order of her doctor.

"Well, it was very selfish of you to let yourself be caught in the rain," Lady Marsdel went on. "I trust you will take better care of yourself from now on. You must not only think of yourself, Lady Quent. There are others who require you."

"So they do," Lord Baydon said, smiling. His smile became a sudden grimace as he sneezed into a handkerchief.

Ivy gave her meekest assurances that her ladyship's advice would be followed. Lady Marsdel motioned for her to sit on the sofa beside her, and Ivy complied. She reached out to pet the little dog. It bared its teeth and emitted a growl, and she hastily withdrew her hand.

"Quit lurking there by the fireplace, Mr. Rafferdy!" Lady Marsdel called out. "I do not know where Mr. and Mrs. Baydon can be or why they presume that they can be late to tea. However, until they arrive to provide us with additional society, you must entertain us. What acts have you passed at Assembly of late? I hope you have made yourself useful."

"Not in the least," he said agreeably, sitting in a chair. "As Lord Baydon is my witness, I have not done one constructive thing in Assembly."

"On the contrary," Lord Baydon said, his voice hoarse after his sneezing fit, "you have helped me to my seat several times, Mr. Rafferdy. And that has been very useful to *me*."

Lady Marsdel appeared unimpressed. "You must take your duties more seriously, Mr. Rafferdy There is a great deal to be done. Do you know that a box of porcelain plates I ordered from the Principalities has failed to arrive? Now I have a letter from the importer telling me that the ship was harried by Murghese corsairs and was forced to dock in Torland. Nor will I ever see the porcelain now. You can be sure the Torlanders have made off with everything—though what people who choose to dwell in hovels should want with fine things, I cannot imagine."

Mr. Rafferdy shrugged. "Perhaps they decided that if their plates are going to be empty, they might as well be pretty to look at."

"And why should their plates be empty?"

"Because they have chosen guns over grain," Mr. Baydon said, striding into the parlor. "Until the rebels at the border put down their arms, the king's army is maintaining a blockade. And I say the soldiers should not let a single wagon of wheat into Torland. If you give a rat a crumb in the garden, then he will only come into the kitchen seeking a loaf. My only concern is that the king is not keeping nearly enough soldiers in the Outlands. You will do something about that, won't you, Rafferdy?"

"On the contrary, I am going to propose to have the king send not soldiers, but a regiment of cats to Torland," Mr. Rafferdy said with a grave look. "Perhaps that will solve the problem with the rats."

"Now you're being willfully absurd, Mr. Rafferdy."

"One is always willfully absurd, Mr. Baydon. If one does not say silly things with a purpose, then he is merely an idiot."

Lady Marsdel opened her fan for the sole purpose that she could then snap it shut. "You are late," she said to her nephew and his wife.

"Captain Branfort took us for a drive all the way around the city," Mrs. Baydon said, for she and the captain had entered the parlor. Her cheeks were very bright and her hair rather mussed. "I have never ridden so fast in my life. Every moment I thought the carriage was going to turn over and all of us would break our necks. I was quite terrified! Lady Quent, you must come with us next time."

"Because you wish her to be terrified as well?" Mr. Rafferdy said, raising an eyebrow.

"No, because it was marvelous."

"You enjoyed being afraid, then?"

Mrs. Baydon shook her head. "I would not say I enjoyed it. Rather, I would say that I felt very alive."

"By being nearly killed? That is curious. I suppose next you will say frost makes you feel warm."

"But it does, Mr. Rafferdy, as soon as one comes inside." She gave him a triumphant smile.

"I believe she has gotten the best of you, Mr. Rafferdy," Captain Branfort said with a jovial laugh.

Mr. Rafferdy made a bow in his chair, as if to surrender.

Mrs. Baydon went to Ivy and clasped her hands in greeting. "I'm so glad you could come today, Lady Quent. And you as well, Mr. Rafferdy. Indeed, it is a particular delight to have you *both* here at once."

Mrs. Baydon fixed him with a pointed look. However, before Ivy could wonder what it purported, Captain Branfort crossed the parlor to bow before her. He was not clad in his regimentals today, but rather a blue coat that made a dashing contrast to his ruddy cheeks and ginger hair. Ivy had met the captain on several occasions, here at Lady Marsdel's and at the Baydons' house on Vallant Street. Ivy was certain that Lily would like him a great deal. Ivy liked him as well, very much.

"I will echo Mrs. Baydon's sentiments," the captain said. "I wish you could have come with us, Lady Quent. We had room for one more in the surrey. Next time, I hope you will join us."

"I will certainly consider it," Ivy said, smiling. "That is, if I feel I have the nerve."

"I am sure you can muster the courage, Lady Quent. Despite what Mrs. Baydon says, I do not drive so very fast. Besides, I have heard that you are uncommonly brave."

Ivy was taken aback by these words. She did not know that she was particularly brave. Certainly she had known great fear when she faced the highwayman Westen and the magicians of the Vigilant Order of the Silver Eye. Only, she had never recounted details of either of these happenings to Mrs. Baydon. So how could the captain know of these events?

But no—he could only be referring to her mother's passing, which Mrs. Baydon had certainly relayed to him. Ivy had faced such extraordinary trials in recent times that she sometimes forgot about the more natural, if no less distressing, ones. She thanked the captain and told him she would certainly like to go driving with them sometime.

"Before you make any further commitments, Lady Quent, you must also agree to return here three umbrals hence," Lady Marsdel said. "I am having a dinner, and your presence will greatly enliven the proceedings. I need someone dependable to invite, for there are others I can never rely upon these days." She gave her fan a flick in Mr. Rafferdy's direction.

Ivy started to express her thanks, and to say that she would be very happy to attend. Only then a realization struck her.

"Oh, but I won't be able to come!"

"Of course you can come," Lady Marsdel said, frowning. "Surely you are recovered, if you were ever very ill."

"It's not that, your ladyship," Ivy said. "I am already engaged by a prior invitation."

This resulted in a great agitation of her ladyship's fan. "A prior invitation? How could you commit to such a thing when you know you are so often invited here, Lady Quent? You should have consulted with me first, to see if you were needed. Regardless, you must break the engagement."

"I cannot," Ivy said, though it pained her greatly.

"What do you mean you cannot? Who is this person you are engaged with whose claim to your presence could have greater precedence than mine? Go on, then—speak this person's name!"

So ordered, Ivy could only obey. "It is Lady Crayford. The viscountess has invited me to a party at her home."

These words were greeted by a look of astonishment on her ladyship's part, and at the same time Mrs. Baydon let out a gasp. Ivy gripped the edge of the sofa, so as not to slip off.

"Well, that is a most remarkable thing," Lady Marsdel said rather breathlessly. "If I did not know you so well, I would think perhaps you were making up a story to avoid having to attend my affair. But I know that sort of deceit is something of which *you* are not capable. Still, I do not know what to think! How did this come to be?"

Ivy's cheeks were hot as she explained how she had encountered the viscountess at the Citadel the day of Mr. Quent's ceremony, and then again the other day. Lady Marsdel appeared satisfied by this explanation, though far from pleased, and she made no further effort to convince Ivy to rescind the invitation.

Mrs. Baydon sighed, but the look she gave Ivy was fond. "So you are lifted up even further, Lady Quent. Not that you do not deserve it. Nevertheless, I fear you shall soon be so far above me that I will no more likely be invited to a party at your house than that of the viscountess."

Ivy shook her head, not knowing what to make of these words.

"You cannot know it, but you have dealt Mrs. Baydon a grave blow," Mr. Rafferdy said. His expression was serious, though his brown eyes were merry.

"In what way?" Ivy said, her distress growing. That she should in any way cause harm to her friend was terrible to consider.

"You could not be more wrong, Mr. Rafferdy," Mrs. Baydon said. "That any happiness Lady Quent might gain should somehow cause *me* to suffer is impossible." She looked at Ivy, her expression wry yet rueful. "However, I have always heard it said that the viscountess gives the most wondrous parties, and though I know it speaks ill of me to hope for such a thing, it is the case that I have long wished to receive an invitation to her house myself."

"Your disappointment on that account is my fault," Captain Branfort said, his usually cheerful face now marked by regret. "I have not had an occasion to see Colonel Daubrent recently."

It was explained to Ivy how the captain had once served in a company under the colonel, who was the viscountess's brother.

Mrs. Baydon smiled at Ivy. "There, you must not have a care! While Mr. Rafferdy would have you think I am so low as to be peeved at you, he is utterly wrong. I am delighted beyond compare that you are going to the viscountess's party. There is only one thing I ask of you—that when it is over, you will walk with me and tell me everything that happened while you were there."

Ivy thought only for a moment, then she sat up straight. "No, I don't believe that I will describe the party for you, Mrs. Baydon."

Her friend stared at her, as did the others.

"You see," Ivy went on hastily, "I won't have any need to tell you what happened, because you will have seen it all for yourself.

Lady Crayford gave me leave to bring a guest, and as my husband will be away from the city, I would ask you to come with me instead. If you will, that is."

Mrs. Baydon's blue eyes went wide in an expression of wonder and delight, only then she shook her head. "But what of your sisters?"

Ivy reminded her that they were not yet out, and so it would not be proper for them to attend such an affair without their father or Sir Quent to accompany them. Assured that she would not be usurping another's place, Mrs. Baydon readily accepted.

Tea arrived then, and the next hour proceeded in a cheerful fashion. Captain Branfort recounted more about their adventure driving around the city that day, and Ivy did wish she could have been with them. It had been so long since she had been out of Invarel, since she had seen the countryside and inhaled fresh air such as was never to be had in the city.

At last, due to the exertions of their ride in the country and the excitement of the invitation to the viscountess's party, Mrs. Baydon was forced to retire from the parlor with a headache, though not before kissing Ivy's cheek and telling her they must confer on what they were going to wear, so as to appear neither too disparate nor too similar.

She departed, and as Mr. Baydon was now engaged in a discussion of politics with his father, and Captain Branfort was gallantly listening to Lady Marsdel describe again the misfortune of her porcelain, Ivy suddenly found herself alone with Mr. Rafferdy. He made a gesture, and the two of them strolled to the far side of the parlor. It was, she realized with a start, the first time the two of them had had a moment to speak alone since the day they encountered the magicians in the house on Durrow Street.

Ivy did not know what to say.

"It is said that women cannot do magick," Mr. Rafferdy said, breaking the silence. "However, I would question that, for you have performed quite an enchantment today, Lady Quent."

His eyes went in the direction Mrs. Baydon had just departed, and she smiled.

"It was nothing. Besides, I will feel far less afraid going to the abode of a viscountess with Mrs. Baydon at my side. I am not sure I would have been able to summon the nerve to enter, otherwise. You see—I am far less brave than Captain Branfort would have me!"

"That is not so," he said, "for I have seen you face things the likes of which the good captain could not imagine, and which would send many a stout soldier fleeing."

A shiver passed through Ivy, but it was more a thrill than a tremor of dread. It occurred to her that it was not simply Mr. Rafferdy's company she had missed these last months. She had told Mr. Quent everything that had happened to her—even the things she had not told Mr. Rafferdy, such as her ability to call on the power of the Wyrdwood. However, Mr. Rafferdy had been in the house; he had stood against the magicians and had glimpsed the dark, ravenous things through the crystalline artifact. That was what she had been missing—the companionship of someone who knew what it was like to have been there that day.

"It has been far too long since I have seen you," she said.

While at the same moment he said, "I have been very busy of late."

Ivy felt suddenly foolish. He had the weight of all his responsibilities at Assembly to bear, as well as concern for his father's health, and she had made it sound as if she were scolding him.

"When you are occupied by serving our nation in difficult times, Mr. Rafferdy, I can hardly fault you for not coming to have tea with my sisters and me. It would not be very patriotic!" She smiled up at him.

He did not return the expression. Instead, he gave her a look the meaning of which she could not quite fathom. His eyes seemed very bright.

"No, you are wrong, Lady Quent. Nothing in Altania could be more important than having tea with you and the Miss Lockwells, and in *that* duty I have been remiss. Tell me when I should come, and I will bring Mr. Garritt with me, if he can be rummaged up."

It had not been Ivy's intention to make him feel a compulsion to call on her and her sisters. Yet she could not say she was sorry.

Lily and Rose would be happy to see him—the former especially so if Mr. Garritt was brought. A plan was quickly made for him to call next quarter month.

After that they spent some time exploring the far end of the parlor. They did not speak of anything weighty, but instead enjoyed the pleasure of idle talk and agreeable companionship. They examined a stone sphinx with lapis eyes, which Mr. Rafferdy said had been exhumed by Lord Marsdel from the sands of the Murgh Empire. There was a similar sphinx at Asterlane, he said, for Lord Rafferdy and Lord Marsdel had served in the army together as young men, during the time after the last war with the Empire.

They reached the door of the library, and Ivy remarked that she had never been inside. The room was usually the purview of the men; besides, she was generally expected to remain within sight of her ladyship. Of course, upon hearing this, Mr. Rafferdy at once suggested they enter. Ivy began to say she did not think they should presume. Only then, through the door, she caught a glimpse of a shelf of books.

"Come on, then," Mr. Rafferdy said in a conspiratorial tone. "Before we are seen."

He took her arm, and she let him lead her through the door into a room that was all she would expect of a library of a great house. There were many shelves of tomes bound in leather, but the books were almost incidental to the variety of objects that filled the room. Maps adorned the walls, and antique compasses and sextants cluttered the mantelpiece. There were jade gryphons from the Principalities, urns glazed red and black in the Tharosian style, and bronze figurines of animals whose primitive and expressive design made her believe they must date to the era before the first Tharosian ships landed on Altania's shores.

Despite these curiosities, it was the books that most interested Ivy. She went to a shelf **and** perused the titles there. Many concerned sea voyages or travels to far-off lands. However, as she ran a finger over their spines, there was one that caught her eye. It was bound in black leather with silver writing on the spine that read *Arcane Sites in the Murgh Empire*.

"I see you have not abandoned your interest in magick."

Ivy realized she had taken the book from the shelf without thinking to do so. It was an impertinent act; she had not been given leave to examine the books. Yet for so long it had been her habit to look at any book on magick she could find, hoping to find a way to help her father. Even now, when it was in science that his hope lay, the old habit remained.

"I suppose not," she said, somewhat embarrassed, though she did not put the book back. "Just because I cannot work magick does not mean I cannot read about it."

"Indeed, just as priests like to read from the Testament even though they seem unable to practice the virtues espoused within."

"Mr. Rafferdy!" she exclaimed, but she could not help laughing. "But what of you? While I might have an interest in magick, it is you who has a real ability. Have you done any magick since I saw you last?"

He tucked his right hand into his pocket. "No, not even the smallest spell."

Ivy could not deny she was saddened by these words. For so long she had wished that she could work magick, only to be denied the opportunity by the circumstance of her sex. That Mr. Rafferdy, who possessed the talent, should show no interest in developing it further was difficult for her to understand. However, she did not express these thoughts. Instead, to conceal any look of disappointment that might have registered on her face, she lowered her head and opened the book in her hands.

"Oh!" she said as a stiff sheet of paper slipped out.

Mr. Rafferdy caught it before it could fall to the floor. "Well, that's a rich bookmark," he said, looking at the square of silvery paper.

Ivy shook her head. "What do you mean?"

"It's an impression. Such things don't come cheaply—as many a person who has acquired one has announced in a loud voice at a party. Generally, if someone has such a thing, they don't hide it in an old book. Rather, they display it in a frame on the wall, as an extravagance can only be really enjoyed when it is viewed by others."

Ivy had heard there were illusionists who could hold an engraving plate in their hands and somehow transfer a scene they pictured in their minds onto the plate, from which copies of the picture could then be printed.

"May I?" she said, curious to see such a thing.

Mr. Rafferdy handed her the impression.

"Oh," she said again, but it was a murmur this time. She studied the image on the paper, rendered in fine shadings of ink. In it, three young men stood together, clad in regimental coats but with turbans upon their heads, arms around one another's shoulders. In the background were the blurred shapes of date trees and sand dunes.

Mr. Rafferdy was looking at her now, not the impression. "What is it?"

It took Ivy a moment to find her voice. She had seen an impression like this before, the day she entered the forbidden room at Heathcrest Hall. Indeed, the image was so identical it could only have been produced from the same engraving plate. She turned it over. On the back, written in faded ink, were the words *The Three Lords of Am-Anaru*.

"That's just what was written on the other one!" she exclaimed.

Mr. Rafferdy gave her a puzzled look, and she explained to him how she had seen this very same impression at Heathcrest.

"Wait a moment, can I see that again?"

She handed the paper back to him.

Now it was his turn to look astonished. "Yes, I'm sure of it now. I've seen paintings of him when he was young, in the royal army. It can only be him."

"Who do you mean?"

"My father, Lord Rafferdy. That's him on the right."

Ivy looked again at the picture. Two of the young men were grinning, but the one on the right had a more serious look about him, his dark hair curling down over his brow. Now that she knew it was Rafferdy's father, she could see the resemblance to him. She was about to remark on this when Lord Baydon entered the room.

"There you are!" he said, huffing for breath. "I knew it would not matter where I began my search, for I was confident you would be in the very first place I looked. My sister is wondering what became of you. What are you doing in here?"

Ivy's cheeks flushed. "We didn't mean to . . . we were only . . ."

"We were only looking at an old impression we found by chance," Mr. Rafferdy said.

Lord Baydon clapped his hands. "Capital! I do so like looking at impressions. Uncanny things. They make me feel very queer, but in a pleasant sort of way. Do you mind?"

Mr. Rafferdy handed him the silver paper.

"Well, it's not chance at all you found this, Mr. Rafferdy. For there's your father, Lord Rafferdy, looking very young. There beside him is Lord Marsdel. They served together in the army long ago, you know. I couldn't join up with them. You wouldn't know it now, but I was very sickly as a young man, and had not the strength!" He patted his bulging waistcoat.

Ivy was intrigued by this news. "But who is the other man?"

"That would be Earl Rylend, of course," Lord Baydon said. "He whom your own Sir Quent used to serve, as I imagine you know. He and Lord Marsdel and Lord Rafferdy were all three inseparable when they were young. I remember how they used to come and go, always off on some adventure or another. How I wished I could go with them! They were such a merry band. Well, except for your father, Mr. Rafferdy. He was the solemn and sober one. I think they might have marched right off the end of the world in their travels if your father had not reined them in with his counsel. What did they used to call themselves? They had a name for their little band, but I can't quite remember it. . . ."

"The Three Lords of Am-Anaru," Ivy said.

"Yes, that was it! But how could you know that, Lady Quent?"

She showed him the back of the impression, and explained how she had seen a copy at Heathcrest Hall with a similar caption.

Lord Baydon was delighted by this. "How marvelous! I suppose they each must have had a copy made when they were in the Empire, just after the war. I'm surprised they found an illusionist to make it. The Murghese don't go for *that* sort of thing, you know."

Ivy was surprised as well. Yet perhaps it was no great mystery. After all, wherever soldiers went, others followed to serve their needs in exchange for coin—the lure of profit proving greater than fear of war's perils.

"What a jolly band of rogues they were!" Lord Baydon went on. "Yes, the Three Lords of Am-Anaru—that was what they took to calling themselves after they came back from the south. I never did find out why. It must have been some place they went together when they were there. They had other names as well, one for each of them. What were they, now?" Lord Baydon shook his head. "I fear I can't remember. You might ask Mr. Bennick, if you can find him. I am sure he would know, for all the time he spent with Lord Marsdel or went out to the country to Earl Rylend's house."

Ivy gave a nod; however, she was quite sure she would never speak to Mr. Bennick again. She placed the impression back in the book, then put the book on the shelf.

Lord Baydon gave a cough, and Mr. Rafferdy took his arm to help him return to the parlor. As they went, Ivy glanced at the sphinx by the fireplace. Mr. Rafferdy said his father had a similar artifact at Asterlane. But if Earl Rylend had been in the Empire as a young man with Lord Marsdel and Lord Rafferdy, why had she not seen a sphinx at Heathcrest? Had the earl not brought back some memento of his journey south?

They were reunited with the others, and Captain Branfort, whose color was even higher than usual, looked very grateful for their return. Ivy decided it was time to relieve the good captain of his post, and so took a turn on duty at Lady Marsdel's side. At last the afternoon waned, and the hour came for Ivy to return to her sisters. Mr. Rafferdy offered to walk her out.

"I will look forward to our meeting next quarter month," he said.

"As will I," Ivy replied with a smile, "though I am sure I will see you in the meantime."

"In the meantime?"

"At Lady Crayford's house. But why do you look at me so?

Surely you are going. I cannot imagine a fashionable party in Invarel to which *you* were not invited!"

"I am glad you cannot," he said, "for that means I am assured I will receive an invitation to any party you might throw. But as for the viscountess's affair—no, I was not invited."

Ivy might have thought he was making a jest; however, his expression was too solemn for that.

"I'm so sorry, Mr. Rafferdy. I thought . . . that is, I believed you . . ."

"You need not be sorry, Lady Quent. The party will benefit far more from *your* presence than mine. Besides, I have other business to attend to. Indeed, I am happy I received no invitation, as it saved me the inconvenience of writing a note declining it. In fact, I should write the viscountess a note thanking her for doing me such a kindness."

He spoke these words with a mock seriousness that could only make Ivy laugh. She clasped his hand warmly, and told him she would look forward to their meeting next quarter month.

As the carriage pulled away, Ivy leaned back in the seat. How good it had been to see Mr. Rafferdy again! It had been far too long to go without the benefit of so special a friend. A smile still upon her lips, she turned to wave at him through the rear window of the carriage.

But the steps before Lady Marsdel's house were empty.

𝒟USK WAS FALLING by the time Ivy returned to the inn. According to the old rosewood clock, night had come a quarter of an hour sooner than the almanac predicted. Yet, as always, the right-hand face seemed in perfect accord with the heavens, for she looked at the clock just in time to see the last sliver of gold vanish as the black disk turned into place.

As improbable as it seemed, there was only one conclusion that could be drawn: whatever errors plagued the almanac of late, there was no fault in the workings of the old rosewood clock, just as the clockmaker's apprentice had said. She marveled, wondering what complex mechanisms resided within the clock that let it calculate, without the benefit of any timetables, just when a lumenal or umbral would begin and end.

"I am sure you could have told me more about how it worked, Father," she said softly as she touched the clock. And perhaps he would one day, if the treatments at the hostel had their intended effect.

She went to the small sitting room to let her sisters know she was back. Lily was thick in the midst of her latest book, and Rose had retired to her room. Even Miss Mew had no need for Ivy, curled up out of reach atop a wardrobe.

Being neither wanted nor needed, Ivy returned to the room she and Mr. Quent occupied. She had hoped Mr. Quent would be here by now, but he was not; he must still be at the Citadel seeing to his work. She knew that every day reports came from the lord inquirer's agents who kept watch on the Wyrdwood around the country, and that all of these must be read and responded to. In addition, work must be done to find funds and materials to effect repairs on the fortifications around every known stand of Old Trees.

Well, she hoped Mr. Quent would be finished soon. In the meantime, she could at last make an examination of her father's journal. It was her idea to go through it, to see if she could detect any evidence that there were hidden words upon its pages. She recalled how several times, when she was a girl, her father had written her secret messages using a vinegar for ink, and she had been delighted when the words appeared while holding the paper over a candle's flame, as if by magick.

"I'm sure you would not have used so simple a trick as that, Father," she said aloud, sitting at the small writing table where the box of Wyrdwood rested. All the same, maybe there was something she could detect if she looked closely enough at the journal.

She opened the box—it required the slightest thought to make the fine tendrils of wood unweave themselves—and took out the leather-bound book within. She opened to the first page, whereupon he had written the dedication to her. She read it again fondly, then turned to the next page. It was blank, as were those that followed. Not knowing where exactly to begin, Ivy thumbed through the pages, all of them fluttering by as white as snow.

A flicker of darkness.

Startled, Ivy ceased moving through the pages of the journal. Then, carefully, she turned back a page, then another, and finally one more.

The page was filled with words.

URSENTUS RISING, ANARES RETROGRADE IN BAELTHUS

There, the deed is done.

I have hidden Tyberion. I do not believe they will be able to find where I have concealed it—though I know with utter certainty that some of them will try. However, it is not anywhere they would expect it to be. They will imagine it is now as far away from here as possible, for that is what they would do to keep such a thing secret; they would never think I would keep it so close.

I wish I might have guarded it with an enchantment. An aura of magick they would sense, and they would try to break whatever protections I might have placed upon it. I am a better magician than most of them, but even I could not make an enchantment to stop them if they worked in unison. Or at least, I could not do so without grave cost—one I may yet have to bear.

But do not fear, my dearest Ivoleyn. I hope it will not yet come to that! Tyberion is safe now. And they never knew about Arantus, for I hid it long ago. There is no chance they will ever seek it, for they do not know of its existence.

How I wish they did not know about Tyberion either. Would that I had never shown it to them! But I hardly understood the true nature of it when Mr. Bennick and I discovered it, and I was giddy with excitement at what we had uncovered. Nor did I apprehend the true nature of those within the order who had intentions besides the pure study of magick.

I can only be thankful for Mr. Bennick, who even then must have had some inkling of the intentions of the others. Why else would he have told me to show them only Tyberion, and to keep Arantus concealed? I am inclined to think the best of others. But Mr. Bennick has ever been of a more practical character, and he possesses a keen insight into the hearts and minds of other men. His advice has, I am sure, saved us from great grief. He is a friend of the deepest and truest sort, and I am fortunate beyond measure to know him.

Well, that is all for now. I will write more when I can, my dearest little Ivy—little now, I say, though you are sure to be far from little as you read these words. Yet so you are at this writing, and even now I am sure you are nestled in your bed at Whitward Street, asleep beside your sisters. Thus I will close this journal, and leave this "awful magician's house" as your mother calls it, and come home to you all.

G.O.L.

Ivy stared at the page. She supposed it was possible that, for all her prior thumbing through the journal, she had somehow missed this page. Perhaps it had been stuck to the page that followed it.

Even as she considered this, she knew that was not the case. She was sure she had turned through every page of the journal before. Just as she was sure it was due to some magick that writing had suddenly appeared on a page that heretofore had been blank. Yet as astonishing as this was, the words her father had written amazed her even more. For it was like hearing his voice in her mind, and being reminded of how he used to be, how he used to talk to her.

Yet it was more than that. To think he had considered himself fortunate to know Mr. Bennick—the same man whose betrayal would force him to cast the very spell he hinted about in the journal, the spell whose cost was his very mind. That Mr. Bennick knew others in the order were not to be trusted came as no surprise to Ivy, for she knew what her father could not—that Mr. Bennick had been conspiring with them all the while. He had tried to seize the Eye of Ran-Yahgren all those years ago. He failed, only later to scheme to use Ivy and Mr. Rafferdy to unwittingly unlock the house on Durrow Street so that the magicians of his order could enter to gain the Eye.

Well, Mr. Bennick had been thwarted, and he had not gotten the artifact. As for the things that her father had described hiding, perhaps Mr. Bennick had never gotten them either. Perhaps he had warned her father about the other magicians in the order because he had sensed they were going to turn against him—something they must have done at some point, for why else would they have taken Mr. Bennick's magick from him?

As for the things her father wrote about hiding, she could only wonder what they were. Tyberion and Arantus—the names sounded familiar to her, but she wasn't sure from where. Her father must have intended to tell her more. And perhaps he had. An excitement rose in her, and again she turned the pages of the journal, going through them one by one.

It took her some time, but at last there could be no doubt. There was no other entry in the journal besides the one. Whatever enchantment had caused it to appear had not affected any other pages.

Ivy's excitement ebbed. Perhaps it was due to the ominous nature of the words her father had written, or to the fact that they reminded her of what she had for so long been deprived—namely, her father's company and guidance. Whatever the cause, a sudden loneliness gripped her. The darkness pushed in through the windows, and the one taper she had lit wavered, as if unable to withstand that ancient force.

Ivy shut the journal and locked it back in the box. Then she rose to light more candles, thinking not of the cost as she spread them all about the room. Then she sat in the midst of them, as if their gold light was an aegis against the night, and waited for Mr. Quent to return.

CHAPTER THIRTEEN

ELDYN SAT AT his desk in the office of the rector, gazing at the blank sheet before him. He drew a breath, then dipped his pen.

The tip clattered loudly against the rim of the ink pot. He tried to blot it, but his hand gave a jerk, and dark drops struck the blotter, spreading outward in a violent stain. Eldyn set down the pen and grasped his right hand, trying to quell its shaking.

But it was no use. As soon as he let go, his hand began to tremble again, as it had ever since he saw that morning's edition of *The Swift Arrow*. A boy had been hawking them before the steps of Graychurch, and Eldyn had bought a copy. However, one glance at the front page and he wished he had saved his penny.

A GRUESOME END FINDS ANOTHER ILLUSIONIST, read the smallish headline near the bottom of the page. The article beneath was brief, but not without salacious details, as lurid pieces were a specialty of *The Swift Arrow*. It described how a young man who was known to perform at the Theater of Emeralds had been discovered in High Holy, dead and bloodied.

Before his remains were heaved upon the steps of the old chapel, read the article, *the unlucky fellow's eyes were plucked from his skull. It was an act some might consider particularly awful, given that it was the victim's vocation to conjure wonders meant to be seen, though we might choose to differ and call it particularly fitting instead. . . .*

Eldyn had read no more; he threw the broadsheet in the gutter and hurried into the church, down to the cool quiet of the room above the crypts. His hands would not stop trembling. Nor could he make his head concentrate on the work at hand. Instead, all he could think of was the sight of Donnebric before the Theater of the Doves, his face a dark, crusted mask. Now another young man had met a similar fate. Had he been indiscreet, as Donnebric had been? Is that why he deserved this *particularly fitting* fate?

"Is everything well, Mr. Garritt?"

Eldyn looked up to see Father Gadby standing beside his desk.

"I'm sorry, I . . ." Eldyn cleared his throat. "That is, I am very well, thank you, Father."

The rector's hands fluttered upward like a brace of pale, plump doves. "Well, we must praise God for the health he has granted us, so we are able do his work in the world. Yet I notice the pace of your own work seems somewhat reduced this morning, Mr. Garritt. Is something amiss?"

Eldyn could not speak of the real reason for his distress that morning. What would he say if the rector asked him why he had any care for illusionists? Instead, he grabbed a slip of paper at random from the box of receipts. "I just wasn't entirely certain what to do with this . . ." he glanced down at the paper, ". . . this note concerning the purchase of several red curtains."

He set the receipt on the desk so it would not reveal the shaking of his hand. The rector leaned over the desk to examine it.

"Why, this is signed by the archdeacon himself!" he exclaimed. "That it is in proper order is assured. Archdeacon Lemarck is aware of every detail about the keeping of Graychurch. There is not the smallest thing that is beneath his attention—not even the work you do, Mr. Garritt. You must record this exactly as it is written."

"I did not mean to question the judgment of the archdeacon in any way," Eldyn said hurriedly. "I wanted only to be certain the work I do reflects his will properly."

The rector smiled and smoothed a few wispy strands of hair over his pate. "Of course you do, Mr. Garritt! And your desire to make yourself *his* instrument in all things is most admirable. We would all do well to trust the archdeacon's wisdom in every matter. Indeed, the Archbishop of Invarel—he who is highest above us all in this world, and closest to Eternum above—relies heavily upon the archdeacon these days. That is why we do not see him here as much as we might wish. Though Graychurch is the seat of his archdeaconry, he is often at St. Galmuth's attending to the archbishop."

Eldyn was not surprised to hear this. It was said the Archbishop of Invarel was aged and frail, and that when he presided over high service in the cathedral his voice could hardly be heard above a mumble.

"There are some who claim the Church is a dusty relic of the past," the rector went on. "Yet you would not say such a thing if you heard the archdeacon give a sermon. What fire, what power there is in his voice. Why, if you saw him, you would think that one of the saints of old had returned to guide us from the shadows in which we have dwelled and back into the light! With men such as the archdeacon to lead us, I believe the Church's most glorious times lay ahead."

"I am sure you are right," Eldyn said.

"Of course I am right, Mr. Garritt!" the rector exclaimed. "Now, do you have what you need to proceed with your work?"

Eldyn assured him he did. Indeed, as the rector waddled away, Eldyn found he was able to hold his pen with sufficient stability to dip it and scribe a row of figures upon the page. He bent over the ledger, and for the next several hours he let himself think of nothing but ink and numbers.

THE LUMENAL WAS short, and as Eldyn walked back to the old monastery the sun slipped behind the buttresses of St. Galmuth's, casting a gloom over all. No longer kept at bay by the industry of work, Eldyn's own gloom was free to return, and a new dread descended over him.

The article in *The Swift Arrow* said the murdered illusionist had worked at the Theater of Emeralds. Eldyn did not know any of the men who worked at that theater; its performances tended toward ribald burlesques that forwent symbolism in favor of obvious vulgarity. *Those* were not the kind of illusion plays Eldyn liked.

However, there had been two murders of illusionists now, and the article had speculated that given the similarity of each case, they had likely been committed by the same hands. If so, was it not possible that the perpetrator would strike again? And what if it was not a stranger who was the victim, but rather someone Eldyn knew?

What if it was Dercy?

Only that was foolish. Dercy knew how to take care of himself. Was he not the one who had said Donnebric had behaved recklessly? Surely this other unfortunate illusionist had done the same. There was no use worrying; Dercy was far too clever to let himself fall into such a perilous situation.

"Good afternoon, Mr. Garritt," spoke a friendly voice—one marked by a soft South-Country accent.

Eldyn looked up as he entered the foyer of the old monastery. A fellow was just coming down the stairs. He was several years older than Eldyn, clad in garb that, though of drab hues, was well-made.

"How are you today, Mr. Fantharp?" Eldyn said.

"Very well, thank you, though very busy. A short day is always good for business, you know."

"I am sure," Eldyn said, managing a smile. Mr. Fantharp, as he knew from their prior encounters in the foyer, was a trader who dealt in the sale of tallow. He was from County Caerdun in the south of Altania, but had a small apartment here in the building where he stayed while in the city on business, as the Church was one of his primary customers.

"And how is Miss Garritt, if I might inquire?"

"You are kind to always ask about her, Mr. Fantharp. She is very well. She busies herself most days by assisting the verger at Graychurch."

"Does she? That is capital, then. Capital!" He rocked on his heels and looked as if he wished to say something more, but did not.

"Well, good day to you, Mr. Fantharp." Eldyn bowed and started up the stairs.

"Do give my regards to your sister, Mr. Garritt, if you will."

Eldyn stopped on the stairs and looked back. Mr. Fantharp's cheeks had gone rather red. A thought occurred to Eldyn—one he was surprised had not come to him before.

Mr. Fantharp was not especially handsome, but his teeth were good and his figure trim. As for his demeanor, it was pleasant, if somewhat monotonous. While he was only a tradesman, it was clear he was well-to-do. That he would be a good match for Sashie was so obvious Eldyn could only wonder that he did not see it before.

"I will tell my sister you asked after her. I am sure she will be pleased to hear it." Eldyn wasn't entirely certain Sashie knew who Mr. Fantharp was; she had never mentioned him. Yet the statement was not a mistruth, for what young woman did not enjoy hearing that a man had inquired after her?

"Thank you, Mr. Garritt. Thank you, and good day to you!"

Mr. Fantharp bowed, then turned to hurry out the door. With a smile, Eldyn continued up the stairs and entered their apartment.

He found Sashie sitting by the window, a book in her hands, her face glowing softly in the last of the daylight that fell through the glass.

"I see you are pleasantly engaged," he said as he entered the room.

She looked up and smiled when she saw him; as always the expression gave him great delight.

"Hello, dear brother."

"I am glad to see you are filling your days not only with work at the church, but rather some amusement as well. Is that a new romance you have found to read? Something with dukes and fair ladies, I hope."

Her smile did not waver, but the slightest trace of a frown touched her brow. "I am sure I would read no such thing, dear brother! I am looking at the Testament, of course."

"I see," he said, a bit surprised.

It was one thing that Sashie enjoyed her work at Graychurch.

After the awful events of last year, the church could only seem the most comforting sort of sanctuary to her. Yet reading the Testament was another matter. The text of it was archaic and not easily comprehended, and he had never in his life known Sashie to take up such a studious endeavor.

"Are you finding it of interest?" he asked her.

"Oh, I am. I am learning a great many things—things that I wish our father had taught us. What peril I have been in and hardly knew it! Did you know it is a sin for a woman to provoke the affections of a man unless she has been betrothed to him? She must not look at him or speak to him in a way that invites his passions, or else she has erred in the eyes of God."

Eldyn raised an eyebrow. "A woman can hardly be blamed for inciting the passions of a man. If she is pretty enough, she need not speak or even look at a man to win those!"

"No, it is very clear." She touched the book on her lap. "Devorah's father told her she must not look at a man with warmth, or else she might incite an awful fire in his heart and so win God's wrath. I know you only wish the best for me, sweet brother. Even so, I must wonder that you let me behave as I did in the past without proper instruction. What danger I was in!"

These words astonished Eldyn. Had he not tried, too many times to count, to alter her behavior? She had indeed been in grave danger when she flirted with Westen, but not the kind she now believed. It was not God's wrath she had been in peril of receiving, but rather the kind of damnation that could be visited only by a mortal man in the flesh.

However, he did not say this. Nor did he speak of his encounter in the foyer. This was perhaps not the propitious time to mention Mr. Fantharp's regard for her. All the same, Eldyn hoped she was not becoming too captivated with religion. While a degree of piety was certainly a virtue, too much of it could be off-putting to a man when considering a wife.

Well, he would keep an eye on her behavior. For now, he asked her how she had spent her day as they took a simple dinner, and he listened to her chat merrily about how she helped the verger oil pews and evict cobwebs from niches as if these were the most pleasant activities.

It had been Eldyn's intention to spend the evening with his sister; but after their meal, it was clear she wished only to resume reading the Testament by lamplight. She did so with a pretty frown upon her face, her lips moving slowly as she read, and so charming did she look as a result that despite his earlier misgivings, he could only smile. Surely, once he had saved enough money, he would have no difficulty finding a suitable bachelor who wished to court her; and once she received such warm attentions from a living man, he had no doubt she would have little interest in reading about long-perished saints.

Tonight, though, she seemed intent on her reading, and he asked, if she was going to be so occupied, would she mind if he went out.

"Of course not, dear brother!" she exclaimed. "I would be dreadful to expect *you* to occupy yourself by watching *me* be occupied. You must engage in some activity to your own liking."

Eldyn was sure he would. The theaters were all dark tonight, as they were once each quarter month. Which meant that Dercy would be free for all manner of other entertainments. He put on his good coat, checked to make sure his hair was properly tied back with a black ribbon, then went to his sister to kiss the top of her head.

She looked up at him, her face aglow in the lamplight, as if a holy illumination indeed welled forth from the book open in her lap. "Have a good evening, dear brother. I am sure you will find some activity just as pleasing to God as my reading."

Eldyn swallowed. "I'm sure no one could please Him more than you," he managed to say. Then he hurried out the door.

A chill had already taken the air, so that his breath fogged as he walked through the Old City. He had been happy at the prospect of seeing Dercy. Even now, the thought of it kindled a warmth in him that repelled the cold. Yet at the same time, a knot had formed in his stomach.

I am sure you will find some activity just as pleasing to God. . . .

He shuddered, and not from the cold. Would God really be pleased with what would surely happen if he found himself alone in a room with Dercy and a bottle of whiskey?

Eldyn knew that working illusions would be forbidden to him once he entered the priesthood. He accepted that as a part of the cost he must pay to gain all the benefits of entering the holy order. True, the thought of giving up his abilities to conjure wonders, so soon after discovering them, left him with a hollow feeling. Yet would they not be replaced by other wonders—ones more pure and sublime?

Besides, he had tallied up all the reasons for his decision. If it was just himself he had to consider, perhaps he could be tempted into a life on Durrow Street. However, what he did reflected upon Sashie, and he could not hope to secure a reputable future for her if he was associated with a place of such iniquity. And it was more than that. All his life, he had believed that he was sullied by his father's actions. But Eldyn knew now that it was his own deeds that mattered, not those of Vandimeer Garritt. He wanted to wash away that taint, and to be something better than his father had been.

So he would be; he was resolved.

Except illusions were not the only activities he had engaged in with Dercy. Nor were they the only pleasures he would have to forsake once he entered the priesthood. . . .

That thought caused a pang in Eldyn's chest, but before he could consider it further, he turned a corner onto the east end of Durrow Street. On nights when the theaters were open, glittering lights and chiming music filled the air while illusionists stood before the various playhouses, crafting small illusions to entice people to enter. Now only a few people slunk down the street past guttering streetlamps.

Usually Eldyn felt a kind of safety within the crowds that thronged Durrow Street. Now, as he looked upon the barren street, he thought of the nameless illusionist from the Theater of Emeralds who had been found dead. High Holy was not so very far from here, and while Eldyn was not Siltheri himself, he had been mistaken for one of them more than once.

A pair of men walked down the far side of the street, laughing roughly as they went; they were not illusionists. With a flick, Eldyn gathered the shadows about himself, then hurried to the Theater of the Moon.

HE FOUND THE actors gathered within, rehearsing a new bit of staging for the scene in which servants of the Sun King pursued the Moon across the bottom of the sea. Given the laughter—and the bottle—that was going around, it was obvious the actors were not applying themselves to the task at hand as much as they were applying the spirits to themselves.

Nor was Eldyn surprised. The players labored hard throughout the quarter month, rehearsing, maintaining the theater, and of course performing. The nights the theaters were dark gave them a welcome respite. Tallyroth, the master illusionist of the Theater of the Moon, clearly agreed, for he smiled as he sat in a chair on the edge of the stage, watching the actors. All the same, he wore his usual wine-colored coat, and his face was powdered and his hair curled just as if it were performance night.

As Eldyn neared the stage, Dercy leaped down and caught him in a great embrace; this Eldyn returned with enthusiasm.

"So the priests let you go for the day, did they?" Dercy said with a laugh. "I'm surprised, for you're just the sort I'm sure they'd like to hold on to."

His embrace grew tighter yet, and Eldyn was aware of the other young man's breath against his neck, and of his lean body pressing close. Eldyn suffered a pang of alarm. The others were surely watching, and they were not the only ones. Did not God see everything?

Eldyn turned his head so that Dercy's lips fell upon his cheek, then stepped away from the embrace. Confusion flickered in the young man's sea-colored eyes.

"Come now, Dercy," Eldyn said, affecting a boisterous tone, "you can't expect me to just stand here while you all pass a bottle around."

Dercy grinned, the confusion in his eyes replaced by a light of mischief. "What was I thinking? That was most uncouth of me to force you to greet me before greeting the bottle!"

He reached up to the stage, the aforementioned bottle was handed down, and Eldyn took a long swig, grateful for the heady rum even though it burned his throat. Would this pleasure be forbidden to him as well? Not entirely, he supposed, for priests did take wine, if only in moderation.

Then again, moderation was not on anyone's mind that night, and for all his plans Eldyn was not a priest yet. Hands reached down and pulled him up to the stage. The bottle was handed back to him, then seemed to return almost as soon as he passed it on.

It was not long before a pleasant tingling danced upon his skin, though whether it was from the effects of the liquor, or from the power and light that shimmered on the air, he could not say. The stage was awash in flickering blue, while schools of fish as bright as jewels darted all around.

Much of it was Dercy's doing, and Eldyn watched him with a growing wonder. He seemed hardly to make any sort of effort as he moved his hands, shaping a glittering ball into a sleek shape. Suddenly a dolphin went racing upward through the ocean of blue light, to the accompaniment of much applause.

"That is very beautiful, Dercy," spoke a voice as the dolphin burst into a spray of silver like a thousand darting minnows, "but I do trust you are being careful."

Eldyn turned around. It was Tallyroth who had spoken.

"We are dark tonight, but tomorrow we perform," the master illusionist went on. His was the voice of an actor: clear, bell-like, the words enunciated so they were crisp and carried easily. "You do not wish to spend yourself."

"Why shouldn't I? A rich man spends freely of his gold. Why should I not spend some of my own riches?"

"You should. You have been given a gift, and it would be wrong for you not to use it. Yet even a rich man may become poor if he spends too much."

"Ah, but I am rich beyond compare," Dercy said with a laugh, and coins fell from his hands, suddenly turning to goldfish that wriggled in all directions. The other illusionists applauded.

"I thought as you did, once," Tallyroth said. He raised an arm as if to conjure an illusion, but his hand trembled in a violent spasm, and he pressed it to his chest. Though Tallyroth was the master illusionist at the Theater of the Moon, it occurred to Eldyn that he had never seen the older Siltheri conjure illusions. He directed the players and oversaw all the staging, but he never performed himself.

"I have a different view now," Tallyroth went on. "Thus I say to you, Dercy, and to all of you—revel in the light, embrace it, but be prudent as well. You know of what I speak."

The blue light flickered and dimmed, and suddenly the ocean was gone, replaced by a bare stage. Dercy's grin had vanished as well. He bowed to Tallyroth, then found the rum bottle and took a long draught.

"What use is there in being prudent?" said a tall illusionist with dark hair and an aquiline nose. His name was Merrick, and he was a little older than Dercy, though far younger than Tallyroth, who Eldyn supposed was well over forty.

"What use is there in saving a portion of ourselves when the whole of our lives can be taken like that?" Merrick snapped long fingers together. "Do you think Braundt was glad that he never overspent himself at the Theater of Emeralds? What use was it for him to have saved anything back? For he will have no chance to spend it now."

At once the mood on the stage went grim, and now Eldyn understood the fierceness with which the illusionists had been drinking rum and conjuring sights of beauty. Braundt—so that was the name of the young Siltheri who had been murdered.

Merrick turned away, and some of the others went to him, putting their arms around his shoulders. Master Tallyroth watched them, a look of sorrow upon his powdered face. Dercy approached Eldyn, bottle in hand.

"Have you heard?" Dercy asked in a low voice.

Eldyn nodded. "I read it in the broadsheet."

"I'm surprised they bothered to report it at all." Dercy's voice was hard. "He was only an illusionist after all."

Eldyn pressed his lips together. What could he say except that there was a truth to his words? *The Swift Arrow* had printed the story not to arouse any sympathy in its readers, but merely to thrill and horrify them.

Dercy glanced over his shoulder at the other illusionists. Merrick had been a friend of Braundt's, he explained. They had both hoped to work at the same house on Durrow Street, but Merrick had not been accepted at the Theater of Emeralds.

Eldyn sighed. That was hard news. He asked if they had any idea who had done the deed. Had Braundt done something indiscreet, as they believed Donnebric had? Dercy didn't know.

"I met Braundt several times," he said. "He was a quiet fellow, modest even. It was his illusions he wished others to see, not himself. It's hard for me to believe he did anything to openly invite this. And yet . . ."

Yet death had found him all the same. And if a man could win the same ill fate being sensible and modest as by being brash and foolish, then was not Merrick right? What did it matter if one was cautious or not?

Except somehow he didn't think it was the sort of danger that had found Braundt that the master illusionist had been warning the others about.

"So what did Tallyroth mean earlier?" Eldyn said. "When he told you to be prudent, and that you knew what he meant. What is it you're supposed to be cautious about?"

"Nothing a clerk needs to worry about," Dercy said loftily. "It's only of concern to illusionists. And, as you're so fond of telling me, you're a scrivener, not a Siltheri."

It was foolish of him; he was giving up illusions. But provoked by the rum as much as Dercy's mocking tone, Eldyn could not resist.

"Is that so?" He gathered his thoughts, then spread his hands apart. A ball of light appeared between them. He concentrated, and it took on shape, leaping toward the rafters in a pewter streak: a dolphin. It was not so perfectly formed as Dercy's had been, nor so well-defined at the edges. However, it was dazzlingly bright.

Dercy's eyes went wide, then he grinned. He opened his mouth, only before he could speak applause sounded behind him.

"That was very nice, Mr. Garritt," a woman's voice echoed across the theater.

Surprised, Eldyn turned to see the speaker walking down the center aisle. She wore a red gown, and her black wig was wrought into an intricate sculpture atop her head, twined with artificial birds and flowers: a creation as fantastical as any illusion.

"Good evening, Madame Richelour," Dercy said. He bowed, as did the illusionists on the stage.

"It grew rather vague toward the tail," the madam of the Theater of the Moon said as she drew near the stage. "A completeness of form is required for a phantasm to be considered perfect. And it vanished a bit too quickly. An illusion must exist for precisely the right amount of time, neither too long nor too short, to have the correct effect. Yet the brilliance of it was quite lovely. What do you think, Master Tallyroth?"

The older illusionist rose slowly from his seat. "Your eye for illusion is keen as always, madam. I would not argue with your criticism, for it is correct. Though I would add, for all its faults, there was a grace to the phantasm, a lightness of quality, that is sometimes lacking in illusions that are more precisely crafted."

Madame Richelour nodded at the master illusionist. "And your eye is subtle as ever, Master Tallyroth. But what are all of you doing here? The theater is dark. It is not an umbral to labor upon the stage. Fly away, all of you! Go amuse yourselves. I am certain you can think of many ways to do this. Here, this should aid you."

She tossed a bag up to the stage, and it jingled merrily as an illusionist caught it.

The young men let out a cheer, then made bows of the most florid and ridiculous manner to the madam, some of them sprouting peacock tails as they did. Then they departed through the wings of the stage. Dercy moved off as well, and Eldyn started to follow, but a touch on his arm stopped him.

"If you have a moment, Mr. Garritt, I would speak with you."

He could not have been more startled if Madame Richelour had struck or kissed him. "Of course," he stammered.

"No, Mr. Fanewerthy, I do not need you," she said as Dercy started back toward them. "Mr. Garritt alone will do. Go after the others, and see that they spend well the coin I gave them. Do not worry. I will send Mr. Garritt after you soon enough."

Dercy raised an eyebrow, but he made no argument. "As you wish, madam." He bowed low, then as he rose he flashed a grin at Eldyn. "We'll be at the Red Jester," he said, then departed the theater, leaving Eldyn alone with Madame Richelour and Master Tallyroth.

"Tell me, Mr. Garritt," the madam of the theater said, "how long have you been working illusions now?"

Dazzled by this attention, he could form no other reply than the truth. "Since last year. But I was awful. It was only when . . . that is, it was about a month ago when I found my abilities suddenly improved."

She smiled. Her face was smooth and white as porcelain, not due to youth, but rather to a careful application of paints and powders. The madam was easily as old as Tallyroth, if not older.

"It is not unusual for an illusionist's abilities to take a sudden leap. Is that not so?" She looked up at Tallyroth, and he nodded.

"I have found it often to be the case," he said. "There comes a point when, after much fumbling, one suddenly understands how to grasp the light, to call it forth, and to shape it. It is as if, after lurching around in a darkened room, one's hand brushes a doorknob, and he thrusts the door open, letting light stream in."

"Yes, it was just like that!" Eldyn said, then was at once embarrassed.

Madame Richelour returned her attention to him. "So how many houses have approached you so far?"

"Pardon me?"

"Come now, Mr. Garritt. There is no reason to withhold. I could hardly be cross. Every madam and master on the street is always looking to win the best new talent for their house. How many theaters have offered a position to you? One, two? Is it more, then?"

He was incredulous at this question. "But none at all have!"

"None, you say?" Her eyebrows rose in thin, perfect arcs above her eyes. "It seems Mr. Fanewerthy has concealed you well. How like a true Siltheri! I will have to give him my thanks for that. If I am the first to approach you, I hope I will also be the last."

Eldyn shook his head. "Approach me?"

The madam let out a rich laugh. "Mr. Garritt, you are the most delightful creature! You tease, yet with utter innocence. Any other young man would have gladly taken the most subtle suggestion, yet you make me speak in the plainest terms. Very well, let me be clear: I would have you work at my theater. As an understudy to begin, of course. There are many who have been here before you, and you have much to learn. Yet I have no doubt, should you accept, that you would soon become, like our own Mr. Fanewerthy, a prized member of our troupe at the Theater of the Moon."

At last Eldyn understood, and he was dumbfounded. Dercy had said the madam of the theater had noticed him, but he had merely ascribed it to Dercy's flattery and encouragement. Eldyn listened as she described the particulars of the offer, and his astonishment was renewed. The wage was over double what he presently earned. How quickly he would be able to save for his and Sashie's futures with such an income!

Madame Richelour looked up at the stage. "Well, what do you think, Master Tallyroth?"

"I think we would be very fortunate to have Mr. Garritt in our troupe. That is, if he is willing to work to improve his craft. While it is the goal for illusions to appear effortless, there is in fact a great deal of effort behind them, Mr. Garritt. I would have you understand that before you join us."

"I have no worry on that account," Madame Richelour said. "Mr. Fanewerthy assures me that Mr. Garritt is the most industrious sort of being. You are currently a scrivener, is that not so?"

"Yes, at present. But I—" Eldyn swallowed the words that followed. He could not tell her what he intended, that it was his plan to be a priest.

"Do not fear, Mr. Garritt." Her voice grew low, and there was a gentleness in her blue eyes. "It is not my intention to force an answer from you this very moment. I know it is a great decision to choose to enter the theater. I ask only that you consider my offer ahead of any you might receive from the other houses on Durrow Street. Right now you should find your friends. Go on, then, before they've spent every last coin I gave them!"

Eldyn could do no more than nod and manage a weak thank-you. His mind was abuzz and his heart fluttered. A kind of fear had seized him, but it was not entirely unpleasant. He hurried to the front of the theater. However, just before he passed through the curtain, he cast a glance back.

Madame Richelour had gone up on the stage. She stood beside Master Tallyroth, who sat in his chair again. He reached up a trembling hand, and she took it in her own, stroking it, stilling its spasms. She smiled at him, only there was a sorrow in the expression, and he gently shook his head.

Eldyn felt keenly that the tableau upon the stage was not for any audience to see. He turned and passed through the curtain.

ELDYN LET THE shadows fall away from him just as he reached the Red Jester. The doorkeeper gave a start as Eldyn appeared abruptly in the circle of lamplight before the tavern, then he scowled and jerked a meaty thumb at the door. Eldyn should have cast off the shadows sooner; however, his mind was still consumed with what had happened at the theater.

He gave the doorkeeper an apologetic bow, then headed into the smoky interior of the tavern. The Red Jester was a frequent haunt of illusionists of the Theater of the Moon not because of its quality or character, but solely due to its proximity to the theater.

A flash of light and a burst of laughter let him know which direction to go, and he followed them to the back of the tavern. The other young men hailed his arrival with raised cups and a spray of multicolored streamers that burst from thin air. Eldyn could only laugh, and some of the tumult in his mind was eased as a cup of punch was placed in his hand.

He took a long swallow, but before he could take another Dercy had his arm and pulled him away into a dim corner. His eyes were alight.

"Well?"

"Well, what?" Eldyn said.

"Don't *you* play coy with me, Eldyn Garritt. Your innocence is an illusion I know how to see through. Something went on after I left the theater. What did Madame Richelour say to you?"

There was no way to say it except plainly. "She offered me a position as understudy at the theater."

Dercy let out a great cry, like the war whoop of an aboriginal from the New Lands. He caught Eldyn in a fierce embrace. Energized by the punch and by the other's enthusiasm, Eldyn could only return it with all his might.

"I knew she was going to do it," Dercy said when at last they drew apart. "I just didn't know when. Madame Richelour has been watching you since the moment I brought you to the theater. I knew she was bound to want you, and Tallyroth, too. She wouldn't have made you an offer if he didn't agree. They're together on everything at the theater."

Eldyn thought of the moment he had witnessed, the way Madame Richelour had held Master Tallyroth's hand. He described what he had seen to Dercy. The other young man's mirth faded a bit.

"She loves him," he said. "We all know it. And he loves her, too. He always has—though of course not in the way she might have once wished for long ago. *That* sort of arrangement could never have happened between them. So she did the next best thing, and she married the theater instead."

Eldyn thought he understood. Illusionists never took wives, at least not that he had seen, yet Madame Richelour and Master Tallyroth had found a way to be together. Only there was something more to what he had seen onstage and the way she had stilled his trembling hand. Before he could ask about it, Dercy's grin returned.

"So what did you tell her, then? What was your answer?"

"She didn't ask me for an answer tonight."

"What's there to think about? You'll accept, of course. You'll be a quick study, I have no doubt, now that you've gotten past whatever it was that was blocking you. Soon we'll be onstage together, and ours will be the finest illusion play on Durrow Street." He grasped Eldyn's shoulders. "Come, let's tell the others."

"Wait," Eldyn said, pulling back.

"Wait for what? There's no reason not to tell everyone. Giving Madame Richelour your answer is a mere formality."

Eldyn opened his mouth, then shut it again. The warmth of the rum vanished, and his dread returned.

Dercy's smile faded. "You *are* going to accept her offer, aren't you?"

Eldyn shook his head. "I don't . . . that is, I haven't decided yet."

But that wasn't true. He *had* decided, hadn't he? To be a Siltheri, to stand upon a stage and craft wonders while audiences gasped and applauded was an idea as intoxicating as the punch in his cup. Yet it was an illusion itself, wasn't it? For all the beauty they conjured, the Siltheri lived in an ugly world—one of ramshackle theaters and grimy taverns and men who would murder them for the simple fact of what they were. A life of squalor and violence was what his father had lived; Eldyn wanted something different for himself.

Dercy's eyes went wide. "By God, you're thinking about refusing. Are you mad, Eldyn? Don't tell me you want to be a scrivener all your life—hunched over your desk, eking out words and a meager living until your fingers are stained black and your mind is as gray as a piece of parchment that's been sanded clean too many times."

"No," Eldyn said. "No, that's not what I want."

"Then what's the matter? You should be leaping at this chance. You might not ever get another. You're already getting old for it, you know. Most have already been in the theater for years at your age."

Eldyn knew he should say the words. Did he not owe Dercy that much for all the other young man had done for him? *I want to enter the Church. I want to pay off the debt of my father's sins, not compound upon them.* Only his jaw would not work; he could not utter the words.

Dercy's brow furrowed. "Well, then? If you have something to say, out with it."

Eldyn could only shake his head.

"What's wrong? Why can't you speak?" Dercy threw his cup on the moldy straw that covered the floor. It shattered. "Must I always tell you what to do, then, like the day I told you how to best that highwayman? You are a good man, Eldyn Garritt. But by God, sometimes you are so mild you drive me to fits. I know you have balls in your trousers, so make use of them for once. Just because you're a Siltheri doesn't mean you have to be a weakling."

At once Dercy snapped his mouth shut. That he knew he had gone too far was clear upon his face. However, the effect of his words was sudden and complete. Eldyn was no longer tongue-tied.

"My father called me weak." He did not speak loudly, yet he knew as he uttered the words that there was a force to them. "So did Westen. But they were both of them wrong. As are you, Dercy. I may be soft, I do not deny it, but I am not weak. And I'm not a Siltheri either—not unless I choose to be. Nor do I need anyone to make that choice for me."

Regret shone in Dercy's eyes. "Eldyn, I'm sorry. I'm drunk and an idiot tonight. You have to forget what I said."

Eldyn shook his head. Despite what Dercy had claimed, his mind was no piece of vellum that could be sanded clean. He had

had enough of run-down taverns and sour punch and illusionists. "I'm tired, Dercy. I'm going home. I must see to my sister."

"No, Eldyn, don't go. Please, not like this."

Dercy reached out to grasp Eldyn's arm, but his fingers closed around empty air. A shadow flickered by the tavern door, then was gone.

CHAPTER FOURTEEN

*I*T WAS THE morning of a middle lumenal, the day after Ivy had gone to Lady Marsdel's for tea, when a note from Mr. Barbridge arrived at The Seventh Swan. Something had been discovered at the house on Durrow Street that Sir and Lady Quent needed to see at once.

They proceeded to the house immediately following breakfast. All the way there, Ivy's imagination explored the most unwelcome possibilities. Had a series of faulty beams been uncovered, or a weakness in the foundation that would require further repairs and delay?

By the time Mr. Quent brought the cabriolet to a halt, Ivy was in a state of agitation. When they entered the house, she could not see anything that was an immediate source of concern. To her eye, the front hall was all but complete. The walls were smooth with fresh paint, and the marble fireplace at the far end had been restored to its original beauty, including the Dratham crest above the mantel.

The double staircase was also finished and formed a sweeping centerpiece to the hall. Though one side of it was new, it had been made to look as rich and detailed as the original. The only differences were the newel posts at the foot of the old staircase, each topped as ever with an orb carved into the shape of an eye.

Mr. Barbridge had taken seriously the command not to alter the unique and peculiar features of the house, even though it had cost him more than a few workers who became unsettled by such things. Those that stayed had evidently grown used to being observed by the house, for the eyes atop the posts were uncovered. They blinked open as Ivy and Mr. Quent proceeded upward, following the sounds of construction. The eyes glanced at them in a disinterested fashion, then snapped shut again.

The state of the second-floor gallery was hard to judge, as it was still draped in cloths. Sun streamed through the windows, which had been greatly expanded, igniting the flecks of dust that swirled upon the air. Mr. Barbridge saw them as they entered, and hurried over. The builder's coat was frosted with plaster dust.

"I am glad you have come, Sir Quent, Lady Quent. I was sure the moment we found it that you would want to see for yourselves."

Mr. Quent regarded him. "What is it you have found?"

"Something we should have discovered long ago, only the cracks were finer this time. It was not until yesterday that I noticed them. However, once I did, I knew it had to be there, and so I had the men tear down the wall."

"But what was it, Mr. Barbridge?" Ivy said, her alarm renewed by this discussion of cracks and walls being torn down.

"Come see for yourself, Lady Quent."

Ivy and Mr. Quent followed after Mr. Barbridge to the south end of the gallery. The dust grew thicker as they went. She started to ask him how long of a delay he thought this would cause.

Then she halted.

"I see," Mr. Quent said beside her. "So there is another."

"I fault myself for not realizing it sooner," Mr. Barbridge said. "But the plasterwork covering this one is somewhat newer, I think, and so the wall has not had as much time to develop signs of weakness. Indeed, the cracks were so fine that if the men had put another coat of paint on the wall, I might never have seen them. Well, Lady Quent, what do you think? Another piece to inspire conversation, wouldn't you say?"

Ivy's throat was too tight—from the dust, and from wonder—to reply. Instead, she moved closer to the wall to examine the thing the men had uncovered.

It was another door.

Like the first, it was fashioned of dark wood with a glossy coating of varnish. This one was not adorned with leaves like the other, on the north side of the gallery. Instead, carved upon the door was a shield and a sword. So intricately was the sword rendered that she could make out the grain of the leather binding on its hilt and fine marks along the edge of the blade as if it had been used in battle. The shield behind was adorned with a fanciful design made up of concentric and interlocking circles.

"It's exquisite," she murmured.

"I presume this one does not go through to the other side of the wall either?" Mr. Quent said.

The builder nodded. "Just like the other. That they are a matched pair, I have no doubt. Though as I said, from the differences in the plasterwork, I don't believe they were covered at the same time."

Ivy marveled that, despite the extent of the restorations, the house on Durrow Street still had secrets to reveal. She and Mr. Quent spent a little while more examining the door, fascinated by its beauty. Then, knowing they were in the way of the workmen, they bid Mr. Barbridge farewell.

As they left the gallery, Ivy glanced at the other door, the one all carved with leaves. She had not seen them tremble again, not since the day she had seen the man in the black mask. He had not shown himself to her since then, and she was beginning to hope that he had heard the words she had spoken in her mind, and that he had chosen to leave her alone.

"I said, Mrs. Quent, did you wish to proceed directly home, or was there somewhere else you wished to go now that we are out?"

Ivy blinked and realized that they stood by the cabriolet.

Mr. Quent's brown eyes grew concerned. "Are you well, Ivoleyn? You seem very distracted."

She managed a smile for him. "I was just thinking about how beautiful the old doors are, and wondering what other secrets we might yet discover in the house."

She said he could return her to the inn, for she knew he still had work to finish at the Citadel before his journey tomorrow. As he drove, Ivy brought up another topic that had been on her mind since yesterday. She described for Mr. Quent the impression she and Mr. Rafferdy had found in the study at Lady Marsdel's, and how she had seen a similar image at Heathcrest Hall.

"I am not surprised Lord Marsdel had a copy of that impression," Mr. Quent said, his hands steady on the reins as he guided the cabriolet through narrow streets. "Earl Rylend did, and I imagine Lord Rafferdy has one as well. The three of them met when they were young men in the army, in the years following the last war with the Empire. They were close friends after that."

"Do you know why they called themselves the Three Lords of Am-Anaru?"

Mr. Quent nodded. "Am-Anaru was a place where the three of them were stationed for a time. It was very remote, on the edge of the desert in the south of the continent, my father told me. He had gone there along with Earl Rylend and the others, you see. They were sent there with their companies to keep watch on the nomadic tribes that inhabited that region, to make sure they were abiding by the treaty between the Murgh Empire and Altania."

"Do you know if Earl Rylend ever brought anything back from the south? An artifact from the Empire, or any such thing?" Ivy described the sphinx she had seen at Lady Marsdel's, and how Rafferdy had said his father possessed a similar one.

"He may have. Though if so, I never saw it, and it is not at Heathcrest any longer. I would know if it was, for I made an inventory of the manor when it came into my possession."

It seemed strange Lord Marsdel and Lord Rafferdy would bring back souvenirs of the south, but not Earl Rylend. However,

Ivy put the subject aside and asked another question that had been on her mind.

"Lord Baydon said Mr. Bennick was often a visitor at Heathcrest Hall," she said. "Is that so?"

Mr. Quent gave her a sharp look. "You are very curious today."

"I am always very curious."

He smiled at her. "So you are, Mrs. Quent, and I would have you no other way." Then his expression grew more serious. "Earl Rylend had his own kind of curiosity, for he always had an interest in magick."

"Indeed?" Ivy was surprised by these words. It was only recently that the study of magick had become fashionable again among the magnates of Altania. A generation ago it would have been regarded more dubiously. But then, the critiques of society could hardly be felt the same out on the lonely West Country moors as in the city.

"Yes, he was very intrigued by magick, though I do not believe he displayed much of a talent for it himself. However, the Rylends could figure their lineage back to one of the seven Old Houses. Thus he had hopes for his only child, Lord Wilden, with regard to magick."

"Were those hopes fulfilled? Did Lord Wilden study magick?"

"He did study magick. It did not turn out as Earl Rylend hoped; not long before the earl's passing, Lord Wilden perished in a fire. We all of us believed it was magick that started the blaze— some spell Wilden had attempted but was unable to control."

Ivy could only be horrified at this knowledge. "His instructor in magick must have been very poor to allow him to attempt something beyond his ability."

"In that you could not be more correct, for Lord Wilden's tutor in magick was none other than Mr. Bennick."

"Mr. Bennick?" Ivy said, astonished anew.

"Yes, Mr. Bennick," Mr. Quent said, and his voice became a growl as he spoke the name. "How Earl Rylend became acquainted with him, I do not know. Perhaps it was through Lord Marsdel. I only met Lord Marsdel on a few occasions, but I knew he had a fondness for famous personages, so perhaps that was what drew him to Mr. Bennick."

Ivy nodded. Though not famous himself, Mr. Bennick was the grandson—though illegitimate—of Slade Vordigan, who was Altania's last great magician. It was historical fact that Vordigan used magick to help defeat the army of the Old Usurper, Bandley Morden, thus saving the nation and preserving the Crown.

Ivy listened with great interest as Mr. Quent described how Earl Rylend had brought Mr. Bennick to Heathcrest to tutor the earl's son, Lord Wilden. For a period of several years, Mr. Bennick was a frequent guest at Heathcrest Hall. Some of his acquaintances also came with him from time to time—men who belonged to the same order of magicians that Mr. Bennick did.

"So that's how you met my father!" Ivy exclaimed, fascinated to learn a bit of the history of the two men in the world she loved most.

He gave the reins a flick. "Yes, Mr. Lockwell came more often than Mr. Bennick's other friends, for which I was glad. Lord Wilden was of an age with me, but Mr. Bennick and his magician friends were several years older. Thus they showed me little interest or regard."

A grimace crossed his face, as if at some unpleasant memory. But it passed after a moment.

"Your father, however, was always very kind to me," he went on. "We spent many hours together rambling over the countryside, for he had a great fascination for all the plants to be found there, and for the structure of the rocks that made up the crags and fells. I had learned about these things from my father before he grew ill, and I was more than happy to share this knowledge with Mr. Lockwell as we walked."

These words filled Ivy with a great warmth. "I am so pleased to know that you and my father were so well-acquainted."

Mr. Quent nodded. "I was always grateful for his friendship, at that time and later. After my father passed, other than Mr. Lockwell, I suppose I had no real companion at Heathcrest Hall except for—"

He swallowed, as if something had caught in his throat.

"Except for whom?"

"Ashaydea," he said in a gruff tone.

"Ashaydea," Ivy said, repeating the name. It was beautiful, and though unfamiliar was certainly feminine. "Who was she?"

It seemed to take him a long time to speak. "She was the ward of Earl Rylend, a bit younger than Lord Wilden and me. The earl brought her back with him from one of his trips to the Empire. She was an orphan, a child of an Altanian lord and a Murghese woman, and she had witnessed her family perish in a violent fashion. Lady Rylend never . . . that was, she was not pleased to have a child of foreign parentage in her house. But Earl Rylend had considered her father a close friend, and so Ashaydea stayed at Heathcrest for many years."

Ivy thought of the large family portrait she had seen on the landing of the staircase at Heathcrest. The elder couple in the painting could only have been Earl and Lady Rylend, and the boy between them their son, Lord Wilden. Then there had been the small figure standing apart from the others, her dark dress merging with the shadows on the very edge of the painting.

"Ashaydea," Ivy said again. "I saw her, I think—in the painting on the stairs at Heathcrest. She was as lovely as her name. But what happened to her after the earl and Lady Rylend passed away? Where is she now?"

For a long moment he said nothing, then a sigh escaped him. "She is here in Invarel."

This statement puzzled Ivy. If his old companion from Heathcrest was here in the city, why did he not go on occasion to see her?

Only perhaps he did, she realized with a sudden astonishment.

What a sad and pitiful creature, Mr. Quent had said that day at the Citadel, when they glimpsed a woman in black on their way out. The woman's hair and eyes had been dark—just like the girl in the painting on the staircase at Heathcrest Hall.

"Lady Shayde!" Ivy exclaimed. "She is Ashaydea, isn't she?"

"She was," Mr. Quent said, his voice low.

Ivy shook her head, thinking of all she had ever heard of Lady Shayde, the king's famed White Lady—how a look from her was said to freeze the blood and make one confess to any sort of crime. Those could only be exaggerations and old wives' tales, of course. Yet it was a fact that over the years, no one had captured more spies or traitors to the Crown.

"But what happened to her?"

"Mr. Bennick happened to her, that's what," Mr. Quent said, his expression grim. "It was years ago, back when we were at Heathcrest Hall. I do not know the details of it. No one ever will, save the two of them alone. He performed some magick upon her—some ancient and abominable enchantment. It made her into what she is."

Ivy could only stare, shocked by this revelation. She thought of the pretty, dusky-skinned girl in the painting, and of the woman she had seen at the Citadel, whose face was as pale as porcelain. Could magick really be used to alter someone so drastically? Perhaps the stories of her abilities were not mere rumors and superstition after all. . . .

Despite the warmth of the lumenal, Ivy shivered. "Why would Mr. Bennick do such a thing?"

"Why would Mr. Bennick do anything?"

Ivy sighed. He could only have done it to advance his own power. After all, that had to be the reason he had schemed to use Ivy and Mr. Rafferdy to gain entry to the house on Durrow Street—in hopes that the magicians of his order would give him his magick back. Similarly, he must have thought he could some-how use Lady Shayde to his benefit all those years ago.

"Only he could not keep her under his control, could he?"

Now Mr. Quent laughed. "No, he could not. And if he had known her then as I did, he would not have thought he could. She was never a pet who could be tamed, as Earl Rylend discov-ered."

A thought occurred to Ivy. "Is Lady Shayde one of the people you've been arguing with at the Citadel?"

He raised an eyebrow and looked at her as he drove. "You are clever indeed, Mrs. Quent. Yes, Lady Shayde and her master, Lord Valhaine, have a different opinion on some matters compared to the inquirers."

"On some matters? You mean concerning how to approach the problem of the Wyrdwood."

He seemed to hesitate. "It is not the Wyrdwood that is the specific item of our disagreements, but rather those who might incite it to rise up."

Witches—so that was the matter they had been arguing over. "But how can she and Lord Valhaine complain?" Ivy said, feeling some indignation on her husband's behalf. "After all, you captured the witch in Torland."

"Yes," he said, gazing forward as he drove. "Yes, we did capture her."

Then what disagreement could there be? Ivy wanted to ask, only at that moment Mr. Quent pulled back on the reins, and the cabriolet came to a halt before The Seventh Swan.

"I must leave you here, dearest," he said. "I fear I must return to the Citadel to have more arguments before I can leave the city tomorrow. Do not worry—I am sure all will be resolved."

Startled, Ivy blinked. So engrossed had she been in the history recounted by Mr. Quent that she had not realized they were already at the inn.

"Of course," she said. "I will not keep you."

He came around to help her from the carriage, and she kissed his bearded cheek.

"When should I expect you tonight?"

"I fear it is best if you do not expect me at all before you retire."

He pressed her hand to his lips. Then he climbed back into the driver's seat, and with a flick of the reins the carriage moved away down the street.

*

𝕴T WAS DEEP in the night when Ivy awoke to find the other side of the bed still empty.

At first she tried to return to slumber. However, while she had been oblivious to Mr. Quent's absence when she was asleep, now that she was awake she was keenly aware of the largeness of the bed and the quietness of the room. Besides, it was one of those umbrals that was just a little too long to sleep all the way through.

Ivy put on a shawl, lit a candle, and sat at the desk in the corner of the bedchamber. She longed for a bit of company, but she had no doubt Lily had stayed up late reading, and that Rose had wandered about in the middle of the night, and that both would be fast asleep now.

"I will look to you for companionship, Father," she whispered.

With a touch and a thought, she opened the Wyrdwood box. As always, a pleasant shiver passed through her as the tendrils unbraided at her beckoning. Not for the first time she found herself wishing she was back at Heathcrest, walking on the moor east of the house, toward the stand of straggled trees behind the stone wall atop the ridge. However, to do so would be gravely perilous. It was best she was here in the city, far away from any stands of Wyrdwood—and from temptation.

She opened the journal, once again fondly reading the inscription her father had written to her on the overleaf. Then she opened it to the middle, to read again the journal entry that had appeared the previous night by means of some enchantment. She wanted to read it again, for she was not sure she had really understood it.

In the entry, her father had described how he had hidden something called Tyberion from the other magicians of his order, and how they had never known about another thing called Arantus, for he had hidden it earlier. But what were Tyberion and Arantus? She could only suppose they were magickal artifacts of some sort, things like the Eye of Ran-Yahgren, that he did not wish the other members of his order to discover.

Only he had told Mr. Bennick of them.

Well, Mr. Bennick was far away in Torland, and whatever the

objects were that her father had described, they were no doubt hidden still. She turned through the pages of the journal.

And turned, and turned. Soon she turned the last page of the book, but she had not come upon the entry.

"I must have missed it," she murmured with a frown.

This time she started from the back of the journal, going page by page, making certain no two were stuck together. Every page she turned was blank, until she reached the very first page with the inscription to her. There could be but one explanation: whatever enchantment it was that had caused the entry to appear, it had expired.

Ivy pressed a hand to her brow and let out a sound of dismay. How foolish she was! She should have known a magick that could make something appear could cause it to vanish again just as easily. Why had she not thought to write down her father's words? Only she hadn't, and now they were gone—perhaps never to appear again.

So once again, Ivy had been deprived of the comfort of her father's companionship. She sighed, then shut the journal back in the Wyrdwood box. A weight of loneliness pressed down upon her. At the same time, the darkness encroached as the candle wavered in a draft. It was useless; such a singular, feeble light could do nothing to hold back the vast and eternal power of night.

Ivy surrendered, and blew out the flame.

SHE MUST HAVE finally fallen asleep, for when Ivy opened her eyes sunlight streamed into the room. Mr. Quent stood by the window. He wore his riding coat, and his brow was deeply furrowed as he gazed outside.

Ivy sat up in bed. "Is something wrong?"

He turned around, then smiled. "I didn't realize you were awake."

"Were you thinking of slipping away without saying good-bye, then?" she said, affecting an impertinent tone.

"On the contrary," he said, crossing the room to sit on the edge of the bed, "I was thinking of all the things I might do while you were insensible, Mrs. Quent."

Her cheeks flushed from the heat of the sun, and from an inward warmth. "In such an instance, I would far rather I had my senses about me."

"As would I, my dearest." He brushed back a lock of her hair and pressed his lips against her throat.

She drew a deep breath and pressed a hand against his bearded cheek. "You do not have to leave soon, do you?"

He kissed her several more times, then drew back with a sigh. "The soldiers are already here with the horses. You would see them if you were to look out the window."

"You are not taking a coach?"

"Riding will be quicker. If we go by horse, and change mounts often, we will arrive a lumenal sooner than otherwise."

"Why must you go so quickly? Surely it cannot matter that much if your surveys in the North Country are resumed one day earlier." However, even as she said this, she thought of the grim manner he had gazed out the window, and the warmth fled her. "There has been some news, hasn't there?"

His brown eyes were somber. "I am not going to the North Country to continue the surveys of the Wyrdwood. Rather, I ride for Torland."

"Torland! But why?" She could not help a gasp. "There have not been more Risings, have there?"

"No, there have been no more incidents, for which I am grateful. However, I must go to see the . . . to see that the work we accomplished there remains in place. We go quickly only because—well, as you know, there are some in the government who do not understand the labors of the inquirers, and we do not wish them to arrive there before us, lest they perform their own investigations and conceive false notions of what was done there."

"Some people," Ivy said, frowning herself. "Like Lady Shayde, you mean."

He did not disagree, and she took that as an affirmation of her guess.

"Do not worry, Mrs. Quent," he said, taking her hand. "It is all merely government rigmarole. Such nonsense only keeps us from work that is of true importance. I am sorry I have to waste my time on it, but that is the way of politics. All the same, there is nothing that need alarm you. I will not return any later than I would have from the northlands."

Ivy *was* alarmed, but she did not say it. If there was something she needed to know, and which it was within his power to tell her, then he would do so. Besides, he had more than enough to concern himself with while he was gone; she would not have him worrying about *her* as well. She did her best to smile for him, and to assure him that she would be very well.

"My dearest," he said, his voice so low she felt as much as heard it. "How much I have asked of you, and continue to ask of you now. Yet you behave as if I have never done you any wrong in your life!"

"Because you never have."

"You can say that even now as I am abandoning you once again?"

"But I am not abandoned! To be sure, I will miss you terribly. However, I have my sisters for company, and Mr. Rafferdy has promised to call on us the lumenal after next with Mr. Garritt."

"Is that so? Well, I am very glad to hear it. I hope Mr. Rafferdy will come often while I am gone. But what of your evenings, when guests are not here and your sisters retire?"

"Well, *this* evening I have the party to attend at the house of the viscountess Lady Crayford. Who knows what other fine people I will meet there, and what affairs *they* will invite me to?" She tilted her chin up. "No, I'm sure I will be very pleasantly occupied while you are gone."

"Not too pleasantly, I trust."

But he was grinning, looking like a mischievous Tharosian faun again, and she could not help laughing at her own little play.

She threw her arms around him and held him close, so that she could smell the scent of heather that always seemed to linger in his coat. He might leave the moors, but they never left him. Too soon they drew apart, and he kissed her once more.

"The men are waiting," he said, then took up his hat and left the room.

*I*VY THOUGHT THE loneliness she had suffered the umbral before would return after Mr. Quent departed. However, she soon found she was too busy to entertain such feelings.

Just after breakfast, a note came from Mrs. Baydon that she was suffering great anguish over choosing a gown to wear that night, for everything she owned was hideous and not fit to be seen in public. Ivy knew that was hardly the case, for Mrs. Baydon had many pretty gowns. She composed a letter suggesting that Mrs. Baydon wear a particular saffron gown and gave the note to Lawden.

Not an hour later came a despondent reply: *that* gown would only make her an object of ridicule. Several more notes were exchanged throughout the morning and afternoon, so that the only thing moving more swiftly than Ivy's pen was the messengers running between Marble Street and Vallant Street.

At last Mrs. Baydon was convinced to take the ribbons she liked from a gown she loathed, and move them to a gown she adored except for its awful ribbons. By then, it was time for Ivy to consider her own attire for the night, only to realize she had given it little prior thought.

At once she was nearly in a panic similar to Mrs. Baydon's. She forced herself to take her own advice and, enlisting the help of her sisters, she removed the pretty lace from an outmoded dress and used it to decorate her favorite, if somewhat plain, gown of green.

"You will be the most beautiful lady there," Rose said as she fixed the lace to the gown with small, neat stitches.

"The second most beautiful, you mean," Lily said as she retied the ribbons on the sleeves. "The viscountess will be there, and I'm sure no one will be prettier than *her.*"

"Ivy will be," Rose said.

"How can you know that when you've never seen the viscountess?"

"You've never seen her either."

Lily opened her mouth but could find no reply for that, so she settled for glaring at Rose.

"You've made me very cross, you know, Ivy," Lily said after a minute. "I shouldn't even be helping you with your gown. I don't know why you're taking Mrs. Baydon to the party and not me."

"You know very well why I cannot take you."

"But it's absolutely mad! Young ladies without handsome suitors are the very sort of persons who need to go to parties. How else are they supposed to find husbands?"

"You will be able to go to parties without Mr. Quent's accompaniment once you are out."

"When will that be?" Lily crumpled a ribbon into a ball and slumped back against the sofa. "Never, I suppose."

Ivy studied her youngest sister. She looked more like a girl of twelve than a young woman of sixteen at the moment. Yet sixteen she was, and it was time for her to be out in the world. Yesterday, Ivy and Mr. Quent had agreed to start preparations for her and Rose's party on his return. Ivy had thought to tell her sisters then, so as not to make them suffer too great a degree of suspense, but perhaps it was best not to delay the news further.

"Never is a very long time," Ivy said. "I would think you should expect to be presented to society significantly sooner than that."

Lily grimaced. "Really? And when should that happen?"

"I am sure it will happen just a moment after Rose is introduced," Ivy said.

"Rose! I am sure I will walk the plank if she is out before she is a spinster!"

"Then we must find a plank for you to walk on. For Rose will be presented at the party Mr. Quent is holding for you both next month. Though since you'll have gone overboard, I suppose it will be just Rose's party."

Lily's jaw dropped open, and Rose let out a gasp. She put her finger to her mouth, having pricked it on the needle.

"Blood and swash!" Lily roared. "You mean it, don't you? We're to have our party at last?"

"Not if you don't stop speaking like a pirate," Ivy said gravely. Then she smiled at her sisters. "But yes, it is past time that you were both out. Only our father's condition and the demands of Mr. Quent's work have delayed it, but it can be put off no longer. We will have the party at Durrow Street as soon as the repairs are complete, and Mr. Quent will present you both to society."

At this Lily let out a crow of delight. Then she took Rose's hands and pulled her up off the sofa, spinning her around in a circle and laughing. At last they sank back to the sofa, breathing hard.

Ivy could not help being delighted at the happiness the news had given her sisters. "I take it you are pleased, then?"

"Blow me down!" Lily said. "I mean, yes, very much. A party at last! And we must make sure all the handsomest young gentlemen are invited. Especially Mr. Garritt. How long did you say Mr. Quent was to be away?"

"I am not certain," Ivy said. "His business is very important. It may take him until next month."

"Well, I cannot wait to talk to him the moment he's back."

"To thank him?"

"That," Lily said, then winked at Rose. "And to ask him to take us shopping for new gowns!"

🍂

IVY WAS PRESSED for time as it was, and once again the lumenal was shorter than the timetables in the almanac had predicted. As a result, a violet dusk was thickening outside the inn by the time Lily fixed the last pin in her hair and Rose sewed one last stitch in her gown.

The old rosewood clock let out a chime as the dark disk covered the gold. At least *it* always knew when the umbral was commencing. Just then a knock came at the chamber door; the carriage had arrived for her.

"The ribbon on your shoulder is still crooked!" Lily exclaimed.

However, there was no more time.

"I must fly," Ivy said to her sisters, kissing them each, then left their chambers to dash down the stairs. As if she were indeed a sparrow, her heart fluttered wildly in her chest.

"She is only a viscountess!" Ivy said under her breath. "And you have met a king. Besides, you have ridden in her carriage before. There is nothing for you to fear."

Even when rational thought urges calmness, there are deeper and more ancient instincts that advocate a different reaction, and the rapid beating of Ivy's heart continued as the footman helped her into Lord Baydon's barouche.

She found Mrs. Baydon inside, if possible in an even more distressed state. Her eyes were wild, and her cheeks were very flushed, though she looked beautiful in a blue gown that matched her eyes.

"Are you well?" Ivy said.

Mrs. Baydon shook her head. "I think I am coming down with a fever."

Ivy smiled at that. "You are simply excited, as am I."

The carriage started into motion, and Mrs. Baydon gave a small cry. "Why ever did I wish to go to a viscountess's party? If anyone looks at me or speaks to me, I am sure I will faint. Though if anyone notices me at all, I will be mistaken for a servant. What was I thinking to wear such a dreadful gown? We must tell the driver to return to Vallant Street at once. He can drive you to the party after you let me off."

Confronted by her friend's trepidation, Ivy's own receded a fraction. "I will have your arm, so you need have no fear of fainting. Besides, I am sure if anyone is mistaken for a servant, it will be me."

"Oh, no one would ever mistake *you* for a servant, Lady Quent," Mrs. Baydon said. "No matter what you wore."

So serious was her expression that Ivy found herself unable to reply. Instead the two sat in silence as the barouche made its way up the Promenade toward the New Quarter. Too soon the carriage came to a halt before a grand house whose facade featured more columns than could be easily counted.

Ivy's trepidation returned as she and Mrs. Baydon departed the carriage and walked slowly up the broad bank of steps. Other revelers passed by them, some in capes and feathered masks, all in finery and moving quickly, as if eager to experience the delights inside. Light shone through the windows of the house, changing hues every few moments. Each time the door opened, the sound of laughter and music spilled forth.

At last they could go no farther without knocking upon the door themselves.

Mrs. Baydon stopped and shook her head. "I cannot go in. It was mad to think I was fit for such an affair. I do not know anyone who will be there!"

Ivy took a breath. "On the contrary, you will indeed know someone at the party."

Mrs. Baydon shook her head. "But who?"

"You will know me, of course."

The two of them clasped hands tightly. Then the door opened, and together they stepped into a dazzling light.

CHAPTER FIFTEEN

RAFFERDY LURKED BETWEEN a pair of columns in the loggia outside the Hall of Magnates, watching as lords passed through the gilded doors.

How he wished he were anywhere but this place! Had he instead been presented with the opportunity to play several hands of Queen's Cabinet with Mrs. Chisingdon, he would have made his choice without hesitation. Instead, he was here, and once again he must sit on a hard bench and listen to countless somniferous speeches, with sleep prevented by the former even as it was induced by the latter.

His only consolation was that he was able to bypass the musty old Robe Room (and its musty old usher), for he wore his new robe of black crepe. Also, there was no need to help Lord Baydon with *his* robe today. The elder lord remained at Vallant Street, for his head cold had been slow to improve. All the same, Lord Baydon had expressed a great degree of certainty that he would find himself completely recovered at any moment, and Rafferdy should not be at all surprised to find him at Assembly before him.

However, Lord Baydon was not here, and Rafferdy could only wonder why he, who considered himself to be so clever, had not thought to play ill himself. Certainly a physician's diagnosis could be purchased for a reasonable sum! Perhaps a doctor could be found on Marble Street. . . .

"Is there somewhere else you need to be, then, Mr. Rafferdy?" a cheerful voice called out.

Rafferdy looked up to see a young man striding toward him. His robe was similar to Rafferdy's, and his hair rose up in a frizzy crown, unconstrained by a wig—if indeed any wig could possibly have constrained it. Shafts of sunlight fell between the columns along the loggia, and each time the young man passed through one there was a flash of crimson on his right hand.

Rafferdy gave a nod as the other approached. "I was simply considering all of the available possibilities."

"Well, I can hardly fault you for that! I can think of any number of things I'd rather do on a fine day than be shut in a room along with a number of Stouts who seem to be as reluctant to bathe as they are to pass any law the king does not support."

"Perhaps they consider it unpatriotic to wash off any of Altania's native soil that might have settled upon them," Rafferdy said, at which Lord Coulten let out a vigorous laugh.

"I can only imagine you're right, Rafferdy. That sounds like something a Stout would say. But why are you lingering out here? Are you waiting on your older companion?"

"Lord Baydon? No, I am afraid he is indisposed today."

"Is he? I'm sorry to hear that. He seems a very genial sort of fellow. I hope his recovery will be swift. In the meantime, you must come sit with us other wigless young lords."

Rafferdy made a bow. "That is kind of you, but you should reconsider your offer. For I am bound to do all of you a great discredit by yawning very frequently and making extensive investigations of the state of my fingernails anytime the High Speaker talks."

"That's nothing, Rafferdy! If you simply remain upright in your seat, you'll be doing better than half of us." Lord Coulten's blue eyes sparkled. "Then again, you may find you have less trouble staying awake this session than you think."

Rafferdy made no effort to suppress a frown. "Forgive me if I am doubtful, but what makes you say so?"

Lord Coulten said nothing. Instead he made a subtle nod toward a man who was just then approaching the doors of the Hall. His long hair was so fair as to be nearly white, and it made a dramatic contrast to his black robe, which was thick with frills and ruffles.

The man must have noticed their gazes, for he adjusted his course, so that in moments he drew near them.

"Good day, Lord Coulten," he said with a deliberate, rather overdone nod. His voice was of a refined timbre, but slightly high in pitch.

"Good day to you," Lord Coulten replied amiably. "Tell me, have you had the pleasure of meeting our newest compatriot in the Hall of Magnates?"

"I do not believe I have. Which is a peculiar thing, for I am sure it is a rule that I am always the first person that any new magnate meets."

The pale-haired man turned slowly, as if in no great hurry to make the introduction. He was taller than Rafferdy, who was in no way short. He did not lower his head, and instead gazed at Rafferdy down the length of his nose. "I am pleased to make your acquaintance, Lord . . . ?"

"Mr. Rafferdy."

The other raised a colorless eyebrow.

"There, you see, your rule is quite intact," Rafferdy said agreeably. "For I am no magnate at all."

"He is occupying Lord Rafferdy's seat while his father is unable to attend Assembly himself," Lord Coulten explained.

"I see," the taller man said. "Then you must at least be very close to becoming a magnate."

This time, Rafferdy's tone was somewhat less pleasant. "On the contrary, I cannot think of anyone who is further from being a magnate in all of Altania than myself."

A long moment of silence ensued.

"You must excuse me!" Lord Coulten exclaimed. "I have forgotten my protocols, despite the Grand Usher's best efforts to pound them into my brain. Mr. Rafferdy, let me introduce you to one of our Hall's most famous members, Lord Farrolbrook."

The taller man extended his right hand in such a way that the ring upon it could not be missed. It was gold with seven red gems, just like the ring that Lord Coulten wore. Rafferdy extended his own right hand, and as he did Lord Farrolbrook's gaze moved down to it. However, if it was a ring he was looking for, he was disappointed; Rafferdy had put on his gray gloves today.

They shook hands briefly, and Farrolbrook pulled away from the gesture no more quickly than Rafferdy did himself.

"I must take my place on the benches," the fair-haired lord said. "I do not want the other members of my party to grow weary from standing."

Rafferdy shook his head. "Well, if they are tired of standing, it can hardly be your problem. They have only to take a seat, don't they?"

Lord Farrolbrook smiled as one might at a child who had asked where the sun sleeps during an umbral.

"I do everything with a particular purpose, Mr. Rafferdy—a

fact the members of my party know well. That includes choosing where I take my seat at the start of each session. It may be there is a lord who I fear may vote upon the wrong side of an issue, and so I will position myself so that I might easily meet his gaze and thus induce him, at the time of the vote, to choose rightly. Or it may be I know I will need to address the Hall to keep it from moving in an errant direction, and so I will select a place that will allow me to be seen by all when I stand and speak. However, you are very new here. *You* cannot be expected to perceive such things." He nodded to each of them. "Lord Coulten, Mr. Rafferdy." Then he turned and moved with languid strides through the doors of the Hall.

Rafferdy was at a loss for words; or rather, he had so many words to utter that, like a group of men trying to exit a door at the same moment, all of them crowded together so that none could get out.

"I will forgo claiming to be insulted," he said at last. "To do so would be to grant him more credit than he likely deserves. For to be convicted of a crime, one must have the wits to have intended to commit it."

Lord Coulten laughed. "Well, I'd say you did rather well. From what I've seen, that was one of Lord Farrolbrook's better introductions."

"Then I would despair to see his worse. Is it true his compatriots wait for him to take his seat before they take theirs?"

"It's quite true," Lord Coulten said. "The Magisters look to him as their leader. I can only believe there are other minds at work within the Magisters, yet he does command a certain attention, and I believe they use that to their advantage."

Rafferdy considered this with some skepticism. That associating with a man such as Lord Farrolbrook could have any sort of benefit was difficult for him to accept, though he supposed fame had its uses.

"So why did you make a nod in his direction? You did so when you said you thought I'd have less difficulty staying awake today."

Now there was a slyness to Lord Coulten's expression. "I've gotten wind that the Magisters are up to something."

"Up to what?"

"I have no idea, really."

Rafferdy waggled a finger at him. "On the contrary, you do have an idea. It is apparent on your face. However, I can see you have no intention of telling me what you've learned, and I am not one to reach for a rumor; for like a ripe fruit, gossip is always at its juiciest when it falls freely from the tree." Rafferdy raised his ivory-handled cane. "Let us go in. We don't want to delay anyone from taking their seat."

"True enough!" Lord Coulten said merrily, and they proceeded through the gilded doors.

DESPITE LORD COULTEN'S assurances, that day's session of the Hall of Magnates was no less dull than before. Yet Rafferdy found that having a companion at one's side made the affair easier to bear.

Disdain, when it is shared, can form a sort of entertainment, and each sigh or groan they emitted, each barely stifled yawn or shifting of the buttocks upon the bench, became an expression of amusement, together forming an ongoing dialogue upon the pro-ceedings. There was no need to exchange words when a low snort served as the most eloquent dissertation upon some old lord's backwards wig or another's propensity for examining the finger that had just explored the interior of his ear.

The High Speaker once again gave a discourse on legislative procedure. Several obscure acts were proposed, debated, and sub-sequently drowned in a chorus of nays. Throughout it all, Lord Farrolbrook sat on the front bench in the most placid manner, his hands upon his knees, his gaze upon whomever was speaking.

At last the proceedings drew toward a close. The High Speaker called for any last business to be presented. One of the Stouts on the far right of the Hall rose to his feet. He was a man who did credit to the name of his political party, being prodigious in dimension from side to side though not from top to bottom. He wore an overlarge wig and his cheeks were as red and wrinkled as last year's apples.

"The Hall recognizes Lord Bastellon," the High Speaker pronounced with a wave of his gavel.

The portly lord gripped the edges of his coat and, instead of speaking immediately, embarked upon an enthusiastic clearing of his throat. Lord Coulten let out a sigh that said, *I thought we were going to escape it this time,* while Rafferdy gave a small cough meaning, *Prepare yourself for the air to become thick and odious.*

Every session since the opening of Assembly, when the High Speaker made his call for final business, the leader of the Stouts had risen to address the Hall. Each time Lord Bastellon had called for debate to be opened on the matter of King Rothard's writ of succession. And each time the Hall had voted against the proposal, with the nays being spoken quickly and loudly by the Magisters and a majority of the lords following suit. So rebuked, the Stouts would leave the Hall in a group, red-faced and fuming.

When at last his lengthy expectoration was concluded, Lord Bastellon once again spoke of the king's desire that Assembly vote upon the matter of his writ of succession—though, despite his efforts at clearing his throat, his words came out with as much phlegm as force.

"The Hall of Citizens has already taken up the matter, and we must do the same," he concluded. "Therefore I call again for debate to be opened on the subject of His Majesty's writ of succession!"

Rafferdy waited for the resounding chorus of nays, preparing to speak along with them. Not that it was his particular wish to defy the king; rather, he simply did not want to vote for anything that would give the Stouts further opportunity to drone on. However, before anyone could speak otherwise, a clear voice rang out.

"Hear, hear! I second the motion."

A low murmur rushed through the hall like a wind. The speaker was none other than Lord Farrolbrook. The pale-haired lord had risen to his feet. Lord Bastellon gaped at him in open astonishment.

The High Speaker banged his gavel against the podium. "The proposal has been seconded. A vote must now be taken on the issue. Shall debate be opened on the matter of the writ of succession of His Majesty, King Rothard? All in favor speak yea!"

This time all of the Magisters stood, speaking their *yeas* in loud voices. Many of the lords in the Hall exchanged baffled looks, but a number of them shrugged and stood as well to join the affirmative. Next to Rafferdy, Lord Coulten jumped to his feet and shouted *yea,* as did several of the young men around them. As he tended to follow Lord Coulten's lead, Rafferdy stood and called out a tentative *yea* himself. Lord Coulten grinned at him.

Now the High Speaker called for the nays, and these were few and uttered in rather confused tones. There was no question; the yeas had it by a great majority. All took to their seats again.

"Debate is now opened!" the High Speaker called out.

Lord Bastellon's astonishment had been replaced by a pleased look. He gripped his coat, striding back and forth as he performed further labors upon the phlegm in his throat. "My good and wise lords, I am pleased. It is past time we grant His Great and Blessed Majesty the due that he deserves and discuss the important matter of—"

"But why discuss it?" a voice rang out, interrupting Bastellon.

Again, all stared at the speaker; again, it was Lord Farrolbrook.

"Since the matter is of such great importance, let us not cause further delay by debating it this way or that," the pale-haired lord said. "Instead, let us see it resolved at once. I call for an end to debate."

All of the Magisters leaped up behind him. The motion was quickly seconded. The High Speaker struck his gavel and called for a vote. Bastellon sputtered, trying to speak, but he was able to produce no words, only spittle. The Magisters called out their yeas, as did many around the Hall, including Lord Coulten. Once again the motion was carried.

"But this is madness!" Lord Bastellon at last managed to cry out. "I will not stand down before I have any chance to speak on the matter."

The High Speaker pounded the podium with his gavel, though he looked as if he would just as readily pound Bastellon's head if needed.

"The motion has carried. Debate on the matter is ended. You will depart the floor, sir!"

Bastellon looked ready to argue, but then the Grand Usher was there at his elbow, a pair of ushers with him, and there was nothing for it; he had to depart. He shook off their hands and stamped to the right to join the other Stouts, who were all stewing in their wigs.

The High Speaker called for a vote on the issue: should the Hall of Magnates ratify and affirm King Rothard's existing writ of succession as the will and law of Altania?

The Stouts leaped out to shout their yeas; these were more than matched by the nays cried out by the Magisters on the left. The middle of the Hall largely joined in the nays, though Lord Coulten did not stand and speak, and so Rafferdy abstained as well. Once again, there was no question about the outcome. The High Speaker's gavel came down, dealing a final, fatal blow to the measure. The proposal had failed.

With this final business so concluded, the day's session was closed. The Stouts rose and marched out of the hall in a group, their faces no longer red but as gray as their wigs. The Magisters departed in a more slow and stately fashion, Lord Farrolbrook at their fore.

"Well, that was a grand entertainment!" Lord Coulten proclaimed as they departed the Hall.

"I suppose I cannot find fault with any measure that keeps the Stouts from speaking," Rafferdy allowed. "All the same, I am not sure I comprehend what you found so delightful in the affair."

Lord Coulten's blue eyes were alight. "Don't you see? The Stouts have wanted to debate the king's writ. Well, now they've had their chance."

"Not much of a chance."

"That's the point. By closing off the debate and calling for a vote, Lord Farrolbrook dealt them a grave blow."

Rafferdy shook his head. "Can it never be voted on again?"

"It can, of course—only not this session. The matter will have to wait for the next session of Assembly before it can be brought up again. I'm sure the Stouts will have learned their lesson by then. They aren't *that* dull. They won't allow the matter to go to debate if they are not confident it has some chance of passing should a vote be called. However, it worked this time, and as a result we won't have to listen to them speak any further on the issue for months. It was, in sum, a clever plan."

"Which means it could not possibly have been conceived by Lord Farrolbrook," Rafferdy said.

"I imagine not!" Lord Coulten agreed. "I can only believe someone else was the author of this play, yet Farrolbrook performed his part very well, which I am sure is his purpose."

They passed through the gilded doors into the loggia. A little way off, a group of lords—mostly Magisters, given the House rings on their hands—gathered around Lord Farrolbrook. They were congratulating the fair-haired man, who wore a pleased expression.

"Yes, it is precisely his purpose, I think," Rafferdy said. "They put forth a posturer as their leader so that others underestimate them—and then promptly fall into their traps. Certainly Lord Bastellon did."

Lord Coulten let out a laugh. "God above, I never thought of it that way, but I'm sure you must be right. I say, you're quite good at politics, Rafferdy. I imagine you'll be giving speeches before the Hall and laying your own snares before the session is out."

Now it was Rafferdy who laughed. "I can assure you no such thing will happen. *His* purpose may be to gain the attention of others, but mine is just the opposite. It is my hope that I will depart this body soon, and that no one so much as notices when I go."

"Well, then, you've already failed, Rafferdy, for *I* will certainly notice your absence."

Rafferdy nodded, but only distractedly. He continued to watch

Lord Farrolbrook from afar. For some reason, he found the fair-haired lord an object of fascination. His mannered gestures, his insipid expression, his overruffled robe—they were all so ridiculous. Did he truly believe that others admired him? Though Rafferdy supposed that some people did, and he recalled all the times Lady Marsdel's nephew, Mr. Harclint, had expounded upon the many talents allegedly possessed by Lord Farrolbrook, from painting to science to magick. Even as Rafferdy thought this, Farrolbrook made a fluttering motion with his hand, and crimson sparked on his finger.

"But can he really be a magician?" Rafferdy said, only realizing he had spoken the words aloud once they were uttered. He looked at Lord Coulten. "That is, I have heard that Farrolbrook has demonstrated magick in public on several occasions."

"Oh, of course he's a magician," Lord Coulten said. "Just as I am a great musician because I tell everyone how much I adore music, how my thoughts are always consumed with music, and how there is nothing in the world so important or worthy of study as music."

Rafferdy raised an eyebrow. "I take it you can't play a note?"

"Not a one! As for magick—I've never seen him do anything that would require an enchantment. They say he called down lightning once, but anyone with a kite and a key and a bit of luck can manage *that* trick."

These words pleased Rafferdy, though he wasn't certain why. What did he care if Lord Farrolbrook was a magician or not?

"All the same, he does wear a House ring," Rafferdy said.

"Well, *that* hardly means anything. They give those out to practically anyone these days." With a wry expression, Lord Coulten raised his own hand and the red-gemmed ring upon it.

Rafferdy gripped the handle of his cane. His glove concealed it, but all the same he could feel the cool weight on his ring finger. "You make a jest of it. Yet I am sure you know that only a magician—or at least, one who *could* be a magician—may put on such a ring."

Lord Coulten shrugged. "I suppose some modicum of magickal ability is required. Yet there is a difference between having a talent for a thing and taking the time and effort to learn to do it—just as there is a difference between speaking about music and practicing an instrument."

Rafferdy gave the other young man a pointed look. "What of you, Lord Coulten? When it comes to magick, are you and your friends more likely to speak or to practice?"

Dimples appeared in Lord Coulten's cheeks. "A magician never divulges his secrets, Rafferdy—at least not in public. You'll have to join us at tavern tonight if you wish to find out the answer to that."

Rafferdy had been so consumed with his despair at attending Assembly, and then with his amusement at mocking it, that he had forgotten entirely the question he had been wanting to ask Lord Coulten.

"Tell me," he said, "is it at the Sword and Leaf that you meet?"

"So it is! But I confess, I am surprised that you know. I am not so mysterious as I hoped."

"I believe I saw you there several umbrals past," Rafferdy explained. "I go to that tavern often. Well, not so often of late, yet often enough. That I have not seen you there before surprises *me*."

"It should not, as we only started meeting there very recently. What's more, we gather in a private room, and we usually come and go through the rear door of the tavern. I came in the front that last time only because I was coming from that direction and was running late. I should have guessed that you frequent the Sword and Leaf. It is said it used to be a favorite haunt for magicians long ago." Lord Coulten gave him an arch look. "But I'm sure *you* knew that."

Actually, it was only recently that he had learned that rumor from Eldyn Garritt. Rafferdy had taken a liking to the Sword and Leaf not for any fact of its history, but rather for the dimness of its booths and the strength of its punch. In all the years they had gone there, Rafferdy had never noticed any magicians or private rooms. Or back doors, for that matter.

He was about to mention this. However, at that moment a voice called out Lord Coulten's name. A group of young lords—

none of them wearing a wig on his head—were waving at them.
Or, more precisely, at Lord Coulten.

"Pardon me, Rafferdy, but I must be off," Lord Coulten said.
"My invitation stands. We will be gathering at the Sword and Leaf
at moonrise. Please join us. You would be most welcome."

Rafferdy explained that he already had plans to meet someone
else for a drink that night. Before he could speak further, the other
men called out again for Lord Coulten. He gave a bow, his tall
crown of hair bobbing, then departed with his companions.

The loggia was all but empty now. Lord Farrolbrook and the
other Magisters were gone; there was not a Stout to be seen. Cane
in hand, Rafferdy started toward the stairs that led down to the esplanade.

A flutter of darkness caught his eye. To his left, a figure
stepped from between two columns into the loggia. She was tall
for a woman and proceeded with a kind of coiled grace, as if her
languid motions might at any moment become swift and forceful.
Her face was as pale as the ivory handle of his cane, and she was
clad in a gown of black like a mourner.

Or rather, like an executioner.

Rafferdy could not guess why Lady Shayde was here. The king
would not address Assembly again until the next session opened,
and was His Majesty not her primary concern?

Perhaps she was looking for more men who bled gray rather
than red. Rafferdy shuddered at the memory. However, as strange
as all that had been, it was not *his* concern. And no matter what
her purpose was, he had no wish for another encounter with
her—or with her hulking companion, Moorkirk, if he was about.

That white visage began to turn in his direction. Rafferdy
wasted no more time. He hurried to the closest columns, slipped
between them, and descended the broad bank of steps beyond. He
found his driver waiting on the street and climbed into the carriage.

"Where to, sir?"

Rafferdy did not know how to answer. He had no wish to return home and be alone. The idea of shopping for new clothes did
not entice him, and it was many hours yet before it was time to

meet Eldyn Garritt. He considered paying a visit to Vallant Street, but he was unsure they were receiving, given Lord Baydon's condition, and a visit to Fairhall Street was not something he would undertake unless commanded by Lady Marsdel.

"Sir?"

"Take me to The Seventh Swan," he said suddenly.

"To the inn down the street, you mean, sir?"

"Yes, that's right."

The plan agreed upon at Lady Marsdel's was that he would call on Mrs. Quent tomorrow. However, that did not mean he could not call on her *today* as well. After all, he had promised Mrs. Quent—that is, Lady Quent—that he would visit her and her sisters more often. Besides, he was sure they would be happy to receive him unexpectedly; and for his part, he wanted to hear how the affair at the house of the viscountess Lady Crayford had gone last night.

To Rafferdy's chagrin, an entire afternoon of writing notes had failed to procure him an invitation to the party. It was paradoxical that, after declining so many invitations in the past, the one time he actually wanted one he could not get it. However, perhaps the two were not unconnected—a notion he had been forced to consider after receiving more than one curt note in which the author stated, if he could not be troubled to ever come to *their* parties, they would not be troubled to help him gain an invitation to another.

Well, it hardly mattered. The only thing about the affair at the viscountess's that would have interested him was seeing *her* there, and hearing about it from Lady Quent would be every bit as satisfying. He grinned, very pleased with his decision, then settled back into the seat as the cabriolet moved down Marble Street.

CHAPTER SIXTEEN

IVY OPENED HER eyes to a dazzle of golden light, and for a moment she wondered if she had never left—if she had simply fallen on a soft velvet chaise to rest her head for just a little while, and that it was still night and she was still there, at the party at Lady Crayford's house.

However, as she sat up she saw the brilliant glints were not from the light of a thousand candles refracting off crystal goblets and diamond cuff links and pendants of topaz that hung low against the décolletage of elegant gowns. Rather, it was only the morning sunlight striking the bits of colored glass that Lily had, on a whim one day, hung from ribbons before the windows in all of their rooms at The Seventh Swan.

Nor were the sounds that had stirred her from her slumber a minuet performed by masked musicians, mingling with the conversation of revelers. Rather, it was the bells of a church tolling the start of the second farthing of the lumenal, and the voices were those of Lily and Rose speaking in the sitting room outside her chamber door.

Even as she listened, the bells finished their carillon. The day was already a quarter over and she was not yet out of bed! And there was much to do with Mr. Quent away. They had begun to receive the furnishings for the house on Durrow Street they had ordered, and there were dozens of accounts for her to reconcile today.

She roused herself from bed and moved to a basin on the bureau to splash water on her face. As she did, she saw her green gown from last night lying over the back of the chair. Bits of glitter still clung to it, sparkling in the sunlight. She picked it up, thinking to hang it properly. Only as she did, the scents of jasmine and lilac emanated from it. She held the gown to her cheek, breathing deeply, and once again she was there, at the house of the viscountess.

Except that, at first, it hadn't been a house at all.

Standing outside in the darkness, Ivy and Mrs. Baydon had been filled with dread at the thought of entering. They had gripped each other's hands so tightly each could feel the rapid rate of the other's pulse. Then, together, they had stepped through the door into—

—a painting.

Or rather, into a whole gallery of paintings. Ivy knew the viscountess was an accomplished artist. She had expected— indeed, had very much hoped—to see some of Lady Crayford's works. What Ivy had not expected was to become a part of those paintings herself.

Yet she and Mrs. Baydon found themselves in a sylvan glade ringed by poplar trees and half-ruined columns and statues that gazed with moss-filled eyes. Everything was brilliantly colored, yet soft and slightly blurred, as if formed from the strokes of a brush. Even as they gaped about them, smiling dryads beckoned to them, drawing them farther in. Fauns walking on crooked legs and carrying silver trays handed them goblets of cool wine. Ivy looked at Mrs. Baydon and saw that leaves tangled in her companion's gold hair. She reached up to her own coif and pulled away another leaf.

If she looked at it closely, Ivy could see that it was not a leaf at all, but rather a slip of green paper. And, if she concentrated very hard, she could see that the dryads and fauns were simply servants in forest-colored garb, and the statues and columns were made of wood and plaster. However, even as she took a sip of the wine, the scene around her softened again, and the servants vanished, re-placed once more by the sylvan beings.

Mrs. Baydon laughed and took her hand, and they strolled about the glade, delighting in everything they saw. To Ivy, it was like being on a hill just outside ancient Tharos. Then they found themselves on the edge of the glade, and once again they stepped forward, into a new painting.

This one was darker, with lanterns reflecting off onyx water and the graceful arches of stone bridges. A narrow gondola glided by as candles floated all around. Ivy had seen pictures of such a place before. It was one of the canal cities on the coast of the Principalities, where people went not by carriage but by boat on the various waterways that served for streets.

Another glass of wine was given to them, this time by a servant in a grotesque yet delightful mask with a beaked nose and decorated with feathers. They had hardly finished it before they were swept into another scene, and another, each as beautiful as the last. They walked upon the parapets of a ruined castle, marveled beneath the golden dome of a Murghese temple, and strolled through a field of brilliant red poppies.

All at once, the poppies gave way to parquet floor, the clouds to chandeliers, and they were once again in Invarel, in a ballroom with grand windows that looked out over the lights of the New Quarter. However, this was in no way less fantastical than the scenes through which they had wandered, for Ivy realized *those* had been only prelude—a means to delight and heighten the senses in preparation for what lay ahead.

Somehow, despite the crowd of people that filled the ballroom, the viscountess found them at once. To Ivy's astonishment—and, she confessed, her great pleasure—Lady Crayford greeted her as if she was the fondest old friend, giving her a warm embrace. In turn she greeted Mrs. Baydon with the most generous expression of warmth. Mrs. Baydon was so amazed she could hardly speak, though she made a beautiful curtsy in reply.

"Come, Lady Quent, you must see my paintings," the viscountess said.

Ivy could only smile. "I believe I already have, your ladyship."

"So you enjoyed my little tableaux, then? I am very glad! Now you must see what inspired them."

She led Ivy and Mrs. Baydon to the end of the ballroom, and

there they all were in gilt frames: the very scenes they had strolled through. There was the old Tharosian villa, the canal city on festival night, and the crumbling castle. So exquisite was the detail of each painting that Ivy could only believe, if she peered closely enough, she would see herself and Mrs. Baydon walking within, their forms rendered in fine brush strokes.

"Now, this is a true enchantment," she said breathlessly, and this won a bright laugh from Lady Crayford.

"Dear Lady Quent, I must make sure my husband hears you say such things. He thinks my hobby perpetually silly. You must come with me to find him. And you as well, of course, Mrs. Baydon. . . ."

What followed then—it was all so brilliant in her mind, just like the viscountess's paintings. Even as words could never really convey the beauty of a work of art, it would be impossible to truly describe it. Lily would press her for details, but how could Ivy explain the way the light had possessed a texture, or the way the music had shimmered on the air?

Nor were Lady Crayford's guests any less extraordinary than the party they inhabited. Perhaps it was the illusory light, but in their finery the revelers had seemed like works of art themselves. The viscountess was unable to find her husband, but she introduced Ivy and Mrs. Baydon to a dozen other people before she was called away by her duties.

Ivy could not believe anyone would find her of interest, and she would have been more than content to stand upon the edges of the party and observe it all. However, once her identity was made known, she found herself an object of constant attention. She and Sir Quent were very famous, she was assured, for he was a hero of the realm, and it was known that she had stood face-to-face with villainous rebels in the country.

How *that* could have become public knowledge, Ivy could not imagine. Yet presented with such an accusation, she could not deny it, though she offered no details of how she had accomplished her escape, and she demurred that she had done nothing remarkable.

So preoccupied was Ivy by all the talk and bright laughter that she did not realize until some time had passed that Mrs. Baydon was no longer beside her. At last, worried about her friend, Ivy extricated herself from those around her. After half a tour around the ballroom, she espied Mrs. Baydon sitting on a marble bench, a rapt expression on her face as she watched, with many others, as an illusionist conjured silver doves and golden sparrows from thin air.

Ivy started to go to her, only at that moment Lady Crayford found her again. The viscountess said there were others who would not be satisfied until they had met the renowned Lady Quent. Seeing her friend was so well-occupied with the illusion play, Ivy let herself be led away.

The night wore on until the first span of the umbral gave way to the second. Ivy spoke with more people, beheld more paintings, and drank more wine. When at last she had a moment to search again for Mrs. Baydon, she learned her friend had grown weary and had departed. Ivy was not to worry, for one of the viscount's carriages would be waiting for her when she was ready to leave.

Only Ivy was anything but tired. Indeed, she could not remember a time when she had felt so vibrant and awake. She let the viscountess lead her on a tour of the various tableaux, and they compared each one to the painting upon which it was based, to see how true it was to the source.

At last Ivy knew she could stay no longer. It was not due to weariness, but rather from a feeling that she could see and hear and experience no more, that her senses were entirely full. She bid the viscountess farewell, and Lady Crayford gave her a fond embrace. Then Ivy walked down the marble steps before the house and climbed into the carriage that waited for her, as if she were some princess in one of Lily's romances.

Now, in the bright light of morning, Ivy realized she was indeed acting like the heroine of one of Lily's books—that is, she was letting sensibility rule over reason. It had been a grand and sumptuous affair, to be sure, but it had only been a party!

In fact, she ought to be aghast at such a lavish display during a time when so many people in the realm had so little. While she could not deny the sights the Siltheri had created were beautiful—nor had she perceived anything inherently unwholesome in the scenes they had produced—that did not mean such things were to be respected. After all, if one could choose to always dwell in a world of imagined beauty, one might never see the true world where so many people lived in want and deprivation. As a result, as remarkable as it all had been, and as much as she had enjoyed herself, Ivy could not entirely approve of the affair.

She picked up her gown to take it to the wardrobe and put it away. As she did, she paused. Then Ivy held the gown up to herself, and she turned around in a circle.

A knock sounded at the door. Startled, Ivy lowered the gown.

"Ivy!" came Lily's voice from the other side of the door. "Ivy, are you awake in there? Rose is beginning to think you never came back last night. She's dreadfully worried that pirates carried you away!"

Ivy cleared her throat. "I'm here," she called through the door. "I'll be out in a moment."

"I'll send down for tea," Lily called back. "We'll wait for you to drink one cup, but after that you must tell us everything that happened last night!"

Ivy dressed quickly, and after a few minutes she was able to enter the sitting room.

She smiled at Rose as she poured a cup of tea. "You see, dearest? I am quite well."

"You were very late," Rose said, her brown eyes wide with worry. "I waited up until the clock struck the third span, but you still weren't back. And Lily told me how she read in her book that pirates sometimes—"

"Of course she was late!" Lily exclaimed as she stole a biscuit from the tray that had been brought for Ivy. "I'm sure if I had been at the viscountess's party, I should have stayed even later. Now, tell us everything that happened, Ivy. And don't leave anything out—for I'll know if you do!"

Ivy obliged her sisters and described the party as she sipped her tea. She did her best to faithfully relate everything she saw, yet at the same time tried not to make it seem too marvelous or delightful. However, it was clear that either her feelings of wonder came through despite her intentions, or Lily's own imagination painted in the color that Ivy purposefully left out.

"Gold and plunder, I want tableaux of paintings at my own party!" Lily glanced at their sister. "I mean at Rose's and my party. But I'm sure she wants tableaux as well. Don't you, Rose? Though that means we'll have to have illusionists, of course."

Ivy set down her cup. "You know that's not possible, Lily."

"But the viscountess had illusionists, and you were there."

"Yes, but I am not a viscountess, and neither are you. Lady Crayford moves in different circles than we and is judged by different rules."

Lily shook her head. "The rules of fashion apply to everyone. For if they didn't, how would we tell who was in mode and who wasn't? And if *she* is doing it, then it must be fashionable."

"No," Ivy said, "we will do what is right, not what is in mode. That is what Mr. Quent expects of us."

Lily knew that tone of voice, and thus knew there was no use arguing against it. Still, she affected a melancholy look and slumped in her chair, as if she had suddenly lost interest in all worldly things.

"Don't worry, Lily," Rose said, taking Lily's hand. "Just because we can't have illusionists doesn't mean we can't have a tableau at our party."

Lily frowned at Rose, though her expression was curious as well. "What do you mean? Of course we would need illusionists."

Rose shook her head. "No, we don't. I'm sure I can sew any sort of costume an illusionist can conjure. Not as quickly as they might weave it out of air, of course, but I think it would be better, for it would be real and couldn't fade away. And no one is more clever at inventing things than you, Lily. I don't think there's any sort of thing you couldn't make with cloth and paints and ribbons.

Unless . . ." Rose shook her head, ". . . unless you think an entire tableau would be too much for us to make?"

"Blow me down, of course it wouldn't be too much!" Lily roared, sitting up in her chair. "Not for me. I can do anything. Well, except for sew very well, but that's what *you're* for, Rose. Now, come with me at once. We have to pick what scene we're going to copy for our tableau. It has to be very beautiful and very famous."

She leaped to her feet and pulled Rose up with her.

"Sorry, Ivy," Lily said. "We don't have time to listen to any more stories about what you did last night. We have to go to a bookshop to look through pages of scenes."

Ivy was in no way regretful to hear this news. After the affair last night, she craved nothing but to be quiet for a while. Besides, she very much approved of Rose's idea. It was good for Lily to remember that the best sort of entertainments were not the ones conjured for you by others, but rather the ones you invented yourself.

After her sisters departed, Ivy savored another cup of tea while Miss Mew curled up on her lap. Soon, however, all the things she needed to do compelled her to set aside her cup. The first order of business was to pen a note to Mrs. Baydon, as she had not had the chance to bid her friend a proper good-bye last night, and she wanted to know if the party had been all that Mrs. Baydon had hoped it would be.

Ivy went back into her bedchamber, Miss Mew padding be-hind, and sat at the writing desk. As she did, her gaze fell upon the Wyrdwood box. Once again she felt a pang at the way her father's words had disappeared from the journal. Yet she felt a curiosity as well. She wondered by what means the entry she had read could have suddenly appeared on a blank page and then, the very next lumenal, vanish again. Certainly it was an enchantment more advanced than writing secret messages in vinegar!

Yet why would her father use magick to conceal words in a journal that, by his inscription, he had intended for Ivy to read? A woman could not do any magick—a fact of which he could only have been well aware. So how could he have expected her to read the journal?

There was only one explanation. Magick had been performed to conceal the words in the journal, but it need not be worked to reveal them. Rather, they would appear on their own, just as she had seen the other night.

Which meant more might have appeared in the meantime.

An excitement caused Ivy's heart to quicken. It was the most unlikely possibility, she admonished herself. It had surely been the rarest and most fortunate of circumstances that had caused her to happen upon the words in the journal, to turn the page to them at just the precise moment they were visible. She could not hope to be so lucky again.

All the same, she reached for the Wyrdwood box, pulling it toward her. With a light touch, Ivy bid the tendrils of wood to release their hold on the lid, and she took out the journal. She opened it just past the inscription, and then began turning through the blank white pages one by one.

And there, not a quarter way through the journal, was a page filled with lines of spidery writing.

While logic had suggested this was possible, still a gasp of wonder escaped Ivy. She was certain that this page had been blank when she last examined the journal. Yet now it was covered with words penned in her father's thin, wandering hand.

LOERUS IN MURGON, DALAVAR RISING
My Dear Ivy,

I have made a dreadful mistake. You are yet small as I write this, and I know in your eyes your father is all-powerful and can do no wrong. But know that is not the case, that I can err like any person. So I have done, for I have trusted someone I should not have, and now it is gone.

But who is the one who could have betrayed my confidence? Mundy, Gambrel, Fintaur, Larken—I am sure it was not any of them who did this. You must understand that Mr. Bennick and I chose them with the greatest care, that we revealed the knowledge only to those whom we were convinced we could utterly trust.

All the same, it is indeed missing. I have looked everywhere, but I knew at once I would not find it. One does not simply leave such a thing lying about! The enchantments upon it were strong and enduring. No, this thing was not carelessly misplaced. Rather, it was willfully taken in the most calculating fashion. But again I come to the question—by whom? Who would take the key to Tyberion?

I do not know. The only thing I am sure of is that the other key is safe with the Black Stork, for I went to him some time ago and gave it to him, and he agreed to keep it. That he could possibly betray us is a thing I know to be impossible. A truer friend there cannot be. As for the others—I know not who in the order Bennick and I can trust now. That someone in our circle did this thing, I am sure. Yet it still might not have been any of those I trusted. There are magicks and arcane devices another might have used to observe our conversations or to seek out its hiding place.

Well, even if I do not know who took the key, there is one thing I do know for certain: I must hide Tyberion. I must conceal it in a place where they would never think to look for it. But where? I will have to consult with Mr. Bennick on this. He will have some good idea, I am sure. He is an exceedingly clever man, Ivy, and a stalwart ally in all I do. I cannot wait for you to grow a little older so you might get to know him. I would introduce you now, but he is something of an imposing man, and not entirely comfortable with—or comforting to—children. Yet one day you will meet him, and I am sure you will hold him in as high a regard as I do.

For now, I must finish this page, for I have work to do. By the time I get to Whitward Street, you will be fast asleep. But if you feel a light touch on your cheek as you dream, have no fear. It is only a kiss from your loving father.

G.O.L.

Again Ivy read the entry, her amazement only somewhat muted by the dire tone of her father's words. So her hypothesis had been proven correct! Whatever enchantment had concealed the entry in the journal also, of its own volition, caused it to appear. And this time, knowing the words would certainly be ephemeral, Ivy would not lose them again. She took out a pen, ink, and a blank sheet of paper, and transcribed the entry that had appeared in the journal. She worked swiftly, half fearing the words would evaporate from the page before she had gotten them down.

Once finished, she compared her copy to the journal. As before, her father had begun the entry not with a usual date, but rather with a description of the arrangement of the stars at the time of writing. He had ever been the amateur astrographer!

Yet it was strange that in this entry he had discussed his intention to hide Tyberion, while in the last entry the concealment had already been done. And this one appeared nearer to the front of the journal than the other. That meant he had written this entry before *that* one. Only this struck her as odd; she would have thought the magick of the journal would reveal the entries in the order they were written.

She finished checking her copy and ruefully noted how her father had placed so much trust in Mr. Bennick. Mr. Lockwell had wondered who had betrayed him and Mr. Bennick, never realizing that it was Mr. Bennick himself who would play him false. Ivy supposed it was he who had taken the key to Tyberion.

What was Tyberion? It was clearly very important. Ivy scanned the lines on the page, but they offered no clue. However, there was something else in the journal that intrigued her even more.

The other key is safe with the Black Stork. . . .

After reading this, the words her father had spoken to her the last time she visited him at Madstone's took on a different meaning.

Has the black stork come to you yet?

She had thought that somehow he knew about the birds that had built a nest at the house on Durrow Street. Only that was impossible, of course, and his words had had nothing to do with the birds upstairs. The Black Stork must have been some friend of his. But who was this person?

Her first thought was that it was the man in the black mask who had appeared to her on several occasions, and who she knew had shown himself to her father as well. Only there was something about that conclusion that did not seem quite right. The man in the mask always appeared at his own whim, but in the entry, her father had described going to see the Black Stork himself. Ivy bent back over the journal, to see if there was a subtle clue she had missed.

The sound of a knock carried into her bedchamber. Someone was at the outer door of the sitting room. Hastily she bookmarked the journal and locked it again in the Wyrdwood box. Then she went out into the sitting room and opened the door. On the other side was a young woman whose white ruffled cap was pulled nearly down to her eyes.

"Pardon for the intrusion, my lady," the young woman said. "The innkeeper bid me to tell you that your people are here."

Ivy shook her head. "My people?"

"Aye, my lady. They arrived in their carriage and are waiting for you to join them."

"But I am not expecting any company," Ivy said. "I'm sure there must be some mistake."

The servant shook her head. "No, my lady, begging your pardon. They asked for you very clearly. I heard them myself."

Ivy wondered if it was perhaps Mr. Rafferdy and Mr. Garritt. However, it was tomorrow that Mr. Rafferdy had promised to pay a visit, and she could not imagine who else it might be. It was not like Mr. and Mrs. Baydon to call without sending a note first.

There was nothing to do but go down, but she was in no state to go out of her rooms. As these visitors had arrived unexpectedly, whoever it was would have to wait for her.

"Please tell them I will be down shortly," Ivy said.

As quickly as she could, Ivy put on a simple yellow dress, made sure her face and teeth were clean, and put her hair up with a few pins. A glance in a mirror confirmed that, while hardly fit for any formal affair, she would at least not inspire horror in anyone who beheld her.

Ivy left her chamber and went downstairs. The innkeeper told her that her callers were awaiting her in the back salon, where they were taking some coffee. Ivy thanked him, then went into the salon.

"Oh!" she exclaimed.

"Good morning, Lady Quent," Lady Crayford said, smiling. The viscountess wore a cobalt gown and a smart hat atop her chestnut hair. "Are you ready for our excursion?"

"But you do not have your hat or parasol," one of her companions said. He was a tall and exceedingly handsome young man with hair the same chestnut color as Lady Crayford's. Ivy had met him last night. This was Colonel Daubrent, the brother of the viscountess. "Would you like me to have a servant go up to your rooms and fetch them for you, Lady Quent?"

"My hat and parasol?" she said, too dumb to think of anything else to say. "Why should I need them?"

"For our drive into the country, of course," replied the other young man who was with them. His name was Lord Eubrey, Ivy had learned last night. He looked very well in a coat of fawn-colored velvet, and an ornate ring, set with a blue stone, sparkled on his right hand.

Again Ivy could only repeat what she had heard. "The country?"

"We have very fine weather for it today," Colonel Daubrent said. He looked at the viscountess. "I am sure even you must find some scene to inspire your eye, Lisenne."

Lady Crayford laughed. "You know perfectly well I can find as much to admire in a foggy scene as a sunny one. Indeed, it is my hope to find something more natural, even wild, to paint today. I am quite weary of depicting tranquil gardens. I wish I could see some of the windswept scenes you described last night, Lady Quent, when you spoke of your time in the West Country."

Ivy was still astonished, but at last she was able to grasp what the others were discussing. There had to be some mistake. And in the gentlest terms, so there was no possibility her words might be construed as an admonishment, she stated that she was unaware there had been any plan to take a drive in the country today.

"But we discussed it in great detail last night," Lady Crayford said. "We were of a mind to go to the country, and we were all in agreement that *you* must come with us, Lady Quent. We spoke of it a great deal. Yet were we all truly so awful as to never think to ask you? It must be so! In which case we are the most wretched sort of beings. You must accept our deepest apologies."

Ivy was aghast. Surely the viscountess did not owe *her* an apology for thinking of her in such a generous manner. She assured them they were very kind to have thought of her.

"On the contrary, we are horridly selfish," Lord Eubrey said. "We did not get our fill of you last night, Lady Quent, having to share you with so many others at the party, and so we wish to have more of you for ourselves."

These words shocked Ivy anew. "I can hardly believe *that* is the case."

"It is very much the case," Lady Crayford said with a bright laugh. "There was no one at the party last night people wished to be near more than you, Lady Quent. I hardly got any chance to speak to you. Thus I concocted a scheme for an excursion in the country to rectify the situation."

The viscountess's mirth was catching, and Ivy smiled. "Well, then, I hope we will soon have an occasion for such a drive."

Colonel Daubrent shook his head. "Are you not going to come with us now, Lady Quent? The carriage stands ready, and we have sent ahead for a dinner at the inn at Corwent Crossing."

The idea of an excursion with such interesting companions was very tempting; Ivy had been in the city so long. To go out into the country, to look at beautiful scenes and discuss how they might be painted, was a marvelous thought.

"I was just sitting down to write a letter to Mrs. Baydon," she said. "And my sisters are out for the morning. They would wonder after me if they returned and found me gone."

Lady Crayford waved a hand. "Think what a more interesting

letter you could write to your friend after a day in the country. You would have such lively things to relate, and so delight and entertain her all the more. As for your sisters, simply leave word with the innkeeper where you have gone, and they will not have any cause to worry."

Ivy could only concede that was true. However, in addition to writing Mrs. Baydon, she had intended to work on the ledger for the house on Durrow Street, for there were many expenses from the refurbishment to record.

"I am not properly dressed," she said. "And I cannot believe I am in any way needed for your amusement."

"I must respectfully disagree on both accounts," Lord Eubrey said. "For I am certain we will have a glum time without you. Lady Crayford will have interest only in scenery, and Daubrent is a dour soul if not properly provoked toward animation—something I'm sure only you can accomplish. Besides, you look perfectly dressed for a drive on a warm day. You want only your bonnet and parasol. I will send for them now."

Ivy could find no further arguments to utter. Within moments her hat and parasol were sent for, and the innkeeper was instructed to tell her sisters where she had gone. Then the viscountess took her arm as they strolled toward the door of the inn.

Now that it had been decided, Ivy felt an excitement growing in her. To see the sun on fields, to feel the wind against her face, and to converse with clever people was suddenly all she wanted.

"You are so good to indulge us, Lady Quent. I am sure you will help me choose the best scene to paint."

"I don't know," Ivy said. "I'm not sure I will know what to look for, or what would make an appropriate subject."

"Your good sense will guide you. Besides, you need not worry. If we do not see a scene today that meets your approval, then we will simply go again tomorrow and the next day."

The young woman who had knocked on Ivy's chamber door earlier arrived just then with her hat and parasol. As Ivy took them, she cast a glance over her shoulder, wondering if she shouldn't go back to her chamber upstairs and attend to the tasks she had planned. Only then the viscountess led her out into the day. In that brilliant light, all worries fled like shadows from the sun. By the time the carriage started into motion, Ivy was laughing, all thoughts of writing letters and sorting receipts gone from her mind.

CHAPTER SEVENTEEN

*I*S SOMETHING AMISS, sweet brother?"

Eldyn looked up from the table in the apartment. Dawn had only just come, but he was already tallying figures in the church ledger. It was his purpose to make a good start on his work, for the lumenal was to be brief, and he wanted to be sure he would have time to speak to the rector.

"And why do you think something is wrong?"

"Because you look awfully serious."

Eldyn set down his pen. "Do not worry, dearest. I am very well."

He meant it. Today he would ask the rector what he needed to do to apply to the priesthood. He glanced at yesterday's broadsheet on the table; however, the words on the page did not rearrange themselves to form a new image. Instead, they kept their places, describing grim happenings in stark black and white. Riots in the Outlands, brigands on the roads, rumors of an army massing across the sea.

He pushed the broadsheet aside; worldly matters meant nothing to him now. A year ago, he had believed it was wealth that would redeem him, that if he could find a way to earn back the Garritt family fortune, he would at last be free of his father's shadow. He knew now how foolish that notion had been. For his father had always been obsessed with finding ways to reclaim the money he had squandered. And the only way Eldyn was ever going to free himself of that tainted legacy was to be something that Vandimeer Garritt never wanted his son to be—something he could never have been himself.

Sashie gave him a kiss on the cheek, and he smiled as he picked up his pen again. Soon both of their futures would be assured.

After a while he put away his work. He and Sashie took their breakfast, then she walked with him to the steps of Graychurch. She had told the verger she would mend any old altar coverings that might still have a use if given some attention. This surprised Eldyn, for he had never known her to have the ability to sew, but he said only that this seemed a pleasant task.

"It matters not if I find it pleasant," Sashie said. "Only that it pleases Him." She cast her eyes upward.

"Yet I hope you do not find it too bothersome," he said. "I am sure the verger doesn't want you to prick your fingers."

"If I spill a bit of blood, why should I regret it? Father Prestus says that a bit of blood given in the service of God is a thing that does not go unnoticed or unrewarded in Eternum."

Eldyn frowned. While at first he had found Sashie's fascination with the Church both understandable and charming, of late he was beginning to grow confounded with her behavior. It was time for his sister to start thinking about practical matters. She was still dressing in the most drab fashion, and she had yet to say two kind words to Mr. Fantharp. Eldyn was beginning to think it might be time he had a talk with this Father Prestus.

Then they passed through the doors of the church, and within the sanctuary of that vaulted space, his annoyance necessarily receded. Despite the brilliance of the morning outside, the smoke of candles made the air dim and rich within. Whispered voices murmured all around.

In a way, Eldyn was reminded of the theater in the moment before the curtain rose, when all the chatter and laughter ceased and the audience fell to a hush, anticipating what was to come. However, it was a different sort of pageantry that would be performed here, one not crafted from illusions. The power of God was not some glamour that faded when the play was over; it was an abiding and ever-present force.

Eldyn started to bid Sashie good-bye for the day, only at that moment he saw the rector hurrying toward them, huffing as he went.

"Good day, Mr. Garritt," he said. "And to you, Miss Garritt."

Eldyn suffered a pang of worry. "Good day, Father Gadby. Were you looking for me? I did not think I was late."

"No, Mr. Garritt. You are punctual as always. I am here for another reason." He affected an expression at once solemn and pleased. "I have heard that *he* will be arriving here at any moment."

For the weight he gave the word, one might have thought the rector was speaking of He who watched from above.

"Word just came from St. Galmuth's to expect the archdeacon," the rector went on, his voice rather high.

Now Eldyn understood Father Gadby's state of agitation. He started to reply, but at that moment the holy gloom of the old church was dispelled as the doors opened and the new light of morning flooded in. A figure all in red strode through, followed by a number of priests in white robes.

For all his months working at Graychurch, Eldyn had never seen the archdeacon; yet there was no mistaking that it was he who moved toward them now. Lemarck was younger than Eldyn would have guessed—no more than forty by his look—and his crimson cassock could not disguise a vigorous frame. He was tall and not unhandsome, but it was not his face that made him remarkable; rather it was his eyes. Once, when they still dwelled at the house at Bramberly, Eldyn had looked out the window after a particularly long and cold umbral, and he had seen shards of ice hanging from the eaves that were that clear, and that blue.

Eldyn expected the archdeacon to stride past them, trailing his retinue of white-frocked priests like a streamer of sparks following a crimson comet, only he paused to greet the rector. Then he turned, and that brilliant gaze fell upon Sashie and Eldyn.

Eldyn would have thought so piercing a look could only induce pain; instead, a warmness came over him, and for a moment he was encapsulated in a golden light. Sashie bowed her head, her cheeks coloring in that amber glow. Eldyn supposed the light of morning had touched the stained-glass windows above, but he could not lift his eyes to look; he could gaze only at the tall, imposing man before them.

The archdeacon inquired who these two beings were, and Father Gadby gave their names.

"So this is the fine young Mr. Garritt who is working miracles with our ledgers!" The archdeacon's voice was rich and clear, no doubt from the practice of many sermons. "You have done us a great service."

Eldyn could not have been more in awe if one of the marble saints had climbed down off his pedestal to bid him good day. "It is nothing remarkable what I do," he said, at once horrified and deeply pleased. "Your eminence," he added, unsure how one addressed an archdeacon.

"On the contrary, Mr. Garritt, our books were previously a daemon's playground. Father Gadby informs me that you have banished the devils and brought a most holy order to the ledgers." He smiled at Sashie, an expression like a flash of sun through dark clouds. "And this can only be Miss Garritt, who has so charitably aided our good verger."

"But, you . . . you know us?" she said, her blue eyes wide.

"The archdeacon is aware of all that happens in his church, Miss Garritt," the rector declaimed.

"It is not my church, Father Gadby. I merely keep it for others who are better and wiser than me."

That anyone could be better or wiser than this man was something Eldyn could not believe. He opened his mouth, wishing he had something to say to such a grand being. He could think of nothing. The priests standing behind the archdeacon fluttered like a flock of pigeons restless to fly.

"Well, there is much work for both of us to do," Lemarck said. "This world will never be perfect, but it is our task to bring it as close to perfection as we may. I am grateful God sent you to be our clerk, Mr. Garritt, but now I have my own, different sorts of ledgers I must go balance. Do come with us if you would, Father Gadby."

The archdeacon started to turn away, only at that moment a compulsion seized Eldyn. Without meaning to—or rather, as if he had no control over his tongue—he found himself speaking in a loud voice.

"I would be more than a clerk, sir. I would be a cleric in God's service!"

The archdeacon turned around. The rector and the priests stared at him. Sashie gasped, her eyes shining.

It was the rector who spoke first, his hands flitting about like a pair of overfed starlings. "That is a commendable sentiment, Mr. Garritt. I can see you have been moved by your service to the Church to give even more of yourself. Yet you must know that you are needed where you are."

Eldyn's cheeks felt hot. His wits and his words were his own again, but there was no point in retracting what he had uttered— or rather, what had been uttered through him by some unknown power—for it was true.

"I know, and I am grateful, Father. But I want to offer an even greater service—that is, to give my very being to the Church."

He cast a nervous look at Sashie and was steadied by her beatific smile.

"Well, this is unusual, Mr. Garritt," Father Gadby said, jowls waggling. "A young man typically comes to us upon the recommendation of a priest who knows him well and chooses to sponsor him. Then there is the matter of the portion that must be paid. It is a rather . . . that is, it is not inconsiderable. Then again, these things hardly matter, as you are too old to enter the priesthood, Mr. Garritt. Far too old!"

Eldyn stared, unable to speak, or hardly even to breathe. In an instant, all his hopes of leaving behind the sorrows and sins of the past, and of finding a bright future for himself and Sashie, vanished. It seemed a tall, brutish figure stood behind the rector, a sneer on his bearded face. However, it was not the specter of Vandimeer Garritt lurking there; it was only a statue of St. Marbeck the Hermit, half in shadow.

The rector nodded to him. "Now, if you'll permit us, Mr. Garritt, we have a great deal of business to attend to. I know you do as well."

Eldyn shrank back. It was all he could do to resist the instinct to throw the shadows around himself and run away through the church. Even so, the dimness thickened about him a bit, and he had to will away the gloom to keep it from coalescing around him.

"Forgive me," he murmured. "I only thought . . ."

He could manage no more, and he groped numbly for Sashie's hand to lead her away.

"Wait a moment," Lemarck said.

Did the archdeacon intend to further chastise him for his impertinence? Eldyn hardly required any further mortification! However, he could not disobey a command from that voice. He looked up at the taller man.

"Tell me, Mr. Garritt, why is it you wish to become a priest?"

Eldyn's instinct was to say nothing, or to profess that it had been a foolish whimsy. Only again a gold light fell upon him, and its warmth steadied him. Besides, how could speaking damn him any further?

He drew a breath. "I have not lived a perfect life, your eminence. I am . . . that is, I have often been lost in darkness. Much of that has been my own doing, I confess, and some has been due to the circumstances to which I was born."

His voice grew stronger as he spoke. He was aware of many eyes on him, but he kept his gaze on the face of an angel carved upon a nearby column.

"When I was young, my father would often take me along with him on his business dealings. I had little understanding of what he did, save that I knew the men he met with were cruel, brutish, and sometimes murderous. I did not question my father, or ask him why he did not do something else for a living. You see, as grim and violent and wretched as that world we dwelled in was, it was the only world I knew. Except then . . ."

The memory came upon him, almost as strong as if he was living it again.

"One day, on his way to one of these meetings, he left me at the steps before a building and told me to wait. I did not know what the building was that my father had left me outside. He had never taken me to such a place. I waited for him as I was told.

"Only then I heard the tolling of bells and the murmur of voices. I was drawn by these things and went up the steps to peer through the doors. Within I saw such things as I had never before imagined—such wondrous things! I saw a place of order and peace, and I saw men acting gently and benevolently. It was a church, of course. Only I didn't know that, for I had never seen such a thing before. I didn't know there could be a different world than the one I had been raised in, a world filled not with money and blood and anger, but with music and beauty and light.

"After that day, whenever I could steal away by myself, I would go to the entrance of a church. I would never venture inside, but I would watch through the doors as the priests performed their mysteries, and I would breathe in the scent of candles that came through the door. It was the knowledge that such a world existed, even if I could not enter it myself, that helped me to endure in the world in which I lived."

Eldyn heard murmurs go among the priests who stood behind the archdeacon. What was he thinking, to speak like this to such important men? He felt suddenly small and naked beneath the ponderous vaults of the church.

"I'm sorry," he murmured. "Please, forgive me." He turned away.

A strong, gentle hand on his arm halted him. "No, you should not be sorry, Mr. Garritt. Rather, you do us all a great service to remind us of what we can sometimes forget in the busy course of our daily work. There is a darkness, one that we must ever do battle with—one that even now seeks to undo all of the good of God's work in the world. And in this battle, we need every warrior we can find on the side of the light." The archdeacon smiled down at Eldyn. "No matter at what particular age they come to us."

It took Eldyn a moment to realize what had just happened. The rector's eyebrows rose up, and his hands gave a flutter, but he did not look displeased. On the contrary, delight shone on his round face. Eldyn glanced to his side and saw Sashie gazing at him with a look of such admiration that he felt his heart swell in his chest.

If there was any doubt yet remaining in his mind, it was erased as Archdeacon Lemarck exchanged brief words with Father Gadby. The rector would see that Eldyn's petition to enter the priesthood was submitted, and the archdeacon himself would be considered his sponsor. There were only some small details to sort out. Eldyn must work with the priests at Graychurch to achieve a basic understanding of the Testament before he could formally enter the priesthood. There was also the matter of the portion that must be granted to the Church upon his entry.

The Church maintained many ancient traditions, and the granting of a sum when a man entered the priesthood was such a custom; it was a symbol of his willingness to give up worldly things. Nor could the amount be waived for some and not for others, the archdeacon explained. *That* would not be just, as he was sure Eldyn certainly understood.

However, there were some funds set aside for such instances when a worthy man came from modest circumstances. Thus, the archdeacon said, the portion in Eldyn's case would be halved from the usual.

"I must depart now," Lemarck said. "Father Gadby, will you remain a moment with Mr. Garritt and make sure his questions are answered? You can meet us in the chapter house when you are done."

The archdeacon nodded to Sashie. "Good day, Miss Garritt. And, Mr. Garritt, I am sure I will see you again. Until then, remember that though the world in which you have dwelled has been filled with darkness and fraught with imperfections, that does not matter here. What you have done before you enter the Church is of no importance. For when you become a priest, it is as if you are a babe again, born anew into the world. Let that thought be a comfort to you as you await your entry into the Church."

With that the archdeacon left them, moving into the dimness of the nave like a crimson firebrand passing through the night, and the white-robed priests followed in his wake like pale embers.

"Well, a great honor has been granted to you, Mr. Garritt!" the rector said after a moment of silence. "I should be quite astounded by it all, save that nothing that *he* does astounds me anymore. That he is the savior of our Church, I am certain. And that he sees you as part of his plan I am certain as well, for he does nothing by chance."

Eldyn could only concede this was indeed astonishing. For the first time in his life a door had not been shut to him because of his past or circumstance; rather it had been opened, and soon he would step through.

Even as elation rose in him, it was weighed with concern. "Father Gadby, if you don't mind me asking, what is the usual portion that must be granted upon entry into the priesthood?"

"Well, it is usually a thousand regals. But it your case it will merely be five hundred, Mr. Garritt." He gave a reassuring smile. "I know that might seem a considerable sum, but with your diligence—and the matter of your age no longer a factor—I'm sure you will have it soon enough."

Eldyn nodded, but inwardly he cringed. Five hundred regals! Even halved, the portion was a greater sum than he had expected; all his prior calculations were awry. At his rate of earnings, it would be years before he could save enough for Sashie's portion and his own.

"Well, as you heard the archdeacon say, there is much work for us to do," Father Gadby said. "I will see you presently, Mr. Garritt. Good day, Miss Garritt."

"Oh, dear brother!" Sashie exclaimed when they were alone. "I always knew it was your wish to occupy yourself with good works, but I had no idea your intentions were of the very highest kind. There could be no better occupation than to give yourself to God's service, nor anything you could do that would make me love or admire you more!"

She threw her arms around him, plying him with kisses and words of praise. At last she took her leave, for the verger would be expecting her, and she moved away through the church.

Alone, Eldyn again looked at the serene angel upon the column nearby. As a child he had stood outside at the church of St. Andelthy, looking at the statue of the martyred saint beyond the iron fence, wishing he could know that same holy peace. Now he could finally have the chance—

—except for money. Five hundred regals! It might as well have been a thousand. Or ten thousand. The archdeacon said age did not matter. Yet it would if Eldyn died of old age and toil before he could save enough to enter the Church. No matter what Eldyn did, he could not wash himself of the sins of Vandimeer Garritt—not without five hundred regals, at any rate. And where was he going to get that? He was not going to earn it on the wages of a scrivener.

Yet what about the wages of an illusionist? Eldyn lifted his hand. His palm was empty. However, it took only the slightest thought, and suddenly he held a handful of thick gold coins.

Good God, what was he doing, working illusions in a church? Did he want to make his lot more impossible yet by compounding his sins? Except it didn't matter. *What you have done before you enter the Church is of no importance,* the archdeacon had said.

Eldyn gazed at the shining coins on his hand. He could not pay his portion to the Church in illusory regals. This was not a dark tavern where they wouldn't notice a silver penny going copper in the drawer. But there was another way that illusions could give him money—real, hard coin. The wage Madame Richelour had offered him was double his wage as a scrivener, and she had said that when he moved from understudy to performer, his wage would double again.

Nor would he have to give up his work clerking at Graychurch. For he could do one job by day and one by night. Yes, sleep would suffer, but that was a small sacrifice. He did a quick cipher in his head. With his combined wages, he could save all he needed for himself and Sashie in no more than a year's time. Nor did he have any reason to fear that working at the theater might irreparably tarnish his soul; the archdeacon himself had assured Eldyn it did not matter what he did before he entered the Church.

A thrill passed through Eldyn at the idea of standing on the stage with Dercy and crafting illusions together. True, he would have to give it all up when he entered the Church, but it would be easier then, for he would have had an entire year to experience life in the theater. No doubt by then he would be quite weary of it, and more than ready for the quiet life of a priest.

Until that time, he had coin to earn. He would go that very evening to the Theater of the Moon and tell Madame Richelour he would gladly and gratefully accept her offer.

Even as he decided this, a thought nagged at the back of his brain. Was there not something else he was supposed to do that night? His pleasantly distracted mind could not seize upon what the thing was. Besides, what could be more important than this?

Eldyn tossed the glittering coins into the air, and with a flash they became a flock of doves which fluttered up to the vaults above.

CHAPTER EIGHTEEN

THOUGH IT WAS not a far length down Marble Street from the Halls of Assembly to The Seventh Swan, Rafferdy's spirits had traveled to an entirely different realm by the time the carriage neared the inn. By then, all thoughts of Stouts and Magisters and White Ladies had gone from his head, replaced by more pleasant notions. Soon they would sit and have tea, or go for a stroll, while her combination of good wit and good sense amused and delighted him in a way politics never could.

Why had he ever conceived to deprive himself of Lady Quent's company? He supposed he had dreaded the pain of seeing her again; and indeed, he had suffered a severe discomfort upon their meeting at Lady Marsdel's house. However, as was so often the case, the anticipation of a hurt was far worse than the hurt itself, and like the sting of a thorn, it passed almost as soon as it was removed. He now had no qualms at all about seeing her.

The carriage came to a halt before the inn. Rafferdy did not wait for his driver to come around, but rather opened the door and bounded out, cane in hand.

"Will you be long, sir?" his man asked.

"I have no doubt of it!"

The driver bowed, and Rafferdy proceeded into the inn. He found himself in a parlor room that was appointed in a fine but staid manner. It was in every way respectable, and in every way dull. No doubt she would tell him how practical it was to stay in such a modest but sufficient place, and how both propriety and funds were preserved. However, he would make it his particular purpose today to induce her to admit how stuffy and boring it was! Amused already by this idea, he found the innkeeper and asked him to tell Lady Quent she had a visitor.

"I'm sorry, sir," the man said, "but her ladyship is not here at present."

Rafferdy shook his head. He had not accounted for this possibility, and thus it was difficult to comprehend. "Not here?"

"Just so, sir. She went out a little while ago."

"But when is she expected back?"

"I cannot say, sir. She didn't say. Though I do think she might be gone for a good while. She and her visitors were to take a drive in the country, I understand. And it's a fine day, isn't it?"

A fine day? No, not any longer. Rafferdy felt his spirits returning to their previous low state. That was foolish. He had come on a whim and could hardly fault her for not being here. Besides, he had their visit tomorrow to look forward to.

Yet that offered scant solace when he wished so much to see her *now*. Besides, who could she have gone for a drive with? Hadn't she mentioned that Mr. Quent was to be gone from the city? It couldn't be the Baydons. Mrs. Baydon would surely have included him in such a scheme.

"Should I tell her you called, sir?"

Rafferdy supposed there was no harm in letting her know he had come. In fact, it might make her think of him, and thus serve to remind her of their visit tomorrow. Not that *she* would ever forget such a thing.

"Yes, please do."

"And who should I tell her called?"

"My name is—"

"Mr. Rafferdy!"

Both he and the innkeeper looked up as a pretty young woman with an oval face flounced down the steps. It was the youngest of Mrs. Quent's sisters. She came to him directly, made a florid but comely curtsy, and then proceeded to seize his arm in a vigorous manner.

"Mr. Rafferdy, it is so marvelous to see you! You've been away so long. Why didn't you tell us you were coming? It is very rude of you to come so unexpectedly. And where is Mr. Garritt? Is he not with you?"

Rafferdy managed a smile. "If it is rude of me to come unexpectedly, Miss Lily, would it not have been twice as rude to bring a guest?"

"No, it would have been just as rude, but far more considerate."

"Well, I will see if he can be brought tomorrow."

"But you must bring him! Do not even think to come to call tomorrow without Mr. Garritt."

These words rankled. Was he not of any value himself, that he must bring another with him to earn his entry? He maintained his smile. "Where is your sister today?"

"Rose? She's upstairs, of course."

"I don't mean Miss Lockwell. Rather, I am referring to Lady Quent."

Lily's face lit up. "Oh, she is out with the viscountess!"

Rafferdy was not astonished by anything that went on in In-varel these days, but these words did surprise him. "You mean Lady Crayford?"

Lily nodded. "Yes, Ivy attended the viscountess's party last night. Then this morning Lady Crayford and some of her companions came to take Ivy for a drive in the country."

"Her companions? Who was with her?"

A hint of a frown clouded Lily's otherwise exuberant expression. "I don't know. Rose and I were away at the time. I only heard it from one of the maids. I do so wish I could have gone with them." She sighed, but then quickly brightened. "Well, I'm sure I'll be able to go the next time. No doubt Lady Crayford will take Ivy on many drives in the country. Ivy and the viscountess are the very best of friends now."

The best of friends? Rafferdy didn't know what to think of this. He supposed he should be happy that Ivy had made such a high and valuable connection. In the course of barely a month she had been made a lady and had been welcomed into the most fashionable circles of society in the city. Yes, he should be very happy for her.

But it was all he could do to keep some vestige of a smile upon his face. "Very well, I will see you tomorrow, Miss Lily, and I will look forward to hearing about your sister's drive in the country."

"Yes, Rose and I will be very glad to see you. And Mr. Garritt, of course. I'm sure we will have a grand time. Only you shouldn't expect Ivy to be here. The maid told me that the viscountess said they would all be going out for a drive again tomorrow to find more pretty scenes to paint. Lady Crayford is a very accomplished artist, you know."

Rafferdy took a step back, as if struck a blow. "But tomorrow—are you sure?"

Lily gave an emphatic nod. "Very sure. If Ivy had the chance to go for a drive with the viscountess, could you imagine her doing otherwise?"

The dim interior of the inn had suddenly grown oppressive and cloying. It was difficult to breathe.

"Excuse me," he said, forcing the words through clenched teeth. "There is . . . I must go see to something now."

"Are you going to see Mr. Garritt, you mean?"

He stared at her stupidly. "Mr. Garritt?"

"Yes, to tell him he must come with you to see us tomorrow."

Rafferdy was beyond words. Instead he made a stiff bow. Then he put on his hat, gripped his cane, and fled out the door.

HIS CARRIAGE WAS not before the inn. However, that was to be expected; he had told the driver he would be a while, and the man had no doubt gone to find a pint to pass the time.

It was just as well. Rafferdy could not sit still; he needed to move. Cane in hand, he walked along Marble Street, his mind awhirl. There had to be some mistake. He could not believe Mrs. Quent would either forget or disregard a prior commitment. It was entirely against her character. Mrs. Quent would never do such a thing.

But what of Lady Quent? It was impossible to separate a person from their circumstances. One's position influenced everything that one perceived or thought or said. You could take the same infant and place him in the house of a chimney sweep or a lord, and by the time he was a man he would be a chimney sweep or a lord himself. Who was to say, just because Mrs. Quent would not do such a thing, that *Lady* Quent would not do it without equivocation?

In any case, why should she forgo such an outing with a viscountess to endure a visit with him? What had he ever been able to offer her other than the false hint of a promise he never had the power to make or to keep? Mr. Quent had offered her something of real value. Now so had Lady Crayford. What use was Rafferdy to her anymore—if indeed he had ever been any?

"Hey now, watch where you're going!" a man called out.

Rafferdy snapped his head up, for he had been gazing at the

ground as he went. Now he saw pale spires rising up before him; he had walked nearly all the way back to the Halls of Assembly.

He looked around, fearing he was about to collide with someone. However, the shouted admonition had not been for him. Ahead, a group of people lurched and stumbled in all directions as a man moved hurriedly down the side of the street, for if they had not gotten out of his path it was certain he would have careened into them. The man's coat of blue velvet was cut in the latest mode, and he held the brim of his hat with a gloved hand so that it shadowed his face.

The man made a quick turn to avoid a boy who was hawking a stack of broadsheets. As he did, he clipped a plump woman in the gray dress of a servant, knocking the basket from her hands and sending apricots rolling across the cobbles. She gave a cry as she lost her balance, and she reached for him to keep herself aright, clasping at his free hand.

He gave his right arm a violent shake, freeing himself of her grasp, then dashed into Marble Street. At that moment a carriage was racing up the street. The driver cried out, pulling on the reins. The hooves of the horses struck visible sparks, and the wheels made a horrible din. Rafferdy thought the carriage would surely run down the man in the blue coat as the other flung up his right hand in a warding gesture.

Rafferdy drew in a breath of astonishment, and not only because the carriage managed to swerve and just avoid striking the fellow. The plump woman must have stripped off his glove when she grasped at his hand, for it was bare now, and as he held it before him Rafferdy saw the black, angular lines that marked the palm.

In an instant it was over. The carriage rattled down the street; people continued on their way as the woman in gray retrieved her basket. There was a flicker of blue in the entrance of a narrow lane across Marble Street. Rafferdy stared, mouth agape.

Then, making sure no more carriages were coming, he hurried across Marble Street.

Rafferdy stepped into the lane where he had seen the man in

the blue coat vanish. Why he was doing this, he could not entirely fathom. After seeing the body of the traitor on the opening day of Assembly, the last thing he wished for was to be reminded of the awful encounter. However, the markings he had glimpsed on the corpse's hand that day were the same as those he had just seen on the palm of the man in the blue coat. He was certain of it. Only what did the marks signify? They reminded him of some of the symbols he had seen in the ancient book of magick at Mr. Bennick's house.

The lane curved past a row of brick houses that quickly became drab as he left behind the bustle of Marble Street. It occurred to him that what he was doing was far from prudent. The man in the blue coat was likely a rebel and a murderer. Or perhaps he was something worse. Rafferdy would never forget how gray fluid had seeped from the corpse's neck that day. A shiver crawled across his skin. All the same he kept moving, wondering where such a being might be going in so great a hurry.

He reached an intersection with another lane, and he looked both ways. Each direction was devoid of people. All he could hear was the muted rumble of Marble Street and the noise of his own heart.

Then he caught it—the echo of footsteps receding down the lane to his left. Rafferdy started in that direction, increasing his pace as he went until he was nearly at a run. He turned a corner just in time to see a figure in blue pass between two buildings and vanish into the dimness of an alleyway. Gripping his cane, Rafferdy pursued.

"Stop!" a gruff voice called out.

Rafferdy was so startled that he could only obey. He turned around. A hulking man had just rounded the corner and now moved toward Rafferdy with swift strides, a pair of redcrests marching behind him.

"Stay right there," the man growled as he approached.

He was clad in various shades of gray, and his clothes were of a fine, even rich, cut. But there was nothing fine about the cut of the man who inhabited them. He had a thick, bullish neck, over-sized hands, and a deeply cragged brow. In moments he was upon Rafferdy.

"Mr. Moorkirk!" Rafferdy exclaimed.

The other's eyes were small and set close together, but there was a keenness to them. They flicked down toward Rafferdy's hands.

"Hand me your cane."

Again Rafferdy was too astonished to do anything but comply. He held out his cane, and it was jerked from his hand.

"Now remove your gloves."

Rafferdy shook his head, mute with a sudden dread. The soldiers reached for the hilts of their swords. Moorkirk's expression darkened into a glower of menace.

"I said remove your gloves, Mr. Rafferdy!"

A sick feeling stirred in Rafferdy's stomach as at last he understood. He fumbled with his kidskin gloves, tugging and jerking at the fingers as quickly as he could. First one glove then the other fell to the street. Moorkirk snatched Rafferdy's right hand, turning it over so quickly that Rafferdy experienced a sharp pain. This action was repeated with the left hand. For a moment all of them were still as stone.

Moorkirk let out a breath. The soldiers released their swords.

"I saw him," Rafferdy managed to utter. It was difficult to draw a breath.

Moorkirk glared at him. "Who did you see?"

"The man in the blue coat. You were following him, weren't you? He had marks on his hand like the—like the other did at Assembly. I saw him go between those two buildings. It was just a minute ago."

He pointed to the place where the man in blue had vanished. Moorkirk studied him for a long moment; Rafferdy willed himself not to flinch or look away.

The larger man glanced at the soldiers. "Go," he said.

At once the two redcrests dashed down the street and headed into the mouth of the alley.

Moorkirk returned his gaze to Rafferdy. "So, once again when I am investigating one of *them* I come upon *you* as well, Mr. Rafferdy. It is a curious thing."

Rafferdy moistened his lips. "I saw him on Marble Street. He ran into a woman, and he must have lost his glove, because I saw the palm of his hand. Then he was nearly run over by a carriage. Only he wasn't." Rafferdy knew he was babbling, but he could not stop himself. He finished describing how he had followed the man in the blue coat to this lane.

Moorkirk raised a dark eyebrow. "You followed him, Mr. Rafferdy? Why would you do such a thing, knowing what they are?"

A chill coursed through Rafferdy. "They? You mean there are more of them—the men with gray blood?"

Moorkirk seemed to think for a moment. "Yes," he said in a low voice.

"And they all have that same symbol on their hands?"

"The ones we have found all bear the same markings, yes. Nor can I believe it is chance that it has become popular fashion to wear gloves just when such men have appeared in the city. Gloves just like you were wearing."

Rafferdy blinked, then his wits cleared a bit. It was one thing to be suspected of being a traitor to the kingdom; it was another thing altogether to be accused of following a mode rather than setting it.

"I assure you, I have been wearing gloves since well before it became popular to do so!"

"Have you indeed?"

Some of Rafferdy's indignation receded. He realized that statement might not serve to lessen any cloud of suspicion that lingered over him.

"Yes, I have. However, it has become too popular for my taste now. I am sure I will not wear gloves again."

Moorkirk nodded. "You would do well to adhere to that, Mr. Rafferdy."

"I will. As for that man, I was only following him out of curiosity. I can assure you that I have nothing to do with his sort."

"That's what *she* said."

He did not need to say her name. Rafferdy knew Moorkirk could only be referring to his mistress, Lady Shayde.

"I have never known her to be wrong," the larger man went on. "All the same, should you see another one of these sort of men, I would advise you not to follow."

Rafferdy shook his head. "What should I do?"

"You should go the other way. For if I catch you in the vicinity of one of them again, I might have to believe that you are indeed involved with them—no matter what she says. I think you understand me. And I know I do not need to remind you to speak of this to no one." He held out the cane. "Consider it our secret, Mr. Rafferdy."

Rafferdy took the cane in a numb hand. Moorkirk moved past him, following the soldiers into the alley.

Blue shadows crept down the lane, and Rafferdy shivered. God, but he needed a cup of punch. Fortunately, the sun was already sinking, and it would not be long until he was to meet Eldyn Garritt at tavern.

And if he arrived there early, and had a pot before Garritt arrived—well, that could be his secret as well.

AS IT TURNED out, he was not so very early to the Sword and Leaf.

By the time he found his driver and returned to Warwent Square, he was exhausted. He laid down to rest for a few minutes, and he fell into a fitful sleep, one inhabited by awful dreams. In one of them, the Lady Shayde came to him and asked to examine him. She pricked his finger with a needle, and instead of blood a colorless fluid oozed out of the wound.

So troubling was the dream that he was half tempted to stab his own finger when he rose to make sure it resulted in crimson. Upon glancing in the mirror and seeing the red lines that marked the whites of his eyes, such a test was rendered unnecessary.

Given the hour, his man said he had time to take supper. However, Rafferdy was without appetite. Besides, his man had to be mistaken, for it was already dark outside. Instead, he put on his coat, called for his driver, and proceeded to the Sword and Leaf.

As Rafferdy entered the tavern, the doorman gave him a sharp look.

"You're early," he said.

How the doorman could presume to know when he had intended to arrive, Rafferdy did not know or care. He did not reply, and instead made his way back to their usual booth in the rear corner.

It was empty. He asked the tavern keep the time and discovered that, despite the thick of night outside, it was in fact not yet the appointed hour of his meeting. That was good, as it would give Rafferdy a chance to get a drink in him—something much needed after the day's events. He ordered a pot of punch, along with lemons and sugar, and when it arrived fixed himself a cup. He did his best to drink it slowly, but by the time it was drained there was no sign of Eldyn Garritt, so he made himself another cup. A sensation began to spread through him that, while not exactly cheerful or pleasant, was at least satisfyingly numb.

"Time for another pot, then?"

"Garritt!" he exclaimed. "Where have you been?"

As he looked up, he saw that it was not his friend, but rather the tavern keep. Rafferdy stared a moment, then nodded. To his surprise the first pot was drained, and he didn't want Garritt to know he had drunk a whole pot of punch without him.

The tavern keeper returned. As tempted as Rafferdy was to fix another cup, he did not. Every time the door of the tavern opened he looked up, but on each occasion it was someone other than his friend who stepped through. His mouth felt dry and his head began to hurt as his numbness dissipated. When the tavern keep passed by, Rafferdy again asked what the hour was.

"It's two hours past moonrise, sir." He glanced at the still-full pot on the table. "Is there someone you're waiting for?"

Rafferdy drew in a breath. "No, it's only myself tonight. I just didn't want to drink too quickly."

The tavern keeper laughed. "Well, you're a noble fellow! But not too noble, I hope. Otherwise, I fear you're in the wrong place, and there's a church down the street." He winked at Rafferdy, then went on his way.

Rafferdy stared at the pot of punch. What use was there in saving it? Now that he had sobered up a bit, it was all too clear. In all their prior meetings here, Garritt had never been tardy. Which could only mean one thing.

He wasn't coming tonight.

He must have forgotten their appointment. Except that wouldn't be like Garritt, who always had a pen with him and seemed to write everything down. Rather, there must have been something more pleasant or enticing to attend to. For hadn't Garritt looked uncharacteristically well of late?

Yes, there was something he had found that was giving him great pleasure—a pretty young woman, or a merry new gang of friends. But why had he not mentioned it? Did he fear his new acquaintances were too low to be introduced to Rafferdy?

Or was it that, with fine new friends, he had no need of a dull old one?

That was the more likely explanation. What did Rafferdy have to offer except witless talk of new coats and dreary complaints about Assembly? Garritt could have no use for such things; and so, just like Lady Quent, he had found more worthwhile companions.

And what did Rafferdy have? Coats and canes and a dwindling number of invitations to parties he never attended. He had seen the awful result of the power that some men wielded over others, and he had never wanted any part of it. It had always been his intention to be utterly harmless. Yet in so doing, he could only concede that he had also made himself irrelevant.

Or was it even worse than that?

The man who does the greatest harm is the man who does nothing at all, Mrs. Baydon had told him by the sphinx in Lady Marsdel's parlor.

What solace might he have been able to offer Lady Quent had he not selfishly avoided her? What assistance might he have been able to give Eldyn Garritt when he was struggling to find some business to support himself and his sister? Rafferdy would never know. And was it any wonder, now that both of them had risen in life, that they would leave behind one who had never offered to lift them up?

No, it could only be expected. So here he was, alone in a dank tavern. This was what all his efforts to be harmless had won him. Well, if he was here, he might as well get drunk.

Rafferdy reached for the pot of punch. Only then he halted, staring at the ring on his right hand. A spark glimmered within the blue gem.

"Good evening, Mr. Rafferdy!"

Rafferdy looked up to see a man with a plain yet cheerful face and a tall crown of frizzy hair.

"Lord Coulten!" he said, astonished. But why should he be surprised? Lord Coulten had said he was going to meet with his magician friends tonight. "Don't you usually come in the back door?"

"Indeed, I do. But I confess, you had mentioned you had an appointment tonight, and I hoped it might be here, as I know you have come to this tavern before."

Rafferdy shook his head; it felt dull from the punch. "You hoped to find me here?" Before he could say anything more, his House ring flashed again. At the same time he caught a blue glint behind Lord Coulten.

"I see yours is a ring of good quality," Lord Coulten said with a grin. "It detects when there is another of the same House nearby. Lord Eubrey is descended of House Gauldren as well."

Only then did Rafferdy see that Lord Coulten had a companion. He was a handsome young man with dark hair. Rafferdy recognized him as one of the wigless young men Lord Coulten often sat with at Assembly.

Lord Eubrey smiled and nodded. "It is good to meet you, Mr. Rafferdy. Lord Coulten has told me much about you. And it seems that we are cousins of a sort." He held up his own ring, which glittered blue like Rafferdy's.

Rafferdy rose—a bit unsteadily—to give a bow of greeting. He hoped he did not appear as dreadful as he felt; he gave his coat a tug to straighten it.

"I'm afraid we cannot tarry," Lord Coulten said. He glanced at his companion. "Lord Eubrey was late returning from an outing today, so we must be off to our meeting. Only I see you are unaccompanied at present. Is your appointment for the evening already over, then?"

Rafferdy glanced at the pot of punch. "Yes," he said. "Yes, it is."

Lord Coulten and Lord Eubrey exchanged a look, and each nodded.

"Then perhaps we could entice you to join us at our meeting tonight," Lord Eubrey said. "Our society is always looking for men of quality, wit, and . . . talent." His gaze moved to Rafferdy's ring.

Lord Coulten laughed. "Why, that's a capital idea. What do you say, Rafferdy—will you come with us? You need never come again if you don't find our little society to your liking."

Rafferdy opened his mouth to offer a polite refusal. He had never asked to be descended from one of the seven Old Houses, nor had he asked for this awful magician's ring.

Of course, he had never asked to be the son of a lord either, yet that did not mean he could avoid becoming one someday. Besides, Lady Quent and Eldyn Garritt had both found new things with which to occupy themselves. Why should he not have something as well? As he thought this, Rafferdy recalled the sensation he had experienced when he used magick to open the locked door at Assembly. It had been a warm and satisfying feeling, even better than that imparted by rum or whiskey.

"I'll come," he said, astonished to hear himself say the words. Yet as he did, a new certainty filled him. It was time to stop being harmless, and to start making something of himself. "I'll come with you to your meeting."

"Excellent!" Lord Coulten exclaimed. "I am very glad to hear it, Mr. Rafferdy. But we had best hurry. We do not want to be late!"

With that, Lord Coulten and Lord Eubrey made their way to

the back of the tavern. Rafferdy followed after, leaving the full pot of punch on the table. They entered the dank corridor Rafferdy had investigated before and came to a halt before the iron-bound door at the end of the passage. Lord Coulten reached out to grip the iron handle.

"But it is only a blank wall on the other side!" Rafferdy exclaimed.

He saw both young men grin in the dimness.

"So you have tried the door yourself," Lord Coulten said. "I see you have already been curious about us."

Rafferdy suffered a pang of chagrin, but Lord Eubrey laughed warmly.

"Do not worry, Mr. Rafferdy. We think no less of you for it. On the contrary, such curiosity will serve you very well beyond this door."

Before Rafferdy could say anything more, Lord Coulten gripped the iron handle. As he did, the ring on his right hand flashed crimson, and a murmuring sound rose on the air.

It was Lord Coulten. He was chanting in a low voice. Lord Eubrey had joined him. Rafferdy couldn't understand what they were saying, but he recognized a few words here and there. They were speaking in the tongue of magick—a language that, Mr. Bennick had once told him, was older than mankind itself.

The incantation ceased. Two blue sparks had joined the red. All of their rings were shining now.

"The way is ready," Lord Eubrey said.

And Lord Coulten opened the door.

CHAPTER NINETEEN

RONZE ORBS SPUN and crystalline spheres turned as Ivy worked the various handles and knobs of the celestial globe. Her hands began to ache, and a stiffness crept up the back of her neck so that her head throbbed. If only she was as skilled at using the globe as her father had been! As a girl, she used to watch in fascination as he manipulated its gears and workings.

Look, Ivy, I have the whole of the heavens right here in my study, he would say, and she would gaze at the rotating spheres until her head grew light and it felt as if she were whirling among the planets herself. Now she wished that, instead of dreaming, she had paid better attention.

Ivy bit her lip as she adjusted a lever. Some months ago, she had used the celestial globe to solve a riddle her father had left for her, and in so doing had discovered the key to the house on Durrow Street in a hidden compartment. Now it was another kind of riddle she was trying to solve.

She gave a knob a quarter turn, and a yellowish ball suspended at the end of a brass arm moved a corresponding amount. The word *Loerus* was engraved on the ball. Loerus was one of the eleven planets—or rather, one of the twelve, now that the red planet, Cerephus, had returned to view.

Ivy took up a thin metal rod and used it to measure a line between the yellow ball and the great sphere of crystal in the center of the globe. Fine dots were etched on the glass, and next to each was a name. She peered at the sphere, reading the name next to the point where the rod had touched it.

Murgon Prime.

Yes, that made sense for Murgon Prime was the brightest star in the constellation Murgon. Ivy moved around the globe. She located the brass circle that represented the horizon, then read the names etched on the glass sphere that were just above the brass line. Andareon. Rikus. Castani.

Dalavar.

A thrill passed through her. She turned and picked up a piece of paper from the table. It was the sheet on which she had transcribed the second entry that had appeared in her father's journal. *Loerus in Murgon,* the entry had begun. *Dalavar Rising.*

She was right. Instead of dating the entries in the journal in the usual fashion, he had described key features in the heavens. How like her father, to have done something in such an arcane manner! Or had there been a greater purpose to it than mere cleverness or amusement?

Again she looked at the celestial globe, counting the tick marks around the central brass ring to determine the position of the sun and the moon. Then she went back to the table and picked up the almanac she had brought with her to the house. She turned the pages, going from back to front, searching for the day when the positions of the sun and moon were the same as those she had read from the globe. If she could find them, then she would know on what day he had written the entry. The idea had come to her that morning just as she woke, and so she had left The Seventh Swan after breakfast and had gone directly to Durrow Street.

And there it was, close to the start of the almanac, almost exactly ten years ago. That was the day he had written about how the key to Tyberion—whatever it was—had gone missing.

Ivy wished she could recall the star positions he had written for the first entry she had found in the journal. If so, she could know how much time had passed between the writings. However, she could not remember, and she had not copied that entry.

Yet she was sure more messages from her father would appear. It was highly unlikely she had happened to open the journal just when the only two entries in it had become visible. Thus logic suggested that more entries would appear over time; she had only to make sure to check the journal regularly, and she was sure to see them.

But what was the purpose of the enchantment that he had placed upon the journal? What scheme was there to the manner in which the writings showed themselves? She could not believe it was random or without order. *That* would not be like her father at all.

She would have to think more about it later. Mr. Rafferdy would be coming to call that afternoon. Wondering how long the day was to be, she turned the almanac's pages to the table for the present month. She saw it was only to be a middling lumenal today, which meant she had better return to the inn. She started to close the almanac—

—then halted as an entry caught her eye. It was yesterday's listing. Slowly, making sure she was not in error, she turned back to the listing from ten years ago.

No, she was not mistaken. The positions noted for the sun and moon were the same for both entries. There was no possible way it could be chance. The entry in the journal had appeared when certain objects in the heavens were arranged in exactly the same way as when it had been written ten years ago.

Ivy marveled at the nature of this enchantment. Only why had her father gone to such trouble? Why not simply let her read all the entries in the journal at once, in the order he had written them?

There was no time to speculate. Mr. Rafferdy had promised to come just after midday, which meant she needed to proceed back to the inn at once. She left her father's study, being sure to lock the door and take the key. This was the only room the builder had been instructed to leave untouched. The chamber that held the Eye of Ran-Yahgren lay behind it, and *that* was a secret of the house she had no wish for Mr. Barbridge to uncover.

She descended the staircase to the front hall. It was quiet and dim, the drapes pulled shut and the new furniture covered in cloths. The workmen were gone. After months of labor, all was ready. As soon as Mr. Quent came back to the city, they would leave the inn and return to Durrow Street.

Ivy was more than ready. They had only dwelled in the house a short time, but even in that little while it had become her home. She longed to return to it—to all the little things that reminded her of her father. She was tempted to pull the sheets from the furniture, to throw open the drapes, and to linger awhile.

There was no time. She cast one fond look at the hall, then hurried out into the late morning.

B Y THE TIME the bells of a church near the inn sounded the start of the third farthing, they were ready.

Ivy had arranged for an extra chair to be placed in the little sitting room, so there was space for all of them in the event Mr. Rafferdy brought Mr. Garritt with him, and a maid had just delivered the tea as well as a plate of biscuits and sandwiches. Rose perched on the sofa, afraid to move for fear of mussing her dress, while Lily peered out the window.

"Blow me down, the sun is past the yardarm," she said. "If they're late, I'll make those scalawags walk the plank!"

"I'm sure a plank won't be necessary," Ivy said in response to Rose's look of alarm.

After a quarter of an hour had passed, it was clear their caller was indeed late. Not that this was entirely out of character. In Ivy's experience, Mr. Rafferdy's notion of time was somewhat flexible.

After another quarter hour the tea was sent back, to be replaced with a hot pot. Lily had grown tired of watching out the window and fidgeted with the ribbons on her dress. Rose remained frozen on the sofa.

By the time the old rosewood clock struck an hour past midday, the tea had been drunk, and the tray was devoid of a large portion of its biscuits and sandwiches. Rose at last got up from the sofa, but as she did she caught the pocket of her dress on the arm, tearing it. She burst into tears. Ivy went to comfort her, and assured her the damage could be easily repaired.

"Where can they be?" Lily said, pacing now before the window, apparently too perturbed to bother with speaking like a seaman any longer. "I hope they don't think we're going to send for more biscuits!"

Whether more biscuits were needed was the least of Ivy's worries. She hoped something ill had not happened to keep Mr. Rafferdy away. "Perhaps he forgot about our appointment," she said.

"That can't be," Lily said. "I reminded him about it just yesterday."

Ivy stared at her. "Yesterday? What do you mean?"

"Avast!" Lily exclaimed. "I suppose I completely forgot to tell you."

"To tell me what?"

"About how Mr. Rafferdy came here yesterday. He had stopped in to see if by chance you were to be found, but I told him that you were out with the viscountess, and how you two had become the best of friends."

Ivy stood, aghast at these words. "Lily, that was hardly a truthful thing to say! I have only just met Lady Crayford."

"So? How long you've known each other doesn't mean anything. You can fall in love with just a glance—all the books I've read agree that you can. And isn't friendship a sort of love?" Lily flopped onto the sofa. "Besides, last night you could hardly stop talking about your drive in the country. It was all Lady Crayford this and Colonel Daubrent that!"

Ivy could not deny that she had greatly enjoyed the outing yesterday. That anyone was more well read or could make more interesting observations than Lady Crayford was inconceivable, and her brother was an expert driver. As for their friend, Lord Eubrey was such a wit that soon even the stoic colonel was laughing.

No less than in the lively company, Ivy had delighted in the sight of the green hills and the feel of wind and sun on her face. They had paused to examine various prospects and vistas, to determine which ones were worthy of the Lady Crayford's brush. To Ivy every one of them was, and the viscountess declared that, while she had felt such bucolic scenes no longer held anything of interest to her, in Ivy's eyes she could apprehend a sublime beauty she had never before seen in them. She declared she would return to the country with her paints and canvas as soon as possible.

As evening fell, Ivy had returned to the inn filled with a sort of excitement she had not felt since her time in the West Country. After describing the day's events to her sisters, she had proceeded to write a lengthy letter to Mr. Quent, telling him all about her experiences.

"Well, I wish you had told me about Mr. Rafferdy's visit," Ivy said. "Yet if you spoke to him about our plan for today, he couldn't have forgotten."

"I should say not! Indeed, I was very adamant when I told him he had to come even if you weren't here."

Ivy shook her head. "What do you mean if I wasn't here?"

"Well, the maid told me that the viscountess said she would most likely need you again today."

A horror began to blossom within Ivy. "And you told Mr. Rafferdy this?"

"Of course! I told him that he must still come with Mr. Garritt even if you wouldn't be here." Lily frowned. "Really, Ivy, I'm very surprised you didn't go out again with the viscountess today. Everything I've read says that best friends can't bear to be apart from each other for even a short while. I'm sure if the viscountess were *my* friend, I should not abandon her so!"

At last Ivy apprehended the whole truth. Because of Lily's thoughtless words, he could only have come to the conclusion that she had chosen to cast aside their prior plans in favor of the chance to go with the viscountess. How callous he must think her!

"I must go to him at once," she said. "I must offer him my sincerest apology. He can only believe I had broken our engagement."

Lily shook her head. "Why should you apologize? It's he who should be sorry for not coming. After all, I told him Rose and I were still going to be here today. It was very rude of him not to come!"

Ivy did not answer. It was clear that Lily was insensible to the harm she had caused, and Ivy did not have the time or desire to explain it now. She went to retrieve her cloak and bonnet, then returned to the sitting room. Lily was nowhere to be seen, and the door to the room she shared with Rose was shut. Rose stood by the window, Miss Mew in her arms.

"Do you think Mr. Rafferdy will be very angry with us?" Rose said, her brown eyes still bright with tears.

Despite her distressed state, Ivy managed a smile for her sister. "No, not *very* angry. Not when I explain what happened."

There was no time to have Lawden ready the cabriolet, so instead Ivy asked the innkeeper to summon a hack cab. There was one right outside the inn, and Ivy instructed the driver to take her to Warwent Square. She hoped she would find Mr. Rafferdy at home, but if not, she would wait for him until he returned.

Marble Street was crowded that day. The carriage moved slowly, and after only a little way it came to a halt. Ivy opened the window and leaned out to see what was causing the delay. There seemed to be some commotion ahead, but she could not see what the problem was, for a large fountain decorated with marble sirens and dolphins blocked her view. She leaned farther out the window.

One of the dolphins slapped the water in the fountain with its tail. The sirens turned their heads to avoid the resulting spray. One of them looked at Ivy and smiled.

Ivy clutched the edge of the carriage door, staring at the stone figures frolicking amid the splashing water. Then a flicker of black caught her eye as *he* stepped from behind the fountain. His black mask was wrought in a grim expression.

Go to Durrow Street, he said. Though as always his mask did not move, and the voice sounded not in her ears, but in her mind.

"To Durrow Street?" she managed to whisper. "Why?"

You will find the Black Stork there. His time grows short. You must go to him while you can.

"The Black Stork?" So she had been right in thinking it was not the man in the mask. "But then who is he?" she said aloud.

Another splash rose up from the fountain, and when the spray cleared he was gone. The sirens and dolphins perched above the water, motionless once more. The hack cab lurched back into motion.

Ivy gazed for a moment at the place where the man in the mask had stood. Then she pounded on the roof of the carriage. Again it came to a halt, and in a moment the driver stood outside the door.

"What is it, madam? The jam's finally cleared in the street."

"You must turn around," she said, trying to keep her voice steady.

"Turn around? But that's not the way to Warwent Square, madam."

"I know. I'm sorry to have given you the wrong direction, but I need you to take me somewhere else."

"As you wish, madam. Where is it I should drive?"

Ivy swallowed, and a feeling rose in her that was at once anticipation and dread. "To Durrow Street," she said.

ℐT TOOK LITTLE more than a quarter of an hour. Ivy paid the driver his fee, then pushed through the iron gate into the garden before the house. She did not know what she expected to see. The last time the man in the peculiar black garb had told her to come here, the magicians of the Vigilant Order of the Silver Eye had been on their way to seize the Eye of Ran-Yahgren. Had someone come now to try the same—perhaps some of those other magicians the man in the mask had spoken of the last time he appeared to her?

It occurred to her this was foolish. If there were magicians here, what would she do against them? Besides, the house had its own defenses; Mr. Rafferdy had awakened them. And had she not told herself that she was done with the strange man and his cryptic warnings?

Yet her father had said in his letter to listen to him.

Ivy moved farther into the garden. It was quiet except for a faint hiss through the leaves of the twisted hawthorns. She moved among the trees and began a circuit around the house, looking for any sign of the one she was supposed to meet with.

She had nearly completed her circle around the house when she came upon a dark heap in the grass. It lay beside a bush off the north side of the house. In life, its wings would have spanned as wide as her outstretched arms. Now they were crumpled beneath its body like black rags. Ants crawled across bedraggled feathers; its eyes were small, eaten pits.

Ivy clapped a hand to her mouth. Was this what the man in the mask had meant for her to find? If so, it was a strange and horrid jest. She had felt badly at depriving the storks of their home. Now it seemed that, ill or injured, one of them had tried to return here to its previous roost to find safe haven. Only the window had been repaired; it could not get in. By the odor, the bird had perished several days ago.

A black stork brings black luck, Mrs. Seenly had once said.

But for whom? Surely the creature's own fate had not been a lucky one. Nor did she comprehend how the masked man had known about the incident with the storks, or why he had wanted her to see this.

Well, Ivy didn't care what his reason was. Whoever the man in the mask was, he was no one she wanted to have anything to do with again. She would go back to the inn and write a note to Mr. Barbridge, asking him to send one of his men to see to the poor creature. She would request that it be given a decent burial here in the north garden. That much, at least, she owed it. Resolved, she made her way back around to the front of the house.

And stopped.

In the street, beyond the iron gate, was a carriage. It was not a hack cab. Instead, its wood was a glossy black decorated with gilded trim, and before it stood four dappled grays.

Something moved in the window of the carriage. It was a thin hand, beckoning to her. A dread descended over Ivy. She wanted to turn, to flee into the house, like the stork searching for a haven.

Again the hand beckoned, and she passed through the gate to approach the carriage. The driver stepped down from his bench.

He tipped his hat to Ivy, then opened the carriage door. In the dimness within she caught a glimpse of something as withered and crumpled as the bird lying in the garden.

"Can you help me?" came a dry voice.

At first Ivy thought the words were directed at her, and a revulsion seized her. But it was the young driver who responded. He reached into the carriage and with strong, sure motions that suggested prior practice, helped a man through the door and down the step.

Now a new kind of horror came over Ivy, but it was at once tinged with sorrow and pity. When she had seen him last year, he had been an older gentleman on the verge of corpulence. Now he appeared ancient rather than old, and thin—so terribly thin. He seemed lost within his dark suit and hat, like a child who had donned a grown man's clothes for amusement.

With the driver's help, he crossed the short distance to Ivy in shuffling steps. Deep grooves etched his face.

"Lord Rafferdy!" she uttered at last.

He smiled—and despite the ruin of his face, she saw something of the good-tempered man she had met last year.

"I am surprised you recognize me at all, Lady Quent." His voice was hoarse, yet carried real feeling. "I know that I am much . . . altered since our last meeting."

Now any horror or revulsion she had felt passed. Those had been sensations of the most selfish kind, borne out of consideration of only her own feelings. Ivy moved to take his hand. It was like grasping a bundle of twigs; she held it gently yet warmly.

"I would always know you, my lord." She did not turn her gaze aside, but instead looked at him directly. "How could I not recognize one who has given so much to my husband, and thus to myself as well?"

He nodded. "I am pleased to hear you say so. Yet I have given nothing so great to your husband as what *you* have given him, Lady Quent."

Ivy knew not what to say to those words.

"I was going to send you a note," Lord Rafferdy said, "yet I see you are already here. Keeping an eye on the final arrangements for the house?"

"No, I came because the . . ." Ivy hesitated, unsure what to say. "But it does not matter. I am only glad that I am here to meet you. But why have *you* come here?"

He gazed past her. "I saw you examining something in the garden over there, Lady Quent. You seemed very intent upon it. What was it, if you do not mind my asking?"

"I fear it was nothing good," she said, and she explained how it was a dead stork—presumably one of the ones that had been driven from the house. The lord inquirer seemed to stagger a bit as she described this, and the young driver steadied his arm.

"It was a black stork, you say?"

Ivy nodded. "It was."

Again his blistered lips curved in a smile, but this time it was a rueful expression. "How strange that one should be here! Only perhaps it is fitting somehow. It was what my closest friends called me, you know—when I was a young man serving in the army."

Now Ivy did stare at him, only out of astonishment rather than horror. "It is you! You are the Black Stork!"

He tilted his head to regard her. "So you've heard that name before?"

Her mind abuzz, she explained how she had seen an illusionist's impression of three young lords at Lady Marsdel's house, and also how her father had mentioned the Black Stork in something he had written.

"The Three Lords of Am-Anaru," he said, shaking his head. "It was Earl Rylend who named our little band. How like him to devise something so ostentatious. The Gold Crane—that was Rylend. And Lord Marsdel was the Blue Fisher. How grand and remarkable we thought ourselves! But that was long ago. They are years gone now, and Sir Quent's father with them, Eternum rest his soul."

As he spoke, his withered hand had slipped into the pocket of his coat, and it seemed he gripped something within.

"Lord Rafferdy?"

His eyes had gone distant, and his lips moved, though they made no sound. At last, he shook his head.

"Forgive me, Lady Quent." He withdrew his hand from his coat. "Like all old men, I am easily lost in recollections of the past. But now that you have called me back to the present, I have a question for you. Do you know where I might find my son? I went to his home earlier, but he was not there."

Ivy confessed that she did not know where Mr. Rafferdy could be found. She described that he had come to The Seventh Swan yesterday, though she had not seen him herself.

"So he is in the city, then. Very good."

"Is that why you came to Invarel, Lord Rafferdy? To see your son?"

"One of the reasons." A grimace crossed his face. "But I can stand out here no longer, Lady Quent. Though my girth is far less than what it was, still my legs find it difficult to bear. Please—let us go inside."

"Of course!" she exclaimed. "But surely you know—no doubt he has made his plans known to you—that my husband is not in the city. I do not expect him back for some time."

"I know, Lady Quent. It is quite all right. You see, it is not Sir Quent that I came to Invarel to see. Rather, it is you who I wish to speak with."

Again she found herself staring. "Me? But about what matter?"

He turned toward the driver. "I am sure that Lady Quent can help me walk to the house. You may wait here."

The young man nodded and stepped away. As he did, Lord Rafferdy laid a hand upon Ivy's arm. His touch was dry and hot.

"Come, Lady Quent," he said. "Since you have heard of the Three Lords of Am-Anaru, it is time you learned what it was they discovered beneath the sands of the Empire."

And while it was he who leaned upon her arm, to Ivy it felt as if she was the one drawn forward toward the house. As they approached the door, he cast a glance at one of the stone lions that kept watch to either side. He seemed to give a small nod, then they passed into the dimness of the empty house. They made it as far as a bench beside a window, and this he sank to before she could even remove the sheet that covered it. He gestured for her to sit beside him, and she did, still wondering what matter he could possibly wish to speak to her about.

"So this is Lockwell's house," he said, looking around with pale gray eyes. "It is an exceedingly handsome edifice. Though I am sure it did not look quite like this when your father dwelled here."

Despite the peculiarity of this meeting, Ivy smiled. "No, I fear it did not. My father was a doctor, and he was always far more interested in books and instruments of science than he was in housekeeping."

"Yes, such was my impression of him," Lord Rafferdy said. "But he was more than a doctor, and he was interested in more than merely science, was that not the case, Lady Quent?"

Surprised, Ivy could only answer with the truth. "Yes, he was also a magician of some ability. But I confess I am puzzled, Lord Rafferdy, for you speak almost as if you knew him."

Now it was toward her that he directed his gaze. "That is because I did know Gaustien Lockwell."

Ivy stared at him, trying to comprehend these words. She had always believed it was only due to Mr. Bennick's machinations that she had ever had a connection with Mr. Rafferdy. Last year, Mr. Bennick had used her cousin, Mr. Wyble, as a means to bring Ivy and Mr. Rafferdy into association in the hopes that together they would open the door to the house on Durrow Street—a thing they in fact accomplished.

However, even as she thought about all this, she realized she should not be so astonished. After all, her father had been a friend of Mr. Quent's, and Mr. Quent had long served the lord inquirer. That at some point Lord Rafferdy and Mr. Lockwell had encountered each other was hardly out of the question. All the same, it was something she had never considered.

At last Ivy found her voice. "Is that why you came here—to tell me that you knew my father?"

"Not precisely. Rather, I come to do something that Mr. Lockwell once asked me to do. It is a duty I should have discharged long ago." He drew in a rattling breath. "Yet first, if my voice will bear it, I think I should tell you about what happened at Am-Anaru, for you have brought the matter up, and it will help you understand how I came to know your father."

Ivy could do no more than give a mute nod. He paused, as if gathering his strength, and once again he slipped a thin hand into his coat pocket. At last he spoke, his words echoing in the stillness of the front hall, and Ivy listened with equal measures of dread and wonder as he described how three young lords, stationed deep in the southern continent in the years following the last war with the Murgh Empire, had come upon the ancient cave.

It was Earl Rylend who had led them there. Up to that point in their lives, Lord Marsdel had had no more than a passing interest in magick, while Lord Rafferdy had usually played the skeptic when it came to the topic. This was despite—or perhaps because of—Rylend's insistence that Rafferdy was descended from a distinguished line of magicians.

In his studies, Rylend had stumbled upon knowledge of an ancient artifact of power that was said to be hidden in the southern wastes of the Empire, in a place called Am-Anaru. It was a name that did not exist on any map. However, during the time the three were stationed at a remote outpost on the edge of the desert, Rylend became convinced that Am-Anaru was a real place, and that it was one and the same with a dead oasis known as Jadi Hawalfa, or "the hungry mouth" in the language of the nomads who inhabited those wastelands.

At last, after great travails crossing blazing expanses of sand, the three young men had come to Jadi Hawalfa in the company of several porters as well as Mr. Quent—the father of her own Sir Quent—who was Earl Rylend's faithful steward. There they discovered a dark mouth in a cliff face.

"The Murghese porters refused to enter the cave," Lord Rafferdy said, his voice rattling. "They claimed the place was *d'waglu*."

Ivy repeated the peculiar word. *"D'waglu?"*

"It means *accursed* in their language. We thought nothing of it. We were Altanian men of reason! We would not make ourselves subject to any sort of foreign superstition, and so we entered. We ventured deep into the cave, until the desert heat gave way to a constant chill, so that our breath began to fog as if we walked in the depths of a greatnight. Then, in the very blackest part of the labyrinth, we glimpsed a light. Rylend saw it first—a faint crimson spark." He nodded at her. "I suppose you can guess what the thing was, Lady Quent. After all, it lies now within this very house."

A gasp escaped her, for she did realize the answer. "It was the Eye of Ran-Yahgren!"

"Yes," he said with a grave nod. "Rylend told us that was its name, and he insisted we take it from the cave."

So the earl had in fact brought something back from the south, Ivy realized. Only it was not an old stone sphinx. Rather, it was the crystalline orb that now was locked in her father's secret study upstairs. Fascinated, she listened as Lord Rafferdy recounted the rest of the tale.

Removing the artifact was a great labor. However, after much wresting the four of them brought the orb out of the cave— wrapped in cloth so that the Murghese porters could not see what it was. The thing was loaded upon a camel and taken back across the desert. Not long after that their time in the royal army was done, and the Three Lords of Am-Anaru—as they styled themselves after the expedition—returned to Altania, along with the elder Mr. Quent. The artifact went with them and entered into Earl Rylend's keeping.

Only something else went with them as well, and as Lord Rafferdy recounted the events of the following years, Ivy shuddered to consider its nature. Was the cave truly cursed, as the Murghese porters had claimed? Or was it simply some ancient poison or contagion that had lingered on the air within, waiting long eons for someone to breathe it in? Either way, the result was the same. All four who entered the cave were afflicted.

The first symptoms began to appear in the years after their return to Altania: a wasting of the flesh accompanied by violent trembling, a difficulty of breath, and lurid hallucinations. They discovered that the effects of the malady could be greatly ameliorated through the application of treatments both medical and magickal, and so the four were all able to maintain enough of their health to fashion lives for themselves.

As the years wore on, the effects of the affliction grew harder and harder to keep at bay. The elder Mr. Quent was the first to succumb, some twenty years after their return from the Empire. Earl Rylend wasted and died a number of years later. After that, the Eye of Ran-Yahgren should have passed into Lord Marsdel's possession, for Rylend had made the other two men swear they would see to its safekeeping. However, by then Lord Marsdel was very ill and could not take it. As for Lord Rafferdy, he knew he did not have the magickal faculties to guard such a thing. But Earl Rylend had often had magicians at Heathcrest Hall, and during Lord Rafferdy's visits there he had come to know one of them whom he trusted.

"It was my father," Ivy said.

Lord Rafferdy nodded. "While I did not always care for the magicians Rylend associated with, I felt differently about your father. As did Sir Quent, who recommended his character to me. Thus we saw that the orb was given into Mr. Lockwell's care. Not long after that, Lord Marsdel succumbed. Of the four of us who entered that cave, only I have continued to endure all these years, and no doubt far more robustly than I should have."

His hand moved inside his coat pocket, as if he touched something within.

"Yet at last the curse of that place has found me," he went on, his voice barely above a whisper. "I can stave off the curse of Am-Anaru no longer. I have but a few more things to do. And this is one of them."

He withdrew his hand from his pocket and, trembling, held something out toward Ivy. She hesitated.

"Go on," he said, as if the words caused him great pain.

Slowly, she reached out and took the thing from his palsied fingers. Even as she did, a rasping breath escaped him, and he slumped on the bench. At the same moment, Ivy let out a gasp.

She gazed at the object in her hand. It was small enough to fit easily between a thumb and finger, thick as several regals stacked together, and triangular in shape. However, its edges were not sharp; rather, they were pleasingly smooth, as if polished from being rubbed for countless years. The thing it most resembled was a worry stone, but one made of wood.

That it was a piece of Wyrdwood she was certain; there was no mistaking it. She could feel the memory of life within it, like the subtlest resonance.

"But what is it?" she asked.

With great effort, he raised his head. "I haven't the faintest idea. All I know is that it was very important to your father. He asked me to keep it safe for him. I confess, I could have returned it to you long ago. I should have done so. For the most selfish reasons, I have delayed discharging my duty. You see, I think it has somehow helped to preserve me all these years. How else can I explain how I endured so much longer than the others?"

"Then you must keep it!" she cried, holding it out toward him.

He shook his head. "No, nothing can preserve me now. Besides, if some goodness indeed abides within this thing, then you will have need of it in the times ahead. Perhaps that was why your father asked me to give it to you. Perhaps he thought it would—"

His words were lost as a fit of coughing wracked him. Hastily, Ivy tucked the piece of Wyrdwood into the pocket of her dress, then put an arm around his shoulder, supporting him. In the coolness of the front hall she felt a heat emanating from him, as from sun-warmed stones after evening fell.

At last his coughing subsided, but he appeared spent from the exertion, and he was unable to speak. He motioned toward the door with a shaking hand, and Ivy understood. She rose and went outside, hurrying down the walk and waving until she caught the attention of the driver. The young man leaped down from the bench of the carriage, and moments later the two of them dashed into the front hall.

To Ivy's relief, Lord Rafferdy had not fallen from the bench. Indeed, he was able to speak now, and he told his man it was time to depart. The driver helped him to rise, and slowly they made their way from the house back to the four-in-hand. The driver opened the door and, with practiced motions, helped the older man inside.

"Thank you, Lady Quent," Lord Rafferdy spoke from the dimness inside the carriage, "for indulging me today."

Ivy had to draw a breath to steady herself, lest she be overcome with tears. "What will you do now?"

"I must go to my son," he said. "Time grows short, and night is falling. Farewell, Lady Quent."

The driver shut the door and climbed back to the bench. Then, with a flick of the reins, the four-in-hand rattled away down the street. She watched it go. And it was only when the carriage was out of sight that, recalling his final words, Ivy thought to look up at the sky.

The sun shone high above; it was broad daylight.

BOOK TWO

The Sword and The Leaf

CHAPTER TWENTY

ELDYN TURNED A silver coin in his fingers, its two faces catching the sunlight that slanted from the window high above his worktable beneath Graychurch. First a laughing moon came into view, embossed on one side of the coin, then the mien of a stern, fiery-maned sun appeared on the other. Again and again, over and over—moon then sun then moon again.

But never the two of them at once.

A weary smile curved upon Eldyn's lips. These days, he knew more than a bit what it felt like to be two things in constant alternation and never both of them at the same time. He had been aware from his prior calculations that his schemes would make him a busy man. However, it was one thing to total up a number of hours and quite another to actually expend the sum.

His work on the ledger at Graychurch required a meticulous application of concentration as well as ink, and it was endless. There were days when his hand was as cramped and stained as after a shift sitting with the other clerks at the tables of Sadent, Mornden, & Bayle.

Evenings found him being taxed in other ways that, while far more engaging, made more than just his scribing hand ache. Eldyn had never imagined that performing in an illusion play would be so demanding an enterprise. When he finally discovered the ability to conjure phantasms, they had come to him with little exertion—especially when Dercy was present to encourage him. However, the glamours he conjured had never been of a size to fill a room, let alone an entire stage.

What was more, he had never appreciated how much the players at the Theater of the Moon moved about during their performances. Seldom did they stand in one place as they worked their craft. Instead, they rushed, leaped, and clambered across the stage as they enacted the Sun King's pursuit of the silvery youth.

Eldyn had known this, of course; he had seen the play at the Theater of the Moon dozens of times. Yet it was not until he was onstage himself, following Master Tallyroth's directions to run house left or hurry downstage, all the while maintaining the illusory existence of a dozen pearlescent stars or ripples of blue light that surged like ocean waves, that he fully appreciated how physical the roles were.

As he was an understudy, it was his task to learn not just one part, but several of them, for there was no telling who he might need to replace some night due to an illness or injury. So far such an occasion had not occurred—and Eldyn hoped it would be a good while before it did.

True, after a month of rehearsing, he felt he had grasped the basic requirements of the roles to which he had been assigned. He knew his cues and how to position himself on his mark, and he had practiced the required illusions over and over, so he could form them with sufficient detail and symmetry to gain Master Tallyroth's approval.

This was a thing that was not easily won. The slightest deviation from the prescribed form—a wave that was too greenish, or a comet whose tail was not just the right length—would result in a critical observation.

"A star should generally twinkle rather than glow, don't you think, Mr. Garritt?" the master illusionist of the Theater of the Moon would say, an arch expression on his powdered face. Or, "A squarish cloud might be interesting, I concede, but as nature cannot really be improved upon, I always suggest one does not try."

Though gently uttered, these admonitions provoked Eldyn's resolve to do better more than any shouted rebuke. He would re-double his efforts, willing the phantasms into more precise forms with every repetition. By the end of the rehearsal he would be trembling and damp with perspiration. However, if Master Tally-roth gave him an approving nod (and so far he always had), then it was more than worth the effort.

Performances were no less strenuous than rehearsals. It was the duty of an understudy to help the other illusionists apply the necessary tints and powders to their faces, and to assist them as they changed in and out of their costumes. Eldyn also served as a stagehand, helping to move about those parts of the set that were not fashioned of air and light but rather of lumber and cloth and metal and paint.

There were, in fact, a large number of these. Watching the play gave an impression that everything one beheld was as ethereal as a dream. In truth, a great deal of what was onstage was physical rather than phantasmal, and after an evening of pushing and turn-ing various platforms and flats on cue, the ache in Eldyn's back would attest to their very real bulk.

Despite their exertions, the players were always ready to ven-ture to some drinking establishment as soon as the theater closed. In the past, Eldyn had always wondered how, after giving their all during a performance, they could go to tavern and conjure more illusions simply for the joy of it. Now, though he had yet to per-form for an audience, he had begun to understand. Previously, his perception of Siltheri was that they were free and merry, even a bit wild; toil and drudgery were not for such fey beings, he had thought.

His experiences as an understudy had changed that opinion. After so many hours of rigorous practice, crafting illusions to the master's exacting ideals, it was not so much a whim he and the others experienced as it was a desperate need to fashion something free and foolish and delightful. Thus as the drink flowed so did the phantasms, until at last punch and coin purses and energy with which to conjure were all thoroughly depleted.

After that, Eldyn would stumble with Dercy back to his room, arm in arm, laughing all the way. Within they found other, no less vigorous activities to engage in, and no matter what had happened at theater or tavern that night, or how exhausted they were, it seemed they always discovered the needed reserves.

At last he would make one final effort—rushing home in the small hours of a long night, wrapped in shadows, or in the swift, silver dawn of a short day, in order to be back to the apartment before Sashie rose.

Once she did, he would spend an hour listening to her chatter as they took their breakfast. Then it was time to go to Graychurch to begin his labors anew. If during all of it he had any bit of free time to himself, then it was spent reading a snippet of the Testament, to make sure he continued to rehearse for a different sort of performance in his future—one far more important and demanding than any illusion play.

While he sometimes felt expended from it all, this was hardly an issue. Coffee imbued him with the power to do his work in the morning. The energy of the stage filled him and buoyed him up in the evening. Rum and his exertions with Dercy brought him back down so he could sleep for a few short hours. So the lumenals and umbrals passed swiftly and in a most agreeable manner, and this, Eldyn had begun to think, must be what happiness felt like.

"Counting your savings, are you, Mr. Garritt? Usually our Lord in Eternum frowns upon the coveting of wealth. However, I am sure you are eager to know how close you are to gaining your portion to enter the Church. And since it is for such a holy purpose that you are amassing a sum, I am also sure that He would make an exception in this instance."

Eldyn looked up to see Father Gadby standing beside the table, clad in a cassock whose length and width were of similar proportions.

A sudden alarm caused his heart to miss a beat. The coin he had been turning was not a quarter regal but rather one of the silver coins that was used by the theaters of Durrow Street. Such coins were granted to the players to give to their friends, or were passed out by the madams of theaters to court favored guests, for nothing was so good for a theater's business as to have famous people attend its play.

Eldyn forced himself to draw a breath. He could not imagine Father Gadby would recognize the true nature of the coin. How would a priest know of such things? All the same, with a deft motion, he spirited the token into a pocket.

"I am not counting my fortune, Father," he said, affecting a smile. "Rather, I am counting the good fortune with which I have been blessed."

Father Gadby clasped a plump hand over his heart. "You have been blessed indeed, Mr. Garritt. To have won the favor of the archdeacon—why, it is hardly less than to have won the favor of Eternum itself! But then, it can only be due to divine notice that you then were directed into *his* awareness."

Now Eldyn's smile was no longer an illusion, but rather a genuinely felt expression. "So I believe, Father Gadby. Though why I have won any notice at all, I confess, is a thing beyond me."

"It is beyond any mortal man, Mr. Garritt. However, the eyes of Eternum see all, and they have perceived in you something that deserves so particular an attention."

A warmth suffused Eldyn—a glow not unlike the radiance he had experienced on the occasion of meeting Archdeacon Lemarck. Despite all the debts against his soul—those heaped upon him by his father, and those he had earned by himself—somehow he had been deemed worthy to receive such gifts. That the divine was anything other than the most benevolent and forgiving of forces, he would never again doubt.

"I shall let you return to your work, Mr. Garritt. One day you will help to wrest men's souls from the grasp of sin, but for now it is that wicked ledger upon which you must force a more holy order."

The rector moved to the other end of the long room and there proceeded to busy himself with the usual tasks that occupied him throughout the day—these being chiefly the moving of pieces of paper from one heap to another and then, after some consideration, back again.

Eldyn returned his attention to the ledger before him. He had let himself be distracted by daydreams, and the beam of sunlight from above was moving with a perceptible speed across the table. He would have to hurry if he was to be out of receipts before the lumenal was out of hours.

A SUDDEN GALE had clotted the sky with clouds, casting a pall over the world, by the time he walked from Graychurch to the old monastery. However, the bells of St. Galmuth's were not yet ringing, which meant the sun had not set on the lumenal.

Or rather, the sun was not yet *supposed* to have set. An article appearing on the front page of all the broadsheets a few days ago confirmed what had already been the subject of conversation all over the city for the half month prior. The almanacs were in error. The tables printed in them—and reprinted daily in the broadsheets—which for so long had reliably predicted the duration of lumenals and umbrals, could no longer be trusted.

The discrepancies had been small at first, such that people hardly detected them; or if they were noticed, they were ascribed to a faulty clock or a misreading of the almanac. Though minor, the variances had begun to compound. A few seconds of disparity became a minute, then several minutes, then more. So far, the greatest amount the almanacs had been in error had been not much more than a quarter of an hour. Yet the variances were only likely to increase as time went on.

According to the article he had read in *The Swift Arrow,* the Royal Society of Astrographers had convened to discuss the matter, and they had determined that the movements of the celestial spheres that contained the moon and the eleven planets had become altered from their previously immutable patterns. The cause of this was almost certainly the new planet, Cerephus, and its increasing proximity in the sky.

The changes had been subtle, but the heavens were large, so even the smallest deviation in their movements resulted in a significant effect. It was like a great clock in which one gear was sped up or slowed down, causing all of the other workings in the clock to change in accordance. The astrographers were laboring to calculate revised timetables, and the king had bid them to pursue the matter with all possible haste. However, they would likely have to observe the new motions of the heavens for some time—perhaps even years—before they could rework their calculations. In the meantime, there was no telling how much things might change.

This was a cause of some concern. Much commerce depended upon a reliable foreknowledge of the length of umbrals and lumenals. Even the theaters on Durrow Street would not be unaffected, for how would they know when they needed to be ready to open their doors if they did not know when evening was to fall?

Eldyn could imagine a great deal of inconvenience resulting from this unpredictability. That said, he did not see how it would cause any real harm to not know the exact length of days and nights. Perhaps it would be better if men were not so slavishly devoted to the clocks that divided their lives into sharp little slivers. Besides, if one wanted to know how the day was progressing, could one not simply look upward?

He did so now, watching the clouds roll before another gust of wind. Then he ducked into the old monastery just as a few large, cold drops of rain began to patter to the ground.

Upon entering the apartment, he found Sashie sitting by the window, reading a book in the dim gray light. She seemed not to have heard him enter, for she remained intent upon the book on her lap.

As usual, her lips moved slightly as she read. She wore a plain gray shift, and her hair was not loose as she usually wore it, but rather pulled back in a tight knot. It was not, he thought, a flattering style. No doubt she had put it up to be out of her way as she worked at some dusty task set for her by the old verger.

He shut the door behind him, and she looked up at the sound. Seeing him she smiled, and the expression imparted to her face a soft loveliness that could not be diminished by a dull dress or a harsh arrangement of her hair. Eldyn smiled at her in return.

"I'm glad to see you're back from the church already," he said. "It's beginning to pelt down rain out there. If you were coming back now, you'd have gotten very soaked."

She appeared to think about this a moment, and a slight frown creased her brow. "It can only be God's choosing when it rains. So I could not complain if I got caught in a storm, for it would be His will."

Eldyn resisted an urge to frown himself. Why would she ever think God would wish something ill to happen to her? "Well," he said, making his voice cheerful, "then it's clear, in His benevolence, that He wished you to be warm and dry today."

Now her smile returned even brighter than before. "I suppose you must be right, dear brother. Oh, but of course you are! You are wiser than I in such matters, and will soon become far wiser still."

Despite his misgivings, her approval could only please him. He took off his coat and laid it carefully over the back of a chair. "Did you happen to encounter Mr. Fantharp as you came in?"

She shrugged. "You mean the tallow seller? No, I did not."

"I met him on my way out this morning, and he expressed some concern that he has not seen you of late. I assured him you were very well, and that he must have simply missed your comings and goings. As you know, he is a busy man, for he does very well in his trade. It was kind of him to ask after you, don't you think?"

"I suppose so." Sashie opened the book on her lap and continued to read.

Eldyn's compulsion to frown returned. He had done everything he could to encourage Sashie to take an interest in Mr. Fantharp's attentions, but so far to no avail.

He moved across the room to her. "Are you reading from the Testament again? You have been very diligent with your study of it lately."

"Far less than you, I am sure!" she exclaimed. "I fear I must read things several times before I begin to comprehend them even the littlest bit. But I am a woman, and so must work harder at such things, as Father Prestus reminds me. I am sure understanding comes far more easily to *you*, brother."

He merely nodded. In truth, he had been too busy to read much of the Testament of late. But he would.

As for Sashie, lately he had begun to think that she was perhaps reading too much of the old book. Some of the words written by the ancient prophets could be alarming in tone, especially to an impressionable young mind that might tend to interpret them too literally. Was it this Father Prestus who was encouraging her to make such a study of it? Eldyn kept meaning to find the priest and speak to him, but given all his duties both day and night, he so far had not had the chance.

Well, he would do so soon. And tomorrow, if time allowed, he would go to a bookshop and find something more frivolous for Sashie to read. He could only think it would be good for her spirits to look at something lighter in tone—the latest romance, perhaps.

For now, she seemed intent to keep reading from the Testament, and as the last of the daylight would soon fail, he did not make an issue of it. Besides, he was too tired to strike up an argument. He could bring up the matter of Mr. Fantharp later. Perhaps he would suggest inviting their neighbor to attend the next Brightday service with them. Surely his sister could find no objection with that idea, and he was sure Mr. Fantharp would readily agree. No doubt being close to each other at the church would lead them to a natural and engaging discussion on the topic of the day's sermon, and thus help to acquaint them with each other.

Pleased with this scheme, he sat at the table, intending to pour himself a small cup of wine to ease the aches in his hand and shoulder. As he did, he saw that a note had come for him. Immediately he recognized the handwriting on the front as belonging to Rafferdy.

Last month, Eldyn feared he had angered his friend. It wasn't until the day after he had gone to the Theater of the Moon to accept Madame Richelour's offer that he recalled he was supposed to have met Rafferdy at the Sword and Leaf the evening prior. In the excitement of his encounter with the archdeacon, the engagement had gone right out of his head. However, that was no excuse; he should not have shown his friend such disregard. The next day, he had sent a long note to Rafferdy that, while not going into the particulars, apologized profusely for failing to show up for their appointment.

Several days passed, and Eldyn had begun to fear his friend was indeed perturbed with him, perhaps irrevocably. At last a reply from Rafferdy had arrived. It had been brief, and by its appearance hastily written, but it had assured him not to worry, that he was in no way insulted or annoyed. Eldyn had been greatly relieved.

Since then, Eldyn had exchanged several notes with Rafferdy, but so far they had not managed to find a time to reschedule their engagement. Eldyn's duties by day and night consumed nearly all of his hours, and Rafferdy was occupied with attending Assembly and taking care of his father's business. Yet hopefully they would find a time soon when they could meet. Eldyn missed his friend's amiable chatter; and now that he thought about it, it had been some time since Rafferdy's last message. Eager to see his friend's latest proposal, Eldyn broke the seal and opened the note.

His hopes faded with the last of the daylight outside the window. No, it was not possible Rafferdy would have time for drinks at tavern and frivolous talk anytime soon. His responsibilities would now be greater than ever. His father, Lord Rafferdy, had passed from this world.

It had happened earlier that month, after a sudden and precipitous decline in the state of his health. Now Rafferdy had returned from Asterlane, where he had been setting his father's affairs in order. There was still much to do, and Assembly remained in session. However, he hoped to be able to see Eldyn at some point, and would write again when he had time.

Gold light pushed back the gloom. Eldyn looked up as Sashie set a candle upon the table.

"You look very solemn, dear brother. Is something amiss?"

He folded the note and set it aside. He would write a reply to Rafferdy tomorrow. In the meantime, there was no reason to burden his sister with ill news about a person she had never met.

"No, nothing is wrong, dearest. I was just giving my eyes a bit of a rest, that's all."

"I am sure you are weary from all your work, dear brother. You deserve a reward for your labors. I will set out supper for you."

While he had not told Sashie the whole truth, neither had his words been a lie. His eyes were indeed tired from peering at the ledger all day. He sat in his chair and rested while Sashie set out a cold pork roast, a loaf and butter, and an apple tart. When she was done, they took their meal in warm light conjured by several beeswax tapers.

To burn multiple candles should have been an unattainable luxury, what with their price of late. However, Mr. Fantharp had given them several boxes, and so they had a good supply. Eldyn made sure to remark how kind it had been of their neighbor to give them all of the candles, and how Mr. Fantharp must be doing very well these days, given the preciousness of tallow. Sashie only smiled as she ate a large slice of tart.

By then it was very dark, and no matter what the almanac said, Eldyn was certain it was time to head to the theater. But after she cleared away the supper dishes, Sashie seemed intent on reading more of the Testament by candlelight. Eldyn occupied himself by brushing his two coats and polishing his good pair of boots, all the while trying not to keep glancing at the candles to see how far they had burned.

At last his sister closed her book and rose from her chair. She kissed his cheek, then retired to her room. Eldyn waited for the click of the latch, then he leaped into action. He put on his newly polished boots, donned his good coat, and examined the state of his hair in the mirror. With that he was out the door, locking it behind him.

Once outside, he walked briskly through the crooked lanes of the Old City. The storm had passed, and the stars were out, their light reflecting on the still-wet cobbles. He considered the idea of hiring a hack cab. It was not to be a rehearsal tonight, but rather a full performance, and he would be expected to arrive well before the curtain rose to help the actors into costume.

As usual, now that he wanted for a cab there was not one in sight. Besides, if he was to save for his and Sashie's futures, he must conserve his funds. Thus he redoubled his pace, drawing the shadows in close around him as he went, to be sure he was not delayed by any unsavory persons who might otherwise be tempted to accost him.

Turning onto the east end of Durrow Street, Eldyn saw that the theaters were just opening their doors. This sight relieved him, for that meant it was yet half an hour before curtain rise. He went around behind the Theater of the Moon and passed through the rear entrance.

He had hardly taken three steps before Dercy was upon him.

"There you are!" he said, seizing Eldyn's arm. He was not yet in costume, but his face and short blond beard were already painted silver.

Eldyn raised an eyebrow. "And good evening to you, too, Dercy."

The other young man shook his head. "Where have you been? Master Tallyroth is clucking about like a hen who can't find all of its chicks. We were about to send someone to your home to fetch you."

Eldyn's good humor wavered as he suffered a pang of dread. What would Sashie think if an illusionist were to show up at the door of their apartment?

"You could have no cause to do such a thing!" he said. "I am sure I am not late. The doors of the theater just opened. There is plenty of time to help everyone into their costumes."

"What of Riethe's costume? Surely there are alterations to make. Riethe is a whole head taller than you are and half again as broad! It will take more pins than I can count, I fear. We will have to hope it holds."

Now it was no longer dread Eldyn suffered from, but rather

confusion. The usual pandemonium that preceded a performance was not helping him clear his thoughts. Actors were laughing and talking excitedly as they put on their face paints, while stagehands dashed about, working cables and pulleys and levers as they put all the set pieces in place.

"What are you talking about?" Eldyn said. "Why would Riethe's costume need alterations?"

"Because he won't be in it. *You* will."

It felt as if one of the bags of sand that counterweighed the curtain had dropped from its pulley and struck Eldyn on the head.

"Where is Riethe?"

"Over there, the damnable idiot. He got into a brawl today with some fool in a tavern. I gather the fellow said a few stupid things about Siltheri. As if we care what some stinking lout thinks of us! He should have just left it. But you know Riethe, he never can."

Eldyn *did* know Riethe. He was a strapping young man with a fiery temper who did not take kindly to epithets being hurled against illusionists. This was not the first tavern fight he had gotten in, and Master Tallyroth had warned him that if he did not cease such activities, he might lose his place at the theater.

"What happened?" Eldyn said.

"Well, Riethe broke the man's nose, but it was the fellow's friends he hadn't considered. They heaved him out the tavern door, and when he landed on the cobbles it was his own hand that got smashed. He'll be lucky if it heals well enough so he's not a cripple. Regardless, there's no way he can go on tonight. Which means *you're* going to perform in his stead."

Eldyn put a hand to his head, making sure a sandbag indeed had not struck him. "Me? You mean perform onstage?"

"Where else would you perform? In a closet? Under a stone? Of course I mean onstage!"

Eldyn felt a tremor pass through him. He had known this day would come, but he had hoped it would be a little while longer. There was so much more he had to learn.

Dercy's silver face waxed into a broad grin. "Come now, Eldyn

Garritt, don't you worry. I've seen what you can do. We all have. You'll be brilliant, I know it. You couldn't be anything else."

As if Dercy were indeed the moon, a silver light surrounded Eldyn. Bathed in that radiant glow, he could only smile in return. Did not some claim the light of the moon induced madness? So it seemed to him, for fear gave way to an intoxicating anticipation. Power seemed to shimmer on the air, and his fingers tingled, as if wonders were ready to burst from them.

Eldyn squeezed Dercy's arm. "Thank you," he said. "For always being so sure of me."

Dercy let out a rich laugh. "Don't thank me. Thank Riethe and his fool's temper. Now come on, we have but a quarter hour to make you into a comet."

CHAPTER TWENTY-ONE

*O*N THE PAST, after a visit to Asterlane, Rafferdy had always been greatly relieved to return to his house on Warwent Square. From the moment he left the house of his father, the coach could never travel the roads fast enough, and the distance behind it was never great enough to satisfy his craving for flight. Not for a moment, during all the hours as the countryside passed outside the window of the coach, would he know any tranquillity or comfort. Not until he was back in the city, amid all his usual surroundings, would he at last allow himself to draw a breath, exhale it, and believe that he had once again made his escape.

"May I take your hat and cane, Lord Rafferdy?"

Rafferdy recoiled a little. He was not yet accustomed to those words being spoken to him.

"Yes, thank you," he managed to say, handing the objects to his man. "And I'll have a brandy. Make it a generous pour."

The steward bowed and retreated from the parlor, leaving Rafferdy alone. He looked around the room and despite its familiarity, this time it offered him no comfortable refuge. There would be no fleeing now. He had left Asterlane and was back in the city, but he would never again escape from Lord Rafferdy's house so long as he lived, for *he* was Lord Rafferdy now.

He crossed the parlor to his writing desk. The warm light of a long afternoon spilled through the window, falling upon its empty surface. Not so very long ago, upon returning from a visit to Asterlane, he would have found the desk heaped with letters of greeting and a multitude of notes asking for his presence at various dinners and parties. However, the only thing that covered the desk now was a thin layer of dust.

Not that this deficit of correspondence surprised him. One could turn down only so many invitations before they ceased to come at all. Everyone wishes to secure the attendance of a guest who is known to attend only the most fashionable parties. Unless, of course, that person never attends *their* parties, in which case the other is wholly unneeded. Discerning persons, Rafferdy had learned, are only wanted when they offer themselves to anybody.

Despite the lack of invitations, he felt no regret. He no longer had dinners or fetes to divert him. These days it was often the case that he had another sort of gathering to attend when evening fell. And while the people he met there frequently sent him messages, these missives did not come by the usual routes of post or messenger.

His man returned with the brandy, which Rafferdy accepted gratefully. He sat in a chair and took a long sip, then another. It was only when he set down the empty glass that he realized he was sitting in the very chair where he had last seen his father alive. Had he unconsciously chosen it for that very reason? While it was the grandest chair in the room, and the most lordly with its arms carved like lion claws, it was far from the most comfortable.

No, it was only a result of chance and weariness that he had sat here. For if he had thought of its previous occupant, he would surely have chosen somewhere else to sit. Only now that he was here, he did not rise. Instead, he laid his hands on the chair's carven arms. They were warm to the touch, as if the seat had been recently occupied. But it was only from the sun streaming through the window, of course.

"Why did you do it?" Rafferdy muttered aloud. "You had to know what the strain would do to you. Why did you come all the way to the city?"

Surely it could not have been just to tell Rafferdy the things he had. Such matters could have waited for his son to travel to Asterlane in answer to a summons. Yet Lord Rafferdy had chosen to make the journey despite the dire effect that hours spent jostling in a carriage would have upon his body.

Rafferdy had pleaded with his father to remain in the city, fearing he could not withstand the journey home. He would write to Asterlane, he said, and bid his mother to travel to Invarel to be with them. Lord Rafferdy would not hear of it. Lady Rafferdy loathed travel. Besides, he had done what he had come to the city to do, he said, and so he left.

Only a few minutes after his father's departure, a knock came at the door of the house. Rafferdy had rushed to it himself rather than waiting for his man to get it, thinking that his father had reconsidered and had ordered his driver to return to Warwent Square. However, when he threw open the door he saw not his father on the other side, but rather a messenger. The boy had a letter for him. It was, he saw as he looked at it, from Lady Quent.

Rafferdy gave the boy a penny, then went to his parlor to open the letter. Lady Quent had begun her note with an apology, and an explanation of how Rafferdy might have come to think she had intended to break their engagement the prior lumenal. However, as he read her words, he realized that it was he who should be making the apology. What had made him think that Lady Quent would ever neglect a promise? It was entirely against her character. He had allowed his most foolish and selfish fears to be encouraged by the youngest Miss Lockwell's silly words. Rafferdy nearly set down the letter right then to compose a reply, expressing his own remorse.

Only then he had turned the page over, and at last he understood the real reason his father had come to the city. With fascination he had read her account of her conversation with Lord Rafferdy, and her description of the object he had given her. That his father had gone to Lady Quent to return something that had once belonged to Mr. Lockwell was a fact that would have greatly puzzled him only an hour before. After his own conversation with his father, Rafferdy could not be astonished.

She closed the note with an expression of hope that he would forgive her, and that they could make another attempt at a meeting soon. Rafferdy had at once written her a reply, stating that no apology was necessary, for he was the one at fault, and that he would be willing to call upon her again at any time of her choosing.

Only they had never gotten another chance to meet for tea. Less than a quarter month later, the letter Rafferdy both dreaded and expected arrived. His father had fallen into a fever upon his return to Asterlane. He had soon slipped into unconsciousness. Then, in the depths of a long night, he had passed silently beyond the bounds of this world.

At once, Rafferdy had departed the city for Asterlane. Whatever shock or grief he might have suffered, it was set aside upon his arrival to attend to all of the necessary business, and to comfort his mother.

Lady Rafferdy had faded a bit with each passing year, growing ever thinner and more brittle, like a flower kept between the pages of a book. Now it was as if the last tinges of color had been leached from her. She said little, and wept not at all that Rafferdy witnessed; instead she sat silently in the parlor, looking out the window at the lands around Asterlane.

Rafferdy spent as much time as he could with her, though he was also much occupied with his father's agents. There were numerous papers to review, and he had to set out his intentions for all of his father's holdings and incomes. However, none of it was truly difficult. The lawyers advised him where and what to sign, and his father had left his affairs in excellent order. In the end, becoming a lord required very little bother on his part.

The funeral was no more difficult. He had only to choose his coat and to support his mother on his arm as they walked into the parish church. After that, his only task was to stand outside the church and suffer the condolences of countless people he did not know. Most were local gentlemen and ladies and clergy. There were some baronets and lords from the nearby counties, and a few magnates from the city. There were also several men whom Rafferdy knew to be inquirers who had worked under his father.

Given the presence of these men, he should not have been surprised to see *her* that day. All the same, he was. He nodded as he clasped the hand of a portly vicar, not hearing a word the fellow said. Then he turned to greet the next person in line—

—and could neither speak nor move. Even dressed all in black, she was lovely, her gold hair tucked beneath a brimmed hat, her green eyes bright with sympathy and concern. So fate had found a way for them to meet after all, if not for tea.

It was she who broke the spell of silence upon him.

"Lord Rafferdy, I am so sorry for the loss of your father. I cannot imagine what a terrible burden it must be for you and your mother to bear."

To hear the words *Lord Rafferdy* from her lips jarred him to his senses. It was exceedingly strange. But then, had her own name not similarly changed of late?

"I know that you have no need to imagine it, Lady Quent," he said, clasping her small hand in his. Had she not been recently deprived of a parent herself? "Yet any burden is easier to bear with you here. And you as well, Sir Quent."

Her husband stood beside her, and Rafferdy was hardly less glad to see his grim, craggy face than her lovely one. It was comforting to have these solid, familiar beings before him. They spoke for a little while—not of anything of importance. Lady Quent commented that she had never been to this part of the country before, and Sir Quent asked Rafferdy's advice about places they might drive for the best prospects for viewing the landscape.

This pleasant exchange lasted but a few minutes, for there were other people who had a need to shake his hand, no matter what *his* needs might be. As far as he could tell, funerals were intended neither for the departed nor the bereaved; rather, their purpose was to be tedious and dreary ordeals, and thus give everyone else a reason not to feel guilty that nothing was wrong in their own lives. Rafferdy thanked Sir and Lady Quent for their presence, and he expressed his desire to speak to them more later.

At this Lady Quent met his eyes, and he thought he understood the meaning of the look. If only they could have some time alone to discuss the things Lord Rafferdy had told her. In turn, he could describe his own peculiar conversation with his father. Only then she and her husband moved on, and Rafferdy found himself being consoled by more esquires and aldermen he could not recall ever having met.

While he hoped to invite the Quents to Asterlane to dine while they were in the country, that night his mother required him, for now that the funeral was done her silence had at last broken, and she had wept long and bitterly. In truth, he was relieved, and spent the night sitting with her. The next lumenal was occupied with further business regarding his father's holdings. It was not until the next day that he managed to dispatch a note to the inn where the Quents were staying, only to learn when a note came back that they had just departed for the city, as Sir Quent was required at the Citadel.

Those next lumenals passed quickly as Rafferdy finished setting his father's estate in order. His mother's demeanor improved, and she began to take up her usual pastimes of arranging flowers from the garden and inviting other ladies to the house for tea. Though she remained somewhat wan, she assured him that he need not fear for her.

"I knew when I became Lady Rafferdy that I would have him only for a time," she told him one day toward the end of his visit. They walked together in the garden amid brilliant blooms. "Indeed, I got to keep him for longer than I had hoped, and for that I am grateful."

At this he had given her a startled look. Perhaps his mother had known more than he had given her credit for. Had she been aware of the curse that had afflicted all those who entered that dark cave in Am-Anaru? However, she could not know of the letter he had gotten from Lady Quent, and so he said nothing about it.

After that, Rafferdy no longer had such a grave fear to leave his mother. Which was good. Assembly had been in recess most of the time he was away, but it would be convening at the start of the month for another session. That he would look forward to attending Assembly again was impossible. Yet now that there was no chance of him giving up his seat, he was more resigned to sitting in it. Once a fate cannot possibly be avoided, however horrible it may be, it loses something of its powers of dread.

Besides, it was a fact that there were some people at Assembly he was looking forward to encountering. Thus, as the month drew to a close, he made his farewells to his mother and commenced the journey back to Invarel and everything he knew.

Only now that he was here, he wasn't certain he really knew anything at all. Or rather, it was as if nothing he had known was truly what he thought it was. Not the city. Not society or the government.

Not even his father.

THINGS ARE NOT as men have long believed," Lord Rafferdy had said, crumpled in the great lion-clawed chair in Rafferdy's front parlor. Surely almost any other seat in the room would have been more comfortable for him. However, he was yet a lord and, whether it was by instinct or habit, he had chosen the most commanding chair.

"The balance has been altered, perhaps forever," he went on, his voice thin and quavering. He seemed to speak not to Rafferdy, but to some person standing behind his son. "The occlusion draws nearer far more rapidly than we ever allowed ourselves to think."

Rafferdy had no idea what to make of these words—or of his father's unexpected appearance in the city. That Lord Rafferdy's health had continued to worsen was apparent as soon as the driver helped him out of the carriage. Rafferdy had hurried to him, supporting his father's weight as they went inside, only there was little to bear. The black suit Lord Rafferdy wore seemed to house not a man, but a few bundles of straw. Not long ago he had been hale, even portly; what remained now was no more than a withered scarecrow.

"A darkness is coming," the elder man said. He trembled, as if cold, though sunlight bathed the chair where he sat. "A great darkness . . ."

Rafferdy shook his head, trying to understand these ramblings. "Do you mean all this business with the planets and the monstrously long umbral that some people say is coming? But that can hardly be a concern. I am sure it is a lot of blather meant to agitate people and sell more broadsheets."

"I would that were true," Lord Rafferdy said. "However, it is more than that."

His eyes were overly bright, and it seemed there was a fear in them. Rafferdy wondered if he should call for the doctor. He worried that his father's illness was making him morbid.

"Well," he said, trying to keep his voice light, "I suppose I will simply have my man buy more candles."

"Will you? If you believe that all it will take to endure this darkness is a few more candles, then you are mistaken."

This response shocked Rafferdy. His father spoke as if he knew something about it.

"Good God, do you mean it's true, then?" he exclaimed. "But how long is it to last?"

Lord Rafferdy let out a rattling sigh. "Perhaps twice the length of a greatnight. Or three times or four. Or perhaps . . ."

"Perhaps what?"

His father looked out the window at the golden afternoon. "Perhaps it will never end."

Rafferdy could only gape. If the world was frosted with snow after a greatnight that lasted thirty hours, what would happen if there was an umbral several times that length?

"That's impossible," he said.

"Impossible? You mean like new planets appearing in the sky?"

Rafferdy did not reply. These could only be the delusions of a fevered brain. His father continued to tremble, and the glassy orbs of his eyes darted this way and that, as if he saw things in the room that were not there. That his father was not in full possession of his faculties, Rafferdy was sure. All the same, this talk of an endless greatnight had stirred a creeping sort of dread in his chest. He went to the credenza and poured a cup of wine.

"It was because I knew what was coming that I did it, you know."

Rafferdy turned around. "That you did what?"

"That I did what I could to keep you apart from Lady Quent when she was yet Miss Lockwell." His hands twitched upon the arms of the chair, clasping at the carved wood. "Always I did everything I could to make certain the two of you were never introduced to each other. Fate—or someone acting on its behalf—had other intentions. Yet even after my efforts proved vain, and you were made known to each other, I did what I had to in order to ensure your acquaintance did not advance in what might have been its natural direction. At least in *that* I had some success. Nor do I regret having done this. Yet you must not ever think I was gladdened by it."

Rafferdy gripped the glass in his hand, unable to drink from it or set it down. He was struck dumb, and a pain stabbed at his chest. Were these words also the phantasms of an ill mind? Only it seemed that there was a horrible truth to them, and Rafferdy could only listen, paralyzed, as his father spoke in a rasping voice, describing how he had met Gaustien Lockwell years ago in the West Country, at Heathcrest Hall.

Lord Rafferdy and Lord Marsdel had long been friends of Earl Rylend, and Mr. Lockwell was a friend of Mr. Bennick, who tutored the earl's son, Lord Wilden, in the subject of magick. Mr. Lockwell had come with Mr. Bennick to Heathcrest with some regularity, and Lord Rafferdy had met him on several occasions.

"You knew Lockwell?" Rafferdy at last managed to say.

His father's eyes seemed to clear a bit, and his voice grew louder, as if recalling these memories had steadied him somehow. "Yes, I always enjoyed my encounters with him. He was a powerfully intelligent man. Yet in him this did not lead to an inflated self-regard. Rather, his intellect was tempered, and thus made stronger, by a modest nature and a strong sense of principle. I admired him very much."

At last Rafferdy managed to take a gulp of the wine; it only induced an uncomfortable churning within him. He put the glass down. "But if you admired *him,* then why did you discourage me from knowing *her?*"

"For every reason I told you at the time. Appearances must be maintained—now more so than ever. I fear that a time of great suspicion and incrimination comes. I hope that I am in error, that we as a nation are better than that. However, if we are not, then soon everyone will look for any reason to accuse another."

A throbbing had begun to form in Rafferdy's head. "I don't follow you. Accuse them of what?"

"It does not matter. To be different will in itself be a crime. When people fear an enemy they cannot see, then anyone can be that enemy. So it is vital that you do not set yourself apart from your class and your peers. Yet there is more to it than that. There is another reason I never wished you to meet Miss Lockwell. You see, while I never had any interest in it myself—much to Marsdel's everlasting disappointment in me—I know what runs in our lineage. And I had no wish for you to fall in with magicians."

Rafferdy slipped his right hand in his coat pocket. Only what was the point? No doubt his father had seen his House ring before this. He forced himself to withdraw his hand. There was a glint of blue as sunlight caught the gem on the ring. However, last night it was not the influence of sunlight that had caused the blue gem to glow. Rather, it had been in answer to the score of other House rings, worn by the other young men in the secret meeting room beneath the Sword and Leaf tavern.

"I don't understand," Rafferdy said. "You said yourself that you admired Mr. Lockwell, and you clearly knew him to be a magician. So why did you not wish for me to associate with magicians?"

"Why? Because magick has been used for great ill—for perhaps the greatest ill that ever was done in all the history of this world. It was an act of great wickedness, one committed by your own forebear—the one whose name is carved upon that ring you wear now. And there are some who would use magick for ill yet."

An indignation welled up within Rafferdy. He thought of what he had done to help Lady Quent thwart the magicians of the Silver Eye, and what her father, Mr. Lockwell, had sacrificed to do the same. "Not all magicians would use their power for ill. What of Slade Mordigan turning back the Old Usurper at Selburn Howe? Surely some magicians have done good."

"I am sure that some of them have. But that does not mean they have done *only* good. Besides, I believe you have witnessed what power can do even to a good man. Indeed, I know you have seen it. I believed myself a good man once. I wish to believe I still am. Yet do not think I was not aware of how you regarded my decision to enclose my estate."

The corners of his mouth pulled down, as if he suffered some sudden pang. Rafferdy suffered one himself. As he still sometimes did, he thought of the people he had helped to remove from his father's lands, recalling the empty looks on their faces, in their eyes. No, he had no wish to wield any sort of power. At least, not then.

The thin lines of Lord Rafferdy's lips drew themselves into a rueful smile. "Well, perhaps I am wrong. Perhaps my fears will not come to pass. Marsdel and Rylend always complained that I only ever saw ill ends. That's why they called me the Black Stork. For

'a black stork brings black luck,' as they say in the Westlands."
A spasm erased his smile. "But then, I endured longer than either
of them did, and I have seen a great deal more."

His hands dropped to his lap as he spoke these last words, and
his fingers moved, as if he fidgeted with some object, only his
hands were empty. For a long moment he was silent—so long that
Rafferdy began to wonder if he was lost in some sort of daze.

"I suppose you can only despise me," Lord Rafferdy said at last.
"Perhaps it would have been better had I never told you all this. I
suppose I have not done it for your sake, but rather for my own.
Come, then—I shall soon be gone, so there is no need for you to
withhold the truth from me. What do you think of me now? I
would hear your thoughts."

Rafferdy turned away and leaned on the credenza. That he
should experience outrage and revulsion was more than war-
ranted. To learn that his father had done more than merely dis-
suade him from proposing marriage to Miss Lockwell, but had in
fact conspired for years to prevent him from meeting her, was an
astonishing revelation. Outrage should have been his reaction.

However, much had changed in the months since he had
thought to make Miss Lockwell into Mrs. Rafferdy. *He* had changed,
and time had allowed him to regard the man he had been with a
degree of disinterest. Was it not the case that he had fancied Miss
Lockwell not only for her great charms, but also because he had
known a connection with her would never have been possible? It
is easy and amusing to make promises one knows one can never
keep, but to offer an oath when one knows it must be obeyed—
that is courage. While Rafferdy believed he had many good qualities, he was not so deluded to believe that bravery was one of
them.

He turned around and regarded his father, willing the anger to
come. However, looking at the small, spent being before him, he
could summon no rage. Rather, he could feel only pity, and dread.

"You say the motions of the planets will bring a long night,"
Rafferdy said in a low voice. "If that is indeed the case, then what
am I supposed to do about it?"

Lord Rafferdy looked up. The anguish on his face had not lessened; indeed, it seemed to deepen as did the lines beside his mouth. All the same, his expression was one of gratitude. Then he shook his head.

"Now that you have asked, I would that I could answer you. Yet both law and duty forbid me to do so. You are my son, but you are not an inquirer. Thus I cannot tell you any more than I have. Yet perhaps it is just as well. The Gray Conclave would give much to learn what we have discovered. It is only because we answer to the Crown directly that we are preserved from their interference. But Lord Valhaine's agents are ever prowling about. If they knew that one who was not an inquirer, one who did not have the Crown's protections, had knowledge they wished to possess—"

Again a shuddering wracked his body, and for a moment he could not speak.

"It is better that you remain where you are," he finally managed to say, "apprehending only what you do. In time, events may occur that will cause you to learn everything of our labors and what we have tried to do. Until then, I ask only this of you, Dashton: that you listen to Sir Quent."

Rafferdy shook his head, astounded by these words. "Sir Quent?"

"Yes, that is why I have come to you, to ask this one thing of you. I fear perhaps you owe me no debt. Yet if you never grant me anything else, I beg you grant me this. I will feel an ease, and will know that I have not abandoned you, if you have *him* to go to." His eyes were shining again with a feverish light. "Swear to me, if Sir Quent has need of you, you will do everything you can to aid him."

Rafferdy stared. Could his father know what he was truly asking—to have Rafferdy pledge himself to the man who had deprived him of the one thing in the world he had ever truly wanted? It was too cruel!

All the same, Rafferdy found he could not deny this wish. Besides, to aid Sir Quent was to aid *her,* was it not?

"I swear it," he said.

At this Lord Rafferdy sighed, and he slumped back in the chair, as if suddenly relieved of a tremendous weight. "There, do you see? There is yet a reason to hope, even as the Black Stork reckons things."

He spoke the words faintly, and Rafferdy had the sense that they had not been directed to him. His father's head bowed then, and he seemed to fall into a doze, exhausted from all his efforts. Rafferdy took a shawl from the back of the sofa and laid it about his father's shoulders. As he did, he noticed that Lord Rafferdy's right hand moved, his fingers twitching as if they sought to grip something that was not there.

Rafferdy touched them, stilling their movements. Then he departed the parlor, leaving his father to his shadowed dreams.

$\mathcal{L}$ORD RAFFERDY?"

Rafferdy looked up, startled. The day had perished outside the window, and a gloom had stolen into the parlor of his house at Warwent Square. How long had he been sitting in the chair? This time it was not his father, but rather he who had been lost there in dark musings.

"Yes, what is it?" he said to his man.

"A note just arrived for you, my lord—from Fairhall Street."

Rafferdy took the folded paper from the silver tray. So his return to the city had not gone unnoticed! Like a spider, Lady Marsdel must have detected a trembling in her web once he entered the city. He turned the note over in his hand but did not break the seal.

"Should I bring another brandy, my lord?"

In no way did he need it. His head ached, and his mind felt dull.

"Yes, do," he said.

After his man departed, Rafferdy rose from the chair. He set the note from Lady Marsdel on his desk, then opened a drawer and took out a book. The book was covered in black leather and bore no mark or writing on its spine or cover; it was bound with a thick silver hasp.

Rafferdy set the book on the desk, then with a finger he drew several runes in the dust all around it. A circle of binding was not really necessary for such a small spell, but he was weary, and from what he had learned it was when they were tired that magicians usually made their mistakes. He had no wish to speak the wrong words by accident and allow something more than evening shadows to enter the parlor.

He uttered the spell, the sharp-sounding words coming to his lips with an ease that continued to surprise him, then touched a finger to the silver hasp. The gem in his House ring flashed blue, and there was a *snick* as the clasp sprang apart. As always, he felt a kind of cool shimmer, as if from a passing breeze. It was not a displeasing sensation.

Rafferdy opened the book. Its pages were filled with writing penned in what appeared to be dark, silvery ink. However, it was not by means of a quill that words were entered into this book.

The tome had been given to him upon his acceptance into the Arcane Society of the Virescent Blade. Each magician in the society had a similar book. In addition, there was a master book, residing in the possession of the magus, the leader of the society. Such was the enchantment placed upon the other books that if a thing was written in the master book, then it appeared in all of the other books simultaneously, whether they were opened or closed, and no matter how far apart they were. It was by means of the books that news and messages were passed through the society.

He turned through the book until he reached the last page with writing upon it. As he read the words, he had the uncanny sensation that they squirmed upon the page like thin, silvery serpents.

We will gather at moonrise on the second umbral of the month. The runes for this meeting are Targoth, Aegon, and Saradir. As always, do not be late or the door will be closed to you even if you should know the runes.

Rafferdy shut the book. So there would be no meeting of the Society tonight. It was just as well, as he felt far too stupid to learn any new runes or spells. All the same, he suffered a pang of disappointment.

With his hand he smeared away the dusty runes on the desk, then he closed the book. The two halves of the silver hasp fit together with an audible sound, and he felt a tingling as the magickal lock was renewed. Rafferdy put the book back in the drawer, then took up the note from Lady Marsdel. He hesitated for a moment, then broke the seal. It was an invitation from her ladyship requesting his presence that very evening.

His man returned to the parlor.

"Your pardon, my lord," he said as he set a full glass of brandy on the desk, "but the messenger has not left. He says that he was commanded not to return to Fairhall Street without an answer. Would you like me to inform the man that you cannot attend?"

Rafferdy reached for the glass, then pulled his hand back.

"No," he said, looking up. "Tell the messenger that I will accept her ladyship's invitation. And have the carriage brought around. I will go to Fairhall Street tonight."

The steward raised an eyebrow, but he only bowed and said that he would call for the carriage at once.

Rafferdy wondered if he was mad. He was weary from his journey. However, he had no wish to remain here alone. There were too many shadows. Besides, if there was to be no meeting of the Arcane Society of the Virescent Blade tonight, then at least he could attend another sort of gathering and enjoy the familiar, if dull, enchantments of company and conversation.

CHAPTER TWENTY-TWO

$\mathcal{I}$VY WALKED IN dappled light. The long afternoon had brought with it a warm zephyr, and the leaves of the New Birch trees around her shimmered green and silver, speaking in a whispering language she felt she could almost understand.

Like the majority of people in Altania, particularly those who dwelled in the Grand City, Ivy had seldom been among trees. She had seen them all her life, of course; elms and beeches and plane trees arched over numerous streets in Invarel, and hazel, laburnum, alder, and cherry trees could be found in abundance in the city's gardens. Then there was the old stand of Wyrdwood near Heathcrest Hall, whose stone wall she had stood outside.

Yet it was one thing to see a tree, or a row of trees; it was quite another to venture within a whole grove of them, to feel them close in around one, and hear their murmurings in all directions. Only once before could she remember doing so. She had been eight or nine years old, and Mr. Lockwell had taken her to Lorring Park on the east edge of the city.

In the center of the park was a stand of New Ash. She had spent a happy hour in the green light beneath the trees, pretending she was Queen Béanore hiding in the forest from Emperor Veradian and the Tharosian soldiers, and shooting stick arrows to drive them off. At one point she had pressed her ear to a trunk near the edge of the grove and shut her eyes, wondering if trees had heartbeats like people did.

Just when she thought she was beginning to hear something— a sort of low, thrumming sound—it was drowned out by the sound of a man's angry voice. She opened her eyes to see a priest in a black cassock standing nearby, making motions for her to move away from the tree. Then her father was there, taking her hand and leading her away from the grove.

And that was the last time they ever went to Lorring Park.

Now the only voices Ivy heard besides the whispers of the trees were the sounds of bright conversation and laughter that drifted on the breeze. At Lady Crayford's suggestion, a small party had driven again that day to the countryside beyond the city's edges.

As the weather was exceptional, no one could find fault with the plan. They took two curricles, one driven by Colonel Daubrent and the other by Lord Eubrey, while Captain Branfort rode alongside on a beautiful chestnut mare. Ivy's only regret was that Mrs. Baydon was not with them. However, the party had arrived at the house on Durrow Street hardly a quarter hour after the note describing the plan. As a result, there had been no time to send a message to Vallant Street.

In any case, there was no room for Mrs. Baydon, as the curricles seated but two each, which meant Mr. Baydon would have been required to drive his gig. That would never do, as a gig was drawn by one horse and a curricle by two, Colonel Daubrent explained, and so the gig would not be able to keep up with them.

When Ivy suggested they might ride more slowly, Lady Crayford had laughed. *Her* brother could go but one speed, she said, and that was as fast as possible. Besides, Captain Branfort assured her that Mr. Baydon would never be ready to venture out so soon after the midday repose of a long lumenal, and Ivy had to concede, given what she knew of Mr. Baydon's habits and his general difficulties in rising, that this was likely the case.

As it turned out, Ivy was glad they had no reason to go slowly. Once they were beyond the city, the men drove the curricles at a pace that she found at once terrifying and thrilling, and she was forced to hold on to her bonnet lest it fly off her head.

They soon discovered a picturesque spot on a rise above a little valley dotted with farms and small copses of New Trees. They spread blankets on the ground and drank wine and basked in the sun as the viscountess set up her easel and took out her brushes.

After a time, Ivy quietly rose. While Lady Crayford painted and the men discussed the topic of hunting, she slipped away to the west, drawn by the stand of New Birches there. A compulsion had come upon her to be alone for a while. This was not because she did not enjoy their little party. Rather, it is the case that sometimes one must step outside of a joyful moment in order to truly appreciate it, and Ivy had much to be appreciative of at present.

Mr. Quent had returned to the city last month, his work in Torland finished once again, and they had at last made their return to the house on Durrow Street. While Ivy had witnessed the regular progress of the refurbishment these last months, it was not until they again dwelled in the house that she truly realized the thoughtfulness, the extreme delicacy and care, that had guided the work.

Everywhere she went in the house, there was some wondrous thing to discover, like how the patterns made by the light as it fell through the windows of the upstairs gallery transformed the floor into a great chessboard. Or the way the frescoes of griffins that adorned the spandrels in the front hall were painted in such a clever manner that, if one moved swiftly through the hall, the sequence of paintings blurred into a single image that seemed to yawn and stretch its wings as one went.

That the house had been restored to the fullness of its original splendor, Ivy was convinced; indeed, she wondered if the house might now be even more glorious than it had been when Mr. Dratham originally built it. She supposed the carved eyes would know, for they had seen everything that had passed in the house over the centuries. However, as they could but watch and not speak, that was something they could not tell.

Ivy's sisters were no less captivated with the house. That it would make a marvelous setting for their party next month, both of them exclaimed at once upon entering. And Lily went on to say that, now that the whole of it had been opened, it was so large they might each have their own wing. At this, Rose had expressed concern that she might get lost by herself in the vastness of the house. Ivy pointed out that she would only have to follow the sound of Lily's pianoforte to find them, and so could never be lost for long, at which point Rose became relieved.

There was only one thing missing that would have made their return to Durrow Street entirely complete, and that was the presence of Mr. Lockwell. How Ivy wished to be able to bring him home, to have him witness all the improvements that had been made to the house, and to be reunited there with his daughters!

Yet it was because of Ivy herself that he was not there now; it was all her doing.

For half a year, Ivy had wanted nothing more than to be able to remove her father from the Madderly-Stoneworth Hostel for the Deranged. Then, on the day after Mr. Quent's return to the city, the message that they had so long awaited finally arrived. Their petition had been granted by King Rothard. His Majesty had signed a dispensation allowing Mr. Lockwell to be removed from Madstone's; they could bring their father home at once.

For a few moments after receiving the message, Ivy had experienced the greatest of joys. If her father was living here at Durrow Street with them, then she could never want for anything more. Only, sometimes what one thinks of as love is in truth a kind of selfishness. While having her father with them at the house was what suited *her*, it was not necessarily what was best for *him*.

In recent weeks, each time Ivy went to see Mr. Lockwell at the hostel, she had found him improved compared to her previous visit. The application of the electrical shocks was continuing to have a profound effect upon him. His eyes were clearer; he was able to feed himself and dress more ably; he spoke more, sometimes in full sentences, and seemed to recognize her at times. While she had been horrified to learn of the treatment at first, she had to confess that her reaction had been based upon a deficit of knowledge as much as a surplus of mistrust for the wardens at the hostel.

She could not allow ignorance or prejudice to stand in the way of something that benefited her father. So it was the case that, even as Ivy read the message from the Citadel, she knew that they could not remove Mr. Lockwell from Madstone's—not when there was hope the treatments would continue to help him.

Mr. Quent had agreed with her decision. As difficult as it was, her feelings were assuaged by the knowledge that they still possessed the petition signed by the king, and it had no expiry. If she ever felt the treatment was no longer helping her father, or that he was being harmed, then she would remove him from the hostel at once. In the meantime, Ivy was beginning to really hope it would be science that would at last undo the ill that magick had afflicted upon Mr. Lockwell, and restore him fully to his senses.

Her father was not the only one whose condition had improved. Mr. Quent had seemed in high spirits ever since his return to the city. He often smiled, and even laughed at times, and kissed Ivy at what seemed like every opportunity. What was more, he had been especially indulgent of Ivy's sisters; anything they expressed a wish for was theirs, to the point where Ivy no longer feared they might be spoiled, but was rather convinced of it.

The night of his return to Invarel, when they at last were alone together in their chamber, Mr. Quent had told her that he had accomplished all that he could in Torland. Ivy could not help being curious about what he had done in his time in the far west, and if any of it had involved Lady Shayde, but she did not ask him about it. For all the confidences that existed between married beings, there were other oaths that bound him—namely those to the Crown. Besides, if there was something she needed to know, and it was within his power to tell her, then he would do so. Until then, she would not bother him like a gossipy wife.

For a while after his return, Mr. Quent spent many more hours with Ivy and her sisters than they were accustomed to, and they enjoyed his increased presence immensely. He read aloud to Ivy in the upstairs gallery, and listened thoughtfully to Lily play the pianoforte, and even let Rose use his hands for a loom as she wound skeins of yarn.

Recently, that situation had changed, and now he was at the Citadel even more often than before. Of course, that was only to be expected after the loss of the lord inquirer. Nor could Ivy complain, for when Mr. Quent was at home, his attention remained devoted to her and her sisters. Indeed, he seemed intent upon spending every moment he possibly could with them, and in their brief span of time together, Ivy had never known him to be so tender and affectionate.

Now Ivy sighed and pressed her cheek against the smooth bark of a birch tree. It seemed awful of her that she should be happy when so many others endured such sorrow. Every time she opened a broadsheet, she read of people in the country who suffered deprivation and uncertainty. Not that she had to look far afield for people who had suffered. Poor Mr. Rafferdy! And poor Mr. Quent as well. The former had lost his father, and the latter his master and friend. What was more, in losing the lord inquirer, she suspected the nation of Altania had been deprived of one of its staunchest defenders.

No, she was sure of it.

Despite the warmth of the afternoon, Ivy shivered. Even now, in this idyllic place drenched in sunlight, she felt a chill when she recalled what Lord Rafferdy had told her that day at the house on Durrow Street: the cave deep in the southern deserts of the Empire, and the fate that befell, one by one, all who entered that lightless and ancient place. She had written to Mr. Rafferdy the next day, describing for him her conversation with his father, and she hoped they would soon be able to discuss it in person. There had been no opportunity to do so when she and Mr. Quent were at Asterlane.

At least she did not have to bear the awful knowledge alone, for almost as soon as he arrived in the city, she had told Mr. Quent everything: how she had encountered the man in the black mask, how he had told her to go to the house on Durrow Street, and how she met Lord Rafferdy there. When she was finished, she had shown Mr. Quent the small piece of Wyrdwood that Lord Rafferdy had given her. He had not known what it might be, only that if her father had charged Lord Rafferdy with its care, then it must be important.

Did you know about the curse? she had asked her husband as they lay together in bed that night, aching too much for each other's company to allow themselves to sleep.

I suppose I did know something of it, he had said, his voice a low rumble. *That is, I knew they had discovered some terrible thing in a cave in the desert. I knew it was because of what befell them there that my father grew ill, and then the others. Though for all these years I have not known what it was they found inside the cave—not until you told me just now.*

Again Ivy shivered; it seemed the light of the sun had gone thin, as if veiled by a cloud. She slipped a hand into the pocket of her dress, and her fingers found the small, smooth bit of wood. Perhaps it was because it had once belonged to her father, but ever since Lord Rafferdy had given her the object, she had kept it near to her.

Or perhaps there was another reason she had kept it close. For even as she touched it, the sunlight grew warm and bright again, and the murmurings of the trees seemed to become a little louder. . . .

"Lady Quent, there you are!"

Ivy gasped and turned around, pulling her hand from her pocket. As she did, Lord Eubrey stepped into view from between a pair of birches.

"I thought we'd quite lost you," he said, then smiled. "And perhaps we did at that. For I say, you look very content!"

Now that her momentary shock had passed, Ivy could not help smiling in return. Lord Eubrey's expressions of cheer were every bit as contagious as they were frequent.

"How could I not be content? For I cannot imagine a more serene place."

He gave a shrug. "I will have to take you at your word. As you know, I utterly lack your and Lady Crayford's sensibility. I believe she brings me along solely because if I think a thing is worth looking at, then it must have no artistic value whatsoever, and so she knows not to paint it."

"I am sure that's not true!"

"On the contrary, it's terribly true. Just as it's true she wishes for you to come along because she knows that if your eye finds a thing intriguing, then there must be something of worth in it."

Ivy would not be accused of possessing abilities she did not. "I know very little of art! I only say what I think."

"Precisely. As most people say what they believe others think, that makes you a very rare and precious commodity, Lady Quent! And one that the rest of our party are wanting for. They wondered where you had gone and so headed off in all directions, looking hither and thither for you. However, once I saw this patch of trees, I knew at once to look for you here."

"What makes you say that?"

"Why, you have an affinity for trees. If we come near any in our ramblings, you are ever drawn to them—at least your gaze is, if not the whole of yourself. I am sure you are quite taken up with trees!"

A chime of alarm sounded within Ivy. For a moment she felt as she did when she was eight years old, standing by the New Ash in Lorring Park as the priest called out to her.

She did her best to make her tone light. "I suppose I do like them, for they are very picturesque."

He laughed. "Like them? On the contrary, you are quite smitten with them! Nor is there any reason to deny it. I have no doubt that if I liked looking at trees and prospects rather than at sleek horses and fast carriages, then I would be both a better and a richer man."

Unlike the priest all those years ago, Ivy detected no hint of suspicion in his words or on his face. All the same, she found she no longer wished to be among the trees.

"I am sorry I caused a commotion," she said. "We had better return to the others at once."

He offered his arm, and together they made their way from the grove. As they started across the field beyond, Ivy caught sight of a man in a blue coat waving at them.

"I believe Captain Branfort has seen us," she said.

"I'm sure he has. I've never met a man with keener eyes."

"Then it is good he is with us."

"Yes, it is. I'm glad his duties allow him to accompany us on occasion. And it is good that Colonel Daubrent and your friend—Mrs. Baydon, is it?—have taken him in. Goodness knows he could use a bit of congenial society. Poor old Branfort!"

Ivy shook her head. "What do you mean, 'Poor old Branfort'? Twenty-seven is hardly old! And I can think of no reason to call him poor." She thought of something Mr. Rafferdy had said once. "He is not *so* lacking in height."

This seemed to bemuse Lord Eubrey. "Height? No, I was not making a reference to his stature. He's a good-looking fellow, and handsome adds half a head. Rather, his deficit is one of companionship."

"Companionship? But as you said, he has made the acquaintance of the colonel as well as Mrs. Baydon, and they cannot be his only society. I am sure such an agreeable man must have a number of friends."

"Must he?" Eubrey gazed across the field. "A military man moves about a great deal. I have not known him for long, but from my conversations with the captain I gather that he has less often been stationed at a lively place such as Point Caravel and more often at remote forts and outposts, ones that housed few men of comparable rank."

Ivy could only concede that, depending on where he was stationed, it might be difficult for an officer to find appropriate society, and there was no Mrs. Branfort.

"What of his family? Surely they must provide Captain Branfort with some companionship."

Lord Eubrey looked down at her. "His family? But don't you know about Captain Branfort's family, Lady Quent?"

"No, he has never spoken of them that I've heard."

"For good reason. You see, his family settled at Marlstown."

Ivy could not hide her horror. "Marlstown?"

Lord Eubrey nodded, his face solemn. They walked more slowly now, and Ivy tried to comprehend this revelation. While the New Lands were thought to be vast, the Altanian colonies were limited to the islands situated off the western coast. To date, all attempts to establish a permanent colony on the shores of the main continent had failed.

The most recent of these attempts had been at Marlstown. A colony of three hundred souls was founded there over twenty-five years ago. According to a missive from the founders carried by one of the ships on its return voyage to Altania, the new colony was thriving. The land was fertile, the climate mild, and contact had been made with the nearby aboriginals, who were found to be curious and peaceable.

After that, no more missives ever came from the colony.

When at last an Altanian navy ship was able to sail down the coast to Marlstown half a year later, they discovered a terrible scene. The stockade that housed the colony had been burned to the ground, as had all the surrounding houses. There had been no sign of any of the colonists. Nor, when the men explored away from the coast, had they found any of the aboriginals. Instead, they had come upon only empty campsites.

The men attempted to go deeper inland but soon found themselves rebuffed by the deviously thick forest that covered the land in all directions. In the years that followed, several more ships went to Marlstown in an attempt to learn what had happened to the colony. However, no clue as to the fate of the colonists was ever found.

There had been rumors, though. Ivy remembered hearing some of them when she was small: how a navy lieutenant had returned stark mad from an expedition along that section of the New Lands coast, and had raved about a bottomless lake whose shores were strewn with skeletons but no skulls. And how the captain of a trader ship, blown ashore near Marlstown by a storm, had encountered a wizened aboriginal man who had told him not to venture into the forest "lest the spirits there take his head."

Ivy supposed these were no more than stories fabricated by

people fascinated with a terrible and inexplicable incident. In subsequent expeditions, no such lake had ever been discovered, and no native people were encountered in the vicinity. All the same, in the years since the destruction at Marlstown, there had not been any other attempts to establish a settlement on the mainland of the new continent. The forest was too vast and impenetrable, it was said, and the natives there too hostile.

"I don't understand," Ivy said at last when she found her voice. "How did he survive what occurred at Marlstown?"

"He was not there," Lord Eubrey said. "I learned about it all from Colonel Daubrent. Captain Branfort was sickly as an infant, having been born too soon, and did not make the journey with his parents. Instead, he was left with a distant relative who planned to send him over when he grew stronger. Of course, that never happened. Though later, Captain Branfort did indeed go to the New Lands, during the campaign at Aratuga."

Aratuga was one of the island colonies, a place where much sugar and rum were produced, and so of great value. Among the southern islands were several corsair states that had broken away from the Empire in decades past. One of these had attempted to gain control of Aratuga some years ago, but had been defeated by Altanian forces.

Lord Eubrey quickened his pace. "Come, Lady Quent, I can see the others are waiting for us. And if you would, don't mention to Captain Branfort that I told you of his history."

"I would never think of it!" she exclaimed.

To speak of such things could only bring up the most distressing memories, and that was something Ivy would never want to do. Lord Eubrey nodded, but he said nothing more, for by then they had come upon the rest of their little party.

"There now, I should have known it would be you who would find her, Eubrey!" Colonel Daubrent said, taking several long strides toward them. "But no doubt you had an unfair advantage, and used some sort of magick to deduce her whereabouts."

Lord Eubrey affected an aggrieved expression. "On the contrary, I did nothing of the sort!" He made a deliberate gesture with his right hand, so that the blue gem of his House ring caught the sunlight.

"Well, however you found her, we are grateful," Captain Branfort said. "Though I wonder what we did to drive you away, Lady Quent. I hope you didn't find our company tedious."

"Of course she found it tedious!" Lady Crayford exclaimed. She wore a gown the color of periwinkles that brought out the violet hues in her eyes. "How could she not find it so? I was fussing over my painting, while you men were speaking of guns and dogs and all manner of topics a woman of any measure of sensibility would find dreadful. It's a wonder Lord Eubrey was able to convince her to come back to us. But now that you have, Lady Quent, you must tell me what you think of my painting."

She took Ivy's hand and led her to her easel. Ivy gazed upon it with great wonder and delight. It was as if the sunlight itself had somehow been condensed into a kind of pigment, which the viscountess had then applied to the canvas in bold strokes.

"It's beautiful!" Ivy said, or rather gasped.

"I had not thought it to be particularly good." The viscountess gazed, not at the canvas, but at Ivy. "Yet I know that your eye is excellent, and that you are capable of speaking only truth, so I must concede there is some worth in the composition. Still, I do not believe you have spoken the *entire* truth. There is something amiss with it—I can see it in your expression. Do not deny it, Lady Quent, for I am as discerning of faces as you are of country scenes!"

So addressed, Ivy could only nod. "Yes, but it is the littlest thing. The birch trees on the left are lovely, but you have made them somewhat too perfect, I think. They are more crooked in life, and they lean a bit to one side."

Captain Branfort peered at the canvas, then regarded the distant prospect. "I believe she may be right."

"Of course she's right, Branfort!" Lord Eubrey said with a laugh. "I am quite sure Lady Quent is an expert on trees."

"I am nothing of the sort!" Ivy said, and felt her cheeks glowing.

"Do not protest, Lady Quent, for modesty when it is false is no virtue," Lady Crayford said, misunderstanding the source of Ivy's discomfort. "You are exactly right. I had felt there was something wrong with that side of the canvas, only I did not know what it was. I see now that I was painting the trees how I thought they should be, rather than how they are. Yet as ever, the imperfect is more fascinating than the idealized. For though the scene is tranquil now, the leaning of the trees speaks of winds that have blown at other times, and will surely blow again. I shall change them at once."

At this Colonel Daubrent shook his head. "Must you change them, sister? I rather like the trees the way they are."

"You mean all standing straight in a row like good soldiers?" Lord Eubrey said, his eyes sparkling. "You would make a regiment of them if you could, and have them march all about on your order."

"Now you're speaking nonsense, Eubrey," Colonel Daubrent said, a scowl darkening his handsome face, "as you so often do. A grove of trees can hardly march here and there."

Lord Eubrey smiled, though it seemed a rather sly expression. "Oh, they can't?"

The sunlight seemed to go white around Ivy. She was suddenly too warm, and the moist air, thick with the scent of honeysuckle, was cloying.

"Lady Quent, are you well? You look very flushed of a sudden."

She blinked and saw Captain Branfort before her. He took her arm, steadying her.

Ivy managed what she hoped was a light tone. "I'm sorry. I think perhaps I walked too far, that's all."

"Glory above, Eubrey!" Daubrent exclaimed. "What were you thinking, dragging her all the way across the field like that?"

Ivy tried to protest, and to tell them it was hardly Lord Eubrey's fault that she had ventured off across the fields. Only, it was difficult to breathe. She let Captain Branfort lead her to one of the chairs they had set up, and he dutifully held her parasol to shade her while the colonel brought her a cup of wine.

Ivy felt some mortification at being fussed over so, and by cap-

tains and colonels besides, yet she could not say she entirely dis-
liked it. The wine and shade revived her, and she was soon able to
relieve the captain of the parasol, which appeared to greatly relieve *him*.

That a man with such a troubled history could have such a
kind and goodly nature was a thing of amazement to Ivy. A life deprived of the comforts of family and close companionship would
have left many men surly or ill-adapted for gentler society. Not so
Captain Branfort.

After that, Ivy was content to sit beneath her parasol while the
others spoke and the viscountess painted. As was often the case in
present company, the conversation turned to a discussion of what
amusements to engage in next, and it was soon decided that the
viscountess would host an affair at her house three lumenals
hence. It would not be a grand party, but rather an afternoon tea,
with perhaps only four dozen invited.

"I am sure you men are bound to find the idea of a tea very
dull," the viscountess said as she mixed colors on a palette with a
brush. "Therefore, we will give it the theme of a hunting party. We
will have it out in the garden. I will summon Lord Crayford's
huntsman from the lodge out in Starness, and he can give a parade
of the viscount's best dogs. We will tap a cask of cider right there
on the lawn and will have plenty of tobacco on hand. What's
more, we can release a cage of quail or grouse into the air, and you
men can make what sport with them you will."

"We cannot shoot our guns in the city," Colonel Daubrent said
sternly. "It would cause a hazard."

Lady Crayford tapped the handle of her brush against her
cheek. "Would it? I suppose it must. Well, we can at least hide the
birds about and have the dogs fetch them for a little play." Lady
Crayford turned to smile at Ivy. "And do not fear, Lady Quent. I will
raise a pavilion so we ladies can enjoy finer fare and amusements
than what the men will be engaging in."

Ivy could only smile in return. She had never seen a hunting
party before, and even a mock affair here in the city was bound to
be a thing of great interest and enjoyment. Except . . .

"What is wrong, Lady Quent?" the viscountess said. "You look awfully grim of a sudden. Do you detect some flaw in my scheme?"

Her smile had wavered, Ivy realized. It seemed ill of her to not express enthusiasm for the plan. Indeed, it sounded delightful, like all of the viscountess's parties. Over the last month, Ivy had beheld so many marvelous sights, and had made the acquaintance of so many marvelous beings, all due to the generosity of Lady Crayford. Who was she to presume to comment on one of the viscountess's affairs?

"You must not think I disapprove in any way!" Ivy said, hoping her earnestness could be heard in her voice and seen upon her face. "It sounds like the most wonderful theme. It is only . . ."

"It is only what, Lady Quent?" Lord Eubrey said, raising an eyebrow.

Ivy hesitated, but she knew she could not withhold her thoughts now. "It is only that I wonder if it is entirely prudent to have another party so soon after the last. Sometimes I think . . . that is, the parties at your house are such grand affairs. Everyone is always dressed in the smartest fashions, and if a visiting royal from one of the Principalities was to sit at the dining table, he could hardly be displeased with anything that was served."

"I fail to see your criticism in this, Lady Quent," Colonel Daubrent said, his dark eyes intent upon her.

Ivy made herself regard him directly. "It is only that there are so many these days who want for so much—not just in the Outlands, but in the city as well. Each time I look at the broadsheet, I see stories of people who have no land or no work, and even those who want for food or shelter. Yet we ourselves have so much. It doesn't seem . . . that is, sometimes I fear that some ill must come of all of it."

Ivy cast her eyes down. Who was she to speak to these people so—people who had treated her in the most disinterested manner, who had given her so much while asking for nothing in return?

She felt a light touch on her cheek and looked up. Lady Crayford stood above her. There was no annoyance in her expression; rather, she wore what seemed a thoughtful smile.

"Dearest Lady Quent, this is why we adore you so. Your sensibility directs our hearts just as it does my brush. Sometimes I am so used to seeing a thing that I hardly see it at all. Yet as with these country scenes, in this matter you encourage me to regard familiar things with a novel eye."

She returned to her canvas, brush still in her hand. "I do sometimes forget how our affairs might look to those observing from the outside. Yet I ask you to consider what should happen if we, who are so fortunate, did not hold parties? If, in these troubled times, we chose austerity? Then who would the fowler offer his birds to, and how would the vintner sell his wine? You speak of those who have no work or food. Think how many more would lack these things if we who have so much chose to live in a frugal manner!"

Ivy felt her cheeks glowing. Her father had always told her to examine arguments from all sides, but in this case she had thought the matter through poorly.

The viscountess considered her painting, then made a small daub with her brush. "We must each live according to our means, Lady Quent, however great or small—not above them, but neither below. Our society functions only when we all do so."

Ivy nodded. "Sir Quent once told me much the same thing."

The viscountess turned away from her painting. "Did he? Well, your husband is a wise man, and a great defender of our country."

Lord Eubrey clapped his hands. "Excellent! You make it sound quite patriotic to have a party, Lady Crayford."

"You say it mockingly, yet I say it in all earnestness: I do not believe there could be a more patriotic thing to do!"

"In that case, I suppose as good soldiers it is our solemn duty to attend," Captain Branfort said. He looked to the viscountess's brother. "What say you, Colonel?"

Colonel Daubrent answered with a bow. "If it serves Altania, then I shall give it my all."

"Well, I will not be singled out as a traitor to my nation," Lord Eubrey said. "Thus I will attend as well. What of you, Lady Quent? Will you give your best for Altania along with the rest of us?"

So confronted, Ivy could only laugh and acquiesce. Of course she would attend the party three lumenals hence—for their sake, and for Altania's.

"Oh!" Ivy said, making a sudden realization. "But I'm sure that's the same day I promised Mrs. Baydon I would next visit with her."

"Then by all means you must bring her with you," Lady Crayford said.

Ivy smiled. She knew Mrs. Baydon would be delighted to have another opportunity to go to the house of the viscountess. She had adored the party there last month, and her only disappointment, she had told Ivy as they walked in Halworth Gardens some days later, was that she had not been able to endure longer than she had. After suffering so much anxiety beforehand, and then being overwhelmed with numerous wonders upon arriving, she was after a few hours utterly exhausted, and so had been forced to depart the party early.

"And do prevail upon Sir Quent to come as well," the viscountess went on. "There are many who would much like to meet him."

Ivy promised she would ask him, though she noted his business for the Crown occupied a great deal of his time these days.

With the matter of their next affair settled, everyone resumed their previous activities. Lady Crayford returned to her painting while the men partook of tobacco and continued their discussions of hunting. Ivy was content to sit in the chair, basking in the warmth of the congenial company and the afternoon sun.

Yet every now and then, when the wind was just right, she could hear the birch trees from across the field, murmuring in secret voices.

CHAPTER TWENTY-THREE

ELDYN GRASPED THE hands to either side of him as he and the other illusionists on the stage took another bow. The audience continued to thunder its approval, letting out sharp whistles and stamping boots against the floor until the entire theater trembled. Another bow was demanded. The players complied again, and again.

At last the crimson curtain sped shut over the proscenium. However, even as the roar of applause dwindled, the excited talk of the illusionists welled up in its place.

"Did you hear them out there?" Dercy said, wearing a grin upon his silver face as he gripped Eldyn's arm. "By God, I half feared they were going to bring the house down over our heads. Only it was worth it to hear such applause. And it was yours, you know."

Eldyn could only laugh. "Mine? I hardly think that's the case! I'm very sure it was *you* they were applauding for. The Moon is the hero of the show, and I don't think you've ever shone brighter than you did tonight. You were a marvel."

Dercy made a florid bow. "You will get no argument from me on that point. I was better than I've ever been tonight. However, it was only because *you* made me so."

These words astonished Eldyn. He did not know what to say. His roles had been important, yes, but all secondary—conjuring comets during the action in the firmament or glittering schools of fish in the scenes in the sea.

"I'm sure people hardly even noticed anything I conjured tonight."

"That's exactly my point."

Now Eldyn was puzzled as well as surprised. "Did all the accolades turn your head? You're making no sense at all."

"On the contrary, for once Dercy is making perfect sense," Hugoth said, taking off his spiky gold crown and scratching his crimson beard. He was one of the oldest illusionists in the troupe, being near to forty, and always brought a weight of maturity to his performance as the jealous Sun King.

"The best performer does not claim the center of the stage for himself," Hugoth went on. "Rather, he makes everyone around him shine the brighter. The reason the audience could fix all of their attention upon Dercy and me was because everything else in the scene was so perfectly wrought. They had no need to concentrate upon it and wonder what this thing or that was supposed to be. Dercy's right—we all earned a portion of the applause, but tonight it belonged especially to you, Eldyn."

The other players around called out their agreements, and Eldyn was beyond words as a warmth enclosed him. Merrick, who seldom seemed to smile these days, did so now and gave him a deep bow, while Riethe clapped Eldyn on the back—with his left hand, for the right was still swathed in bandages.

"That was fine work you did out there," Riethe said. "I don't mind saying it, though it means I might not be getting my roles back even if my hand does heal up all right."

"Don't worry, Riethe," said a small, slightly built illusionist with brown hair. His name was Mauress, but everyone just called him Mouse, given his size and the propensity for his nose to wrinkle up when he was nervous. "You'll always have a place here at the Theater of the Moon. There's always a need for a big dunderhead to hoist the sandbags to the rafters."

"It's you who'll be hoisted to the rafters if you keep talking like that, Mouse," Riethe called back cheerfully.

"I'm sure the roles will be waiting for you as soon as your hand is better," Eldyn said to Riethe.

The other illusionist shrugged broad shoulders. "If so, it's because by then you'll be on to bigger things."

The illusionists continued to talk excitedly of the performance.

A bottle was passed around, and Eldyn took a fiery draught, though whiskey could hardly have made him more intoxicated. Then whoops and whistles rang out as Master Tallyroth, clad in his customary black, stepped from the wings.

"Did you see us, Master Tallyroth?" Dercy said gleefully.

"It is my legs that give me a bit of trouble these days, Dercy," the elder illusionist said. "My eyes function quite well. But to answer your question—yes, you were all quite splendid tonight."

Leaning upon his cane, Master Tallyroth approached Eldyn. "I heard the others congratulating you, Mr. Garritt. As they should. Yours was an excellent performance."

"Thank you," Eldyn managed to say. As always, a few words from the master illusionist meant more than any amount of applause.

"Though I did notice you deviated from the stage directions in the scene atop the mountain. The direction called for falcons, yet I saw that you conjured doves instead."

Eldyn no longer felt so warm. "I'm sorry, Master Tallyroth. I'm not sure why I did it, exactly. It was only . . . well, the scene is about how the birds untie the Moon's bonds and help him escape the king's men. Only, falcons are birds of prey, while doves are a symbol of the soul's freedom in . . ."

He started to say *in the Testament,* but quickly swallowed the words.

". . . that is, in many stories they stand for freedom," he finished.

"Well, I thought it was brilliant," Dercy proclaimed. "It was more beautiful. Don't you agree, Master Tallyroth?"

"I do," the master illusionist said. "However, next time, Mr. Garritt, I would ask that you not improvise during a performance. Rather, if you have an idea to improve something, let us rehearse it first to make certain it does not alter the intent of the scene."

"Yes, Master Tallyroth," Eldyn said, ducking his head.

What had he been thinking, to make a change to the play like that? Had not Master Tallyroth devised every bit of staging himself? Yet Eldyn had been so caught up in the scene on the mountain, and as he conjured the birds he had thought of a passage he had recently read in the Testament, describing how St. Galibran had escaped his own captors when a flock of doves untied the ropes that bound him.

"There now, have no fear," Tallyroth said, leaning close and speaking in a voice that only Eldyn could hear. "You did exceedingly well tonight, Mr. Garritt. I am very pleased, as is Madame Richelour."

Even as he spoke this, the madam of the theater arrived on-stage, clad in a gown hardly less flamboyant and colorful than any costume worn by the illusionists. She spread kisses around, as well as many silver quarter regals, and told them to go celebrate and make merry—though not too much, or too late. For once word of tonight's performance spread along Durrow Street, they were sure to gain an even larger audience for the next show, and she wanted it to be just as good as this one.

A QUARTER HOUR later, just as at every house on the east end of Durrow Street, illusionists spilled out the back of the Theater of the Moon, having lost their costumes but not their thirst. They proceeded at once to a nearby tavern, parading through the door in a spirited throng.

Their kind was not an unusual sight at this particular establishment. While a few scowls greeted them, there were a greater number of cheers, and these were rewarded by bouquets of poppies that suddenly burst up from ale cups or hummingbirds that flew out of unkempt beards—much to the surprise and amusement of their respective owners.

The illusionists took over the booths in one corner and called for whiskey and punch. Given the tavern's proximity to Durrow Street, the barkeeps here knew to bite a coin before taking it as payment. Illusion might trick the eye, but not the tooth. Fortunately, Madame Richelour had given them more than enough to fuel their revel, and soon laughter and phantasms welled forth.

The flow of their merriment ebbed only once, when a trio of

young men entered the tavern. They wore green velvet coats trimmed with lace, and their faces were powdered as white as their wigs. Several of the players from the Theater of the Moon hailed the newcomers and called out cheerful greetings. The young men waved back, but they did not come over; instead, they sat apart at a table and hunkered over their cups.

"So who are those three over there?" Eldyn asked, gesturing with his own cup.

It was Merrick who answered. "They are players at the Theater of Emeralds."

Now Eldyn understood why the laughter had quieted. All of them had read the story in *The Swift Arrow* last quarter month— how the body of a young man had washed up on the shores of the Anbyrn down in Waterside. The story described how the corpse could not be identified, for it had been decomposed, and its eyes consumed by fish.

Except they all knew that wasn't the case—that the young man's eyes had surely been gone before his body was heaved in the river. What's more, *The Swift Arrow,* which always had a penchant for lurid detail, had described how shreds of fine lace and green velvet clung to the corpse.

For all the brightness in Eldyn's own world over these last months, a darkness had continued to stalk around the edges of Durrow Street. In that time, a number of illusionists had gone missing. How many exactly, no one could say. It was not unusual for the young men who worked in the theaters to leave the city without warning—perhaps whisked off by angry fathers who had discovered what mischief they were up to, or going of their own accord to escape debts or warrants.

Yet more illusionists had vanished than could be accounted for by the usual comings and goings, and no one had forgotten what had happened to Donnebric or Braundt. Whispers rippled along Durrow Street. Currents of fear ebbed and flowed among the theaters.

And then the dead body had washed up from the gray, lapping waters of the Anbyrn.

Merrick bowed his head over his cup. Several of the others gripped his shoulders. All of them knew his friend Braundt had also been a player at the Theater of Emeralds.

"Two missing from one house," Riethe said, letting out a heavy breath. "By God, that's cruel luck."

"And now two more have quit the theater," Mouse chimed in. "I heard about it yesterday. It was those dark-haired twins who performed there—they went back to the country."

"But why would they quit the theater?" Eldyn asked.

Mouse's nose wrinkled up. "Well, why do you think? They left the city because they don't want to be the next ones pulled out of the river."

"Hush, Mouse!" Dercy said, glaring at the smaller illusionist. "That's not the sort of talk we need tonight. We're here to celebrate. No one wants to hear your morbid ramblings."

"I have a right to say what I want," Mouse protested.

Riethe jerked a thumb at a piece of paper tacked to the wall. "Not according to the Rules of Citizenship, you don't. I believe Number Seventeen prohibits acting like an utter prat. You don't want us to call for the redcrests and have them haul you to Barrowgate, do you? I'm sure the Black Dog could use a hot poker to prod all sorts of interesting secrets out of you."

Mouse scowled and opened his mouth, but before he could say anything more, Merrick looked up from his drink.

"Mouse may be a prat, but what he heard is true. Teodan and Jerris did quit, and now the Theater of Emeralds is down by four players. I've heard they might have to shut their doors."

Riethe let out a snort. "Surely they have understudies. And they can always find another player if they have to."

"Can they?" Mouse said, crawling past Riethe onto the table and taking up the pitcher of punch. "New players of quality are hard to come by. Why do you think Madame Richelour was so keen to nab Eldyn? Besides, everyone knows that the master illusionist at the Theater of Emeralds has fallen deep into the grips of the mor—"

"Mouse!" Dercy said, angrily this time. "I said, enough. We're here to make merry. Understand? So get to it."

Dercy wrested the pitcher of punch from Mouse, filled a cup, and thrust it into the young man's hands. Mouse made a mocking bow, then sat cross-legged on the table and took a deep draught. As he did, long whiskers sprang outward from either side of his nose and a thin gray tail uncoiled behind him. This resulted in a burst of laughter all around.

With that, the ill mood was dispelled. More punch was called for, and before long a number of the young men were belting out bawdy songs, proving they were not nearly as skilled at singing as at making illusions. After some encouragement Eldyn joined in, and he found himself singing about less than savory ladies and sailors with unusual appendages. It was only after some time that he thought to glance across the tavern at the place where the three illusionists from the Theater of Emeralds sat.

The table was empty; the three young men were gone.

ELDYN AWOKE TO moonlight.

He turned his head on the pillow. Dercy lay next to him on the narrow bed, one arm flung above his head. The wan illumination washed all color from his skin and hair, and he might have seemed a thing carved of marble were it not for the steady rise and fall of his chest.

Moving quietly, Eldyn sat up against the plain wooden head-board. Some hours ago, having conjured an excess of heat, they had thrown open the shutters of the one small window in Dercy's room. Now the air flowing through the opening was cold against Eldyn's skin.

He slipped from the bed and moved to the window to close the shutters; then he paused. The moon was full, shining in the firmament like a silver coin that had just been minted. Despite the chill, he basked in its light and beauty.

It had been less than a year since he'd first seen an illusion play at the Theater of the Moon. Now he was performing there himself. Nor did finding out what went on behind the curtain in any way lessen the wonder of the play for him. Rather, it was all more marvelous than ever.

With only the slightest flick of his finger, Eldyn brought forth an illusory dove. The bird perched upon his hand, its feathers exquisitely formed and as luminous as the moonlight itself. He could not help a pleased smile. For some reason, illusions were always especially easy for him to summon after he and Dercy had amused themselves upon the bed.

Eldyn tilted his hand, and the dove hopped down to the windowsill, puffing its chest as if readying itself to burst into song. Though of course that was not possible; the Siltheri had the power to conjure illusions only of light, not sound. Instead, the illusory dove stretched its wings. As it did, a slight tinge of crimson colored its white feathers.

Eldyn looked up. The heavens had continued their ceaseless turnings, and now another body had appeared in the sky, glowing a rusty red. The new planet, Cerephus, had grown so close that even to the naked eye it could be perceived as a tiny disk rather than a single point. Its proximity was what had caused the lumenals and umbrals to go all mad, and had made a jumble of the timetables in the almanac.

Well, at least there was an explanation for the increasing unpredictability of the length of days and nights. Yet what was it that was making everything else go mad these days? It seemed that every day brought a fresh report of rebels or traitors being shot down in some skirmish in the Outlands or getting hanged by the neck right here in the city. Yet it was paradoxical that the more traitors to the realm that were dispatched, the more of them there seemed to be. It was similar to the way the broadsheets continually reported shortages of land and work and food and candles, yet there never seemed to be a shortage of ink or paper to print grim news upon.

That's why the work we do is needed more than ever, Dercy had told him the other day when Eldyn, gloomy from looking through a copy of *The Fox,* had expressed these thoughts. *People need something to help them forget all the darkness, and to remember how to see light and beauty.*

Eldyn wanted to believe that was true. After all, when his own life was not so happy as it was now, illusion plays had allowed him to escape his troubles, at least for a time. Yet if the world needed illusionists so much, why were they being found bloodied on the steps of abandoned chapels and floating in the waters of the river?

He shivered, then gave his finger a flick, and the dove sprang off the sill to wing into the night sky, heading upward until the white bird was lost against the white moon. In the play, in the scene when Eldyn summoned the birds, the Moon was able to escape his captors. Yet his escape was only temporary; in the end, the Sun King still caught up to him.

Eldyn thought of the twins who had left the Theater of Emeralds and had returned to the country. Had they really escaped? Who was to say they would not be discovered for their nature there, and find themselves in the power of those who did not care for their kind?

Well, he hoped that would not be the case, for them or any others. In the meantime, Eldyn would be careful himself, and he would make liberal use of shadows if he was ever alone in unsavory places. Then, soon enough, when he had earned his and Sashie's portions, he would leave Durrow Street behind to take his place in the Church, and there, within those blessed walls, it was impossible that any harm should ever come to him.

"What are you doing over there?" spoke a sleepy voice.

"Just closing the shutters," Eldyn said softly. "The night is long, and has gotten cold. Go back to sleep."

"Great God, it is cold," Dercy said, shuddering as he pulled up the bedcovers. "I can half see my breath. Come back here, will you?"

Eldyn pulled the shutters closed. Now only a thin sliver of moonlight passed into the room. In the gloom he returned to the bed and climbed beneath the covers. But though he willed them to do so, his eyes did not shut.

Dercy leaned up on an elbow to look down at him. "Are you

certain you're all right? I know that look—the way that small line appears just above the bridge of your nose." He yawned, then touched Eldyn's brow with a finger. "Something is troubling you, isn't it? Well, go on, then, tell me what it is. You know neither of us will get another wink until you do."

Eldyn could only concede this was true, for he knew Dercy would not stop pressing him until he confessed to something. However, he didn't want to talk about the missing illusionists.

"What was Mouse talking about back at the tavern?" he said instead.

Dercy frowned. "Why should you care about anything Mouse said? If he utters a thing, then it can only be nonsense."

Eldyn sat up, trying to recall the little man's words. "He said there was something the matter with the master illusionist at the Theater of Emeralds. He started to say what it was, only you interrupted him." A thought came to him. "It's the same thing that's wrong with Master Tallyroth, isn't it?"

Dercy didn't answer right away, and by that Eldyn knew he was right. "What is it?" he said. "Master Tallyroth can only walk with the help of a cane. His hands are always shaking, and I never see him craft an illusion."

With a sigh, Dercy laid back down on the pillow and stared up into the darkness. "You've had enough to think about these last weeks, what with learning the craft and then taking to the stage. I didn't want you to be bothered by thinking about it. But now that you're Siltheri, you have to learn about it eventually."

"I have to learn about what?"

"About the mordoth."

The window was fast shut, but all the same Eldyn shuddered. "The mordoth," he murmured, the word strange and unpleasant on his tongue. "What is it?"

"It's an affliction. Some call it the Gray Wasting."

"I've never heard of an illness called that."

Dercy let out a snort. "That's no surprise. Nobody but illusionists speaks of it, because nobody but an illusionist can be affected by it."

"It is very contagious, then?" Eldyn said, his chest growing tight.

"No," Dercy said firmly, sitting up. "No, it's not contagious. You can't catch the mordoth from anyone else. Which means it's nothing you need to have any worry about—not if you're careful."

"What do you mean, if I'm careful?"

Dercy leaned back against the headboard and seemed to think for several moments; then he looked at Eldyn. "When you conjure an illusion, do you know where it comes from?"

Eldyn considered this; it was a question he had wondered about this last month. "I'm not really sure. It feels like I'm gathering the light around me and shaping it into something."

"That's right. Even at night, here in this room with the shutters closed, there is light for me to shape." He held out his hand, and a ball of soft blue illumination appeared on it. "There's the moonlight and starlight seeping through the crack in the shutter, and a bit of light from the streetlamps making its way in. But even if you were to seal the window, and cover it with a black cloth, and plug every chink in the wall so that not the slightest beam of light could enter, and the room was utterly dark—even then you would still be able to conjure an illusion."

Eldyn reached out, taking the glowing ball of light into his own hand. Now he was sustaining the phantasm, not Dercy. "How is that possible? How can I shape an illusion when there's no light to shape?"

"Because there is always light in here." Dercy tapped a finger against Eldyn's chest. "Or rather, there is a power that can become light. It's the same power that causes your heart to beat and your lungs to draw breath."

"It's life, you mean."

Dercy nodded. "Yes, it's the force of your life. And every time you create an illusion, like that light you're holding there, you must give up a portion of that power—but only the tiniest bit. Think of an oyster making a pearl. Just like an oyster can only form a pearl around a grain of sand, so you must give up a fragment of yourself around which to fashion the phantasm."

These words astonished Eldyn. "You mean I must give up some part of my life every time I make an illusion?"

The sphere of light wavered on his hand. It would have sputtered and gone out, only Dercy took it back, and it resumed its soft, steady glow.

He gave a low laugh. "Come now, don't look so shocked. Doesn't everything that is good in this world come at a price? Besides, it takes only the littlest amount of your power—a single grain from a mountain of sand. And you're young, so you've got plenty to give. If it means you might endure a handful fewer years in your decrepitude when you are an old man, what of it? Is that really too much to give up in exchange for all this?"

Dercy tossed the ball into the air. It split into a dozen tinier spheres, and they floated gently above the bed like fairy-lights.

In the gentle glow, Eldyn looked down at his hands. Instead of smooth, he imagined them thick-knuckled and knotted with veins. It was not a pleasant exercise. To see his hands—and the whole of his body—wither with age was not an idea he relished. If he could exchange the final few years of his life, which were sure to be plagued by pain and decay, for the power to craft illusions now, was that not a fair bargain?

He closed his hands and looked up at Dercy. "If it's normal for illusionists to give up a bit of themselves when they craft phantasms, then what's the mordoth?"

"It's what happens to Siltheri who are not careful. It only takes a tiny grain for an oyster to make a pearl—as long as you are patient. Just so, it only takes a bit of your power to make an illusion. However, you can give it more if you want to. Much more."

"I don't understand. Why would someone do such a thing?"

"It takes hard work to learn to shape light properly." Dercy flicked his finger, and the fairy-lights danced and wove in the air above them. "And the bigger, brighter, and more elaborate the phantasms, the more time and practice it takes to learn how to conjure them. It's easier to shape the light that comes from within you compared to the light around us—because it's your own light after all."

Eldyn felt a pang of horror. "You mean some illusionists use up their own life just to make grander illusions?"

"They do," Dercy said, his voice going low. "I think you can understand the temptation. On Durrow Street, to conjure the grandest illusions is to win the greatest accolades—and the most gold regals. You might even become a master illusionist. But as with all things, there is a cost to be paid. Some use up too much of their own light too quickly in their pursuit of greatness. They become spent and weak; they begin to waste."

"And if they keep conjuring illusions?"

"Then they die."

Eldyn hugged his knees to his chest. "There is no cure," he said, not really asking a question, for he thought he already knew the answer.

"No, there is no remedy. A man only has so much light, so much life, within him. Once it is spent, it is gone forever."

They were quiet for a minute, and Eldyn tried to comprehend what he had learned. Illusions were so beautiful—how cruel that to create them should cost so much! Why would God grant a man such a wondrous ability and then punish him so terribly to use it? It seemed the most awful sort of jest.

All the same, the cost did not have to be so great. Dercy had said that only the foolish squandered their own light when conjuring illusions. Skill that could have been properly earned through diligent practice was instead bought in the most cavalier fashion at the cost of one's own life. It was madness, of course, but men did many mad things for money or glory.

"Only, I can't imagine Master Tallyroth being so foolish," Eldyn said. "How could he have been one who fell prey to such temptation?"

Dercy gave a sigh. "Sometimes knowledge is won only at great cost. Master Tallyroth is wise now, but he was not always so. From stories I have heard, as a youth he was a libertine who led the most profligate sort of existence, and he likely would have died very young had it not been for the influence of Madame Richelour."

A sadness filled Eldyn, and he wiped dampness from his

cheek. "I do not care what Master Tallyroth did when he was young. He is good now, and I do not want him to die."

"There, don't be so glum," Dercy said, circling an arm around Eldyn's shoulders. "What's done is done, so there's no use mourning it. Master Tallyroth knows that better than anyone does. Besides, Madame Richelour is watching over him. She convinced him to give up crafting even the smallest illusions, which means he's bound to endure for years and years."

Eldyn had more questions to ask—how much light did he have, and how would he know if he was using too much?

Dercy touched a finger to his lips. "Come now, we're wide awake and the room is cold. We might as well warm it up."

After that, they had no breath for words. Instead they bent all their attention to conjuring different sorts of wonders while the fairy-lights danced above them in wild circles.

CHAPTER TWENTY-FOUR

O, ROSE, YOU'VE got your trident all crooked," Lily said. "Hold it straight beside you. And lift up your chin! No one will be able to see your face if you keep staring at your feet like that. Remember, you're a princess."

Rose shook her head. "But I'm not really a princess."

"Yes you are, as long as you're in the tableau." Lily adjusted the tiara made of pasteboard and tempera that crowned her head. "Now hold yourself in a way befitting a daughter of the sea king."

Rose adjusted the white sheet that draped her shoulder and drew herself up, looking at once pretty and awkward, and thus also very sweet. Ivy put a hand to her mouth to conceal a smile, for she knew her sisters were being quite serious about this business.

Indeed, the industriousness Lily had displayed regarding the affair of the tableau had astonished Ivy. That morning, upon rising in the dark toward the end of an umbral that was a bit too long to sleep all the way through, Ivy had gone downstairs to find Lily already risen and poring over a book of Tharosian myths by candlelight. Rose appeared soon after, and they had hardly finished their breakfast when, at Lily's command, the two of them proceeded up to the second floor gallery to continue their work.

While Lily and Rose had been laboring over their tableau for nearly a month, there was already some degree of concern that the scene would not be done in time for their party. For one thing, they had lost a number of lumenals making attempts at other scenes. After some initial effort was put in, Lily had found a flaw with each one. The illustration was not dramatic enough to sustain a tableau, she decided, or the theme had the proper weight and effect but did not lend itself to being presented with the materials they might reasonably obtain.

There was a period of several lumenals when Lily was alarmingly determined to stage a tableau that required the presence of an actual, living horse. That lasted until Mr. Quent declared that anyone who was responsible for bringing a horse into the house was also responsible for removing anything it might deposit inside, at which point that scene was discarded.

At last Lily settled upon depicting the Annunciation of Cassephia and Hesper. It was a scene taken from Tharosian myth. In the story, two beautiful young sisters fled the Bull King of Belethon, who intended to make sacrifices of them in his effort to win the favor of Vrais, the god of battle. With nowhere left to run, they leaped off a rocky cliff into the crashing waves of the ocean rather then let themselves be a cause of war.

They would surely have perished, only the sea god Ureyus, enchanted by their beauty and goodness, took pity on the sisters. He bore them up on a blue wave and crowned them with sea foam, announcing to all the world that they were henceforth to be protected as his own daughters. Thus the Bull King's schemes of war were thwarted. And to this day, situated off the coast of the Principalities, there were two small islands named Cassephia and Hesper, both of which were said to be lovely and peaceful.

Ivy thought the theme was appropriate for two young ladies being presented to society, and she approved of its choice, as did Mr. Quent. In the time since, Ivy had become increasingly impressed with Lily's ability to invoke the mood and grandeur of the scene using not the skills of Siltheri illusionists, but only her own ingenuity. Shimmering silks of blue and green were hung and arranged in the most clever way to suggest surging waves capped with white gauze. Craggy rocks formed of paper and wire were given the most naturalistic look through the liberal application of plaster and paint, and there were even real shells affixed to their surfaces.

Despite Lily and Rose's progress, there was still a great deal to do to complete the scene, and their costumes were not even begun, hence the sheets that draped them at present. Before they started the costumes, Lily wanted to know exactly how they would be standing in the scene, so that their garb could be designed to both permit and flatter the proper poses. It was this task Ivy had agreed to help them with that morning.

"Put your shoulders back, Rose. No, not *that* far back. You'll get a crick. Remember, left hand on your hip and the trident held straight in your right. Now, imagine that you can feel a bracing wind fresh off the sea."

Rose gripped the broom that was serving as her trident. She drew a breath, and suddenly upon her face was such an expression that it seemed she did feel the touch of some unseen breeze.

"That's it!" Lily cried. "Don't move an inch, Rose. While you hold yourself in that pose, I will stand just so."

She affected her position quite easily and naturally, and Ivy could only imagine she had practiced it many times before a mirror.

"Quickly, Ivy. Pin our sheets in place before either of us moves! And do not pull the cloth too tight. It must look like it is caught in a wind."

Ivy hurried to the task, beginning with Rose. Fortunately, Mrs. Seenly arrived in the gallery at that moment, and at Lily's prompting she gladly helped with the task. Soon all the pins were in place so that the arrangements of the sheets might be re-created when the costumes were sewn.

"Don't you both look regal," Mrs. Seenly said as she took a step back from the platform where the two stood. "I feel just as if I had stepped into a picture in a storybook."

This comment elicited a pleased expression on Lily's round face, though she only said, "Oh, we are not at all regal now—not compared to how we will look when the tableau is done."

Ivy helped her sisters climb down from the platform and remove their sheets, which were carefully folded so as not to disturb the pins. These were then given to Mrs. Seenly to take to the parlor, where Rose would work on sewing the seams later.

After this was done, Lily declared that the paper and plaster rocks did not look natural enough and so would require bits of seaweed; this she was certain Rose could make very easily by knitting green yarn, as long as Lily directed her how to shape the strands. As the two busied themselves with this new task, Ivy walked toward the north end of the room. It was difficult for her to pass through the gallery without making an examination of the two doors that had been uncovered during the renovation.

The door at the south end of the gallery, with its carving of a rune-covered sword over a shield, was certainly remarkable. However, it was the northern door, the one carved with leaves, that fascinated her the most. As she approached it, the wooden leaves carved upon it seemed to ripple as if they, too, felt the wind that Lily had imagined for Rose.

Indeed, so pronounced was the effect that Ivy wondered if *he* was near, but when she glanced out the nearest window she saw that the garden below was empty save for the little hawthorns and chestnuts that grew there. It was merely an effect of the light filtering through the gauze curtains that made it appear as if the leaves on the door were trembling.

The man in the black mask had not shown himself to her since the day she had spoken with Lord Rafferdy. Why the stranger had wanted her to find the Black Stork that day, she did not know. And while the things Lord Rafferdy told her had been fascinating, she did not know how they could be important to *him*. Still, as she had done his bidding, perhaps the mysterious being was done with her now. She hoped that was the case.

Wishing to see how her sisters were progressing, Ivy started to move away from the door, only then she turned back. Increasingly of late, a peculiar feeling had come over her when she studied the door—an impression that something was missing from it. This hardly seemed possible, of course. The door had been so perfectly fashioned by its maker that she could not imagine a flaw would have gone unnoticed or uncorrected.

All the same, she had sensed it again just now as she was turning away. When she was a girl, her father had taught her that the very faintest stars were actually easier to see when you looked at them out of the corner of your eye rather than gazing at them directly. Perhaps there was something about the door that was similar in that regard. . . .

"Well, Ivy, what do you think of it?"

"I don't know what it could be," she murmured.

"Avast, what do you mean you don't know what it could be? It's seaweed, of course!"

Ivy blinked, then turned her head to see Lily standing beside her, holding a thick green strand.

"I think Rose did a very fine job," Lily went on. "That is, once I told her how it must be shaped, for she had it all wrong at first. 'It has to be crooked, Rose, not straight,' I told her. 'Otherwise it will not look at all natural.'"

Ivy smiled. "It looks very authentic. I should fear it was going to drip seawater on the floor if I did not know it was made of yarn."

Lily appeared very pleased by this. "I'm not surprised you

should think such a thing. It's quite convincing. Now we must make a dozen more." She glanced at the windows. "Blast and blunder, can the sun already be so high? If we keep having such short lumenals, we'll be slaving by lamplight to have the tableau done in time."

She hurried back across the long room to Rose to continue their labors. Deciding her assistance was no longer needed, Ivy departed the gallery and proceeded downstairs. As she drew near the door of the library, the wooden eye carved in the lintel above opened with an audible *snick,* then turned to peer down at her.

"And good morning to you," Ivy said, looking up.

The eye gazed at her for a moment, then snapped shut. Ivy gave it a fond smile, then entered the library. This was a spacious room populated with many comfortable chairs and whose large windows let in plenty of light to read by. It was, in Ivy's opinion, the best room in the house.

There was a cherrywood writing table beside one of the windows that offered a view of the garden. It was here that Ivy liked to compose letters or work on the house ledger. And it was here as well that she performed another task each day and night.

Ivy took a key from her pocket and unlocked a drawer beneath the table. She removed the Wyrdwood box and, with a light touch, unbound the tendrils that held it shut. Since discovering the secret of her father's journal, she had made sure to look through it at least once each lumenal and umbral, or twice if they were especially long. She would go through the pages one by one, turning each carefully, and if she came upon a new entry she would transcribe it on a fresh sheet of paper.

In this way, she had discovered at least half a dozen more entries written in her father's thin, wandering hand. As with the first two she had found, each entry was preceded not with a date but rather with a description of the position of certain celestial objects. From her experiments with the celestial globe, Ivy knew that an entry appeared in the journal only when particular stars and planets were aligned in the heavens just as they had been when her father originally wrote the words.

It was a remarkable enchantment. Yet why had he placed it on the journal? He had written to her in his foreword that the knowledge contained therein must not come into the possession of others—presumably the magicians in the Vigilant Order of the Silver Eye. But surely locking it in the box of Wyrdwood would have sufficed in that regard. Besides, she could not think she was so clever that others would not be able to discover the secret to the puzzle if she could. There had to be some other reason her father had enchanted the journal.

Unfortunately, the recent entries she had discovered had cast no light on the matter. Nor had they made any mention of Tyberion and Arantus. What these objects were, Ivy still did not know. For a while she had begun to wonder if they might in fact be the two doors that had been discovered in the second floor gallery. After all, despite their beauty, both doors had been deliberately covered up. What's more, her father had described Tyberion and Arantus as having keys, and he had stated it was important they not be opened—both of which suggested doors of some sort.

However, she could not recall seeing a keyhole on either of the doors in the gallery, and a thorough examination confirmed this fact. Besides, neither of the doors was locked, and there was nothing on the other side of them save for stone walls. Thus, disappointed, she had been forced to admit that she had no idea what Tyberion and Arantus might be, or where they were.

All the same, there was one thing she had learned about them. She had thought she had seen the names before, and after going through some of the books of Tharosian myths Lily had brought into the house, Ivy had discovered she was right. Both of them were lesser Tharosian deities. Tyberion was a god of vengeance, while Arantus, his sister, was a figure associated with hunts and the bow. They were two of the numerous children of Dalatair, who himself was one of the greater gods of the Tharosian pantheon, being the master of fates and chance.

Dalatair was also the name of one of the eleven planets. It was at times the brightest planet in the sky, and its motions were the most complex. Through further reading, Ivy had discovered that two of Dalatair's many moons were named Tyberion and Arantus. That was fitting, given their association with Dalatair in myth. But what did any of this have to do with the things her father had written about in the journal?

Ivy didn't know. She hoped she would come upon more entries that would explain what these objects were. Lately it was her impression that the journal entries she found had all been written at a time prior to the events involving Tyberion and Arantus.

This was not to say she was in any way disappointed with what she had discovered within the journal's pages. It was fascinating to gain a glimpse of what her father had been like years ago. As a child, she had been aware only of those qualities of her father that affected her: his gentle manner, his sternness if she was naughty, and the stories he told her that caught and enflamed her curiosities about myth and science and magick. How much more there had been to him than what a small girl could apprehend!

Some of his entries had concerned his arcane studies, which had been even more extensive and varied than Ivy had guessed. As she long suspected, he had first gained an interest in the subject of magick from the older magician who had sold him the house on Durrow Street. On other pages, he discussed his own research into the history of the house. The identity of the house's original owner had been known to him, and in one particularly fascinating entry he had written about the latest bit of information he had discovered about the man Dratham.

From the box, Ivy took the sheets on which she had transcribed the entries in the journal. She looked through them until she found the one he had penned about Dratham.

I have learned he belonged to a magickal order as I do, her father had written, the slant of his hand suggesting his excitement. *Of course, in those days such societies had to take greater precautions for remaining concealed than we must in this modern age. Magick might be somewhat disreputable now, but in that time it was criminal. So they met in a hidden chamber, one locked by magick, which was situated be-*

neath a public house or tavern. I know not the name of this establishment, only that the tavern was located on Durrow Street—closer to what is now its more disreputable end, I presume.

Ivy wondered how much more her father had learned of the house's history, but so far she had encountered no further entries in which he had discussed the topic. Which meant she would simply have to continue her own research into the house's past. Now, however, it was time to commence her daily task. Ivy took the journal from the box, opened it, and began turning the pages one at a time.

Almost at once she came upon a page that was filled with words.

Her heart gave a leap, for she was certain this was a page of the journal that had heretofore always been blank when she examined it. Eagerly she read the lines scribed in her father's hand, the letters as thin and wispy and prone to fly away as the hair on his head had always been.

REGULUS AND ACREON DIRECT IN CASSIADES

Bennick and I opened the chamber and showed it to the others today. Well, to some of them at least. Mundy wouldn't so much as set foot in the room! He was quavering in his boots and said he had no need to look at it, that he could feel it well enough. But Fintaur, Larken, and Gambrel all went in, for which I was glad; I value their opinions more than that of anyone save for Bennick. They all of them agreed with our conclusions, so there can be no uncertainty about the matter now—the Eye is quiescent no longer.

Not that I had any doubt. The red light is no longer a faint spark at its center, visible only when the room is absolutely dark. Instead it has brightened and dilated by a significant degree. Though there seems to be a slow periodicity to it, like the rhythm of the most torpid pulse, sometimes contracting inward, at others expanding outward from the center of the crystal.

A few times, when the glow has been at its most pronounced, I have had the sensation that there were things moving within the orb, like black flecks of ash floating above the embers of a fire. I feel I might almost be able to tell what they are if I was to look closer, but I know better than to peer within its depths! Mr. Bennick has warned us all of the grave peril of gazing into the Eye, and I would warn you the same, Ivy. Do not gaze into it! To do so is to invite madness. Or perhaps to invite something even worse.

However, if you are reading this, then it means my house is in your possession, and the Eye is safe within the enchanted wards around it. So bound, I do not believe it can cause great harm. What's more, the stand of Wyrdwood upon which it rests seems to have an innate property that allows it to resist and even contain the influences of the orb.

I had hoped that would be the case; that was why I commissioned the stand prior to the Eye's removal from Earl Rylend's house at Heathcrest. The stand was made by a young man—or boy, really, for he could not have been more than fifteen—whom I had the good fortune to meet at Heathcrest Hall. He had a talent for gleaning fallen twigs and branches from outside the wall of a local stand of Wyrdwood and shaping them into the most marvelous objects—baskets and chairs and the like.

Seeing examples of his work, I asked him to make a sturdy frame— though I did not tell him what it would hold, and merely described the required dimensions. This he did. He also made the box of Wyrdwood in which you found this journal you are reading now. It was made with the cleverest hasp that, once shut, could never be opened again save for one who could bend and shape Wyrdwood like the box's maker.

Like you, Ivoleyn.

As for the Eye of Ran-Yahgren, I am grateful it is well guarded by the order of magicians to which I belong. Why the crimson light within it has been growing now, after being quiescent for so many eons, I am not certain, but I have a hypothesis. If I learn more, then I will be sure to tell you of it. Someday I will tell you as well how the thing came to be in the house on Durrow Street and under our care.

Only I will save that tale for another time. As I write this, it is deep in a greatnight, and the world is too dark to recount such a tale. Instead,

I will set down my pen, tread upstairs, and kiss you and your sisters lightly so that you do not wake. Then I will lay my own head down to sleep. If I can.

G.O.L.

Ivy looked up from the page. So her first impression of the Wyrd-wood box had been correct! When Mr. Quent brought it to her, she had been reminded of the bent willow chair in her attic room at Heathcrest Hall, the one made by Mr. Samonds when he was a youth, before he traded working wood for iron and became the farrier at Cairnbridge. The box had also reminded her of the stand of Wyrdwood on which the Eye of Ran-Yahgren rested, and which—by means of some property of the Wyrdwood itself—helped to contain its arcane energies. Now she knew that Mr. Samonds had made both the box and the stand at the request of her father.

Fascinated, Ivy read the entry again. This must have been one of the earliest entries in the journal. If the Eye was only just begin-ning to brighten, it meant that Cerephus was still far beyond the sight of even the most powerful ocular lenses. Yet somehow her fa-ther had known about the existence of the planet—she was cer-tain that was the hypothesis he had alluded to.

From a drawer she took out a pen, a bottle of ink, and a fresh sheet of paper. Then, being sure she did not miss a word, she tran-scribed the entry. *Someday I will tell you as well how the thing came to be in the house,* she copied the words. *Only I will save that tale for another time. . . .*

Ivy set down her quill. She wondered if her father had ever written another entry describing how his order had come into possession of the Eye of Ran-Yahgren. All the same, even if he never did set down the tale, it was a story she now knew because of the Black Stork.

Again, she could only marvel at the events Lord Rafferdy had recounted. How much more closely bound with a history of magicians Mr. Rafferdy was than he had ever thought! And how much more closely he and Ivy were bound to each other than they could ever have suspected. Last year, after learning from Mrs. Baydon of Mr. Rafferdy's engagement, Ivy had condemned herself as foolish to ever have wished for a connection with him.

Only it hadn't been foolish at all; they *were* connected, she knew now, through the mutual history of their fathers. This was a thought that gave her real pleasure. In the end, it was utterly natural that they had become acquainted; indeed, it was likely inevitable.

Ivy looked over the words she had copied from the journal, making sure she had not missed any. *As for the Eye of Ran-Yahgren, I am grateful it is well guarded by the order of magicians to which I belong. . . .*

Only in the end, the artifact had not been safe after all. Over time, some of the magicians in the order who had sworn to protect the Eye instead came to covet it. Was it Mr. Bennick—perhaps jealous that the Eye had been given into her father's care rather than his own—who had whispered to the others, giving the desire to use the Eye? Or was it some terrible influence of the artifact itself that had corrupted them?

Likely it had been something of both. Either way, their first attempt to seize the Eye of Ran-Yahgren was averted twelve years ago when Mr. Lockwell sacrificed himself to bind the artifact with magickal wards and seal the house on Durrow Street. The more recent effort of the magicians to gain the Eye had similarly been thwarted through Ivy's and Mr. Rafferdy's efforts.

Now the enchantments guarding the artifact had been renewed, and the members of the order who had tried to seize it were perished or locked up at Madstone's. As for Mr. Bennick, he was far away in Torland, she supposed. Besides, his magickal power had been stripped from him. Without his former compatriots to aid him, what power could he have against the enchantments that warded the Eye?

Ivy sprinkled sand on the sheet she had written to dry it, then set it aside. Though she did not expect to find any more entries in the journal, she turned through the remaining pages of the book. As she did, she wondered what had become of the other magicians her father had written about, the ones in the Vigilant Order of the Silver Eye he had trusted most—Gambrel, Fintaur, Larken, and Mundy.

The last one she was acquainted with, of course, for she had been in his shop of magickal books and items. At the time she had not known of Mr. Mundy's associations with her father, and she could not imagine there was any way he had recognized her. For if he had ever seen her before, it would have been when she was very small.

It was difficult for Ivy to imagine her father having a friendship with the little toad of a man. She could only suppose the events that broke apart the order affected him gravely. Though, in the passing references her father had written in the journal, it sounded as if even then Mr. Mundy's nature had tended toward a natural sourness.

As for the others her father had been closest to, she could not know what had become of them. At the least, Ivy knew that none of them had been among the magicians who had attempted to seize the Eye of Ran-Yahgren last year. On a recent visit to Madstone's, she had managed to engage one of the wardens in conversation, and through flattery and a feigned interest in his work, she had gotten him to discuss the magicians who had been brought to the hostel last year.

From the warden, she had learned the names of all the magicians who had gone mad gazing into the Eye, and there was not a Fintaur, Larken, or Gambrel among them. Another of the magicians had perished that day at the house, but Ivy recalled that he had been a youngish man—far too young to have been a contemporary of her father's.

She reached the last page of the journal. As she had expected, there were no more entries. Ivy returned the journal to the Wyrdwood box and started to close the lid, only then she paused. She reached into the pocket of her dress and drew out the piece of Wyrdwood that Lord Rafferdy had given her. As always she marveled at the pleasing smoothness of its surface.

In one of his journal entries, her father had written that he had given the key to Arantus to the Black Stork, but the triangular bit of wood hardly looked like any sort of key. If she had had her wits about her that day Lord Rafferdy came to talk to her, she would have asked him if her father had ever given him any sort of key that he knew of. Only she had not had the presence of mind to do so, and now it was too late.

Ivy sighed. She supposed it was just one more mystery her father had left for her. However, she had lost enough of him, and she did not wish to lose this thing as well. Somewhat reluctantly, for she enjoyed its touch, she put the bit of Wyrdwood inside the box for safekeeping. She put the pages she had written in the box as well and locked it in the desk.

Then she rose and departed the library, to see if her sisters needed more help.

CHAPTER TWENTY-FIVE

𝕿HIS TIME, THE conflagration occurred in the dead of a long umbral. Nor was it an old war monument that bore the brunt—though this structure, too, was a thing of symbolic importance.

Just as the bells of St. Galmuth's rang the start of the third span of the night, a gout of blue flame was observed jutting into the air from the east end of Marble Street. The fiery column rose so high as to equal or even surmount the altitude of the highest turrets of the Citadel, and it was bright enough that for a moment the whole of the Old City was lit up as clearly as if it were midday. Except the light was not warm and yellow as sunlight, but rather possessed a cold, unnatural hue. That there was some sort of enchantment behind it was rumored almost as soon as the spire of flame died away.

The precise location of the occurrence was not known at once. At first some said it was the Office of the Royal Exchequer that had been consumed by the fire, for traitors meant to cripple the nation by rendering it penniless. Others claimed it was Assembly itself that had been destroyed. However, by the time the sun rose over the Old City, turning the sky a sickly orange due to the acrid smoke that still infused the air, the truth was generally known. It was the Ministry of Printing that had been the subject of the attack.

The ministry was responsible for the publication of all official government documents, from books of laws and regulations to all manner of official bills and notices. However, there was one document in particular that these days used more of the ministry's presses, and consumed greater quantities of ink and paper, than any other. The document was the Rules of Citizenship—that ever-present list of directives to be obeyed by every good citizen of the nation, and which by decree of the king's Black Dog, Lord Valhaine, was posted in every shop, tavern, coffeehouse, and place of public gathering.

Such was the frequency with which the Rules were revised and expanded—as well as the frequency with which they were defaced or torn down—that a vast number of copies were required. Thus an entire wing of the ministry had been given over to the printing of this one single document, and the presses there hardly ever ceased their labors. In Altania, people might sometimes go without food or candles or a roof to cover the head, but they would never want for instruction concerning the proper and lawful way to behave.

Only now the endless flow of ink and paper had ceased. With apparent ease, the perpetrators had breached the outer wall of the ministry even though it was well guarded by redcrests. Once within, they might have taken down the entire edifice, along with the governmental buildings to either side. Yet it was only the part of the ministry that housed the presses responsible for printing the

Rules of Citizenship that was consumed in the eruption. Thus the designers of this deed had posted their own message for all to read. It was not buildings or men they sought to destroy, but rather words.

All the same, the incident had not been without a cost in both life and property. A redcrest posted outside the wall of the ministry was killed by a stone that was hurled into the sky and fell back down, dashing in his head. In addition, one of the instigators had been unable to escape as nimbly as he had entered and had also been slain by the blast. If there was any doubt, given the lurid color of the flames, that magick had been involved in the attack, it was removed by the ring that was discovered upon the corpse's hand—a ring whose gem was said to have still been sparking with an eerie blue light when the first witnesses arrived at the scene.

Despite the late hour, a crowd soon began to assemble, but it was dispersed by a band of soldiers who arrived in the company of the Black Dog himself. The Lady Shayde was said to be with him as well, and at the sight of her pale face the onlookers quickly departed. It was said the White Lady could know a man's guilt just by looking at him, and even men who had never committed a crime in their lives had no wish to meet her gaze. For what fellow, even the most law-abiding, had never thought about doing something wicked once or twice?

Indeed, Rafferdy was considering something wicked himself at this very moment. He noted that Mr. Harclint's full wineglass was situated perilously close to the edge of the dining table. All it would take was a flick of a fork, a motion so slight that no one would ever notice it, and the glass would topple over the edge directly into Mr. Harclint's lap.

It would be awful of him, of course. But desperate times required desperate deeds, and for the last quarter hour Lady Marsdel's nephew had been plying Rafferdy with ceaseless questions about Assembly—or rather, about one specific member of that honored body. That was, how many times had he seen Lord Farrolbrook there? What laws had Lord Farrolbrook voted for? And had Lord Farrolbrook done any sort of magick?

"I cannot fathom why you would still profess an interest in this Lord Farrolbog," Sir Earnsley exclaimed.

Rafferdy had never imagined he would ever be grateful that Lady Marsdel had invited the bluff old baronet to dinner. He was at that moment, though, for Mr. Harclint directed his watery gaze across the table.

"Farrolbrook," he said with exaggerated enunciation. "It is Lord Farrolbrook."

Sir Earnsley made a dismissive gesture with a capon's leg. "Bog or brook, one is as wet as the other. Either way, I wouldn't think after all that has happened you would still profess such a keen interest in magick."

Mr. Baydon, who sat beside the baronet, scowled. "Why should he not maintain such an interest?"

Sir Earnsley blew a snort through his drooping mustache. "Come now, Mr. Baydon! Surely you can no longer think that your magicians are to be the saviors of our nation."

"On the contrary, I am as convinced as ever that they will be."

"How can that be? I have seen the stories in the very broadsheets you hew to so loyally. It was magicians who blew up the Ministry of Printing. Do not tell me you can doubt that fact."

"I do not doubt it," Mr. Baydon said, his tone sharp. "Magick was surely used to accomplish the deed. I can only suppose it was a band of university students who did this mischief, and nor were they very wise to have done it. Surely one of them paid a far greater price than they expected. All the same, it is hardly the first time a prank got out of hand."

Sir Earnsley waggled the capon leg at Mr. Baydon. "So when the doers of such a deed are thought to be Morden men, they are hoodlums and traitors, yet when it turns out they are magicians, then they are merely making mischief and playing pranks. As I recall, you were greatly put out when the cenotaph in Trawlsden Square fell. Or have you changed your mind and decided that was a jolly prank as well?" He took a bite of capon.

The ever-present furrows in Mr. Baydon's brow deepened. "And as I recall, Sir Earnsley, you have long professed that magick is no more than an affectation. Yet now you yourself have admitted that magick has power enough to bring down a building."

"I said I did not believe in magick," the old baronet said, his voice going low. "I did not say that I doubted its existence."

"Well, it most certainly does exist," Mr. Harclint sputtered, finally managing to get in a word. "Lord Farrolbrook says it is magick that keeps the Wyrdwood from rising up."

"Does it now?" Sir Earnsley said, glowering. "And what would you say to those in Torland who lost their lives in the Risings there?"

"I would say it was their own fault!" Mr. Baydon exclaimed. "The Torlanders could only have done something to provoke the attacks. There can be no doubting the effects of the magick Gauldren placed upon the Wyrdwood all those centuries ago. Were it not for the Quelling, men should never have been able to build a civilization upon the island of Altania. We would all still be living in wicker hovels, huddled over stinking fires and trembling every time the wind shook the branches of the trees. Surely you cannot deny *that,* Sir Earnsley."

The old baronet set down the capon leg, as if he had lost his appetite. "Aye, the Quelling was worked with magick. But I wonder—can magick quell those who would seek to put Bandley Morden on the throne? Or will it rather help them to do so?"

"I cannot think magicians would have any sympathy for a Morden," Mr. Baydon said with a sniff. "It was our last great magician who drove Morden's grandfather from the shores of Altania, as you'll recall."

Sir Earnsley did not answer. This prompted Mr. Baydon to give a satisfied nod, and he returned his attention to his supper. At the same time Mr. Harclint turned toward Rafferdy as if to continue his line of questions. Rafferdy edged his fork closer to Mr. Harclint's wineglass.

Before he had need to wield the utensil, Mrs. Baydon asked Lady Marsdel what she thought of the weather of late. This elicited a lengthy discourse on the part of her ladyship, superseding all other conversation at the table. Rafferdy gave Mrs. Baydon a grateful

look, and she smiled in return. Listening to her ladyship's complaints about the dreadful quality of the air in the city was far from
a pleasant entertainment, but it was preferable to Mr. Harclint's
attentions.

As Lady Marsdel went on, Rafferdy looked down at his hand.
His House ring—which bore the sigil of Gauldren, the very magician who had worked the Quelling long ago—winked blue in the
lamplight. By all the accounts, a similar ring had been seen upon
the hand of the magician who had been found dead at the ruins of
the Ministry of Printing. But for what purpose had he been there?
If it was truly a prank, as Mr. Baydon insisted, it seemed a great
length to go for a bit of amusement.

Whatever their reasons, Rafferdy hoped none of his acquaintances had been part of it. Certainly he had never heard anything
at their meetings that made him think others in the society harbored such intents. However, in the days since the conflagration at
the ministry, there had been neither a session of Assembly nor a
meeting of the Arcane Society of the Virescent Blade.

Would that there was a meeting of the society tonight! Then he
would have had an excuse to forgo dinner at her ladyship's.
He had come to Lady Marsdel's that first evening he returned to
the city on a foolish impulse to avoid being alone. Since then, each
invitation had led to another, for it was not as easy to decline her
ladyship in person as by pen.

That was not to say Rafferdy had submitted to Lady Marsdel's
demands for his recurring presence without a hope that he would
gain some benefit by doing so. Of course, that hope had proved
false. None of the times he had come since his return to Invarel
had Lady Quent been here. He supposed she was otherwise occupied with her new acquaintance, Lady Crayford.

With both dinner and Lady Marsdel's exposition upon the
weather concluded, the party retired to the parlor. They were a
small group that night, and so became dispersed once they
attempted to occupy the vast room. As a result, Rafferdy found himself a reassuring distance from Mr. Harclint but rather close to Mr.
and Mrs. Baydon. The pair were engaged in their usual activities:

she frowning over a picture puzzle while he frowned over that day's edition of *The Comet*.

"I presume from his absence at table that Lord Baydon is still not recovered," Rafferdy said.

"I'm afraid that's so," Mrs. Baydon said.

"How are his spirits?"

"Very high." She turned a piece this way and that in an attempt to fit it in a gap. "As you know, my father-in-law is ever of good cheer. Each day he is certain that he will be better the next." She sighed and set the piece aside in favor of another.

"I have no doubt that is *his* belief. What do the doctors say?"

"They are concerned by his continued weakness and tremblings. Yet they watch him closely, and they do not feel he is in great danger."

Rafferdy picked up the piece she had discarded and set it into the puzzle, an act that elicited a sound of first delight, then dismay.

"I am very dull tonight!" she exclaimed. "I tried that piece a dozen times. You didn't use magick to fit it in, did you?"

"No, I wouldn't dare. I would not want for Sir Earnsley to call the redcrests and give them a report of magicians brandishing spells." He took up another piece and set it into the puzzle. "Where is your captain tonight? I did not think a good soldier such as he would neglect his duties."

"He is not neglecting his duties, Mr. Rafferdy. Rather, he is seeing to them. I have it from Colonel Daubrent that Captain Branfort had to return to the West Country to see to some matters there, but I believe he is due back anytime."

Rafferdy raised an eyebrow. "Colonel Daubrent, you say? Have you been seeing the viscountess's brother often of late?"

"Oh, not *often*," she said, and gave a coy smile.

Mr. Baydon folded over his broadsheet. "What Mrs. Baydon means to say is that she has seen him precisely once of late, when he stopped by our house to deliver a note on behalf of his sister. He did not set foot through our door, and he lingered no more than a minute, for he was merely passing by."

"It was more than a minute, I am sure!" Mrs. Baydon said. "For

I looked at the invitation while he waited, and you know I am not a swift reader. I must sound out everything in my mind—I can't help it."

Rafferdy turned another piece in his fingers. He could see where it fit, but he was waiting until Mrs. Baydon placed one first.

"The colonel brought an invitation, you say?"

"Yes, to Lady Crayford's tea the lumenal after next. You are coming, of course, aren't you, Mr. Rafferdy?"

He set the puzzle piece back down on the table, very close to the place it belonged and in the correct orientation. "No, I'm afraid I have other matters I must attend to that day."

"That's a pity," Mrs. Baydon said. "I'm sure it will be a very marvelous affair. And the colonel told me Lady Quent will be there. Oh!" She plucked up the piece Rafferdy had set before her and put it in the puzzle. "It seems I am clever after all, for that was the most awful piece to discover."

"Indeed it was," Mr. Rafferdy said, and sank back into his chair.

A man came by with brandy. Rafferdy took one, drained it, set the empty glass back on the tray, and took another. The servant turned to Mr. Baydon, who set his broadsheet on the table to take a brandy himself. Rafferdy's gaze strayed idly to the paper, not drawn by any words he saw, but rather by the vivid image printed on the paper.

The picture was rendered in such lifelike detail that it could only be an impression. Rafferdy did not understand why it was scandalous for respectable persons to go to a theater on Durrow Street, yet no one thought a thing if a respectable paper printed the work of an illusionist. Then again, was not the business of a broadsheet publishing one person's sins for others to enjoy? It was what they called *news*.

The picture was upside down, and all Rafferdy could make out were a pile of rocks and what looked to be several redcrests, given their plumed helms. Idly, he reached out to turn the broadsheet around to get a better look.

A horror came upon him. He saw now that the rocks were in

fact broken building stones, and the redcrests were shouting, their arms raised, at people who must have stood just out of view. On the ground lay the crumpled figure of a man. The corpse—for it could only have been such—was partially obscured by the rubble, but a limp arm protruded from the wreckage, ending in a pale hand.

Rafferdy leaned over the table, peering closer at the impression. The illusionist must have been one of the first to the scene; he had to have gotten very close to have seen everything so clearly that his memory of it could later be imprinted on an engraving plate with such exacting detail. Rafferdy could see the ring upon the man's hand. There was something else on his hand as well.

Several sharp black lines arranged in a familiar pattern.

Mr. Baydon set down his brandy and took up the broadsheet again. Rafferdy stared at the table for a moment, then slumped back in the chair. A pain throbbed in his head, and his mouth had gone dry.

Twice before he had seen that same symbol on the hand of a man. Each time it had made him think of a magickal rune of some sort, and this man had been wearing a House ring. The other men could have worn one as well, for a magician's ring might be worn on any finger of either hand. Which meant the explosion at the Ministry of Printing was not the first attempt by magicians to disrupt the workings of the government.

Yet why? Surely Mr. Baydon was right; magicians could have no enthusiasm for Huntley Morden, and not just because the magician Slade Vordigan drove Bandley Morden from the shores of Altania seventy years ago. After all, most magicians were gentlemen or magnates. They already ruled Altania, so they could have no affection for someone who intended to usurp that rule.

Then again, even if these men were magicians, they were not men like Rafferdy and his companions in the society. No, they were not like any sort of men at all—at least not when they were cut and bled. And according to the Lady Shayde's man, Moorkirk, there were more of them out there. . . .

Mrs. Baydon set another wooden piece in place. "Come now,

Mr. Rafferdy," she said in a chiding tone. "You are being no help at all. It is *you* who is dull tonight, I think."

"You're right, Mrs. Baydon," he said, the dryness in his throat making his voice hoarse. "I fear I have no head for puzzles tonight."

He glanced at the ring on his right hand. Then he held up his empty glass to call for another brandy.

꧁ PECULIAR THING occurred the following morning. Upon rising—at an unusually early hour after only a middle umbral—Rafferdy discovered that he was anxious to go to Assembly.

Such was the novelty of this sensation that Rafferdy gave in to it entirely. He took a breakfast consisting solely of coffee in his bedchamber, then dressed without waiting for his man to assist him. Downstairs, he called for his carriage and was standing on the doorstep by the time it arrived. The driver did not proceed with speed enough to suit him, and he rapped with his cane on the roof several times to let his displeasure be known.

Despite his driver's leisurely pace, Marble Street was not yet crowded, and he soon departed his carriage before the stairs that led up to the Halls of Assembly. He took the steps two at a time, his black robe billowing out behind him.

He entered the Hall of Magnates through the main doors to find it largely vacant save for a group of Stouts who sat on one side. They were arranged in a tight knot despite the emptiness of the chamber, as if they anticipated some assault and so had formed a defensive phalanx to be ready.

Rafferdy proceeded to the upper benches where the wigless young lords habitually gathered. Lately, he had sat there himself, for Lord Baydon had not attended Assembly in over a month due to his health. However, none of Rafferdy's usual companions was there, and as he sat, he realized it was from this source that sprang his desire to attend Assembly that day. He wished to make certain that all his acquaintances in the Arcane Society of the Virescent Blade could be accounted for.

Fortunately, he did not have to suffer from anxiousness for long. Soon Lord Coulten entered the Hall. Lord Eubrey followed a few minutes after, as did the several young men who customarily sat with them, and who were also members of the society. All of them looked well and sound. Though, Rafferdy noted, they also all wore gloves.

Rafferdy's own hands were bare.

"I say, Rafferdy, you're here awfully early," Lord Coulten exclaimed. His frizzy crown of hair was, if anything, taller than ever, and his face was cheerful and pink-cheeked. "Eager for Assembly to meet again so you can cast a vote on the Act Regarding Standards for the Excellence of Pork Fat or the Measure Providing More Methods for Gouty Old Lords to Acquire Money?"

As usual, Rafferdy found it impossible not to return Coulten's grin. "Aren't those acts the same thing? But no, I was not anxious to get to Assembly so much as I was to see you. I was hoping you would all be here."

"Why shouldn't we be?"

"After recent events . . ." Rafferdy cleared his throat. "Well, I didn't feel I could be entirely sure."

Lord Eubrey affected a scandalized look; indeed, he was so convincing that Rafferdy wasn't certain he was acting.

"How now, Rafferdy—are you saying you thought we might have been involved in the business at the Ministry of Printing?"

Now that his fears had been revealed, Rafferdy was rather embarrassed by them. "Forgive me, it was ill of me to think that anyone in our circle might have been involved in such a thing."

Coulten let out a merry laugh. "There is no need to apologize, Rafferdy! Indeed, I'm delighted you thought that we are of sufficiently devious and dastardly character to have possibly been involved in such a matter. It allows me to fancy that I am more intriguing than I am, and I have always wanted to be notorious. How about you, Lord Eubrey?"

"I concur. It's very amusing to think that I could have been out in the black depths of the umbral sneaking around and working wicked spells, when in fact I was at home and fast asleep in my bed.

I fear that truth incriminates me more than could any involvement in the affairs at the Ministry, as it proves beyond doubt that I am criminally dull."

Rafferdy was grateful for these good-natured comments from his companions. "On the count of dullness you will never be convicted, Eubrey. I have seen you at tavern, and can attest to that! Besides, I can only think there are better ways to prove one possesses an interesting character than to blow up buildings. The magicians who did it should have chosen otherwise."

"What makes you believe it was magicians who did it?" Coulten said. He was no longer smiling.

Rafferdy shook his head. "All the reports say magick was involved. There was the preternatural color of the flames. There was also the fellow they found who . . ." He clipped his words short. He had no wish to describe the dreadful impression he had seen in the broadsheet.

Lord Eubrey shrugged. "Perhaps it was magick. Or perhaps it was something else. I do not know of an arcane society or magickal order that would wish to call such attention to itself."

Rafferdy was not one to overly subscribe to the notion of logic, but Eubrey's words had an air of reasonability about them. Did not the group to which they belonged go to great lengths to keep their meetings secret? Magick had started to come back into fashion these days, but that did not mean its practice was considered entirely acceptable.

What was more, from what he understood, it was the habit of arcane societies for each to keep its research and accomplishments unknown to other such orders and groups. A society could attract the best talent to its ranks only if magicians thought it possessed insights into the arcane that could not be gained elsewhere.

"Well, perhaps they were intoxicated," Rafferdy said. "Or maybe things went awry."

"Perhaps," Lord Eubrey said. His dark eyes glanced away, then back. "Or perhaps whoever did it, it was their wish to make it *appear* as if magick was involved."

This statement baffled Rafferdy. Who would wish to make an act look as if magick had caused it when it hadn't, and for what purpose? Before he could voice his question, an audible hiss whispered around the chamber, as of many breaths being drawn in at once.

"If it was the perpetrator's goal to bring the practice of magick under suspicion, then their deed has done so," Coulten said, his typically jovial tone now low and sober. "Look there."

Rafferdy turned to follow Coulten's gaze. While they had spoken, magnates had continued to enter, and the Hall was now nearly full. All had ceased their progress in finding and settling onto the benches, and instead they were still, watching as another figure entered.

Like the magnates, this figure was clad all in black, though not in a robe; rather, she wore a black dress that was gathered tight about the neck and wrists. The gown was fashioned of some stiff material that hardly seemed to move as she walked. She wore a small hat with a veil that obscured the upper part of her face. All that was visible were a pointed chin and a pair of lips. These latter were so dark they were a blue-black against her talc-white skin, and they were ever so slightly curved to offer the suggestion of a smile.

As all looked on, the Lady Shayde ascended the steps behind the High Speaker's podium. With deliberate motions she took a seat that afforded her a view of the entire Hall—or rather, one that afforded all a view of *her*.

Sounds filled the Hall again as the magnates returned to their conversations and to the task of finding their seats, though the din was more subdued than it had been before.

"Now the White Thorn comes to watch us," Lord Eubrey said.

Rafferdy could not tell from his expression if he was alarmed or intrigued. Perhaps it was a bit of both, for Rafferdy himself was interested by the appearance of the White Lady—even if he had no wish to be subjected to her sharp gaze. He knew what it was like to suffer her attention, and he hoped never to do so again.

"Look there at the Magisters," Coulten said. His grin had returned, and a light danced in his blue eyes. "So much for their prideful airs. They are no different from the rest of us now!"

Rafferdy looked down at the benches where the members of the Magister party customarily sat. At first he did not notice what was altered about them; certainly their haughty expressions were no different than before. Then one of them, a young lord with a large nose, took out a handkerchief to wipe that prominent proboscis, and Rafferdy saw what had changed.

The young magnate was wearing gloves. Rafferdy looked and saw the same was true for all of the Magisters. Each of them wore gloves upon his hands. There was not a House ring to be seen.

Had Lord Farrolbrook adopted this same affectation? Rafferdy supposed that must be the case, for he could not imagine the Magisters doing something their proclaimed leader did not. Only, as Rafferdy searched among them, he saw no sign of the fair-haired lord. This was odd, for had not Lord Farrolbrook crowed that the other Magisters would not take their seats until he took his? Yet they were all of them seated now.

Even as Rafferdy wondered at this, Lord Farrolbrook strode into the Hall, his pale, flowing hair as notable as his elaborately ruffled robe. He moved at a pace that, while still stately, had a slightly hurried cadence to it. He made a bit of a stumble as he stepped on his hem, then adjusted the ornate garment as he took his place among the Magisters.

"I daresay Lord Farrolbrook had difficulty getting into his robe today," Lord Eubrey said with obvious delight. "Perhaps he is still getting accustomed to wearing such singular attire."

Rafferdy glanced at Eubrey. "What do you mean? I thought Farrolbrook always had a penchant for such ostentatious clothes."

It was Coulten who answered. "Actually, it is a recent affectation. He did not used to dress so outlandishly, though his father always had a penchant for such attire—all ruffles and gores and frills. It was dreadful stuff—a costume out of some moldy old play, you would have thought. Then, when the elder Lord Farrolbrook passed on a bit over a year ago, our Lord Farrolbrook quite sud-

denly adopted his father's mode of dress. Though at least he seems
to have had new robes made, so even if they look as dreadful as his
father's, they don't *smell* as dreadful."

Rafferdy supposed it was not unusual for a son to more closely
emulate his father once the elder man had passed. Was not Rafferdy
himself doing something he had never thought he would now that
his own father was gone—that was, taking a permanent seat in
Assembly? It was a peculiar fact that parents sometimes had
greater influence over the behavior of their children after they
departed the world than before.

As Rafferdy watched, Lord Farrolbrook rearranged the frills
and ruffles of his robe. His cheeks seemed bright, and his hair was
not quite so smoothly arranged over his shoulders as usual.

"I imagine you're glad that you aren't sitting down there next
to him, Coulten," Eubrey said, nudging their companion with an
elbow.

Rafferdy gave Eubrey a curious look. "Why might Coulten be
sitting next to Lord Farrolbrook?"

"Because he almost joined the order that Farrolbrook and a
number of the other Magisters belong to, that's why."

"I did no such thing!" Coulten protested. "I never received an
invitation from the High Order of the Golden Door, and nor did I
wish for one. I merely had a few conversations with Lord Farrolbrook, that's all." Coulten looked at Rafferdy. "He approached me
shortly after I took a seat in the Hall of Magnates, for we are both
descended of House Myrrgon."

Eubrey clapped him on the back and grinned. "Fortunately for
Coulten, I came to his rescue and convinced him to join our little
society instead."

A pounding noise rang out, drawing their attention to the front
of the Hall. The High Speaker was exacting a stern punishment
upon the podium with his gavel, and the Grand Usher was waving
his overlarge golden key at the offending magnates like a herdsman
flicking a switch at errant cows. Gradually all took their seats.

"So how long do you think the Stouts will wait before they
bring it up?" Eubrey whispered to Rafferdy's right.

"I'm sure they will show great patience on the matter," Coulten replied from Rafferdy's left. "That is, they will wait at least an entire minute before they start blathering on about it."

"Before they blather on about what?" Rafferdy asked.

Eubrey stifled a laugh. "If it's a minute, it's only because it will take Lord Bastellon that long to straighten that greasy old wig of his and heave himself to his feet. See? I told you—there he goes already."

Even as the High Speaker was setting down his gavel, a thick-set old lord in a matted wig rose to his feet—with surprising alacrity despite his bulk—and bowed toward the High Speaker.

"The Hall recognizes Lord Bastellon," the High Speaker said in a distinctly pained tone.

"My fellow magnates," Lord Bastellon began, then coughed several times to clear his throat. "These are times fraught with peril and consequence. And as our body convenes again for a new session, I call for a debate to be opened upon the matter of—"

Another series of coughs ensued. As the old Stout worked upon the phlegm in his throat, the Magisters leaned forward on their benches, as if eager to leap to action.

"—upon the matter of each and every sort of action that must be taken to ensure the future safety and prosperity of our nation!"

A murmur went about the Hall. The Magisters leaned back on their benches, and several of them affected looks of annoyance.

Coulten gave a soft laugh. "Well, old Bastellon isn't as much of a lump as he looks. He's learned from his mistake, it seems."

"How so?" Rafferdy whispered back.

"Remember what happened the last time Lord Bastellon brought up the subject of the king's writ of succession?" Eubrey replied. "The Magisters closed the debate as soon as it was opened, then called for a vote, knowing the Stouts didn't have the yeas to carry the measure."

"So why don't they do the same this time?"

"That's just it—they can't. Bastellon has called for debate not on the matter of the writ of succession, but upon every matter that affects the future of Altania. The Magisters can't very well close debate on *that* issue, for then nothing at all could be discussed for the remainder of the session. Which means the Stouts will be free to bring up the writ of succession. They can't call for a vote on it—that would require bringing the specific measure up for debate—but at least they can speak about it now. Really, I'm surprised the Magisters let them get away with it."

"Farrolbrook must be losing his edge," Coulten said.

Eubrey gave a sniff. "If he ever had one. Just because a blade is brightly polished doesn't mean it's sharp."

Coulten grinned. "I think that goes for all of the Magisters!"

"Indubitably," Eubrey said, tugging the wrists of his fawn-colored gloves. "I've learned that the high magus of at least one society populated largely by Magisters has approached our own magus in hopes of forming a brotherhood of orders. No doubt they simply need help working any kind of magick. I doubt most Magisters could formulate an enchantment to bind shut a hatbox!"

"Well, that would be more magick than I have seen worked at gatherings of our own society," Rafferdy observed dryly.

So far, the meetings Rafferdy had attended had been ponderous with discussion about magick and light on the performing of actual spells. There were the doors that led to the secret room beneath the Sword and Leaf, of course, which could only be opened by speaking the prescribed runes. And there were the enchanted journals by which messages were passed among members of the Virescent Blade. However, other than those things, Rafferdy had not seen the working of any kind of magick at the meetings of the society.

"Oh, there is magick done within our society that far surpasses the opening and closing of hatboxes," Eubrey said. He leaned in close and placed a hand beside his mouth so that his words would not carry over the tumult in the Hall. "Coulten can attest to that fact, for he's seen through the Door."

"Only just the once," Coulten said. "But Eubrey here has peeked in three times now. Haven't you, Eubrey? No doubt the next time, you'll be handed a gold robe and get to step through."

It was generally Rafferdy's aim to appear bored with all things.

However, these words sent a thrill through him. There was only one door his companions could be referring to. Rafferdy had seen it each time he had attended a meeting in the secret chamber beneath the tavern; or rather, he had seen the curtain behind which he knew a door stood. That was, *the* Door.

The Door was one of three doors in the chamber. The first was the one that opened into the interior of the Sword and Leaf. The second one Rafferdy had not yet been through, but he knew it was the door behind the tavern that many of the members of the society used to enter the meeting chamber.

Then there was the third. Rafferdy had never seen anyone pass through the Door; the initiates were always dismissed before it was opened. Only the sages—those who had been admitted to the innermost circle of the society—were allowed to pass through the Door. However, those initiates who were candidates to be raised to that higher rank were sometimes allowed to stay in the chamber after the others had been released, and to peer through the Door as it was opened.

What lay beyond, Rafferdy could not imagine; perhaps it was nothing at all, and was merely meant to arouse curiosity to encourage new members to stay in the society.

Except he doubted that. Sometimes, during their meetings, Rafferdy would feel a draft of chill air and catch a queer, metallic odor. At such times, he would look up to see the black curtain that covered the Door stir ever so slightly, as if under the influence of a breath of strange air.

"So you have seen magick performed beyond the Door?" he said, unable to prevent an eager tone from creeping into his voice.

Eubrey winked at him. "You know we can't tell you what's beyond it. Our tongues would be turned to slugs if we tried."

"Don't worry, Rafferdy." Coulten put a hand on his arm. "You're sure to get a peek beyond the curtain soon. You're the sharpest new magician we've gotten in a long while. The sages have their eyes on you, I'm sure of it."

Rafferdy laughed. "How can you know? They're always wearing hoods!"

"In the outer room, yes," Eubrey said. "Not beyond the Door. But if you do not feel you've seen enough magick, Rafferdy, then make a date to come on a little excursion with me next quarter month."

"An excursion?"

"Yes, it's not very far from the city. A ride of no more than half a middle lumenal. Coulten is coming with me."

"For what purpose?"

"I really don't think I should say anything more about it," Eubrey said, then gave a subtle nod.

Following Eubrey's gaze, Rafferdy looked across the Hall. The Lady Shayde sat above the High Speaker's podium, her white hands folded on her black dress. Her eyes were still hidden behind her veil—yet were no doubt watching all the same.

On the floor of the Hall, Lord Bastellon proceeded to drone on, and various magnates after him, but Rafferdy heard nothing they said. Instead he fidgeted with the House ring on his finger and wondered just what sort of magick it was that Eubrey intended to do.

CHAPTER TWENTY-SIX

*I*VY WOKE IN the colorless light before dawn. The umbral had been brief, and its few hours had offered her scant rest. Her dreams had been vague and fitful—shapeless, gloom-filled interludes haunted by wordless murmurs and the sighing of a distant wind.

At one point, she had awakened certain she heard the sound of voices speaking in cadence, like the sibilant whispers of priests across an empty cathedral. She nearly sprang from the bed to throw open the chamber door. However, it must have been a phantasm from her dreams. Surely Mr. Quent would have awakened as well if there had indeed been noises intruding through the door.

Mrs. Lockwell is greatly relieved to have departed the house on Durrow Street, her father had written in an entry that had recently appeared in the journal. *Our new abode on Whitward Street is much more to her liking. She complained that the old house was always watching her, and she claimed that she often heard noises—particularly a far-off soughing. I confess, I have not noticed such things. But then, neither my sight nor my hearing is so keen as hers, and it may be that over the years I have grown accustomed to such qualities that must be characteristic of any house inhabited for so long by those who study the arcane. Besides, I do not think it is so very ill if a house has life to it. And this house—the house you now inhabit, I hope—has more life than most dwellings, I think.*

Ivy had loved her mother dearly, but even Ivy had to admit that Mrs. Lockwell had not always been the most logical of beings. She had been given to frights and starts. Surely dwelling in an old house, one prone to creaking and filled with the peculiar trappings of generations of magicians, had impressed itself upon her senses. As for Ivy, had she not seen something herself yesterday—something that no doubt had found its way into her dreams and affected them?

Therefore, she would not do as her mother and ascribe to fact what logic told her must have been imagined. All the same, she moved her arm beneath the bedclothes, reaching for the solid presence of her husband.

Her hand found only the smooth flatness of the linen sheet.

Ivy sighed. Though the hour was early, Mr. Quent was already risen and gone—off to the Citadel, no doubt. She wished she had some urgent purpose as he did to propel her from bed, or that she had the ability to go back to sleep. However, neither was the case, so she would rise early herself, and for no reason at all.

She drew her robe over her nightgown, then moved to the window to push the drapes aside. Ivy glanced at the garden below. Nothing stirred in the pallid light. This did not surprise her; she had not expected to see anything there. Then again, she had not expected anything yesterday morning either, when shortly after breakfast she looked out a window in the front hall to see *him* standing on the other side of the gate.

The expression on his onyx mask had been flat—neither frowning nor smiling. He had said nothing, and had stood there for but a moment. Then he turned and departed in what seemed a great haste, his elaborate cape billowing behind him like black wings.

Why had he bothered to show himself so briefly? She did not know. Perhaps his purpose had been simply to remind her of his presence. In which case he had succeeded, and she was sure she had to look no further for the source of her ill night's visions than the sight of the man in black.

Well, if he could not be bothered to tell her why he had shown himself, she would not be bothered to think of him.

The sky was brightening by the time she finished readying herself for the day and went downstairs. It was still too early for breakfast, and Mrs. Seenly was not yet in the kitchen, so Ivy poured herself a cup of cold tea from the pot on the stove, then proceeded to the library.

A quick glance at the almanac showed that the night had ended nearly half an hour sooner than it was supposed to have. However, as always, the old rosewood clock was unerring, and it let out a chime just as the first pink rays of light fell through the library's windows. On the right face, the black disk had turned just enough to reveal a sliver of gold.

Ivy sat at the writing table, took out the Wyrdwood box, and opened it with a touch. Making her usual careful perusal, she turned the pages of her father's journal. It was her hope that she would find something he had written about the man in the black costume. In his letter, he had told Ivy to trust the stranger, but how could she trust someone who revealed so little? She could not know his purposes, or what he wanted of her. Some words on the subject from her father would surely help to assuage her unease.

As she turned the last page, Ivy sighed. All of the pages in the journal were blank today. She returned the book to the box, then took out the small piece of Wyrdwood that Lord Rafferdy had given her. Even though it had been shut away in the box, there was a warmth to it, as though someone had just been worrying it in their hand.

Was there some quality about it beyond that echoing hum, that memory of life that was inherent in all wood hewn of Old Trees? Ivy could not say. All she knew was that it was different than the wood from which the box had been fashioned. The box had been made of twigs and small branches woven cleverly together, while the triangular piece of Wyrdwood was harder and more thickly grained. Had her father acquired it from the same person as the box? She supposed there was no way to know.

Or was there?

She recalled the last entry she had found in her father's journal, concerning his description of the Eye of Ran-Yahgren and the wooden frame it rested upon. *The stand was made by a young man . . . whom I had the good fortune to meet at Heathcrest Hall,* he had written. And, *He also made the box of Wyrdwood in which you found this journal you are reading now.*

Reluctantly, for she found its smooth surface pleasing to touch, Ivy returned the piece of Wyrdwood to the box. Then she took paper and ink from the drawer. She cut a fresh quill and dipped it. For a moment she hesitated, wondering where to begin. She had not been in contact with him since leaving County Westmorain and returning to the city. Yet she could not think he would find a letter from her unwelcome. He had shown her nothing but kindness in her time in the West Country. Resolved, she tapped the tip of her pen against the ink pot, then set it to the paper.

Dear Mr. Samonds, she wrote.

AFTER THE LETTER was sealed with wax and given to a servant to be delivered, Ivy turned her attention to the seemingly endless task of placing her father's books in order on the shelves. She had been at this task just long enough to become engrossed when she heard footsteps behind her.

"Would you be so kind as to bring me a cup of tea?" she said without looking up, supposing it to be Mrs. Seenly.

"Whatever you wish, your ladyship," spoke a gruff voice.

Ivy let out a gasp and turned around, then smiled. "But you are back so soon! Once I saw you were gone, I did not expect to see you all day."

Mr. Quent affected a solemn look. "I came back to make certain you were not deprived of your morning tea."

"Do not mock me!" she said with a laugh. "For I have not had anything today but cold tea, and I do not think I will ever be able to sort out these books without the benefit of another cup or two." She set down her burden on the desk and crossed the room to kiss her husband. "Yet I imagine you have had nothing yourself today. That would be very like you to rush off to see to the needs of the Crown without seeing to any of your own."

"This is all the sustenance I need," he said, and kissed her again.

For a minute he held her in his arms, and Ivy was surprised, for there seemed an unusual fierceness to his action. Not that she could say she was discontent to let him encompass her so, or to lean her head against his chest and listen to the solid beating of his heart.

At last it was not only the sound of his beating heart she heard, but also the noise of his stomach. She commented upon this, and he reluctantly agreed that he might in fact need something other than kisses to sustain him. A maid was called and given instructions to ask Mrs. Seenly to bring a tray, and soon the two of them sat at a table in the library, taking a little breakfast together.

While they might have saved Mrs. Seenly trouble by going to the dining room, Ivy confessed it was pleasant to have Mr. Quent to herself—and to not have to listen to more of Lily's chatter about her and Rose's progress on the tableau. All the same, Mr. Quent had some curiosity on that particular subject, and she assured him that the tableau was bound to be impressively elaborate and theatrical.

"I do hope Lily will not be worn out by the time the day of

their party arrives," Ivy said, pouring him more tea from the pot. "I want her to be able to enjoy the affair."

"On that account I can have little worry," he said, and put three lumps of sugar in his cup. As Ivy had learned in their time together, he possessed something of a sweet tooth. "That said, I will be sure to admonish her to conserve herself if I observe her to look in any way tired or spent upon my return."

Ivy set down her own cup with a clatter. "What do you mean, upon your return?"

He said nothing, but his expression was enough to answer her and confirm her fears. "You are going away again! That's why you came back so early from the Citadel—to get ready to leave."

"I confess, that is the case."

A sudden panic came upon her. She knew it was ill of her to protest—what could it accomplish save to make his task more difficult?—yet she could not prevent herself. "You said you had accomplished what you needed to on your last venture to Torland. Surely there is no reason for you to return there. And it is so far— you will never return in time for Lily and Rose's party!"

He reached across the table and took her hand. She tried to snatch it back, but he tightened his grip on it, holding it with a force that, though gentle, was beyond her power to break.

"I am *not* going back to Torland," he said, his voice low, and his brown eyes intent upon her. "There is nothing more that I can do there. I am only going so far as Mansford in the south. I must meet with another of the inquirers there. He has some papers belonging to the lord inquirer that were in his keeping, and I must retrieve them."

Ivy's dread receded somewhat. Mansford was not so terribly distant. If he took a swift stage, and did not linger long, he would be no more than a quarter month. All the same, that would have him returning very near to Lily and Rose's party.

"Cannot this other inquirer bring the papers to the city?" she said.

"He is not at liberty to do so. His business lies in the other direction. Nor are these things that could safely be sent by post."

Ivy sighed, and the last of her fear was replaced by resignation. "It is just . . . you have already been at the Citadel so much of late."

"I know." He stroked the back of her hand with his thumb. "There has been much to do since our loss of Lord Rafferdy."

"Then the situation can only be improved when there is a new lord inquirer appointed. Therefore I will hope that day comes soon."

"You may not want to express such a hope!"

"Why should I not?"

He withdrew his hand from hers. "Because I fear that it is I who will be nominated for the post. Indeed, the papers I go to re-trieve may confirm that very thing. All that has been wanting is to know what Lord Rafferdy's mind on the subject was, and I have reason to believe that among these letters is one that expresses his intent that I succeed him. Thus you can now be assured that it is only with the greatest reluctance that I leave you to go on this journey."

Ivy's astonishment was so great that for a long moment she could not speak. "But you must go!" she exclaimed at last. "This is marvelous."

He leaned back in his chair. "Is it marvelous? That is hardly the word I would have chosen."

"Yet it is the word I choose," Ivy said.

She gazed at him. In that moment, all her dreads and anxieties and selfish cares, while they did not depart, became so light that she could easily pick them up and set them aside. She stood and went around to him, resting her hands upon his thick, sloped shoulders.

"Do not think that I am not sensible to what this portends. It means I will be able to claim an even smaller part of you than I already do. Yet you must ignore all of my silly complaints. How can I be jealous of Altania? For in serving *her,* you serve all of us, including myself. Besides, I would rather possess a fraction of a great and good man, rather than the whole of one whom I did not so greatly admire, and so greatly love."

He said nothing. Instead, he caught her hand in his—the

maimed one this time—and pressed it to his bearded cheek. They stayed that way for a while. Then, at last, he let go.

"Well, perhaps it will not come to pass," he said, though he did not sound very hopeful.

"If not, then no one shall be more glad than I. And if it does come to be, then no one shall be more proud than I." She shook her head. "Yet I confess, this is a wonder. It does not surprise me, given your abilities and your dedication, that you would be considered for such a post. Still, I did not think a baronet could attain such a position."

"He cannot," Mr. Quent said grimly.

Ivy stared at him stupidly.

"Oh!" she said as understanding at last came upon her. Then she went back around the table and sat in her chair.

Now dread and wonder were replaced with a kind of cold numbness. She could hardly comprehend what he meant—not because his meaning was not clear, but rather because it did not seem possible. Was it not enough he had been made a baronet? Would he now be raised to a magnate as well? Such a thing was scarcely heard of in modern times.

Now it was he who rose and came around the table to her.

"Let us not think about things that have not come to pass," he said, touching her hair, "for they may never do so. Besides, I have a little time before I must depart, and I can think of more pleasant ways to pass it."

He brushed aside her hair, exposing the nape of her neck, then bent to press his lips against it. Ivy sighed, and while she knew they would no doubt return, in that moment the chill of worry vanished from her, replaced by the most pleasant warmth. Shutting her eyes, she reached up, touching the side of his face, and leaned against him.

"As you wish, my lord," she murmured.

𝕿HE CARRIAGE CAME to a halt before a grand house in the New Quarter. She was here already.

Ivy sighed and leaned back against the bench. Since bidding farewell to Mr. Quent earlier that day, her spirits had been very low, and she was not in the proper frame of mind to attend a party. However, he had admonished her that she must in no way give up her plans to attend the affair.

If he was in fact to be the next lord inquirer—a position that would raise him even further—then it was all the more important that they appear fitting and worthy of such a grand benefit. In this regard, her behavior was as vital as his; or, he had told her, even more so. She was seen by society much more often than he was, and their observations upon her could only be used to infer judgments about *him*.

With such thoughts in her mind, Ivy could hardly look forward to the tea at Lady Crayford's—a thing that previously had sounded so amusing—with much anticipation. She reminded herself that Mrs. Baydon would be present, and seeing her friend was something she could always look forward to. Thus, when Lawden opened the carriage door, Ivy found the will to take his hand and descend to the street.

The viscount's house looked no less magnificent in daylight than by moonlight. Its marble columns gleamed like the stones of some classical Tharosian ruin. Ivy took the steps slowly; there were a great number of them, and she did not wish to look flushed upon her arrival. Besides, she was in no great hurry to be in the company of others who would expect her to speak and be charming.

Only then she was there, and the door opened before she could lay a hand upon the knocker. She was whisked within and led down a long gallery and through a pair of glass doors. Beyond was an airy colonnade, and once past that she came into the garden behind the house.

Except it was more like a park: a great lawn bordered by tall plane trees. The tinkling of water filled the air, for all around there were fountains and little springs that tumbled over rocks. The garden had been made to look like the most natural place, yet it was clear it was all carefully tended and arranged to appear so.

"There you are at last, Lady Quent!" called Lady Crayford, hurrying across the lawn in her direction.

This greeting left Ivy perplexed. She was certain she was in no way late; and even if she was, she could not imagine the party had been waiting upon *her* arrival. However, any momentary vexation she suffered vanished as the viscountess took her arm and led her across the garden, talking brightly all the way.

Upon reaching the others, Ivy discovered that she was in fact the last to arrive. Mrs. Baydon was already there, happily engaged in conversation with Captain Branfort, while Lord Eubrey was gesturing in an exaggerated manner, apparently attempting to win some sort of response from Colonel Daubrent. The viscountess's brother had folded his arms over his broad chest and seemed unwilling to surrender his phlegmatic demeanor.

There were a number of others there as well—some Ivy recognized from other affairs at Lady Crayford's, and some were new to her. While there were many there she did not recognize, she was astonished to find that everyone present seemed to recognize *her*. What was more, they all wished to approach her at once, and she was immediately subjected to a lengthy series of greetings and introductions with various lords and ladies, sirs, misters, misses, and madams, and even a stray earl.

At last Ivy was rescued by the sound of muskets.

All conversation was suspended as Colonel Daubrent led Captain Branfort and several other men in a display of their firearms. While no shot was loaded in the muskets, they made the most alarming and delightful noise all the same. Soon the servants released the hounds, which prowled about the bushes hunting for the pheasants that had been hidden there. With the smoke of gunpowder drifting on the air, and the men looking so handsome and imposing in their hunting coats, rifles in hand, Ivy could indeed believe she was part of a birding party out in the country.

"Isn't it all marvelous!" someone said, taking her arm, and Ivy was delighted to discover it was Mrs. Baydon.

"It is a very convincing facsimile."

Mrs. Baydon sighed. "Mr. Baydon hates hunting with the

greatest vehemence, but I have always wanted to be able to go out with a hunting party. Though I confess, the sound of the guns is very startling. I believe I need a glass of wine to settle my nerves."

As another musket volley sounded, they proceeded to one of the tables set up on the lawn. There they sat and were brought wine and a luncheon of savory and sweet things that Ivy was certain were far more elaborate than anything men might consume on a hunting trip, which she guessed would consist of tobacco, whiskey, and little else.

Soon they were joined at their table by Captain Branfort and Colonel Daubrent, who had set down their guns, and Lord Eubrey followed after. Ivy expected Lady Crayford to sit with some other of her guests, but it was the viscountess who took the last seat at their table. Glasses were raised, and the talk that ensued was like the wine they drank; that is, it flowed freely and was deliciously heady, even if it provided scant substance. Ivy listened to tales of this party or that affair, who was at each, and more important, who was not. All the while, Mrs. Baydon watched with blue eyes aglow.

"But where is the viscount today?" Captain Branfort said after a time. "I had intended to show him my new rifle. He had expressed an interest in seeing it when last I spoke with him."

"I have no idea where he is," Lady Crayford said. "Engrossed in some dull affair of business, I have no doubt. I told him how marvelous our party was to be, but he said such an affair could not interest him—that it would have to offer something truly novel to entice him."

Ivy was disappointed by this news, as she had hoped to meet the viscount as well. She expressed this sentiment, and Lady Crayford's violet eyes flashed as she set down the apricot she had been nibbling.

"If you wished to meet the viscount, I imagine it is within your power, Lady Quent. For of course he has heard all about you from me, and he told me the other day that he was quite interested to attend your next affair."

"My affair?" Ivy said, and took another sip of cool wine.

"Yes, of course—the party for the occasion of presenting your sisters."

Ivy set down her glass; had she imbibed so much that she could not hear clearly? "The party for my sisters?"

"Yes, Mrs. Baydon told me all about it. I confess, I am astonished you did not inform me of it yourself."

Ivy suffered a sudden pang of alarm. "I assure you, it was not my intention to keep such news from you! It is simply that it never—" She took a breath, thinking how best to phrase it. "You see, it will be only a modest affair. That is, it will be nothing remarkable compared to a party such as this."

"Well, I don't believe that at all," Colonel Daubrent said, a frown on his handsome face. "One hardly needs all this mummery my sister favors to host an agreeable affair. I have been to parties in canvas tents in the Outlands where all we had were tin cups and a cask of ale, and I found them to be perfectly entertaining."

Ivy knew the colonel was being serious, yet she could not help smiling at his description, and some of her dread receded. Lady Crayford seemed amused as well, rather than perturbed, by her brother's words.

"I have no doubt that is just the sort of party you military men favor," she said.

"The colonel does not speak for us all!" Captain Branfort declared. "I for one would greatly prefer an affair at Lady Quent's to just about any sort of gathering. I had the occasion to ride by your house on Durrow Street the other day and caught a glimpse through the gate. It is the most handsome sort of old edifice. Indeed, so pleasing are its proportions and the air of solidity about it that I wonder why people ever abandoned the Old City in favor of the New Quarter."

Lord Eubrey was idly folding a piece of paper into the shape of a swan. "No doubt people will begin to return to the Old City once word circulates of the affair at Lady Quent's excellent house," he said. "I wager that within a quarter month it will be seen as the most daring and marvelous thing to leave the New Quarter and take up residence on Durrow Street."

"I am certain that will not be so!" Ivy said, astonished.

He raised an eyebrow. "Are you? Well, if you think that to be the case, there is only one way to test your hypothesis. You must invite us all to your sisters' party."

Now Ivy was beyond astonished; she could find no capacity for speech.

"Unless, of course, you do not think the Miss Lockwells would wish to have so many guests who are unknown to them at their affair," Captain Branfort said seriously.

"No!" Ivy at last managed to cry, and so gallant and absurd were the captain's words that she could not help laughing. For who would Lily more wish to have at her party than the very sort of people sitting at this table? It would be, for Lily, like a chapter from one of her romances. "No, they would both be delighted if you all came, I have no doubt. But you must do so only if it is something you truly wish to do, not out of any sense of regard or duty. I warn you again, it will be a very modest affair."

They would judge that for themselves, her companions at the table declared. For they would all surely attend, and Lady Crayford was confident her husband would be enticed to go as well. For what could be more novel than to attend a grand party at a grand house that had not seen such an affair in centuries?

So overwhelmed was Ivy that she could only nod and take another sip of her wine. Beneath the table, Mrs. Baydon squeezed her hand.

The afternoon wore on. They left the tables and sat on blankets on the grass, eating strawberries and gazing at the trees that swayed gently overhead while Lady Crayford made little drawings of all their profiles in her sketchbook. A great contentment came over Ivy; she could have wanted for nothing else, save to share this all with Mr. Quent.

On the blanket beside her, Mrs. Baydon let out a sigh. The afternoon light shone gold upon her hair. "It is so lovely here," she said. "Yet it fills me with a longing to go on a real trip to the country. Somewhere far away from the city—somewhere wild."

"Somewhere wild?" Lord Eubrey said, his chin held high as he posed for the viscountess. "Somewhere like Madiger's Wall, perhaps?"

Mrs. Baydon gasped and clapped her hands. "Oh, but I have always wanted to go to the wall and see the Evengrove!"

"You have never been?"

She shook her head. "My husband has always refused to take me."

"Perhaps it's because of that slow gig of his," Lord Eubrey said with a laugh. "It would take a long lumenal indeed to get all the way to the Evengrove if you were to take a gig. But a good number can fit in the viscount's four-in-hand, which is wickedly fast. Why, the colonel's curricle would be hard-pressed to keep up with it. And I can meet you all there."

"Why would you not just come with us?" Colonel Daubrent said.

"I have a plan already to travel there tomorrow with some associates of mine. If you were all there as well, it would make for a merry outing."

The others concurred that it would no doubt make for a great adventure, and the details of a plan were quickly formulated.

"But do you think it is very wise?" Ivy said.

The others looked at her, and the anxiousness that had been growing within Ivy throughout this conversation increased further. Long ago, the Tharosian emperor Madiger had commanded the wall to be built to protect the outpost of Invarduin from incursions of the Wyrdwood. In the centuries that followed, the wall was strengthened and expanded; over the same period, the old Tharosian fort grew into the Grand City of Invarel. As a result, the greatest expanse of primeval forest in the nation was not far out in the country, but was rather a journey of but a few hours from the city.

In recent years, making a tour of Madiger's Wall had become a popular entertainment. Ivy, however, had never been there; Mr. Lockwell had never taken them to the Evengrove. Nor did this surprise Ivy, knowing what she did now of her own heritage.

The others still gazed at her, and with some difficulty she drew in a breath. "I mean only, since the events in Torland, I cannot imagine people are going to the Evengrove much anymore."

"On the contrary, I'm sure they go now more than ever," Lord Eubrey said brightly. "I imagine a great number of people are curious to gaze upon the very sort of trees that caused the Risings, and to think what it might be like to see them stir of their own accord."

"Oh, that's a dreadful thought!" Mrs. Baydon exclaimed, though her eyes were shining.

"I would say it's perfectly natural to wonder about it," Lady Crayford said. "While it might cause a shiver to consider such things, there can be no harm in it. I am sure it is perfectly safe to go to the Evengrove. No doubt the soldiers are watching it night and day."

Her brother said this was indeed the case.

"Do you see, Lady Quent?" the viscountess said, turning toward her. "Even one as sensible as yourself must be satisfied that everything can only be perfectly safe with so many soldiers about."

Ivy had to concede that was likely the case. All the same, her every urge was to tell the others that they must go without her. But what would she give them for a reason? She could not say Mr. Quent had forbidden it, for he was not in town. Nor could she very well tell them the reason for her dread—that she was a witch, and to go near so great a stand of Wyrdwood could only be perilous for her.

"There!" Lady Crayford said triumphantly. "You can offer no reason against it, Lady Quent. So it is decided, then—we will all go to the Evengrove tomorrow."

The others continued to devise a scheme for the trip. They would leave early, so there would be plenty of time to linger at the wall when they arrived. Now that it was decided, and there was no chance of refusal, Ivy's dread began to recede. For Lady Crayford was right—what harm could possibly come to them there? It was not as if Ivy would be able to pass beyond the wall. Indeed, she would not venture near to it at all.

Which meant there was no cause for any sort of worry. Besides, now that it was beyond her power to refuse, she was in truth eager to lay eyes upon the Evengrove. She had always wished to see it, as it was a place of such importance in the history of Altania. It was held by some historians that the Evengrove was the very patch of forest into which Queen Béanore had vanished after she used her bow to inflict a fatal wound upon the Emperor Veradian, thus driving him from Altania. To behold such a place would be fascinating.

Her thoughts thus pleasantly occupied, Ivy sipped her wine as the others spoke, and she gazed up at the plane trees, watching their branches weave against the sky.

CHAPTER TWENTY-SEVEN

*I*T WAS A full house again that night.

In recent years, the Theater of the Moon had been one of the least popular theaters on Durrow Street. It was smaller and more dilapidated than most of the other houses, and it was often overlooked, half-hidden as it was at the end of the row. What was more, the illusion play performed there was not a fantasia or a burlesque, but rather an esoteric piece that offered little appeal to patrons seeking diverting idylls or sights of passion.

Now that had changed. The only thing that traveled faster on Durrow Street than news of a poor performance was news of a great one. Thus word of that first remarkable performance at the Theater of the Moon spread rapidly. The following night a small crowd had assembled outside the door of the theater by the time it opened, and such is the nature of people that, if they see others gathering, they will join in themselves. Soon people were flocking to the newest sensation on Durrow Street, and theatergoers had to be turned away for want of available seats.

Those who had been lucky enough to gain entrance tonight were not disappointed, and their applause continued as the curtain fell. Behind the tattered velvet, the illusionists laughed and embraced one another, sweating and bright with energy.

"Splendid!" Master Tallyroth said as he thumped his cane against the boards. "That was splendid work! I do not believe I have ever seen a finer performance upon this stage."

"Why, thank you, Master Tallyroth," Dercy said, a grin splitting his blond beard as he spread his arms and gave a florid bow.

"I do not think you can claim sole credit for the success, Mr. Fanewerthy," the master illusionist said in a scolding tone, though he smiled as well. "You were excellent tonight, I grant you, but so was everyone else. And a special mention must be made, I think, of Mr. Garritt's improvements to the final scene, for I believe they worked greatly to heighten its effect."

Dercy gave a wave of his hand, and suddenly a beam of shimmering white light shone down upon Eldyn. The other young men laughed and clapped him on the back, and Eldyn experienced a warmth that could not be attributed to the illusory illumination.

He was pleased to have his idea so praised. It had occurred to him that when the Sun King finally captured the Moon Prince, the king should not smite the prince down to the stage. Rather, Eldyn had suggested, the Moon should be bound and raised up on high; in that way, when he was consumed by fire, the flames would radiate out from him like a golden corona.

It was again something Eldyn had read in the Testament that made him think of the idea—how St. Mirzan, convicted of heresy, was lashed to a tall post and left to a lingering death. Only God sent to him a sparrow with a berry from the Tree of Flame, and when Mirzan ate the berry, he was consumed from within by a brilliant fire, so perishing swiftly and mercifully.

"I could feel every gaze in the house upon me while I was hanging up there," Dercy said, his grin softening a bit. "And did you hear how everyone drew a breath when the flames surrounded me?"

"I swear, I felt it like a wind rushing into the theater," Riethe said. His right hand was healing badly, and he was working the front door these days. "How did you conceive of it, Eldyn?"

Eldyn thought of the fable of Mirzan and the holy flames that released him from his pain.

"It just came to me," he said.

The noise of the audience had at last ceased beyond the curtain. The illusionists made ready for their own exit from the theater, and their plan to proceed directly to tavern was benefited by the arrival of Madame Richelour. The mistress of the theater opened the box with that night's receipts and proceeded to hand out coins.

"I must give some of this away," she declared, "for otherwise I will not be able to close the lid!"

Eldyn happily accepted some of this largesse along with the other illusionists. However, as he gazed at the coins in his hand, his mirth dwindled. "It seems strange," he said softly.

Dercy, who stood close beside him, cocked his head to one side. "Strange? How so?"

He looked up at Dercy. "Strange that our theater should know such success when others have had to close their doors."

Dercy's expression grew solemn. The news had flown down Durrow Street just yesterday that the Theater of Emeralds had gone dark forever. They had lost too many illusionists—those who had vanished, and those who had left the city—and their master illusionist was perilously ill. The mordoth would take him soon, it was whispered.

"Some rise while others fall," Dercy said, his sea green eyes thoughtful. "That's the nature of the world. Besides, there's some good in it all. No player from the Theater of Emeralds will have trouble finding a place at another house, not if he wants one. Besides, if our play draws so many people that we must turn them away from the door, it only means they'll go to one of the other theaters. So you see, our good fortune helps the whole street."

Eldyn had to admit his friend's words sounded like wisdom. Still, he could not help but wonder how many other theaters would have to close if more young men went missing or fled the city.

Dercy looped an arm around Eldyn's. "Come on, let's be the first to the tavern. That way we can buy ourselves a round of punch, and then when the others come they can buy us another!"

That sounded like a merry plan. All the same, Eldyn gently disengaged his arm from his friend's.

"Unfortunately, I must go home," he said. "Even if the almanac's error is in my favor tonight, it will still be a short umbral, and I am needed early at Graychurch tomorrow."

"You are needed, you say? What of our need to celebrate our glory? It is your solemn duty to raise a glass with your fellows."

Eldyn let out a laugh. "It is also my solemn duty to show up to my work in a few hours sober and able to hold a pen. And as the one duty will earn me regals while the other will cost them, for all Madame Richelour's bounty, I think my choice is made."

"Why are you still so concerned with thoughts of money?" Dercy said with a frown. "You're earning a full player's wage now. And if you need more, just ask Madame Richelour. I'm sure there's enough in her box to give you another regal or two."

"You forget that I'll need more than a regal or two to save up a portion for my sister if she is to be married respectably. And then there's the amount I'll need for—" Eldyn clamped his jaw shut.

Dercy's green eyes narrowed. "The amount you'll need for what?"

"For her wedding party and such," Eldyn said hurriedly.

Dercy seemed to study him, then at last he shook his head. "I hardly understand you sometimes, Eldyn. You've discovered you can conjure wonders that bring audiences to their feet, yet you seem perfectly content to sit in a musty old crypt and scribble numbers on paper for a few pennies."

"It's more than a few pennies," Eldyn said. "Besides, it won't be for much longer."

"I suppose. All the same, sometimes I begin to think you rather enjoy working for the Church."

Eldyn suffered a pang of alarm. "What do you mean?"

"The idea of lifting me up on high just came to you?" Dercy let out a snort. "You forget I was a priest, Eldyn. I wasn't one for long, I grant you, but it was enough to learn about all the saints, Mirzan included. And the doves in the scene on the mountain—that's right out of the Testament. It's all brilliant, of course, and it gives me more than a little pleasure to think how red-faced the priests at St. Adaris would be if they knew scenes from the holy book were being used to improve a profane illusion play on Durrow Street." Now his grin returned. "Why, it's so perverse I don't know why I didn't think of it myself. So go on, then—keep working at the Church to find ideas to steal. I won't tell Master Tallyroth the secret source of your improvements."

A horror came upon Eldyn. He had not considered that it might be sacrilegious to include holy symbols in their performances. What if what he had done had caused an insult to God? Except he could not believe that. Theirs was not some ribald display. Besides, the archdeacon himself had assured Eldyn that what he did before he became a priest was of no matter. All would be forgiven at that moment.

Still, he thought perhaps he would consider it more carefully if another idea for improving the illusion play came to him while reading scripture.

"I will see you tomorrow," he told Dercy. "Tell Merrick and Mouse to have a drink for me. Tell Riethe to have two." He gave Dercy an embrace that, while strong, was so brief it left Dercy no time to reply.

He passed through the front door and out into the night. Durrow Street was not so busy as he had imagined it would be. The crowds had dispersed quickly after the illusion plays let out. A few people walked here and there, and several carriages sped by, wheels clattering loudly against the cobbles. From somewhere down the street came the bubbling sound of laughter. Or was it a sound of suffering?

Eldyn could not help thinking of the illusionists who had been found murdered. Even as he did, a tall man clad all in black—alone, the brim of his hat pulled low—came striding down the street. A sudden desire to not be seen came over Eldyn, and he reached out for the shadows, drawing them in close and wrapping them around him like a soft, comforting cloak.

The man walked past him without so much as a glance. Eldyn let out the breath he had been holding, then hurried down the street.

Soon he came to the edges of High Holy. Usually he went around the infamous section of Durrow Street. While he might cloak himself in shadows and so pass unseen, the shadows could not prevent *him* from seeing the sights of wretchedness and degeneracy all around. However, the umbral was to be brief, and passing through High Holy was the quickest route back to the old monastery.

With a thought he redoubled the shroud of darkness around him. He kept his gaze down as he went, only now and then casting a furtive glance to either side to see if anyone noticed him. Men with slack faces huddled in doorways or warmed their hands over fires burning in barrels. A trio of whores, their skirts hiked up to reveal their pantaloons, were drinking gin and cackling with laughter on the steps of the abandoned chapel. No one looked Eldyn's way.

He left the decrepit chapel behind and drew near the statue of St. Thadrus the Elder, whitened by pigeons, which marked the east end of High Holy. A man stood beneath the statue, clad in a ragged cape whose hood was pulled up to cover his head against the night chill.

The man moved back and forth in front of the statue, his head swaying from side to side as he went. A wheezing emanated from within the hood, as if from labored breaths being drawn. Having no wish to catch an illness from some vagrant, Eldyn gave the man a wide berth as he passed by the statue of St. Thadrus.

There was a hissing noise, and the hood turned in Eldyn's direction.

Eldyn's step faltered. It was almost as if the hooded man had seen him. But that was impossible, concealed as he was in shadows. As for being heard, the noise of his footsteps could only be lost amid the harsh laughter and moans that echoed throughout High Holy. Assured he could not have been detected, Eldyn continued on.

The hooded head swung around, following him as he went.

A seed of dread germinated in Eldyn's heart, then quickly blossomed into horror as the man took a step in his direction. He pulled down a thick curtain of darkness before him, and slowly, soundlessly edged away.

The black pit of the hood turned slowly as well, moving just as Eldyn did. The man reached out a pale hand. A finger uncoiled and thrust itself forward, pointing stiffly ahead.

Pointing at Eldyn.

The curtain of darkness fell to tatters as Eldyn lost his grip on the illusion. No longer did he care if others saw him pass. Instead, he turned and ran east along Durrow Street, his heart pounding in time with his boots against the cobbles. The horrible noise of wheezing was loud in his ears.

But it was only his own labored breaths he was hearing, and when he cast a glance over his shoulder, the street behind him was empty.

𝒯HE BELLS OF St. Galmuth's were tolling the coming of dawn when Eldyn left the old monastery, though it was still nearly dark as night, for the sky was a leaden gray, and a fine rain was misting down from the clouds.

Despite the dreary weather and queer happenings after leaving the theater last night, Eldyn's spirits were bright. He was still filled with the afterglow of their last performance, and a little rain could not douse such a light. As for the peculiar occurrence in High Holy on his way home, it did not seem so disconcerting when considered in the light of morning as it did when alone in the dark of night. The hooded man could not possibly have seen him. The derelict had been mad or ill or addled with gin, that was all, looking for things that did not exist and pointing at things that were not there. It was simply chance that his finger had happened to point in Eldyn's direction.

So there was nothing to worry about. As long as he was careful, and made liberal use of shadows as he went to and from the theater, he had no reason to fear any harm would come to him. Besides, his time on Durrow Street was to be shorter than he had thought. The receipts at the theater had quadrupled from what they were before, and now he was getting a full player's share. As a result, it would be a matter of months before he had amassed funds enough for his and Sashie's portions. Which meant, even if murderous beings continued to stalk along Durrow Street, Eldyn would soon have no cause to fear them.

Yet what of the other players at the Theater of the Moon? And what of Dercy? Eldyn might be safe within the walls of a church; however, as long as illusionists continued to go missing, or to turn up floating in the Anbyrn, no one at any of the houses on Durrow Street would be safe.

While the rain could not dampen Eldyn's spirits, this thought did. How could he be content in his secure and happy life as a priest knowing that his friends might at any moment be preyed upon by those who wished harm to their kind? Even worse, what if more theaters, including his own, were forced to close in the near future? The loss of that income would ruin all of his plans for him and his sister. There had to be some way to find and bring to light the perpetrators of these awful acts.

Only he did not know how. The redcrests cared nothing if a few Siltheri were found dead; wicked things happened to wicked men, was all they would say. Nor could the Crown or Assembly be expected to do anything about it. Eldyn imagined they could only be glad if all the theaters were closed; to them, it would be the welcome removal of a blemish upon the Grand City. But then who was there left who could help them?

The bells of the cathedral tolled the final notes of their carillon, and Eldyn's gaze was drawn up to the spires that reached toward the gray sky. He knew the Church frowned upon the activities of illusionists. Yet God loved the wretched and lowly as much as he did the high and noble, or so he had read in the Testament. Perhaps there was some way the Church could intervene on behalf of the Siltheri. After all, if its purpose was to save men's souls, did not their lives need to be saved first?

His spirits buoyed once more, he turned up the collar of his coat against the chill and hurried across the street and up the steps of Graychurch to commence his work for the day.

Soon Eldyn was bent over his writing table in the rector's office, his pen scratching rapidly against paper. As usual, the box of receipts and demands was overflowing. Eldyn was continually amazed at the busy nature of the church's accounts. Surely they surpassed those of any private company. Indeed, so numerous were the purchases to record in the ledger that he began to wonder if all the items were really needed.

Even as he thought this, Eldyn took from the box a receipt for several sets of red curtains. It was not the first time he had seen such a purchase, yet he was sure he had never seen red curtains anywhere in Graychurch or St. Galmuth's cathedral, or in any church he could think of. More than likely they were lining some priest's private chambers!

Well, it was not for him to question. Like so many of the purchases he recorded in the ledger, this one must have had all proper sanctions, for it had been signed by Archdeacon Lemarck on behalf of the archbishop.

Eldyn could not be surprised that the archdeacon was doing so much of the archbishop's work; it had long been known that the Archbishop of Invarel was infirm. What was more, an article in a recent edition of *The Swift Arrow* had repeated rumors that it was more than age or illness that afflicted him—that in fact the archbishop was prone to fits and spells, and that he had fallen under the grip of a derangement of the mind.

According to the article, persons who had managed to get near to the archbishop reported that he was suffering hallucinations. He often claimed he saw daemons and fell beasts prowling outside the cathedral—creatures formed of tooth and shadow that lurked on the edges of the light, hungering to feast upon the souls of men.

Eldyn hoped the article in *The Swift Arrow* was in error, and that the archbishop was not so mad as that. All the same, that he was ill was not in doubt; even Father Gadby had said as much. This caused Eldyn some worry, for the Archbishop of Invarel was the Primate of the Church of Altania. Of course, the Church was fortunate to have a man such as Archdeacon Lemarck on whom to rely in this difficult situation.

Eldyn had been at his labors for some hours and was preparing to start on another box of receipts when Father Gadby complained that he was in need of some air, and he asked Eldyn if he wished to go up and sit for a while outside. Eldyn readily agreed. His neck ached, and his hand had become cramped from holding the pen.

Soon the two of them were happily ensconced on the steps before the church, though it had required some effort on Eldyn's part to help lower the portly rector so that he might take his seat. The clouds had burned off, and the day had become fine. The cooing of pigeons drifted on the air, along with the calls of a boy hawking copies of *The Fox* across the street.

"I do wish that young hooligan would move along and take his mischief elsewhere," the rector said with a frown.

"The boy is doing no harm that I can see," Eldyn replied. "He is only selling broadsheets."

"Broadsheets! He is selling woe and misery. There can be nothing good contained in those newspapers. A man should better spend his time reading the Testament."

Eldyn could not disagree with that. "Still, I would think it is good for a person to know what is going on in the world."

"Well, if one wishes to know what is happening in the world, one should see it for oneself. Perhaps King Rothard would not tolerate such wicked and profligate behavior in our nation if he were to come down off of his throne once in a while and go out among the people."

Eldyn could not help a laugh. "I can only imagine people

would cease behaving in wicked and profligate ways the moment they saw their king approaching."

"Well, then he ought to leave his crown and go about in plain attire," the rector said. "That way he would be able to observe how people truly are when they are at their ease, not when acting on their best behavior. That is what the archdeacon does to discover what is happening within his demesne."

"You mean he goes about dressed as a layman?" Eldyn said, astonished by this news.

The rector's jowls waggled. "No, not as a layman! That would hardly be proper for a man who has taken the vows. I have heard from reliable sources that the archdeacon sometimes goes about clad in the garb of a simple priest. Dressed in that manner he attracts little notice, and so he can better see how his flock fares. However, now that I think about it, I believe that I perhaps should not have told you this. So I will ask you to keep this in confidence, Mr. Garritt. Were it known widely that this was his practice, he might not be able to go about so anonymously."

Eldyn promised that he would keep this knowledge to himself, and the rector was greatly relieved.

"I am glad the archdeacon is here among us to work so much good," Eldyn said. "But I fear there will never be a lack of woeful news to print in the broadsheets. It is man's nature, is it not, to be weak and wicked?"

"It is the nature of *some* men," the rector said with a sniff. "Which is why, if they must print anything at all, they should be printing stories of saints and not villains. When the broadsheets reward criminals with fame and attention, is it any wonder that other men are moved to become criminals themselves? Now the newspapers have given great attention to the affair at the Ministry of Printing, and I can only worry that rather than causing young men to scorn and condemn magick, it will cause them instead to pursue it in an effort to gain notoriety."

"I grant you, what was done at the ministry was dreadful," Eldyn said. "Yet they could have easily used black powder instead of a spell to do the deed. It does not mean magick itself is wicked."

"On the contrary, it is dreadfully wicked!" the rector exclaimed. "You can be forgiven for not knowing, Mr. Garritt, for I am sure *you* have never dabbled in such awful things as the arcane."

No, Eldyn had never dabbled in magick and never would. Yet he knew that Rafferdy had—that his friend was descended of one of the seven Old Houses and was these days something of a magician.

"Why is magick so awful?" he asked.

"Because it deceives men. Magick convinces them that they can wield power over daemons and devils. Only that is a trick. There is only one thing that can help man fight against unholy forces, and that is the power of God in Eternum. There is nothing else that can preserve men from evil—anything else which would promise to do so is a lie."

Eldyn had never considered it like this. He could see how some magicians might be fooled into thinking they had power over the dark things they summoned and thus forsake God's protections, but he could not imagine Rafferdy ever falling for such a ruse—he was far too clever.

"Well, as awful as magicians are, they are not nearly so awful as illusionists," Father Gadby said.

Eldyn stared at the rector. "What's that?"

"Look, there go a lot of them now."

The rector's round face, usually soft and cheerful, had gone suddenly hard. Eldyn followed his gaze and saw a group of young men walking along the street before the church. Their coats were gaudy with lace and brocade, and their faces and wigs were powdered white. Any doubt that they were Siltheri was removed when one of them held up a hand and a silvery dove appeared upon it. The bird flitted upward to circle around the spire of St. Galmuth's before vanishing into the sky.

It was far too early in the day for the illusionists to be on their way to a rehearsal or a performance. Nor was Graychurch near the east end of Durrow Street. Eldyn could only suppose the young men had come this way to taunt the priests in the cathedral. He knew from Dercy that some illusionists enjoyed such activities as a sport. Eldyn did not know which house these men were from; none of them looked familiar. All the same he lowered his head for fear one of them might recognize him.

Out of the corner of his eye, he saw one of the illusionists wave a handkerchief in their direction.

"Those vile sinners!" Spittle sprayed from the rector's lips as he spoke. "There is no pit in the Abyss deep enough for their kind. To make men see things that God Himself did not bring into being—why, it mocks God's own creations. And as if that was not enough . . ." He shook his head. "Well, you must know they lie with one another in the most foul and pernicious ways."

Despite the warmth of the sun, a trembling had come over Eldyn, and he clasped his hands together so Father Gadby would not detect it. What a fool he was to have thought that the Church might somehow help to discover who was preying upon the illusionists of Durrow Street. Eldyn's own happiness at the knowledge he would soon enter the Church had caused him to forget what he knew. Now he recalled the words the priest outside the old church of St. Adaris had shouted at him that night a year ago.

Begone, daemon. By all the saints, I command you. Go back to your houses of sin and trouble us no more. . . .

No, the illusionists could not look to the Church for help. The Siltheri were already damned, in its opinion.

Yet was not the greatest revelation of the Testament the knowledge that all men could be forgiven for their sins? The archdeacon himself had said that what Eldyn did in life before he entered the Church did not matter. Surely that meant even an illusionist could find grace.

Except they would have to give up being Siltheri, wouldn't they? Just like he was going to have to do himself one day. Eldyn couldn't imagine that many of the young men at the Theater of the Moon would willingly give up conjuring illusions in exchange for the blessings of the Church. Not Mouse or Merrick or Riethe. And especially not Dercy.

The illusionists disappeared around a corner, and the rector heaved himself to his feet.

"Come, Mr. Garritt. I have quite lost my desire to be outside. Let us return within and continue our labors for God."

He waddled through the doors of the church, and Eldyn followed after him—though not before casting a glance in the direction where the illusionists had disappeared from view.

CHAPTER TWENTY-EIGHT

IVY RESTED LITTLE the night before the excursion to Madiger's Wall. Anticipation made it difficult to sleep, and when she finally did manage to shut her eyes, her repose was once again interrupted by the faint murmurs of voices and the moaning of a distant wind.

Certain these noises had not been dreamed, she put on a robe, took up a candle, and left her chamber to make a survey of the house. However, she found nothing out of order; the only things that stirred in the house were the wooden eyes that opened drowsily as her candlelight fell upon them, and then closed again as she passed.

At last she climbed the stairs to return to her bed. Only then, as she was passing the gallery on the second floor, she again heard the soughing sound of wind. She went to the window, but in the moonlight all the trees in the garden were motionless.

As she gazed at the disheveled little chestnut and hawthorn trees below, she could not help but feel wonder. Yesterday evening, after returning from the tea at Lady Crayford's, she had made her usual perusal of her father's journal, and she had come upon a new entry.

In it, he had described some experiments he had performed with a number of seeds that he had acquired in the West

Country—seeds that were purported to have been gleaned on the edges of a stand of Wyrdwood. Mr. Lockwell had made repeated attempts to germinate the seeds to see if they might be grown into seedlings whose properties he could study, but he had never had any luck getting them to grow.

Until he brought Ivy to the house.

It was not two months after I brought you here as a small child when I saw the first sprouts, her father had written. *They were growing in the garden in the very place where you most liked to run about and play. After all my failed attempts, I knew it could not be ascribed to chance that the seeds germinated almost at once after you came to the house. I hardly needed further proof; but if I did, I had it once I removed us to Whitward Street. Not long after we did so, I returned to the old house and noted that the saplings had become sickly and withered. Ever after that their growth was stunted, and they were always shedding their leaves. Yet they did not perish, and I have often wondered how they would fare if you were to return to the house. . . .*

To think, here in their very garden were Old Trees! It was strange to think of the little trees, which did not have even as many years as she did, as *Old*. Yet they were of the same primeval stock as the Wyrdwood.

Ivy was sure Mr. Quent would be displeased to learn this fact. In the country, such trees would never be allowed to take root near a dwelling, though she could only think that any peril *these* trees presented was not significant. Did not the power of the Wyrdwood come from the manner in which the roots spread and twined beneath the soil, thus permitting the trees to communicate with one another? She was certain there were no Old Trees near the city with which these small specimens might converse. All the same, she would be sure to tell Mr. Quent what she had learned.

As to her father's question—since their return to the house, the little hawthorns and chestnuts in the garden had begun to thrive and grow, and while they still had a tendency to shed their leaves, they were always gaining new ones.

Yet those leaves were not moving now. So where had the noise of the wind come from?

Ivy turned, and as she did the candlelight danced over the surface of the door in the northern wall. The carved wooden leaves seemed to stir as if they felt a breath of air. But it was only an effect of the flickering shadows cast by the candle; and though she stood there for several minutes, listening, the sound did not come again.

After that Ivy returned to her room. Despite the early hour, sleep was beyond her now, so she made herself ready for the day. Once this was done, she went downstairs and, to pass the time, worked at organizing her father's books in the library. She must have become absorbed in the task, for when a loud noise echoed through the door of the library, she gasped and nearly dropped the book in her hand.

The noise came again. It was the sound of someone briskly knocking at the front door. They were here! Ivy hastily slipped the book into place on a shelf, then hurried from the library.

She reached the front hall in time to see Mrs. Seenly open the door. A moment later Captain Branfort stepped over the threshold. He was handsome in his blue coat, and his hat was tucked under his arm. When he saw Ivy approaching, he gave a deep bow.

"Good morning, Lady Quent," he said, rising up. "Are you eager to be off on our expedition?"

Now that the moment had arrived, Ivy realized that she *was* eager to go. "I am," she said. "Very much."

He offered his arm. "Excellent! Then let us be off. I can't tell who's chafing more at the reins being held—Colonel Daubrent's horses or the colonel himself!"

WHICH PASSED MORE swiftly, the horses or the time, Ivy could not say.

She spent the first part of the journey riding in the viscount's four-in-hand with Lady Crayford and Mr. and Mrs. Baydon. For much of this time, the viscountess and Mr. Baydon were engaged in a lively argument upon the theme of which was the more vital matter, politics or art.

He claimed that it must be politics, for the very endurance of

the nation of Altania depended upon the decisions being made by
Crown and Assembly. But, claimed she, art was of greater importance; for a work of art could endure long after the nation where
it was created fell to dust. Were there not masterworks of
Tharosian sculpture displayed in the Royal Museum? Art, she declared, was above any government.

"What do you think on the matter, Lady Quent?" the viscountess asked after it was clear she and Mr. Baydon were at an impasse.

"It is evident great art can endure long beyond the civilization
where it was birthed," Ivy said, choosing her words with care. "But
I would also say that the highest forms of art cannot be birthed at
all except when given the nurturing and protection of a great civilization."

Mr. Baydon opened his mouth, but he could seem to find no
reply to that, and Lady Crayford arched an eyebrow.

"Lady Quent," she said, "you have negated all our arguments
of the prior two hours with a mere two sentences."

"I'm so sorry," Ivy said, her cheeks growing warm.

"But you mustn't apologize!" Mrs. Baydon exclaimed. "For
you've proven that they are both of them right."

Now the viscountess laughed. "Well, that is our Lady Quent;
she is as sensitive as she is sensible. I do believe any cause we had
to argue has been removed, Mr. Baydon. We will have to speak of
the weather instead."

To which he could only concur.

After several hours they stopped the carriages and took a rest,
as well as a cup of coffee, at a charming inn along the road that
catered to travelers to the wall. When they resumed their journey,
their positions were changed, and Ivy found herself riding with
Colonel Daubrent in his curricle. The light little carriage fairly
flew down the road, though Ivy suffered no fear. By now she was
confident in the colonel's ability as a masterful driver.

The viscountess's brother was not one for making idle conversation, but Ivy in no way minded. She was more than content to
watch hills and fields and stone crofts pass by. It could not be
more different than her first journey to the country. That had

taken place in the darkness of a long night, cramped within the confines of a coach. In contrast, even allowing for errors in the almanac, today was to be a lumenal of over twenty hours, and the land all around basked in warm sun.

At last, just when the ache in her legs began to suggest it would be good to stop driving across the countryside, and instead to get out and walk through it, they crested a low rise.

And there it was, not two furlongs before them.

Ivy had read countless descriptions of Madiger's Wall, and she had seen engraving plates that showed detailed etchings. She knew it was twenty feet high and ten feet thick, and that most of its gray stones had been hewn from a quarry in the mountains of Northaltia and carted here along Tharosian roads.

While it was one thing to *know* something, to see it was another matter altogether. For all her reading, she had not conceived just how massive and forbidding the wall would appear, or how ancient. Its surface was shaggy with moss and mottled by lichen. Even the sunlight seemed heavier here: a rich bronze tinged with green, like an ancient coin dug up from the leaf mold where it had lain for a thousand years.

Movement caught her eye, and Ivy looked up. The wall was so high that only the crowns of the Old Trees showed above. Their highest branches swayed and bent in the breeze like gnarled fingers trying to reach over the top of the wall. Above, crows circled against the sky.

"I said, Lady Quent, are you ready to depart the carriage?"

Ivy blinked and looked down to see Colonel Daubrent standing on her side of the carriage, his hand extended.

"Of course," she said hurriedly, and allowed him to help her from the curricle. The viscount's four-in-hand had stopped close by, and the others had already climbed out.

It appeared Lady Crayford had been right when she said Madiger's Wall was bound to be more popular than ever. Theirs were hardly the only carriages there. In fact, there were so many—from plain country surreys to glossy cabriolets—that Ivy could not easily count them all. Numerous people walked along the path that led to the wall, while others strolled along its boundaries. They looked very small against it, Ivy thought.

Everyone in their party was eager to see the wall, and it was determined they should walk to it at once while the driver and the maid set out a luncheon. Mr. Baydon seemed especially enthusiastic.

"I am anxious," he said, "to see if it is right to have some confidence in this decrepit old structure, which is all that protects Invarel from so malevolent a thing."

"Malevolent!" Ivy exclaimed before she could think not to. "Why do you choose that particular word, Mr. Baydon? You make it sound as if the Wyrdwood has a will to cause harm."

"Does it not?" he said, the ever-present furrows in his brow deepening. "I imagine all those poor fellows in Torland who were deprived of their lives would say so if they could."

The others were looking at Ivy. She should not have spoken, but Mr. Baydon's words had shocked her. "It is perilous, of course," she said carefully. "I do not mean to imply otherwise. Yet even though something has the power to do harm, it does not mean it has the malice to do so."

Her gaze went again to the crowns of the trees above the wall. "The Wyrdwood is queer, I grant you. It is far more ancient than men, and I suppose as such it has little care for them. Yet, while I do not mean to detract from the terrible things that happened in Torland, I cannot help but think that no one would have been harmed if people had given the Wyrdwood the proper berth." She lowered her gaze to regard Mr. Baydon. "There are a great number of people in Altania these days, and there are very few Old Trees left. From that I would surmise, if all things are summed, it is *we* who have been the more fearsome."

"Very true!" Lady Crayford exclaimed before Mr. Baydon could reply. "Which means we had best go and see the Evengrove before someone decides it must all be cut down."

The viscountess took Ivy's arm, and Ivy was grateful for her humor; for some reason Mr. Baydon's words had unsettled her. As they walked down the path, though, Ivy's spirits lifted. She was walking toward the Evengrove and Madiger's Wall—a place out of so many stories she had read and loved as a girl. If she had not known the others would think her mad, she would have taken up a switch and pretended she was Queen Béanore fending off Tharosian soldiers with her hazel bow.

"There are so many people," Captain Branfort said as they went. "I wonder how we will find Lord Eubrey."

Even as he uttered this, they saw just ahead the figure of a slim, dark-haired man waving toward them. It could only be Lord Eubrey. He was walking in their direction, while two young men followed just behind him. It was Ivy's impression that one of them was wearing an exceedingly high hat, only as they drew near she saw that it was in fact a tremendous crown of frizzy hair. The other young man was tall and, she thought, cut a very fine figure in a gray coat as he walked along, swinging the cane in his hand.

The cane ceased its motions just as Ivy let out a gasp.

"Mr. Rafferdy!" she exclaimed.

"Lord Rafferdy, you mean," Lord Eubrey said with a smile as he drew near. He cocked his head to one side. "Yet I can only presume that you and Lord Rafferdy are already acquainted?"

Behind Eubrey, Mr. Rafferdy appeared every bit as astonished as Ivy, only then he smiled. "Indeed, Lady Quent and I are very well-acquainted." He bowed deeply.

Lord Eubrey clapped his gloved hands. "Well, this is splendid. We shall make for a merry party indeed. We had only just arrived ourselves and were walking to the wall when we saw you, so we have not yet been all the way there. Shall we proceed?"

Now that Ivy's initial astonishment had passed, she could feel only great pleasure that Mr. Rafferdy was here. She had longed to see him ever since their return from Asterlane. However, as the party walked along the path, there was no opportunity to speak about any topics other than those that were appropriate in general company.

As they went, Ivy was introduced to Lord Eubrey's other companion, Lord Coulten, whose temperament was as exuberant as his hairstyle. Ivy could not help wondering if the latter was somehow encouraged by the former, for his spirits seemed as high as his coiffure. She was informed that the two of them habitually sat with Mr. Rafferdy in Assembly.

"Of course, we meet at other times besides," Lord Eubrey said—rather mysteriously, Ivy thought. Lord Coulten let out a burst of laughter, but for his part Mr. Rafferdy gave Lord Eubrey a perturbed look.

There was no time to wonder what this meant, for by then Lady Crayford was demanding a full account of how Ivy and Mr. Rafferdy had come to be acquainted. An explanation was provided, with the two of them speaking in alternation—and each of them, Ivy knew, attempting to speak only what was strictly necessary. They had met through a mutual acquaintance of Lady Marsdel's, Mr. Rafferdy said, and their fathers had known each other in the past, Ivy added.

"Indeed?" Lady Crayford said. "And here I had, in the most vain and prideful sort of way, allowed myself to think that I could claim to have given society the first and happy opportunity to become acquainted with you, Lady Quent. Yet now I learn that you were already exceedingly well-connected. It seems I have done you no service at all!"

"But you have!" Ivy said, alarmed by this speech. "You have given me so much—more than I can conceive, I am sure. I am greatly in your debt."

Lady Crayford stopped her progress down the path, her expression thoughtful. "Dear Lady Quent, I can claim that you are in my debt no more than I imagine Lord Rafferdy can claim such a thing. It is *we* who have benefited from your society. If any debt is owed at all, then it is we to you. Would you not agree, Lord Rafferdy?"

"Completely, your ladyship," he said, his expression suddenly so grave that Ivy could only imagine it was feigned for some sort of jest.

The party continued along the path, and soon Madiger's Wall loomed before them. Now that they were close, the wall looked even more massive and more ancient. She was surprised to see that people were strolling right at its very foundation, and some were reaching out to touch its mossy walls.

She supposed there could be no real danger. There was ten feet of solid stone between them and the Old Trees on the other side. No branches had been allowed to droop down over the wall, and a number of redcrests marched in twos and threes among the pleasure walkers. Indeed, the presence of so many people could only mean that if there was any sudden change in the wall—a loose stone or a crack—it would be noted at once, and any peril it might present corrected.

"To think, we are truly here," Mrs. Baydon said. She took Ivy's hand in her own and squeezed it. "I feel as if I have stepped into another of Lady Crayford's paintings. Isn't it the most quaint and beautiful sight?"

Yes, the Evengrove *was* beautiful, and it was sad as well. Once, almost all of the island of Altania had been covered with deep, shadowed forest such as this. Then men had cut it back with fire and ax, and had quelled it with magick so it could be cut further. Now all that remained of the Wyrdwood were small patches scattered about the countryside, bounded by their own walls—and this single large grove.

Not that the Evengrove was really so very large in extent. Madiger's Wall made a rough circle some twenty miles across. Yet when one considered that of old the Wyrdwood had stretched for hundreds of miles in all directions, it was not so great at all. The Evengrove was a mere remnant—an emerald lake that was all that remained of a deep green sea.

Even so, it was wondrous: a grove of Wyrdwood a hundred times larger than the stand near Heathcrest Hall! Why had this great swath of trees been allowed to endure when every other one in Altania had been reduced to a tiny patch—or cut down altogether? Ivy did not know, yet she was grateful for the fact. She listened, and in the murmuring of the leaves she imagined she could hear an echo of that ancient green sea. . . .

"Ivoleyn?" She felt a pressure against her hand.

Ivy blinked, and the air around went from green back to gold. "Yes," she said, and squeezed Mrs. Baydon's hand back. "It's very beautiful."

Mrs. Baydon smiled at her, and they continued walking. Soon they reached the path at the base of Madiger's Wall, and they joined the other parties who strolled along it. The day was growing warm, but a pleasant chill emanated from the wall as if it recalled the touch of night. A longing came over Ivy to reach for the mossy stones, to cool her fingers against them.

Instead, she kept her hands at her sides.

Their party soon became drawn out along the path, as a few rushed along toward some interesting sight, while others lingered to examine a feature of the wall. As a result, Ivy found herself after a little while walking alongside Mr. Rafferdy and at some distance from the others.

Now that she had an opportunity to speak to him with some privacy, Ivy was not certain what to say. She supposed he might have questions about her conversation with his father, which she had described in her letter to him. Yet that was a topic of considerable gravity, and in the brilliant sunlight of a long afternoon, and after such a long time since their last meeting, she could not quite bring herself to broach it.

"I believe I owe you an apology, Lord Rafferdy," she began instead.

He winced at this. "I know that is a title I cannot now escape, Lady Quent, but I was wondering if you might do me a kindness and instead address me as Mr. Rafferdy. It would give me great comfort to hear those words from *you*. Namely, it would remind me of a simple and happy time!"

She gave him a fond smile. "I have happy memories as well of a time when you bore no other title. I will gladly honor your request—but on one condition only. That is, that you refer to me as Mrs. Quent in turn, so I might be similarly reminded."

This arrangement was readily agreed to, much to their mutual satisfaction.

"But I am rather confounded, Mrs. Quent," he said, giving her a quizzing look. "While I can easily think of a hundred things I should apologize for, no matter how hard I think on it, I cannot conceive of anything you ever have done that would require an apology to *me*."

"There is in fact something, though perhaps you do not recall it. You see, once when you were walking with my sisters and me, I told you that one can truly know a thing through reading about it in a book."

That elicited a smile. "You did say such a thing when I suggested otherwise. As I recall, you corrected me with some zeal."

"I am sure I did! That is why you are owed an apology, for I know now that I was wrong." She gazed at the rough stones above them. "I have read a great deal about Madiger's Wall—of its history and dimensions and the manner of its construction. I thought I had mastered all there was to know about it. Yet now that I am here, I see how woefully I was mistaken. You see, I did not know how even on a long lumenal one would be able to feel the coolness of night coming off the stones. That was a fact that was never contained in any volume I ever read on the subject. Therefore you were right to tell me one cannot really know something by reading it in a book."

"But I cannot accept your apology!" he said with a laugh.

"What reason could you have to refuse it?"

"Because you were right." He swung his ivory-handled cane as they walked. "Prior to meeting you, Mrs. Quent, I never thought that anything of real worth could be gained from a book. I have come to see how witless and conceited that notion was. Indeed, I have learned that there are some things that can be gained *only* through the pages of a book—for there is no other way in which a mind might ever have an opportunity to apprehend them."

This speech both delighted and astonished Ivy. She could not recall ever hearing him speak in such a manner. "I can only think, Mr. Rafferdy, that we have had an influence upon each other. For my impression of books has been lessened even as yours has been raised. Yet as ever, I suppose the truth lies somewhere in between the extremes. Even if books cannot reveal all to us, they can impart knowledge and experience—even wisdom, I would go so far as to say." She shook her head, bemused. "Yet from the way you speak, I would almost think you are studying magick again."

He cast a glance over his shoulder, then returned his gaze to Ivy. "I am," he said in a low voice.

Once more there was a seriousness to his expression. When they had first met, Ivy had thought Mr. Rafferdy to be good-looking only when he smiled. Sometime over the last year that had changed. Perhaps it was simply that he was a year older and was coming into his own as a man. Regardless, he looked very good at the moment—even lordly, she might have said; and so solemn was his expression, without any hint of a satirical purpose, that she was forced to concede that he spoke the truth.

"Mr. Rafferdy!" she exclaimed, laying a hand on his arm, and stopping them both in the path. She saw his gaze dart past her; she had spoken loudly. Hastily, she lowered her voice. "This is the most remarkable news. I do confess, I am to a degree surprised to hear it. I had not thought it was your inclination to continue to make a study of the arcane. I am very pleased to discover I was incorrect—I am very pleased."

Now his smile returned, though it was muted compared to before. "I was not certain until I told you just now that I would even impart this knowledge to you. Yet now I have done it, and I suppose I had some idea that you would appreciate hearing it. Lady Crayford says we all owe you a debt. It is certainly true that I owe any interest I have in magick to you."

"If that is the case, if I can claim to have encouraged you in some small way, then I am happy indeed," she said. "But I cannot claim any more due than that. The talent you have for the arcane is entirely your own, and any progress you have made in pursuing it is because of your own diligence. But I am curious, how are you going about studying magick? Have you returned to university, .then?"

He shook his head. "I believe one goes to Gauldren's College to learn how to affect the air of a magician rather than how to become one. Rather, I am meeting with a private society. I probably should not have just told you this, as it's all meant to be very secret. Yet I believe you heard Lord Eubrey allude to it earlier, for he and Lord Coulten are also part of the society."

"A society of magicians, you mean? That is marvelous!"

"On the contrary, you must not think so much of it. I have in fact seen very little actual magick done in any of our meetings. Further, we gather in the most low and humble sort of environs, a place that could not be more mean. That is, we meet in a room beneath a tavern."

Ivy's fingers tightened around the sleeve of his coat. "You say that you meet in a tavern?" These words were rather breathless, and she could feel her heart beating rapidly in her chest.

"Yes, that's what I said. Why do you look at me like that?"

Her head had grown light, and she made herself take in a breath. Then, in as few words as she could manage, she explained to him how she had been looking into the history of the man who had built her father's house, and how she had discovered that Dratham had belonged to a society of magicians who met beneath a tavern on Durrow Street.

"Now I see," he said when she had finished. "That you should have reacted as you did is perfectly understandable, but now I am given the unhappy task of disappointing you. I'm afraid the tavern we meet beneath is not situated on Durrow Street. While it is in the Old City, it is a quarter mile at least from Durrow Street. So I do not think it can be the same establishment where your man Dratham once mingled with magicians."

His expression was filled with real concern, and Ivy at once assured him that she was in no way disappointed. She had been startled by the coincidence, that was all, and so had leaped to an unwarranted conclusion. Nevertheless, she was very pleased that he was continuing his magickal studies, and she was curious to know more about the matter—how he had found this society, and what sort of things he was learning there.

Even as she asked these things, they heard the sounds of Mrs. Baydon and Captain Branfort behind them. Mr. Rafferdy gave a slight shake of his head, and Ivy understood. Discussions of secret arcane orders were best left to a time when others were not nearby. They continued along the path, and turned their conversation to topics that could be more safely overheard.

"It really is wonderful to see you, Mr. Rafferdy. I know you have been much occupied, but I fear Lily is convinced you no longer like us." She affected a light tone so he would know she was teasing. "Or perhaps it is simply that we were only amusing to you when our connections were scandalous, and now that we have become respectable you find us necessarily dull."

This elicited a laugh on his part. "What was dull was being required to listen to your cousin expound upon his theory that romance and lawyering were closely akin. Be assured I will always find *you* amusing, Mrs. Quent. Besides, I cannot fault your current society—it is far better than what I keep! If I had not met you last year, then I would never have a hope to do so, as I imagine you soon will be far above me."

These words shocked her. "I will never be any such thing, Mr. Rafferdy! Besides, given the connection between our fathers, I am sure it is impossible that we would not have met. Rather, it is the most expected thing that we are acquainted."

"Of course," he said, but he looked away as he said this, and for a little while they were quiet as they walked.

"How is Mr. Garritt?" she asked at length.

"I have not seen him much of late, though we have traded some notes. I gather he is very busy. He is clerking for the rector at Graychurch these days."

Ivy was glad to hear this news, at least to a degree. "That seems a very respectable sort of occupation. All the same, he is such a kind and thoughtful man. I cannot help wishing that he could rise higher."

"As do I. I cannot conceive of anyone who would deserve it more. It seems to me that many who deserve to inhabit high positions are ever denied them, while so many who are anything but deserving can claim them by mere circumstance. It is exceedingly cruel, yet not unexpected. I have come to believe that there is a force in the world, a natural order that constantly labors to keep us all in our places."

"An order, yes, but there is nothing natural about it!" Ivy exclaimed. "Why should one person be elevated above another? There can be no reason, of course, for we are all of us the same."

His brown eyes sparkled. "Why, Mrs. Quent, I wonder if I should call out for the redcrests. You sound like a regular anarchist."

Ivy felt her cheeks grow warm. "I am no such thing! I do no more than repeat the wisdom of the Testament, which tells us we are all of us the same in God's opinion."

He waggled a finger at her. "You will not so easily convince me of your innocence, Mrs. Quent. That we are all the same is a very insidious notion—one that kings and generals have long fought to stamp out. For why would a man follow a king, or a soldier a general, if he did not believe that other was greater than he? As for God . . ." He shrugged. "Well, if all men were identical in His eyes, would they not all enter into Eternum upon departing this world? However, *that* is not the case, and I am sure any priest will tell you that a vast number of souls are bound to end up somewhere else."

He spoke all this merrily, clearly intending to make a jest, yet it did not provoke laughter in Ivy. Instead, his words unsettled her, though she wasn't entirely certain of the reason. Perhaps it was because, even if society were to consider all men to be alike, a woman would still never be like to a man. Only why? If there was a natural order that kept all in their places, why did it make sure that a woman's was always beneath a man's?

A rushing sound drew her attention upward to the crowns of the trees that rose over the wall. They swayed as they felt the touch of a zephyr, their crooked branches bending this way and that, but unable to reach beyond the stones that encircled them. . . .

"Hello there, Rafferdy!" called out a voice. "Come here and tell us what you think of this."

Ivy lowered her gaze and saw Lord Coulten and Lord Eubrey a little way ahead, standing beside the wall. She and Mr. Rafferdy walked in their direction and soon joined them.

"What is it?" Mr. Rafferdy said.

"A very curious thing," Lord Coulten replied. "Look at this stone here. Do you see how it is different than the others in the wall?"

Mr. Rafferdy stroked his chin. "I suppose it is a different color than the other stones."

He was right. The block of stone Lord Coulten had pointed out, which was perhaps a foot on a side, was not gray like the others but rather was a deep, reddish hue. It was a color that Ivy at once found familiar, as it was very like the ruddy stones that formed the outer walls of the old house on Durrow Street.

"Is that the only difference?" Lord Eubrey said with a grin. "You're not looking very closely if that's all you see."

Mr. Rafferdy shook his head, evidently at a loss for words.

"There is no moss on it," Ivy said.

Lord Eubrey raised an eyebrow. "It seems Lady Quent's powers of observation are keener than yours, Rafferdy." He turned his attention to Ivy. "As you say, there is no moss on *this* stone, while all the others are covered with it. I believe you possess a methodical mind, Lady Quent—do you have any hypothesis of why that might be so?"

Ivy hesitated. Lord Eubrey's initial query had not been directed to her, and she had spoken without meaning to. However, he had now posed her a question, and so she could not ignore it.

"Perhaps the stone, given its different color, has been an object of curiosity among the walkers here. As such, it would have been frequently touched, which would discourage any moss to grow upon it. Or . . ."

Lord Eubrey tilted his head. "Yes, Lady Quent?"

Ivy took a step nearer to the wall. The red stone was speckled with darker flecks, and it was smoother than the rough blocks that surrounded it. "Perhaps," she said, "the nature of this stone is unique in some way, and its surface does not provide a hospitable place for moss to grow."

Lord Coulten clapped his hands. "I say, well done, Lady Quent! Those are both very plausible notions."

"Yet it's the second that I think the *most* plausible," Lord Eubrey said, though he did not give any reason for this conclusion. "Coulten and I are going to see if there are other stones like this one. It will be an amusing pastime as we walk, don't you think? You must come with us, Rafferdy."

Ivy would have liked to search for more stones herself, to see if there were others in the wall that looked like the stone from which her father's house had been built. However, she noted that an invitation had not been extended to her.

Rafferdy seemed to perceive this as well, for he gave her a concerned look.

"I should go back to the others," she said before he could speak. "Our maid and driver were setting out a luncheon for us, and I imagine it is ready by now."

In fact, when she glanced back, she saw all of the others in a group, and Captain Branfort waving vigorously in her direction.

Rafferdy gave her a smart bow. "I am certain we will encounter you this afternoon."

"Of course we will see Lady Quent later," Lord Eubrey said. "After we are done with our little exploration."

He gave her a cheerful smile, but once again Ivy had the impression of a certain slyness about his eyes.

"Well, are you two coming along, then?" Lord Coulten called back, for he was already proceeding down the path that went along the wall.

The other two men followed him, and there was nothing for Ivy to do but turn and start back toward her companions.

CHAPTER TWENTY-NINE

AFFERDY WATCHED AS Mrs. Quent walked away down the path, her figure as lithe as a willow switch in her gown of pale green.

He gripped the ivory handle of his cane. *I am sure it is impossible that we would not have met,* she had said as they strolled together. *Rather, it is the most expected thing that we are acquainted. . . .*

If only she was aware how in error that statement was! But she could not know how his father had conspired to keep the two of them from meeting. No, it was not at all expected that they were acquainted, but was instead the most unlikely phenomenon. For all Mr. Bennick's villainy, Rafferdy could still be grateful to him for this one thing: that through his machinations, Rafferdy and Ivy had come to know each other.

Yet it should never have had to happen in that fashion. How might things have been altered had the two of them been allowed to meet in the *expected* manner? The Lockwells would not have been so very low then, before her father fell ill, and Rafferdy's family would have lifted hers up by association. She could have been properly introduced to society and allowed to rise on her own ability and merits—just as she had done in the most easy and natural manner now that she had been given the opportunity. Once society had become acquainted and charmed by her, a union between their families might not have been out of the question, and her name would not now be Lady Quent, but rather Lady Rafferdy.

"Come along, Rafferdy," Lord Eubrey called out. "We'll lose sight of Coulten if we don't hurry after him."

Rafferdy hesitated. A compulsion came over him to go back

down the path, to take her arm and walk with her to the carriages. That impulse, though, was at odds with another—to discover just what it was Eubrey was about. He had been exceedingly mysterious on the journey here, and in the carriage he had refused to divulge even the slightest hint as to his reason for wishing to come to the Evengrove.

If only *she* could accompany them! Then both of his desires would have been fulfilled. Besides, he had no doubt that she would very much enjoy seeing magick being done. However, given Eubrey's secrecy about the whole affair, he knew that was not possible.

In the distance, her pale green figure vanished beyond a bend in the wall. Rafferdy sighed; then, cane in hand, he turned and followed after Eubrey. He had to go at a fair jog to catch up.

"Make it lively now, Rafferdy! I don't think it's a good idea for us to let Coulten get too far ahead. I would not want him trying a spell on his own."

"Why is that?"

"Because he doesn't take it seriously. Not like you or I do. To Coulten, it's all an amusing diversion. Yet he has ability—considerable ability, in fact. I would be very dismayed if he attempted something without using the proper preventatives and got himself into a dire circumstance."

"Attempted what?"

Lord Eubrey grinned at him. "You'll see," he said, and continued walking briskly down the path.

After proceeding only a little way, they encountered a band of several redcrests on patrol. The soldiers showed no sign of breaking their stride, so Rafferdy and Eubrey were obliged to step off the path. As the other men passed by in their blue regimental coats, Rafferdy tipped his hat. The redcrests made no reply, their faces stern as they marched at a rapid pace in the direction Rafferdy and Eubrey had come from.

"I say, you're very daring, Rafferdy," Eubrey said after the soldiers had gone.

Rafferdy shook his head. "Daring? How so?"

"Your House ring is in plain sight, that's how."

"I don't see how that matters to a band of soldiers."

Eubrey raised an eyebrow. "Have you forgotten what took place at the Ministry of Printing? Even if you have, I am certain the king's Black Dog has not! He is Lady Shayde's master, so it must have been on his order that she showed herself at Assembly, and you can be certain the king's soldiers have similar orders to keep watch."

"To keep watch over what?"

"Over us, of course! Or rather, over any magicians. You would do well to put on your gloves like the rest of us."

Rafferdy looked down at the ring on his right hand, its blue gem throwing sparks in the sunlight. He recalled the man he had followed from Marble Street that day two months ago. The man had been wearing gloves until one was torn off, revealing the arcane symbol that marked his palm—the same symbol that the White Lady's brutish servant, Moorkirk, had said marked the hands of all the men with gray blood.

Nor can I believe it is chance that it has become popular fashion to wear gloves just when such men have appeared in the city, Moorkirk had said to him that day. *Gloves just like you were wearing . . .*

Rafferdy lowered his hand and looked up at Eubrey. "No, I don't believe I will put on gloves," he said. "I'm quite done with that fashion—it's become far too popular for my taste."

Eubrey studied him for a moment, then shrugged and continued down the path. Cane in hand, Rafferdy followed after.

By now they had lost sight of Coulten altogether, and they walked at a pace that was so swift Rafferdy soon felt short of breath. Just when he was on the verge of suggesting they stop to rest a moment, they rounded a sharp bend in Madiger's Wall, and there was Coulten, standing beside the wall a little way ahead. They quickly closed the distance to him.

"There you laggards are!" Coulten exclaimed. "While you two have been loitering about, I have been at our task. Look at what I've found."

He stepped back from the rough surface of the wall, and Eubrey clapped his gloved hands.

"Excellent! Well done, Coulten."

Coulten gave a bow, his cheeks a rosy color from the sun.

"Well, Rafferdy," Eubrey said. "What do you think?"

Rafferdy took a step closer. This time it was not a single red stone in the wall, but rather a number of them. Like the one that they had seen earlier, these stones were free of moss and lichen. They were arranged in a rectangular shape a little higher and broader in extent than a man; and the whole looked like nothing so much as a door that had been closed up at some point with red stones. Rafferdy lifted his cane and tapped the end of it against one of the blocks.

There was a bright flash from his right hand, and a line of blue sparks traveled down the length of his cane.

"Careful there, Rafferdy!" Eubrey said. "You wouldn't want to open it without taking a few precautions."

Rafferdy hastily lowered his cane, then gave the others what he had no doubt was a startled look. "You mean it *is* a door?"

Eubrey moved closer to the wall. "Of course. Every wall has a door, Rafferdy; one only has to find it. That's what magicians do We seek out doors and open them."

"I believe there's but one door you're bent on opening, Eubrey," Coulten said with a laugh, "and it's not this one."

Rafferdy frowned; the other two men were being far too abstruse for his taste. "Speak clearly, Coulten—what door do you mean?"

"I mean the Door, the one in our meeting room beneath the Sword and Leaf, behind the curtain."

Now Rafferdy understood. Only the sages—those who had been admitted to the inner circle of the Arcane Society of the Virescent Blade—were allowed to pass through the door in the meeting room. What took place beyond, Rafferdy had no idea, but one thing was certain: it was Eubrey's ambition to be the next initiate to step through the Door. And from what Rafferdy understood, a magician was invited to become a sage only after he had proven his ability to help the society further its aim of discovering magickal secrets.

Rafferdy examined the stones more closely, though he was careful not to touch them. There was something familiar about their reddish color, though he was not certain what it was.

"If it is a door, then why is it here?" he said. "I thought the whole point of Madiger's Wall was to keep the Evengrove contained within. It seems to rather defeat the purpose to go and put an opening in it."

"Does it?" Eubrey paced back and forth before the wall. "What prison does not have at least a few small windows so that one can peer inside and see what the prisoners are doing? And even the strongest, most impregnable prison always has at least one door."

Coulten's usually open expression compressed into a frown. "I don't know, Eubrey—I think perhaps Rafferdy is on to something. I can see how someone might want to remove a stone from the wall now and then to take a peek at what's going on in the Evengrove. Yet what need would there ever be for something larger than that? If even the strongest prison has a door, as you say, it's only so that more prisoners can be tossed within. However, trees grow where they are, and cutting them down destroys them. Which means I cannot imagine that anyone would ever have a need to open the door and throw more inmates into this particular prison!"

"What makes you think it is the trees that are the prisoners in the Evengrove?" Eubrey said in a low voice.

For a moment both Rafferdy and Coulten stared at their companion; the only noise was the drone of locusts in the fields beyond the wall.

"Do you know something about the Evengrove?" Rafferdy said at length.

Eubrey shrugged. "Know? We can only truly know what we have seen for ourselves. Yet I have read some things."

"Read some things? Where?"

"In a history of the wall written by a magician long ago. It is a very rare volume, one that recently came into the possession of the sages, and which they have shown to me. In his account of the wall, the magician noted seeing a number of stones that exhibited peculiar qualities, and he postulated a theory that they might be intended to serve as openings in the wall."

Coulten let out a laugh. "Or perhaps they are here because some fellow making repairs used stones from the wrong heap, and the man who wrote that account wasn't a real magician at all. Where did the sages come by this book?"

"It was given to them by the magus of the High Order of the Golden Door," Eubrey replied.

This answer surprised Rafferdy. "The Golden Door? But isn't that Lord Farrolbrook's order?"

Eubrey gave a sniff. "Farrolbrook belongs to it, yes, though I wouldn't go so far as to say it was *his* order. I have no doubt that some people believe he's its leader, but I know for a fact that he is not the magus of the High Order of the Golden Door."

Now Rafferdy could not claim he was surprised. While the Magisters might use him to effect by presenting him as their leader in public, there would be no need to maintain that ruse when meeting in secret, and surely it was an impossibility that Lord Farrolbrook could lead an arcane order.

"Anyway," Eubrey went on, "it is not unheard of for one magickal society to share a piece of arcane knowledge with another, if they are given something in return. I do not know how the magus of the Golden Door obtained the book, but no doubt they realized that to make a proper investigation of its mysteries, they would need not a lot of Magisters who play at working enchantments, but rather real magicians. And so here we are." He gestured to the wall. "Rafferdy, would you be so kind as to speak a few runes of revealing?"

Rafferdy was taken aback. "Me? But I'm sure *you* could work the spell better than I, Eubrey."

"Perhaps I could—or perhaps not. Regardless, I do not want our good skeptic, Coulten, to think I am somehow manufacturing things or making them appear as they otherwise are. If *you* work the enchantment, then I am sure he can have no doubt of the result."

Rafferdy hesitated, then approached the red stones in the wall. He glanced in either direction, but there were no other parties in sight. The three of them had come a considerable distance along the wall—farther than most people usually ventured, he would guess, as the path here had narrowed to no more than a thin, half-overgrown track. The only sound was the droning of the insects. There was not a breath of wind.

While Rafferdy tended to complain that at meetings of the society magick was more likely discussed than practiced, it did not mean that they had not done any magick at all. For one thing, they had practiced reading magickal runes, as well as how to pronounce them.

Some magicians held that the language of magick was older than mankind itself, as it contained sounds that the human mouth did not seem to have been designed to produce. Despite this, Rafferdy found that with some effort he could utter any of the runes that were put before him, and he could not help noticing that speaking words of magick appeared to come easier for him than it did for many of the other initiates.

The sages had also spent some time instructing the initiates in the matter of magickal principals. At first, Rafferdy had decided he would be very bored with these discussions. The sages would sit at the front of the chamber draped in gold robes and their heads covered with hoods. It was the custom that magicians, once admitted to the inner circle of the society, thereafter never revealed their faces to the initiates; only when they stepped through the Door that lay behind the curtain would they lower their hoods.

Of course, Eubrey and Coulten had known some of the magicians when they were still initiates, and so recognized a few by their voices. To Rafferdy, though, they were all strangers, and listening to men he did not know, their voices muffled by hoods, ramble on about this magickal axiom or that arcane principle was something he was certain could only be tedious.

Only instead, it was engrossing. The magicians spoke of the three pillars of magick upon which all of the arcane arts were founded—that was, Knowledge, Power, and Will. Like a table with three legs, they explained, without any one of these things a magician was bound to fail. They spoke also of the purpose of magick—of opening doors, as Eubrey had said, and also of binding them, and of hiding and revealing them.

Yet it was more than that; doors were not the only things that could be concealed or bound. Or rather, there were many sorts of doors. For what was a door but merely an opening from one place or thing to another? A window was like a door, as was a box. Yet those were simple comparisons; others could be made. Were not eyes like windows, the magicians posed, or books? Was not the human heart like a four-chambered box? If one did not constrain the mind by limiting it to what was obvious, and instead strove to see that which was subtle and obscure, then there was almost no limit to the things upon which magick might be worked.

"Well, Rafferdy?" Coulten said. "Are you going to show us if there's something here or not? I will if you do not!"

Rafferdy shook his head. "No, I can work the spell."

It would not be difficult. The enchantment to reveal that which was hidden was one of the most fundamental of a magician's spells. Whether it would reveal something was an entirely different matter. While the spell itself was not complicated, it would be countered by any spell of concealing that might have been used on the stones.

He gripped his cane and pointed it at the wall. The cane itself was superfluous, but he found that if he imagined the force of the spell traveling down its length, it helped to focus his will. For a moment he gathered himself, recalling the words of the spell to his mind. It would not do to speak any of them incorrectly. If he uttered gibberish, the spell would merely fail. However, if in mispronouncing the runes he accidentally uttered the words of a *different* spell, then there was no predicting what might happen. Many a magician had perished that way, he had been told.

At last, satisfied he had recalled it properly, he uttered the spell, concentrating to form each harsh sound firmly and precisely. Then, as he spoke the last word, he touched the tip of the cane to the wall.

He felt it as well as saw it: crackling lines of power spiraling down his cane and striking the stone, spreading over them in a shimmering blue spider's web. His House ring gave a bright flash. Then the lines of power faded, and his ring went dark. Rafferdy lowered his cane.

Coulten crossed his arms. "Either Rafferdy is not so talented as we thought, or your notion is incorrect, Eubrey. There's nothing there."

"No, you're wrong. Look."

Eubrey reached out with a gloved hand and brushed one of the stones. Rafferdy moved closer, peering over Eubrey's shoulder. They were faint in the sunlight, but once he saw them they were unmistakable: small, fine runes shimmering on the surface of the stone.

By the widening of his eyes, Coulten saw them as well. "Good show, Rafferdy! You've bested whatever magician it was that hid these runes."

Rafferdy knew that wasn't entirely the case. He had possessed the Knowledge—that was, the correct spell—and the sum of his Power and Will had exceeded that of the concealing enchantment that had been placed upon the stones, but that was not as great a feat as it sounded. Unless rare and powerful magicks were worked, it was the nature of any enchantment to weaken over time. Which meant Rafferdy hadn't been required to match the Power and Will of the magician who had hidden the runes long ago, but only the fraction of the enchantment that remained.

"It's some sort of spell of opening, isn't it?" Coulten went on as he examined the wall. "I recognize most of the runes, but not every single one, I confess."

"You would know them all if you had been paying attention at our last meetings at the society," Eubrey replied. "But yes, it is a spell of opening."

"Capital! But do you really think you can count on this discovery to get us admitted through the Door?"

Eubrey let out a laugh. "It will get *me* admitted, I am sure! I believe you have a bit more to do to earn the regard of the sages, Coulten. You are making some progress toward that end, I think. Though if you don't apply yourself, you may find Rafferdy will be admitted before you!"

Rafferdy could not believe *that* was the case, though he made no reply. Sometimes by attempting to refute an assertion, one only served to lend it an air of credibility. "Now what?" he said instead.

Eubrey traced a gloved finger beneath the line of shimmering runes. "Now we follow the instructions that have been left for us."

These words shocked Rafferdy. He had assumed that discovering the presence of the runes was the purpose of Eubrey's mission for the sages, not actually invoking them. Before he could question the wisdom of the act, Eubrey was already sounding out the words of magick one by one.

Despite his astonishment, Rafferdy said nothing. Now that Eubrey had begun, it would not do to interrupt him. He heard Coulten draw a breath, as if to make some exclamation, but Rafferdy gave him a firm look, and Coulten clamped his jaw shut.

A tension grew upon the air as Eubrey spoke the words of magick, like when clouds gather and threaten a storm. Rafferdy read the runes silently to himself while Eubrey uttered them. As far as he could tell, Eubrey pronounced each one correctly and with the appropriate inflection. Rafferdy knew he could have done no better.

As Eubrey spoke the last of the spell, the air seemed to darken several shades around them, and the sunlight went thin. Rafferdy gave a quick glance up, but saw no clouds in the sky save for a grayish smudge to the south, above the crowns of the trees.

"By God, I can see right through them!" Coulten exclaimed.

Rafferdy looked back down and uttered his own oath. Fortunately, there could no longer be a concern of disrupting the spell, for it was complete, and its result was apparent. Coulten was right; the red stones had faded in color, and vague shapes could be glimpsed through them. Even as Rafferdy watched, the stones grew lighter and lighter, becoming translucent as glass.

Then they were gone altogether. All that remained was the line of runes, floating in midair. They flickered with crimson light, as if afire.

"Rafferdy, may I borrow your cane?" Eubrey said.

Such was his astonishment that Rafferdy did not think to question this request. He handed over his cane. Eubrey took it, then extended it into the empty space that moments before had been solid wall.

The tip of the cane passed through the opening with no resistance. Beyond was a rough tunnel several paces long, and past that a dim greenish light that seeped among crooked shadows.

Now that his initial shock had passed, Rafferdy could only be impressed. "The stones are gone," he said.

Eubrey shook his head. "No, not gone. Rather, they are . . . somewhere else."

"No matter where they are, the result is quite the same," Coulten said. "Great gods, Eubrey! I didn't think you were going to open it."

Eubrey turned to give Coulten a pointed look. "What else does one do with doors?"

"Sometimes one knocks to announce oneself," Rafferdy said dryly.

Eubrey laughed. "And I have found that, for some parties, it is best to arrive unexpected."

He held out the cane, and Rafferdy took it back. Now that the door had been opened, he could only be fascinated by it. How long had it been since a way had been opened in Madiger's Wall? Surely the magician who put this door here had opened it, and perhaps other magicians since then. Yet for all they knew, they were the first to look through this gap in the stones in a hundred years, or in five hundred.

Rafferdy moved closer to the opening. At the far end of the passage was a dense tangle of roots and branches and crooked black trunks. The ground was covered with a carpet of decayed leaves, and every now and then another withered specimen drifted down to add itself to the mold below.

For all its age and history, the appearance of the Evengrove was decidedly unimpressive. To Rafferdy, the trees looked more spindly and decrepit than they did great or ancient. All the same, this was the Wyrdwood. It was this—this gloomy forest, these hoary old trees—that had impeded man's and civilization's march across the island of Altania.

Yet Rafferdy could not say he felt any sort of menace emanating through the passage in the wall. Rather, it was a sort of melancholy he felt as he looked at the disheveled trees. A listless breeze passed among them, and they gave a weary sigh. Then they fell still again.

A raucous noise drifted from above. Several crows wheeled in circles overhead. Rafferdy glanced in either direction, but as before there was no one in sight. Yet what if the soldiers were to come back this way? If they did, he could not imagine they would be pleased with what they saw.

"Magick is not just the opening of doors, Eubrey," he said, regarding the other young man. "It is also the binding of them as well. Do tell me you have some idea how to close this door again?"

"Of course! For all that it was hidden, it is quite the usual sort of spell. Invoking it in the reverse will do the trick, I am sure. I will close it shortly—but not before I have a chance to work an experiment."

He moved closer to the opening, so that the toes of his boots were even with its edge.

Coulten crossed his arms. "I don't know what you are about, Eubrey, but I do hope you're taking care. You always tell me I'm not properly sensible to the perils of working magick."

"That's because you're not. But I am." Eubrey moved forward another step; he was now within the passage in the wall.

Rafferdy suffered a sudden impulse to reach out and take Eubrey's arm to pull him back.

"So what is this experiment you're planning?" he said instead.

"I'm going to work the Quelling."

"You're *what*?" Coulten and Rafferdy both exclaimed at once.

Eubrey glanced back at them, his expression roguish. "I believe you heard me clearly enough."

Rafferdy *had* heard him, but that made Eubrey's words no easier to comprehend. As children, everyone had listened to tales of Altania's first great magician, Gauldren, and how he had worked a great enchantment over the forest that covered all of Altania, stilling the trees.

Only they hadn't merely been tales, as everyone now knew. The Wyrdwood had indeed fought the first men who tried to settle the island of Altania, just as the groves had recently lashed out in Torland. It was only Gauldren's spell, his Quelling, that had finally allowed men to press from the island's edges and into its interior to build their forts and keeps, their castles and towns, without fear of reprisal from the forest.

"How can you work the Quelling when it was already worked ages ago?" Coulten said, giving voice to the question on Rafferdy's mind. "Besides, while I warrant you're good, Eubrey, you're not even a member in full standing in our society, and Gauldren was one of Altania's greatest magicians."

"One of the greatest, yes," Eubrey said. "But not *the* greatest—meaning no disrespect to you, Rafferdy, for I know that you are a scion of that particular House. As remarkable as the Quelling was, the enchantment was not perfect—as I believe the people of Torland can attest. The Wyrdwood was cast into a slumber, but it is a fitful doze, and one from which it can still be awakened."

"Which is precisely why we should not provoke it!" Coulten said, casting a wary glance past Eubrey.

"Do get ahold of yourself, Coulten. I'm not going to provoke it. Rather, my experiment will have only a further pacifying effect—if it has any effect at all. It was, I confess, more than a bit conceited of me to say I will work the Quelling. In fact, no one really knows what old Gauldren did when he worked his enchantment, but over the years various magicians have had ideas about how he might have done it, and the sages have charged me with testing one of the more plausible notions."

Eubrey took another step down the passage. He was over halfway through it now.

"It is not an entire spell," he went on, his voice echoing out of the opening in the wall. "Rather, it is but a fragment of one—a sequence of runes that might have been one portion of the Quelling, though far from the whole of it. Yet it is a beginning, and if I were to observe the spell to have some sort of mollifying effect on the Old Trees, the sages believe it would lend credence to the idea that it had been used by Gauldren in working the Quelling."

Rafferdy stood with Coulten on the very edge of the doorway, but he did not step through. "That's all very interesting, Eubrey. But why should anyone want to know how the Quelling was worked?"

"Because if we can learn what it was that Gauldren did, then we may be able to strengthen the Quelling, to perfect it. The sages are very concerned with the Risings."

"The Risings?" Coulten called out. "Why should the sages care about the Risings in Torland?"

"They haven't told me," Eubrey said, taking another step along the passage. "At least not yet. However, I am sure I will find out more when they admit me into their circle—a thing they are bound to do if I succeed here today."

Coulten laid a hand on the rough gray stones and leaned through the doorway. "Really, this is madness, Eubrey. Rafferdy is right—the redcrests could come by at any moment. Surely by opening this door you've discovered enough to prove yourself to the sages. There is no need for you to do any more. Now come out of there!"

"This will only take a moment," Eubrey said, and he reached the tangle of branches at the end of the passage.

Coulten looked at Rafferdy, his usually ruddy face grim and gray. "Good God, he actually means to do something. And he says I'm the foolish one!"

Rafferdy hesitated for a moment, then he stepped into the passage. It was not long, being only as great in extent as the thickness of the wall, which was perhaps ten feet. At once he felt an oppressive sensation, like a kind of pressure pushing him back. He moved halfway down the passage and stopped. Eubrey was just over an arm's length away.

"Eubrey, I don't think you should—"

Rafferdy bit his tongue, for the other young man was already speaking words of magick, his hands before him. He had stripped off his gloves, and the ring on his right hand flared bright. Quickly, the words of the spell rose to a crescendo. As he spoke the final runes, blue sparks flew outward from his hand, striking one of the trees at the end of the passage, coiling and sizzling all around its trunk.

The words of magick echoed off the stone walls, then fell to silence; the blue sparks dimmed and were gone. The trees at the end of the passage stood as they had before, motionless. Rafferdy let out the breath he had been holding.

"I don't think the enchantment did anything," he said.

"We cannot know until we test it." Eubrey took out a small pocketknife and unfolded it.

"Whatever is that for?" Coulten called out.

"I am going to test if the spell had any effect."

"How so?"

"Like this," Eubrey said. And with a single thrust he plunged the knife into the trunk of the tree.

Behind Rafferdy, Coulten let out a shout. Rafferdy nearly did the same. A shudder coursed up the trunk of the tree; at the same time a shower of dead leaves rained down from above. Rafferdy lunged forward to grab Eubrey's arm, then hauled the other man back out of the passage into the sunlight.

To his great consternation, Eubrey was laughing.

"It worked!" he exclaimed, sounding not unlike the crows that circled in the sky above. "Do you see? The tree made no reaction at all despite my attack upon it."

"It shed a number of leaves," Rafferdy said.

Eubrey waved a hand. "No doubt those were already dead, and so were loosened quite naturally when the tree shook. But the tree did nothing in and of *itself*."

Rafferdy peered down the passage. In the dim green light he

could see that the flurry of leaves had ceased. The tree Eubrey had struck was immobile, the knife lodged in its trunk.

He glared at Eubrey. "What do you think it should have done?"

"I'm not certain, but so assaulted it should have done *something,* don't you think? If the historical accounts are true—and given recent events in Torland, we must believe they are—the Old Trees are capable of resisting assaults. Only this tree has done nothing at all. The spell must have had some effect on it, rendering it quiescent. The sages will be very interested to learn this, I am sure. Now, if you'll release me, Rafferdy, I'll go retrieve my knife."

Rafferdy tightened his grip on Eubrey's arm. "I'll buy you another. I think instead you should close the door."

"I concur!" Coulten said, glancing nervously about them. "I can only believe the redcrests will be returning this way at any moment."

In fact, Rafferdy was surprised they had not done so already. The soldiers had been patrolling in both directions along the wall earlier. Why had they not come back this way?

Eubrey scowled. "Suit yourself, Rafferdy. However, it's an excellent knife of Murghese steel and has a pearl handle. It will cost you dearly to replace it. And do not think I will settle for something of inferior make!"

The crows continued to circle above, making a racket.

"Just close the door," Rafferdy said.

Eubrey studied the runes that blazed in the empty air of the opening. Then, as before, he incanted the words of magick, only this time speaking them in reverse. As he uttered the last one, his House ring gave a flash of blue, and a moment later the stones became faintly visible upon the air. They grew rapidly more opaque, until Rafferdy could no longer see through them. At the same time, the magickal runes flickered and were snuffed out.

Rafferdy gripped his cane and tapped its end against the red stones. They seemed quite solid. He gave a satisfied nod.

"Good, it is closed," Coulten said, his relief plain. "Now let us be away from here."

This received no argument, and together the three young men

turned from the wall and started back down the path. They had gone no more than a few steps when they heard a sound behind them: a rushing as of a wind through leaves.

Rafferdy glanced at the ground. The tall grass beside the path drooped in the heat of the long afternoon, unstirred by any breeze.

The rushing swiftly grew into a roar. It was accompanied by a groaning so low it was more felt than heard, as well as a high-pitched creaking that to Rafferdy sounded almost like voices crying out in pain. As one, the three young men stopped and turned around.

"By the hosts of Eternum!" Coulten cried out.

While Eubrey said, in a lower voice, "Now I understand what it was they meant."

Rafferdy thought this a peculiar thing to say, but it was quickly forgotten as a dread came over him—or rather, a sort of terrible awe. Above the top of the old wall, the crowns of the trees were tossing violently back and forth.

"Perhaps . . . perhaps it is a storm," Coulten called over the din, though these words sounded far from confident. "There's a dark cloud over there."

"No, it can't be a storm," Rafferdy called back. "There's no wind. Besides, that doesn't look like any usual sort of cloud." He held a hand to his brow, shading his eyes as he studied the smudge to the south. It was thicker than before, billowing up into the sky in a black pillar.

"May I suggest we retreat a bit farther?" Eubrey said, loudly now.

The tops of the trees continued to heave to and fro, as if propelled by a capricious gale. Then, as the groaning grew louder, branches bent and lashed, clawing against the top of the wall like thin black fingers.

Coulten's eyes were wide, and his usually ruddy cheeks had gone pale. "I don't think the trees cared for your spell after all, Eubrey. You had better undo it right this moment."

Eubrey made no answer. He only gazed at the trees, as if fascinated by them. The branches bent farther, making an awful creaking as they strained to reach over the top of the wall. Leaves fell all around like black snow.

Coulten grabbed his arm. "Don't just stand there, Eubrey! It was your spell that did this. Speak another spell to put a stop to it!"

"He can't," Rafferdy said.

"What do you mean he can't?" Coulten shouted.

Rafferdy held out a hand. One of the black leaves settled upon it. He rubbed it with his thumb, and it smeared into a sooty streak across his palm. The raucous noises made by the crows drew his gaze back up.

"Look there, above the trees."

The others did so. The black cloud had grown larger yet. Only it wasn't a cloud at all, Rafferdy knew.

"Eubrey can't stop it," he said, "because it wasn't his spell that did this."

And even as they watched, the column of smoke reached higher in the sky as the crows darted and wheeled.

CHAPTER THIRTY

𝓣HE LONG AFTERNOON seemed to stand still. There was not a cloud in view, and in the fields all around poppies drooped their heads. It was as if all the world had fallen into a golden drowse, lulled by the drone of locusts.

Mrs. Baydon took a sip of wine and gave a sigh. "I really believe nothing could be conceived that would be more marvelous than this. Wouldn't you agree, Ivoleyn?"

Ivy could not deny it was all very pleasant; or rather, she knew that she *ought* to have found it pleasant. The maid and the driver had strewn blankets on the grass and heaped them with cushions, so that all of the party were able to arrange themselves in the most comfortable fashion. There were niceties to partake of, and there was a plentitude of wine, poured from bottles that had been kept cool in moist clay pots. Ivy should only have been content.

Instead, her own glass of wine remained full in her hand, and her attention kept roving down the path to the gray-green curtain of Madiger's Wall. She wondered what sort of things Lord Rafferdy, Lord Eubrey, and Lord Coulten had discovered in their exploration. In particular, she wondered if they had come upon any more red stones. Ivy was curious how a stone block that looked just like the ones her father's house was built from had come to be a part of Madiger's Wall.

"Ivoleyn?"

Ivy realized she had been staring at the wall again. "Of course," she said, and gave her friend a smile. "There could be nothing more lovely than this."

"I knew you would agree," Mrs. Baydon said, only then her own smile altered into a frown. "Do not be so greedy with the cherries, Mr. Baydon! I am sure others might wish to taste them."

Her husband responded with a look of indignation, though its effect was significantly lessened by the red stain on his chin.

"We must be sure to invite Lord Rafferdy with us on our next outing," Lady Crayford said. She was making a sketch in her book of a bouquet of poppies that Captain Branfort had brought her. "He would be a natural addition to our circle, given that both you and Lord Eubrey are already acquainted with him."

Ivy could only be pleased by this suggestion. "Captain Branfort knows him as well. And I would not be surprised if the same was true of your husband."

Lady Crayford looked up from her book. "What would make you say such a thing, Lady Quent?"

"I was only thinking it is possible that Lord Rafferdy has encountered the viscount at Assembly."

"But that is not possible at all!" Lady Crayford exclaimed. "The viscount never goes to Assembly. It is his belief that there are other and better ways to affect affairs in our nation."

"What other way could there possibly be?" Mr. Baydon said, lowering a cherry he had been about to pop in his mouth.

At this, Colonel Daubrent, who was reclining on his back to gaze at the sky, gave a rare laugh. "Politics are far from the only way to affect the course of nations. Wouldn't you concur, Branfort?"

"I would," the captain said.

Mr. Baydon scowled. "You are both military men, so I can only presume you mean to imply that war can alter the fate of a nation. Yet you forget that all wars come about for some reason of politics or another."

Captain Branfort slapped his knee. "I do believe he has us there, Colonel! What can we poor soldiers do but go whither and fight whoever our government commands us to? We have no choice in the matter."

"No, we do not," Daubrent said. "Not unless we were to become the government ourselves."

Ivy supposed this statement was meant to be humorous. Except the colonel was not one for making jokes. She considered asking him to explain further, but at that moment Mrs. Baydon let out a sound of dismay.

"What ill luck!" she said. "I want only to linger here all afternoon, but I do believe a storm is coming. Look how the trees are blowing, and there is a dark cloud over there."

Ivy had been doing her best not to be fascinated by the wall, and to instead pay attention to her companions. Now she did look that way and saw that Mrs. Baydon was right. Above the wall, the crowns of the trees were tossing back and forth, and a dark smudge stained the sky.

Captain Branfort stood and lifted a hand to shade his eyes. "I say, that doesn't look like any sort of cloud."

Ivy felt a prickling on the back of her neck and her arms. She looked at the fields of poppies around them; the flowers still drooped on their stalks, motionless. There was not a breath of wind.

Yet the trees moved as if propelled by a violent gale.

Even as understanding came to her, she heard the first shouts. The others must have heard as well, for they all followed Captain Branfort and leaped to their feet. Now people were rushing up the path, fleeing away from Madiger's Wall in the most chaotic fashion.

"What's all this now?" Mr. Baydon exclaimed.

Ivy looked upward. The black stain continued to spread over the sky, and at the same time a terrible sound rose on the air: deep groans punctuated by a shrill creaking. There were no words in the sound, but Ivy comprehended it all the same. It was an expression of shock and pain.

And of anger.

Several redcrests went dashing by, running not away from the wall but toward it.

"Ho, there!" Captain Branfort called, stopping one of them with a raised hand. "Can you give me a report?"

The soldier eyed Branfort's coat and nodded. "You had best get your people away from here, sir."

"Why should we leave?" Mr. Baydon said, his voice pitched rather high now. "I demand to know what is going on!"

The redcrest kept his attention on Captain Branfort. "We have a report that someone has made an attempt to lob torches soaked with naphtha over the wall, and there's a fire. Nor have they caught whoever did it."

"A fire!" Ivy said, a horror coming over her. "You mean in the Evengrove?"

"No, as far as we can tell none of the torches made it over the wall. It was too high for that, but the field and bracken all along the wall is ablaze. And the trees, they . . . I had believed it of course, all the stories in Torland, only I never really . . ."

The man shook his head, at a loss, but Ivy understood him perfectly. The Old Trees, beaten back by flame and ax for so many centuries, had perceived the acrid smoke and the heat licking against the stones of the wall. They felt the fire was near.

And they had awakened from quiescence.

"I must take my leave, sir," the soldier said. "I only left to fetch more men. There is a water tower near the wall. We are to form a brigade."

Captain Branfort gave a firm nod. "The colonel and I can lend a hand, can't we?"

"Of course," Daubrent said grimly.

"Mr. Baydon, please escort the ladies a safe distance from the wall," Captain Branfort said. "Several furlongs at least. Mr. Baydon!"

Mr. Baydon blinked, then managed to look away from the wall and the thrashing trees. "Yes, of course. At once."

Captain Branfort touched Ivy's arm. "Do not be afraid. The wall is very thick. It has withstood the forest for over a thousand years. There is no way they can get beyond it."

Ivy's breathing was rapid; her heart raced in her breast. Only she was not frightened. Rather, a wonder had come over her, and an exhilaration. The soldier started back down the path after his compatriots. Captain Branfort and Colonel Daubrent followed.

All around now were shouts and cries of alarm. The horses were wild-eyed, having smelled the smoke, but there was no hope of getting the carriages any farther from the wall; as people fled from the Evengrove the road had become a snarl of traffic worse than the busiest day on Marble Street.

Instead, the driver freed the horses from the harnesses. He took the team from the four-in-hand, while Mr. Baydon grabbed the reins of the colonel's pair. They led the beasts away from the wall while Mrs. Baydon and Lady Crayford hurried after, along with the maid.

Ivy hesitated. Smoke billowed into the sky, and ash had begun to rain down like gray snow. Above the top of the wall, the trees still tossed to and fro. She was astonished by the violence and speed with which they moved. Even as she watched, she saw the first branches reach out and scrabble against the topmost stones, straining to reach past.

"Lady Quent, what are you doing?"

Only when she heard Mr. Baydon's shout did Ivy realize she had taken several steps down the path toward the wall. She nearly collided with a knot of people fleeing along the path.

One of them, a young man, flung up his hand to keep from colliding with her. His palm was marked with black lines, and she wondered if he had gotten too close to the fire. Indeed, the sleeves of his coat were scorched in several places; only the marks on his hand were too sharp to have been formed by smears of soot.

In an instant, the group was past her, and Ivy forgot all other thoughts as she saw three figures hurrying up the path.

"Mr. Rafferdy!" she cried out, running toward him.

Lord Eubrey and Lord Coulten were with him, and such was their pace that she had gone only a few steps before they were upon her.

"Mrs. Quent, are you well?" There was great concern in his eyes.

"I am!" she said, rather breathlessly. "I had feared you were still near the wall. I am so relieved you are away. It is . . ."

"It is a Rising," Lord Eubrey said, his expression more one of interest than dread.

In hurried words, Ivy explained how Captain Branfort and Colonel Daubrent had gone to aid the soldiers, and the others had gone with the horses away from the wall.

"Then let us join them," Lord Eubrey said, starting in that direction. Lord Coulten said nothing as he followed after, his face the color of whey.

"Come, Mrs. Quent, we must go."

Mr. Rafferdy took her arm. At that moment came the terrible sound of a man's screams. They both turned to see a dreadful sight: a soldier caught in a tangle of black branches, being lifted into the air.

How the branches had managed to reach so far down, Ivy did not know. Perhaps it was a place where, due to long years of weathering or some other damage, the wall was a little lower. Or perhaps the boughs of the trees were extending in length somehow. Whatever the reason, it was enough for the branches to just reach a soldier as he ran along the base of the wall, a bucket in hand.

"Do not look, Mrs. Quent!" Mr. Rafferdy cried. "Turn your head."

As he said this, he took her in his arms, and with one hand pressed her cheek against his coat to avert her eyes. However, he had not been so swift that she hadn't seen the soldier's limbs flop about like those of a doll shaken by a child, or how he was cast twenty feet back to the ground.

For a moment both she and Mr. Rafferdy were motionless, though she could hear the thudding of his heart in his chest. It felt different than when Mr. Quent held her close. Mr. Rafferdy's arms were perhaps not so powerful, but he was taller, and was able to easily enfold her in his embrace, so that she felt no less secure.

"Good God," Mr. Rafferdy said in a low voice. "I did not believe they could reach so far. I think the poor fellow is . . ."

He did not finish speaking, nor did he need to. She had no doubt that the unfortunate soldier had perished in the fall, if not before. How many others would share a similar fate before the fire could be put out?

A thought occurred to her, one that left her feeling giddy. The Old Trees were lashing out because they were fearful; she could hear it in their wordless voices. But what if they could be told that they had no reason to be afraid, that they were safe within the bounds of the wall? Was there not at least some possibility they might listen?

Only she had to get closer. She had to touch them.

"Mr. Rafferdy," she said, pushing herself away from his grasp. "I must get closer to the wall."

His expression was startled. And at first, she was not certain it was her words that had astonished him, but rather the fact of their embrace. However, after a moment it was clear her words had indeed impinged upon him.

"You are in a state of shock, Mrs. Quent! It has made you morbid. You must come with me at once."

Beyond him, she could see soldiers running toward their fallen comrade, axes in their hands. This only convinced her further.

"No, Mr. Rafferdy. There is something I must do there, though I know you cannot possibly understand."

"No, I cannot understand!" he exclaimed. "You've just seen a man perish. Would you have yourself be the next?"

"No, I would try to ensure that no more come to harm."

"How is such a thing possible?"

"I do not know that it is possible! But there is some hope it may be if I can get to the wall." Then she shook her head, her thoughts racing. "Except it won't be enough to be close to the wall. I must find a way to get *through* it. Yet how could that be done? Perhaps it is hopeless after all."

His expression was startled anew. She laid a hand on his arm.

"What is it, Mr. Rafferdy? There is something you almost spoke just now. What was it? I beg that you tell me!"

He drew in a shuddering breath. "There is a door in the wall, one locked by magick. Eubrey had read of it, and Coulten discovered it."

"When?"

"Just a little while earlier."

"And you opened it with magick?"

He hesitated, then nodded. "At first I feared it was our own actions that disturbed the trees. Only it wasn't—it was the fire."

A thrill passed through her, and she tightened her fingers around his arm. "You did not cause this, Mr. Rafferdy, but perhaps you can help to ease it if you take me to the door."

He shook his head and tried to recoil from her, but she would not release him from her grasp.

"How could I do such a thing?"

Ivy drew in a breath. There was so much to explain to him,

only there was no time. The crowns of the trees continued to heave violently; the air was choked with smoke and ash.

"Mr. Rafferdy," she said, keeping her voice low, and meeting his gaze with her own. "I know you recall our encounter with the magicians of my father's order at the house on Durrow Street. Yet there is something about that day you do not know—something that I did. You did not see due to the enchantment they placed upon you, but it is something you will witness now if you take me to the door, and then you will understand."

He stared at her, his expression one of horror. Yet there was a glint of curiosity in his eyes as well—she was certain of it.

"Please, Mr. Rafferdy! You know I would not ask you such a thing if it must not be done."

A shudder passed through him, and he held a hand to his brow. "Your husband will have me hanged if he learns of this." Then a wan smile touched the corners of his lips. "Yet how can I argue with you, Mrs. Quent? You have ever been the sensible one, not I."

She squeezed his arm. "Thank you."

"This way, before I come to my senses," he said, and he led her down the path toward the Evengrove.

IVY CLUNG TO Mr. Rafferdy's arm as they cut across the open fields. Rather than take the path along the wall, their intention was to keep their distance from the Evengrove as long as possible to avoid both the trees and the soldiers who might question them.

"There," he said, pointing to the wall. "I can see the red stones from here."

Now that she knew to look for them, they were easy to see against the gray-green curtain of the wall: red stones arranged in the shape of a door. The wall was reassuringly high at this point, and the trees above, while they swayed back and forth, were not moving nearly as violently as those to the south, closer to the smoke of the fire. This gave her some hope that to approach would not be exceedingly dangerous.

Yet she could not deny there was some peril in doing so. She recalled the rain-lashed evening when, as governess to Clarette and Chambley, she had followed the children to the old stand of Wyrdwood east of Heathcrest Hall. She would never forget the way the branches had reached down over the wall to bar their passage.

Only they had raised back up when she commanded them to do so.

They slowed their pace as they approached the wall. Ivy looked around, fearing soldiers might see them and tell them to get back. However, they were beyond a bend in the wall now, and for all the smoke she could see little more than a furlong. No, it was not soldiers they need be concerned with.

"They move even though there is no wind," Mr. Rafferdy said as he gazed up at the trees, his brown eyes wide. "I knew it was possible, and I see it before me, yet still I can hardly believe it."

He was right; there was no wind. All the same, the sound was like that of a gale through the boughs of the trees. So deafening was the noise that Ivy was nearly overcome by it. They had felt the heat of fire; they had seen the bright flash of axes. The Old Trees had encountered these things before, they knew what they portended, and they would fight back.

She would fight back. . . .

"Mrs. Quent!"

Ivy shook her head, and the air around her went from green to ash gray.

He was looking at her, a grimace on his face. "I say, you have an unusually forceful grip. Could you please . . . ?"

Ivy snatched her hand back. There was a red weal around his wrist. He raised it and rubbed it with his other hand.

"Are you still certain you want to do this?"

She gave him a mute nod.

"Very well," he said, and he crossed the last distance to the wall.

He did not look up as he went, but instead kept his eyes upon the red stones of the door. The bravery of this act astonished Ivy.

It was not that she had any reason to believe Mr. Rafferdy was *not* brave; indeed, he had shown great courage when they confronted the magicians at the house on Durrow Street. It was only that she wondered when in his life, prior to the events of last year, he had ever been required to display such a character.

With so fine an example to follow, Ivy could only do her best to summon her own bravery and approach the wall. Unlike Mr. Rafferdy, she kept her eyes on the trees.

You have no cause to fear us! she cast the thought outward. *We wish no harm to you!*

She had no idea if these unspoken words had any effect, but while the trees continued to toss about, and a few branches scraped the top of the wall, none reached downward.

By the time she reached Mr. Rafferdy, he was already speaking harsh, ancient words. As he did, a row of crimson runes flickered to life, like flames dancing across the surface of the stones.

Her dread was momentarily superseded by curiosity. For as long as she could remember, she had been fascinated by magick, and here was a spell being worked before her. She wondered what sort of enchantment it was, and how he had known what runes to speak. However, she kept these questions to herself lest she disturb him as he worked the spell.

He ran a finger below the runes, as if making a quick study of them. Then he began another spell—the one inscribed in the fiery runes, she presumed. This one was longer than the first and seemed more complicated. Lines creased his brow as he uttered the words, and some were of such strange sound and inflection that merely hearing them made Ivy's head start to throb.

Mr. Rafferdy spoke one last word with great force and struck the end of his cane against the red stones. A blue flash traveled from his hand down the length of the cane.

The stones vanished.

He turned around. The ring on his right hand still threw off blue sparks, and his eyes seemed to do the same. "There, it is open," he said, only then he shook his head. "Yet now that it is, how can I let you step through it?"

"You must, Mr. Rafferdy."

For a moment he gazed at her, then he sighed and stepped aside. Ivy approached the opening in the wall. Beyond was a rough stone passage, and at the far end was a tangle of green and black.

"I will be directly behind you, Mrs. Quent."

"No, you must stay out here. I cannot be sure you will be safe if you go within."

His expression was one of shock. "Then it cannot be safe for you either! How will I reach you if something goes amiss?"

She looked up and met his gaze. "If something goes amiss, Mr. Rafferdy, then you must close the door as quickly as you can."

Before he could say anything more, she stepped into the passage. It was cooler within, and quieter, for the stones muffled some of the furor of the wood. The air was moist and thick with the scent of decaying leaves. She felt a faint wind moving through the passage, first inward, then out, as if the Evengrove was breathing. She exhaled a breath herself, then proceeded down the passage, trailing a hand along its rough sides to steady herself.

She would not have to enter the grove; at least she did not think so. There was a large tree just past the end of the passage. All she had to do was get close enough to touch it.

The passage was not long, and she quickly reached the end. Beyond, a dim green light found its way through a crooked labyrinth of branches and trunks. Leaves rained down from above, along with small twigs and acorns. She ignored these things and instead fixed her attention on the tree before her. It was an Old Ash, its trunk thick and speckled with moss. The tree was less than an arm's reach from the end of the passage. She could remain within the protection of the stones and still touch it.

Yet what would she do when she did? Now that she had reached the end of the passage, the sound of the trees was once again a roar in her ears. What if their voices were the greater, and drowned out her own?

Before she could consider this question, she noticed a glint of silver. Protruding from the trunk of the tree was a knife with a pearl handle. A horror came over Ivy at the sight. Quickly, she reached out and grasped the knife, trying to pull it from the tree, only it was stuck more firmly than she thought. Her second attempt wrenched it free, but she lost her balance in the act. The knife dropped from her hands to the ground as she flung her arms out to catch herself. She stumbled as her foot caught a snag—

—and her hands fell upon the trunk of the tree.

At once a green veil descended over her vision. Ivy tried to retreat into the mouth of the passage, but her feet seemed to take root in the ground. She thought she heard a shouting behind her, but any words it carried were swept away by the furious chorus that filled her ears. The voices spoke in no human language, yet all the same she understood them.

Pain—there had been pain. Only now the cold, sharp prick of metal was gone. Yet there was danger still. Flame and bright metal—they were close by. Ivy rose upward, stretching toward the sky, straining to see where they were. Men—it was men who had done this. It was always men who came, who cut and burned and destroyed.

And men would suffer for what they had done. . . .

An awful sort of delight came over Ivy. Her face grew tight, and she perceived that she was smiling.

Yes, I can tell you where the men are, Ivy thought. *I can tell you from which direction they come. And there is something more—a gap has been made in the wall that has long imprisoned you.*

She felt their interest, their desire to know more, and her smile grew broader.

I can show you where it—

"No!" Ivy cried out.

She snatched her hands back from the tree as her eyes flew open. The force of the sentiments that had come over her, and their suddenness, had nearly overpowered her. How easy it would have been to let herself be swept away, as if on a surging green sea. For a moment she had wanted nothing more than to tell the trees how to escape the bonds of the wall.

However, Mr. Quent had warned her of the danger the Wyrdwood posed to a witch. The first Mrs. Quent had perished because he had failed to do so, and he had not made that same error with Ivy. She had known she would be entranced by the trees, and she had guarded herself against it.

Even so, she had nearly been overcome. Without the benefit of such knowledge, how could the first Mrs. Quent have ever hoped to resist the call of the remnant of old forest so near to Heathcrest? And how could Merriel Addysen have done anything but provoke the trees with her own agony and rage that day men, their will bent on awful acts, pursued her to the grove atop the hill north of the village of Cairnbridge?

The thought of Gennivel Quent and Merriel Addysen lent Ivy a new strength. *They* had not known what they were when the trees called to them, but Ivy did. The voices of the trees, though still a roar in her ears, no longer overwhelmed her own thoughts.

"Mrs. Quent!" she heard Mr. Rafferdy's voice behind her. "You must come away from there!"

She shook her head. "Not yet," she murmured, and once again she laid her hands upon the tree.

This time, while the sensations were no less powerful than before, she was not subsumed in them, and it was not their will that shaped her thoughts, but rather her own.

There is no peril to the wood. The man who set the fire is gone. The flames cannot reach through the wall. The men beyond are putting out the blaze. You must not harm them. There is no peril to the wood. . . .

Again and again she repeated these thoughts, over and over. She encircled the tree with her arms. She pressed her cheek to the roughness of its bark and felt the violent shudder of its throes. The noise of the trees filled her head, so that she could not hear herself think. All the same, she kept repeating the words in her mind, until at last she fell into a kind of stupor in which she heard nothing, and saw nothing, and thought nothing at all.

"Mrs. Quent?"

"There is no peril to the wood," she murmured through dry lips. "The man who set the fire is gone. . . ."

"Mrs. Quent, can you hear me? Are you harmed?"

With great effort Ivy opened her eyelids a crack. She saw a circle of pale light, and in the midst of it the dark shape of a man, like one of Lady Crayford's silhouettes.

"Mrs. Quent?"

She blinked, and the silhouette resolved into the familiar sight of Mr. Rafferdy. He crouched beside her at the base of the tree, where she must have collapsed. On his face was a peculiar expression: wrought at once with concern and, she thought, a keen curiosity.

Ivy craned her neck, looking upward. Above, the boughs of the Old Ash were motionless. The air of the grove was heavy and still.

"They've stopped," Mr. Rafferdy said, looking upward as well. "All of the trees have, as far as I can tell. Yet I do not know why they should have ceased their movements."

"Don't you?" she said, lowering her gaze to look at him.

He met her look, held it, and after a moment she saw understanding blossom in his eyes. And now that he understood, he would recoil from her as if from the most loathsome thing, and she would never in her life see him again, unless it was as her accuser before a magistrate.

Only he didn't do these things. Instead, he took her hands in his own and helped her regain her feet. She was dizzy for a moment, then her head cleared a bit. She could not bear to look at him now, so instead she brushed the leaf litter from her gown.

"You are full of many surprises, Mrs. Quent. Now I wonder what you did that day at your father's house when the magicians saw fit to put me under an enchantment. I had thought the orb itself did them in all of its own, but I suppose that's not the case."

She plucked a small twig from her gown and held it in her fingers. "The stand that held the Eye was made out of Wyrdwood. My father believed that there was some power of the wood of the Old Trees that helped it to resist and contain the influence of the orb. Only, the Wyrdwood the stand was made of had another power as well, one that I was able to awaken."

"Ah," he said. And then, after a moment, "Ah!"

Yes, he understood now. There was no more use in hiding what she was. With a thought she awakened the bit of life that still lingered within the twig, causing it to coil around her finger like a tiny brown serpent. Then she willed herself to look up at him.

"I am sorry, Mr. Rafferdy. I know in the past you have regarded me with affection. For you to now discover such a thing about me—I can only imagine what a horror you must be suffering."

"Why should I suffer a horror? Because you have some peculiar ability that most others do not?" He raised his right hand. The blue gem of his House ring shone dimly in the gloom of the grove. "If that was the case, I should have to be horrified of myself, don't you think? And as I am sure you are aware, Mrs. Quent, I am in fact rather fond of myself."

Ivy could hardly believe this reply. "But in history, witches have always been regarded as the most abhorrent beings!"

He gave a shrug. "You know how little I read, Mrs. Quent, and how ignorant of history I am. I suppose it's true that men have always had a wish to keep women from having any sort of influence over affairs. I am sure this is because, in general, women possess superior sense compared to men. If they were to have greater strength as well, then men would have no advantage over women whatsoever."

His gaze went to the tree behind her. Then he looked at her again, and the hint of a smile curved his mouth. "All the same, I cannot help but think that if anyone in this kingdom should have power, it should be *you*, Mrs. Quent. If we were all under your benevolent influence, I have no doubt Altania would be the better for it."

Ivy could form no response to these words. Her heart had swelled, leaving no room in her chest for her to draw in a breath. So she squeezed his hand instead, and only let go when she at last had to wipe a dampness from her cheek.

"Oh, Mr. Rafferdy!" she was able to say at last.

Now he did appear uncomfortable, and he quickly turned away. "We had better go. The others will be concerned for us."

He stooped to retrieve the ivory-handled knife from the ground and put it in his coat pocket. Then he moved back through the passage. For a moment Ivy felt a compulsion not to follow and to remain in the grove. She ignored the sensation and moved after him.

They emerged on the other side of the wall. The smoke was now only a thin blue veil upon the air; the men must have succeeded in putting out the blaze. At once, Mr. Rafferdy began speaking words of magick.

As he did, a coppery glint caught Ivy's eye. She bent down and picked up something from the ground. It was a gilded button, and by its shiny surface and lack of tarnish it had not lain here long. One of the soldiers must have lost it while running to and fro by the wall. A fear came over her, but when she glanced around she saw no one in sight.

"There, it is shut," Mr. Rafferdy said.

Ivy looked and saw that the red blocks had indeed reappeared in the wall, sealing the opening. The runes flickered crimson for a moment, then they faded and were gone.

"Let us hurry," he said. "I am sure our parties are wondering what has became of us."

This received no argument from Ivy. She took his arm, and they started back through the grass and poppies. They had gone only a little way when they saw Captain Branfort striding toward them across the field. His short, sturdy legs moved swiftly, and he was quickly upon them. His blue coat was open, and his face and shirt were smudged with soot.

"By God, I am glad to find you!" he exclaimed. "We were all of us in a dread when I returned to the carriages and learned you were missing. Where were you?"

"We could not see for all the smoke and got turned around," Mr. Rafferdy said, his tone so easy and convincing that Ivy nearly believed him. "Once it began to clear we discovered we had quite gone the wrong way. Is the fire out?"

"Yes, the men got a train of buckets going from the water tower. It's all extinguished now."

"That must be what calmed the trees in the Evengrove."

Captain Branfort frowned as he regarded him. "Indeed, what else could possibly have done it?"

"Nothing, of course," Mr. Rafferdy replied quickly. "I am very glad a Rising was averted."

"Was it averted? Three men have lost their lives today." The captain shook his head. "Forgive me, now is not the time to discuss such things. Come, Lady Quent—Lady Crayford and the others will be very glad to see you."

He extended his arm. While this was a gallant gesture, it was another's arm Ivy might have preferred to lean upon. Instead, she accepted the one proffered and let Captain Branfort lead her across the field while Mr. Rafferdy walked alongside.

CHAPTER THIRTY-ONE

OLDYN PICKED A bit of lint from the sleeve of his gray coat, then looked in the small silver mirror to check the arrangement of his hair. He ought to do his best to make a good impression, for it had been many months since he had last had occasion to see Lady Quent. Indeed, she had not even been a *Lady* when he saw her last.

Now she was one, and her husband a *Sir,* and he had no doubt there would be all manner of fine beings in attendance at the party that night to see the remaining Miss Lockwells introduced. To a degree, he had been astonished when the invitation arrived for him several lumenals ago. If she had not deemed him to be of a station suitable to the affair, he could neither have argued nor taken offense. Yet her note had been written in the warmest fashion; and in it she had expressed a fond hope that he would attend the party, and also that he should bring any guest he liked.

Such a considerate invitation could only be accepted, and he wrote back to express his thanks and assure her he would indeed attend. Now Eldyn had to hope his gray coat was fashionable enough, and that he would not seem out of place or bring discredit to Lady Quent with his appearance. He saw that a lock of his hair had escaped the ribbon behind his neck, and he started to tuck it back. Then it occurred to him that it was not only Lady Quent he would be seeing for the first time in a long while, but also her sisters—including the youngest one.

Perhaps, he thought, it would be good not to look *too* well. He left the stray lock as it was, and turned from the mirror.

"Are you sure you won't change your mind, dearest?" he said. Sashie sat by the window, reading her copy of the Testament in the dwindling light of the brief day. "I'm certain you would have a very good time at the party."

"I am certain I would have no such thing!" she said, not lifting her eyes from the book. "For I have little doubt that there will be young ladies there dressed in all the vile sorts of gowns that are popular these days, and young men begging them to engage in the most lurid dances, such as one can hardly imagine are permitted in public. I know propriety requires *you* to attend no matter how shameful it is, dear brother, given your prior association with these people. Yet you must know it would be the most wicked thing for me to attend such an affair." She turned a page of the Testament; the edges of its papers were growing frayed.

Eldyn was vexed with this reply, though far from surprised. She had made her case against attending very strongly the day the invitation arrived. All the same, he had hoped she might reconsider. He thought it would be a great benefit for Sashie to engage in the society of other young ladies. It would give her an opportunity to see that just because they wore pretty dresses and smiled did not mean they were not in every way respectable.

It was difficult to reproach the avidness with which she had engaged in her activities at Graychurch these last months. Then again, a virtue pursued to the exclusion of all else is no such thing, and it was high time for his sister to begin thinking in a practical manner about her future. It had been a while since Mr. Fantharp had inquired about her, and Eldyn feared that, without any reciprocation, the man might give up. Going to the party and seeing other young women vying for the interest of eligible young men, he had hoped, might awaken a similar and natural compulsion in Sashie.

However, there was no use in arguing. She had bent back over the book, her face sharp and colorless in the wan light. Besides, how could he have taken her anyway? Yesterday he had looked inside her wardrobe to see what gown she might wear to the party, only to discover she had thrown away all of the pretty dresses he had bought her. All that remained were those plain, ash-colored garments she wore every day to the church.

Resigned, he went to her and kissed her cheek. "It is probably best if you do not wait up for me, dearest."

"If I am up in the night, it will be only to pray."

"Pray?" he said, startled. "For what?"

She did not answer, and instead turned another page of the Testament. He left the little apartment, shutting the door behind him, and went out into the cooling evening.

It would be best to take a hack cab later tonight, for the affair would no doubt end late. Thus he had decided to save paying a fare twice and walk to the party. The air was gentle, and it was not very far. He made his way past the cathedral and soon turned onto the east end of Durrow Street.

"Penny for a paper!" a boy cried, holding a broadsheet. "Today's copy of *The Fox*—only a few left!"

Such was the way the boy waved the newspaper that Eldyn could not help but read the headline. EVENGROVE WATCH CONTINUES, claimed the headline, and beneath that in large type, *No Persons Allowed Near Madiger's Wall*. Taking up much of the rest of the front page was an image of a high stone wall before a ragged line of treetops. Even in the dimming light, the picture was rendered so vividly it seemed to glow with its own light, and Eldyn knew it had to be an impression.

How some illusionists mastered the trick—holding an engraving plate and willing upon it the image of some scene in their mind—was one Eldyn did not comprehend. As far as he knew, only a few Siltheri had the capability to do such a thing. No one at the Theater of the Moon could work such a feat, not even Dercy. However, at tavern one night after a performance, he had met a young illusionist from the Theater of Mirrors who made a good bit of money selling his work to the various broadsheets.

Would that Eldyn could make impressions, for then he would be able to save portions for himself and Sashie all the sooner! But he could not, so instead of making money he would instead save it by forgoing a paper.

Not that there was any need to read more than the words of the headline. The news of the happening at the Evengrove had been shocking. It was one thing to hear of Risings in Torland; it was quite another to have such a thing take place so near the city. However, in the quarter month since then, there had been no more news, nor did he expect any. No doubt the soldiers would keep any other mad individuals from attempting to light fires and provoke the trees.

He waved the boy aside, walked around Béanore's fountain, and continued down the length of Durrow Street—from the direction of the theaters, and past houses that grew larger and more ancient as he went. Many of these edifices were dilapidated shadows of the grand edifices they had been in the days when this was the fashionable part of the city, before the New Quarter was constructed.

Before too long, though, near the end of the street, he approached a dwelling whose windows were ablaze in the gloaming, and which appeared not the worse for its ancientness, but rather all the more handsome and majestic. The house was set off from the street by a wild garden and bordered by hedges and a fence of wrought iron, which lent it almost the appearance of some keep in the moorland. Eldyn gave his coat a tug to straighten it, then started toward the gate in the fence.

His way was blocked as, from out of the dusky air, Dercy manifested with a flourish and a grin.

"I was wondering when you would appear," Eldyn said.

Dercy laughed. "And I was wondering when you were going to notice me. I've been following you for half a mile!"

"Oh?" Eldyn said, affecting a bored tone. "I hadn't bothered to look."

Dercy gave him an affectionate punch in the arm. "Don't pretend you weren't surprised when I showed up just now."

In fact, Eldyn wasn't surprised. The other night he had told Dercy about the party, how he could bring a guest, and how he was disappointed that his sister was refusing to attend. Given this, and what he knew about Dercy, Eldyn would have been more surprised if he *hadn't* appeared, his beard trimmed, his blond hair rakishly tousled, and wearing his most dashing coat.

"Besides, you should look about when you go out walking at twilight," Dercy went on. "There's no telling who might be prowling up behind you with the most awful of intentions. You don't want to be the next to go missing, do you?"

Though the evening was balmy, Eldyn could not help a shudder. Just yesterday there had been whispers on Durrow Street of another illusionist who had not shown up at his theater for a performance and had not been seen since. True, he may have simply left the city to escape a bad debt or return home to the country. Or he might wash up on the shores of the Anbyrn, his eyes gone from his skull.

"You shouldn't make a jest about such things," Eldyn said.

Dercy's grin went dark in the gloom. "You're right. It was a poor joke. Why don't you let me make it up to you by buying you a cup of punch before we go to the party?"

"You can't expect that I'm taking you to Lady Quent's affair!" Eldyn exclaimed. "You will embarrass me, I have no doubt."

"On the contrary, I will save you from embarrassing yourself. Indeed, I already have. You were about to approach the gate, and the sun has only just set. Everyone knows a formal affair starts an hour after sunset."

Eldyn hadn't known that fact, but he did not want to admit it. "I did not wish to be late."

"That's your second error," Dercy said, grinning again. "The most desirable guests to a party always come late. Indeed, the more desirable they are, then the later they come. Therefore, if we wait a good while, everyone will wonder who we are and wish to speak with us when we do arrive, believing us to be very important personages."

Eldyn looked past Dercy at the house. It was true that he did not yet see any carriages out front or people approaching the gate.

"All right," he said. "You can buy me a punch while I wait. But you are not coming with me to the party!"

"Whatever you say, my lord," Dercy said with a mock bow, then rose and held out his arm.

Eldyn hooked his elbow around his companion's, glad the matter was settled.

"Except I *am* coming," Dercy said with a laugh, and he pulled Eldyn down the street in the direction of the nearest tavern.

CHAPTER THIRTY-TWO

 VY COULD NOT be startled when the door of her bedchamber suddenly burst open, for even the most violent and abrupt noise lost its ability to induce alarm if it occurred often enough.

"My new pink ribbon has gone missing!" Lily exclaimed as if Murghese soldiers were storming the walls of the house. "I've looked everywhere and I can't find it."

"Have you looked in Rose's hair?" Ivy said without glancing up from the broadsheet she was looking at as she sat near the window. "That is likely where it is, as you told her this morning at breakfast that she could wear it."

"Nonsense," Lily roared. "Why would I ever have done such a ridiculous thing?"

"I think it was to return the kindness she has shown in so faithfully laboring on your tableau to have it ready for tonight."

"The tableau is both of ours, which means Rose should have to show a kindness to me as well. I will tell her to give me the ribbon."

Now Ivy did lower the broadsheet, and she gave Lily a stern look. "A kindness rescinded is no kindness at all, but rather a cruelty. Besides, I think a blue ribbon would best suit your hair."

"It might best suit my hair, but it does not best suit *me,*" Lily said with a sour expression. "But I suppose you're right—I can't very well take the ribbon from Rose, for she would have to do her hair over again, and she will hardly be done in time as it is. It always takes Rose a hundred years to get ready for anything."

Ivy conceded there was some truth to this. If they were all going somewhere, she usually told Rose they were about to leave an hour before Ivy actually wished to depart.

"What of you, Ivy? You aren't even in your gown yet, and the party is hardly an hour away!"

"My hair is ready, and it does not take me an hour to put on my gown," Ivy said. "Besides, it is more than an hour until the party will begin. The sun has not yet set."

"I am sure that it has set," Lily said despite the apricot-colored glow that colored the panes of the window. "And wherever is Mr. Quent? I have not seen him yet."

"He will be here shortly," Ivy said, keeping her voice light.

Just after breakfast a note penned in a hasty hand had arrived at the house. It was from Mr. Quent. His trip had taken him longer than planned, but he had at last arrived in the city that morning. He had to make a report at the Citadel before he could return to the house, but he had assured Ivy that he would arrive in good order for Lily and Rose's affair.

"How can Rose and I be presented if there is no one to present us? There will be no party at all!"

"He will be here," Ivy said. "Have you ever known Mr. Quent to disregard a promise?"

Lily frowned, but she said nothing. Nor could she, for Mr.

Quent always kept his word. All the same, Ivy could not help
sharing some of Lily's despair. She had no doubt that Mr. Quent
would arrive before the party began, but it would have soothed all
of their nerves if he had been there already.

These last days, the rapid approach of the party had induced a
great deal of anticipation and apprehension in the household—so
much that Ivy could, to a great degree, forgive Lily's behavior.
Rose, too, had been overcome more than once. Earlier that afternoon, Ivy had had to console her, for Rose had expressed a terror
that she would not know what to say to people she met.

"No one ever caused offense by smiling nicely and saying 'How
do you do,'" Ivy said, and this had seemed to reassure her.

Evidently there was nothing more to complain about, because
Lily departed the chamber. Ivy looked down at the broadsheet in
her lap. It had come into the house that morning, and all day she
had been fascinated by the picture of the Evengrove on the front
page. It was an illusionist's impression, and so perfectly was the
picture rendered that she could almost see the crowns of the trees
swaying above the top of the wall.

The news of the Rising at the Evengrove and the deaths of
three of the king's soldiers had resulted in a sensation in Invarel.
Yet for all the commotion, things in the city proceeded in much
the same way as before, and Ivy had known there could be no talk
of delaying her sisters' party.

Only everything wasn't the same. Or rather, Ivy wasn't the same.
Ever since that day, she could hardly go an hour without recalling
what it had been like to touch the rough bark of the Old Ash, to
hear the voices of the trees, and to feel the vast and ancient will of
the Wyrdwood—a will that *she* had been able to alter and direct.

For the last quarter month, she had wanted nothing more than
to speak to someone about what had happened. However, she
dared not write about what had taken place to Mr. Quent for fear
of who might see the letter. The only other person she could have
spoken to about that day was Mr. Rafferdy. Yet she had not seen
him since then, and while she had every expectation he would be

at the party tonight, she doubted there would be any opportunity for them to speak together in private. All the same, merely to exchange a look with him was something she would be grateful for.

Ivy set the broadsheet down and rose from her chair, but she did not put on her gown just yet. She did not want to be in the midst of dressing when Mr. Quent arrived, for she wished to greet him as soon as he entered the house. With this thought, she left her bedchamber. The umbral had begun, which meant it was time to check her father's journal again. She could not count on getting another chance that night, for the party might go very late.

She descended the stairs, passing bustling servants making the last preparations for the arrival of the guests, then proceeded to the library, which was dim and quiet. Soothed by the tranquillity, she sat at the desk, opened the Wyrdwood box, and took out the journal.

"I wish you could be here tonight, Father," she murmured. "How delighted you would be to see Rose and Lily all grown and ready to enter the world!"

Though she smiled, she also suffered a pang of regret. Yet she had every hope that she would bring their father home soon, and then they would all be together. Consoled by this thought, she opened the journal and turned through the pages.

And there it was, a little over halfway in: a page filled with spindly letters. Ivy read, at first in delight, but then in growing dread.

LOERUS IN AGNATHON RISING

My dear, you are small as I write these words, and you think me to be infallible—stronger and wiser than any man. It is natural for a child to believe this about her father. However, as you read these words you are now a woman grown, and I fear I must inform you that I am as imperfect as any man. While I have often thought myself to be clever, I know now there is another much cleverer, for I have been most profoundly deceived!

I suppose I should have seen it, yet I was blinded by affection and loyalty. I always knew he had ambition; he never attempted to dissemble when it came to that fact. He comes from an old family, and he often made a jest that if a large enough number of his relatives were to perish, he would find himself a magnate of high degree one day. Now I wonder if he means to assure this event happens! I knew it was his aim to rise high, yet I did not know before to what lengths he would go to do it.

Now I do. It was Gambrel who stole the key to Tyberion. And he intends to use it.

Yet for all his scheming, that is something he will not be able to do. Mundy, Larken, and Fintaur all knew of the key, as did Gambrel; Bennick and I needed their aid to help bind the enchantment to protect it, and we chose them carefully for that reason. Little did I know that Gambrel had sown the seeds of the spell's undoing in its very casting. He was ever a sly and subtle magician. Yet he does not know where Tyberion is hidden; that is something only I and Bennick have knowledge of.

Gambrel was aware of this fact, and he went to Bennick, thinking he could get the secret out of him. Being that most perceptive judge of character that he is, Bennick must have sensed Gambrel's duplicitous intentions. He gave Gambrel the impression that he would indeed reveal the location of Tyberion. And so, once Gambrel had stolen the key, he went at once to Bennick. Thus the theft was revealed to us.

Bless Mr. Bennick! Once again I am deeply in his debt. I hope that you have come to know him, Ivy. If you have, then I am sure you admire and trust him as I do. I will not make him out to be something he is not—his demeanor can be as sharp as his intellect—but he is the truest of friends.

Because of Bennick's foresight and actions, Gambrel's duplicity was revealed, and he has fled. Though he is a powerful magician—the best of us all, I have no doubt—still he cannot face the wrath of Bennick, Fintaur, Larken, Mundy, and myself all at once. Where he has gone to, we do not know. It does not matter. He may have the key to Tyberion, but he has no idea of Tyberion's whereabouts.

Even if he did—if he was to learn that it is in fact here in this very house—still he would not be able to reach it to place the key upon it. I am sure you are familiar with the Arcane Eyes all about the house, Ivy. I have warned them of Gambrel, and they know to watch for him.

Should he ever try to enter the house, the eyes would raise such an alarm that his presence would be known at once.

Again, I must chide myself for not realizing sooner what Gambrel's intentions were. I should have known that it was not merely out of polite interest that he made all those enquiries concerning my research into Waywrend Dratham and the Sword and the Leaf.

Well, even if the key is gone, Tyberion itself remains hidden and safe. Nor do any of the others, save for Bennick, know of the existence of Arantus. Thus its secret is well-guarded. You must know how important Tyberion and Arantus are. No one can ever be allowed to use them, for fear of what hideous powers might be unleashed through them.

These have been trying days, my dearest Ivy. I am greatly fatigued from all the magicks we have been forced to work. I am very glad you are safe in your bed at Whitward Street. I will make certain all of the eyes in this house are properly enchanted with all the correct wards, and then I shall come home to you, and give you a kiss as you sleep. Then I shall lay my own self down. I pray I shall not dream.

G.O.L.

Ivy set down the journal. Though the words her father had written had set her mind awhirl, there was no time to peruse the entry again in a slow and careful fashion to comprehend what it all meant. Instead, she took out pen, ink, and paper and transcribed the entry as hastily as possible, caring not if she made a spot or smudge as she went.

All the while, her thoughts worked as swiftly as her pen. So it was not Mr. Bennick after all who had taken the key to Tyberion! Yet surely he must have put Gambrel up to the deed—why else had Gambrel gone right to him after stealing it? Only somehow Bennick's scheme had gone awry, and Mr. Lockwell had discovered the theft before Tyberion could be used. While Gambrel still possessed the key, he had been banished from the house and could not enter, for it was under the watch of the arcane eyes. What's more, having been betrayed himself, Gambrel had no doubt refused to relinquish the key to Mr. Bennick. Thus Tyberion was and remained safe. Only what were Tyberion and Arantus? Ivy still didn't know.

Or did she? Maybe she had known all along.

Ivy glanced over the words she had transcribed. *I should have known that it was not merely out of polite interest that he made all those enquiries concerning my research into Waywrend Dratham and the Sword and the Leaf. . . .*

A thrill coursed through her. The Sword and the Leaf—what else could her father be referring to but the doors she had uncovered in the second floor gallery? Both of them had been hidden, the one sometime earlier than the other, Mr. Barbridge had said. Besides, what else did one open with a key in order to let something through but a door?

True, she had dismissed this notion earlier, for she had not observed a keyhole in either of them. But in the entry he had referred to the key not as a thing to be inserted into the door, but rather something to be placed upon it. Which meant, perhaps, that her notion of what the key should look like had been limited by conventional notions.

A great fascination came over Ivy. She wanted nothing more than to go back through the entries she had transcribed from her father's journal, and to delve once again into the history of Waywrend Loerus Dratham. However, such things would have to wait. How she would manage to keep her mind on a party that night, she didn't know! Only she must.

Ivy sprinkled sand upon the paper to dry the ink, and at that very moment she heard the distant sound of the door in the front hall opening and shutting. Had guests already begun to arrive? Then a moment later she heard the deep sound of a voice, and the thump of boots approaching.

Quickly, Ivy shut the journal in the Wyrdwood box and put it away. Then he stepped into the library. At once everything in the room seemed to shift a bit, as if to accommodate his solid presence, and all thoughts of keys and doors and magicians fled Ivy's mind.

Who moved more swiftly, she or he, was impossible to say.

Within a moment, all distance between them was removed. Neither uttered a word. What could they say that a caress of the cheek, the touch of the hand, and a kiss of the lips could not speak far more eloquently?

"But you are trembling so!" he exclaimed at last.

It was true. A shuddering had come over her, and though she held him fiercely, and he fashioned a circle around her with the strength of his arms, she could not stop.

"Is something amiss, Mrs. Quent?" he said, his voice low with concern. "Are you well?"

"I am well now," she said, and her trembling began to subside. "You must forgive me. It is only that, since you've been gone, there have been . . . that is, so much has . . . ." She shook her head. For the last quarter month she had wanted nothing except to be able to speak to him. Only now that he was here, words were beyond her.

He pushed her away a little, so he could look down at her, but did not release her from his grasp. "You say you are well, but I cannot believe it! I can see in your eyes there is something wrong, and I would know what it is so I can set it aright. I beg you, Mrs. Quent, tell me what has happened while I was gone."

"It's what happened at the Evengrove," she managed at last.

A heavy sigh went out of him. "The news came to me in the south. By then the Rising had been averted, and other inquirers were already at the wall to make investigations and keep watch. Thus I did not hasten my return and finished my business. I knew from the reports that there was no threat to you and your sisters, that you were safe here in the city."

"But I was there that day!" she cried, unable to keep the knowledge from him any longer.

"There?" He stared down at her, and his grip tightened on her arms. "Is this true—you were at Madiger's Wall the day of the Rising?"

She drew in a gulping breath and nodded. "I went there on an excursion with Lady Crayford. We were there when it all happened."

Even as she watched, his face went gray behind his beard. He released her arms and took a staggering step back. "Did you hear them?" His voice was low and hoarse, and his brown eyes were intent upon her. "Did you hear the trees calling to you?"

A terrible dread filled her, and she started to tremble. Did he think that she had caused the Rising?

"But it wasn't me!" she gasped, reaching out toward him. "I did not provoke them!"

He shook his head, then his expression of shock became one of anguish instead. In a swift motion, he moved back to her, taking her hands and holding them tight in his own.

"Of course you didn't! I would never have thought such a thing, Ivoleyn, even if I hadn't already known what caused the Rising. I read the reports, and I know it was a man who set a fire near the wall that caused the trees to lash out."

The relief Ivy felt was so acute it was like a pain in her chest, but it was a welcome ache. As they gripped hands, she spoke quietly of how she had come to be at the Evengrove that day, and what took place there—how she had called out to the trees, and they had listened.

"I should have known it," he said, wonder upon his craggy face. "From the report I read, I knew there was something peculiar about this Rising. Given the size of the Evengrove, the Rising should have continued to grow as more and more trees communicated their fear and anger to the others. Only it ended so suddenly. I had wondered how more people were not harmed. Now I know the reason. It was *you*, dearest."

He released her hands and touched her cheek, smiling down at her. Only after a moment his expression grew troubled again, and with a heavy breath he turned away from her, and he leaned upon the back of a chair.

"You protected all those people at the wall that day. And where was I?" His shoulders slumped downward. "You were in grave peril, and I was halfway across the country."

She went to him, laying a hand on the broad surface of his back. "You were seeing to your duty."

"I am your husband," he said, his voice gruff. "My duty is to protect you. How many of them have I labored to keep safe at all cost? I went all the way back to Torland to make certain that she was protected." He bowed his head. "Yet I left you here, and so did nothing when you were in peril."

These words filled Ivy with concern. Yet she could not help feeling a curiosity as well. "She? You mean the witch in Torland—the one who caused the Risings?"

"Yes, I mean her."

"But what protections could she have needed? She is in the custody of the Crown, is she not? You said you captured her."

"I did capture her." He turned around to gaze at her, and there was a strange light in his dark eyes. "I captured her, and then I let her go."

Now it was Ivy who stared, and who staggered a step back. "Why?" she managed to utter.

For a long moment he was silent. "I made a promise to her," he said at last, and as he spoke his voice grew steadier. "I promised that if she would cease to provoke the Old Trees, I would swear upon the authority granted me by the Crown that no harm would come to her."

Ivy listened, fascinated, as he described what happened in terse words: how, following hearsay and rumor, he had at last tracked her down to a grove of Wyrdwood deep in Torland, and how he called out to her again and again, until at last she came to the wall to meet him. He came near enough that she might have bid the trees to snatch him up and break him. Or she might have called to the rebels she had been harboring in the grove to bring their guns. Instead, she had listened to him.

"But I don't understand," Ivy said when he paused. "Why would she heed your words?"

"I think because something of my reputation proceeded me, and so perhaps she believed she could trust me. But more than that, I think she knew as I did that if the Risings did not end, more would come to harm."

Ivy shook her head. "More Old Trees, you mean?"

"No," he said, his voice low. "More witches."

Slowly, Ivy sank down onto a sofa, sitting on its edge.

"It is not only the work of the inquirers to investigate Risings, and to prevent them from happening," Mr. Quent went on, pacing before her now. "Much of our effort goes toward finding those women who have heard the call of the Old Trees, and getting them to safety—not only so they do not provoke the Wyrdwood, but so they are not harmed themselves.

"Nor is it only from the ancient forest that they face peril. While the matter of the Wyrdwood—and therefore the matter of witches as well—is under the purview of the lord inquirer, there are those within the government who have made it their purpose to seek out all threats to the Crown, and they have long desired to come into the possession of a witch."

Ivy shuddered. "You mean Lady Shayde."

He nodded. "Or more properly, her master, Lord Valhaine. I am loath to even think what they might do to a suspected sibyl who was delivered into their keeping—what methods they might use to try to draw knowledge from her, whether she was truly a witch or not. Thus the inquirers have always labored to be the first to any Rising, or better yet, to reach them before they can ever have a chance to occur—and before agents of the Gray Conclave can get there themselves."

Ivy tried to comprehend these words. "So that's why you went to Torland this time." She looked up at him. "To free the witch before Lady Shayde could get to her."

"She was already free. I went only to make sure she was safely away from the Wyrdwood—and in a place she could not be found."

Ivy felt a thrill that the witch had escaped. Only was that right? Should she not be horrified instead? "But people perished in Torland. And to let her go after what she had done—was it really the only way?"

He gave a grim nod. "It was the only way to achieve an immediate end to the Risings. If they did not cease, and quickly, it was only a matter of time until a woman who was thought to be a witch was brought to harm. And you know what would happen then."

Ivy thought of Merriel Addysen. It hadn't been her intention to cause a Rising. It had happened against her will, after she was violently accosted by a pair of vagrant men. And then the stand of Wyrdwood was burned down while she was still within it.

"If she felt anger," Ivy said softly, "or fear or pain, and if there was a grove of Wyrdwood near, then it would hear her."

"Yes. And hearing such a thing would only cause the wood to lash out more violently. The witch I met with understood that as well. She had accomplished what she wished, I think—to remind people of the power of the ancient wood. But she knew further Risings would only put other women like her in peril, and so she agreed to depart. So you see, if I had not let her go, the Risings could only have grown worse, until people at last resorted to taking up ax and fire against the Wyrdwood."

"I can hardly be surprised they would!" she exclaimed.

"Yet at all cost, they must not do so." He rubbed his thumb over the scar on his left hand—all that remained of the last two fingers. "The more that the Wyrdwood is fought, the more it will resist— and the more women it will call to, summoning them to its aid."

Ivy could only shudder. How many women would hear such a call, and answer it? Some might be aware of their own natures. But others would not understand. They would listen to the Wyrdwood and heed it without knowing why. And they would find themselves in grave danger.

Just like Merriel Addysen. And just like Gennivel Quent, who had left a party at Heathcrest Hall to run across the moonlit moors—and then perished when she fell from the wall that surrounded a grove of Wyrdwood.

And yet there was hope. For were there not inquirers to keep the Wyrdwood from Rising up and calling to those women who could hear? Ivy knew he had saved Altania in Torland, but now she knew that he had saved *her* as well—her and other women like her. The cold dread Ivy had suffered was now burned away by a fierce love. She went to Mr. Quent, threw her arms around him, and held him with all her might.

"You did protect me from harm," she said, pressing her cheek against his chest.

"But I was not with you!" he cried. "Just like that night at . . ."

His voice trailed off, but he did not need to finish. She understood. How could she not? He had been distracted at the party that night over a dozen years ago; he had failed to protect the first Mrs. Quent. Only he had not known then what he did now.

"You were not here," she said, holding him more tightly yet. "Only it doesn't matter. No matter where you go, the work you do protects me. It protects all of us."

She listened to the beat of his heart. Ten she counted, while he stood there, motionless. Then at last he drew a deep breath, and he returned her embrace, and kissed her.

At last they drew apart, and he looked down at her. "I am hardly deserving of you, you know."

"On the contrary," she said, astonished by his words, "you are deserving of far greater rewards! Altania owes you everything after what you have done."

"Does it?" He shook his head. "Not all would agree with you on that account, I fear. If it came to light that I had struck a bargain with the witch who caused the Risings in Torland . . . well, some might decide it is not a reward that I deserve."

"But how could they question it? What you did was done with the authority of the Crown, and it caused the Risings to cease. Besides, if you do become the next lord inquirer, I am sure such persons will be in no position to do anything against you."

She spoke this adamantly, and at last he gave a nod. At that moment, the old rosewood clock let out a chime.

"The party!" Ivy exclaimed, remembering what was to occur in just a little while. "Lily has been fretting for your arrival."

All at once he let out a deep laugh, and the sound was like that of a bell, resonating upon the air and clearing it of all dread and worry.

"I have no doubt that she has!" he roared. "Well, I am sorry to have caused her distress. I will go to her and let her know I've arrived, then ready myself. I suspect you must do the same."

She did. And while before she had had plenty of time, now she would indeed have to hurry. They proceeded upstairs, enjoying this brief moment together, for she doubted they would have much chance to be with each other once the evening's affair began. All too soon they reached the third landing, and with a kiss they parted ways. He went off to find Lily, and she proceeded to her dressing room, humming a song to herself as she did.

Only then some unknown instinct caused her to glance out the window, and the music perished on her lips. The light was dying outside, and his black garb merged with the shadows in the garden below. It was too dim to fully make out the expression on his black mask. It was, she thought, a grimace, like an expression of pain.

Before Ivy could wonder more, she heard his voice as if he were standing in the room beside her, and his words were no less queer than the means of their conveyance or his sudden appearance.

You must conceal Arantus, he said.

CHAPTER THIRTY-THREE

HE STARS WERE beginning to appear in the purple sky as Lord Baydon's four-in-hand made its way down the length of Durrow Street.

"Mr. Baydon, set down your broadsheet!" Mrs. Baydon said to her husband on the opposite bench. "We are nearly to the party."

"That's precisely why he is reading so furiously," Rafferdy said. "As he is about to be subjected to all manner of amusements and pleasantries, he must absorb as much dreariness and tedium as possible. If he does not take care to gird himself, he might find himself overcome with merriment."

Mrs. Baydon was overcome herself at this, and she laughed.

"Have no fear, Mrs. Baydon," her husband said, folding up his newspaper. "I assure you I will endeavor to be the most cheerful and insipid being at the party. I will think nothing of all the grave troubles that beset our nation. Instead, I will speak only of the weather and how I am certain everything I have bought of late cost less and is of superior quality to anything that anyone else has bought."

"Perfect," Mrs. Baydon said with an affectionate smile, and reached across to straighten his collar.

He gave her a confounded look, but by then the carriage had halted. Rafferdy climbed out, followed by Mr. and Mrs. Baydon, and as the carriage departed another pulled forward to take its place before the gate, with more lined up.

"So many carriages!" Mrs. Baydon exclaimed. "I would my father-in-law could see this. He would find it greatly amusing, I think."

While Lord Baydon's condition had improved somewhat of late, he remained too ill to leave the house. According to Mrs. Baydon, though, he had encouraged her to go to the party, and he had told her not to be surprised if, upon arriving there, she found him already dancing.

"It is very thrilling so many are coming to see the Miss Lockwells presented," she went on. "Or at least, I am thrilled. I am sure *you* can only be bored with the prospect of a party, Mr. Rafferdy."

Usually that would be the case. But then, usually when he went to a party *she* could not be expected to be encountered there. True, it was likely he would not in fact encounter her tonight, as she was certain to be occupied with all of her other guests. Yet even to glimpse her across the room for a moment was a reward for which he would willingly suffer through an entire evening of drab conversations or tedious party games.

Besides, even if he did have a moment with her, what would either of them say? They would not be at liberty to broach the one topic he knew they would wish to discuss. How captivated she had been last year when he had demonstrated his ability with magick for her! Yet he was not the only one with a power, was he? And while the city seemed thick with magicians these days, *hers* was a far more remarkable ability.

It was an axiom that the more commonplace a thing was, then the less interest it held for Rafferdy, which explained why, for the last quarter month, nothing had fascinated him more than thoughts of what he had witnessed at the Evengrove.

He could vividly recall the way she had taken up a twig and, by some silent command or thought, caused it to wriggle like a living creature and loop around her finger. Yet it was more than merely a twig whose bidding she had commanded that day. He had watched as she threw her arms about one of the trees and called out for them all to cease their violence.

And they had done so.

Rafferdy was not so ignorant of history that he did not know what this meant concerning her nature. While a year ago he would have scoffed at the suggestion such beings had really existed, now he knew better than to question the veracity of old legends. For a while after that day, he had wondered if that was the real reason his father had not wanted him to have an association with Ivoleyn Lockwell. Had he known what she had the capacity to do?

Perhaps. Or perhaps it was simply as his father had said, that he had not wanted his son to become entangled with the family of a magician. Either way, there had to be some imperfection in Rafferdy's understanding of the histories, or in the histories themselves. Were not witches supposed to have incited the Wyrdwood long ago and caused the Old Trees to lash out at men? Yet she had done no such thing. Instead, she had accomplished what all the soldiers there with their swords and buckets could not.

She had put a stop to a Rising.

It was not only the fact that she had accomplished this feat that intrigued him, but also the fact that she had known there was at least some possibility she could do such a thing. How long had she known of this affinity she displayed for the Old Trees?

For some time at least, he was sure. He recalled again the way the twig had writhed in her fingers like a little brown serpent, and he thought perhaps he indeed had a better understanding of what had befallen the magicians that day, how they came to gaze into the crystalline orb and were made bereft of their minds. After all, the large frame upon which the artifact rested had been fashioned of braided Wyrdwood, for the wood of the Old Trees had some power to resist the energies of the artifact. And if she could shape a twig with her thoughts, what might she have been able to do with all the wood that made up the stand?

"What are you lingering there for, Mr. Rafferdy?" Mrs. Baydon called back through the open gate. "Come along!"

Rafferdy realized he was still standing on the street while men in fine coats and ladies in fluttering gowns moved past him. He hurried to catch up to Mr. and Mrs. Baydon, and together they proceeded through the twilit garden and into the house.

Rafferdy had been inside the house of Mr. Lockwell on two prior occasions, but the first time had been after the house had endured a period of long neglect, and the second had been before the renovations were very far along. Nothing of what he had seen then had presaged what he now beheld. In any modern edifice in the New Quarter, everything would have been marble and crystal and gilt, all meant to dazzle the eye. No such artifices had been employed here. The beauty of this house came not from the trappings that had been placed within it, but rather was a property that arose from the very form and shape of its construction.

The front hall would have been more than capable of housing a large party; however, it served as no more than an antechamber that night, for people were ascending the double staircase that curved upward to the second floor, chattering in a lively fashion as they went.

Rafferdy followed Mr. and Mrs. Baydon to the steps, ascending toward gold light and the strains of music. Yet as they neared the top, Rafferdy felt a peculiar hesitation and slowed his pace. It was not because he dreaded any tedium that lay ahead. Rather, it was a sudden concern that this affair was above him, that others would regard him in astonishment and wonder how *he* had come to be invited.

Only then they reached the top of the steps, and such was the eagerness of those who came behind him that he was swept up along with them, into the gallery beyond.

"Oh!" Mrs. Baydon exclaimed. "How magnificent!"

Whether she referred to the room itself, or the multitude of people, Rafferdy did not know. Nor did it matter; on either account she would be right. For all the grand halls and ballrooms he had entered in his life, he could not recall one so handsome or inviting as this. The harmonious lines and sturdy proportions gave one a sense of grandeur as well as comfort.

The guests who filled the long space of the gallery were no less remarkable. Perhaps it was the solidness of the room that made their finery all the more striking, or perhaps there was something in the way the light was reflected off the rich wood all around, glazing the air like a honey-colored varnish. Whatever the reason, everyone's attire seemed more vivid in hue than he had ever seen before. Gowns and coats were not yellow or blue or green; they were saffron, cerulean, and brilliant viridian.

"I feel as if I have never seen a party at all before now," Mrs. Baydon sighed.

Rafferdy could only agree. In the past he had been so conceited as to think that *he* was the most interesting guest one would likely encounter at a party. That was not the case now. Here were not merely city gentlemen, country sirs, and a stray lord and his lady. From the crests and medals and jeweled diadems he saw flashing around him, here also were viscounts and viscountesses, earls and countesses, marquesses and marchionesses. There was only one thing that exceeded Rafferdy's astonishment upon seeing just how far above him in society Mrs. Quent—*Lady* Quent—had truly risen. And that was his great delight, for who could have deserved to be raised in such a manner more than she?

At this thought he laughed—a sound of real pleasure—and Mrs. Baydon smiled at him. Then she looked to her husband.

"Do you not think it magnificent, Mr. Baydon?"

"I would think it considerably more magnificent if I could find the quiet salon where men might sit and take tobacco and discuss the stories in today's edition of *The Comet*." With that he took his leave of them, off to discover such a place.

Mrs. Baydon paid him little heed as he departed. "Look there," she said, pointing across the gallery to a small platform that had been covered with a white curtain. "That must be where the Miss Lockwells are to appear. I have it from Lady Quent that they have conceived some manner of surprise for the party. I must go find Captain Branfort. I want to see his expression when we find out what it is—and if he thinks the Miss Lockwells very pretty!"

With that, she moved farther into the gallery and was at once lost among the multitude of guests.

Rafferdy had his own people to look for. He made a tour along the gallery, keeping to the edge of the room as he went, casting his gaze out over the party. A hope came upon him that he would see Eldyn Garritt, whom he expected to be here tonight. It had been a long time since they had met at tavern for a drink, and he wondered how his friend was faring.

It was Lord Coulten he saw first. Or rather, it was Lord Coulten's hair, rising above the heads of the people all around. With his gaze fixed upon that landmark, Rafferdy navigated his way through the crowded gallery.

"There you are, Rafferdy!" Coulten said, his cheeks ruddy and his blue eyes sparkling. "I was wondering if I would need to use a spell to reveal where you were."

Rafferdy raised an eyebrow. "Would that have been very wise? After all, Eubrey claims we magicians are all under the watchful eye of Lord Valhaine and the White Lady. Who knows if one of their agents is here? Besides, I see you still wear gloves."

"Well, I'm sure I will soon have no reason to wear them. For they are bound to need us."

"Need us? What do you mean?"

Coulten leaned in close, holding a hand beside his mouth and speaking in a conspiratorial tone. "I mean, who else can put a stop to all these Risings? You saw what Eubrey accomplished at the Evengrove. They will need us to strengthen the Quelling on the Wyrdwood one day—perhaps sooner rather than later. Then we will show off our House rings without a care!"

Rafferdy doubted Eubrey had accomplished anything at all. It was not Eubrey's knife that had raised the ire of the Old Trees, nor was it his spell that had soothed them. Only he did not speak these thoughts aloud.

"Some of us magicians do still show our rings," he said instead, raising his right hand so the blue gem caught the light. "Speaking of Eubrey, where is he? Did he come on his own rather than accompany you here?"

"He did neither, for he is not coming at all," Coulten said, and his eyes twinkled as they always did when he was about to impart some interesting news. "Eubrey is to receive his reward tonight."

"His reward?"

"Yes, quite. The sages are going to open the Door for him, and not merely so he can look through it. He has been invited to step beyond."

Rafferdy could not conceal his surprise. "So he finally did it, then. He has gotten himself admitted to the inner circle of the society."

"Indeed, the next time we see him at a meeting he will be one of the magicians in hoods. What's more, he says he will put in a good word for me. So with luck I may be the next one in a gold hood!" Coulten gripped his shoulder. "Don't look so glum, Rafferdy. We can all still be companions when we're not at gatherings of the society. Besides, with your talents, I'm sure it won't be long before *you* are invited through the Door."

Coulten had misread the look upon his face. It was not any sort of envy or regret that had caused Rafferdy to frown. Rather, it was simply difficult to understand why Eubrey had been granted entry to the inner circle of the Arcane Society of the Virescent

Blade. Surely the sages did not believe Eubrey's spell had had some effect on the Rising at the Evengrove. Or was it simply the case that for all their hints of occult secrets, there was nothing at all beyond the curtained door but another room beneath a dank tavern?

Before he could respond to Coulten, a voice called out his name, and despite all the sounds of conversation and music, the words carried as clearly across the gallery as if it were her own parlor.

"Lord Rafferdy, do come here at once and present yourself!"

He turned, and through a gap amid the revelers he saw Lady Marsdel sitting a little way away. She beckoned to him with her closed fan, and he could not refuse. Achieving lordship, it seemed, had done nothing to change the arrangement of their stations. He approached, and Coulten followed.

"Good evening, your ladyship," he said with a deep bow.

As he rose, he could only be impressed. Lady Marsdel was far from the highest magnate in attendance tonight, yet somehow she had won what was arguably the finest seat at the party. It was situated at the southern end of the room and offered an excellent view of the gallery. What was more, the chair was situated close to the most beautiful old door.

The door, which was shut, was fashioned of dark wood and was fabulously carved with a sword and a shield. The former was decorated with runic inscriptions, and both were rendered so skillfully that it was easy to fancy reaching up and taking them from the door like artifacts that had been hung upon the wall. Such a remarkable piece was bound to attract interest, and any who came to examine it would be setting foot directly in Lady Marsdel's web of influence.

A number of people had already been thus ensnared, among them Mrs. Baydon, Captain Branfort, and Colonel Daubrent.

Lady Marsdel nodded in response to Rafferdy's show of obeisance, then she turned in her seat to regard the tall figure of the colonel. "As I was saying, Colonel Daubrent, I think it is awful when common people rise up too quickly. It is of no benefit to them. For how can they be expected to possess the proper traits needed to successfully navigate among all of the intricacies to be found at the highest levels of society?"

"You make it sound rather perilous," Colonel Daubrent observed in a dour tone.

"It could not be more perilous!" Lady Marsdel exclaimed, spreading her fan for emphasis. "Is it not far more dangerous to lose one's balance while standing upon a high precipice than a low bench? Lady Quent is sensible and clever, I grant you. Yet I am not sure that all in her family can claim to share these same characteristics, and there are some abilities that can be gained only by being born into the correct lineage."

Colonel Daubrent frowned. "If that is the case, then I wonder what is the origin of these peculiar abilities you refer to. For I am certain, if you go back far enough, we all must possess an ancestor who was the first in our lineage to be raised up, and therefore was born a commoner himself."

"The Marsdels have always been magnates," her ladyship said, and her fan snapped shut.

"Even when they were striking rocks together in a cave, no doubt," Rafferdy said cheerfully.

The others laughed, and Rafferdy prepared himself to endure a look of displeasure from Lady Marsdel. Instead, she gazed at him with what seemed to him an unusually thoughtful expression.

"Nobility does not come from acquiring fine houses or rich clothes, Mr. Rafferdy," she said. "Nor can it be escaped by spurning these things. Rather, it is something that one either possesses or does not."

Rafferdy found himself without any sort of witticism or clever remark with which to respond. He was suddenly aware of his bare hand and the ring upon his finger, and he put his hand in his pocket.

Thankfully, any attention was drawn away from him as the others proceeded to make an examination of the door.

"It's really remarkable," Mrs. Baydon said. "Both lovely and terrible all at once. I want only to examine it more closely to see every detail of it, yet I fear I should prick my finger were I to touch the blade on accident. What do you think of it, Captain Branfort? As a martial sort of man, I imagine you must find it quite fascinating."

He gave a shrug. "I hadn't considered it."

"You hadn't considered it? On the contrary, Captain, your eyes have strayed to the door a dozen times since we've been gathered here. I do hope you have not taken to emulating our Lord Rafferdy and are pretending to find a thing dull so you will seem more interesting yourself." She gave Rafferdy a teasing smile. "Let me put you on the spot, Lord Rafferdy. You must tell me the truth—do you not find this to be the most striking sight to behold?"

"Yes, it's a very striking sight," he said.

However, it was not the door he was looking at. Rather, his gaze had gone past Mrs. Baydon to the slender figure dressed in a leaf green gown who was approaching them. Mrs. Baydon affected a puzzled look, but then when Rafferdy bowed she turned around.

"Lady Quent!" she exclaimed, and took the other's hands and kissed her cheek. When these greetings had been warmly returned, Mrs. Baydon went on. "I was telling Captain Branfort earlier that I am sure this is the most lovely party that has ever been seen in the Old City."

Lady Quent smiled. "As its name implies, the Old City is very ancient. Therefore I imagine it has seen parties of every variety and quality. But I am happy you find *this* affair to your liking."

"I do! The Miss Lockwells must be so pleased. They will be the envy of all other young ladies in the city tomorrow. And I simply cannot wait to see what surprise they have arranged for the occasion."

"You will not have to wait much longer," Mrs. Quent said with a smile. "They will be making their appearance shortly."

She glanced at the far side of the room, to the white curtain draped before the north wall. For a moment there was a cast to her green eyes that made Rafferdy wonder if there was something about this unveiled surprise that worried her.

The moment passed, and as Mrs. Baydon continued to make exclamations about the party, her expression became one of pleasure. Rafferdy could only wish it was to *him* that happy face was turned. After just a few minutes, Mrs. Quent regretfully said she must take her leave of them, for she needed to hurry to attend to her sisters.

"But you will never be able to hurry to them if you attempt to cross the gallery alone!" Lady Marsdel declaimed. "A hundred people shall accost you and make you speak to them. Where is your husband to escort you?"

"I fear he has been accosted himself," Mrs. Quent said with a rueful glance across the gallery. There was the stolid figure of Sir Quent, back against the windows, bravely facing the gauntlet of half a dozen lords who were repeatedly shaking his hand.

"Well, then, Lord Rafferdy must accompany you. Do what is required to see her swiftly to the Miss Lockwells, Lord Rafferdy, even if it requires some sort of enchantment!"

Rafferdy liked to think that he had seen so many things in his existence that astonishment was beyond him, but at that moment he could only look at Lady Marsdel with real shock. Yet her command was delivered in such a way that it could not be ignored. Mrs. Quent took his arm, and they started across the gallery.

"I am so glad you're here tonight, Mr. Rafferdy," she said as they walked. "So much has happened of late that I sometimes feel as if I'm in a carriage drawn by runaway horses, and all I can do is look at the scenes flashing past the windows. It is a comfort to have such a dear and familiar friend here tonight."

Rafferdy was aware of many eyes turning in their direction, and he could not help feeling pleasure at being singled out by the most desirable person at the party. No doubt they wondered how he had come to be so distinguished; he rather wondered at it himself. Yet he was not about to protest, and he attended to his duty, skillfully turning Mrs. Quent away from anyone who looked as if they were about to attempt to approach her.

"I am looking forward to seeing the Miss Lockwells," he said.

"And they you! We shall all of us have to gather together with Mr. Garritt. It will be just like our time in the parlor at Whitward Street."

He laughed as he glanced around at the grandness of the gallery and its current denizens. "Yes, just like it—with a few small differences, perhaps. But where is that elusive Eldyn Garritt? I have not yet seen him tonight."

"He is here. I encountered him only a little while ago, along with his friend Mr. Fanewerthy. Do you know him?"

Rafferdy could only confess that he did not. "I am not surprised he has been required to find new companions. Given my duties, I have not had an occasion of late to meet Mr. Garritt at the Sword and Leaf."

He was forced to stop, for she had suddenly come to a halt.

"The Sword and Leaf!" she gasped and looked up at him, her green eyes very wide.

Rafferdy could only wonder at this reaction. "It's our usual haunt—the tavern where Mr. Garritt and I have often met." Belatedly he wondered if her response was due to the fact that bringing up a house of drinking was not an appropriate topic for this occasion.

"You are certain that is the name of the tavern?" she said, gripping his arm.

Now his wonderment was redoubled. "Yes, the Sword and Leaf. It's the same tavern beneath which the members of the magickal society I belong to gather and meet."

"It cannot be chance," she said, then shook her head. "Only you told me that the tavern where you meet is not on Durrow Street. So it cannot be the tavern where Dratham used to go."

She glanced again at the white curtain at the north end of the gallery, which they were now very close to. He saw a hand extend beyond the cloth, beckoning in an urgent fashion.

"It cannot be the tavern where who used to go?" he said.

But at the same time she said, "Forgive me, Mr. Rafferdy, I must go to my sisters."

Before he could ask more, she disengaged herself from his arm and vanished behind the curtain.

Rafferdy stared a moment, his mind as blank as the white drapery. Then he turned and wended his way back across the gallery. As he went, his startled mind calmed a degree and began to assemble useful thoughts. Dratham—she had mentioned that name at Madiger's Wall, he recalled now. He was the man who had built this house centuries ago, and who had belonged to a magickal order that met beneath a tavern on Durrow Street.

"There you are, Rafferdy!" Lord Coulten said, slipping through a knot of revelers to come upon him. "I was wondering if you wished to join me in asking some of these excellent ladies to dance. But I say, you look awfully confounded. Is something amiss?"

Rafferdy leaned in close to Coulten, so his voice would not carry. "Tell me, do you know of any taverns on Durrow Street beneath which other orders of magicians might meet?"

"Well, I can't speak about other orders," Coulten said with a frown. "There is only ours that I know of."

Now Rafferdy was startled anew. "What do you mean, *our* order?"

"Don't you know?" Coulten said, only then he let out a laugh, his cheeks brightening. "Of course—you always make a habit of coming in through the tavern proper. You like a nip of rum before our meetings, don't you, Rafferdy? Can't say I blame you."

"What are you talking about?" Rafferdy said, growing perturbed now. "What don't I know?"

"About the other door, the back entrance to our meeting room."

"What's there to know? It's the back door, so it must be in the alley behind the Sword and Leaf."

Coulten waggled a gloved finger at him. "Haven't you been paying attention to the sages, Rafferdy? A magickal door doesn't have to behave like a usual one. Just because one side of a door is on the inside wall of a building doesn't mean the other side of it has to be on the outer wall. It can be . . . well, it can be anywhere at all."

"Anywhere?" Rafferdy said, and at last understanding dawned upon him. "You mean like Durrow Street."

"Now you've got it!" Coulten said, his tall head of hair bobbing as he nodded. "I'm not sure exactly why the outside of the door is on Durrow Street. I suppose it was put there long ago, when arcane orders were all considered a bit more dodgy than today."

Now that Rafferdy considered it, this arrangement made a great degree of sense. Anyone who saw magicians entering the door wouldn't know where it was that they were really meeting, and without the correct runes they would not be able to follow. They could tear apart the building that contained the door and still not discover the room where the magicians gathered. It was a clever way to keep their meeting place secret in a time when magickal societies were frowned upon or even outlawed.

"So our order does meet beneath a tavern on Durrow Street," he said.

"Or a tavern reached from Durrow Street, I would say. But why is it so interesting to you of a sudden?"

Rafferdy didn't know how to answer that, and before he could think of what to say, the music rose to a crescendo, rising above all conversations. Then the musicians ceased their work, and all in the gallery turned toward the north end as a deep voice—one which could only belong to Sir Quent—thundered out over the room.

"Permit me to introduce to you," he intoned, standing beside the white drape, "a scene of the Annunciation of Cassephia and Hesper."

And the white curtain fell.

CHAPTER THIRTY-FOUR

*I*VY FELT LIKE a leaf afloat on a windswept sea. Her wishes were of no consequence, and as the revelers surged all around her, she could only go where the ebb and flow of their movements took her.

"Your sisters' tableau was magnificent," someone told her. "What a surprising and charming sight," said another. And exclaimed someone else, "How lovely the Miss Lockwells looked!"

Though Ivy's thoughts were awhirl in her head, she managed a smile and a thank-you to everyone who approached her. Yes, the tableau had been all the doing of her sisters, she assured them, and she agreed it was remarkable how very well it had turned out.

In fact, it was more than remarkable; it was extraordinary. The tableau had been a far greater success than Ivy had ever imagined it would be. She had not seen Lily's and Rose's final preparations, for they had kept the tableau secret from all in the house but themselves. Even so, she had been confident that their scene would be met with at the very least polite approval, and perhaps even some amount of genuine delight.

What occurred when Mr. Quent pulled the rope and the curtain fell was something else altogether. Ivy could not say what it was—the illumination of so many candles and lamps, or the way it reflected off the jewels and finery of all the partygoers—but the light in the gallery had appeared to gather about the little stage like a gauze, imbuing all the trappings upon it with a pearlescent sheen and granting them an astonishing verisimilitude, as if they had indeed been just raised up from the sea.

The light had wrought no less of an effect upon Lily and Rose. Dressed in their classical Tharosian costumes, their cheeks and lips tinted coral pink, they were the very image of young goddesses. As the curtain fell to reveal the scene, a gasp had passed through the gallery like a zephyr, followed by a rising gale of murmurs, which quickly broke loose in a storm of hand-clapping that went on and on. All the while Lily beamed upon the stage, never straying an inch from her perfect pose; while Rose, clearly dumbfounded, wore an expression of sweetness that was so natural, and so unaffected, even the most skilled actress could never have hoped to duplicate it.

In all, the scene rivaled any of the tableaux Ivy had ever seen at Lady Crayford's house, and perhaps even surpassed them all. For what could ever be more marvelous to behold than youthful and innocent beauty?

All these thoughts, however, passed fleetingly through Ivy's head, as she was swept to and fro. Instead, it was the words Mr. Rafferdy had spoken to her that kept returning to her mind.

Given my duties, I have not had an occasion of late to meet Mr. Garritt at the Sword and Leaf. . . .

How strange that he should happen to speak such a thing tonight! Her father had used the same words—the Sword and the Leaf—in the entry she had read in the journal just before the party. From her father's words, she had realized that her earlier hypothesis, which she had previously dismissed, was in fact true: Tyberion and Arantus were the two doors that had been discovered in this very gallery. Then, as if somehow knowing what it was she had read in the journal, *he* had appeared to her, the man in the black mask.

Such had been the way he had spoken the command—or rather, how it had sounded in her mind—that for all the suspicion with which she had regarded him and his motives of late, she did not question. Besides, it could not do any harm to conceal Arantus, and she now had no doubt that great harm could arise if it was revealed to the wrong persons.

You must know how important Tyberion and Arantus are, Mr. Lockwell had written. *No one can ever be allowed to use them, for fear of what hideous powers might be unleashed through them.*

For a moment a dread came over her. What if there was someone in this crowd of people around her who sought to use the doors? Only that could hardly be possible. Almost everyone who had been in the Vigilant Order of the Silver Eye was either dead or locked away in Madstone's. Mr. Mundy remained, of course, but she would recognize the toadlike little man on sight, and from what her father had written in his journal, Mundy had remained true to Mr. Lockwell, as had Fintaur and Larken. As for Mr. Bennick, he was in all likelihood far away in Torland. Besides, he no longer possessed any magickal ability with which he might open the door.

Though it was his intention to alter that fact, she was sure. Last year, Mr. Bennick had sought to gain entry to the house, in order to deliver the Eye of Ran-Yahgren to members of his order—no doubt in the hope they would restore his magickal abilities to him in return. Had it been his intention to tell them of the doors as well? Or had he intended to keep them secret and use them himself once he had regained his power as a magician? Ivy could only imagine it was the latter case, before she and Mr. Rafferdy had thwarted his plans. And anyway, he did not possess the key to either of the doors.

The only other magician who had known of Tyberion was Mr. Gambrel himself, for he had fled and escaped after his duplicity was revealed. However, her father had made this treachery known to all the arcane eyes in the house. If Gambrel were ever to try to enter here, they would surely raise an alarm. But they were all of them closed, or silently observing the party.

Which meant the doors were safe.

So why, then, had the man in the black mask told her to hide Arantus? And why had he not told her to hide Tyberion as well? Ivy didn't know, for he had vanished as soon as he spoke that single command. Besides, there would not have been time to arrange a way to conceal both doors. She had gone at once to Mrs. Seenly,

directing her to have the servants move the stage for the tableau—
quickly, before the first guests arrived. Then she had hurried back
to her room to finish dressing for the party.

She returned to the gallery just before the first guests began to
enter. To her relief, the servants had just finished moving the
stage, concealing the leaf-carved door at the north end of the
gallery. Mr. Quent noticed this change and asked her why she had
had it done. Quickly, she had told him how she had seen the man
in the mask again. It was clear from his expression that this news
troubled him, but there was no more time to discuss it, for by then
the first guests were arriving. The gallery rapidly filled, and in the
excitement of the party, thoughts of the journal, the doors, and the
man in black were driven from Ivy's mind.

Only then Mr. Rafferdy had mentioned the Sword and Leaf,
and it had all come back to her.

Yet what did it mean? Her father had written that Gambrel had
been interested in Dratham and the Sword and the Leaf. Only what
did that have to do with the establishment where Mr. Rafferdy met
with his fellow magicians? *That* tavern was not on Durrow Street,
so it could not be Dratham's.

More people called out to Ivy, approached her, spoke to her,
and she was buffeted this way and that about the gallery. She
looked for Mr. Quent, craving the solid anchor of his presence,
and also for Mr. Rafferdy—for she wanted to ask him more about
the Sword and Leaf. However, she could find neither of them. At
one point, she caught a fleeting glimpse of Mr. Garritt from across
the party, only to see him and his handsome, blond-haired friend
exit down a corridor that led from the gallery. She hoped Mr. Garritt was not leaving so soon, for she wished to speak to him more.

Despite her efforts, she was unable to move in that direction.
Instead, a surge in the flow of the partygoers, followed by a sudden ebb, deposited her near to her sisters. A bit of the shimmering
light still seemed to cling to the two of them. Or perhaps it was
they themselves who were glowing. A number of young men had
gathered around them, paying them great attention.

Lily seemed to be captivating half a dozen of them at once,

successfully engaging them all in bright conversation, while Rose spoke to the young men in turn, saying to each "How do you do?"

Ivy smiled at this scene, and the tumult of her thoughts began to calm. This was what mattered most tonight. The sight before her now was everything Mrs. Lockwell could ever have hoped for; indeed, it could only far exceed what had been even her loftiest fancies.

"I wish you could see how beautiful Rose and Lily look, Mother," she said quietly to herself. "And how handsome all of the young men are! You would be so pleased."

"I have no doubt that she would be pleased," spoke a gentle voice.

Startled, Ivy turned around to see Lady Crayford standing beside her.

"You must forgive me, Lady Quent," the viscountess said, her violet eyes concerned. "It was not my intent to impose upon your private thoughts. I had been biding my time, hoping for a chance to speak with you. When I saw that for a moment you were not being monopolized by others, I thought I would be so bold as to seize my chance and approach you."

These words shocked Ivy. "But *you* must never wait your turn to speak to me. For whom could I ever wish to speak to more than you? I cannot imagine such a being!"

"You may soon find that not so difficult a thing to conceive," Lady Crayford said, smiling now. "This may be the Miss Lockwells' party, and the young men are no doubt captivated by them. Yet for many people here tonight—for the most consequential people, I would say—there is only one person they wish to speak to."

"You mean my husband."

"No, Lady Quent. I mean *you*."

Ivy did not know what to say to these words; she was baffled by them.

"I know you are in great demand," Lady Crayford said, "but will you walk with me for a few moments?"

"You need not even ask!" Ivy exclaimed.

Indeed, she suddenly had a desire to speak to no one else at the party save for Lady Crayford; and if they walked together arm in arm, and kept their heads close to each other, they might hope to go uninterrupted for a little while.

"I would be horribly envious, of course, if you were not so dear to me, Lady Quent."

This thought seemed so absurd Ivy could only think her companion was making a jest. "For what reason could you be envious of anyone?"

The viscountess sighed, though her smile did not diminish. "It does seem very ill of me, doesn't it? But you see, I still recall what it was like to make my first entrance in society. The grand affairs, the people, the conversations—everything was so bright, so novel in the beginning. Alas, it is a fact that things can only be new once. Therefore I envy you that pleasure I once had, and which now lies before you."

"Well, if one can expect to find novel things at each circle of society," Ivy said, "then surely you have much to look forward to as well."

Lady Crayford gave a shrug. "I cannot say. It is true that my husband is something of an ambitious man, so perhaps it will be as you predict."

"But is he not here tonight?" Ivy glanced around them. "I was hoping he would be able to come."

"As was he! I fear that something has conspired to keep him away. Yet he sends his regards to you, and also his assurance that he will call on you very soon."

"Then I will look forward to it."

"I believe you have a great deal to look forward to, Lady Quent," the viscountess said, and now her smile took on a mysterious aspect.

"What do you mean?"

"Only that my husband has told me of the whisperings he has heard."

Ivy could only stare. "Whisperings?"

"The viscount may not attend Assembly or make a habit of frequenting parties, but he is very clever in his manner of gaining knowledge. He has learned that your husband is almost certain to be nominated for the post of lord inquirer. And for that to happen, yet another title must be bestowed upon him. While that might seem extraordinary, these are extraordinary times, and as history has shown us, one certain way to rise is to be a great man in a time of great troubles. Who can say what other titles and ranks will be granted to your husband if Altania continues to face dire times?" Her violet eyes were bright as she regarded Ivy. "So you see, Lady Quent, you have much to look forward to indeed."

Ivy hardly knew how to respond to these words. "I do not harbor any hopes for myself in that regard," she managed to say at last. "Already I find myself in a position I could never have conceived even a year ago. Yet if such a thing is bestowed upon my husband, then it will only be because he earned it through his own merits."

Lady Crayford hesitated a moment, then gave her head a slight shake. "No, that is not entirely correct, Lady Quent. He has risen through his own actions, yet I do not believe his actions would be enough to gain the rewards I speak of were you not at his side. You are part of what makes Sir Quent a thing of such charm and fascination. While his deeds might call for the bestowing of new titles, it is *your* presence that assures he will be gladly welcomed into those higher ranks."

"*My* presence?"

"Do not look so astonished! Everyone wishes to be close to you, Lady Quent. You are the talk of all Invarel. There are countesses and earls and even dukes who greatly desired an invitation to this affair tonight. They would never admit to it, of course. To do so would be to reveal they wanted a thing they could not gain, which no one who wishes to maintain their position in society would ever willingly do. But you must trust me that it is true. So do you see? Your husband's rise would be impossible without your own; rather, it entirely depends upon it."

Now Lady Crayford lowered her voice, so others could not possibly hear. "And with your assistance, your husband can only rise higher. With the perils that our nation faces, and the importance of his service, can you not expect him to become an earl, a marquess, or even more? Yet he is so modest! It will be up to you to assure he strives to place himself in a position best able to aid Altania in her time of need. Without you, I fear Altania may be deprived of its most likely hero. You must encourage him to reach as high as possible, so that he will have the necessary vantage to see what needs doing and the force to have it done. It may not be a natural thing for him, but if you encourage him, I know he will do it."

Ivy wanted to say this could not be the case, but she was dumbfounded. Except it was not simply shock that kept her from protesting. Her father had always encouraged her to place reason before sensibility, and Ivy could not deny that there was a logic to what Lady Crayford had said.

Mr. Quent was not a man to seek out power or position. However, if she was able to encourage her husband to strive toward higher positions, would it not be to his benefit? Earlier that evening, he had suggested that there were those in the government who might turn against him if the truth of all he did in Torland was revealed. Yet if he was in a greater position of authority than they, they could not possibly challenge him. And if it was within her power to help him achieve such a thing, how could she not do so?

Again Lady Crayford sighed, though it was a wistful rather than mournful sound. "Do you see now why you are the object of my envy, Lady Quent? It is not for what you have, but because there is so much that lies ahead of you! If you wish it, I believe you will one day find yourself to be a great lady—indeed, one of the greatest ladies in all of Altania."

Ivy was shocked anew. This was an impossible notion to consider. Or at least, it *should* have been.

Before she could speak, Lady Crayford gently disengaged her arm.

"I must relinquish you now, Lady Quent. There are many waiting to speak with you. I will say but one more thing. That is, in the future, when you can command the attention of anyone in Invarel no matter how high they might be, I hope that you will still choose to cast your gaze down a bit and notice me from time to time."

The viscountess smiled again. However, for a moment there was a look in her violet eyes that, to Ivy, seemed almost like a kind of regret. Then, before Ivy could wonder more, Lady Crayford turned to thread her way easily among the crowd that filled the gallery and was gone.

Now that Ivy was no longer so intimately engaged, a number of people hastily approached her. It was Lily who reached her first. Her cheeks were very bright:

"Ivy, it is all so marvelous!" she said, then lowered her voice to a false whisper. "Have you seen how many young men have come to speak to me and Rose? There are at least half a dozen for Rose, and twice as many for me, and each one is more handsome than the next. Sink me if I could fathom how to choose among them!"

Ivy could only smile, despite Lily's continued habit of speaking like a pirate, and was happy to consider such a simple topic for a moment as choosing the best-looking young man. "Indeed, they are all very handsome," she said.

"But I have yet to see Mr. Garritt," Lily continued without drawing a breath. "Have you seen him anywhere?"

Ivy hesitated. She liked Mr. Garritt very much, and she doubted, for all the good-looking young men here tonight, that any could be considered more handsome than he. Yet even when they dwelled on Whitward Street, Mr. Garritt would not have been a suitable match for Lily. And now that their station had been elevated, and might become even higher still . . .

Yet those were unkind thoughts. Mr. Garritt was a friend, and Ivy wished only the best for him. Besides, once Lily saw the benefits that a young man of high standing could offer, her interest in Mr. Garritt would naturally recede. Until then, this was her night, and she should be able to speak to whomever she most wished.

She nodded across the gallery. "I saw him depart down the south corridor just a little while ago. I was hoping he wasn't looking for a discreet way to depart the party."

"Without speaking to me first?" Lily said as if this was the most scandalous suggestion. "I should think not! Knowing Mr. Garritt, he is simply looking for a quiet spot away from all these people to contemplate some bit of poetry."

"I suppose you're right at that," Ivy said, smiling.

But Lily was already weaving her way across the gallery, moving faster than any young man who might have thought to come near her, and vanished from sight.

Now that Ivy was unengaged, there was nothing to prevent the sirs and lords and earls, the ladies and countesses, from approaching to speak with her. Yet, strangely, Ivy found she no longer minded. Why should she not speak with them all?

If you wish it, I believe you will one day find yourself to be a great lady—indeed, one of the greatest ladies in all of Altania. . . .

A warmth came over her, and the dazzling light of the party seemed to become even brighter yet, as Lady Quent smiled and in the most charming and gracious fashion greeted all who came to her.

CHAPTER THIRTY-FIVE

QUICK, THIS WAY!" Dercy whispered as he pulled Eldyn by the hand down the corridor, away from the noises of music and conversation.

"Why are we going down here?" Eldyn whispered back, casting a worried glance over his shoulder.

"To find the real party, of course," Dercy said, flashing a roguish grin. "Everyone knows the best amusements are to be found away from the main affair. There's always a room where people who grow bored with a party gather to take part in more, let us say, engaging diversions."

"I don't think this is that sort of party," Eldyn said with a frown.

"On the contrary, it's precisely that sort of party. The more proper the affair, the more likely it is some people will have slipped away to seek out their own sorts of entertainments."

Eldyn wanted to say that he didn't have to slip away to be content, and that he had been enjoying the party greatly. Just at that moment a woman in a crisp gray dress appeared from around a corner ahead of them, a stack of linens in her arms. The linens blocked her face from their view—and kept the two young men from *her* view—but the knot of red hair atop her head was shot with gray, and Eldyn recognized her as the housekeeper, from his one prior visit here. Before he could think what to do, Dercy grabbed him and pulled him into the corner between a large cabinet and the wall.

"The shadows!" he hissed.

On instinct, Eldyn pulled a dark veil over the two of them— enough to obscure their shapes, but not so much as to result in a darkness that would look out of place. They held their breath, and the housekeeper passed them by without so much as a glance, disappearing in the direction of the party.

Dercy let out his breath, along with a fit of laughter. "Come on," he said, pulling Eldyn from their hiding place and back down the corridor. He tried a door, but it was locked.

"How do you know which room you're looking for?" Eldyn said.

"Oh, I'll know."

He tried another door, but it, too, was locked. Then he went to the one across the corridor from it and turned the knob. The door swung open.

"Here we are!" Dercy said triumphantly. "This is the place."

Eldyn did not think it was appropriate behavior to go prowling about Lady Quent's house. Before he could protest, Dercy gave a jerk on his arm, pulling him into the room and shutting the door behind them. The air grew suddenly dark, then brightened again as a sphere of pearlescent light appeared upon Dercy's outstretched palm.

"What do you mean this is the place?" Eldyn said, looking around at the small sitting chamber. "There's nobody here besides us."

"Precisely," Dercy said, stroking his blond beard in a devilish manner. "As I said, there's always a room at a party where people go off to find more pleasurable diversions."

With that he pulled Eldyn to him, and kissed him.

Eldyn was rather peeved by this revelation, but after a moment he could no longer pretend he did not like what Dercy was doing, and he returned the embrace as the silvery orb of light rose in the air above them. Others joined it, filling the room with soft luminescence.

Dercy looked up at the lights. "Very pretty," he said. "As was the Miss Lockwells' tableau. It was an enormous success, don't you think?"

"As if you don't know the reason for that!" Eldyn said with a laugh.

"I suppose I do," Dercy said, flopping down into one of the chairs. "But it was actually surprisingly good to begin with. I find it hard to believe the Miss Lockwells devised it all themselves."

"I don't find it hard," Eldyn said. "Lily—that is, the youngest Miss Lockwell—is very imaginative, and she has a fine sensibility. I know she reads plays a great deal."

"Well, she's clearly learned something from them. The staging was better than what you'd find at more than a few theaters on Durrow Street. It wasn't difficult at all to make it nearly as good as a scene from a proper illusion play—just a little bit of light here and there was all it needed."

Eldyn winced. He had felt just a little bit awful when Dercy whispered to him in the gallery just after the curtain fell, suggesting they add a few illusions to the tableau, but the temptation had proved impossible to resist. As Dercy had said, the staging was already excellent, and at once Eldyn had seen how its effect could be heightened with only a small amount of light in hues of pearl, coral, and aquamarine.

Besides, they had made only the subtlest improvements. Their intent was not to make it into something it was not, but simply to enhance what the Miss Lockwells had already achieved. Given the gasps and applause that had gone through the gallery, and the expression upon Lily's face, they had succeeded in that task, and any guilt Eldyn might have suffered was assuaged by a pleasure that he had done something to increase the happiness of the youngest Miss Lockwell, for whom he retained a fondness.

It had been good to see her and her sisters, particularly Lady Quent. Given her station, and the great demands upon her attention, he was flattered that she had taken a few minutes to greet him. They had reminisced fondly about the day he and Mr. Rafferdy had visited their house on Whitward Street and they read from the first act of *Alitha and Antelidon*.

There was only one peculiar thing about their conversation, and that was how, as they spoke, Eldyn had begun to discern a faint green light around her. At first he thought it was simply candlelight radiating off her dress of emerald satin. Only the more he paid attention, the more he thought it wasn't from the gown that the green light emanated, but rather from her hands, her throat, and her face. He wondered if Dercy had seen it, and he asked so now.

"Oh, you noticed that, did you?" Dercy said, swinging a leg over the arm of the chair in a cavalier fashion.

"So you saw it as well?"

Dercy nodded. "A few times in the past I've seen a glow such as that around a woman I've passed on the street, but it was always a good deal fainter than that. The illumination around Lady Quent was very bright."

"What does it mean?"

Dercy shrugged. "I haven't any idea."

"But why could we see it?"

"Why can I see the light around you or other Siltheri?"

Eldyn shook his head. "I can't see light around illusionists, not like you do."

"Are you so certain of that? Over time, many illusionists find they can do so—at least those who have a fine sensitivity to our natural light. All you have to do is try."

Eldyn wasn't so sure about that. All the same he gazed at the other young man, concentrating. Then he let out a gasp. For a fleeting moment, it had seemed as if a faint corona, like copper and gold flames, flickered around Dercy.

"Are you doing that?" he said.

"Doing what?" Dercy said. Then he sat up and raised an eyebrow. "You can see the light around me, can't you?"

Eldyn hesitated, then nodded. "I'm not sure—I think so."

"Well, if you're not certain, come here and get a closer look."

This was a suggestion Eldyn willingly took. He crossed the room to Dercy, who took his hand, pulling him downward into a kiss. Eldyn shut his eyes, but he could still see the coppery light. In fact, it was brighter now that he was blind to all other lights, and as if the flickering illumination was indeed from a fire, the most marvelous sort of warmth coursed through him.

A creaking noise sounded behind him.

Even as Eldyn realized what it was from, what was happening, a voice called out.

"Hello, are you in here, Mr. Garritt? Ivy said she saw you come down this way and—oh!"

Hastily Eldyn broke away from Dercy. However, when he turned around, he saw that he had been too slow. Lily Lockwell stood in the open doorway, her brown eyes wide in the pretty oval of her face. Her gaze went to Dercy in the chair, then returned to Eldyn, and the color drained from her cheeks.

"Miss Lily!" Eldyn exclaimed.

Slowly, she shook her head and took a step backward, still clutching the doorknob.

"No, please don't go." He reached a hand out toward her. "Lily—"

She clapped a hand to her mouth to stifle a sobbing sound, then spun around and fled back into the corridor, her white costume billowing like sea foam behind her. Eldyn took a staggering step toward the door, then halted. It was no use; he would never be able to catch her. Even if he did, what would he say to her? The warmth had drained from him, leaving a terrible coldness in his chest.

Behind him, Dercy let out a heavy sigh. "Well, I admit, I hadn't expected *that*. I should have remembered to bolt the door. Only I hadn't thought anyone would have a reason to come in here. Anyone besides us, that is. Well, it's no matter." He held out his hand. "We can continue our little play, for Miss Lily has run off."

"No wonder she ran," Eldyn said. His heart was working at a rapid pace, and it was difficult to draw a breath. "Who would not turn away in the greatest shock from such a sight as she saw? I dread whom she is speaking to even now of what she witnessed."

Dercy scowled. "I certainly would rather she had not seen us, yet I doubt she will speak of it to anyone. You have told me she fancies you, does she not? Thus I am sure she would do nothing to cause you distress. Besides, you speak as if we were doing some awful thing."

A shudder passed through Eldyn. "But it *is* awful, isn't it? At least in the eyes of many people. You cannot deny that. And the Testament says it is—"

Dercy let out a snort. "Pray tell me, who cares what the Testament says? It is beyond me why anyone would think it is a reasonable thing to take instruction from a book that claims the stars are pinpricks in the black bowl of the sky and that milk gotten from a goat during a greatnight will curdle. What a lot of rubbish! Besides, *you* seemed to be enjoying what we were doing. You didn't feel like you were up to something awful, did you?"

Eldyn could only speak the truth. "No, I didn't. It was . . ." At last he was able to draw a breath. "It was wonderful, actually."

Dercy's sea green eyes shone. "There, do you see! You are better to trust to your senses rather than your brain."

As usual, when Dercy was grinning at him, it was difficult for Eldyn to worry about how the Testament or society might view the things the two of them did together. Besides, it didn't matter anyway. All that he had done in his life would be forgotten the moment he entered the Church. So why torment himself now?

He returned Dercy's grin. "I suppose you're right."

"As I ever am. Now come here and let us finish the first act of our little play before we begin the next."

Eldyn felt his fear recede. Dercy was right. It was regrettable that Lily Lockwell had witnessed them together, but he could not imagine she would ever speak of what she had seen. Indeed, more than likely she did not even comprehend what she had glimpsed. Reassured by these thoughts, he went to Dercy and bent down. However, Dercy pressed a finger to Eldyn's lips.

"Are you certain you are not afraid of committing some awful sin?" he said, his tone gently mocking. "I know you are a favorite of the archdeacon's, and I don't want to cause any difficulty between you and your employer."

"You have no worry there," Eldyn said with a laugh. "For I have it from Archdeacon Lemarck directly that it is of no concern anything I might do before I enter the—"

Eldyn clamped his teeth down upon his tongue so hard a taste of metal filled his mouth, but the sacrifice of his blood was in vain.

"It is no concern what you do before you enter what?" Dercy said, his eyes narrowing.

"Before I enter Graychurch each day," Eldyn said. However, even to him the words sounded lame.

Dercy leaped up from the chair. "Do not lie to me, Eldyn. You know that you have no aptitude for it. You mean to enter the priesthood, don't you? That's why you've been scrimping and saving like some miserly old crone. You have been saving for your portion to pay the Church." He ran a hand through his blond hair, so it stood on end. "I should have realized it before. I knew you were up to something! Yet I never guessed it to be this."

"It's not what you think it is!" Eldyn blurted out.

"No, it's precisely what I think," Dercy said, and he prowled around Eldyn. "All this time you have been deceiving me—you have been deceiving all of us. It has never been your intention to be a member of our troupe at the Theater of the Moon. You've been using us to gain a bit of coin, that's all. And if you could have a little amusement along the way at my expense, well so much the better. Then, as soon as you have the money you need, your intention is to avert your gaze from us like so much offal in the gutter while you stride through the doors of the cathedral."

Eldyn's eyes stung, and his cheeks were hot. "No, that's not true!"

"I told you not to lie," Dercy snapped.

Now some of Eldyn's anguish was substituted with anger. "You chastise me for deceiving, you tell me not to lie," he said bitterly. "Well, isn't that all that illusions are? Lies made out of light? How am I supposed to build a future for myself and my sister upon that?"

"Illusions aren't lies," Dercy said. He gave his hand a flick, sending the glowing orbs spinning around the room so that they cast wild shadows. "They are not some unseen, unheard, formless notion that people slavishly mumble prayers to, or which they cite to excuse whatever awful acts they were going to do anyway. Illusions are something we can behold ourselves. Their beauty can illuminate even the darkest life."

"But they're not real!" Eldyn cried.

"And you think the Church is? Did you not hear anything that I told you of the priests at the church of St. Adaris?"

"Graychurch isn't like that."

"All churches are like that. The only difference is how big they are. I'm telling you, Eldyn, the priesthood isn't what you think."

Eldyn held a hand to his brow; it was throbbing. "No, you're wrong, Dercy. I know what you told me about St. Adaris, but the archdeacon is a great man. He has given me a chance—one I could never even have imagined I would get—and I have to seize it."

Dercy was staring at him now, an expression in his sea-colored eyes that Eldyn could not name.

"Don't you see?" Eldyn went on. "I'm weary of living my life hidden in the shadows. I don't want to merely conjure light—I want to dwell in it. This is the only way I know how—it's the only way I can build a happy future for myself and my sister."

At last Dercy spoke, and his voice was low. "I thought we *were* happy. What a fool I was: a Siltheri tricked by phantasms. I see now that it was all just an illusion. And after all that I gave you to—" He shook his head.

Eldyn was trembling now; he couldn't stop. Once before when he was shaking, that night after they saw Gerivel holding Donnebric's body before the Theater of the Doves, Dercy had held him until the spasms passed. Now the other young man stood at arm's length.

"Dercy, please, you have to understand." Eldyn took a lurching step toward him.

At the same moment Dercy took a step back.

"I understand perfectly now, Eldyn." He let out a breath. "To think, once I thought you were an angel standing there in the night."

All at once the illusory lights were snuffed out so that blackness took the chamber. Eldyn fumbled, forcing his shaking hands to be steady. Only by the time he finally managed to conjure a single, wavering light, its pale blue glow revealed what he already knew.

He was alone in the room.

CHAPTER THIRTY-SIX

RAFFERDY HURRIED UP the marble steps before the Halls of Assembly, his robe snapping behind him like a black sail. He wasn't certain if it was due to the fact that he had awakened late after a restless umbral, or if it was because the lumenal had dawned a good deal earlier than it was supposed to have. Either way the result was the same.

He was late.

Not that he would be barred from the Hall for arriving after the High Speaker's gavel had fallen. Members of Assembly generally made a practice of coming and going at all times during the session—as well as eating, sleeping, taking tobacco, and gambling with dice in the wings. The only time it really mattered if one was on the bench was when a vote was called for. All the same, Lady Shayde had continued to observe the proceedings of Assembly of late, and Rafferdy had no wish to straggle into the Hall and thus be singled out for her attention.

To his relief, the bells in the spire that rose above Assembly began to ring out just as he dashed up the final steps, and he fell in with a number of other magnates who were streaming into the Hall. Doing his best to make himself anonymous within the throng, he proceeded to the upper benches where he and the other wigless young lords sat.

He found Lord Coulten already there. The other young man waved and gestured to the seat beside him, which Rafferdy took.

"There you are at last!" Coulten exclaimed.

"I'm sorry," Rafferdy returned. "Were you waiting for me?"

"You know perfectly well I was waiting for you." He lowered his voice and leaned his head toward Rafferdy. "I have been eager to know what you thought of our meeting last night. I wished to speak to you once it was over, only you departed the tavern before I had the chance."

"I was too tired and stupid for conversation," Rafferdy said, and this was true, if not exactly the whole of the truth. "Besides, you seemed happily engaged in speaking with the rest of the initiates."

Coulten grinned, then held a gloved hand beside his mouth as he spoke. "Yes, we were all of us speculating which of the sages was Eubrey."

"Did you determine which one he was?"

"Not at all! We could not any of us agree. I thought he was the second one from the left, for that one fidgeted a bit, as Eubrey is wont to do. But the others said it could not be *him*, that he was too tall to be Eubrey. I suppose they were right at that." Coulten raised an eyebrow. "So, which one do you think was Eubrey?"

Rafferdy considered this. Last night had been the first meeting of the Arcane Society of the Virescent Blade since the party at Mrs. Quent's. Thus, when the notice of the meeting appeared in the black leather book he kept locked in his desk, Rafferdy had been eager for the prescribed day and hour to arrive. He had been curious himself to see if he could discern Eubrey from the other sages by his voice alone, and last night he had opened the magickal door at the back of the Sword and Leaf with great anticipation.

In the chamber beneath the tavern, the sages had sat as they always did: in a line before the curtain that concealed the Door to the inner sanctum. Their number was indeed increased by one from the previous, but the gold robes that draped them from head to toe were heavy, so as to obscure any discernible feature. This meant the only way Eubrey might be recognized was through his voice, and Rafferdy thought attempting to do so would be an amusing game.

As it happened, neither his wish for amusement nor his curiosity were satisfied. Throughout the meeting, only one of the sages spoke, and given his sibilant, slightly lisping voice, it was not Eubrey. Rather, it was the one Rafferdy knew only as the magus of the society, his name being a mystery to all of the initiates, including Coulten.

For a long while the meeting passed in a dull fashion. The magus droned on again about the Three Pillars of Magick, and how the initiates could not be admitted beyond the Door into the sanctum until they mastered them. It was only toward the end of the meeting that the magus brought up a new subject—one that had never been discussed before at any of the meetings Rafferdy attended.

The Wyrdwood.

Rafferdy, who had been drowsing in his seat, lifted his head. He listened as the magus discussed how there was no matter of greater importance facing Altania than the recent Risings. Long ago, magicians had striven against the Wyrdwood, and they had won dominion over it. However, the spells with which the ancient forest had been quelled were imperfect, and one day soon they could expect magicians to be called upon again to wield their will against the Old Trees. It was a day they must all ready themselves for.

Eubrey had said that day at Madiger's Wall that the sages were interested in the Quelling. While Eubrey's experiment had seemed to Rafferdy to have had little point, perhaps his report had done something to encourage the sages on the topic of the Wyrdwood.

They must work against the peril of the Wyrdwood in any manner they could, the magus went on, his voice emanating out of the shadows of his hood. They must expect to wield not only the power of magick against it, but the power of politics as well. Spells might be used to defeat the Old Trees, but only if magicians were allowed by law to do so—for how could magicians approach the groves if soldiers would not allow them?

"Yet you must not worry," the magus intoned in that peculiarly soft, lisping manner. "Know that we have many allies in this matter, for ours is not the only magickal order that is concerned with the Risings. I can promise you, very soon this subject will be brought up in Assembly by members of one such order. We will put a stop to the wood, and those who by their very nature would seek to incite it."

The other magicians had seemed to like this statement, and an excited murmur passed among them. Even Coulten nodded, his eyes alight, but these words left Rafferdy with a peculiar feeling. He found himself thinking of Mrs. Quent and what she had done to stop the Evengrove from Rising that day. It had been brave, and utterly remarkable. Yet if her nature was known, would she not be deemed one "who by their very nature would seek to incite" the Wyrdwood?

The more he thought about this, the more troubled he became. Before long, the magus's voice was reduced to a wordless hissing. Rafferdy fidgeted with the ring upon his right hand, and as soon as the meeting concluded, he left the chamber beneath the tavern. All night he had tossed about on his bed, caught half in a dream in which the sheets were black branches coiling around him while Mrs. Quent watched and smiled.

"Well, go on, then," Coulten said eagerly. "You look as if it's on the tip of your tongue. So which one of the sages last night was Eubrey?"

"I couldn't say," Rafferdy said honestly, then glanced at the Hall around them. "So where is Eubrey anyway this morning?"

Coulten grinned slyly, then he opened his mouth to speak. However, at that very moment the High Speaker banged his gavel, calling the Hall to order. Behind his right shoulder, Lady Shayde sat in her customary seat, her face a pale fog behind the veil that draped her hat.

As usual, the High Speaker's gavel had hardly ceased its clatter before Lord Bastellon was off his bench and requesting to address the Hall. This was granted, if reluctantly. Rafferdy would much rather have heard whatever it was Coulten had been about to tell him. Instead, they all had to endure yet another treatise from Lord Bastellon on how important it was, in these uncertain times, that King Rothard's writ of succession be ratified.

As the old Stout continued his exposition, the Magisters all bristled visibly, but there was nothing they could do about it. They had allowed Bastellon to open debate on all issues concerning Altania, including the writ of succession. Thus there was nothing the Magisters could do but listen as the old Stout marched before the Speaker's podium in his crooked wig and cast his words and spittle in all directions.

Rafferdy imagined Lord Farrolbrook must be particularly peeved by the situation, as it was due to his miscalculation that Lord Bastellon's gambit had succeeded. Only, when he looked down at where Farrolbrook sat with the other Magisters, he was surprised to see that the fair-haired lord was paying Bastellon no attention. Instead, he gazed at the domed ceiling above, an absent look upon his usually haughty face, all the while fidgeting with one of the many frills of his robe.

At last Bastellon seemed to have run out of his reservoir of words and phlegm, and he marched back to his seat among the other Stouts.

"You say we must honor the king's will on the matter of succession, Lord Bastellon," spoke a loud voice. "But is that really wise at this time?"

The High Speaker's gavel struck the podium. "The Hall recognizes Lord Mertrand!"

The lord who sat next to Farrolbrook rose and stepped forward. He was tall and impressive in a simple but stylish black robe, and he turned slowly as he spoke, regarding the Hall with a keen, dark-eyed gaze.

"The Wyrdwood stirs as it has not done in living memory," the tall Magister went on. "Risings have taken the lives of men not only in Torland, but also no more than twenty miles from where we stand at this very moment. I hope it will be a long while before we have to worry about who will succeed our king, but that day will come. And when it does, despite the peril we face from the Wyrdwood, Lord Bastellon suggests that we willingly consent to put a woman upon the throne!"

At this mutters and murmurs ran about the Hall, and Lord Bastellon leaped to his feet. However, when he tried to sputter out angry words, he was drowned out by the clamor of the High Speaker's gavel.

"The floor belongs to Lord Mertrand!"

Lord Bastellon glowered at this, but he could do nothing save return to his seat.

"Thank you, High Speaker," Mertrand said with a nod toward the podium. "At this time I would like to relinquish the floor to the leader of my party. That is, to Lord Farrolbrook."

These words seemed to catch Farrolbrook unawares, for he jumped a bit in his seat, then stared at Lord Mertrand. Mertrand made a gesture toward the center of the Hall, and after a moment Farrolbrook blinked, then stood and made his way forward as Mertrand retreated.

"Thank you," Farrolbrook said. "Thank you, Lord Mertrand,

I do have something I wish to say on this matter. These are indeed grave times, and I wish to say . . ." He drew a breath. "That is, it is my belief that . . ."

His words faltered and fell short, and he stood still for a moment, his head slightly tilted, as if he was listening to some far-off sound. Silence fell over the Hall as all eyes gazed at him. Suddenly he shook his head.

"Forgive me, High Speaker, I do not have anything to say after all."

With that he turned and went back to his seat. Noises of surprise rose up all around the Hall, and the Magisters watched the fair-haired lord with looks of confusion—and perturbation. Farrolbrook seemed confused himself. He continued to shake his head as he returned to his seat. Once there, he hunched over and, in a rapid manner, turned the red-gemmed ring on his finger round and round.

"Great God," Coulten whispered delightedly in Rafferdy's ear, "I quite think Lord Farrolbrook has lost command of his wits! Not that he had that many to begin with."

Rafferdy was inclined to concur. But if Farrolbrook had misplaced his wits, Mertrand retained full command of his, and he leaped back from his seat before the floor could be turned over to another speaker.

"Lord Farrolbrook is overcome with worry for our nation," the dark-eyed lord said. "Therefore, I will give voice to his concerns—which ought to be the concerns of every man of reasonable mind in this Hall."

He paced across the floor now, his voice rising so that it commanded attention. "Is it not enough that our nation is beset by outlaws and traitors? Shall we give them a place to harbor themselves as well? It is well known that last year a band of nefarious rebels sought refuge in a grove of Wyrdwood in the West Country. There they made a most unholy alliance with a witch, and so used the stand of Old Trees as a place to hide themselves, and a fortress from which they could strike out to commit all manner of awful crimes. Who knows what other traitors have made similar alliances and even now are concealing themselves in ancient groves, plotting against our nation?"

He turned to direct his gaze at Lord Bastellon. "We cannot know, of course. Which is why, if we truly wish to do something to address the future of our nation in these troubled times, we should not be taking up the king's writ of succession. Rather, we should be voting on an act in favor of cutting down, burning, and forever destroying every stand, every grove, every remnant of Wyrdwood in all of Altania, down to the last tree!"

At once a great commotion broke out in the Hall. There were expressions of shock all around—though not among the Magisters, Rafferdy noted. They evinced no surprise and gazed at Lord Mertrand serenely. All except for Lord Farrolbrook, that was, who continued to slump in his seat and fidget with the ring on his right hand.

The High Speaker struck his gavel, calling for order, and Lord Mertrand spread his arms wide in a gesture that begged for silence.

"Why do you exhibit such astonishment?" he called out, his voice rising above the uproar. "It is no startling thing I suggest. What is startling to me is that we have allowed the Wyrdwood to endure for as long as we have. And why? Because the groves represent some quaint and picturesque relic of our history? I do not believe the men who died in Torland, or the brave soldiers who lost their lives at the Evengrove, would call them such. What purpose can the Old Trees serve? What benefit can they possibly bring to our nation that offsets the peril they pose? Answer these questions, and then tell me why we shouldn't cut down the trees."

Rafferdy had to admit, this was a question he had wondered about himself. Why had remnants of a thing that had long posed such a peril been allowed to remain over the centuries, preserved in patches behind old stone walls? Why hadn't it all been burned and cleared from the land long years ago? Surely it was not out of some sort of nostalgia.

"Why not?" Mertrand called out again, sweeping his gaze across the Hall. "Why not cut down the last of the Wyrdwood?"

An old lord, one of the Stouts, pushed himself to his feet, his face reddened and wrinkled from years of sun and wind. "Because the more the old wood is harmed, the more it will rise up and fight us!" he shouted. "Any fool in the country knows that!"

A number of *hear, hears* followed this, but Mertrand gave a dismissive wave of his hand.

"Well, we all know there are plenty of fools in the country," he said, his lips curving upward ever so slightly.

At this, the face of the Stout who had spoken grew redder yet, but his attempts at a rejoinder were drowned out by a roar of laughter, and he sank back to his bench, fuming.

"Besides," Mertrand went on, "we may soon find we have no choice in the matter. If our good Stouts have their way, and Assembly chooses to ratify the king's writ of succession, we will one day—for only the third time in the entire history of our nation—have a woman upon the throne. We all know what is told of Queen Elsadore, and of Queen Béanore before her. Why should we imagine *this* queen would be different? In which case, will we not be forced to scrub all traces of the Wyrdwood from our fair island? For if we do not, how can we be certain Her Majesty would not hear its call, and perhaps even heed it, just as the only two queens before her are said to have done?"

A great gasp went around the Hall, and suddenly all fell to silence. The air became as the skin of a drum—pulled overtaught, and vibrating with even the faintest cough or scrape of a boot.

At last Lord Bastellon rose again. Previously, when he spoke, there had been something of a buffoonish air about him, in his dowdy robe and yellowed wig. But now his face was grim and anything but laughable.

"You warn us of traitors, Lord Mertrand," he said, and for all that the words were spoken low, they carried throughout the Hall. "Now I will warn you—do not make a traitor of yourself with your words. You may speak against royal acts and royal decrees you believe to be irresponsible. That is our right, our duty even. But to speak against the royal person—by all the laws of our realm, that is a crime of the highest treason."

Mertrand raised an eyebrow. "Do you threaten me, Lord Bastellon?"

"I threaten any who would dare to set himself up as a rebel and a traitor to Altania," the old Stout said. "And I swear it to you, Lord Mertrand, I will do everything in my power to see them each and all hung."

With that, he gave his wig a firm tug, then went back to his bench.

A buzzing filled the Hall, like that of a hive into which a stick has been thrust. Mertrand returned to his place in an unhurried manner, and if Bastellon's words had affected him in any way, he did not show it. Only for a moment did the calmness of his visage alter, and that was when he cast a brief frown at Lord Farrolbrook. This look went unnoticed by its subject, however, who continued to stare at the House ring on his right hand.

It was then that Rafferdy realized Farrolbrook was not wearing gloves like the rest of the Magisters or the other young magicians in the Hall. A flicker of darkness caught his eye, and he turned to see that Lady Shayde had lifted her veil. Her dark eyes were fixed not upon Lord Mertrand as might have been expected, but rather on Lord Farrolbrook.

After these events, a few small pieces of business were brought up, but by then no one was interested in discussing matters of politics in the Hall. Rather, they were ready to talk about them over rum and ale at the Silver Branch. Soon the High Speaker's gavel clattered down, signaling the end of the session.

"Well, that was remarkable!" Coulten exclaimed. "I never would have imagined any topic Lord Bastellon might bring up could lead to so entertaining a display."

Rafferdy wasn't certain *entertaining* was the word he would have chosen, though it had all been fascinating, to be sure.

"I only wish Eubrey had been here to see it," Coulten went on.

"Where is he, by the way?" Rafferdy said as they left their seats. "You were going to tell me when the session was called to order."

Coulten cast several—rather conspicuous—glances around them, then leaned in close. "I don't know precisely. I received a note from him yesterday before our meeting at the tavern. He said only that he had something of great importance to do, some task that had been given to him by the sages."

"What task?"

"He was not at liberty to say, though I suspect it has something to do with his experiment at the Evengrove. Yet that wasn't all he said in the note. He wrote that the sages had been keeping their eyes on me, that they have been making plans with me in mind. Eubrey thinks that I am sure to be the next magician in the society to be invited through the Door." He gave a broad grin. "What do you think of that, Rafferdy? You aren't going to beat me to the inner sanctum after all!"

Rafferdy could only grin back. "I am not surprised, Coulten. You have ever been higher than me!" He directed his gaze at his companion's lofty crown of hair.

This caused them both to laugh as they proceeded down the steps. However, after a moment Rafferdy's mirth faltered. He felt a chill on the back of his neck, and he glanced up. Across the Hall, Lady Shayde had risen from her seat, and her black eyes were directed not at Farrolbrook or Mertrand or any other magnate, but rather at *him*. Despite his efforts to do nothing to attract her notice, he had failed. But how?

Then he caught a glint of blue as a stray beam of sunlight struck his right hand, and he understood. There had been only two men in the Hall who had worn their House rings openly, and one of them was Lord Farrolbrook.

Rafferdy shivered, then he stuck his right hand in his pocket.

"Come on," he said. "There won't be a free bench at the Silver Branch if we don't hurry."

And he led the way out of the Hall of Magnates.

🍂

EVENING WAS JUST falling by the time Rafferdy departed the Silver Branch, and while he had not yet had his fill of rum, he'd had more than his fill of politics.

He had not taken part in any of the discussions himself, but they had gone on all around him and Coulten. Most of the discussions concerned who had gotten the best of the other that day at Assembly: Lord Mertrand or Lord Bastellon. Expectedly, many lords came down firmly on Mertrand's side. But there were a surprising number who scored the day for Bastellon, and not all of them were old Stouts in greasy wigs.

All the same, as the afternoon wore on and the spirits flowed, Rafferdy overheard more and more men echoing Mertrand's question—why hadn't the Wyrdwood been burned down before, and why shouldn't they do so now?

Each time he heard this question spoken, it left Rafferdy with an unsettled feeling, though he did not know why that should be. After all, he had neither interest in nor affection for the Wyrdwood, and he had seen firsthand what awful power it had. He would not soon forget the way the black branches had plucked up the soldier that day, shaking him as a capricious child might punish a doll. It had been a dreadful sight.

All the same, the more he heard men speaking of destroying the Old Trees, the more fretful his thoughts became, and the more rum he craved. After a time, he found himself turning his House ring around and around on his finger. By its blue gem and the runes etched on its side, he was descended from Gauldren, Altania's first great magician, who had placed the Quelling upon the Wyrdwood. Eubrey had said that the Quelling was imperfect, and that was why magicians would one day be needed again.

Yet Rafferdy found himself wondering if that was really the case. What if Gauldren's spell had worked exactly as he had intended it to? Perhaps it had been his wish only to make the Wyrdwood slumber, and there was some reason not to destroy it outright. After all, were there not other ways to control the wood? He thought of what Mrs. Quent had done that day, how the Old Trees had grown subdued at her bidding.

Finally some intoxicated lord had stood up on a table and called for torches to be brought to the Evengrove that very night. He was promptly hauled back down by others, of course; no one was *that* drunk. All the same, Rafferdy found himself no longer in any mood to stay, and he said his farewells to Coulten.

As he walked down Marble Street, Rafferdy found he was in no mood to go back to his home on Warwent Square either. He considered it only for a moment, then he hailed a hack cab and issued familiar instructions.

A quarter hour later the carriage halted on a dingy street before a squat, dingy building. Hanging above the door was a faded sign, barely visible in the light of a sputtering streetlamp, which illustrated a sword piercing the center of a large, curling leaf.

He had checked his black book earlier, and there had been no notice of a meeting of the society tonight. That was just as well, for it was not magick he wished to partake of. Instead, seeking familiar comfort, he entered the tavern and went to his favorite booth in one corner.

To his dismay he found it occupied by a lone figure in gray. Having no wish to attempt conversation with a stranger, he started to turn to go find another table, only then the booth's occupant raised his head.

"Garritt!" he said in surprise.

While at the same time the other exclaimed, "Rafferdy!"

They stared at each other for a moment. At last Rafferdy overcame his astonishment.

"May I?"

"Of course!" Eldyn leaped to his feet and called for another cup. Once this was brought they both sat, and he filled Rafferdy's cup with punch. They both took long draughts.

"So, what are you about tonight?"

Eldyn made a wordless gesture toward his cup.

"Ah," Rafferdy replied.

They sat in silence for a while. For all that he had long been wanting to meet with his old friend, to catch up on affairs in both of their lives, Rafferdy found he had little desire to speak. For his part, Eldyn seemed to share this disinclination for talk. All the same, it felt good to be here in this familiar place, with this familiar person before him. For perhaps the first time since his father had passed, Rafferdy felt at ease.

"Well, how have you been, you rascal?" Rafferdy said at last, when it felt natural to do so. "You looked very well at the party for the Miss Lockwells, I must say."

This seemed to Rafferdy an innocuous statement, but it elicited a grimace from his companion. The last time they had met here, Garritt had been uncharacteristically cheerful—so much so that Rafferdy had told him to affect his more usual air of melancholy when next they met.

Garritt had lived up to this demand. His face was wan, his gaze mournful, and he was prone to sigh every time he set down his cup. Yet now that his friend had become his more naturally glum self, Rafferdy could not say he was satisfied.

"You need not speak of it if you do not wish," he said, refilling their cups, "but has your business you were scheming taken an ill turn?"

Garritt laughed a little at this. "No, on the contrary, it all has gone exceedingly well—far better than I had thought. My plan is nearly at fruition, and far sooner than I expected."

"Well, I am glad to hear it."

"Are you?" Garritt shook his head. "I suppose I should be glad as well, only . . ." He gazed down into his cup.

"Only what?" Rafferdy said.

Garritt looked up at him, his eyes reflecting the smoky lamplight. "Have you ever had to give up something—a thing that was precious to you, which you adored more than almost anything—because there was something else that you had to do instead? Something that you knew to be the right thing, even if perhaps it was not so dear to you?"

Now Rafferdy looked at his own cup, and it was he who grimaced. Asked such a question, how could he think of anything but the day he had wished to go to Mrs. Quent, then Miss Lockwell, and ask her for her hand. Only he had opened his door to find his father standing there, and Lord Rafferdy had convinced him not to do his heart's bidding, but rather to do his duty, which he knew to be right.

Yet had it been?

Rafferdy took a swig of punch. "Yes, I believe I have faced such a situation as you describe. And I will say this, Garritt." He looked up at his friend. "You should not do what you think to be the right thing. Rather, you should act as your wishes and your heart direct you."

"I see." His companion drew a breath. "Only you didn't, did you?"

Rafferdy hesitated, then shook his head.

Garritt let out a sigh. "I suppose I am bound to do the same."

They drank in companionable silence after that, until all the punch was gone. Then, though neither said it, they both knew it was time to go, and they rose to their feet.

"I hope one day you can tell me of your business, and what you decided," Rafferdy said as they clasped hands firmly.

Garritt nodded. "It was good to see you, Rafferdy. Let us not make it so long before our next meeting. I will be . . . that is, I may have news for you then."

With that, they went out together into the night. Rafferdy raised a hand to hail a hack cab that was rattling by, then turned to ask Eldyn if he needed a ride anywhere.

But his friend was nowhere in view, and all he saw were shadows.

CHAPTER THIRTY-SEVEN

HE SCRATCHING OF Eldyn's pen was the only noise to controvert the silence of the vaulted room beneath Graychurch.

He bent over the church ledger in the dwindling light that fell from the window high above his desk, totaling neat columns of figures. In the past, he had always derived a satisfaction from the act of transforming a jumbled box of receipts and demands into precisely aligned rows upon a page. It had let him believe that, with the proper application of intellect and ink, any sort of muddle might be brought into order. Only now, no matter how many times he checked his ciphering, the sums never seemed to work out right.

Other sounds broke the quietude: the thumping of heavy footfalls, and the groan of a door.

"But, Mr. Garritt, you are still here!"

Eldyn looked up to see the plump form of the rector of Graychurch in the doorway.

"Hello, Father Gadby," he said.

"I had come back only to make certain all the candles were put out," the rector said, proceeding in a swift waddle toward him. "I had a sudden fright that I had left one burning. I see I did not, but I am glad I came all the same. It is past time for you to have gone home."

"I was only just trying to finish these last receipts."

The rector clucked his tongue. "I am sure you are anxious to earn your portion to enter the Church, Mr. Garritt, and your diligence is commendable, but tomorrow is another lumenal. What's more, every good priest knows when it is time for labor and when it is time for contemplation. Now, put down your pen, and go to your sister. I'm sure she wants for you."

So directed, Eldyn could only do what the rector asked, and he put up his work.

"Do not look so doleful, Mr. Garritt!" Father Gadby said with a smile. "You will be a priest soon enough. Why, I am quite sure that God already has a task set out for you."

Eldyn only nodded, then ascended the stairs to the church above. The priests were chanting the evening prayers. Often, when his work was done for the day, Eldyn would stand among the saints in the ambulatory and listen for a little while. However, this evening there was a dissonance to the chanting of the priests, as if several of them intoned the words in an off key. What's more, they had thrown too much incense upon the braziers, so that the air was cloying to breathe and made his eyes sting.

He did not pause, passing through the dimness of the nave and out into the twilight.

Usually he would be in a hurry to get to the theater, as following middle lumenals rehearsals typically commenced an hour after nightfall. However, he walked slowly to the old monastery and took the stairs at a deliberate pace. He wondered if he would encounter Mr. Fantharp. Only there was no one else on the stairs, and he soon entered the little apartment.

As usual, he found Sashie reading from the Testament by the dimming window. She did not look up to greet him as he entered. He saw that she had not set out the supper things that had been left by the cooking lady, so he did this himself and lit a few candles—though not so many as he might have before, as they had not had many from Mr. Fantharp of late.

As soon as he finished these actions, Sashie rose, gave him a brief, cool kiss on the cheek, and sat at the table. He asked her how she had occupied herself that day, but then regretted it, for she proceeded to tell him the story of every martyred saint she had dusted in the church. With what seemed great relish she recounted which ones had been shot with arrows by barbarians and which had been made to drink hot lead due to their faith.

"What of you, brother?" she said as she licked bits of an apricot tart from her fingers. "Are you going to stay and read from the Testament tonight? I can show you some verses I believe you might find to be . . . of interest to you."

She gestured to the book on the table, which she must have set there. Compared to her own well-frayed copy of the Testament, his looked as if it were newly printed, and there was a thin layer of dust upon the cover. While he was far from eager to go to the theater, the thought of staying in that cramped room and reading from the Testament with her caused a shudder to pass through him. He pushed away from the table and stood.

"I'm afraid I have business to attend to."

"Do you? Perhaps I am in error, but I thought that your only business was to work toward entering the priesthood." She laid a hand on the copy of the Testament. "Yet you are so often gone at night, and I must begin to wonder, brother, what sort of virtuous business you can possibly have after dark?"

What little food he had managed to consume now churned in his stomach. Her face, despite its roundness, seemed hard, like that of some marble saint glaring from its niche.

"Whatever it is, it is no business of yours and is mine alone!" he cried, and while the words sounded angry, it was more out of a dread that he had raised his voice.

Despite the volume of the words, Sashie did not flinch. "It may not be *my* business, as you say, brother. Yet Father Prestus tells me that all we do in this world is the business of Eternum, else it is the work of the Abyss. I only hope you know which it is you are doing tonight."

With that, she picked up his copy of the Testament and one of the candles and went into her room. For a moment Eldyn stared at the dirty plates on the table. Then he put on his gray coat and, without pausing to check his appearance in the mirror, went out into the night.

He did not draw the shadows around him as he proceeded through the streets of the Old City. Why should he bother when he already felt like a shadow himself? Nor did anyone accost him, and despite his reluctance to go that night, he found himself arriving at the Theater of the Moon just as the rehearsal was commencing.

The last two nights had been performances, and Eldyn had been able to fulfill his role and depart the theater without ever having to encounter Dercy except upon the stage, at which times the play scripted their actions. However, there would be no avoiding him tonight, for it was to be a rehearsal. Eldyn tried to think of what he would say to him.

It did not matter, for Dercy was not there. He had sent a note earlier stating that he was ill, Riethe said when Eldyn asked about his whereabouts. At this news, Eldyn suffered at once a pang of relief and disappointment. He found that he wanted more than anything to see Dercy, and to tell him he did not want to have an argument with him.

Except what use was there in it? In the end it would not change what Eldyn had to do. As he had told Rafferdy at tavern last night, he was bound to do what he knew was right. While he would never have wished for him and Dercy to part in such a manner, it did not alter the fact that they would have had to part soon enough anyway. Perhaps it was better it had happened this way, so that the pain was done with swiftly instead of drawn out.

All the same, as the rehearsal progressed, Eldyn could not help glancing at the wings of the stage, wondering if he would see a young man with a blond beard grinning there. Only he never did, and soon the rehearsal ended—somewhat earlier than usual, for there had been no new staging.

"I am disappointed you have not devised some remarkable new way to present one of our scenes, Mr. Garritt," Master Tallyroth said as the illusionists left the stage. His voice was thin and tremulous, as was the hand with which he gripped his cane, but his gaze was as sharp and bright as ever.

"I'm sorry, I haven't had any good ideas of late," Eldyn said, ducking his head. Before the master illusionist could say anything more, he hurriedly departed the stage with the rest of the young men.

He followed the others down the street and into a nearby tavern, one of their favored haunts. It was not that Eldyn was in the mood for merriment, but he had no wish to return to the apartment for fear Sashie was still up. Besides, he could not deny that he thirsted for a cup of punch.

They took up their usual residence in the tavern. One cup became two, then three. Soon the others were conjuring phantasms with their customary enthusiasm. While Riethe's hand had at last begun to improve, he was making a show of pretending that his injury was yet causing him difficulty in properly forming illusions, and he fashioned daisy-headed mice and fairies with playing cards for wings and all manner of grotesqueries, so that soon even tall, dour Merrick was laughing. Eldyn smiled from time to time, but he could summon no laughter—though he drank his punch with diligence.

It was as Eldyn set down his fourth cup that he noticed a young man sitting all alone on the other side of the tavern. By his powdered face and the folded silk fan tucked into the pocket of his velvet coat, he was an illusionist, but he conjured no phantasms. Instead, he drank whiskey, though he did this with great difficulty. His entire body was gripped by a constant and violent palsy, and he was forced to clasp the cup in two hands to bring it to the thin gray line of his lips.

"Poor sod," Mouse said cheerfully, nodding toward the illusionist. He took the pitcher in front of Eldyn and filled his cup. "It's a pity he isn't already out of his misery. He will be soon enough, I suppose."

The content of Mouse's words astonished Eldyn as much as their indifferent manner. "Do you know him, then?"

The little brown-haired man shook his head. "No. I've seen him on the street from time to time, that's all. But I don't need to know him to know what's wrong with him. It's the mordoth, of course."

Eldyn was astonished anew. "The mordoth? Yet he is not old at all!" Indeed, despite his sunken cheeks and bony fingers, Eldyn would have guessed the solitary illusionist to be no older than he was.

Mouse squelched a swig of punch between his teeth. "You don't have to be old to get the Gray Wasting. You just have to be a chump."

"You mean he's been casting too many illusions?"

"Him? No, he has been on Durrow Street hardly more than a year, I'm sure of it. You could make all the illusions you wanted, and you'd never have a hint of the mordoth in so little time. But I've seen him before, hanging on those painted old scags from the Theater of the Fans, letting them have their way with him, like he hadn't any idea what he was giving up to them."

Eldyn's head was foggy from all the punch. "What do you mean? What was he giving to them?"

"His light, of course. Now he's got barely a spark of it left, like one ember left in the fireplace after a cold, dark greatnight. Soon even that will burn out."

Eldyn must have been groggier than he thought; he could not have heard correctly. "But you can't give someone your light!"

"Of course you can. In fact, you can't help it. Even as we sit here and talk, a little bit of my light goes to you and yours into me. It's tiny, though—not enough to matter in a hundred years. But every exchange between Siltheri is an exchange of light. A touch gives more, and a kiss—well, a kiss is downright perilous between illusionists." He took another swig of punch.

Eldyn stared at him, trying to understand. "But if the light goes back and forth, it can't be all that awful."

"It doesn't work like that," Mouse replied with a sharp laugh. "Someone always comes out the better. There's the kisser and the one being kissed, if you see what I mean—the one as gets the light, and the other as gives it. Then there are perils far greater than kisses. We know how dangerous *those* are. Yet we still can't help ourselves sometimes when we see a pretty lad, can we?"

He winked and gave Eldyn a salacious grin.

"In the end, it all usually evens out. Unless . . . ." Mouse cast a glance at the lone illusionist, and his grin went flat. "Unless you're fool enough to always give, and give again, and never receive your-self. Those pinch-faced old spiders at the Theater of the Fans—

they're always spinning webs for young illusionists they can feed on to make their own illusions grander. As if any amount of light they steal could help their awful themes and staging! But they always seem to find willing idiots. They tell them they'll be lead players one day, that all they have to do is just give up a little of what they have, and a little more. Until they've used up all there is. Then, once there's nothing left to get, they toss what remains of the fool back in the gutter."

Eldyn could only stare at the small illusionist in horror. "Surely people can be selfish and not think of what their actions do to another. But no one can truly be so wicked as to do such a thing intentionally!"

"Of course they can, and worse. I would have thought Dercy had warned you about Siltheri like that. With the wonders you've been conjuring of late—why, I'd think you would draw decrepit illusionists to you like moths to a flame. *You* seem to have more than your share of light."

"And you think they would take it from me?"

"Take it?" Mouse's eyes went wide. "Now *that* would truly be an evil! No, your light must be freely given. But that doesn't mean a man still isn't awful for always receiving and never giving. So keep your wits about you, Eldyn. You don't want to end up like that wretched fellow."

Even as he said this the lone illusionist stood, and in the most feeble and halting steps shuffled out of the tavern and was gone. Mouse drained his cup, filled it again, then turned to laugh at another of Riethe's disfigured phantasms, a rabbit with tobacco pipe ears. Eldyn pushed his own cup away; the punch he had drunk curdled in his stomach.

As he drew his hand back, he saw that it was trembling, not unlike the illusionist with the mordoth. Yet surely he was far from ever having the Gray Wasting.

You seem to have more than your share of light, Mouse had said.

Perhaps he did, but why was that so? Eldyn had never been able to explain it. One day he could conjure no more than the simplest illusions, while the next he could summon wondrous phantasms. Something had changed the night they saw Donnebric lying dead before the Theater of the Doves. The night he and Dercy had first kissed . . .

His trembling worsened, and the punch churned in his stomach. What else had Mouse said?

A kiss is downright perilous between illusionists . . .

"No," he said aloud, though the word was drowned out in the laughter of the others. "No, Dercy, say that you didn't. . . ."

Eldyn swallowed the sour bile in his throat, then heaved himself to his feet.

"Where are you going?" Mouse said, frowning at him. "The night's just begun."

"Back," he said. It was all he could manage without spilling all the punch he had drunk onto the straw that covered the floor. Before Mouse or the others could protest, he lurched to the door and out into the night.

Once outside, Eldyn turned about dizzily, unsure which way to go. Then the cool night air cleared his head somewhat, and he stumbled down the lane. He started to weave the shadows around himself, then stopped. Whose light was he using to craft the illusion? Was it even his own?

He left the shadows where they were, and went naked through the night.

ELDYN WOKE TO brilliant light.

"Dercy!" he cried out, sitting up in bed, blinking against the gold glare that had dispelled the darkness.

Then his vision cleared, and he saw it was not an illusory light that filled the little room above the theater; rather, it was the radiance of dawn. Last night, when he returned to the theater, he had found the room empty. He had meant only to rest on the bed for a little while as he waited for Dercy to return, but he must have fallen asleep as he lay there. Now the lumenal had come, though it had not brought Dercy with it.

Eldyn started to stand, then groaned and sank back to the bed, holding a hand to his temple. His head throbbed from the after-effects of punch. Or was it the awful knowledge he had drunk in at the tavern last night that had induced the pain?

He looked down at his hands. How pleased he had been with himself, how astonished at his newfound ability to conjure illusions. Only all this time, they hadn't been his own. None of them were.

Well, he could not give back what he had taken without knowing, but he would never again conjure phantasms. Today he would tell Madame Richelour that he was quitting the Theater of the Moon. Nor would this greatly delay his plans for himself and his sister. His wages at the theater had been so generous recently that he had amassed nearly enough to pay for both of their portions. There was only one more thing he needed to do here.

The theater was quiet as Eldyn went downstairs, for it was not a habit of illusionists to rise early. Mrs. Murnlout was moving about in the little kitchen, and he asked the cook if she had seen Dercy.

She hadn't, but Dercy would have to return to the theater eventually. He might skip a rehearsal, but he would never miss a performance. Besides, Eldyn would have to come back later himself, to speak with Madame Richelour. For now he drank a cup of coffee that the cook gave him, then left the theater and went out into the morning.

The brilliant light of morning did nothing to improve the appearance of Durrow Street, but rather laid bare its grime and squalor. The theaters, which appeared so mysterious and enticing by moonlight, were exposed by the beams of the sun for what they really were: shabby old buildings with sagging facades, their foundations riddled with rat holes. Eldyn squinted against the morning glare, then made his way down the street.

He was brought up short as a boy dashed before him, holding up fresh copies of *The Swift Arrow* for sale. Eldyn started to wave the boy aside, only then the fragment of a headline caught his eye, and a bolt of fear stuck him.

"Here, I'll take a copy!" he called out.

The boy shifted from foot to foot as Eldyn fumbled for a penny in his pocket. The urchin snatched the coin as soon as it was produced, thrust a broadsheet at Eldyn, then ran down the street. A sick feeling churned in Eldyn's stomach as he raised the newspaper.

ONE ILLUSIONIST NOT SO EASILY DISPATCHED, read the headline in the middle of the page. Quickly, Eldyn scanned the article below. It described how another body of a young man had been dredged from the waters of the Anbyrn, his eyes missing just like those of the others. Only this corpse had differed in one regard, for much to the surprise of those who pulled it from the river, it had begun to move, and then even attempted to speak.

For an awful moment, Eldyn feared that it was Dercy, and this was the reason he had been missing. Only as he read the article, it was clear from the description of the body that it was not Dercy. Nor could it be anyone from the Theater of the Moon, as this had all occurred yesterday evening, and no one besides Dercy had been missing at rehearsal.

Though it was awful another illusionist had met an ill fate, Eldyn could only feel relief that it had not been Dercy or one of the players at the Theater of the Moon. However, his relief vanished as he read the remainder of the article. In its place, a dread came over him.

It had to be a coincidence; such a connection was impossible. Only it seemed so strange, and even as he folded up the broadsheet, he could not stop thinking about it. There was only one way he could be certain.

He had to get to Graychurch at once.

THE SUN WAS rising slowly that morning, and Father Gadby must have been following suit, for when Eldyn tried the door of the rector's office he found it locked. At that moment the verger came tottering down the stairs, and after Eldyn helped the old man to safely climb down the last few steps, he was more than willing to open the door with a key.

Once inside, Eldyn went to the cabinet where he kept those receipts that he had already entered in the ledger. He pulled out a drawer, then began looking through slips of paper.

It didn't take him long to find what he wanted. He went to the table where he worked and set down a receipt. Then he pulled the copy of *The Swift Arrow* from his pocket and unfolded it on the table. Once again, he read the final words of the article on the front page.

We are as surprised as anyone that such a soft and mincing creature as an illusionist should prove so startlingly resilient, the author wrote. *However, to endure after being beaten, blinded, and heaved into the river suggests that at least this particular Siltheri had some strength in him. In the end, though, it was not enough, and an hour after he was taken from the river he expired. Nor, for all that he tried to speak, was anything intelligible gotten out of him, and the only words he uttered that could be made out were something about "red curtains below the crypt." Yet perhaps that was a fitting epitaph. For does not the fall of a crimson curtain signal the end of every illusion play on Durrow Street? And shortly after he spoke those words, this player's final performance was at its end, and it was off to the crypt for him. Bravo!*

Again Eldyn felt a dread that was not simply due to the unfortunate illusionist's fate. He set down the broadsheet and picked up the slip of paper he had taken from the drawer. It was a receipt for a set of red curtains, dated just a few days ago, and was signed by Archdeacon Lemarck himself.

Eldyn had entered at least a half-dozen other receipts like it in the ledger. He had always supposed the curtains were meant for some cardinal or bishop with ostentatious taste. But what if the curtains had some other purpose? He recalled what Dercy had told him once, how only the color red could fully block the light of illusions . . .

"Mr. Garritt! What are you doing here already?"

Hastily, Eldyn slipped the receipt in between two pages of the broadsheet.

"Good morning, Father Gadby," he said, affecting a cheerful expression. "The verger was kind enough to let me get an early start. I need to . . . that is, I have an errand I need to go do, and I didn't want to fall behind on my work."

The portly rector smiled. "That is very diligent of you, Mr. Garritt. Well, go on, then, see to this errand of yours, whatever it is. But don't be too long. I'm sure there is much more for you to do today."

Eldyn promised he would not be long. He folded the broadsheet over, put it in his coat pocket, and hurried from the office below the church.

QUARTER HOUR later, Eldyn came to a halt before a prosperous-looking stone building a short way off of Marble Street. He read the number painted on the corner of the building, then pulled the slip of paper from his pocket to check it. The receipt had been made out to Profram and Sons, Number 7 Weaver's Row. This was the place.

Eldyn drew a breath to gather his will, then went in through the door of the building. At once he was approached by a young man he took to be one of the proprietor's sons. Dercy had told Eldyn that he was not a good liar, and it was likely so. All the same, he did his best to hold his voice steady as he explained how he wished to check on an order for curtains, and he produced the receipt from his pocket.

The young man took the receipt, then compared it against a ledger on the counter. "Ah, yes," he said. "Another set of red curtains commissioned by the Church. They are not finished yet, but they should be done lumenal after next. I assume we are still to deliver them to the usual place?"

Eldyn blinked. "The usual place?"

"Yes, the old chapel in High Holy. I confess, I did not think that church was still in use. But I can only suppose it is being refurbished."

Eldyn could do no more than give a mute nod.

"Very good," the young man said cheerfully. "We will deliver the curtains as soon as they are ready. But if you don't mind my asking, where is the priest who usually manages the orders? I trust he is well."

"The priest?" Eldyn said stupidly.

"Yes, the tall fellow with the sharp blue eyes. I've never gotten his name—I confess, I speak with him little, for he's rather imposing—but he always wears a crimson cassock."

Eldyn could not breathe. It felt as if he had been dealt a blow in the gut. "He is not . . ." He shook his head. "That is, I'm sorry, but I must go."

Before the other man could say anything more, Eldyn turned and hurried out the door. The morning light was warm, but he was shivering all the same. As quickly as his legs would carry him, he walked down the lane, his mind a confusion of thoughts and awful notions. Only, as he went, the facts began to align themselves into a comprehensible order. Red curtains below the crypt—the final words uttered by a dying illusionist. The old chapel at High Holy, where another one of the murdered illusionists had been found. And a blue-eyed priest in a red cassock . . .

It was impossible. It *had* to be.

Yet Eldyn above anyone knew that figures could not mislead; if summed correctly, they always led to the same result, whether one cared for the final total or not. In his mind, he made the tally again. Donnebric had last been seen going to a magnate's house in the company of a priest in a red cassock. And Father Gadby had described how Archdeacon Lemarck sometimes went about dressed as a priest—no doubt in crimson, a striking contrast to his sharp blue eyes. Over and over as Eldyn walked, he went over everything that he knew.

Over and over, the sum was the same.

Eldyn came to a sudden halt, and he was startled to find that it was not the hulking edifice of Graychurch he stood before, but rather the ramshackle building that housed the Theater of the Moon. Sweat ran down his sides, and he was breathing hard from his labors walking here. All the same, he still felt cold inside.

He went through the door and headed up to the little room above the theater. Dercy was still not there, but Eldyn knew he could not wait, that Father Gadby would be expecting him. He went to a little table, rummaged in a drawer, and there found pen, ink, and paper to write upon. Forcing his hand to stay steady, he penned a note to Dercy.

My dearest friend and companion, you were right, he wrote. *I fear that the Church is not what I thought it was. Nor, if what I suspect is true, is the archdeacon the great man I had believed. I have reason to think he is scheming some awful thing beneath the old chapel in High Holy. I intend to know more, and when I do I will tell you everything. Until then, I beg of you—have nothing to do with any priest who may approach you, especially one in red!*

He signed the note and set it on the bed. Then he departed the room and went back outside into the morning.

It was time to go to work.

CHAPTER THIRTY-EIGHT

 LUMENAL PASSED, then an umbral, and still there was no word from Coulten or Eubrey. Now, as morning light fell into the parlor at Warwent Square, Rafferdy took the black book from the drawer of his writing table. He spoke the runes of unbinding, then opened it.

No new message had appeared upon its pages; there would not be a meeting of the Arcane Society of the Virescent Blade that night. Whether he was disappointed or relieved he could not say. He was curious to learn what Eubrey had been up to since being admitted to the inner circle, yet he had no desire to hear more calls for the ruination of the Wyrdwood, given the peculiar feeling such discussions stirred in him.

Thinking of the wood brought Mrs. Quent to mind. As he returned the book to the drawer, he recalled that he had intended to send her a note to tell her what he had learned from Eubrey at the party for the Miss Lockwells. He had no idea why the topic of the Sword and Leaf was of such interest to Mrs. Quent. However, given her curiosity on the matter, he thought she might like to know that the tavern was indeed located off of Durrow Street—if one counted the magickal door that led directly from the street to the meeting room beneath the tavern.

Rafferdy sat at the table, took out paper and ink, and penned a brief note to this effect. He signed the note, began to fold it, then opened it back up and scrawled a hasty postscript.

I hope we might have an occasion to take a walk together soon.

He folded the note and sealed it, then gave it to his man with instructions for it to be delivered at once. After that he put on his coat and hat, and took up his cane. Even if he had looked at the almanac, there would be no way to be certain how much longer the lumenal would last, and he wished to take in some sun before it was gone for the day.

With this purpose he set out from Warwent Square. He went not upward in the direction of the New Quarter, but rather down toward the Old City. It felt good to stroll along the street, and he swung his cane in a jaunty fashion as he went. Soon a plan began to form in his mind; he would proceed to his club, he thought, and take a brandy while he pretended to read the latest edition of *The Comet,* while in fact eavesdropping on the conversations of others. Pleased with this idea, he altered his course and turned onto Coronet Street.

And there, on the other side of the street, was Lord Eubrey.

He was unmistakable, cutting a fine figure in a wine-colored coat as he walked with what seemed great purpose down the street. For days Rafferdy had been left in a state of suspense, wondering how Eubrey was faring in his new status within the society. Now here he was barely a stone's throw from Warwent Square, and he had not even bothered to call on Rafferdy! At once annoyed and delighted, Rafferdy hailed his friend.

Eubrey kept walking along the street, moving with swift strides, his gaze fixed forward.

Rafferdy called out again, but still Eubrey did not stop. Had he not heard Rafferdy's call? Surely it had been loud enough, and Coronet Street was not at all noisy or busy. Vexed now, Rafferdy hurried after him.

Catching up to his quarry was no easy task, as Eubrey continued to move at a rapid pace, and soon Rafferdy's heart kept time to his swift steps. However, just as Coronet Street ran into the north end of Marble Street, several carriages went clattering by. Eubrey was forced to stop short to avoid them, and this gave Rafferdy the opportunity to at last draw near.

"Ho, there, Eubrey!" he said breathlessly as he approached the other young man. "I've caught you at last, you scoundrel."

Still Eubrey gave no indication that he had heard Rafferdy, though he was no more than five paces away. Instead, with deliberate motions, he reached into his coat pocket and took out a pair of kidskin gloves.

By now Rafferdy had become greatly perturbed. "I say, Eubrey, I'm right here behind—"

The words caught in his throat as his feet and his heart both came to a sudden halt. Moving slowly, mechanically, Eubrey put on his gloves. As he did this, Rafferdy glimpsed the sharp, dark lines that formed a rune on Eubrey's right hand.

The symbol disappeared from view as Eubrey finished putting on his gloves. He turned his head, glancing around, and for a moment his gaze passed over Rafferdy. A horror descended, and Rafferdy froze, now fearing Eubrey would see him. However, there was no glint of recognition in Eubrey's eyes. Rather, they were darker than Rafferdy recalled them being, with no glint of light or life in them.

All at once Eubrey tilted his head, as if he heard some sound or voice, though what it might be Rafferdy could not tell. Then, as the last of the carriages passed by, Eubrey sprang forward, dashing down the length of Marble Street at a full run.

Rafferdy tried to call out, but the only thing he could give voice to was a wordless sound of despair. He still tried to comprehend what he had seen, only he knew what it signified, didn't he? A convulsion of understanding and dread shuddered through him. Yes, he knew now what it was that Eubrey had been up to these last days . . .

"Gods, no, Eubrey," he at last managed to speak in a whisper.

Then he was running down Marble Street himself, weaving in and out among the people and horses, wielding his cane before him to clear a path. The spires of Assembly loomed before him as he went.

A lorry bore down on him, and Rafferdy narrowly dodged to one side to avoid being crushed. He caught a glimpse of wine-colored velvet ahead, and despite the pain in his lungs he ran in that direction. By now he was nearly even with the Halls of Assembly. A group of several men were walking down the broad swath of marble steps. One of them was short and thickset, wearing a yellowed wig and old-fashioned yet lordly attire.

A four-in-hand thundered before Rafferdy, and he was forced to stop short lest he be trampled. When the way was clear he saw that the lord in the wig had reached the bottom of the steps. It was, he realized, Lord Bastellon. The door of a black carriage opened, and the old Stout climbed inside. At the same moment a figure in a wine-colored coat appeared from out of the throng on the street and moved toward the carriage.

Rafferdy propelled himself forward through the crowd. "No!" he shouted at loudly as he could. "Stop!"

Only his words were lost in the clatter of wheels and the pounding of hooves against cobbles. Twenty paces away, the door of the black carriage shut. At the same moment the figure in the wine-colored coat—not Eubrey, the thing could no longer be called Eubrey—approached the carriage.

"Get out!" Rafferdy shouted, only his throat was raw, his voice hoarse. "Get out of the—"

A gloved hand touched the side of the carriage. There was a brilliant flash, as from a bolt of lightning, followed by a deafening noise. A moment later a column of blue fire leaped up toward the sky from the very spot where the carriage was parked before the steps.

Rafferdy staggered, thrown back by the force of the conflagration along with dozens of others. Shouts and cries sounded all around him, as well as the terrible screams of horses. The latter were cut short as the livid flames quickly consumed the black carriage, far more swiftly than any mundane fire could have done. Smoke climbed into the sky in a black pillar, forming a shadowed mirror to the spires that crowned Assembly.

An acrid scent spread upon the air, making Rafferdy's eyes smart and water. He took a halting step forward, but there was no use. The flames collapsed back on themselves, dwindled, and died out. Where the carriage had stood there was little more than a smoldering black heap on the cobbles.

There was no sign of a man in a wine-colored coat.

More shouts rang out. Soldiers were marching rapidly down the street. Several more were coming down the steps before Assembly. At their fore was a large, hulking figure dressed all in gray.

A glint of blue caught Rafferdy's eye. He glanced down and saw that the gem in his House ring was glittering. A fresh dread came upon him. He looked up and saw that the brutish man in gray had nearly reached the bottom of the steps. The last thing Rafferdy wanted now was to be caught by Moorkirk, not a dozen paces from the remains of Lord Bastellon's carriage, his magician's ring blazing in echo to the arcane energies that had just been unleashed.

Moorkirk shouted something to the soldiers. The redcrests rushed toward the crowd—to begin accosting people, Rafferdy supposed, though he did not wait to find out. He turned and, pushing his way through the confusion, ran back down the length of Marble Street.

He did not stop running until he reached Coronet Street. Then he was forced to walk, for his lungs and heart would bear no more. Though his body moved more slowly now, his mind continued to race. There was no doubting what he had witnessed, but still it was difficult for his mind to fully grasp it. Why had Eubrey done this thing?

Only it wasn't Eubrey who had done it. It was a thing wearing Eubrey's face and skin—a thing that, had it not been burned up and destroyed in the magickal fire, would have bled not blood but a gray oozing fluid when the soldiers brought it down with their rifles.

Though he sweated inside his coat, he shivered; his skin was clammy, and he felt a sickness churning in his stomach. How had this happened to Eubrey? When had this horrible deed been done to him?

Except he already knew the answer to that question. After all, he and Coulten had not seen Eubrey since he was admitted by the sages to the inner circle of the Arcane Society of the Virescent Blade—since he had passed through the Door into the sanctum beneath the tavern. Coulten had gotten the news from him in a note before the party for the Miss Lockwells.

Coulten! A new dread welled up within Rafferdy. What was it Coulten had told him at Assembly the other day?

Eubrey thinks that I am sure to be the next magician in the society to be invited through the Door. . . .

Dread became a sudden panic. Gripping his cane, Rafferdy forced himself back into a run. He had to return to his house, get his carriage, and go warn Coulten that he was in the gravest danger—and that whatever he did, he must not go through the Door.

Minutes later he reached his house in Warwent Square, panting as he climbed the steps. Once inside he called for his man, then told him to have the carriage brought around, that he needed to go at once to Lord Coulten's abode in the New Quarter.

"Very well, sir," his man said. "Though you may care to read this first, as it just arrived. It is a note from Lord Coulten."

Rafferdy took the note, staring at it as his heart thudded in his chest. Then, as his man left the parlor, Rafferdy sank into a chair and opened the note. It was indeed from Coulten and was very brief.

I have but a moment to write this, yet I wanted you to know the excellent news! I received a missive from Eubrey. He tells me that the sages have an experiment for me to conduct, and that if I can successfully perform it, they will admit me to the inner circle of the society. I don't know what it involves yet—I'm to take direction from the magus himself—but Eubrey tells me it is of great importance to our alliance with another magickal order.

Do not be too envious, Rafferdy, for I am sure you will be the next in line to be admitted to the inner sanctum. I will tell you more when I have more to tell, but for now I must be off to receive my instructions. It's all very secret and exciting, don't you think? I feel positively notorious. Bid me luck!

—Coulten

Again Rafferdy read the note, and his dread was renewed. What mission was it the sages were giving to Coulten? Rafferdy did not know what it might be, only that Coulten must not be allowed to perform whatever task it was.

His man returned to the parlor. "The carriage is being readied for you, sir. Do you still wish to go to the New Quarter?"

Rafferdy stared at the note. He had to warn Coulten that he was in grave peril. Only how could he do that when he had no idea where Coulten was off to? For a mad moment he considered trying to seek out the sages, to demand that they tell him where Coulten was going. Yet he had no idea who the sages really were, and even if he did, they were the ones who had condemned Eubrey to his awful fate. Rafferdy's mind was a fog of confusion; he could think of no way he could possibly find where Coulten was to go.

Then, by some magick he did not fully comprehend, the murk of fear in his mind was transmuted into a clear and crystalline resolve. He folded the note and stood.

"Tell the driver to bring the carriage around at once," he said to his man. "I will go to the New Quarter as planned."

Only, he was not going there for a leisurely drive.

*R*AFFERDY DRUMMED HIS fingers against the bench of his carriage as it made its way up the Promenade. A compulsion came over him to pound with his cane upon the ceiling, to urge the driver to go faster, but he refrained. The broad, winding avenue was busy with people out for a drive or a stroll in the midday sun. The driver could go no faster.

And what if it didn't matter how swiftly he went? What if all Rafferdy accomplished here was to squander what little time he had? However, even as these doubts registered, he dismissed them. In his note, Coulten had written that the task the sages had for him involved an alliance with another magickal order. Rafferdy recalled the words the magus had spoken, at the last meeting of the society, regarding the Wyrdwood.

Know that we have many allies in this matter . . . very soon this subject will be brought up in Assembly by members of one such order.

The matter of the Wyrdwood had indeed been brought up at Assembly—by the Magisters. Rafferdy knew what magickal order many of them belonged to. What was more, he knew by name at least one member of that order.

The carriage came to a halt, and the driver climbed down to open the door.

"We have arrived at Lord Farrolbrook's abode, sir."

Rafferdy took up his hat and cane, then departed the carriage. "Wait here," he instructed the driver. "It is my hope I will not be long."

Gripping his cane, Rafferdy passed through a large gate and walked up marble steps to the door of a grand house. It was an ostentatious structure, with a surfeit of columns, friezes, and winged cherubs that perched upon every available cornice and ledge like so many fat stone pigeons. It was gaudy and absurd—that is, precisely the sort of edifice he would have expected its occupant to dwell in.

He reached the front door and, eschewing the ornate knocker fashioned from a trio of bronze nymphs, used the handle of his cane to rap on the door. After a moment this was opened by a tall but rather stooped manservant.

"I am sorry," he intoned in a dry voice before Rafferdy could utter a word, "but the master is not receiving visitors today." He started to shut the door.

Rafferdy wedged his cane in the gap, then used it as a lever to force the door back. He was not about to be delayed in his task by a haughty butler. "You will take me to Lord Farrolbrook at once," he said, and he raised his right hand so that the gem on his House ring flashed blue in the sunlight.

This action had an even greater effect on the man than Rafferdy had hoped it would, for his heretofore squinted eyes went wide, and he took a hasty step back from the door. Rafferdy seized the opportunity to cross the threshold.

"Thank you," he said pleasantly. "Now, show me to your master."

However, the man shook his head. "I told him I will not have any more dealings with your kind—not after the last time. If you wish to see him, then find him yourself!"

With that the manservant turned and hurried down a hallway, shooing a pair of maids—who had no doubt been eavesdropping—ahead of him. Rafferdy found this all very peculiar, but there was no time to wonder about it. He left the front hall in the opposite way the butler had gone, guessing from the man's reaction that this would be the most likely direction to find the master of the house.

His hypothesis soon proved correct. The first two doors he opened revealed empty rooms beyond, but the third, at the end of the corridor, led to a large parlor. It was hard at first to gauge the parlor's expanse, for the curtains had been drawn over the windows, shutting out most of the daylight.

Gradually Rafferdy's eyes adjusted to the gloom, and he became aware of a vast array of clutter that filled the parlor: tables littered with compasses and sextants and scales, large canvases resting upon easels, and half-finished sculptures that strained and contorted to free themselves from blocks of stone. All manner of books and tools were scattered about, along with numerous trays containing uneaten food and full cups of tea. There was a stale, rather unwholesome smell upon the air.

Rafferdy was about to shut the door when a silhouette, which he had taken to be a pale statue draped in black cloth, suddenly took a step toward him.

"Have you come to deprive me of my magick, then?" spoke a voice—one that for all its weariness had a clear timbre that carried across the parlor. "But you must know by now there is not much to take."

The figure took another step forward. It was not a statue, but rather a tall man with long, pale hair. He wore a black robe that was heavily decorated with frills and ruffs.

Despite the urgency of his business here, Rafferdy felt both pity and curiosity. It had seemed in Assembly the other day that Farrolbrook was losing his wits, and now Rafferdy could only believe that was the case. He took a step into the room. As he did, he passed one of the paintings that leaned upon an easel. It depicted a pastoral scene; or rather it had. Black splotches of paint had been spattered over the image of hills and meadows, as if a dark mold had eaten away at the canvas.

"I don't know a thing about taking anyone's magick, Lord Farrolbrook," Rafferdy said, keeping his tone brisk and light. "I only came here to ask you a question."

The other man lifted a hand to his brow, then moved into a thin beam of light that fell through a gap in the curtains.

"Lord Rafferdy, is that you?"

So he had not entirely lost his wits, then, to recall Rafferdy so well after only speaking to him once—and before Rafferdy was a lord, at that.

"Yes, that's right," he said.

"Did Lord Mertrand approach you, then? Did he invite you into the order?"

Rafferdy shook his head. "Lord Mertrand?" That was the magnate in Assembly who had called out for the destruction of the

Wyrdwood—the same one Lord Bastellon had warned about speaking treasonous things. "No, I've never even met him."

"Well, you can be glad of that," Farrolbrook said, then he let out a soft laugh. "But I should have known Mertrand didn't send you. After all, Lord Rafferdy, you aren't wearing gloves."

Rafferdy could only stare. What did Farrolbrook mean by that?

"Do forgive me, Lord Rafferdy. I have completely forgotten my manners. I'm afraid that I am . . . that is, I haven't been entirely myself lately." He picked up a cup from one of the trays littered about and held it out. "Would you care for some tea?"

Rafferdy managed to swallow. "That's very kind, but no thank you. As I said, I only came here to ask you something. I apologize for calling on you in such an unexpected fashion, but it is a matter of some urgency."

Farrolbrook took a sip from the cup. "Is it about the gray men?"

Rafferdy was so startled he was forced to put down his cane to keep from staggering. "You know about them?"

"Mertrand thinks that I don't. He thinks I have no idea what goes on at meetings of the High Order of the Golden Door after I leave. It is always his habit to flatter me as he sees me out for the evening, and to tell me all that is left to do is uninteresting rigmarole that is beneath me—that he and the sages will send for me at once if they are doing any magick of importance and my expertise is required. And I suppose I have always believed him. That is, at least until recently." He took another sip, then grimaced as he set down the teacup.

Despite the urgency of his mission, Rafferdy could only be fascinated, while at the same time he felt the hair on his neck stand on end. "So you think your order is doing something to its magicians—that it is making them into these gray men?"

Lord Farrolbrook moved to one of the paintings and picked up a brush and a palette. "I suppose I shouldn't tell you. It is all meant to be secret. Only lately they have begun to say things around me as if I am not there. I think they believe that I won't comprehend them."

Rafferdy understood. Their opinion of Lord Farrolbrook was clearly no higher than his own. They had simply been using his popularity in Assembly to further their own ends, whatever those were.

"But they were wrong," Rafferdy said. "You did understand them."

Farrolbrook laughed at this. "Not so well as you might think! You see, I have come to realize that I am not much of a magician after all. You may have heard of all my famous exploits, Lord Rafferdy—how I called down lightning and made objects placed in a cabinet vanish. Well, I am convinced now that I achieved none of those things on my own. It was all *their* doing, weaving enchantments behind my back. They simply made it look as if I were the one doing magick. Only I never was." He ran the brush over the canvas—an idyllic scene of a country cottage—staining it with black paint.

Rafferdy took a step closer to him. "Yet you are a magician."

"Do not try to flatter me as they did, Lord Rafferdy!"

"That is not what I mean. I only note that you wear a magician's ring."

Farrolbrook's brush ceased to move, then he raised his hand to regard it. The gem set in his House ring glinted red in the thin beam of sunlight that passed between the curtains.

"I do not know," he said softly. "I am descended of magicians, for whatever that is worth. Anyway, I suppose it doesn't matter if I tell you about the gray men. Mertrand and the sages are already angry with me—they made that very clear the last time they were here. Besides, you're not the only one who suspects something. Lady Shayde has sent that hooligan of hers to speak to me more than once."

Rafferdy was astonished anew. "Moorkirk? What has he wanted with you?"

"Lady Shayde knows about the gray men," Lord Farrolbrook said, daubing his brush against the palette. "What's more, she's pieced together enough evidence to suspect that at least some of them belong to the same magickal order that I do. I haven't told her anything, though. Not yet, at any rate." He blotted out a cloud with black. "So why was she looking at you at Assembly the other day?"

Rafferdy could only wince. "I've had the unfortunate luck to encounter her and her man Moorkirk while they were in the process of investigating some of these gray men."

"Ah, that is ill luck indeed—though not as ill as that of the men whom Lady Shayde was investigating."

Rafferdy thought of Eubrey, the black symbol on his hand, and his throat grew tight. He could only nod.

"I fear more will be similarly unlucky," Farrolbrook went on, still working his brush. "Lord Mertrand has made some bargain with the magus of another order. Mertrand gave this other magus something of great value, and in return he gets more magicians to turn into gray men—something he needs, for our own order grows depleted, and he cannot recruit young men quickly enough to suit his purposes."

Rafferdy could only shudder at this abominable activity. "But what is his purpose? What are the gray men for?"

"I don't know. To ruin things, I think. And to sow disruption and suspicion in Altania. For so long I thought nothing about what the others in the order did—I cared only for my experiments, my paintings, and my speeches. Only ever since my father passed, a feeling has been growing in me, stronger and stronger every day. It is . . ." He shook his head. "But I cannot explain it. Still, I fear they are doing something awful."

"Something awful?" Rafferdy thought of the words his father had said in their final conversation, how magicians were responsible for working great ill—perhaps the greatest ill ever done in all of history. "But what do they mean to accomplish?"

"I don't know." Lord Farrolbrook's brush went still, and he cocked his head. "No, that's not true. I *do* know. It has something to do with the Wyrdwood. They want to destroy it, to cut it all down and burn it up, only they must not be allowed to do so."

"But why not?"

Farrolbrook pressed a hand to his temple. "I'm not certain. But if it is something they wish for, it cannot be good. And without doubt they are scheming to do it. I heard them talking as they left here. They said the magus of that other society—the one Lord Mertrand has a bargain with—is sending a magician to the wall to perform another experiment."

Again Rafferdy suffered a shock. "To the wall—you mean to Madiger's Wall?"

"Yes, Madiger's Wall, I'm sure of it. I'm not certain what this experiment involves. I believe I heard them say it has something to do with some door that was discovered there." Lord Farrolbrook turned away from the easel. "Only, I have forgotten my manners again. You said you came here to ask a question, Lord Rafferdy—what is it?"

Rafferdy stared past the tall lord at the painting. All traces of the country scene were gone now; the canvas was solid black.

"Nothing important," he said. "I am sorry to have disturbed you. I beg your leave, my lord."

He gave a swift bow, then turned to hurry from the parlor. As he reached the door, Rafferdy glanced back into the room. Farrolbrook had set down his brush, and he stood in the dimness of the room in his ruffled black robe. His lips moved silently as he turned the House ring around and around on his finger.

Rafferdy felt a peculiar compulsion to go back to him, to try to listen to what he was saying, but there was no time for that. The sages had sent Coulten back to the door in the wall. For what purpose, Rafferdy did not know, but it could not be for good. He rushed through the front hall, out the door, and down the steps to his carriage.

"I must leave the city," he said as his driver helped him inside and shut the door. "Drive me to Madiger's Wall at once."

The man appeared surprised by these directions, but he only nodded. He climbed back into his seat and snapped the reins, and the carriage rolled into motion. As it did, Rafferdy slumped back against the seat. It would take at least three hours to get to the wall.

"Good God, Coulten," he said aloud. "Please try not to do anything foolish before I get there."

And he twisted his own House ring on his finger as first the city and then the countryside flickered by outside the window.

CHAPTER THIRTY-NINE

IVY GLANCED IN a mirror, making sure her hair was pinned firmly in place, then took up her bonnet and parasol.

That morning at breakfast, quite to her surprise, Mr. Quent had asked her if she would like to take a drive in the country. Ivy was thrilled by this idea. All the same, she had tried to remain composed, and she said that while a drive sounded very nice, she wondered that he didn't have to go to the Citadel. However, he assured her that nothing could be more important than to take her on a drive, that it was long overdue. He had some correspondence to go through that morning, but come afternoon they would be off.

Now the sound of bells drifted through the window as the church down the street chimed the start of the third farthing. Ivy left her chamber and went downstairs, taking the steps at a swift pace. She could not think of anything more delightful than going out to the country with her husband. Nor did she have to worry about abandoning her sisters, for they had not one but two affairs to attend that day, and so would be well occupied. Her thoughts thus happily directed, she leaped off the last step into the front hall.

Mr. Quent was not there, as she had expected. She looked out the front door, wondering if he had already brought the cabriolet around, but the street beyond the gate was empty. She shut the door and went to his study off the north end of the hall.

And there he was, sitting at his desk, looking at a letter. He glanced up at the sound of her entrance.

"Forgive me, Sir Quent," she said, smiling at him. "I didn't realize you were still working at your correspondence. I will wait in the front hall while you finish."

He set down the letter and stood. "No, Ivoleyn, there is no need for you to wait for me."

At once her cheerful mood went dim. She clutched her parasol and bonnet, as if loath to let go of what they had represented. Only then, slowly, she set them down on a sideboard.

"You have to go to the Citadel after all," she said.

He gave a solemn nod. "I am sorry, dearest. A message just came for me. There was an . . . attack by rebels before the Halls of Assembly a little while ago."

She felt a note of alarm. "An attack? Was someone harmed?"

"I fear so."

"That is dreadful news! Only . . ." She shook her head. "It's just that I would think such a thing was for the redcrests or perhaps the Gray Conclave to deal with. Is such a matter really your business?"

"In this case, I fear that it is." He folded the letter and put it in his coat pocket, then went to her. "I am sorry, Ivoleyn. I know that this means I must ruin our plans. But I promise that I will take you for a drive soon."

Just not today, she wanted to say. Only how could she worry about her own whims and desires when some poor soul had lost their life that day? Besides, if he was truly to rise to an even higher position, and so put himself beyond the reach of any who might seek to reproach him for his actions in Torland, then she needed to provide him with the necessary encouragement, and to reassure him that his duties to the Crown were more important than drives in the country or any other thing she might want.

She touched his bearded cheek. "Be as long as you must," she said. "I will be waiting for you when you return."

His look was one of gratitude and affection. He held her, and kissed her with a great fierceness. Then he departed the chamber.

***

IVY RETURNED HER bonnet and parasol to her chamber, then went back downstairs to the library to turn through the pages of her father's journal, as she had not yet done so that day. However, the pages were all blank. There had not been a new entry in the journal since the one that had appeared just before her sisters' party, the one in which he revealed it had been his friend Gambrel who had betrayed the order and stole the key to the door Tyberion.

How she wished another entry would appear! She wanted to know if her father had ever found Gambrel, or if the traitorous magician was still at large after all these years. She would have felt terrified by the prospect, except that she knew the wards her father had placed upon the house would warn her if Gambrel ever attempted to enter. Besides, those protections had been renewed and strengthened by Mr. Rafferdy's spell. That Gambrel could come inside the house without being invited was impossible.

Ivy returned the journal to the Wyrdwood box, along with the pages she had transcribed and the triangle-shaped bit of Old Wood that Lord Rafferdy had given her. With an absent touch, she bid the tendrils that coiled about the box to entwine themselves, locking it.

She returned the box to its drawer, then took up a folded piece of paper that lay atop the writing desk. It was a note from Mr. Rafferdy and had arrived earlier that morning. Again she read the letter, wondering at the knowledge it contained.

I believe you may find this of interest, he had written. *I have discovered there is indeed a door that, by means of magick, leads from the tavern where my society meets directly to Durrow Street.*

This fact was indeed of interest to her. Yet she did not know what to think. It was utterly improbable that that magickal society

Rafferdy happened to belong to met in the exact place where Dratham's arcane order had nearly three centuries ago. All the same, logic demanded that this must be the case. For all she knew it was the very same society, and had been perpetuated by magicians meeting in secret during the long, dark years when the study of the arcane was in disrepute.

A sudden thrill passed through Ivy. If Mr. Rafferdy belonged to the same occult society Dratham had, perhaps there were things Mr. Rafferdy knew, or that he could find out, that would teach her more about the man who had first constructed the house on Durrow Street.

Ivy took out a fresh sheet, picked up a pen, and wrote a reply to Mr. Rafferdy's note. *I hope we can indeed go walking together soon,* she concluded the note, and signed her name.

She sealed the note, then went out into the front hall, where she found Mrs. Seenly.

"Would you please see that this is delivered as soon as possible?" she said, handing the note to the housekeeper.

"Of course, Lady Quent. I will see that it goes out at once."

"Oh, and Mrs. Seenly, my sisters are off to an affair this afternoon and another one tonight, and I expect Sir Quent will be late at the Citadel. Therefore, once Lily and Rose have gone, I think you and Mr. Seenly and the staff should take the rest of the lumenal off."

At this the housekeeper's eyes shone. "But are you certain, Lady Quent? There will be no one to serve supper."

"It is not very long since I served supper myself," Ivy said with a laugh. "I will do very well if you leave something out for me."

Thus assured, the housekeeper smiled and thanked her, then tucked the note into her apron and bustled off. Ivy proceeded upstairs to see if her sisters had begun preparing for the parties they were to attend.

As she reached the gallery on the second floor, she paused. The door Tyberion commanded the south end of the gallery as usual, the sword carved upon it gleaming in the morning light so that it seemed forged of bronze. At the north end, the door Arantus was still hidden behind the white curtain, for she had not directed the servants to take down the cloth.

The man in the black mask had told her to conceal Arantus, and he had not shown himself to her since. She did not know why he had wanted her to conceal the door, or from whom. And as there were often people in the house—from servants and craftsmen to agents of the Crown who came to visit her husband—she had decided it was best to leave the curtain up until the man in the black costume appeared to her again. That he would do so eventually was something of which she was certain, even if his purposes were a matter of doubt.

A temptation came upon Ivy to go to the white curtain, to lift the cloth, and to look at the door carved all with leaves. However, sisterly duty compelled her to delay no longer, and instead she went upstairs.

It was good she did, for she found her sisters in great need of assistance. They were having much difficulty choosing what to wear for their affairs, for Lily despised each of her gowns as much as the next, while Rose adored all of hers in equal measure.

Ivy did her best to offer aid. Gowns were put on and taken off. A light luncheon was called for. Cakes were eaten, and more gowns were modeled. At last, after a great deal of effort on the part of Ivy, Lily was finally convinced that one of her dresses was slightly less awful than all the others. Rose, in turn, was coaxed into admitting that she found one of her gowns to be just the littlest bit prettier than the rest.

With so much time spent in deciding what to wear, there was little time left to actually put it on, and the lumenal was moving more swiftly than the almanac had called for. All in a rush, bodices were laced, sleeves buttoned, and ribbons tied. Lily and Rose fluttered downstairs like colorful birds, with Miss Mew chasing after them. Then they were in the cabriolet, with Lawden at the reins, his homely face hardly to be noticed for his handsome hat and coat.

Ivy stood outside the gate to see them off. They both looked, she thought, very pretty.

"If you are weary after the dinner, you need not go to the ball," she said. It was not the first time she had mentioned this, as she had been concerned when Lily accepted both invitations.

"Nonsense!" Lily exclaimed, lifting her parasol against the swift-moving sun. "Now that Rose and I are finally out, we may go to as many parties as we wish—and we must meet as many good-looking men as we can!"

Though Ivy was still somewhat concerned about them attending two affairs in one day, she could only admit that she was glad Lily was showing an interest in meeting other young men besides Mr. Garritt. Indeed, she seemed very determined at the task. And now that Ivy thought of it, Lily had not mentioned Mr. Garritt once since the party.

Lawden flicked the reins, and the cabriolet started into motion. Rose turned in the seat to wave at Ivy, her brown eyes shining. Ivy waved back. Then the carriage turned a corner and was lost from view.

For a moment Ivy watched the empty street, then she turned and walked through the garden. She went slowly, as there was nothing to hurry back to. It was not visiting day at Madstone's, Mr. Quent and her sisters would both be late, and the servants were dismissed.

Besides, she might see *him* if she lingered out here. The man in the black mask had only ever appeared to her when she was alone. It was for this reason that she had let the staff go for the rest of the day. She had a hope that, if she was by herself in the house, he might show himself.

Not that this was something she looked forward to, exactly. His recent manifestations had all instilled a foreboding in her. Despite her father's letter urging her to trust the man in black, she could not help but be wary of him and his intentions. Yet it was clear from his warning that he knew something about the doors in the gallery, and if he was to appear, perhaps he would impart further knowledge.

However, as she strolled through the garden, she saw no sign of the mysterious visitor, and the only voices she heard were the murmurings of the little hawthorns and chestnuts.

Though they were dwarfed by the stately ashes and elms that framed the house, the scraggly little trees were the more remarkable specimens. Recently, she had told Mr. Quent what she had learned in her father's journal—that they were in fact sprung from the seeds of Old Trees gathered on the edges of a stand of Wyrdwood. Mr. Quent had been alarmed by this fact, but so far he had been of a mind to leave the trees as they were.

"They are far from the Evengrove," he had said. "Too far for their roots to be in any sort of communication with it. I suspect they could be cut down with little chance of a reaction. Still, I am loath to cause any disturbance at this point, no matter how small the risk might be."

Thus the trees remained for now, and Mr. Seenly had been given strict orders not to trim them, or cut even the least branch. Ivy was glad for this, as the sight of the trees always gave her joy, and they reminded her of her time in the country. What harm could there be in having them here? Could she not soothe them should they ever choose to stir of their own will? Besides, they were all so small and stunted.

Except that was not really true anymore. In the last months, the hawthorns and chestnuts had all grown measurably. And while they still tended to be always shedding their leaves, they had more of them to shed than before. Despite the brilliance of the afternoon sun, a green shadow abided among the little trees, like the cool of a premature twilight. A breeze moved through the branches, and the leaves whispered around her.

The sound reminded Ivy of the last time she had been among trees. Often, since that day at the Evengrove, she had recalled how it had felt to listen to the voices of the trees, and to call out to them in return. Yet she had almost lost her own voice among those of the trees. She had been in grave peril that day, and the thought of ever venturing again into any stand of Wyrdwood—let alone the largest grove in all of Altania—should have been a subject of horror.

Only it wasn't.

Suddenly it was not the day at the Evengrove Ivy thought of, but rather the night of her sisters' party, and her conversation with Lady Crayford.

If you wish it, I believe you will one day find yourself to be a great lady, the viscountess had told her that night. *Indeed, one of the greatest ladies in all of Altania.*

These words had astonished Ivy at first. But she had thought about them over these last lumenals, and she had to concede there was a logic to them. As a lady of consequence, would she not be in a better position to help her husband achieve his aims? After all, politics was worked in ballrooms in the New Quarter as much as it was in the Halls of Assembly. The higher she rose in society, the more she could help win for Mr. Quent the prominence he would need to protect Altania without having to worry about what others in the government might think of his methods.

It was a shocking notion, that a woman might wield such influence. For all of history, it was men who had commanded affairs, who had shaped lives and nations. Yet what had they wrought with all that power? Peace and prosperity?

No, it was very much the opposite. For all men, no matter how good of nature they were, could only ever think of action and advancement rather than calm and continuity. If women were able to share in directing the nation and its affairs, might not a more harmonious balance of powers come to be? Compulsions to build up and tear down might be ameliorated by desires to grow and to tend. Thus the nation would be strengthened and made the wiser, just as a man was made if he married well and heeded his wife.

Another breeze moved among the trees, and they murmured replies to her thoughts. Why shouldn't a woman wield power? She lifted a hand, running her fingers through viridian leaves. . . .

A ringing sounded behind her. Ivy drew her hand back and blinked, and the green shadows seemed to retreat as the sunlight brightened around her. She turned just in time to see the brass bell that hung by the gate cease to swing; the afternoon post had come.

Usually Mrs. Seenly would retrieve the post, but as Ivy was on her own for the remainder of the day, she went to the box next to the gate. Not that she minded doing so herself. Indeed, she missed many of the mundane tasks she had been used to doing.

Ivy opened the box and took out a stack of notes. As she went through them, she saw they were nearly all invitations for Lily and Rose—so many that she doubted even Lily would be able to accept them all, though her youngest sister would no doubt try. Toward the bottom of the stack, Ivy at last came upon a letter that was addressed to her. The directions were written in a hand she did not recognize. She turned it over to see who the sender was, and at once a great excitement came upon her.

Such was her curiosity to read the contents of the letter that she began to open it right there. All at once, the sun dipped behind the roof of the house, casting the garden into a deep shadow. Clutching the stack of notes, she hurried up the walk, past the stone lions, and into the house.

Ivy set all the invitations for Lily and Rose on a table in the front hall. Hastily she turned up the wick on a lamp that had been left burning, then sat in a chair beside it and opened the letter. It was from Mr. Samonds, the farrier in the village of Cairnbridge in County Westmorain, and was written in a neat, rather soft-edged hand.

To Lady Quent, with great Regard and Affection, it began. *You are more than kind to recall your acquaintance with me, especially given your present circumstances, which have been (as you can no doubt imagine) the cause of much discussion and interest here in Cairnbridge. I am deeply pleased for you and your husband, and I am humbled and honored to receive your letter. I hope you will forgive me if I presumed to show it to my aunt, Miss Samonds. However, she speaks of you often, and recalls your conversations with much fondness. She bid me to pass her greetings to you, and her wishes for continued good fortune and happiness, and now that I have written these words I will consider my promise to her fulfilled.*

Ivy could only smile as she read these lines. She recalled Mr. Samonds and Miss Samonds with much endearment. They were, besides Mr. Quent and the children and the maid Lanna, her only real companions during her time at Heathcrest. She shared another connection with Mr. Samonds as well—for he was, like Ivy, a great-grandchild of Rowan Addysen.

As for the question of your note, Mr. Samonds's letter continued, *I believe I can offer you some help, though perhaps not as much as you might have hoped for. I do in fact know of an item such as you describe: a piece of wood from an Old Tree, small enough to fit in your palm, and with three sides. I know of it because it was I who shaped it. There was a gentleman whose acquaintance I made up at Heathcrest Hall years ago, one of those times I was there as a boy. His name was Mr. Lockwell, and only as I read your letter did I finally understand what I should have realized upon meeting you and learning your name—that he was your father.*

Only it had been many years since I had thought of him, or of the things he asked me to fashion from gleaned Wyrdwood. Yet I can recall them clearly now. The one was a box, and the other a frame or stand meant to hold I know not what, though he provided me with very specific dimensions. I did not ask questions, for I knew he was a magician, and that he was a friend of the man the earl sometimes brought to Heathcrest to tutor Lord Wilden in magick. Mr. Bennick, I believe his name was. He was one who always gave me a chill, but Mr. Lockwell—your father—was ever kind to me. I made him the box and the stand gladly. And one more thing I did for him, the last time I saw him.

He gave me a small thing made of Wyrdwood, and he asked me to change its appearance. He did not want it cut or carved in any way, only shaped and molded so that it would remain whole and intact yet might not be recognized for what it was. Though I touch it no longer, I believe you know that in my youth I had some ability for shaping the fallen wood of the Old Trees, and so I did this last task for him. What appears to you as a three-sided piece of wood was, in its original shape, a leaf carved in the most beautiful detail.

So now you know what the object you have once was, though I do not know if that tells you what you wish to know. I can only suppose the

*object had some significance or importance, but what it was your father
did not tell me. I am sorry I can be of no greater help in the matter.*

"But you have been of great help, Mr. Samonds!" Ivy said
aloud, looking up from the letter.

The piece of Wyrdwood Lord Rafferdy gave her had been
carved to look like a leaf! Ivy wanted nothing more than to go to
the library, retrieve the piece of wood from the box, and dash upstairs to the door in the north wall of the gallery. However, she was
nearly to the end of the letter. Then, as she read the last things
Mr. Samonds had written, the room seemed to grow darker, and a
foreboding wrapped around her like a shawl soaked in a cold rain.

*As I have pen already in hand, there is one more thing I thought I
should tell you. It is likely of no consequence, but I did find it peculiar
and so thought I would describe it. In recent months, on at least two occasions, a man has come to Cairnbridge, and also to Low Sorrell, and
has made various inquiries about you. He seemed to want to hear anything that was known about your time spent in County Westmorain. In
particular, he wished to know of any connection you might have with the
Addysen name.*

*I do not know what he might have learned during his visits here. Yet
some are more inclined to speak to outsiders than others. Also, there are
some in the two villages who regard the Addysen name, and any known
or thought to have descended of that family, with little affection. What
significance this has, if any, I cannot say, though I thought perhaps you
should know about it. As for the man himself, I never heard his name,
but he wore the coat of a captain in the king's army. He was short of
stature, though well-made, and had a crown of red hair.*

*That is all the news I have to impart for now. I hope this finds you
and your husband well. And if ever you have occasion to return to
Heathcrest Hall, I and many in the county would be greatly pleased.*

The letter was signed simply, *Mr. Samonds.* However, Ivy
hardly read the last few words.

He was short of stature . . . and had a crown of red hair. . . .

Her lungs couldn't seem to draw a proper breath, and a pain
throbbed in her head. All this time, like Mrs. Baydon, she had

thought him to be so kind, so cheerful and gallant. She had never had an ill thought about him. Yet they had all of them been deceived in the most awful manner!

What Captain Branfort's purpose was in making inquiries about her in Cairnbridge and Low Sorrell, she could not guess, but it could not have been for good, else he would not have so misrepresented himself to her. That she now knew by what means people in the city had learned about the events that befell her in the Westlands, she was certain.

Yet what had been the reason for this act of duplicity? Why had he presented himself as a disinterested friend only to go seeking knowledge of her in secret? She did not know. All the same, given what he had done, there was no telling what other acts of deceit the captain was capable of. That they had profoundly misjudged his character and intent could not be a matter of doubt, and she had to warn Mrs. Baydon to break off her acquaintance with Captain Branfort at once.

She put down Mr. Samonds's letter and rose, moving toward the library, intending to write to Mrs. Baydon. As she crossed the front hall, a loud noise suddenly rang out. After a startled moment she realized it was a knock upon the front door of the house. Someone must have let themselves in the gate and was on the step.

"Mrs. Seenly," Ivy called out, "would you see to the door?"

Her voice echoed into silence. Of course—she had given the servants the rest of the lumenal. No doubt they were all away visiting with their families or otherwise taking advantage of the time.

Again a knock sounded upon the door. Who it was, Ivy could not guess, for she was not expecting any visitors that day. Only then a thought came to her that perhaps it was Mrs. Baydon, for once or twice before she had come to call unexpectedly.

Ivy hurried to the entryway. As she did, a pair of wooden eyes carved in the lintel above the door blinked open. They peered down at her curiously for a moment, then their lids drooped back down as if in slumber. Ivy gripped the brass handle and pulled the heavy door open.

The caller who stood upon the doorstep in the thickening air of late afternoon was not Mrs. Baydon. Rather, he was a gentleman clad in an elegant charcoal-colored suit, dark gloves, and a top hat. He was, she thought, near to her father in age, though he wore the years as handsomely as he did his attire. The gray at his temples, the lines beside his mouth and eyes, and the well-honed edge of his jaw all served to lend him a striking appearance.

"Oh!" Ivy could only say, surprised by the presence of the stranger.

The man quickly removed his hat and bowed. "Forgive me, but I was not expecting you to answer the door, your ladyship."

"I suppose not," Ivy said, and could not help a smile. She imagined few great ladies answered their own doors. "Are we acquainted, then?" she asked, thinking back to her sisters' party. She was certain she would have recalled meeting such a distinguished gentleman.

"I confess, we are not *properly* acquainted," he said. There was a softness to the manner of his speech that made it very soothing to listen to, despite the slight presence of a lisp. "However, I have heard a great deal about you, and I believe you have heard some amount with regard to me. What's more, you have been to my house on more than one occasion."

"*Your* house?" Ivy said, puzzled.

"Yes, at affairs hosted by Lady Crayford."

Now her confusion was replaced by astonishment and delight. "The viscountess's parties were at your house? Then you can only be the viscount yourself!"

He smiled, the lines beside his eyes crinkling in a charming manner. He certainly had as many years over Lady Crayford as Mr. Quent did over her. Yet just as Ivy could not complain about her husband's appearance, she could see that the viscountess had no reason for complaint either.

"My wife tells me you are very clever, Lady Quent, and that few mysteries can withstand the scrutiny of your keen attention. Now I observe for myself that this is so."

"I am sure that is not the case!" she said, and she laughed. "For if I were so good at mysteries, I would have known at once who you are."

He raised an eyebrow. "Oh, but how could you have known?"

She had to concede, there was really no way she could have. "Well, now I do know, Lord Crayford, and I am very pleased."

"As am I," he said. "I was, as the viscountess told you, unable to attend the party for your sisters. I am sorry for that fact, as I have long looked forward to meeting you, as well as to seeing your remarkable house that I have heard so much about."

"It is in no way so remarkable as yours," Ivy said.

"On the contrary, there are things I heard from the night of the party that have made me very interested in seeing it for myself. Just as I have been very interested to meet you. Therefore, I hope you will forgive me if I presume to arrive here today with no invitation."

"You can have need of none!" Ivy exclaimed. Only then she realized that his timing, through no fault of his own, had not been very fortuitous. "Yet, by chance, you come when my husband and sisters are away, and when the staff has been let go for the evening."

He raised a hand, his expression solemn. "You need say nothing more, Lady Quent. I see that I have chosen to present myself at an inconvenient moment. I hope you will forgive the intrusion. I will call some other time that is more appropriate for a tour of the house."

Ivy conceded that, before she opened the door, she had wanted nothing more than to pen a note to Mrs. Baydon, and then take the bit of Wyrdwood to the leaf-carved door in the second floor gallery. But how could she turn the viscount away? It was not only that he was an important man—a man who perhaps could be a valuable ally for her husband—but that he was important to one who had shown her such great kindness. When she owed Lady Crayford so much, how could she do anything but welcome Lord Crayford?

"If you do not mind having me as your guide, then there is no more appropriate time than now," Ivy said. "Please, you must come in."

He regarded her. "Are you certain, Lady Quent? Do not say so if you do not wish it! For if you do invite me, I will certainly come."

"I am very certain," she said as warmly as she could. "Please, Lord Crayford, you are in every way invited and welcome in this house."

Now he smiled again. "Well, if you say it, then it must be so, Lady Quent. I thank you. I believe I will come in, for just a little while."

The viscount approached the door as she stepped back. He seemed to hesitate for a moment, so she gestured for him to enter, to reassure him all was well. Then, hat in hand, he stepped over the threshold.

A high, keening noise stabbed at the air.

So loud and sudden was the sound that Ivy cried out and stumbled back. She clasped her hands to her ears, but it did little to muffle the sharp wail that seemed to spring from all directions. She fought to comprehend what was occurring but could not. The noise was like a needle piercing her brain, making it impossible to think.

Standing just inside the doorway, the viscount appeared curious rather than surprised. He glanced upward, then smiled.

"Ah, Lockwell's little spies," he said, his lisping voice rising to compete with the din. "I had guessed he would direct them to warn against my presence. I see that he did not disappoint me."

Ivy shook her head. What was the viscount talking about? She followed his gaze, looking upward.

A horror gripped her. Above the doorway, the two eyes carved upon the lintel had opened wide, as if in shock or alarm. They rolled in their sockets, looking this way and that, but always coming back to peer at Lord Crayford below. All the while a brilliant blue light emanated from them, as did the keening sound.

She took another staggering step back, then glanced behind her at the grand staircase. The eye atop the newel post at the bottom was open as well, shining blue and emitting the same shrill tone. At last the paralysis that gripped her mind was broken by a shudder of understanding.

I have warned the eyes of Gambrel, her father had written in the journal, *and they know to watch for him. . . .*

She turned back toward the door, and now it was not the eyes at which she gazed, but rather at the distinguished gentleman dressed in ash gray.

"You!" she cried. "You're Mr. Gambrel!"

"The very same, Lady Quent," he said with a bow. Then he straightened, directing his inquisitive gaze at her. "Now, my dear, why don't we proceed with that tour of the house?"

CHAPTER FORTY

𝒯HE LUMENAL WAS far shorter than what the almanac called for, and the sunbeam that fell from the high window seemed to lurch across Eldyn's writing table in fits and starts.

He did little work on the box of receipts. How could he have done! Yet it was easy enough to emulate Father Gadby, and to simply shuffle slips of paper from one heap to another. As long as some activity was taking place, the rector seemed not to notice his lack of progress.

Several times as the brief day stuttered by, Eldyn went back through the ledger. One by one he found them: receipts he had recorded for the purchase of red curtains, all of them signed by Archdeacon Lemarck. Previously, Eldyn had thought it odd there were so many such receipts when he had never seen red drapes anywhere in Graychurch.

Now he knew it was not for this church that the curtains had been intended, but rather for another church within the archdeaconry of the Old City. *I assume we are still to deliver them to the usual place,* the man at the shop on Weaver's Row had said, *the old chapel in High Holy. . . .*

But for what purpose? The theaters on Durrow Street used red curtains before their stages to block out the light of illusion and keep the audience from glimpsing a scene before it was ready to be revealed. However, Eldyn could not imagine a reason why they might be wanted beneath the old chapel. Perhaps it was simply that *he* had a taste for that lurid color, and so robed himself in it, and draped it around him.

Or perhaps it was as the article in *The Swift Arrow* suggested, and he had decided that red curtains formed a fitting backdrop to a place where he lured illusionists to meet their end. Only why? According to the Testament, God would judge them in Eternum. So why had the archdeacon taken it upon himself to condemn them here in this world?

As if a candle had been snuffed out, the shaft of light falling upon the open ledger ceased. He shut it, rose, and went to the stairs.

"Good night, Mr. Garritt," the rector said, adding an extra jowl or two to his chin as he smiled. "I will see you on the morrow, I trust?"

Eldyn drew in a breath. "Good-bye, Father Gadby," he said, then ascended to the church above.

He moved swiftly through the long nave, past rows of glaring saints, having no wish to linger. Previously, he had felt a sense of quietude within the walls of Graychurch. Now it was no longer a lofty sanctuary, but rather a dim, hulking prison from which he only wanted escape.

Despite his urgency, as he drew even with the door that led to the chapel of St. Amorah, he paused. Through the door, he glimpsed a figure in a gray dress standing before the marble form of the saint, her hands clasped tightly in prayer. He approached the entrance of the side chapel, thinking to go in, to tell his sister not to expect him at the apartment that night.

As he reached the doorway his view was improved, and he realized with a start that Sashie was not alone. A priest in a black robe stood beside her. He was somewhat thickset and possessed of a balding pate. Even as Eldyn watched, Sashie took a sliver of wood and caught the flame from a candle. She glanced up at the priest, and he laid a large hand upon her wrist, gently guiding her as she lit another candle before the saint. As she gazed at the candle, he moved nearer, leaning down to bring his nose close to the dark knot of her hair.

Eldyn sucked in a sharp breath. The sound echoed off the stone vaults, and Sashie gasped as she looked up. At the same time the priest took a hurried step back from her. Both of them turned to look at the doorway.

There was nothing within its arch but shadows.

Eldyn backed away from the entrance to the side chapel, weaving the darkness around himself, caring not that he wove illusions beneath the vaults of a church. He was not certain what he had just witnessed. Or wasn't he? After all, Dercy had told him about the proclivities of priests.

Tomorrow he would speak to Sashie and warn her about Father Prestus's motives—if tomorrow found Eldyn still in the world, that was. For now, he turned and passed through the front doors, leaving behind the chanting, the incense, and the brilliant frescoes upon the ceiling.

The evening bells began to ring as he hurried down the steps of Graychurch. He did not look back. As he passed through crooked streets, he kept the shadows around him, weaving them thicker and darker, so that no eye could penetrate them.

Soon he reached the edge of High Holy, and Eldyn moved more carefully. However, while he noticed all the usual denizens of the place—the night ladies and drunks and hard-faced men standing by open blazes in the street—he did not see any figures in hooded robes. Nor did anyone see *him,* and so he came to the old chapel at the summit of the hill.

He made his way past the group of whores who sat upon the chapel steps, and what with their cackling and the bottle of gin they passed back and forth, they paid him no heed. The wooden door of the church leaned crooked upon its hinges, and it was easy enough to press his slim form through the crack, into the chapel beyond.

That he was not the first to have done so was apparent. As his eyes adjusted to the faint haze of moon and fires that breathed through the broken-toothed maws of the windows, he saw that the chapel had been stripped of all its trappings. Over the years, anything gilt or marble that could be pried up had been. There was nothing left but a few rats' nests of blankets that had been wadded up in alcoves by people seeking shelter. Nothing adorned the walls save dark stains that ran down the bare stone.

Still encapsulated in shadows, Eldyn moved to the back of the chapel. There, behind the place where the altar would have once rested, was a hole in the floor. He could make out the first few steps leading down. He listened for a moment, but he heard only the raucous laughter outside. Then, taking in a breath of musty air, he descended the steps into the crypts.

The blackness was complete beneath the chapel, so that he was forced to release the shadows and instead conjure the faintest ball of blue light he could fashion. By its wan emanations, he made his way past niches in the wall that were empty of anything except for bits of splintered wood and, here and there, the pale shard of a bone.

At last he reached the end of the crypt, and there in the wall was an opening blocked by an iron gate. Eldyn gripped one of the stout metal bars and pushed against the gate. It did not budge; a massive lock held the gate shut. He peered through the bars, but his fairy-light illuminated only the first few feet of a rough-hewn passage.

Eldyn retreated to the alcove nearest the door and huddled down inside it. At some point, *he* would come here, with more curtains, or perhaps an illusionist, and he would have to open the gate when he did. Eldyn would wait for him, no matter how long it took. What he would do then, he did not know. Follow, he supposed, if he could.

It was Eldyn's intention to wait all night, and to come the next night if he had to, and the next. However, he had sat on the cold stone no more than half an hour when he heard the echoing sound of footsteps. Hastily he snuffed out the blue wisp of light, realizing he had been sustaining it without thinking. He retreated deeper into the niche, making himself as small as he could against the rotting brick wall.

The footsteps drew closer, accompanied by a wheezing noise. It was not from above that the sounds came, as he had expected; rather, they echoed out of the passage beyond the iron gate. A moment later there was a jingling sound, followed by the groan of metal.

Someone had opened the gate. Then the jingling resumed; they were locking it again! Eldyn sucked in a breath. Only he must have made an audible sound, for the jingling ceased.

"Who is there?" a voice hissed off cold stone.

Eldyn groped against the wall of the niche. His fingers found the edge of a brick and pulled. It came free, along with a rain of rotted mortar that pattered against the floor.

"I know you are there!" said the voice. There came the wheezing sound again, punctuated by a snuffling, and then a low laugh. "There you are—I can see your light. So another has come right to our doorstop. What providence! I will not have to go to Durrow Street to find him one more for tonight."

Those words made no sense. How could the other see him? Eldyn had extinguished the illusory light. Unless it was a different illumination the other had spoken of. . . .

The footsteps drew closer. Eldyn waited until they were nearly upon him. Then he sprang to his feet, and at the same time he conjured an orb of light. It was not a faint wisp he fashioned this time, but rather a blazing sphere. The darkness fled before its rays, and the robed figure before him let out a cry and staggered back.

The other drew in a wheezing breath. "You?" a voice emanated from the depths of his black hood. "How are *you* here?"

Eldyn did not know what this meant, but he did not wait to hear more. Instead he gripped the brick in his right hand and brought it down with all his might against the black hood.

There was an awful *thud,* and in an instant the other crumpled to the floor of the crypt, lying there like one of the wadded nests of rags he had seen in the chapel above. For a moment he clutched the brick, holding it high in case he had to strike another blow.

There was no need. The other's chest still rose and fell, but he otherwise made no motion.

Eldyn dimmed the orb of light to a fainter glow, then knelt down. The man's hood had fallen aside, and his face was visible now. He was not so old as Eldyn had thought, though his cheeks were sunken, and there was a grayness to his flesh. Yet it was not these things that made Eldyn let out a gasp. Rather, it was the man's eyes.

Or rather, the scarred pits where his eyes should have been.

The man was blind, yet he had seen Eldyn there in the dark— just like the robed figure that night he passed through High Holy, cloaked in shadows. But then, surely this was the same man. Only how could he see Eldyn and the light he had conjured when he possessed no eyes?

There was no time to wonder more. The sounds of their struggle might have drawn attention. Straining, Eldyn pulled the limp form into the niche. When his work was done he went to the iron gate.

A ring of keys dangled from the lock. Eldyn took them, then pushed against the gate. It swung forward. A momentary trembling came over him. He started to murmur a prayer to steady himself, but stopped after only a few words. Who was he to ask the help of God?

He entered the passage and locked the gate behind him.

Eldyn maintained the orb of illusory light as he went, though once again he made it as faint as possible, so that it did no more than allow him to see where his next footstep would fall. The passage doubled back on itself several times, and he often glimpsed the first of a flight of steps just before he went tumbling forward. Down, the passage led, and deeper down.

Suddenly it was not rough-hewn stone he passed by; rather, he felt the velvety brush of cloth to either side of him. A shudder coursed through him. He was close now.

Even as he thought this, he saw a light ahead—not the blue glow of his fairy-light, but rather a warm radiance. The passage widened, and he had the sense that he was in a large space now. However, sound and the movement of air were stifled by the many curtains that draped all around. They hung from the ceiling, dividing up the room into dozens of smaller pockets, making a labyrinth of the place.

Eldyn navigated by following the light, the curtains whispering as he passed them. He heard other sounds as well—soft sighs and moanings, and the clanking of chains. He did his best to put these sounds out of mind and kept moving toward the light. At one point he passed a table on which were arrayed a variety of knives, hooks, and other metallic utensils whose purpose he dared not try to fathom. He took up a curved knife and gripped its leather-wrapped handle.

The illumination grew brighter, until at last he saw its source: a gold line gleaming through the crack between two crimson drapes. He crept as quietly as he could toward the gap, though he did not know what noise he might have made, for he could hear nothing over the pounding of his heart. With a shaking hand, he reached to part the curtains farther.

"Be still, Mr. Garritt," spoke a deep, resonant voice. "There will be pain, but it is little to suffer in exchange for the gift you will be given."

Terror froze Eldyn. He had been seen! Only there was something odd. It had not seemed that the voice was speaking to *him*. Despite his dread, he leaned forward and peered through the gap into the curtains.

Beyond was a small space draped all around in red, lit by the glow from an iron brazier. In the center of the space stood the tall figure of Archdeacon Lemarck. Even though Eldyn knew it was him, had even expected it, the sight was still a shock. The archdeacon wore a priest's cassock that was as red as the curtains, and his piercing blue gaze was directed to the chair before him. Sitting in the chair, bound to it with leather cords, was a slender, dark-haired man in a gray coat.

"It will be easier on you if you do not struggle," the archdeacon said. He held a pair of iron pincers over the coals in the brazier, heating them. "Do not fear. It will take but a moment, and when I am done you will be able to see with a holier vision. For I have been told by my lord that you have been chosen to receive this gift."

The man in the chair let out a bitter laugh, and he raised his head to look at the archdeacon. As he did, a confusion came over Eldyn, and his brain struggled to comprehend the scene before him. For the man who was bound to the chair was . . .

. . . Eldyn Garritt.

"God doesn't speak to you," the Eldyn in the chair said, a look of disgust upon his pretty face. "God doesn't speak to anyone. He listens from far away—if he listens at all. That's what the Testament says."

All at once confusion was replaced by clarity, followed swiftly by horror. Illusion could change one's appearance, but it couldn't alter a person's voice.

"I did not say it was God who spoke to me, Mr. Garritt." The archdeacon gave a little shrug. "Well, struggle if you wish. It matters not. In the end, the will of my lord must be done."

In a swift motion he grabbed a handful of dark hair, pulling it back to tilt the other's face upward. The man in the chair let out a moan of pain and fear. Then the archdeacon brought the hot pincers down toward one of those wide brown eyes. . . .

"No!" Eldyn cried out, thrusting the curtains aside.

The archdeacon drew back the pincers and turned his head. For only a moment was his expression one of surprise. Then, quickly, it grew serene again. He ran his blue gaze over Eldyn, then directed it again to the chair, to the other Eldyn who sat there. All at once, he laughed.

"Well, I see that a little trick has been played upon me. How amusing! I confess, it never occurred to me someone would attempt such a thing. I made no effort at all to look for such a ruse. Though now that I do, it is seen through easily enough." He reached out, laying his free hand upon the brow of the man in the chair as if in a benediction.

The other screamed, his back arching away from the chair, straining against the bonds. Then, as if tearing off a mask, the archdeacon pulled his hand away, and the bound man was no longer Eldyn.

In the chair, Dercy shuddered. His blond hair was wild, and his face twisted into a grimace of pain. He turned his sea green eyes toward Eldyn, and they grew large.

"Blast you, Eldyn, what are you—?"

"Silence," the archdeacon commanded.

Again he laid a hand on Dercy's brow, and again Dercy cried out, the leather cords cutting deep into the flesh of his wrists as he strained against them. His skin went gray; at the same time the archdeacon let out a breath, like the sigh one emits upon experiencing some sensation of pleasure. For a moment his own skin glowed with a warm, coppery radiance that Eldyn was sure did not come from the brazier.

Eldyn leaped into the space beyond the curtain, the knife before him. "Stop it!"

"There, I have stopped," Lemarck said coolly as he withdrew the pincers and put them back on the brazier. "There is no need to shout like a hooligan, Mr. Garritt. A priest must speak in quiet, measured words."

Eldyn clenched his hands into fists. "I will never be a priest."

"No, I suppose you won't."

In the chair, Dercy sagged against his bonds, his face ashen and glistening with sweat, and his chest heaving rapidly. His hair was no longer its usual bright gold, but was rather dull and tarnished. He gripped the arms of the chair with white fingers.

A sickness spread through Eldyn. "What have you done to him?"

"I took some of his light," the archdeacon said, as if this was the most inconsequential thing.

Eldyn's brain labored to understand. He recalled his conversation with Mouse in the tavern. "But light can only be given. You cannot take it from someone."

"Perhaps *you* cannot take it, Mr. Garritt. My lord has seen fit to grant me . . . other abilities."

Eldyn took another step forward, the knife before him. "Your lord? You mean God?"

"God?" Lemarck seemed to consider these words for a moment. "At first, I thought perhaps it was God I heard. After all, it was beneath Graychurch, deep in the crypts there, that I discovered the window. Even though it was far below the ground, a red light spilled through it, and I wondered if it was the light of Eternum."

He shook his head. "But it wasn't Eternum I glimpsed through the window, and the voice that spoke to me did not belong to the God to whom this chapel was raised. No, Ul'zulgul is older than that, and far stronger. For eons he has waited for the door to open again. Now the time comes when he and the others will pass from their world into our own, and we must make certain all is ready for their coming. For if we do, we will be greatly rewarded."

Eldyn felt both a wonder and a horror. "You're mad," he murmured.

"Am I?" The archdeacon made a small motion with his hand. "Or is it you who has lost possession of his faculties, Mr. Garritt?"

Lemarck was no more than three paces away. Eldyn tightened his grip on the knife and prepared himself to leap forward; only then he halted, glancing downward in puzzlement.

The floor before him was moving. Its surface undulated like the black water of a pond whipped by a wind. Even as he watched, a number of droplets splashed upon his trousers.

Then they began to move up his legs.

Eldyn bent to look closer, and a cry escaped him. The spots on his legs were not droplets of black water, but rather black spiders. The entire floor was covered with spiders now. They skittered over one another in a thick, writhing mass.

He swatted at the spiders on his legs, but more of them climbed up to take their place. Eldyn stamped his feet, trying to crush them beneath his boots, but it was no use. More spiders crawled up his legs. Others swarmed down the curtains and dropped onto his shoulders and arms from above. In a panic he dropped the knife and tried to brush them off, but it was no use. More spiders crawled over him. He opened his mouth to scream.

"Eldyn, look through it!" a haggard voice called out. "It's not real—it's only an illusion!"

It was Dercy. Somehow, despite the terror that gripped him, Eldyn held out his shaking hands to look at the spiders. For all that they covered his hands, he could not feel their writhing touch against his skin. He willed himself to peer closer.

The spiders faded, so that he could see through them. He looked at the floor, the curtains, and it was the same. If he made an effort, he could see right through the spiders as if they weren't there.

Because they weren't.

"Very good, Mr. Garritt." Again the archdeacon made a motion with his hand, and all at once the spiders vanished. "You possess some wits. That will aid you in your service to Ul'zulgul and the Ashen."

Eldyn took a step back. "You're an illusionist!"

An expression of disgust flickered across the archdeacon's visage. "No, I am not an abomination like the Siltheri. I was given this ability not as punishment for my sins, but rather to strive against sin." He gestured toward Dercy. "You see, I have been shown a way to grant salvation to wicked men such as him. And such as *you,* Mr. Garritt.

"When I saw you that day in Graychurch, I detected a glimmer about you. It was weak, to be sure, but I thought it possible you would do, if I had great need. Events are moving swiftly now, and I have had to labor at a more rapid pace than before. A dark time is coming, Mr. Garritt—a terrible time—and there is much to be done. There will soon be a great need for the tools that I am learning to forge here."

Out of the corner of his eye, Eldyn saw the knife on the floor no more than two paces away. "Tools?" he said. "What tools do you mean?"

"I mean my witch-hounds."

Eldyn did not know what these words meant, but all the same they filled him with a foreboding. "Witch-hounds?"

"A great peril faces Altania, Mr. Garritt. The ancient trees stir, the Wyrdwood lashes out, and it is the witches who provoke it. They speak to it, call to it, and cause it to strike out at men." Though his expression remained calm, the light in his eyes grew brighter and hotter as he spoke. "Illusionists may be abominations, but they are nothing to witches. There is no greater evil in the world than a sibyl of the wood. Too long have we suffered them in our midst, and too long the pyres in Greenly Circle have remained unlit. Yet my lord has told me all that is about to change. And you illusionists are going to play a part in it."

He moved around the chair and laid a hand on Dercy's slumped shoulder. Dercy let out a moan, as if he had been struck. His skin seemed to pale another shade.

"After all, what is an illusionist but the son of a witch?" the archdeacon said, a fascination in his voice. "Only they are stunted. They have something of their mother's power but cannot draw upon the Wyrdwood. So they turn their powers inward, and upon one another, in vile and depraved ways. They are pathetic, loathsome creatures. Only I have discovered something remarkable, Mr. Garritt—a way that illusionists can be redeemed."

These words caused Eldyn to stagger. "Redeemed?" he cried. "You mean by blinding them?"

The archdeacon shook his head. "I remove their eyes, Mr. Garritt, but I do not blind them. Rather, once they are no longer distracted by the mundane sights of this world, they can see with far clearer vision. No witch will be able to conceal herself from them. All that will need to be done is to bring a woman before one of my witch-hounds, and in an instant he will know whether or not she is a sibyl, for he will see the telltale light around her."

A new horror came over Eldyn. He thought of Lady Quent, and of the green emanation he and Dercy had detected around her. Would a witch-hound raise his finger to point at her? Would she be hauled to the pyre in Greenly Circle to be burned?

He clasped a hand to his head, for it was throbbing. "So that's why you've been seizing illusionists and murdering them."

Lemarck squeezed Dercy's shoulder like a father might his son. "No, it was never my intent that they should die. However, there is more that must be done besides the removal of the eyes. To become a witch-hound, the illusionist's mind and soul must be bared to the presence of my lord who is to come, to know his mind, and to understand why all witches must be found. Not many have the strength to endure such a vision, for he and his kin are great and terrible.

"As I told you, time grows short. It is affairs of the spiritual demesne that are of interest to me, but I am in contact with those who shape events in the temporal world. Viscount Crayford tells me my witch-hounds will be needed very soon, and I know he is wise in such matters. You see, it was he who first told me of the window far beneath Graychurch. Thus I have had to perform my work more quickly. It is regrettable that many have not been able to endure the force of their redemption, but it is a necessary cost to pay. And with each attempt, my efforts are perfected. It has taken me long to reach this point, but lately there have been a number of great successes. Indeed, they are all around us now, within these very chambers."

A realization came upon Eldyn. "That's why you have the red curtains—so they cannot see what you are doing in here."

"No, it is so their vision remains keen. Does not even the feeblest light seem brilliant when you have been long in a darkened room? I wish to make certain they can detect even the faintest bit of witch light."

In the chair, Dercy let out a croaking laugh. "And what of your red cassock?" He raised his head weakly, and though his voice was hoarse it was defiant as well. "What other reason can there be for it except to hide what you are—that you are an illusionist just like us? I think we can guess why the Archbishop of Invarel has been having visions. Are you not his closest advisor? You are driving him mad, just as you've driven these poor illusionists chained down here mad. Only in the end it is you who belongs up at Madstone's—you're the one who hears voices."

All semblance of calm departed the archdeacon's expression. "Silence!"

"You couldn't stand it, could you?" Dercy went on, and despite his haggardness he was grinning his old, mischievous grin. "You couldn't bear the fact that you were nothing but a vile, wicked sinner like all the rest of us on Durrow Street. Now it's cracked your mind."

"I said silence!"

He tightened his grip on Dercy's shoulder. Again a golden glow colored his skin, and at the same moment Dercy threw his head back in an awful scream. Then the archdeacon released him, and Dercy slumped forward in the chair, so that only the bonds prevented him from falling. His face and hair were both the color of ash; he was not moving.

Eldyn gripped the curtain beside him to keep from staggering. He searched with his eyes for any sign of movement, then to his relief saw that Dercy still breathed. But otherwise he did not move.

The archdeacon's expression was no longer one of anger, but rather curiosity. "A young man such as he should have had more light to take than that. I suppose he must have been foolish enough to have already given much of it to someone. And I believe I know to whom." Now he turned his blue gaze on Eldyn. "As I told you before, Mr. Garritt, the glimmer around you was feeble— barely enough for me to think you worth keeping at hand should I have need of another illusionist. Yet the last time I saw you at Graychurch I noticed how much brighter your light had grown. Indeed, it is very bright now, and you have conveniently seen fit to present yourself here tonight."

Lemarck took a step toward him.

"I believe *you* will be my next witch-hound, Mr. Garritt."

Eldyn tried to lurch back, but he was too slow. The archdeacon moved his hand, and suddenly the curtained room vanished. Instead, Eldyn stood upon a rocky height far above the world.

Beams of gold illumination streamed through clefts in the dark clouds that swept across the sky. His head dizzy, Eldyn leaned forward to peer over the edge of the precipice. In the depths below, a mass of shadows heaved and roiled like a cauldron of pitch. Even as he watched, some of the shadows broke free of the rest. With alarming rapidness, they began to scale the walls of rock.

Shaking his head, Eldyn tried to will himself to see through the vision. For a moment he thought he caught a flicker of red curtains, and of the ghostly shape of Dercy limp in the chair. Then these things disappeared as the shining figure of the archdeacon walked toward him. He was no longer clad in red, but now in white, and he held a blazing sword.

"This isn't real," Eldyn cried out. "It's an illusion!"

Only all he could see were the windswept clouds and the twisted forms that surged up the sharp cliffs. How much light had Lemarck taken from Dercy to conjure this illusion? The power of his phantasms could not be resisted. They filled Eldyn's eyes, his mind.

"No, this is real, Mr. Garritt," the shining figure of the archdeacon said. His eyes were as bright as ice. He raised the glittering sword. "Or rather, it will be real very soon. A war is coming—a terrible war that will grip all this world in fire and blood. And if you will not fight upon the side of righteousness, then you will be cast into the pits of darkness."

Eldyn cried out in fear, for though he had not taken a step he was suddenly on the very edge of the abyss. The shadowy forms clawed and scrabbled just below him, reaching up with misshapen limbs, opening maws filled with jagged teeth.

"You must choose, Mr. Garritt!" the archdeacon's voice boomed from the sky. "On which side of this war will you fight? The side of weakness, of men? Or will you fight for the forces of strength, for Ul'zulgul and the Ashen?"

At these thunderous words the clouds were rent open, revealing a window in the heavens through which a fierce red point of light shone. Even as Eldyn looked up, the point grew in size, becoming a brilliant crimson disk, like a terrible red eye peering down from the firmament. Eldyn shriveled under its fiery gaze, and he was laid open, as if the eye's gaze had burned through his flesh, so that it could gaze into his very soul.

Eldyn cried out in despair. He did not have the will to resist the archdeacon's voice or the fiery gaze of the eye above. Who was he to question powers that were so superior to him? He could only kneel and pray. His legs buckled beneath him—

—yet he did not fall. Something prevented him from sinking downward, like a tug upon his right arm. Eldyn looked at his hand. It was curled in on itself as if to clench something, only he could see nothing in his grip. Again he pulled his hand, and again he felt resistance. He moved his fingers, and though he could not see it, he felt it: a knot of something soft and pliable clenched in his hand. Something real . . .

Shadows roiled before him, and brilliant light streamed from behind.

"Kneel," the archdeacon commanded. "Kneel and seek supplication!"

Eldyn clenched his right hand into a tight fist. "No," he said through clenched teeth. "I will not pray to your god."

He spun around, pulling with all his might. There was a tearing sound; he felt something heavy give way. Then he thrust his hand outward.

The clouds and the shadows vanished; the crimson eye in the heavens blinked out. He was no longer on the high precipice, but rather in the dank chamber beneath the old chapel.

Before him, the archdeacon struggled within the folds of the red curtain that Eldyn had cast over him. Before the archdeacon could free himself, Eldyn turned and ripped down another one of the drapes and cast it over him. The tall figure stumbled and fell beneath the tangling weight of the cloth.

"This little play is over," Eldyn said.

A glint of metal caught his eye: the knife he had dropped. Quickly he snatched it up, went to the chair, and used it to slice the bonds that held Dercy captive.

With a moan, Dercy collapsed into Eldyn's arms. At first Eldyn thought he was still unconscious, then he saw a thin line of sea green through the cracks of Dercy's eyelids.

Eldyn brushed a hand over his cheek, his brow. "Can you walk?"

"I think so, with a little help," Dercy said faintly, then he grinned. "I've been wobblier after a night at tavern."

Possessed of a strength that surprised him, Eldyn heaved Dercy to his feet. Or was it that Dercy was so much lighter than Eldyn had expected?

"You will be punished for these sins!" the archdeacon shouted, though his voice was muffled by the heavy folds of red cloth, just as the light of his illusions had been.

"Perhaps you are right," Eldyn said, "but I'll leave it to God to judge us both."

He pulled down another curtain, and another and another, so that any more words the archdeacon might have uttered were muted beneath thick, stifling folds of red.

"Let's go," Eldyn said, tightening his arm around Dercy.

"What of the others?" Dercy said as Eldyn helped him limp through the labyrinth of red curtains. "We have to save them."

Eldyn thought of the vision he had glimpsed for only a moment: of the red eye gazing from above, stripping away everything he was, until his soul had been laid bare and quivering—a thing to be plucked, and consumed.

We can't save them, he wanted to say. *They are already lost.*

Instead, he said, "I will send word to the redcrests to search beneath the chapel. They will be found."

This seemed to satisfy Dercy, and he allowed Eldyn to lead him toward the steps. Eldyn would do as he said; the king's soldiers would find the men chained down here. Though they would not find the archdeacon, Eldyn had no doubt. Lemarck would be long gone by then.

Only that didn't matter. For as they passed the red curtains draped all around, an idea began to form in Eldyn's mind.

"Come on," he said, pulling Dercy with him up the steps. "We have to get to the theater."

"Why?" Dercy croaked the word.

Now it was Eldyn who was grinning. "Because we have a play to put on, that's why."

CHAPTER FORTY-ONE

IVY PRESSED HER hands to her ears, but still the keening of the arcane eyes pierced her brain, paralyzing it so that she could not move, could not think.

Before her, the elegant man in charcoal gray took off his gloves, then raised his right hand. On his middle finger was a thick gold ring set with purple amethysts. He uttered several words, and unlike his previous manner of speech, which was soft and sibilant, these words had a queer dissonance. At the same time he made a sharp motion with his hand, and the gold ring flashed with a lurid violet light.

The shrill sound ceased, and the arcane eyes above the door snapped shut. Ivy took a staggering step back. After the high-pitched din, the silence was a shocking thing.

"How?" she managed to say at last, lowering her hands from her ears. "How did you make them stop?"

"I commanded them with a spell," the viscount—that was, Gambrel—said amiably.

"But my father enchanted them to guard against . . ." Ivy's voice faltered as he took a step toward her.

"To guard against me. Yes, that's so. However, the moment you so kindly invited me to enter, the wards that surround the house were lowered to me. Besides, who do you think helped your father to understand the workings of the house's defenses in the first place? Those amateurs Mundy, Fintaur, and Larken? As for Bennick . . ." He gave a small laugh. "I'm not sure he ever was much of a magician, but it mattered not, for by then he didn't have a spark of magick left in him."

Ivy retreated another step. "Because you took it from him, or the magicians of your order did—the Vigilant Order of the Silver Eye. You took it from him to punish him, didn't you?"

Gambrel raised an eyebrow. "Is that what you think?" He shook his head. "No, it was not because of us that Bennick lost his magick. That was all *his* doing. At any rate, I did not come to recount histories. I am here, as I said, to tour the house. I have not seen it in a very long time."

Despite her fear, an outrage came over Ivy. "Not since you stole the key to Tyberion, you mean!"

"So you know about that, do you? You are clever indeed, Lady Quent. Yet do you have any idea why I took the key?" He folded his gloves neatly and tucked them into his coat pocket. "No, I don't think that you do."

Ivy edged back another step. If she could get far enough away from him, perhaps she would have a chance to turn and flee. "It isn't here anymore," she said. "It is gone, and so is the Eye of Ran-Yahgren."

He gave her a stern look. "Lady Quent, I am disappointed. Such petty lies do not become you. Besides, I don't care a whit about the Eye of Ran-Yahgren. It was never a thing that suited my purposes. Some of the others approached me last year with their silly little plan to try to gain the artifact, but I would have nothing to do with it. I had a feeling it would end up just as it did. Though, if I had the knowledge I do now, I would have accompanied them merely to gain entry to the house."

His gaze roved around the front hall. "I never thought he would have been so bold as to hide it here, but that was Lockwell—ever astute." Now he looked at Ivy. "Yes, that's right—I know that the door Tyberion is in the house. It is in the second floor gallery, on the south wall. I know, for Captain Branfort told me he saw it."

Ivy was shocked anew. "Captain Branfort? Then it was you who sent him to the West Country to make inquiries about me."

He cocked his head, a light of curiosity in his eyes as he studied her. "You are your father's daughter indeed, Lady Quent. I see I have been shrewd to approach you in the most cautious fashion, to learn all I can first, and not to make the error of underestimating you."

"To approach me? You mean to send Captain Branfort to spy upon me!" She began to tremble, and her skin grew clammy, as if a fever had seized her. "That was also the true reason Lady Crayford came to me and expressed her wish to be my friend—because you asked her to."

"Of course. She is a good wife, and she obeys her husband."

Ivy clasped a hand to her mouth, but she could not stifle the sobbing sound that escaped her.

"Do not think ill of the viscountess, Lady Quent. Yes, it was because I asked her that she made her first overtures to you. I charged her with learning everything she could about you. However, it was not long before she needed no encouragement at all, for she quickly became fond of you. Lady Crayford cares for you very much."

"That cannot be true! She cannot care for me, not if she would willingly and cruelly deceive me."

Gambrel waggled a finger at her. "Come now, Lady Quent, the heart is not so simple a device as you claim. We are all greatly capable of deceiving those we love. Indeed, the more we love, the more we are compelled to prevaricate and even lie. Were you not yourself greatly deceived by Sir Quent regarding your parentage and history? Yet still you married him."

Ivy clenched her jaw, else she might have gasped as if in pain.

"For my part, I was very fond of your father," Gambrel went on. "I still am. It was he who first sparked my interest in magick. I owe so much of what I have become to him. All the same, I did not and will not allow sentimentality to stand in the way of what I need."

"What you need? You mean the door?"

"No, Lady Quent. What I need lies *through* Tyberion."

"You're mad," she said. "My father hid it for a reason." Again she retreated a pace, trying to increase the distance between them in hopes she might have a chance to escape.

Her movements did not go unnoticed.

"Do not think you can flee or call for help, Lady Quent," Gambrel said. "Now that you have allowed me into the house, you have no power to stop me from doing as I will."

She lifted her chin and gazed at him directly. "Then why are you speaking to me? Why do you not go to the door?"

"The magicks I will be working are best performed after darkness falls. Given the inaccuracies of the almanac of late, I couldn't be quite certain precisely when to arrive. Besides, I am enjoying our conversation. After hearing so much about you from my wife and Captain Branfort, I have been anxious to meet you myself."

He glanced at a nearby window; outside, the last light of afternoon was faltering. "It looks like we have a bit more time, Lady Quent. Come—a curious mind such as yours must be filled with questions. Ask me anything you like. I will tell you whatever you wish to know."

The last thing Ivy wanted was to engage in idle conversation with the man who had betrayed her father, and who had architected the plan to betray her by means of Lady Crayford and Captain Branfort. All the same, her mind schemed, trying to fathom how she might get away; the longer she could delay him, the more time it would give her to think of what to do.

"How is it you are a viscount?" she said. "There were many who stood between you and the title Lord Crayford, were there not? I must suppose you murdered them all."

He affected a frown. "Really, Lady Quent, I am disappointed you would pose such an uninteresting question. There were not all *that* many men in my lineage who had to pass away before the title fell to me, and contrary to what you might think, there were none I did away with directly. Though if there were some who were easily enticed to try a hand at magick, and to attempt things that were beyond their power . . ." He shrugged. "Well, it is not my fault if they lost their minds or their lives through such foolish acts."

Ivy could imagine what encouragements Gambrel might have offered to the men who stood between him and the title of viscount—men who, like him, were descended of one of the seven Old Houses of magick.

He strolled toward the marble fireplace, examining the crest above it, then turned around. "Now, Lady Quent, ask me what is really on your mind. I see you have found a fine example of the Dratham crest. Surely you have questions about *him*."

Despite her dread of this man, and her antipathy toward him, Ivy could not deny that she was indeed curious to know more about Dratham.

"Was it he who made the door?" she asked. "Did he fashion Tyberion?"

"Fashion it?" Gambrel shook his head. "No, he did not fashion it, not precisely. From what we learned, Tyberion was a thing he discovered, and it is exceedingly ancient—a relic from a time long before history began. Yet he did work to shape it, giving it the form of a door it now holds."

"If it is a door, where does it lead?"

"It leads just where you would think from its name—to Tyberion."

She stared at him, fear replaced momentarily by astonishment. "You mean to the moon of Dalatair?"

"Precisely."

"But that cannot be!"

He stroked his chin as he regarded her. "I would not think you would make such a claim, Lady Quent. After all, did you not see through the Eye of Ran-Yahgren a place that was similarly far distant in the heavens?"

He was right. Through the Eye she had glimpsed the world Cerephus. If the artifact was a window to a planet, could not a door open to a moon?

Gambrel nodded. "Good, I see that you comprehend now. As did Dratham when he passed through the door. He discovered that Tyberion was a sort of way station, for on its surface were a number of magickal doors, all of them protected from the frozen emptiness of the aether by a magickal dome. Long ago, the doors would have opened to many different places here on our own world, allowing one to travel swiftly over vast miles."

She struggled to comprehend this. "But why place the way station on a moon? If the doors led to places in this world, why wasn't it here?"

"Who can say what the intentions of the builders were?" Gambrel shrugged. "Perhaps there was some inherent property of the moon that lent a power to the doors, or perhaps the builders wished to keep them in a place that would not be easy for others to reach. Only someone did reach them, for as Dratham and his companions explored, they discovered that the doors no longer functioned—they had been destroyed. Except, after much searching, they at last came upon one door that was not completely broken, and which still retained a fraction of its enchantment. After much time and study, they were at last able to restore the door to working order, and in so doing they discovered that it led to a very interesting place."

A chill came over her. "What sort of place?"

"To a tomb," he said. "The tomb of a god."

"A god!"

He made a small flick of a hand. "Well, to the primitive peoples who knew the power of Neth-Bragga, he was as a deity. The Broken God, they called him, for his shape was so deformed, so twisted and hideous to look upon, that the mere sight of it induced delusions and shattered the mind."

Ivy shuddered at these words. "You said the door led to his tomb. This god—this being—you speak of must be dead."

"Can you really slay a god, Lady Quent?" Gambrel shook his head. "No, Neth-Bragga is not truly dead, not as we know the word. He merely slumbers, waiting for the time when he is awakened by the proper incantations. You see, many eons ago there was a great war—a war in which the stakes were no less than the whole of our world. Some believe that this war was won by mankind, but that is not true. The war never really ended. It has gone on in secret through the ages, even up to this very moment. A time comes soon when the war will no longer be waged in the shadows. It will be played out in the open, and we will all of us be made to choose whether we will fight against them and perish, or join them and be rewarded."

A horror had descended over Ivy as he spoke; the twilight seemed to press in from all around. "Who do you mean?" she said, hardly able to voice the words. "Who must we fight or join?"

"The Ashen, of course."

Ivy thought of the world of Cerephus, which she had glimpsed through the Eye of Ran-Yahgren, and of the dark creatures that had swarmed over its crimson surface. Her heart seemed to freeze in her chest.

"The Ashen," she murmured.

Gambrel glanced at a window. "I believe we have a little more time, Lady Quent. Let me tell you a bit more of the Ashen, and what I am doing to prepare the world for their coming."

One can be sensible to only so much terror. After a certain point is reached, no further fear can possibly be suffered. So it was with a kind of numbness that Ivy listened as Gambrel spoke.

It was her father, he said, who first learned of the door Tyberion, and those he entrusted this secret to—Gambrel, Bennick, Fintaur, Larken, and Mundy—helped him to further his research. In time they learned of the society of magicians Dratham belonged to, which met in a hidden room beneath a tavern on Durrow Street. It was from Dratham's order—the Occult Order of the Sword and the Leaf—that the tavern gained its name.

While the magicians who belonged to the order were gentlemen of modest fortune and family, they all rose to great wealth and prominence. The secret to their rise was the door Tyberion—or rather, what they found beyond it. On the cold, barren moon, they passed through the one working door they found, and so reached the tomb of the Broken God. There, they discovered that the stone from which the tomb was built had remarkable properties. It had the power to increase the potency of any magick; that was surely the reason why it had been employed by the nameless magicians eons ago, during the war with the Ashen, to imprison Neth-Bragga. Where it was hewn from, Dratham did not know, though that its origin was not of this world, he had been certain.

Dratham and the other members of his order found that the stones could be arranged in ways that would greatly increase the effect of any spells they worked or arcane energies they summoned. They knew, with these stones, they could all become very powerful magicians. So they conspired to pry some of the stones from the walls of the tomb and bring them back. This they did by summoning daemons for slaves, and by fashioning a new path from the tomb of the Broken God. At last, by their efforts, they were able to retrieve some number of the stones.

"Did that not weaken the enchantment upon the tomb?" Ivy said, fascinated despite herself.

"Of course," Gambrel said. "They studied the enchantments wrought upon the tomb and decided it was a risk they were willing to bear. In the end, while the Broken God's prison was weakened, still it was not enough that he was awakened."

An idea came to Ivy, one she was suddenly certain was correct. "These stones they brought from the tomb—were they reddish in color, with darker flecks that catch the light?"

Gambrel laughed—a sound of genuine delight. "Once again, you know more than I would have thought you did. You are correct, Lady Quent. Dratham worked a number of stones from the tomb into the walls of this house—that is a great part of the power of its defenses. He hid them in plain view, blending them with stones of a more mundane origin, but which were a similar hue. The others of his order used the stones as well, employing them in various ways. Thus all of them were able to become greater magicians than they ever would have otherwise—though none so much as Dratham himself, for he gained more of the stones than anyone."

"That's why you want to go through the door," Ivy said, her

voice quavering. "You want to gain some of these stones for your-self!"

"I'm afraid this time you do not know as much as you think you do, Lady Quent," Gambrel said pleasantly. "My purpose is not to take stones from the tomb. Rather, my intention is to break open the tomb altogether."

A gasp escaped her. "Surely that will release the Broken God!"

"So it will."

Ivy held a hand to her brow; she felt as if she were the one who had gazed upon some hideous thing and had lost her senses. "You cannot think you could control such a being to use for your own gain. Why then would you seek to release one of the Ashen into our world?"

"Because they cannot be stopped," he said in his soft but com-pelling voice. "Cerephus returns, drawing ever closer in the heav-ens. One day, the Ashen will enter our world again, and the war against them will be waged anew. Only this time they will not be defeated."

"Why not? Reason holds that if they were defeated once, then they can be again."

He shook his head, his expression grave. "No, Lady Quent. The world is a different place now than it was then. This time, the Ashen will be victorious. Which means you can either struggle against them and be destroyed, or you can ally yourself with them and help to shape the future of our world."

A revulsion came over her. "No sane person would help you do such a terrible thing!"

"On the contrary, there are many who are doing so even now. Some of them are great men. There is a cleric I have met—a re-markable man who rises quickly in the Church of Altania. I have had him to my house on occasion. You should see the work he is doing in the name of the Ashen! It is because of men like him that the victory of the Ashen is assured. Your husband could be a great man as well, he could play an important role and be rewarded for it—if only you would encourage him to be so."

Now it was a kind of outrage Ivy felt. Who were these people, to make such decisions that would affect the fate of all people in the world? "If they would do such awful things, then they cannot be wise at all!" she exclaimed. "I do not know who these persons are who are helping you, Mr. Gambrel, but I assure you my husband will never be one of them, and neither will I."

Gambrel let out a sigh. "No, I don't suppose you will. I am saddened, but I cannot say I am surprised. Lady Crayford held out a hope that you might choose otherwise, but I knew if Lockwell had any influence upon you that you would not. Lockwell was never a pragmatist, not like me or Bennick. He was never willing to put aside his own silly notions of what was right and wrong and instead do what circumstance required. I see you are very like him in that regard."

He glanced at a window. "Well, the umbral falls. I'm afraid I must leave you now, Lady Quent. Or rather, *you* must leave me. There's no need for you to take me upstairs—I am sure I can find Tyberion myself."

As he said this, he took something out of his coat pocket and held it on his palm: a piece of wood carved to resemble a gem. It looked, she thought, like just the sort of jewel that might fit in the pommel of a sword.

"Thank you for your hospitality, Lady Quent. I have waited long years to use this key. To think, all this time it has been right above my head!"

She thought surely she had misheard him. "What do you mean?"

"In our meeting room beneath the tavern, there is another door—one that was also created by Dratham. Carved upon it are the shapes of a sword piercing a leaf. The door leads to a chamber we use as our innermost sanctum. Yet that chamber is not, in fact, located beneath the tavern. Rather, by a trick of magick, it lies beneath this very house."

Ivy could only stare, beyond words.

"Dratham wanted the chamber where the order performed their deepest magicks to be near his house," Gambrel went on.

"That way their spells might gain the benefit of the stones from the tomb he had worked into the walls of the house. Magick was not at all tolerated then, so he wanted to make certain any who ever managed to find the chamber would not know where it was truly located. That was why there was no passage leading from the house to the chamber below. Or at least, no passage large enough for a person to move through. I have come upon a tiny hole in the ceiling of the chamber. No doubt he used it to eavesdrop upon other members of his order, for it would have carried sound up here into the house."

He smiled at her. "I hope we have not ever kept you up at night with any of our incantations, Lady Quent. If so, do accept my apology. And now"—he closed his fingers around the wooden jewel—"it is time for you to leave me. I have sent one of the younger initiates in my order on a little errand, and he will be ready by now."

"Ready for what?" she said, edging farther away from him.

"To open a way for me, and then to be consumed by the Broken God," Gambrel said blithely. "Neth-Bragga will be angry after eons of imprisonment, and I do not wish for him to turn his wrath upon me."

Despite the awful things she had heard, this struck Ivy anew. "Turn on you? Should he not reward you instead?"

"No, that will be for the rest of the Ashen to do when they have won the war for this world. For Neth-Bragga will not endure long after he is released. Rather, he will be destroyed. But in his destruction he will work a great deed—one that will shape the events that are to come!"

Ivy could not imagine how the destruction of the being he sought to free could possibly be of a benefit to Gambrel, nor did she ask him about it. For as he spoke, she had edged farther away from him. She eyed the distance to the door of the library, planning the steps in her mind, and how she would shut the door behind her and throw the lock.

Before he could move, she sprang into action. She dashed

across the front hall so rapidly he could not possibly have caught up to her. In a few swift strides she passed through the door to the library—

—and found herself racing across the front hall.

It was as if she had run into a mirror, then had come back out of it just as her reflection might have. She stumbled to a halt. Before her, Gambrel raised his right hand. The ring upon it glittered with purple sparks.

"No, not that way," he said. "I have arranged a little affair for you out in the garden. You may think of it as your farewell party. I trust you will enjoy it. Now good-bye, Lady Quent."

Before she could try once more to flee, he spoke several sharp words and made a motion with his hand.

Again she was racing through the front hall, only this time it was not her feet that moved, but rather the hall itself. The room elongated and contracted around her in jarring spasms. Then, suddenly, she found herself standing on the step outside the front door.

"No!" Ivy cried out.

The sound of her voice was cut off by a thunderclap as the front door swung shut before her. There came the noise of a lock turning, and by the time she reached out to grasp the handle, it was too late.

FOR A TIME Ivy merely stood there, staring stupidly at the locked door, as the purple air thickened in the garden behind her. She could not move, could not think; she did not know what to do and so did nothing.

At last a sudden clatter of hooves drifted from off the street, and as if freed of a trance she drew in a gasping breath. Her heart soared. Mr. Quent had returned! She would tell him everything that had happened; he would know what to do.

Ivy turned from the door and ran past the stone lions, down the steps. Even as she did she saw a broad figure walking up the darkened path. Relief flooded through her.

"Mr. Quent!" she cried, running down the path to meet him. "Mr. Quent, something awful has—"

Ivy stopped short. The moon had just risen over the roofs of the Old City, and a pale beam, tinged crimson by the light of Cerephus, fell into the garden. The short, broad-shouldered figure drew closer along the path, stepping into that sickly light.

Ivy's elation was replaced by fear. She took a staggering step back, then started to turn to run.

"No, don't go!" Captain Branfort called to her, holding out a hand. "Please, Lady Quent, I won't hurt you, I swear it!"

It was not because she believed these words that she stopped; rather, her eyes went to the pistol that gleamed at his hip.

"If you mean what you say, then come no farther," she said, trying to master the trembling in her voice.

He stopped on the path and spread his arms wide. "As you wish, Lady Quent. As I said, it is not my intent to cause you any harm."

She could only be incredulous at these words. "Was it not your intent to cause harm when you went to the West Country to learn about me at the bidding of your master? Was it not your intent to harm when you deceived me as to your true intentions?"

A grimace crossed his handsome face. "It was never my intent," he said, his voice going low. "Yet I own that I did cause you harm, even as I harmed my own honor and reputation."

Now it was not fear she felt, but a most awful sorrow. She had thought him so kind, so gallant; she had thought Lily would favor him. And poor Mrs. Baydon—she was so fond of him. "Why?" Ivy said, and the word was hoarse for the way her throat ached.

"He told me that the Wyrdwood must be destroyed."

Ivy shook her head; she did not understand. "The Wyrdwood?"

His eyes were lost in shadow. "You may already know this, Lady Quent—how all of my family was lost at the colony of Marlstown. I always wondered what had become of them; I thought I would never know. That ignorance was a burden that weighed upon me. Only then Captain Daubrent introduced me to Lord

Crayford. The viscount told me he had discovered the truth—that it was the ancient forest that covers the New Lands that did it, that the Old Trees turned against the colonists. Just as they've begun to turn against people here in Altania."

Ivy could only stare, unable to speak.

"You have to understand," he said, taking a step toward her, his arms still outspread. "I never had the chance to save my parents in Marlstown, nor my brothers or sisters. But after I spoke to Lord Crayford, I thought perhaps I could at least save others here in Altania. So when he asked me to go to the West Country, I did."

"You were deceived!" she cried at last.

He gave a grim nod. "I know that now. He wanted me to learn as much about you as possible. I don't entirely know the reason why, but he told me that it was important. And I believed him after what I learned in the West Country, what I learned about the things you did there."

Ivy shivered. Again her eyes went to the pistol at his hip.

"I know what you are, Lady Quent. I heard rumors about it in County Westmorain, though I doubted its veracity at the time. Only then . . ."

"Then what?" she whispered.

His face was pale and anguished in the moonlight. The buttons of his coat glittered in the pale illumination. It was then she noticed that, while there were four buttons on the left cuff of his coat, there were only three on the right. A button was missing.

One brass button.

"You were there!" she gasped. "At the Evengrove. You saw Mr. Rafferdy and me at the wall."

He nodded, his expression grim. "I did. I looked into the passage, and I saw the way you called to the trees—and how you calmed them. Lord Crayford said that women like you were a danger, that you would incite the Wyrdwood. Only you didn't incite. You stopped it."

He took another step toward her, and this time Ivy did not retreat.

"I know what I did was a terrible thing," he said, his face lined

with sorrow. "I have wronged you in a way that cannot be forgiven, and I know now that Lord Crayford is mistaken. And I
know that, whatever it is you mean to do, Lady Quent, it will
never be ill for Altania."

An ache grew in Ivy's heart, so that she could no longer feel
fear, or sadness, or anger. He had wronged her, yes, and terribly.
Yet he had been wronged himself in the most awful ways, first as
a child and again by Lord Crayford. She hesitated, then slowly she
lifted her hand toward him.

Captain Branfort stared at her, his expression one of shock at
first. Then it was a look of wonder that crossed his face. He took a
step forward, reaching out his hand toward hers. His fingers
brushed her own—

—and a shadow rose up behind him, coagulating out of the
darkness like a clot from black blood.

He must have seen her eyes go wide, for he frowned at her.
Then he turned around to look over his shoulder. As he did, the
shadow spread itself wide, then in one swift motion it wrapped
around him.

Ivy screamed.

All her life, she had felt a peculiar dread when the day ended
and night stole over the world. Sometimes she had the sensation
that the darkness was a conscious thing: ancient, hungry, and possessed of a will to smother all light, all life from the world.

As it was now smothering Captain Branfort.

He struggled as if caught in folds of black, tangling cloth.
What the thing was that held him in its grasp, she could not say,
for its edges melded with the night itself. Here and there she saw
a line like a gaping jaw, or a curve as of long talons, but for the
most part it was formless. Or rather, its form was of such a bizarre
shape, and of such hideous proportions, that her mind could
make no sense of it. It was like trying to see the color of night.

There was a bright flash, followed by a sudden deafening
noise. A shriek vibrated upon the air—a quivering, loathsome
sound that offended the ears as the most noisome offal might
the nose. The darkness folded in on itself and slunk back, pooling

like a black stain upon the ground. It seemed to absorb all moonlight and starlight that fell upon it—save for the sickly gleam of yellow that reflected off a row of jagged teeth.

Captain Branfort staggered back, his pistol held before him.

"Run!" he cried out.

Ivy could not move. The shadows seemed to coil around her feet, rooting her to the ground.

Captain Branfort looked back over his shoulder at her. His eyes were wild; a black fluid ran down his face, but she did not know if it was his blood or some secretion given off by the dark form.

"I only have one more shot before I must reload," he shouted. "You must get in the house, Lady Quent!"

Before him, the shapeless thing began to stir again. It rose up off the ground, unfolding itself as it did, the edges of its form bubbling and rippling. More teeth appeared as its maw widened.

Captain Branfort's gaze locked upon her own. His face was pale, and there was a pleading in his eyes.

"I beg you, Lady Quent," he said. "You must run to the house. Now!"

At last Ivy was freed of her paralysis. She turned and dashed back along the path. Behind her came another flash, followed by a loud report. Again she heard the thing's awful shriek, only this time it was more a sound of fury than of pain. A moment later came another cry, and this time it was the horrible sound of a man screaming.

The sounds behind her ceased. Ivy sobbed as she ran. She had nearly reached the front steps, only then she remembered that the door was locked. There was no safety for her that way. But where could she go? That Captain Branfort could no longer protect her, she was certain, and the shapeless thing was between her and the gate to the street.

She cast her gaze about wildly—and saw thin, straggled shapes to her left. Only for a moment did she think about it, then she ran toward the little grove of chestnut and hawthorn saplings.

As she went, she dared a glance over her shoulder, and a moan

escaped her. A thing of darkness coiled and uncoiled itself in rapid
succession, loping across the garden toward her. She flung herself
forward, into the midst of the trees. As she did she reached out,
gripping the nearest trunk.

Help me! she cried out, though not with her voice but rather
her thoughts. *Please, help me!*

And the trees heard.

Ivy felt anger stir among them like a wind. They knew this
shapeless thing that undulated toward her. Its likes had been seen
before, in the ancient war long, long ago.

Gol-yagru, she heard the word in her mind. *Ashen-slave.*

Yes, they remembered, and they knew what to do. This was
their purpose; it was for this they had grown from a seed and put
down strong roots. They would not let their witch come to harm.

One more time the dark form uncoiled itself, leaping forward,
its teeth glittering like the shards of glass around the casing of a
broken window. Ivy cried out, flinging her hands up, waiting for
darkness to enfold her in its smothering embrace.

Instead, it was rough branches that coiled around her. The
boughs grasped her like hands, tenderly yet with strength. They
bore her up off the ground, and like a child she was carried
through the grove, passed from limb to limb, and then deposited
on the ground at its far edge.

Ivy stumbled backward as the branches released her, and she
watched the moonlit scene before her in horror and wonderment.
The little trees, which had seemed so scraggly and harmless,
whipped back and forth with violent force, their boughs whistling
and cracking like horsewhips.

In their midst, she could make out a ball of darkness that flung
itself against them. Again it did so, and again; but it could not escape the tangling net of their branches, and their blows beat it
back. Even as she watched, the thing's outline began to fray and
tatter. Still the trees whipped and beat at the black shape. Its
piteous keening rose on the air, then was lost amid the cracking
and creaking of branches.

"The daemon that he summoned will not escape," spoke a

voice behind her. "You have awakened the trees. They know their purpose, and they will destroy the gol-yagru."

Ivy screamed and turned around. Before her stood another black form, only this one was shaped as a man. He was tall, and he was garbed not in folds of shadow, but rather ruffs and frills of black cloth. Moonlight highlighted the edges of his ebon mask; it was wrought in a grim expression.

She swooned and might have fallen, but he gripped her arm with a black-gloved hand, holding her upright.

"There is no time for that!" he hissed. "Gambrel has already passed through Tyberion. He will be searching for the door to the tomb of the Broken God. You must get there before him."

Dully, she realized he was speaking audibly, the words emanating from his black mask.

"Go where?" she said.

The mask twisted into a shape of anger. "Did you not hear me? Listen, child, or all is lost! You must get to the tomb before Gambrel. You must keep him from entering it."

She clasped a hand to her head, trying to think. "The house is locked. Even if it weren't, he has already gone through the door. How could I catch up to him?"

"Once he passed through Tyberion, he could no longer maintain his binding on the house. You can pass inside. Besides, you do not need to catch up to him. There is another way to the tomb."

Again she could do no more than echo. "Another way?"

"Do not be so stupid! Why do you think I told you to conceal it?"

"The other door!" she gasped, understanding at last.

Now the mouth of the mask turned upward in a sharp smile. "There, you are not so dull after all. Now come."

He pulled her arm, and she started to follow; only then she halted.

"Captain Branfort," she said. "He is—"

"He is beyond help. It was always his wish to save another, was it not? Do not render his deed meaningless."

Ivy bit her lip, for else she would have burst into weeping. She let the man in the black mask pull her up the steps to the front door. Behind them, the trees had ceased moving; the night was still.

They reached the door. She tried the handle and, as he had said, it was no longer locked. She pushed open the door. The front hall beyond was dark and silent, and she was suddenly loath to enter.

"You have a little time," the man in the black costume said. "But only a little. Gambrel does not know which door on Tyberion is the one that leads to the tomb. He will have to search among them, but he is clever and knows what to look for. It will not take him long to find it. You must go through Arantus at once."

"Go through it? How?"

"Think, child. Did the Black Stork not give you the key?"

Ivy thought of Mr. Samonds's letter. Yes, she did have the key. "Only where does the door go?"

"To the moon Arantus, just as its name implies. Like Tyberion, Arantus served as a way point during the war against the Ashen long ago, and there are many doors upon it. Yet unlike those on Tyberion, the enemy never knew of these doors, and they were never warred over and ruined. They still retain their enchantment. You must find the right one, and go through it."

A new terror came upon her. Could not a magickal door lead anywhere? "How will I know which is the right one?"

Again his mask formed into a smile. "You will know it. It is the one that will take you closest to the tomb."

"But I do not know where the tomb is!"

"Then cease your interruptions for a moment and listen to me. The tomb of the Broken God lies within the Evengrove. That is the reason why so great a strand of primeval forest was allowed to exist all these centuries. That is why the great wall was raised around it—not to imprison the Wyrdwood, but to imprison Neth-Bragga."

A hope sprang up within Ivy. She thought of the little trees in the garden, and how they had recognized the shadowy form and knew what to do with it. Were not the trees of the Evengrove far greater, and far more numerous?

"Surely if Gambrel frees the Broken God, the trees will turn against it," she said. However, her relief was quickly negated by his reply.

"Indeed, they would turn against Neth-Bragga with the greatest force and violence, and that is precisely Gambrel's intention in freeing the Broken God. To have a powerful Ashen awaken in their midst would induce in the trees a terrible fury such as the world has not seen since ancient days. Already calls go out in Assembly for the Evengrove and the Wyrdwood to be destroyed, and this after only a few, pitifully small Risings. Imagine what demands would be shouted if the entire Evengrove were to rise up and throw down Madiger's Wall in a rage to destroy Neth-Bragga?"

Ivy stared at his onyx face, and a coldness gripped her. "It would be burned down," she whispered. "All of it."

He nodded. "That is what Gambrel wants, for that is what the Ashen want—for men to cut down and destroy every last Old Tree, until there is not a scrap of Wyrdwood left in all of Altania."

Ivy thought of how the little hawthorns and chestnuts had fought against the gol-yagru—how they had torn apart its dark form—and she began to understand. The Ashen could only loathe the Wyrdwood, and fear it. Which meant, at all cost, it must be preserved.

She drew in a breath. "What must I do?"

"Go through Arantus, as I said. Find the door that will take you to the Evengrove. Once you reach the tomb, you will see another door—the one that leads to the moon Tyberion. It is through this door Gambrel will come. You must bind it with magick so he cannot come through."

"Bind it? I cannot work magick."

"No, but your friend Mr. Rafferdy is a very powerful magician. You must retrieve him and take him to the tomb. Even now, he and one of his companions wait beside Madiger's Wall, for they were sent there by their order. There is a door there in the wall."

She nodded. "Yes, I've seen it. It opens into the Evengrove."

"Rafferdy's companion has been tasked to open the door. He does not know the reason—to provide Gambrel a way to escape the Wyrdwood. For once the tomb is broken, there will be no way for him to go back through the door to Tyberion. Neth-Bragga will destroy all around it in its fury. Thus Gambrel previously made sure that an initiate could open the door in the wall. There is a path fashioned with the same red stones as the tomb of the Broken God that leads from the tomb to the door. It is Gambrel's only way out."

Ivy shuddered, thinking of Mr. Rafferdy standing at the door as the Broken God was freed and the Wyrdwood rose up in fury. *Neth-Bragga will be angry after eons of imprisonment,* Gambrel had said, *and I do not wish for him to turn his wrath upon me....*

Her eyes went wide. Mr. Rafferdy was in the gravest peril!

"What are you waiting for, child?" The man in the mask gripped her arm, shaking her. "Go! And be sure to lock Tyberion before you go through Arantus. That way he will have no escape."

With that, he pushed her through the door into the house.

She stared back at him. "What of you?"

His shoulders heaved as he drew in a breath. For the first time, Ivy realized that he seemed weary. His ruffled costume was crooked and ill adjusted, as if hastily thrown on. The onyx mask was slightly askew, and there was a slight gap between it and his cowl, from which a stray lock of pale hair protruded.

"I can be no help to you among the trees," he said, his voice haggard. "I do not think Gambrel summoned more daemons, for that is not easily done. Yet he might have, so I will watch for more gol-yagru. Now get yourself to Arantus and through it—quickly, before all is lost!"

He turned in a flutter of black frills and lace. Ivy gazed out the door of the house for a moment, her heart pounding.

Then she turned and ran. She dashed across the front hall, her footsteps echoing, and through the door to the library. With fumbling fingers she opened the desk drawer and took out the Wyrdwood box. As she touched it, her hands grew steadier, and a warmth crept into her fingers.

With a thought she opened the box and took out the little piece of Wyrdwood. Now that she knew what its true shape was, she wondered how she had not seen it before. She closed her fingers around the piece of wood. *Be what you are!* she called out in her mind. Then she opened her hand.

On her palm lay a leaf, perfectly carved of wood.

A sigh of pleasure escaped her; it had felt good to shape the wood—or rather, to unshape it. Gripping the leaf, she turned and dashed out of the library, then up the stairs to the gallery on the second floor.

She went first to the door in the south wall, to Tyberion. As she drew near, she detected an acrid smell, like that which had permeated the air after Captain Branfort fired his gun. There were black marks on the floor. The door was not shut all the way, but rather had been left slightly ajar, so that there was a small crack. Ivy hesitated a moment, then she bent forward and peered through the gap.

A breath of wonder escaped her. Through the door, she glimpsed not a brick wall, but a barren, gray-blue plain, its surface pockmarked and littered with jagged rocks. Above the curved horizon, brilliant stars blazed in the sky alongside an enormous violet sickle shape, like a gigantic crescent moon.

Only it wasn't a moon, she knew. Rather, it was the planet Dalatair, and the place through the door was the face of its satellite, Tyberion. Her eyes roved further, and here and there she saw shapes that stood up from the ground: archways fashioned of the gray-blue stone. They were doorways, though those close enough to see contained only darkness within their frames. Above the doors she detected a faint bluish shimmer against the black void, like a dome of azure glass.

Ivy blinked. How long had she been standing there, fascinated by the sights through the door? Now she remembered her task, and a fresh urgency came over her. She pulled on the door, shutting it with a *click*. Then she examined it in the pale light that came through the windows. After a moment she saw it: the piece of wood carved like a gem. It was, as she had guessed, set into the pommel of the sword carved upon the door. Ivy reached out and gripped the wooden jewel with her fingertips.

The key to Tyberion came away in her hand.

Ivy could not help a small smile as she slipped the key into her pocket. Gambrel would not be coming back *this* way.

Now to the other door. Ivy turned and moved swiftly across the gallery. The shroud that covered it glowed in the moonlight. She cast it aside, revealing Arantus.

Several times before, as she looked at the door, she had felt there was something missing from it, only she hadn't been able to discern what it was. Perhaps it was an effect of the moon's illumination, or perhaps it was because she knew now what it was that was missing. Either way, this time she saw it at once. In the center of the door was an odd shadow: a slight gap in the pattern of the carved leaves. There was just space enough where one more might fit. She took the wooden leaf and set it into the niche in the door.

There was a *click,* and the door swung open.

"Oh," Ivy murmured.

The sight before her was not unlike what she had glimpsed through the door Tyberion, only the surface of this moon was smoother: a pale gray-green marked by ripples and crisscrossed by fine lines. The lavender crescent of Dalatair hung in the sky, though at a different angle, and the stars all around it blazed like diamonds and emeralds and sapphires. Ivy drew in a breath, holding it.

Then she stepped through the door.

At once a coldness bit into her skin, as bitter as the shortest, coldest lumenal. Her breath escaped her in a gasp of surprise, fogging upon the air. She drew in another, stuttering lungful. She had feared the atmosphere upon the moon might be a poisonous miasma. Instead, while there was a stale, metallic taste to it, and it was viciously cold, the air seemed to cause no harm to her. She looked up and, as on Tyberion, saw a faint dome of translucent blue overhead. It was as the man in the mask had said—some enchantment protected this place from the aether of the heavens.

Ivy cast a glance behind her. Through the door she could still see the moonlit gallery. Reassured, she walked across the dusty blue plain. Just ahead, she saw them: stone doorways that scattered the surface of the moon. Unlike those she had glimpsed through Tyberion, these doors led not to empty darkness. Rather, she could glimpse faint light through them.

She approached the first one, and she let out an exclamation of delight, for it was like looking out the window of her attic room at Heathcrest Hall. She saw rolling moors bathed in moonlight, and not far off a line of straggled shapes bounded by a stone wall.

Ivy hurried to the next doorway. This time there was less light, and it took a moment to make out a tangle of black trunks and crooked branches. A rushing sound emanated from the doorway as a wind stirred their leaves. Was this where she needed to go?

No. It was a grove of Wyrdwood, but these trees were not thick and tall enough. She moved on, hurrying to the next door, and the next. Through a few of them she saw other copses of Old Trees, sometimes nearby, sometimes at a distance. However, most of the doors gazed out over empty fields or opened onto cobbled streets.

Ivy began to understand. The man in black had said that the doors on Tyberion all led to various places in the world. By them, magicians could have moved about swiftly. Logic implied that the doors here on Arantus were similar. However, it was her guess that these doors had not been intended to help magicians travel swiftly, but rather witches.

Long ago, she supposed, all of these doors had led to various places within the Wyrdwood. But over the centuries, so many of the Old Trees had been cut down and burned, and villages, towns, and cities had been raised in their place. Had there once been a grove upon the spot where the house on Durrow Street now stood? If so, a new grove now sprouted where the old had once grown.

She kept moving. Then her heart leaped as she came to another door that opened into a grove of trees. Though crooked and shedding their leaves, these trees were tall and powerful, woven into a dense fabric that had never been cut, never been frayed or torn.

The man in the black mask was right. She *did* know.

Ivy cast a glance behind her. She could still see the door she had come through in the distance, and even a glimpse of the gallery beyond. However, it was to another place she had to go.

It was for this purpose that the way station had been constructed eons ago—so women just like her might move among the groves. The builders had placed it here, far removed from the world, so that the enemy would not know of it. While, in the end, the Ashen had discovered the way station on Tyberion, and had destroyed the doors there, it was clear they had never found what had been hidden on Arantus. Ivy turned to face the door. For a moment she stood there, bathed in the purple light of Dalatair.

Then she stepped through the doorway.

Ivy let out a breath of dry, frigid air one moment, then drew in one rich and moist and warm with life the next. She thought of the way the trees in the garden had lifted her up to bear her upon their branches. Then she reached out, touching the rough bark of the ancient trunks around her.

There are two magicians by the wall that bounds you, Ivy called out with her thoughts. *Hurry—you must take me to them!*

And the Wyrdwood listened to its witch.

CHAPTER FORTY-TWO

THE MORE RAFFERDY watched the landscape out the window, the slower it seemed to creep by.

He slumped back against the upholstered bench. His head ached from the incessant vibrations of the carriage, and his throat was dry from lack of anything to drink. An hour ago, the driver had brought them to a halt at an inn by a crossroads, and he had climbed down to ask if Rafferdy wished to stop for something to eat. However, Rafferdy had no appetite, not after the things he had witnessed that day. And while he would gladly have drunk down several glasses of whiskey, if given the chance, it was better that he kept full command of his faculties. There was no telling what he would have to do when they arrived at Madiger's Wall. He told the driver to climb back up to his perch, and to continue on with all haste.

He winced as the carriage was jolted by a particularly deep rut. Outside, the hills and fields were beginning to fade from gold to ash gray.

"Come on, hurry it along," he said through clenched teeth, even though he knew the horses could go no faster than they were.

Besides, in his note, Coulten had written that he still had to go to the magus of the order to receive his instructions. Nor was it possible that he might travel to the wall any more quickly than Rafferdy; horses could only run so fast. Which meant Coulten could not be very far ahead of him. All the same, Rafferdy leaned forward in the seat, as if to be sure to arrive not a moment later than possible.

Ever since leaving the city, a dread had been steadily growing in him that he was already too late—that when Coulten went to the magus he had been taken to the inner sanctum to be made into one of the gray men. Or perhaps he had been delivered to Mertrand and the sages of the High Order of the Golden Door. As peculiar as Lord Farrolbrook had acted earlier that day, his words had all possessed a ring of truth, and he had said it was the Golden Door that was the source of many of the gray men.

By what terrible enchantment it was done, Rafferdy could not imagine, though he could guess Lord Mertrand's methods well enough. Young men who could trace their ancestry to one of the seven Old Houses would be recruited, enticed with promises of power, and eventually invited into a secret chamber. There, an eldritch symbol would be drawn upon their hand. Then, by means of some unspeakable magick, a daemon would be summoned and placed within the vessel of their body. Surely that was what had happened to the man who had tried to harm King Rothard at the opening of Assembly, and to the man who had destroyed the Ministry of Printing.

And it was what had happened to Eubrey as well.

That the person who had heretofore resided within that mortal shell survived this process was impossible. Rafferdy had only to recall the dead look in Eubrey's eyes to know it for a fact. A shudder passed through him, and he wondered—would he see the same flat, empty expression in Coulten's gaze if he did find his friend at the wall?

Only, he could not think that way. According to Farrolbrook, Lord Mertrand had made a bargain with the magus of another order—the Arcane Society of the Virescent Blade, Rafferdy was sure. Farrolbrook had said this magus was sending a magician to Madiger's Wall to perform an experiment, and it could only be Coulten. Eubrey had not yet been made a gray man when he was sent to the wall to do his task, and Rafferdy had to hope it was the same for Coulten.

The carriage gave a violent lurch, and Rafferdy supposed they had hit another rut. Only then the fields ceased to move outside the window, and the rattling of the carriage ceased. They had come to a halt.

Rafferdy was out the door before the driver could climb down from the bench. A purple gloom was thickening on the air. Across the fields, a quarter mile away, he could see a dark line surmounted by ragged shapes.

"I'm sorry, sir," the driver said from his perch, "but I don't believe I can go any closer. I've heard reports that no one is being allowed near Madiger's Wall, and I can see soldiers ahead."

Rafferdy could just make them out in the gloaming. There were several redcrests standing beside a wooden barricade that lay across the road. The men were lighting lanterns against the coming dark.

"Turn the carriage around," Rafferdy said. "Go back around the bend until you're out of sight of the wall, and then stop there."

The driver nodded, and Rafferdy climbed back into the carriage, going about it slowly to be sure the soldiers had seen him get in. The driver brought the horses around, and the carriage turned, going back down the road and away from the wall. Then it came to a halt, and Rafferdy climbed back out. The barricade and the soldiers were no longer in sight.

"Now what, my lord?" the driver called down. "Do we make back to the inn, or all the way to Invarel?"

"Wait for me," Rafferdy said, and without waiting for a response, he struck out across the fields, cane in hand.

He walked through the tall grass, going a full furlong perpendicular to the road before he turned to start making his way back toward the Evengrove. After some distance he crested a low rise and saw it again before him—the long line of gray stone, crowned by straggled shapes. He was now out of view of the barricade across the road, but in the gloom, he could see points of light bobbing as they moved to and fro. There were soldiers patrolling back and forth along the base of the wall. Rafferdy let out an oath. How was he going to get past them without being seen?

Even as he considered this, a column of blue light shot upward, cutting a livid gash in the dusky sky. For several heartbeats the column glowed hotly in the distance, somewhere past the soldiers' barricade, then it fell back on itself and was abruptly snuffed out. Rafferdy heard the faint sound of shouting. Now all the points of light along the wall were moving in one direction—toward the place where the gout of blue fire had sprung up.

Despite his dread, he let out a laugh. Coulten was cleverer than Rafferdy sometimes gave him credit for. In a recent meeting of the society, the sages had described how certain volatile chemicals might be placed in two chambers of a box, with a magickal barrier between them. If the enchantment was fashioned carefully, it would expire after a prescribed period, at which point the two chemicals would mix and react.

That Coulten had used this very method to arrange the diversion, Rafferdy was certain. What's more, it meant that Coulten himself could not yet have reached the wall. The soldiers would have kept him at bay. Only now all of the points of light had moved off into the distance, past the barricade. Along the section of the wall before Rafferdy, there were no lights at all, only gloom and shadow.

Gripping his cane, Rafferdy started toward the wall at a rapid pace. He imagined Coulten had stationed himself as close to the door as possible, ready to dash to it once the soldiers all ran off toward the commotion. Which meant Coulten would likely get there first.

Rafferdy was right. He was still a good fifty paces from the wall when he saw a line of crimson sparks flicker into being. Glancing down at his ring, he detected a faint glow within the blue gem— an answering echo to the magick that had just been worked up ahead.

"Blast you, Coulten," Rafferdy growled under his breath. "Don't you dare step through that door."

Rafferdy picked up his cane and broke into a run as he crossed the last distance to the wall. He arrived just in time to see the last of the red stones fade away, leaving the crimson line of runes hanging in midair. A man with a tall crown of hair stood before the opening. He started to step toward it, only then he turned around at the noise behind him.

"Rafferdy!" Coulten cried, pressing a hand to his chest, then hurriedly lowered his voice. "Good God, but you gave me an awful fright. I thought that you were a soldier come upon me."

Rafferdy let out a breath, not only from exertion, but also from relief. Even in the dimness, it was clear from his words and the expression on his face that this was still the Coulten he knew.

"No, all the soldiers ran off in the other direction, thanks to your little diversion."

Now Coulten grinned, his teeth glowing in the light of the rising moon. "Did you see it? I must say, I thought it went off splendidly. And here Eubrey says I never pay attention at meetings."

Rafferdy could only cringe at the mention of Eubrey's name.

"Only, I say, Rafferdy, what the devil are you doing here?" His eyes went wide. "Did the magus send you here to help me? But that's capital—it means you're to be admitted to the inner circle of the society with me! Well, come on, then. We'd best get through before the soldiers come back. The magus says there is a path through the door."

With that, he turned and stepped through the opening in the wall. Not knowing what Coulten intended—or had been ordered—to do, Rafferdy hurried after him. The rough stone passage was dark inside, but it was no more than a dozen feet long, and they quickly reached the end of it. Beyond was a tangle of black branches limned in silver moonlight.

Before them was the tall tree Eubrey had stuck with his knife, while past it was something Rafferdy had not noticed that lumenal. Perhaps the green shadows of day had made it blend in with the forest floor. Now the stray moonbeams that slipped through the branches gleamed off the red stones upon the ground.

Rafferdy followed the line of stones with his eyes. While the trees grew right up to the path, none of them grew over it. Instead, it ran straight through the forest, vanishing into the darkness. Given the color of the stones, Rafferdy could only suppose the path had been put here by the same magicians who had made the door in the wall. Yet for what purpose did they need a trail leading into the Evengrove?

"You're not intending to follow that path, are you?" Rafferdy said, laying a hand on Coulten's arm.

"Of course not, Rafferdy! The magus's directions were very clear—to open the door and wait for him at the start of the path. But didn't he tell you the same thing?"

Rafferdy only shook his head. "We have to go, Coulten. We have to leave and close the door. Now."

"What are you talking about?" Coulten said, his frown dimly visible in the gloom. "We can't leave before the magus gets here. If we fail at the task he gave us, then he won't admit us to the inner circle of the society and make us sages like Eubrey."

Rafferdy clenched his jaw. "Eubrey isn't a sage, Coulten. And they're not going to make us into sages either. That was never their intention."

Coulten shook off Rafferdy's hand. "Now you're making no

sense at all, Rafferdy. Of course Eubrey's a sage! We saw him ourselves at the last meeting of the society."

"Did we? We saw a number of men in gold robes and hoods,
but did we really see Eubrey that night?"

"I'm certain one of them was him," Coulten said, though in
fact he sounded less certain now.

Rafferdy drew in a breath. There was so much he had to tell
Coulten. Only how could he begin? He didn't know, but he had to.

"Coulten," he said in a grim voice, "there's something you have
to know. Eubrey is—"

A rushing sound filled the air, quickly rising to a roar, drowning out Rafferdy's voice. He looked past Coulten, at the tangled
forest, and he was gripped by a sudden dread.

"By all of Eternum!" Coulten called out. "Not again!"

Beyond the tunnel, the trees swayed back and forth, their
boughs shaking as if from the winds of a storm. Yet crazed beams
of moonlight darted between the branches as they danced about;
the night sky was cloudless.

"Come on!" Rafferdy shouted, and he seized Coulten's arm,
pulling him back through the tunnel.

This time Coulten needed no encouragement. The two men
dashed through the tunnel, out the entrance, and stumbled a
dozen paces from the wall before turning to look back. Rafferdy
lifted his gaze to the crowns of the trees. Just like before, the
branches trembled and tossed. Only there was something different
about their motions this time. They were not so violent and furious as they had been that day.

"Is it another Rising?" Coulten said.

However, at that moment, the agitation of the branches began
to slow. The roaring noise dwindled. Then, with one last rustling
sigh, several branches bent down and, with what seemed a strangely
gentle motion, set something down on the top of the wall. Then a
stray moonbeam gleamed off golden hair, and Rafferdy drew in a
breath as wonder filled him.

"No," he murmured, "it's not a Rising."

Coulten had been looking through the tunnel. Only now, following Rafferdy's gaze, he began to lift his head to look upward. Despite Rafferdy's shock and confusion, one clear thought occurred to him: Coulten must not see what had alighted atop the wall.

"Great gods, look there!" Rafferdy exclaimed, turning to point behind them. "Are those soldiers coming?"

Coulten's eyes went wide, and he spun around. "Where?" he said, peering away from the wall, toward the darkened fields. "I don't see any—oh." His words ended in a soft exhalation as he slumped to the ground.

Rafferdy gripped his cane, whose ivory handle he had just applied with some force to the back of Coulten's skull. Then he knelt down to make sure the other young man was yet breathing, and that he had not fallen in an awkward position. These things were readily confirmed. Coulten would be fine—though he was bound to have an awful headache once he woke.

"Do forgive me, my friend," he said in a low voice, "but I couldn't let you see her."

Even as he said this, he heard a rustling of leaves behind him. He stood and turned around. The top of the wall was empty now, and the crowns of the trees were motionless. Then a slender figure stepped out of the opening in the wall and into the moonlight.

"Mr. Rafferdy," she said with a smile, as if they had just encountered each other by chance while out for a stroll on the Promenade.

For his part, Rafferdy was beyond astonishment. "Mrs. Quent," he said, and gave an elegant bow.

Now she hurried toward him, her smile replaced by an expression of concern. "But what have you done to Lord Coulten?"

"I didn't think it prudent that he see you here," Rafferdy replied.

She hesitated, then nodded. "I suppose it is for the best that he didn't. But will he . . . ?"

"He will be fine enough when he wakes. Though he will also be very angry with me, I imagine. Only that doesn't matter right now." Rafferdy took a step toward her. "What in the world are you doing here, Mrs. Quent? And more important, *how* are you here?"

"I can explain everything, Mr. Rafferdy. But you must come with me. We don't have much time."

"Come with you? Where?"

She held out a small hand toward him. "Into the Evengrove."

ONLY SCANT MINUTES had passed since Mrs. Quent had stepped out of the door in the wall, but everything had changed in that brief time. He had listened in both horror and fascination as she described all that had happened to her that evening. Now, despite the balmy night, Rafferdy suffered a terrible chill. Yet if she could be willing to do this, he must do the same. He gathered his courage, such as it was, then followed Mrs. Quent into the stone passage.

"Should I bind the door shut behind us?" he said, his words echoing off the stone. "I don't want Coulten following us if he wakes up."

"No, don't close it," she said, touching his arm. "The man in the mask said it cannot be opened from this side. That's why Gambrel needed someone here to open it for him."

Rafferdy nodded. He knew now that was the real task Eubrey had been sent here to do that day—to make sure an initiate could open the door in the wall. Only, then Eubrey had been used for a different purpose, and so another initiate had been needed to perform the duty.

"I can make sure Coulten does not follow us," she said as they stepped from the passage and into the forest. She turned, then laid her hand on the trunk of the large tree that stood before the opening. The tree gave a shudder, then all at once its branches bent down, weaving together in an impenetrable curtain, blocking the passage through the wall.

Rafferdy watched all of this with fascination. "It seems magick is not the only way to bind doors," he said dryly.

"I suppose you're right," she said, giving him a fleeting smile. Then her expression turned grave. "We must hurry, Mr. Rafferdy."

"Of course," he said, and started down the stone path.

"No, not that way," she said behind him. "Walking will be too slow. We would never reach the tomb before Gambrel."

He turned to regard her. "Then how do you propose we get there?"

"Just as I got here," she said, reaching up to entwine her fingers with leaves and twigs. "The trees will know the way."

And before he could ask her what she meant, a number of branches reached down and plucked Rafferdy up off the ground.

He let out a cry of alarm and struggled to free himself, only it was no use. Strong green tendrils coiled around his limbs, and in a moment he was borne thirty feet off the ground, up to the very tops of the trees. The stars and moon glittered overhead.

"Don't be afraid, Mr. Rafferdy!" a voice called out.

He looked around wildly, then saw her only a short distance away. She seemed to float on the very tops of the trees, held aloft by the swaying motions of the branches.

Her statement was obviously absurd. How could he not be afraid when he was being torn limb from limb by trees that could move of their own will? Only, he realized then, the branches weren't pulling him into pieces. Rather, he was being held up in the most careful manner. Indeed, the less he struggled, the more gentle the motions became.

Now his fear was replaced by amazement. "Are you doing this?" he called out to her.

She smiled at him. "Brace yourself, Mr. Rafferdy."

And all at once they were moving as they were passed from branch to branch and carried along the treetops.

Rafferdy cried out again, only this time it was not due to fear but rather exhilaration. The night air rushed past them, and he and Mrs. Quent sped across the tops of the trees like flotsam blown upon an emerald sea. He did not fight against the motions of the branches, but rather moved with them, shifting his weight from one to the next as they carried him along. That they were moving far faster than a horse could run, he was certain.

Soon he became aware that he was grinning like a mad fool, only he could not help himself. As strange as this was, for some reason he could not name, it felt peculiarly natural as well. It seemed to him that there was a kind of *rightness* to the notion of a witch helping to bring a magician to a place deep in the Wyrdwood.

Suddenly a glint of blue caught Rafferdy's eye, and he looked at his hand. The gem in his magician's ring was glittering with an interior light. Before he could wonder why, he felt himself being carried downward. The stars vanished as branches closed around him. Then, a moment later, he felt a hard surface beneath his boots as he was deposited upon the ground.

The branches raised themselves up to reveal Mrs. Quent standing beside him. Even in the gloom he could see that her gown was askew and her hair was a gold tangle.

"Are we there?" he said.

She shook her head. "I don't know. The trees . . . they were reluctant to take us any farther."

As she said this, he saw the line of red stones upon the ground, leading forward. "This way," he said.

This time it was he who went first as they walked down the stone path. After no more than a dozen paces the trees gave way to either side, and they found themselves on the edge of a vast clearing in the forest. The clearing was at least a furlong across, unnaturally circular in shape, and entirely devoid of trees. The ground within the circle was black and barren, and the trees along its edge all leaned away from it, as if unwilling or unable to grow another inch nearer. Rafferdy was loath to enter the clearing himself. His ring continued to throw off blue sparks, and the air was thick and foul with, it seemed to him, a terrible power or presence.

Just then the moon sailed higher in the sky, edging over the crowns of the trees. By the pale flood of its light they could see that the clearing was not empty. Rather, a massive structure hulked in the very center of the circle. It was a sort of pyramid shape, like something that might be illustrated in a book concerning the ruins in the deserts of the Murgh Empire. However, its sides were tilted at such a bizarre angle that the structure was discomforting, almost painful, to gaze upon. It was fashioned of stone that, even in the moonlight, was the color of dried blood.

"That has to be the tomb you spoke of," he said, only he winced as his words died upon the preternaturally still air.

Next to him, Mrs. Quent only nodded, as if she was loath to break the awful silence.

Rafferdy took another step along the path. How long had this pyramid stood here, concealed in the center of the ancient grove of trees? Many eons, he supposed. Yet here it was, no more than twenty miles from the greatest city in Altania, and no one had ever known about it.

Except that was not true. There were some who had in fact known about it—the magicians who built this path, and who put the door in the wall. And perhaps the emperor who built the wall in the first place. He took another step along the path, moving farther into the clearing. As he did, he realized that Mrs. Quent was still behind him. He glanced back. Her face was wan and tight in the moonlight.

"Come along," he said. "Gambrel can't have come through yet, or there would be an awful commotion here. He must still be on Tyberion, looking for the right door. Which means we still have time."

Mrs. Quent started to take a hesitant step, then stopped and shook her head. "I don't think I can, Mr. Rafferdy." Her words were faint and breathless. "There is something here that . . . I cannot say what it is. But I do not think it will allow me to enter the circle."

Rafferdy stared at her. Yet, after a moment, he thought that perhaps he should not be so astonished. After all, some dreadful magick prevented the Wyrdwood from encroaching upon the circle, just as the Old Trees disallowed it from escaping. Her natural abilities could only be at odds with the arcane energies that permeated this place.

"Go on," she said, her voice strained. "You have to shut the door before Gambrel can come through it."

Now his shock was renewed. The idea of entering the clearing and approaching the tomb by himself was one that caused him to shudder. He wanted only to dash along the path through the forest, to find his way back to the door in Madiger's Wall.

"Please, Mr. Rafferdy," she said, meeting his gaze with her own. "I know it is within your power. Only you can do it."

Despite the chill dread that pooled within him, he felt a sudden spark of warmth in his chest. He squared his shoulders and gave a crisp bow. "As you wish, my lady," he said.

Then, gripping his cane, he turned and made his way along the path, deeper into the clearing. At once his confidence wavered, and the warm spark in his chest was snuffed out. The air grew thicker and more oppressive with every step he took, and colder as well. He began to feel a queer tickling in his chest, a sensation that crawled up into his throat, until he was forced to clench his jaw to resist the compulsion to scream.

The moon rose higher still, and by its light he saw it standing there in the shadow of the pyramid: a stone archway, perhaps ten feet in height. The path led directly toward it, and as Rafferdy took several more reluctant steps along it, he could see that the stones of the arch were carved with runes.

That it was the door, he had no doubt.

Pushing his cane against the ground with every step, Rafferdy slowly approached the arch. The pyramid loomed above him, and an awful presence emanated from the structure—an energy that spoke with such force and malice that it had become a kind of constant shrieking in Rafferdy's brain. On his right hand, his ring flickered with azure fire.

At last, with one final push of his cane, he reached the arch. Now a new dread came over him—a fear that at any moment the door might sparkle with arcane power and Gambrel would step through it. However, all Rafferdy could see through the stone arch was blackness. The door had not opened. And he would make certain it never did.

The runes carved on the stones were dark and sharp in the moonlight. He circled around the arch and saw there were runes on the other side as well. As quickly as he could, he made an examination of the ancient writing, and gradually he began to understand the function of the arch.

A spell of opening was inscribed upon each side of the door. If entered from one direction, he surmised, the door could be used to travel to the way station on Tyberion, while passing through the other way would take one into the pyramid itself. But for the door leading into the tomb to function, it appeared that the door on Tyberion would have to be activated as well. Which meant one could only get to the tomb by coming from the way station on Tyberion. No doubt the magicians who had built the pyramid had put these precautions in place to make the pyramid difficult to open. Even if an enemy gained control of this door, it would still not be enough to open the tomb.

Yet difficult was not impossible, and according to Mrs. Quent, Gambrel had already reached Tyberion.

Hurrying now, Rafferdy returned to the front of the arch, again reading the runes there. As he had learned from Mr. Bennick, a spell of opening could also be used as a spell of closing and binding. Only what was the proper order to speak the runes in? If he spoke them incorrectly, he could fail to bind the door shut. Even worse, if Gambrel had already activated the door on Tyberion, Rafferdy might inadvertently open the way into the pyramid and set the Broken God free, just as Gambrel intended to do. For a moment a panic seized Rafferdy. He could not move.

Only then he thought of the way Mrs. Quent had regarded him at the edge of the clearing, and the confidence in her expression. If she believed it was within his power, then it had to be so. After all, she was the sensible one, not he.

Rafferdy drew in a breath, then lifted his cane and pressed the tip against the arch. As quickly as he dared, he uttered the runes carved upon the stones. As he spoke them, a faint purple glow appeared within the blackness of the archway. The light rapidly brightened into an amethyst sparkle, and in its midst was a shadow, almost like the silhouette of a man. At that moment, Rafferdy uttered the final rune. His ring let off a brilliant flash. Blue sparks coursed down the length of his cane and struck the arch, sizzling as they spread out across its stones.

There came a deafening *crack*. Black lines appeared upon the stones and snaked across their surfaces. The arch gave a violent shudder. Then, all at once, it collapsed in a heap of rubble, throwing up a cloud of dust. Rafferdy stumbled back, then stared at the pile of stones. Gradually, a comprehension of what had happened came to him. The arcane power that suffused the air in this place had made his enchantment far stronger than he had intended, and his spell of binding had instead become a spell of breaking.

It was just as well. Now it was assured that Gambrel could never pass through the door. The Broken God would remain asleep in its tomb—and the Evengrove would continue to guard its secret.

His task finished, Rafferdy turned to start back down the path. Now that he was moving away from the pyramid, he found that he could not go swiftly enough. He broke into a run, not caring one whit how undignified it might make him look. At last, his heart beating rapidly, he reached the edge of the clearing.

And there she was, standing among the trees, smiling at him.

"Oh, Mr. Rafferdy!" she cried, and she took his hand, squeezing it tightly. As she did, he felt an energy that had nothing to do with magick run tingling up his arm.

"It is done," he said, surprised at how haggard his voice sounded. "Let's leave this place, and may we never return."

She nodded, her face still pale and drawn.

"You had better take me back to the door in the wall," he said. "I fear Coulten will wake soon, if he already hasn't by now, and I don't want him to get in trouble with any soldiers."

She placed a hand on the trunk of a tree, then looked at him. "Are you ready, then?"

"Very ready," he replied.

And this time, he was not the least bit shocked when the

branches reached down and plucked him up off the ground. Rather, despite the awful nature of this place, he laughed out loud. In moments the two of them were lifted up to the crowns of the trees, and there they were propelled along at a thrilling pace while the moon and stars glittered above.

All too soon, Rafferdy caught a glimpse of a thick gray line through the branches. They had reached the wall. The branches slowed their motions, lowering him to the ground, and there released him. However, they continued to twine about her, holding her aloft a dozen feet off the ground.

"I think it is best if I return through the door to Arantus," she called down to him. "If Lord Coulten is awake, it is perhaps prudent that he does not see me."

"I think he would be struck unconscious again if he did!" Rafferdy called back brightly.

Cane in hand, he moved to the wall. As he did, the branches lifted from the mouth of the passage, clearing the way. He turned, looking up at her, and gave a nod.

"Good-bye, Mrs. Quent."

"Only for now, Mr. Rafferdy."

She smiled down at him, a stray moonbeam illuminating her face. And as she floated there amid the branches, like some ethereal being, he thought that he had never in his life seen a woman more beautiful.

Then came a rushing noise, like a wind, and she was gone.

CHAPTER FORTY-THREE

ONCE AGAIN, THE illusionists joined hands on the stage and bowed as thunderous applause shook the theater. The house had been full that night, as it had been every night of late. These days, there was not a person who came down to Durrow Street with a quarter regal in hand who did not want to see the illusion play at the Theater of the Moon.

The play there had already been the talk of Durrow Street for the past month. However, when a new scene was added, its first performance caused a sensation to sweep along the street and into the city at large. The broadsheets quickly printed stories about it, and by the very next lumenal it was a matter being discussed in every tavern, club, and house in the Grand City of Invarel—even by those who would never think of doing something so scandalous as to attend an illusion play.

The scene in question had appeared at the very beginning of the second act. Usually, at that point in the play, mercenaries in the employ of the Sun King pursued the youthful Moon through locales in the far south of the Empire. However, as the red curtain opened that night, it was not an exotic Murghese city that the audience saw. Instead, it was a perfectly wrought scene of Invarel, and the soldiers who pursued the silver-faced youth were a band of redcrests clad in blue coats.

In the center of the stage were two churches, and for all that they had been shrunk to fit within the confines of the proscenium, they retained their imposing presence. On the left soared the pale, graceful spires of St. Galmuth's cathedral, while on the right sulked the charcoal walls of Graychurch.

It was to St. Galmuth's that the Moon went. He pounded upon its doors, calling out for sanctuary. After a moment those doors opened, and he was let inside.

Just then the soldiers who had been pursuing him arrived. They shouted out, demanding to know where the Moon was hiding. In response to their words, the doors of both churches opened, and a figure appeared on the steps of each. Before St. Galmuth's on the left, dressed in a snowy robe, was an old man with a long white beard and an angelic expression on his face. While on the right, upon the steps of Graychurch, was a tall figure with fierce blue eyes, wearing a cassock of livid crimson.

At this a murmur ran through the audience, and many shifted uneasily upon their seats. That the man in white was meant to be the Archbishop of Invarel, while the figure in red was the Archdeacon of Graychurch, was clear to everyone. However, so fascinating was the scene that all in the audience watched with hardly a blink or breath.

Again the soldiers shouted out, demanding that the Moon be surrendered to them. The priest in red claimed he was not in Graychurch, so the soldiers advanced toward the steps of St. Galmuth's. As they did, the cleric in white held up a hand. *You shall not bring your swords within these holy walls,* he said, *for he has claimed sanctuary here.*

So rebuffed, the soldiers could not enter. However, at that point the priest in red scowled and rubbed his hands together. He descended the steps of Graychurch, and now the scene shifted and moved around him as he walked across the stage, and by the sights flickering behind him all could see that it was down Durrow Street he walked.

Now the audience's nervousness was released in peals of laughter, for the actor who played the priest in red made him at once a sneering and foppish figure. He used a handkerchief to bat away soiled urchins who begged for coins, plucked fastidiously at the hem of his robe as he stepped over drunks and offal in the gutter, and recoiled from voluptuous women who batted their eyes at him, as if they were the most hideous things.

At last the scene changed again, showing a dilapidated chapel that rose on a hill above an unsavory street. In the way that only illusion could manage, the scene rippled and blurred, following him as he went into the chapel, down to the crypts, and below, to a labyrinth walled by red curtains.

There he came to a place where several men sat bound to chairs, heads drooped as if in slumber. The priest took a crystal orb out of his red robe. Then he went to one of the men and, with a motion such as one might make when pulling a thread out of a frayed seam, he pulled a silver cord from the man's brow, then touched it to the orb. The man screamed, then fell still. The priest went to the next man, and the next, pulling a silver cord from each one's head and touching it to the orb.

At last he laughed, holding up the orb. Through the power of illusion, the orb grew for a moment, until it seemed to fill the stage, and all could see the hideous scenes that flickered within it: images of fire and blood, fear and death, and lumbering, monstrous forms. They were nightmares, all knew at once, taken from the dreams of the men and placed in the crystal.

The orb shrank to its previous size, and the priest ascended from the maze beneath the old chapel. The scene changed once more, so that the forms of St. Galmuth's and Graychurch once again dominated the stage. Still the soldiers stood before the cathedral, rebuffed by the white-robed cleric.

Only then the priest in the red cassock approached, and he ascended the steps of the cathedral. He smiled, an awful expression, and held out the orb of crystal to the other priest. The white-bearded man smiled in return, then looked into the orb.

His expression became one of horror. Silver threads sprang outward from the crystal, passing into his forehead. Then he turned and rushed down the steps, his eyes wild, his hair standing on end. For a minute he ran to and fro upon the stage, clutching his head, raving about the scenes of doom and destruction that had been revealed to him, and the audience gasped, for they knew he had been driven mad.

Upon the steps of St. Galmuth's, the priest in red smiled again, and he tucked the orb into his robe. Then, gesturing for the soldiers to follow him, he walked through the doors of the cathedral.

At the same moment, the silver-faced figure of the Moon appeared from behind the cathedral; he had slipped out the back. He looked both ways, then dashed offstage. After that the play continued just as it always had. However, throughout it all the audience whispered about the scene they had watched, and their whispers became a roar as they left the theater.

By morning, the rumor was being repeated all over Invarel, from Waterside to Gauldren's Heights to the New Quarter: that the Archdeacon of Graychurch was some manner of sorcerer, that it was he who had caused the Archbishop of Invarel to become insane, and that he had done this so he could become archbishop himself.

These charges were as astonishing as the fact that the play at the Theater of the Moon had intimated them. While it was not uncommon for a play to lampoon or tease a famous figure for the amusement of the audience, to so clearly imply one had committed a heinous deed was another matter altogether, and usually a theater would have been shut down by the Crown for such libelous acts.

That might have happened in this case, except that Lord Valhaine, no doubt in an effort to dispel the rumors, dispatched a few soldiers to investigate beneath the old chapel at High Holy. There they found horrible things: a labyrinth of red curtains, and men who were chained to chairs, some long rotten, others alive but quite mad, and all with their eyes burned or plucked out. At the same time, a number of receipts were delivered to the publisher of *The Swift Arrow* by an anonymous hand. The receipts were for the purchase of red curtains, and they were all signed by Archdeacon Lemarck.

After this story was published, the Black Dog himself went to Graychurch, and the archdeacon was led away to the Citadel to be questioned. He was kept there for several days, and though he confessed nothing, it was noted by the priests at St. Galmuth's that during this time the archbishop's condition rapidly improved. His eyes grew clear, he became lucid, and he no longer claimed to see any sort of visions. It was as if he had awakened from a nightmare, he was reported to have said.

Previously, the archdeacon had been known to visit the archbishop at least once each lumenal and umbral. Now, after just a few days without these visits, the archbishop's madness had ceased.

As if this was not damning enough, just as this news reached the Citadel, one of the soldiers guarding the chamber where the archdeacon was being held suddenly turned upon his fellows, hacking at them with his saber, shouting that there were shadows inside them he had to cut out. He slew two men before he himself was shot dead.

No further proof could be needed. Upon Lord Valhaine's order, the archdeacon was swaddled all in red cloth, with a red bag covering his head, and was hauled to Barrowgate. He was placed in a cell deep in the bowels of the prison, in a room with no windows, into which not the faintest scrap of illumination might seep. It was utterly lightless. These things were done, it was said, based upon advice received from a number of illusionists on Durrow Street.

There the archdeacon had been left to await his trial. However, earlier today, a new and shocking story had appeared in the broadsheets. When the door to the archdeacon's cell was opened to deliver food to him, he was found not to be moving. At last the prison's guards dared to light a candle, and what they saw was a gruesome scene. Archdeacon Lemarck was dead, his flesh gray and sunken against his bones.

The broadsheets stated that the cause of the archdeacon's demise was a mystery. Only it was no mystery to any illusionist on Durrow Street. Down there in the dark, he had been unable to resist the temptation to conjure visions for himself. Or perhaps he had simply gone mad and could not help summoning phantasms. Either way, the results were the same. As there had been no light in the cell to draw upon, he had instead drawn upon his own. He had used every last bit of his light, until it was utterly gone, and so the Gray Wasting had taken him.

Throughout all these investigations, the play at the Theater of the Moon only increased in popularity; everyone wanted to see for themselves the scene that had incriminated the vile Archdeacon of Graychurch. Tonight's audience was no different. However, after today's grisly news, Eldyn knew that tonight's performance of the scene had been the last.

The players stepped back as the red curtain closed. Merrick, Mouse, Hugoth, Riethe in his red cassock, and all the other men embraced and laughed, and they shouted out in delight as Master Tallyroth and Madame Richelour appeared from the wings to share the largesse of that night's bulging receipts box.

Eldyn did not take part in the merriment. Instead, he slipped quietly away. He paused for a moment before a mirror, using a cloth to wipe away the silver paint from his face. Then he climbed upstairs, to one of the small rooms above the theater. The door was ajar. He hesitated a moment, then he knocked softly and entered.

Dercy looked up from the chair where he sat. His beard—its bright gold now flecked here and there with gray—parted as he smiled. "Well," he said, "how did it go tonight?"

Eldyn smiled in return. "It was a great success, of course. Madame Richelour could hardly carry the moneybox. Everyone loves your scene."

Dercy made a dismissive gesture with a thin hand. Eldyn could not help noticing the way the back of it was traced with blue veins, and how it trembled as he moved.

"It's not my scene," Dercy said. "It was your idea to do it."

"Yes, but it was *you* who schemed up how we would accomplish the staging."

"Well, I suppose so. But the embellishment and execution were all *yours*, Eldyn. And it was brilliant. I could never have given so great a performance."

"Yes, you could have," Eldyn said. He went to Dercy, knelt beside him, and gripped one of his hands, stilling its trembling.

Dercy started to protest, only then a cough wracked him. At last his paroxysm subsided, and they were both silent for a time.

"You won't be doing the scene again, I suppose," Dercy said at last. He glanced toward a broadsheet that lay on the bed. ARCHDEACON OF GRAYCHURCH MEETS GHASTLY DEMISE, the headline read.

Eldyn shook his head. "No, I don't think we will."

"Good" was all Dercy said.

Eldyn stroked that pale hand, and at last he dared to ask the question he had wanted to ask all during these last days. At first Dercy had been too ill, confined to his bed while Master Tallyroth and Madame Richelour tended to him. As he grew stronger and passed out of danger, Eldyn had still found himself reluctant to speak of it; he had wanted Dercy to think only of getting well, not of what had brought on his illness.

Now, though his eyes were too bright, and his cheeks were grayish and hollow beneath his beard, Dercy was sitting upright, and his trembling was not so awful, confined mostly to his hands. It was time.

"Why, Dercy?" he said softly. "I couldn't work illusions. Oh, I could manage small glamours well enough, but no real phantasms. You knew that I couldn't. Only, you gave me your light all the same, all those times we were here in this room together. Why did you do it?"

Dercy did not look at him. A grimace crossed his face, like a spasm of pain, only after a moment it became a smile.

"I did it because I wanted you to be with me, here at the theater."

These words caused a pang in Eldyn's chest. "Even at so great a cost to yourself?"

Dercy shrugged. "It was not so very great." He reached out and touched Eldyn's cheek. "What was giving up a year or two of my life to spend all those that remained making grand illusions with you?"

"But I can't work illusions!" Eldyn cried. "It was all you—it was all your light, not mine. Now look what's become of you!"

Dercy shook his head, and his expression was stern. "That's not true, Eldyn. I helped you, yes. I showed you what you were capable of. But as time went on, I gave you less and less. You were learning to find your own light. By the end, I was lending you the barest glimmer. And now . . ." He sighed. "Well, I certainly wasn't helping you tonight, was I? That was all your own doing. Which means what I told you all those months ago was true. No matter what you thought you might be, you *are* an illusionist, Eldyn Garritt."

Eldyn's eyes stung, and an anguish gripped his throat.

"Besides, it was not because of anything I gave you that this has befallen me." Dercy withdrew his hand and held it up, so that the palsy that shook it could not be hidden. "You know who did this to me."

"You're getting better, though," Eldyn said, finding words at last.

Dercy grinned, and the expression had something of his usual mischief in it. "Yes, I'll live. So Master Tallyroth assures me, and I suppose he should know. He told me earlier tonight that my mordoth is not even as bad as his, and that we both have many years left in us, as long as we are careful."

At these words a relief flooded through Eldyn. He leaped to his feet. "We will be careful. We'll make sure you do nothing that might cost you any light at all."

Dercy drew in a breath. Then, slowly yet deliberately, he rose from the chair. "No, Eldyn. *We* won't be careful. I will. It's up to me, and to me alone. I will take care not to do anything that might worsen my mordoth. But you—you have many illusions yet to conjure."

Before Eldyn could ask what these words meant, there was a knock upon the door. He turned to see one of the stagehands standing there.

"The hack cab is here for you, Mr. Fanewerthy," he said. "I've handed your bag to the driver. He is ready to take you to the station to catch the post."

"Thank you," Dercy said. "I'll be down at once."

The man nodded and left. Dercy took up a wooden cane and, leaning upon it, started toward the door.

"What are you doing?" Eldyn cried out in shock.

Dercy did not look at him. "I'm going to the country to live with my cousin for a time. He is the vicar of a small parish and has the living there. I wrote to him, and he told me I could stay with him as long as I wish."

"You can't leave," Eldyn said, and madly he searched for a reason why this was the case. "It's dark out there."

"The stagecoaches care not if it is an umbral or a lumenal," Dercy said. "They always keep to their timetables."

Then Eldyn spoke the one reason that mattered to him. "But I don't want you to go! I want to be with you."

Dercy turned to look at him, and in his sea green eyes was an expression of sorrow and affection. "I want to be with you, too, Eldyn. More than anything. But I can't. If I stay here, if I stay with you, the temptation to work illusions will be too great. I know myself. I'll tell myself I'll behave. Only I'll see what you and the others are doing, and I won't be able to help it in the end."

Eldyn took a step toward him. "I'll give you my light, then."

Dercy smiled. "I know you would, Eldyn. But you'll need it all yourself, to do the great things that I know you're bound to do."

Eldyn opened his mouth, to speak the words that would convince Dercy to change his mind and compel him to stay. Only, he could not think of what those words might be.

With halting steps, Dercy came to him. He brushed his lips against Eldyn's cheek, so that Eldyn felt the roughness of his beard, and the warmth of his breath.

"Well," Dercy said, "my coach is waiting." Leaning on his cane, he walked slowly through the door and was gone.

Eldyn went to the bed, and he sat there for a time in the moonlight that spilled through the window, trying to decide where he should go. He could not return to the apartment in the old monastery. It had been granted to him as part of his remuneration for working at Graychurch, but he did not work there anymore. It was strange that, as a Siltheri, he had been so beguiled by illusions himself, but he had seen through them now. Just as Vandimeer Garritt had said, his son would never enter the Church.

But his daughter would.

The day after the events beneath the chapel in High Holy, once he was certain Dercy was out of immediate danger, Eldyn had gone to the apartment, thinking his sister would be worried that he had been away all night, and that she would be relieved and thankful to see him. Instead, the rooms were empty. There was only a note upon the table, penned in her childish hand.

She had sought sanctuary in Graychurch, Sashie had written. She now knew the truth of what he was, for at her request Father Prestus had followed him one night, and he had seen everything. As a result, Sashie wanted nothing to do with Eldyn ever again.

You need not pray for me, brother, she had closed the letter. *I do not know what will become of me, but I will trust my fate to God. And for my part, I will not pray for you, for I know that you are beyond the help of any prayers now.*

For a long time Eldyn had sat there, staring at the letter. At last he set the paper down, then went into his room and, from a hollow in the wall behind the headboard of his bed, he withdrew the box where he kept his savings. After that he went back to the outer room, sat at the table, and composed a letter himself.

To the rector of Graychurch, it began. *Enclosed is a sum of a thousand regals to pay the portion to the Church on behalf of one Sashie Garritt, lately a frequent visitor to Graychurch, that she might enter whichever nunnery is deemed most in need of her devotion and service. If Miss Garritt should ask where the funds for her portion came from, tell her only that it came from an unknown benefactor who wanted to do good.*

Eldyn read back over the letter. Then he dipped his pen and signed it, *An Anonymous Soul.*

He folded the letter and placed it in the box, then left the apartment just as dusk was falling. Cloaking himself thickly in shadows, he crossed the street and one last time passed through the doors of Graychurch. Moving unseen, he stole down the stairs to the rector's office, slipped through the door, and set the box on Father Gadby's table while the portly priest's back was turned.

Then, like some ghost exiled from the kingdom of Eternum, he crept from the room above crypts and drifted from the church.

What exactly would happen to Sashie, and where she would go, Eldyn didn't know, but it was no longer his concern. His sister was in God's hands now.

As for the matter of where he should go himself, Eldyn supposed *this* room was free now. He looked around the little chamber, and a faint smile came to his lips. It was small, and rather bare, but it was as good a place as any. He would speak to Master Tallyroth in the morning, and ask if he could stay here.

Even as he thought this, there came the heavy sound of boots. He looked up and saw Riethe standing in the doorway.

"There you are, Eldyn! Everyone's wondering where you went. We're all off to tavern, and our pockets are full of regals!" The strapping young illusionist frowned at him. "Well, what is it? I can't wait here all umbral. Are you in or are you out, Eldyn Garritt?"

Eldyn reached in his pocket and drew out a penny. He ran his thumb over it, then he flipped it in the air, and by the time he caught it, the coin had turned from copper to gold.

He looked up at Riethe, then laughed.

"It looks like I'm in."

⚜

ⲦHE HONEYED LIGHT of a long morning filled the parlor at Rafferdy's house in Warwent Square. He glanced out the window and saw his driver was already waiting with the carriage. It was past time to put on his robe and go. A session of Assembly was convening that day, and he knew that there would be a great amount of discussion and debate, as it was the first time the Hall of Magnates would come to order since the murder of Lord Bastellon.

All the same, he did not put on his robe just yet. On a sudden whim he had sent his man out on an errand that morning, and Rafferdy was waiting for his return.

To pass the time, he sat at his writing desk and looked again at the note that had arrived for him several days ago. It was written in a careful yet lovely hand. He smiled as he read the final words.

I hope we can indeed go walking together soon. . . .

She must have written it that very same day, before Gambrel came to her house, and even as Rafferdy was chasing after Coulten to Madiger's Wall. Little did he know, when he set off that afternoon for the Evengrove at a mad pace in his cabriolet, that he would see Mrs. Quent that very night. While it was not precisely a walk, they had in fact gone on a sojourn together—one of a most extraordinary character.

"I hope we can indeed go for another walk soon, Mrs. Quent," he said, and smiled.

Rafferdy set the note down. Then, from his desk he took out a book bound in black leather and opened it with a whispered rune. As he suspected would be the case, no new words had appeared on its pages.

A few days after their return from the Evengrove, Rafferdy and Coulten had dared to go to the meeting chamber beneath the Sword and Leaf. It had been empty. The curtain that always before had concealed the way to the inner sanctum was askew, and the Door itself had been open. They had passed through, feeling a cool shiver on their skin as they did, stepping into a room that Rafferdy knew was located not beneath the tavern, but rather beneath Mrs. Quent's house.

The chamber was empty save for a circle of power etched in silver on the floor. He had imagined the sort of rituals that had been conducted here, and he'd shuddered. That Gambrel, as magus of the Arcane Society of the Virescent Blade, had been the prime instigator of it all, Rafferdy did not doubt. Only he had needed others to help work spells in the name of the Ashen, and so the other sages—and even other magickal orders—had been enlisted to aid him. What had Gambrel promised them? Power, most likely, and money.

Who they were, Rafferdy did not know—with one exception. Rafferdy did know the name of one of the men who had aided

Gambrel. In Assembly, he and Coulten had already begun to cir-
culate whispers among the younger magicians that Lord Mertrand
and the High Order of the Golden Door were to be avoided at all
cost. However, the sages of the Arcane Society of the Virescent
Blade were still at large. And there may well have been other magickal orders allied with Gambrel. Which meant more young men
might yet be tricked by promises of wealth and power.

Well, if Rafferdy and Coulten could not prevent such things
from happening, they could at least prevent them from happening
here. They shut the door to the sanctum, binding it with the most
powerful spells they could manage. They bound as well the two
doors that led to the meeting room—the one from Durrow Street
and the one in the rear of the Sword and Leaf. Then they sat in
the tavern to have a drink, and to raise a glass in memory of Lord
Eubrey.

Now, with a sigh, Rafferdy returned the black book to the
desk. He rose and put on his robe, then he took up a pair of
gloves.

Since the attack upon Lord Bastellon—an act obviously
worked with magick—magicians and arcane societies had come
under even further scrutiny. It was said that Lady Shayde had
made an appearance at Gauldren's College, and that agents of Lord
Valhaine had been asking questions about the city, seeking information concerning secret magickal orders. These days, it did not
seem like a prudent thing to go about with a magician's ring in
plain view on one's hand.

Rafferdy started to put on the gloves, only then he drew them
off again and set them back down. Despite his father's words, he
could not believe that magicians could only be wicked. After all,
without magick, there would have been no way to thwart Gambrel's plan. He had wished to free the Broken God from its tomb,
to provoke the Wyrdwood to rise up so violently that men would
become determined to cut it all down. After what Rafferdy had
seen, he knew that could not be allowed, that the Wyrdwood had to
be preserved, for there was some innate property in it that allowed
it to resist the power of magick, and of the Ashen.

Only now Lord Bastellon was dead, and over these last several days Rafferdy had wondered who in Assembly would stand up to Lord Mertrand and the Magisters. Who would take to the floor of the Hall of Magnates to challenge the calls to destroy the Wyrd-wood and argue forcefully against them? Then, just as Rafferdy was taking his breakfast that morning, an idea had come to him.

Footsteps sounded behind him, and his man rushed into the room, a box in his hands.

"I was able to find what you wished, Lord Rafferdy," he said breathlessly, and he set the box on the desk.

Rafferdy clapped his hands together. "Excellent! Tell the driver I'll be out in a moment."

His man nodded and hurried from the parlor. An eagerness filled Rafferdy. He found he was now very anxious to get to Assembly that day. He could not wait to see the look upon Coulten's face. And perhaps he would suggest that they not sit upon the very back benches this time, but rather, closer up front.

With this in mind, Rafferdy opened the box. He took out the powdered white wig that lay within and put it upon his head, tugging it firmly into place. Bastellon was no more, but Rafferdy would make sure there was at least one lord in Assembly who would argue against the Magisters. He glanced in a mirror to make sure the wig was square upon his head. Then, satisfied, he turned and departed the room.

It was high time Lord Rafferdy got himself to the Hall of Magnates.

THIS TIME IT was Ivy who slipped from bed in the gray light before dawn, while Mr. Quent still slumbered.

She drew a light robe around her shoulders against the slight chill in the air, then departed their bedchamber. It was not a noise that had awakened her. Her sleep had not been disturbed by the sound of voices these last umbrals, and while from time to time she still heard a faint soughing like a far-off wind, even when the trees were motionless in the garden, this caused her no distress. She would simply shut her eyes and imagine stone archways through which green leaves fluttered.

Now the house was silent as she moved down the stairs to the second floor gallery. She went first to the north wall, touching the carved leaves upon the door there, and she smiled. To her great relief, it had still been open when she passed through the door from the Evengrove back to the way station on Arantus. She had hurried across the impossible moonscape and with a sigh stepped into the warm familiarity of the gallery. Magicians might think nothing of going this way and that through doors, but she found it all rather disconcerting.

She had shut the door and removed the leaf-shaped key, which she put back in the Wyrdwood box in the library. Arantus was locked once more. Yet it pleased her to know that, perhaps one day, she would open it again, and gaze through the doors at other stands of Wyrdwood—that she might even step through into those whispering groves. For now, she was content to think of the door as merely a beautiful object to gaze upon.

Ivy turned and proceeded to the other end of the gallery. There she saw that Mr. Barbridge and his men had done their work well. The construction had been completed just yesterday, and the wall at the south end of the gallery was now smooth and unbroken. Nor was there any sign that a door had ever been there.

She had told Mr. Barbridge simply that she found the design upon the door to be too martial in nature for a room intended for parties and balls, and she wanted it covered again. If he had wondered why she did not simply hang a curtain over it, but instead had him layer upon it brick and lath and plaster, he did not ask, and he performed the work as instructed.

Ivy pressed her ear to the wall, listening. Once or twice, before Tyberion was covered, she had thought she heard sounds through the thick wood of the door: muffled shouts, and a distant knocking. Now all she heard was the sound of her own breathing. She would speak to Mr. Seenly later that day, and tell him to hang a painting here.

A pale apricot glow colored the windowpanes, and Ivy went to one of the windows to gaze down at the garden. The crooked branches of the hawthorn and chestnut trees were still. However, it was not hard for her to picture them whipping and cracking with motion as they had that night. Her father had placed many magickal protections on this house, yet she could protect it in her own way, she knew now.

Several times over these last days, she had gone into the garden and had searched for any signs of the struggle that had happened there. Exactly what the shadowy being had been, she was not certain. The man in the black mask had called it a gol-yagru, a daemon. To her it had looked like the hideous black forms she had glimpsed through the Eye of Ran-Yahgren. They had swarmed over the crimson face of Cerephus, devouring one another, their number beyond counting.

This one could not have come from Cerephus, she was sure. If a door to *that* place was open, then there would have been far more than a single daemon. Rather, the creature must have been a remnant of the ancient war of the Ashen, imprisoned in some tomb or chamber from which Gambrel had freed it, just as he had wished to free the Broken God.

The daemon was not so great and terrible a being as Neth-Bragga, of course. All the same, the thing would have destroyed her if it had not been for the trees in the garden, sprouted from the seeds of Old Trees. Now that she had felt their fury and hatred for the gol-yagru, she could understand why the Ashen desired to have the Wyrdwood burned down.

Which was why those scant fragments of the ancient forest that remained had to be preserved. Ivy would never again complain when Mr. Quent was forced to stay late at the Citadel, or to go off into the country in his duties as an inquirer. His work was more important than ever. The people of Altania must not be made to fear the Old Trees!

Despite her time spent searching in the garden, she never did find any sign of the gol-yagru. The trees had utterly destroyed the daemon. Nor did she find any traces of the other for whom she searched, except for a single brass button lying upon the ground.

It had been crusted with a dark stain. However, she had carefully cleaned and polished it, and now it resided in the Wyrdwood box, along with the button she had found at the Evengrove.

Mrs. Baydon had been greatly distressed at the sudden disappearance of Captain Branfort, but Ivy had decided there was no purpose in telling her friend of the way the captain had deceived them all. Instead, she had told Mrs. Baydon that Captain Branfort had no doubt removed himself from Invarel due to the scandal surrounding Lady Crayford and Colonel Daubrent.

The news of the unspeakable crimes committed by the Archdeacon of Graychurch had been the subject of much print in the broadsheets of late, and once the ink began to flow, it soon stained other people. Lord Valhaine seized the archdeacon's papers, and once these were gone through his association with several other important personages in the city was exposed. Chief among these was a relationship with Lord Crayford. Servants at the viscount's house were questioned, and several confessed to having seen a priest in a red robe there on several occasions, often in the company of illusionists, and their descriptions of the priest matched those of the archdeacon.

The viscount's abrupt disappearance from the city only served to incriminate him further. He could only have fled the country, the stories in the broadsheets speculated, and in all likelihood he was now in hiding in one of the Principalities. Until he could be apprehended, he could not be properly charged and brought to trial. Thus, Lady Crayford continued to dwell in her husband's house in the New Quarter.

While before it had been the scene of many fashionable parties, it was now the case that no one went to the house of the viscountess except for a small number of servants. Nowhere she went in the city would anyone speak to her, or even meet her gaze. She, whose invitations had once been desired by the highest beings in the city, was now shunned by even the lowest.

A few days ago, Ivy had glanced out an upstairs window, and she had seen a figure in a dark violet gown standing on the street outside the front gate, her face concealed by a veil that draped from her broad hat. Though the figure lingered beyond the gate for some time, Ivy did not instruct the servants to go address the other and invite her in.

At last, as evening fell, Ivy had glanced out the window again, and the street beyond the gate was empty.

Ever since the reports linking the archdeacon and the viscount had appeared in the broadsheets, Ivy had done her best to comfort Mrs. Baydon. Captain Branfort was a kind and honorable man, she had said. No doubt he had deemed it best to keep his distance from Ivy and Mrs. Baydon, so that his intimate association with Lady Crayford's brother and the viscount's household could not possibly taint them.

While Mrs. Baydon still missed the captain, these words tempered her sorrow. Of course the captain would do such an honorable thing, she had said. And lately, her spirits had been greatly improved.

Now a pink tinge colored the windows in the gallery. Whether it was to be a long lumenal or short, Ivy had no idea. There was no use consulting the almanac anymore; the timetables could not be relied upon. However, she would go look at the old rosewood clock in the library later, and listen to the whirring of its gears. While the almanac could no longer be trusted, the clock never failed to chime just when a lumenal or umbral began. Like her father's celestial globe, its inner workings were somehow calibrated to understand the new, altered motions of the heavens. How that could be, she did not know, but perhaps an entry would appear in his journal, explaining it to her.

At this moment, however, a yawn escaped Ivy, and she went back upstairs to return to bed for a little while. She slipped quietly into her bedchamber and found that Mr. Quent still slept soundly, for which she was glad. She knew he was greatly tired from his work. Then again, he had not seemed in any way weary last night, and her cheeks grew warm as she recalled the most ardent and pleasant way he had embraced her.

Indeed, there had been a fierceness to it, just as there had been with all of their embraces ever since she had told him about the events concerning Gambrel and the doors. She had told him that very night, upon his return from the Citadel, even though she had been reluctant to do so. She could only recall his great distress to learn she had been at the Evengrove the day of the Rising. All the same, she had told him everything: her encounter with Gambrel, how the saplings in the garden had destroyed the gol-yagru, and how she had commanded the trees of the Evengrove to carry her to Mr. Rafferdy, and then to the tomb of the Broken God.

For a long time after she finished, Mr. Quent was silent. At last he had asked to look through Arantus, and she had taken him to the door, using the leaf key to open it, and he gazed through at the moonscape beyond. Then he had told her to shut the door, and to keep the key safe in her Wyrdwood box. Also, he had agreed with her idea to cover up the door Tyberion, so that Gambrel could never escape from the way station there.

And that was all. She had feared he would grow angry with her, or scold her for placing herself in such peril. Instead, he had only said he was grateful Mr. Rafferdy had been with her. Then he'd taken her in his arms, holding her so tightly her breath was forced out of her in a gasp—though she made no motion to free herself.

Since then, they had spoken little of it all. Though she noticed he had not been at the Citadel as much these last days, and instead had been spending a significant amount of his time with Ivy and her sisters, something for which they were all happy and grateful.

Now, upon the bed, Mr. Quent stirred as the first rays of sunlight touched his face. He made a low sound, speaking in his sleep as he sometimes did. Ivy leaned closer to catch his words.

"No, Ashaydea," he murmured. "You must let her go."

The warmth faded from Ivy, leaving her cold despite the sunlight coming through the window. She remembered what he had told her the day of her sisters' party—how Lady Shayde very much wanted to question a witch, and how there were forces in the government that would not view it favorably if it was discovered Mr. Quent had let the witch who caused the Risings in Torland go free.

"No," he sighed again, and Ivy wondered who was there in his dream with Lady Shayde. Was it the woman in Torland? Or was it some other witch . . .

There was a sharp sound as he drew in a sudden breath of air. Then he opened his eyes, and his expression became a smile as he gazed up at her.

"Well, good morning, Mrs. Quent," he said gruffly. Only then the furrows deepened again on his craggy brow. "But why do you look at me so intently as that! Is there something you wish to tell me?"

Despite the chill that crept through her, Ivy made herself smile.

"Only that you look very handsome this morning," she said, and she leaned down to kiss him.

OUTSIDE, THE SUN lurched into the sky in fits and starts. The people of Invarel rose and began to go about their daily work, hurrying just a little and casting glances at the sky now and then, for there was no way to know just how long the lumenal would be.

Some of those who happened to gaze upward noticed that the sun was not the only light above. Rather, a faint red speck could be perceived as well. No longer was it visible only in the dark of an umbral. It had grown so bright that even the light of the sun could not entirely banish it from the sky. Those who saw it shuddered a little despite the warmth of the morning, then lowered their heads and continued on about their business.

Then, all at once, a ringing noise echoed out over Invarel. High upon the Crag, the bells of the Citadel were rolling and clanging. Unlike the bells of the churches in the city, which tolled the farthings of the day, there were only two occasions when the bells of the Citadel were ever rung. One was to announce the birth of a new prince or princess.

The other was to announce the death of a king.

Everywhere in the city, people ceased their hurried labors, listening to the tolling of the bells, understanding what that somber clarion portended. However, unlike the small beings who inhabited the city below, the heavens did not cease their motions, nor even so much as pause.

Instead, the celestial spheres continued to wheel, turning like the gears of a great clock, counting toward some soon impending hour.

ABOUT THE AUTHOR

What if there was a fantastical cause underlying the social constraints and limited choices confronting a heroine in a novel by Jane Austen or Charlotte Brontë? GALEN BECKETT began writing *The Magicians and Mrs. Quent* to answer that question. The author lives in Colorado and is currently at work on the next chapter in this fabulous tale of witches, magicians, and revolution, *The Master of Heathcrest Hall.*

ABOUT THE TYPE

The text of this book was set in Berkeley, designed by Tony Stan in the early 1980s. It was inspired by and is a variation on University of California Old Style, created in the late 1930s by Frederick Goudy for the exclusive use of the University of California Press at Berkeley. The present face, in fact, bears influences of a number of Goudy's fonts, including Kennerly, Goudy Old Style, Deepdene, and Booklet Oldstyle. Berkeley is notable for both its legibility and its lightness.